EX LIBRIS

VINTAGE CLASSICS

ALMS FOR OBLIVION: VOLUME I

Simon Raven was perhaps known as much for his controversial behaviour as for his writing. Born on 28 December 1927, he grew up reading and studying the classics, translating them from Greek and Latin into English and vice-versa. He was expelled from Charterhouse School in 1945 for homosexual activities, having first been seduced at the age of nine by the games master (an experience he described as giving 'immediate and unalloyed pleasure') and went on to join the army. Following his National Service, Raven attended King's College, Cambridge to read English. Raven later returned to the army but was asked to resign rather than face a court-martial for 'conduct unbecoming'. It was at this point that he turned his focus to writing. The publisher Anthony Blond paid Raven to write and to move away from London to Deal, Kent. His works span a multitude of genres including fiction, drama, essays, memoirs and screenplays. Simon Raven died in May 2001, having written his own epitaph: 'He shared his bottle – and, when still young and appetising, his bed.'

OTHER WORKS BY SIMON RAVEN

Novels

The Feathers of Death
Brother Cain
Doctors Wear Scarlet
Close of Play
The Roses of Picardie
An Inch of Fortune
September Castle
The Troubadour

Alms for Oblivion sequence

The Rich Pay Late
Friends in Low Places
The Sabre Squadron
Fielding Gray
The Judas Boy
Places Where They Sing
Sound the Retreat
Come Like Shadows
Bring Forth the Body
The Survivors

Belles-Lettres

The English Gentleman
Boys Will Be Boys
The Fortunes of Fingel
The Old School

Plays

*Royal Foundation and
Other Plays*

Autobiography

Shadows on the Grass
The Old Gang
Bird of Ill Omen
Is There Anybody There?
Said the Traveller

First Born of Egypt sequence

Morning Star
The Face of the Waters
Before the Cock Crow
New Seed For Old
Blood of my Bone
In the Image of God

SIMON RAVEN

Alms For Oblivion

Volume I

The Rich Pay Late
Friends in Low Places
The Sabre Squadron
Fielding Gray

VINTAGE BOOKS
London

Published by Vintage 2012

2 4 6 8 10 9 7 5 3 1

The Rich Pay Late
First published in Great Britain by Anthony Blond Ltd in 1964
Copyright © Simon Raven 1964

Friends in Low Places
First published in Great Britain by Anthony Blond Ltd in 1965
Copyright © Simon Raven 1965

The Sabre Squadron
First published in Great Britain by Anthony Blond Ltd in 1966
Copyright © Simon Raven 1966

Fielding Gray
First published in Great Britain by Anthony Blond Ltd in 1967
Copyright © Simon Raven 1967

First published by Vintage in 1998

Vintage
Random House, 20 Vauxhall Bridge Road,
London SW1V 2SA

www.vintage-classics.info

Addresses for companies within The Random House Group Limited
can be found at: www.randomhouse.co.uk/offices.htm

The Random House Group Limited Reg. No. 954009

A CIP catalogue record for this book
is available from the British Library

ISBN 9780099561323

The Random House Group Limited supports The Forest Stewardship
Council (FSC®), the leading international forest certification organisation.
Our books carrying the FSC label are printed on FSC® certified paper.
FSC is the only forest certification scheme endorsed by the leading
environmental organisations, including Greenpeace.
Our paper procurement policy can be found at:
www.randomhouse.co.uk/environment

Printed and bound in Great Britain by Clays Ltd, St Ives Plc

Contents

THE RICH
PAY LATE

Part One

1

'That's all very well, my dear,' said Donald Salinger; 'but we should need money. At least seventy thousand, I'd say.'

Jude Holbrook pursed his lips, passed a comb quickly through his hair, and walked over to the window. A thick yellow fog was settling into Chancery Lane for the night like a cat into its basket. The lights from the windows opposite shone as from a far country; there was neither sight nor sound of the street below.

'We could find seventy thousand,' Jude Holbrook said.

'You mean, my dear, that *I* could find seventy thousand.'

'No, I don't,' said Holbrook, turning peevishly from the window. 'I mean that we, this firm, could easily find, say, fifteen thousand in cash and offer excellent security for the rest.'

He gestured round the dingy office as though it had been a palace.

'We don't even *own* –'

'– But we do own the printing works and the plant.'

'We're still paying for it.'

'Nevertheless –'

'– My dear Jude,' said Salinger, gently reproving. 'After six years we are within sight, no more, of stabilizing our position. Salinger & Holbrook are now known and respected for their reliable printing and distribution of high quality advertising material. But although substantial orders are beginning to come in –'

'– Troy Cinemas are worth at least three hundred a week, and when Tanner & Tanner give us their stuff –'

'– *If* Tanner & Tanner give us their custom, we are still in no position to stretch ourselves. We must consolidate. Finish paying for the plant, assess what regular income we may depend on, and then, and only then, consider how far we can afford to expand.'

Holbrook flicked finger and thumb very quickly several times.

'You don't understand, Donald. These days one must expand, expand all the time, or die. We can't *wait* to consolidate or count the cost, because if we do someone else will jump in ahead of us. We must have faith – faith in our future.'

'We must also have money.'

'Where there is faith, and the energy to proclaim it, money always follows. You're taking just the kind of attitude you took six years ago. Where's the money to come from, you said; we mustn't go too fast, you said; what about the bank, who'll give us contracts, the *accountant's* having a *fit* in the *lavatory* . . . If it hadn't been for me, we'd never have got off the ground at all.'

'If it hadn't been for *my* money –'

A middle-aged and shrewish woman with a shawl over her shoulders opened the door without knocking and said:

'Letters, Mr. Salinger. You too, Mr. Holbrook.'

'In a few minutes, Miss Beatty,' said Holbrook waving her out.

'I want to get them signed and posted. There's a fog outside in case you hadn't noticed.'

'*In a few minutes*,' Holbrook snarled, and came towards her as if to put her out by force. Miss Beatty gave a shrug of resentment and slammed the door.

'Never keep staff that way,' said Salinger smugly.

'You leave the staff to me. Now listen, Donald, and then for God's sake do some thinking over the weekend. Salinger & Holbrook now has a definite and growing reputation. It is therefore high time to expand. Now, this magazine I've been telling you of –'

'That's just it,' said Salinger: 'why a magazine? We're not publishers. Our business is to print and distribute the advertising material sent to us for an agreed fee. Magazines are speculative ventures and generally lose money.'

'Not this one. *Strix* is not really a magazine. It is a serious journal of industry and commerce, with a circulation which has risen steadily since it was started nine months ago.'

'But what do *we* want with it?'

'Let me spell it out to you once more. A and one, we could print and distribute it ourselves, thus saving money in publication and increasing profit. B and two, we could let it be known that advertisers who employ us to prepare their stuff would be sure of advantageous rates in *Strix*.'

'Is that such an inducement? Now, if it were *The Sunday Express* –'

'– For Christ's sake,' said Holbrook twitching with temper: '*Strix* is a high-class journal of commerce and is therefore a good place for prestige advertising which will draw attention in the right commercial circles. And this brings us to the most important point: C and three, if we own *Strix*, we shall be in a position to propose and influence policy. Quietly and tactfully but with increasing pressure we can emphasize, we can even initiate, business trends that will prove to our own advantage.'

Salinger's look changed from patronizing amusement to mild dismay. He removed his spectacles with great care, blinked pathetically, and started to polish the lenses with a damp looking handkerchief.

'Is that ... er ... ethical?' he inquired.

'You're not going to be priggish on top of everything else?'

'Even supposing I'm not, *why Strix*? There are other journals, trade papers, which –'

'– Because *Strix* enjoys intellectual prestige and therefore gives first rate cover for what we intend.'

'We?'

'And because there is a way in. It is edited by your chum Somerset Lloyd-James.'

'Is it now?' said Salinger, who knew this perfectly well. He replaced his glasses, which were now smeared with mucus, and manfully assumed what he liked to think was the cautious but enlightened manner of one born to high responsibility which only conscience forbade him abrogate as modesty suggested. In fact, he was beginning to be badly put out: why did Holbrook want to raise such an issue at 4.30 on a Friday, and this Friday of all? Scepticism was now replaced by apprehension, the apprehension of an ageing and privileged hen who fears, in time of scarcity, lest she may after all be marked for the pot.

'You're . . . you're quite serious, Jude?' he said. 'I mean about using this . . . *Strix* . . . to . . . er . . . *apply pressures?*'

'I was never more serious in my life.'

Ambition, reflected Salinger crossly, as Holbrook launched into yet another appraisal of the possibilities of *Strix*. Something of the kind had always threatened, as he had known from the beginning, and if he'd had any sense he'd have been prepared for it, ready to stamp on it the moment it appeared, instead of sitting on his bottom prevaricating when all he wanted to do was collect Vanessa Drew and get out of London for the weekend. What a pity Holbrook hadn't raised his scheme a year, even six months, before; because then he could have said straight away and with absolute conviction that there was no question of risking more money or in any way committing the firm beyond its day to day struggle to exist. But now, as they both knew, things were different; after six years hard they had suddenly begun to see the fruit of their labour. Their debts and mortgages, always adequately secured, were now almost paid off; they were making good money and receiving new orders on the strength of a growing reputation for prompt and accurate work; they had cash in the bank and a bank manager ready and eager to lend them a great deal more.

And of course he had Holbrook to thank for this. When in 1949, they had come down from Oxford, Holbrook had suggested that an alliance of Salinger's money with his own energetic taste for business might prove profitable to both of them. At first Salinger had hedged, but later on, guilty at having no occupation and resentfully conscious that a third class degree in English would not qualify him for any professional career worth the name, he had accepted Holbrook's proposition. He would arrange for money and guarantees amounting to £50,000 over four years, and would sit in the best office with dignity and hold a watching brief: Holbrook, with whom all profit was to be shared fifty-fifty, would do the rest.

As indeed Holbrook had. From a tatty office in Bayswater and a single contract for the advertisements of a small chain of cinemas they had graduated, *via* Chelsea and Soho, to two floors in Chancery Lane and a staff of nine in the office alone – most of whom, although the odd survivors from early days (like Miss Beatty) did not have quite the tone now required, were young, trim and quick-witted. The mean little cinema circuit which they served in 1949 had grown into a screen empire for which they now displayed luscious posters over half England; and this was only one of several advertising projects for the conduct of which they were responsible and the material for all of which was produced in a small but streamlined printing works of which they themselves now enjoyed almost unencumbered ownership. It was a proud achievement – if only, thought Donald Salinger, Jude would just give us time to enjoy it.

But no. No sooner had they finished one climb than Jude Holbrook was proposing the next. Instead of taking his ease on a comparative eminence and admiring the coloured counties below him, Donald was being nagged on to the next gradient. Saddle the mules, onwards and upwards . . . and of course at increasing expense. Yet he knew very well, and Holbrook knew that he knew, that they could bear the expense – and the more easily as the death of Donald's mother four months previously had transformed him from a middling rich young man to a definitely wealthy one. This had enabled him not only to buy a house in the country and to procure for himself full membership of Lloyd's but also to make available, putatively at least, funds for the immediate consolidation of the firm. He could have paid off the small loans still outstanding tomorrow if he'd wanted to, and saved paying interest by so doing; what prevented him was a temperamental preference for proceeding slowly, a wish, almost a need, to relish at leisure the final stages whereby a hazardous undertaking was being brought to a safe conclusion.

It was just this pleasure which Holbrook was now spoiling. A

bit of peace and quiet in which to gloat and congratulate one-
self: this – he might have known it, indeed always had really
known it – was exactly what the restless and greedy Holbrook
would never allow. 'Expand or die': Donald wanted to expand
all right – for three months in the Mediterranean sun with
Vanessa Drew by his side.

'Are you listening, Donald?' came Holbrook's sharp, insis-
tent, rather common voice. ('My dear,' Jonathan Gamp had
said to Donald only the other day, 'are you *sure* he was at
Winchester?')

'Yes, Jude. I'm listening.'

'Well then. To sum up . . . *Strix* means profit in itself, it
means a cheap way of conferring a bonus on clients and so
attracting new ones, and it means a prestige organ for putting
across whatever we want to put across. There's a man on the
spot – Somerset Lloyd-James – who's known to you. And the
price, for what we'd be getting, is not a heavy one. *Not yet.* But
Strix is gaining ground, and the price therefore rising, with
every minute that passes.'

'Seventy thousand is already quite enough . . . Anyway, what
makes you think they'd be interested in an offer if they're
doing so well?'

'Young Philby, the new proprietor. They tell me he's more
interested in ready cash than anything else. A tactful approach
– through your chum Lloyd-James - and he'd off-load quick
enough. A nice hunk of lolly – and to hell with daddy's dreary
old paper and a few measly hundred at a time.'

'I wonder the old man didn't tie things up a bit tighter. . . .'

'*Strix* was only a side-line, a hobby for his old age. The big
stuff's sewn up good and close, don't you worry. Which is just
why his little lordship will be glad to sell anything he can sell
when he starts running short of sweeties.'

'And is he . . . running short of sweeties?'

'The rate he's going he must be. And he's got trustees as
tough as rhino hide. Not a penny of principal will they let him
pinch.'

'Well, I'll think about it, Jude. But now I must sign my

letters and go, because Vanessa –'

'– Never mind Vanessa for a few minutes. Not only must you think about it, Donald, you must get ready to –'

There was an off-hand knock, after which a round and querulous face of indeterminate sex appeared through the door.

'Come in, Ashley,' said Donald quickly and hopefully. 'I'm just off, but if there's anything –'

'It's Jude I want,' said the face. A yellow sweater and green corduroy trousers followed it through the door, arousing a presumption, no more, that it was masculine.

'Not now, Ashley,' said Holbrook, quivering, clenching and unclenching his fists.

'It won't take a moment, boy. These designs that Marjoram and Tape have sent in for their tooth-paste campaign. *They are hideous*. Can I send them back for revision?'

'No,' said Holbrook, as sharp and nasty as a cap-pistol, watching Donald slyly press the bell for Miss Beatty. 'I've told you a thousand times. Our job is reproduction and distribution. Let the clients or their agencies send in whatever copy or designs they choose. It's no business of ours if it's crap.'

'But if the campaign flops –'

'– It'll be their fault. We shall have done, and be *known* to have done, what we are *paid* to do, which is to print the stuff and stick it up where we're told.'

Miss Beatty came po-faced through the door and made for Donald's desk with a pile of typed letters.

'But Jude. I cannot make a decent job of this. Look.'

Ashley thrust in front of Holbrook a crude drawing of a girl in early adolescence who was brushing her teeth in an unbuttoned pyjama jacket, thereby revealing half each of two copious breasts and somehow suggesting that she wasn't wearing trousers.

'What's the matter with that?'

'Twenty-five-year-old breasts under a twelve-year-old face. That's what's the matter with that.'

'We are not required to be anatomical experts.'

'Taste –'

'– Nor are we custodians of taste.'

'It will look damned ridiculous and *we* shall be blamed.'

'If you ask me,' said Holbrook with cold fury, 'every normal male in this country between eight and eighty will get a bloody great rise the moment he looks at it. Which is presumably what Marjoram want. Just because your own tastes –'

'– Let's not be spiteful, Jude.'

'Let's not make difficulties, Ashley. Adjust those dugs a bit, if you really must, but get that thing lined up for the works by first thing Monday.'

Donald, who had been signing away hysterically at his desk, now rose and tip-toed quietly towards the door.

'Just a minute, Donald, *if you please*. All right, Miss Beatty, I'll be along to sign mine later. Remember, Ashley: Monday.'

Miss Beatty and Ashley shrugged in concert and withdrew. Donald turned ingratiatingly to his partner.

'Jude dear, Vanessa will be waiting.'

'Before you go, I want you to promise that you will not let this chance slip.'

'But is it such a chance? After all, Somerset is only the editor. He may have no pull with Philby at all. And there's bound to be some kind of board to cope with.'

'From what I hear, Somerset Lloyd-James is a man people listen to. They may not like him much, but they listen.'

'And the money?'

'Take away the fifty thousand you put up at the start, and half of everything this firm is worth is mine. Right?'

'I suppose so.'

'You know bloody well so. Then don't tell me that we can't raise thirty-five thousand each.'

'It's too much for safety.'

'*Safety*.'

Vanessa. No one became so readily impatient. God, God, would there be no end to it? He must yield something or Holbrook would never let him go. Reconciling haste with prudence, Donald said:

'I'm prepared to agree that the firm find forty thousand. The other thirty must be raised from outside – fifteen thousand by each of us.'

That'll do you, he thought. Even if this preposterous paper is for sale, you couldn't find fifteen hundred outside your interest in this firm. And that you can't cash up on or dispose of without my agreement.

'All right,' said Holbrook casually.

'You'll find fifteen thousand from outside then?' said Donald, winded slightly. '*If* the paper's in the market, of course.'

'The paper will be in the market, Donald, and I shall find fifteen thousand from outside.'

'Just one more thing,' said Donald, deciding to assert himself before he left but being uncertain quite how. 'I'd be grateful if you'd be nicer to Ashley Dexterside. It's bad enough when you're rude to an old employee like Miss Beatty, but it's worse with Ashley, who's an old friend. That kind of thing, you know, is just not done.'

'Balls,' said Holbrook, and left the room without farewell.

Donald sighed, shrugged, put on his British Warm, his blue silk scarf with white spots and his bowler hat, took up his umbrella and his brief-case, put his brief-case down again as being unwanted until Monday, checked his face for pimples in a hand mirror, stuck his bottom firmly out behind him, and started down the narrow staircase to the street. Would Vanessa have got tired of waiting? And supposing she had? She could hardly have made new plans for the weekend in the last half hour, particularly as she hadn't got a telephone. Come to that, if she *had* got a telephone he could have rung her up and reassured her, so it was her own fault if she was worried. Worried? But that was the trouble with Vanessa: she never got worried, not about him at any rate, she just went off and did something else. With somebody else. Ten to one, if she'd got bored with his non-appearance, she'd have picked up a head scarf and taken the first taxi she could find to the first of her friends whose name came into her head. It might be a man and

it might be a woman, and she might stay with whoever it was
anything from three seconds to three weeks. It was most unsatisfactory, most improper: she had no adult sense of how to conduct a relationship and didn't care whom she hurt. He must
either put a stop to the whole thing or Vanessa must toe the
line. One must be firm. He imagined himself proceeding down
the steps to Vanessa's basement to find, as so often, a locked
door, darkness and desertion, and for a moment he became so
sick with misery that he almost had to sit down on the stairs.
But no. One must be firm. If she was not there, this time was
the last; if the little bitch could not treat him (not to mention
his money) with proper respect, then she deserved to lose him.
(But could he bear it? Firm, Donald, firm.)

   Emerging into the fog, Donald was somewhat reassured.
Vanessa must realize that on such a night no one could be
punctual – and would surely think twice before going out herself. But here was another problem which, because of Jude's
thoughtless behaviour, had not yet received proper attention.
What were they going to do for the weekend? The plan had
been to drive down to Chevenix Court, his new house in the
country, stopping for dinner on the way. But in this? He could
hardly see three yards in front of him, cars were crawling down
Chancery Lane like wounded rats, it would take at least three
quarters of an hour to drive to Vanessa, it would be torture getting out of London, it might be even worse when they did, oh
God, God, November in London, why weren't they in Rome or
Athens or Beirut? (No, not Athens, the food was really too disgusting.) Steady, think. As always in moments of agitation,
Donald's left knee quivered and sweat broke out beneath his
buttocks. Now then. Leave the car for the night, take a tube
train to Earl's Court, go to Vanessa and say, 'Let's spend the
night in London and drive down in the morning if it's better.
We'll stay Sunday night to make up.' Obvious good sense; but
then Vanessa, who would change her own plans for anyone
else's at the drop of a silk stocking, hated change when it was
suggested by others. Well, she'd just have to put up with it.
Donald started up Chancery Lane towards the Underground

Station. If she made a scene it would be the last. Always assuming, of course, that she was there at all. Oh God. But surely . . . in this fog? She'd be huddled over the electric fire thinking, 'Thank God I'm safe in the warm, I do hope Donald's all right.' No she wouldn't. She'd be thinking, 'If Donald's not here in five minutes, I'll walk round the corner to Jonathan Gamp. He may be queer but he's always glad of a quick blow.' That's what she'd be thinking, the dirty slut. Oh Vanessa, Vanessa, your thin legs, your little breasts, your thighs: your firm boy's thighs. This really would not do. Frantic with lust and anxiety, Donald stumbled down the steps into Chancery Lane Station (have to change at least once, hell). Whether or not Vanessa was there, something must be decided (no small change, queue, hell), yes, something must be decided for good. Black hair, brown eyes; thin legs, boy's thighs: Vanessa, oh Vanessa; Vanessa Drew.

After Jude Holbrook had walked from Donald's office to his own (smaller but twice as comfortable) he thought of four things. First, and very briefly, of Vanessa Drew, with whom he, like almost everyone else he knew, had conducted a spasmodic affair over the last three years: which was to say that whenever he met her at a party he tried to manoeuvre her into the bathroom for ten minutes and was usually, provided she hadn't been manoeuvred there by someone else within the last half-hour, successful. Donald, typically, had been the last of all his friends to catch on to the amenities which Vanessa offered; and having done so was now, equally typically, taking her with deadly seriousness and getting possessive about her curriculum. Which, thought Holbrook, would be uphill work for Donald, a novelty for Vanessa, and a bore (should Donald succeed in inhibiting her) for all her old acquaintances.

Secondly, he thought about his wife and son. Little Donny (Salinger's godson) was beginning, at four, to be pert, pretty and interesting; while Penelope, after four years of marriage, was vainer, duller and, despite the money she made as a model, greedier than she had ever been. It was high time to get rid of her, a proceeding which her persistent and open infidelities would make very easy: he was simply waiting until she did something so gross that he himself would be awarded care of Donny, even in the unlikely event of Penelope wishing to keep the boy. Having allowed two minutes for these and similar sentiments, he telephoned his flat and told the German girl who had current charge of Donny to inform Mrs. Holbrook that he must be away for the weekend on an unexpected matter of business. The German girl seemed distressed to hear this, and it emerged that Donny had been talking the whole day of his father's promise to take him to the Round Pond on Saturday. Wincing slightly, Holbrook asked for Donny to be put on the line. The other end was all confusion and heavy breathing; then a shy little voice,

'Daddy?'

'Hullo, Donny. Look, old chap. Daddy's got something very important to see to. Something sudden, which must be done tomorrow. It can't be helped. You do understand, don't you?'

'Daddy?'

'Yes, Donny?'

'When can we go to the Round Pond?'

'I expect Fraulein . . . Fraulein . . . er will take you.'

'I meant me and you. Can we go tomorrow?'

'You haven't understood, Donny. Daddy's very busy tomorrow, something sudden –'

'– Too busy to take me to the Round Pond?'

'Yes, I'm afraid so . . . No, God damn it all, of course I'll take you tomorrow. I'll be back for lunch, Donny, and we'll go immediately after. Got your boat all ready?'

'Yes, yes, Daddy, yes.'

'See you tomorrow at lunch then. I'm looking forward to it, Donny, really looking forward to it. . . .'

Having apprised Fraulein . . . er of the new arrangement, Holbrook started to think, thirdly, of Angela Tuck, who was going to be very put out by this interruption of their weekend. However, since Miss Beatty now appeared with his letters he decided to play that one off the cuff. Utterly dismissing both Donny and Angela, he passed his comb through his hair and

turned to a swift but ruthless examination of the letters before
him. After he had signed six and told Miss Beatty to take three
more away for alteration, Holbrook thought, fourthly and
finally, about money.

Fifteen thousand pounds. He himself couldn't, his bank
wouldn't . . . or would it? 'Of course you realize, Mr. Sangster,
that half of Salinger & Holbrook is mine. For obvious reasons
I don't want to sell out, but as security?' 'Possibly, Mr.
Holbrook. But presumably you have some form of agreement
with Mr. Salinger, whereby you can only sell your share of the
firm with his consent?' 'Yes.' 'Then by the same token we
should require his agreement before accepting it as security.
. . .' No. Not the bank. A lending house? Bigger interest, same
objection. There was only one thing for it. It was high time his
father handed over some money, if only as a precaution
against death duties, and now at last his father must be made
to realize this. Holbrook senior had been sitting on his inherited capital for the last twenty years, allowing it to decline
amidst opportunities enough to treble it, and now at last he
must be made to realize that equity, duty, common prudence
required that he assist his son – who had not had a penny from
him since the last instalment of the meagre allowance he was
paid at Oxford. Yes; but *how* to make him realize this? Fifteen
thousand pounds represented perhaps a quarter of what the
old man was worth; and when Holbrook had suggested, six
years before, that even two thousand pounds would help him
to get started, he was bluntly told that he had received a first-
rate education and could expect nothing more. His father had
some curious idea that he was going to live for ever: 'It's my
money,' he had said, 'and I'm going to need it all. You've got
your youth.' There was no reason to suppose – quite the contrary from what little Holbrook had seen of him – that six
years had made any change in this attitude.

Then how? Play on the old man's greed? Tell him the money
would only be a loan and would bring in a substantial profit?
But Holbrook senior, though occasionally duped by the flattery
of plausible strangers (he had once lent a man £2,000 to play

an 'infallible' roulette system), was eminently mistrustful of his own flesh and blood. So how? There was only one possible way: through his mother. In financial matters, Holbrook père mistrusted his wife as much as he did any of his relations, but he was dependent on her to organize his home, to prop his dubious health, to administer strong drink in quantities which would comfort yet not kill. Without her guidance and control the old man would be dead in a year – and knew it. If she insisted that he give his son money, he would curse her for a fool and give. But would she insist? His mother had an inborn contempt of all business matters; the daughter of a Professor of Latin in a Northern University, she regarded commercial profit, not as morally or socially wrong, but as unmentionable, aesthetically loathsome. She loved her son, and if he needed money to save him from disgrace, she would doubtless procure it; but if asked to finance a business venture she would turn away with a pained smile, just as she had when he first told her about Salinger & Holbrook, and talk of something else. Very well; his course was quite plain; he must simply tell his mother that he must have £15,000 because he would go to prison if he didn't. If people would adopt such silly and unworldly attitudes, if they wouldn't listen to common sense, then one must manage them how one might.

As Holbrook contemplated, with some annoyance, the visit to his parents which this scheme would necessitate, Miss Beatty came in with the amended letters. Once again, while Miss Beatty regarded him wolfishly from the other side of his desk, he read them through meticulously.

'"If it *were* possible",' he said, rapping the bottom sheet, 'not, "if it was". But I don't suppose Messrs. Carghill's chief draughtsman worries much about subjunctives, so we'll let it go. Time to let you go too, Miss Beatty. Sorry to have kept you so late.'

'That's all right, Mr. Holbrook. I'll just get those into the post.'

Holbrook handed her the signed letters and gave her what Jonathan Gamp used to call his 'fallen angel' smile.

'I hope you've not been anxious because of the fog.'

'Anything to oblige *you*, Mr. Holbrook. After all these years. You see, I don't have a very exciting home life, so all this has been rather an adventure for me. Starting in that horrible little office at Bayswater . . . and now *this*.'

'And it won't stop at this, Miss Beatty.'

'I'm sure I hope not.' She giggled coquettishly. 'And I want you to know that I never mind when you're a bit sharp with me, because I realize the pressure you're under . . . and, if I may say so, that you don't get . . . all the help . . . which you might expect.'

'I'll be all right so long as I've got you, Miss Beatty. Good night.'

'Good night, sir,' said Miss Beatty, blushing with pleasure.

What Donald doesn't realize, thought Holbrook as he reached for his camel-hair coat, is that he is so consistently polite to them all that he bores them to death. But push 'em about a bit, shout and make drama, and they know that it's for real and they're a part of it. That woman enjoys her work because there's change, excitement, even violence. She'll go back and tell her old mother, 'Mr. Holbrook threw me out of Mr. Salinger's office this afternoon, but he was awfully sweet later on. There's something up there, I wouldn't wonder.' So she'll hardly be able to wait for Monday, to see what happens next. Not that anything much will, but the last trump wouldn't keep her from the office. Whereas if it were just poor old Donald, she'd stay away a week every time she got the curse.

He ran down the stairs, immediately spotted the only free taxi within a radius of a mile, and gave the driver Angela Tuck's address in Holland Park.

There he goes, said Miss Beatty to herself as she sealed the last of the letters. If only he wanted me, I'd lie down for him in the corridor. I wonder what he's really like. Kisses fierce and hirsute? But a tender tongue? This won't do, Beatty. Lock up for the weekend and go home. Home to Mother . . . But can I trust him? Donald Salinger, he's soft, yet you know where you are with him. But Jude . . . ah, Jude . . . if it served his turn he'd throw you out like an old sock. If Donald would let him. A good thing Donald's here, really. I wonder what *he's* really like. Rather dainty . . . shy . . . nervous and slow? More dependable and nicer, giving you time to breathe? But I know which I'd choose.

Ashley Dexterside, in duffle-coat and fur-lined suede boots, paused on the pavement, wondered which of six possible bars to go to, and decided on the Cavalier, where he could cash a cheque. Which reminded him. He must talk to Donald and Jude about his promised increase in salary – promised last March and unmentioned since. He was about to indulge his favourite pastime, which was conducting imaginary dialogues, bitter and contemptuous, with his grovelling employers, when someone bumped into his back. Miss Beatty.

'Good night, dear.' You putrid old cow.

'Good night, Mr. Dexterside.' You nasty little faggot. All the same, I wonder what *you're* really like. Dirty underwear, *I'd* say.

2

At about this time, in a house at the far end of Gower Street, Somerset Lloyd-James, a bald and spotty young man of twenty-seven winters, was correcting the galleys of next week's issue of *Strix*. The internal telephone, ringing to announce the arrival of Tom Llewyllyn, gave no pleasure at all; but before the receptionist could be instructed to turn Tom off, the door opened to reveal a cascade of dripping curls on top of a decomposing mack.

'Books, dear. Booooooks.'

'I told you on the telephone yesterday, Tom. At the moment there's nothing for you to review.'

'Anything'll do. War, travel, adventure, how to succeed as a royal mistress without really trying –'

'– Tom. The limited review section in this journal comprises books about economics, commerce and industry, and occasionally political or sociological works which have some bearing on the above.'

'Righty-oh. Bung over the latest load of bollocks about the expanding economy. Tom Llewyllyn, all-purpose intellectual, at your service. Turn knob to indicate amount required, then press button for instant high-quality copy.'

'Everything I want done for the next three weeks has already gone.'

'What's the matter?' said Tom huffily, and sat down, still in his mack, on a pile of corrected galleys. 'Didn't you like my last bit?'

'Very much. Would you please take that revolting garment off my proofs?'

'Well then?' said Tom, handing Somerset the galleys, which had already been badly affected by the mackintosh.

'It's just that I need some serious and substantial pieces,'

Lloyd-James said. 'Yours tend to flippancy, which in these circles is not always acceptable.'

'What you mean is that I take the piss out of money, which offends all the pompous businessmen.'

'Partly. And I've got my board to cope with.'

'But now the old man's dead? Don't tell me young Philby gives a damn.'

'Apart from Lord Philby, there are three others on the board . . . or will be when we've filled the vacancy.'

'And they don't like my stuff?'

'They don't like your tone to predominate. I'll have more for you to do, Tom. But not for a few weeks.'

'I see.' Tom took off his mackintosh and arranged it, with the help of two chairs, into a kind of tent over the electric fire. 'Listen, love,' he said. 'I am broke. B-R-O-K-E. I owe Tessie for God knows how long in rent, and the poor old bag is getting bothered. She's got a new accountant who comes in every day to tell her to throw me out. She's been dead loyal, bless her rotten old heart, but I must give her some money *soon*. So if you can't give me work, give me a pile of this muck' – he indicated the dusty, reproachful left-overs stacked round the room – 'and I'll flog 'em to Gaston for what I can get.'

'Sorry, Tom.'

'But this is all old stuff. You're not going to review any of it now.'

'I have to keep a strict record. At the end of the financial year all unreviewed books will be sold *en bloc* and the proceeds sent to the accounts department for banking.'

'Mean hounds. They might at least give the staff a cut. *The Listener* does.'

'Lord Philby – *old* Philby – didn't believe in gratuities.'

There was a silence, during which Tom sniffed the fumes rising from his mack and Lloyd-James returned pointedly to his proofs.

'What am I to do, Somerset?' said Tom at last.

'Sell your car?'

'Uneconomic. It's a fair running proposition – by my

standards – but no one would pay me twenty quid. Anyhow, I'm fond of the old thing.'

'Will Stern give you any more on your book?'

'I'm three months behind with the revised typescript. Lucky if it's finished by Christmas.'

'And the last one?'

'Had every penny. Lend me some money, love. Please.'

'I don't lend money, Tom.'

All the same, he thought, there is an exception to every rule. Tom was already putting on his mackintosh, but Lloyd-James signed to him to sit and under the pretence of consulting his review-schedule took thirty seconds to think. Tom's first book, a political novel published four years previously, while garish and extravagant, had yet enjoyed high critical favour as well as substantial sales – so substantial as to keep even Tom in drink and women until about six months ago. The second book, a project upon which time, research and publisher's money had been lavished for the last three years, was to be a history of Communist expansion since 1945; and granted the combination of sales and serious acclaim which the first had achieved, the auguries were clearly set for a popular prestige success of a kind which might go into ample American and foreign editions. It was common talk that Gregory Stern, the publisher, was preparing to mount a lavish publicity campaign just as soon as he had received Tom's final typescript, against the delivery of which he was deliberately keeping Tom short of funds. Which, things being so, now was the time to buy in at a low price.

'Tom. This book of yours. I could be interested.'

'If you want to serialize it, I'm afraid you'll have to deal with Stern. In which case he'd hang on to the cash against advances already iss –'

'– Not for *Strix*, it's not quite our thing, but for myself.'

'Yourself?'

'A secured loan, Tom, I'll advance you £500, at the rate of £100 a month from now until March, against the promise to pay me half of every cheque you receive for the book when it's published.

'You old *Jew*.'

'The risk, Tom, is considerable. The book may never be published for all I know. And what with the advances you've already had, it'll be a long time before you see any royalties.'

£500, Lloyd-James reflected, was a big enough sum to tempt Tom in his present condition, while the method of spread payment would ensure against too prolonged and work-disrupting a celebration. All in all, he inclined to regard his offer as one of generous and enlightened patronage.

'It's enough,' he pursued slyly, 'to let you finish the book without worry and keep you comfortable for some time afterwards. As I say, I don't lend money; so look on this as the measure of my faith in your abilities.'

'You unctuous old extortioner.'

Tom grinned across the table at Somerset, who smiled sedately back.

'All right,' said Tom. 'Art for art's sake but money for God's sake. Can I have the first hundred in cash? No good putting it into my bank. It'd just dissolve on sight.'

'Open cheque?'

'Scrummy.'

'Then sign this.'

Tom signed without reading the succinct agreement which Somerset had already drawn and which confirmed his title to fifty per cent both of royalties and rights.

'You do bank in London?' he said as he signed. 'I'll need some cash tomorrow morning – I've got to visit my constituency.'

'Coutt's, Piccadilly . . . You're wasting your time down there, Tom. You can nurse that constituency for a hundred years; they'll never return a labour member.'

'If I do well at the next election they'll give me something more favourable.'

'You make a success of this book, and you'll have better things to think of.'

'I like politics. And I believe in Socialism.'

'Then you're about the only Socialist who still does. You

may like politics, Tom, but they're never going to like you.
You're at once too sincere and too disreputable. Stick to what
you're good at; I like to have confidence in my investments.'

'Next hundred on December one?'

'Come round here. I'll have some reviewing for you as well
by then. And now if you'll excuse me, Tom. . . .'

'Ta, Somerset. Night-night.'

When Tom left Somerset's office he hailed the first taxi he
saw, forgetting that apart from the cheque the only money he
had was a few coppers and a sixpence.

'Buttock's Hotel, please.'

'*Where*, guv.?'

'Buttock's Hotel. Cromwell Road – near the Natural
History Museum.'

On the whole, Tom thought, he had done a good afternoon's
work. It had always been his instinct to snatch at ready money
when it offered; and as Somerset said, he would now have
enough to finish his book without worry. (Only two chapters to
go, though the last, predicting possible trends for the future,
was very dicey and would need a lot of revision.) Privately, he
did not expect much in the way of sales – he was more interested in the reactions of the few informed critics he respected
– so he considered it unlikely that he would have to repay much
money to Somerset, despite the latter's extortionate terms. If,
on the other hand, he did strike lucky, then so long as the lolly
kept rolling in he would pay Somerset half and welcome. It was
not Tom's way to worry about the niggardly details; so long as
he could put his hand in his pocket without thinking twice. He
believed his finances to be entirely healthy, even if he was in
hock to every money-lender in London.

Tomorrow, he thought, that dreary constituency: so be it –
tonight pleasure. There was a new girl at the Tin Tack who was
worth every penny of the customary ten pounds, even if she did
keep on about her brother being an officer in the R.A.F. But of
course this programme would mean turning Somerset's
cheque into cash that very evening. Well, Tessie would just
have to lend him some on the strength of it. Thirty pounds

would do the trick – fifteen for the Tin Tack's disgusting
drinks, five for dinner first and general expenses, ten for
Norma or whatever the hell she was called. Then tomorrow he
would give Tessie back her thirty quid plus another fifty, which
would take care of the arrears and leave him paid up for the
next fortnight. That only left twenty – money seemed to melt
in one's hand – but he could always borrow a bit on the
strength of Somerset's next hundred.

The taxi drew up outside Buttock's Private Hotel. Tom felt
in his pocket, cursed softly, and told the driver to hang on. But
his luck was in: in the hall and as large as the bank was Tessie
Buttock, sitting on the fender in front of the open fire and
combing her terrier, Albert Edward.

'Tessie darling, I've got a hundred pounds.'

'Very nice too, dear,' said Tessie, blinking two huge watery
eyes behind her glasses; 'and I hope some of it's for me. Mr.
Jaffé the accountant says –'

'Fifty for you, Tessie. But there's a taxi outside waiting and
I need thirty quid to be going on with.'

'I thought you just said –'

'– A cheque, Tessie. I can't cash it till the morning.'

'Or ever, I dare say.'

'It's quite all right. It's Somerset Lloyd-James's.'

'And who might he be?'

'You know perfectly well.' As indeed she did, for Somerset's
family had been staying at Buttock's whenever they came to
London for the last forty years.

'Tell you what I'll do, dear,' Tessie intoned giving him a
shrewd look, 'I'll ask Albert Edward. Woozie, woozie,' she said,
kissing the repulsive brute on the nose. 'Woosums give
naughty Tom some money?'

She placed her ear to Albert Edward's mouth and listened
intently while he stuck his tongue into it.

'Albert Edward says we can give you twenty quid in cash,
dear, so long as you turn your cheque over to us now. That'll
put you square and nicely paid up for a while to come.'

'But, Tessie, I'll be needing some of it myself.'

'You'll have the twenty quid, won't you?'

'Yes, but –'

'– Suit yourself, dear. It's all one to us, isn't it, woosums, woosums.'

'Twenty-five in cash?'

'Twenty, dear. And don't forget to endorse the cheque.'

There was only one thing for it, thought Tom as Tessie waddled off to her office: Norma would have to take a cheque. Most girls at the Tin Tack did if you asked nicely. It would certainly bounce, but he could make it up later in cash. It was a long time since his bank had let him have a proper cheque book, but luckily he had been able to buy a book of elegant mauve cheque forms from a stationer who supplied them to smart restaurants. Surely Norma would not be able to resist a mauve cheque? The trouble was that even so he would now be out of cash by the morning. How was he to get down to his 'Constituency' in Kent?

Tessie came back with a pile of filthy ten shilling notes and a five pound bag of sixpences.

'Albert Edward says not to spend it all at once, dear.'

Tom kissed Tessie on the cheek (the conventional way of thanking her for such services), retched slightly and went to pay his driver. All right then, he thought, so I won't have enough money to go to Kent. I can send them a wire and say I'm ill. With this fog they can't expect much, and anyway Somerset's probably right: I'm wasting my time down there. But whatever the score I'm going to have another good go with Norma: it's been a long, hard day and I've earned it.

When Somerset had finished his proof-correcting, he walked to his bed-sitting room in Russell Square, paid his landlady, in cash, the four guineas he owed her for a week's lodging with breakfast, changed his clothes but washed only his face and hands, took from his selection of hats an elegant grey bowler, and caught a tube train from Goodge Street to the Strand. Thence he walked across Trafalgar Square, raised his hat as he passed Nelson's column, though little more than the pediment was visible in the fog, and proceeded down Pall Mall to the Infantry Club, where he was to dine as the guest of Peter Morrison, M.P., an old school friend with whom he used frequently to swap intelligence.

The Hall Porter told him that Mr. Morrison had telephoned earlier to express his regrets at being held up outside London by the fog, and would Somerset meanwhile join 'the other gentleman', who was waiting in the library? Somerset would, and discovered in the library Captain Detterling (also M.P., and also, though thirteen years older than Somerset, of his old school), one of the group of younger Tories among whom Morrison's influence was regarded as paramount. This group, which was just beginning to make a name for itself and to attract the attention of the press, had imprecise aims which might best be summed up in the words 'decency' and 'straight speaking'; it consisted mainly of country or professional gentlemen and tended to exclude the business element of the party as being unclean. Indeed, it had very nearly excluded Captain Detterling, who was connected with Lloyd's; but Lloyd's, after all, did not carry the stigma of most 'business', Detterling as a full member drew his money without ever going near the place, and his ten years' service as a regular officer had been allowed as a final and decisive factor in his favour. It was, as it happened, Morrison's distrust, not to say detestation, of the business members of his party which led him to consult Somerset whenever he wanted information on commercial or financial matters. Somerset was objective; though frankly interested in monetary processes, he did not make unctuous moral or patriotic claims on their behalf; and he could and did tell Morrison more about the real motives and machinations of the money-makers in ten minutes than they themselves would have disclosed in ten years.

Detterling was wearing a dinner jacket, in marked contrast to the tweed suit which Somerset had considered suitable for a club dinner on a Friday evening (on the ground that it hinted discreetly at a forthcoming country weekend). What was more invidious than their difference in attire was that Detterling appeared not to recognize him. True, they had only met twice, respectively ten and two years ago, but twice should have been enough when the person concerned, Somerset felt, was of Somerset's distinction.

'Good evening,' he said to Detterling; 'I think we've met.'

'Ten years ago,' said Detterling after some thought: 'on School Terrace after that Memorial Service.'

'You were wearing uniform with red trousers.'

'Cherry trousers.'

'But more recently too, I think.'

'Perhaps. I find that my memory works better these days at long distance. What happened then seems more worth remembering.'

'You're having dinner with Peter and me?'

'Yes. We want to consult you,' said Detterling rather primly, 'about property speculation. It seems to be getting popular.'

'You disapprove?'

'That I shall know better after we've heard what you have to say.'

'What shall you do if you should disapprove?'

'My dear – er – er –'

'– Lloyd-James –'

'– My dear Lloyd-James. Members of Parliament don't *do* anything, other than answer their constituents' foolish letters. They just make speeches . . . not even that, as a rule . . . *they give things to be understood*, after which their reputations are debited or credited according to the impression created.'

'It's rather the same,' Somerset said, 'with property speculators. Only their final credits are in money. Somewhere along the line a theoretical value is actually realized as hard cash.'

'Somebody else's hard cash,' said Detterling thoughtfully.

'In the same way as your pretty speeches, and the credit you earn for them, must be backed sooner or later by somebody else's hard deeds. Some wretched civil servant, probably.'

'But of course we get all the kicks if things go wrong. What happens to property dealers when things go wrong?'

'They go to prison for fraud,' Somerset said.

'Just where some of our chaps ought to be. For fraudulent
utterance of worthless words. . . . We met quite recently, you
say?'

'A party of Donald Salinger's. Two years ago.'

'You're a friend of Donald's?' said Detterling sceptically.

'His mother and mine were brought out together.'

'It's odd to think of anyone in Donald's family being brought
out. His father was – er – well, just *er*.'

'His mother was a Trench.'

'So that's why he bought Chevenix Court with her money?'

'I think,' said Somerset, 'that Father Salinger made most of
it. He may have been . . . *er* . . . but he was good at making
money.'

'How?'

'Old-fashioned and more reputable type of property speculation. Which is to say he bought within his means and so
didn't come unstuck if he had to sell short occasionally. He
was worth what he said he was worth.'

'They don't come like that these days, it seems . . . *Peter*. My
dear chap, I hope it's not been too frightful getting here.'

How fit Peter looks, thought Somerset enviously as
Morrison exchanged greetings with Detterling. Summer and
autumn in the country, that's what does it. Fresh air and exercise. Happily married too; regular and uncomplicated sex.

'My dear old Somerset,' Peter said: 'so what's the dirt from
Gower Street?'

'You name it, we've got it.'

'Property speculators?'

'I've just been telling Detterling here –'

'– Let's wait till we're settled. Dining room upstairs.'

It was typical of Peter Morrison that although he had provided a liberal dinner with plenty of wine he had not thought
it necessary to offer his guests a drink first. In the formal
aspects of his behaviour he belonged to an era sixty years gone
when everyone endured the half-hour before dinner without
even a glass of sherry to keep him going. In most other ways he
was an enlightened man: he was known, for example, to favour

independence for the remaining colonies and to have an
interest in the reform of the homosexuality laws, an interest
encouraged by the member of his group next prominent after
himself (a lawyer called Carton Weir) but regarded as politically premature by Detterling and others. The truth was – and
in this again he reverted to the nineteenth century – that
Morrison was a man of conscience and goodwill, a wealthy,
landed young man who conceived it his duty to take a part in
public life and there to advocate, without regard to the yapping of the Whips or protest from hide-bound constituents,
whatever he believed to be right. Flexible enough to compromise over most issues of opinion, he would never condone a
palpable falsehood or injustice; he was not a careerist politician but a gentleman assisting in the Councils of his Sovereign,
and he would accept promotion, should it come, in the same
modest and unambitious spirit as he would have accepted the
Presidency of his local cricket club. It was one of the things one
did, not without interest but with no calculation of personal
profit. The important thing was to do it with honour; and if
honour proved (as sooner or later these days it was most likely
to) an embarrassment to Party, then the only course would be
to show his contempt with a shrug and return to his Norfolk
fields.

From all of which the activities of his group were easily predictable. They were set against three things: the fudging of
issues to save ministerial or other faces; undue deference to
public opinion; and the dishonesty, back-biting and cringing of
those to whom politics were their chief livelihood. Morrison's
associates, in what was beginning to be called both with mockery and respect 'The Young England Group', were mostly
junior M.P.s of the same ample background as himself, men
with the 'clean' money which came from wide and prudently
managed acres. There were exceptions; Detterling was older
than most of them, Carton Weir poorer; but by and large, of
the two essential prerequisites of political integrity – youth
and private fortune – the Young Englanders enjoyed both.

It was Somerset's fancy to support this group in the pages

of *Strix*, hoping in turn for their friendship against the day when he himself would be seeking a Parliamentary seat. Since the group's indifference to political careers as such might assist its speedy dissolution, the gamble was manifest; but although at first sight it might seem odd in Somerset to court so small and volatile a faction, his reasons were well grounded. During the long period of Conservative rule which he now expected it seemed likely that elements of morality or endeavour would be few; any group, therefore, that had some claim to dedication would achieve notice out of all proper ratio to its importance, in which case the Prime Minister might think it wise to accord recognition and a few minor offices. In three or four years' time, which was when Somerset saw himself embarking into politics, his friends of 'the young England Group' might be so placed as to be very helpful indeed; so that now was the time for Somerset to get himself rated *persona grata* for discreet and reliable services of the kind which he was rendering at dinner this evening. He gave a clear exposition of the principles (or the lack of them) which lay behind some notorious recent deals, pointed out ethical objections and economic flaws, named some powerful and tainted names, and finally leaned back to drink his port with satisfaction and to receive thanks.

Detterling expressed his with restraint and rose to go.

'I'm sorry,' he said; 'but I have someone – er – waiting.'

'You know who?' said Somerset when Detterling was gone.

'Susan Grange?' Peter had a shrewd and uncensorious taste in gossip.

'So they say. And harmless enough. Little Lady Susan leads her men a dance, but she doesn't cling or make trouble when the dance is over. I'm glad he's gone in any case. I've got a proposition to put to you.'

'Oh?' said Peter, smiling in faint deprecation.

'There's a vacant place on the Board of *Strix*.'

'And so?'

'Let me explain. The Board consists of five people: the so-called proprietor, young Lord Philby, who has inherited a 70 per cent interest; the editor, who has his salary but otherwise no interest; and three members, each of whom enjoys a 10 per cent interest during tenure, but cannot, of course, touch the principal. In other words, if you joined the Board you'd get 10 per cent of the profits – which are small but growing – in return for your services.'

'And what would those be?'

'Basically, to attend a monthly meeting to consider the financial position of the paper and to express your opinions as to past performance and future policy.'

'To dictate to you, in fact?'

'To *discuss* with me. And the rest of the Board, of course.'

'And it would suit you to have a friend there?'

'Candidly, yes,' said Somerset smirking. 'His Lordship doesn't often come and I'm on reasonable terms with the other two, but it would be nice to see an old friend at the table.'

'How did the vacancy come about?'

'Resignation of General Peterson. Gaga.'

'I see,' said Peter thoughtfully; 'but it's hardly my thing, is it? I have no business interests and don't know the first thing about it all unless I ask you.'

'That's just the point. The articles drawn up in old Lord Philby's time provide that the editor and other members of the Board must be without any direct commercial or industrial commitments – must have no financial axe to grind. Otherwise they might try to use the paper to put their own stuff across.'

'I see. Like the *Spectator* not appointing anyone who holds political office?'

'Roughly, yes.'

'But the Philbys themselves have a financial axe to grind?'

'Yes. . . . But Insurance on that scale is so massive it's above suspicion. It's like running a bank – there's no need to start getting smart in a trade journal. Anyway, old Philby was the soul of integrity and young Philby doesn't give a twopenny curse so long as he gets his cash and isn't bothered. I might add that there are very strong provisions in the articles against the

Proprietorship passing into unsuitable hands. If Philby wanted to sell, you and I as members of the Board are bound, and are empowered, to prevent him selling to someone who might make undesirable use of the opportunities.'

'I'm not a member yet,' said Peter gently.

'Look, Peter. This is your chance to learn about these things, to get inside information without being involved or getting your hands dirty. I know you hate the money boys, but you of all people will need to learn their language and how to cope with them. *Strix* covers everything from economic theory to the disposal of reject golf balls.'

'And if I say "yes", what then?'

'I'll put your name forward at the board-meeting next week. Philby's in America, but three's a quorum, and I'm pretty sure I can carry the other two.'

'Who are they?'

'Both *ex officio*. Harry Dilkes, as secretary to the Institute for Political and Economic Studies, and Robert Constable, as Professor of Economics in the University of Salop – old Philby was a Shropshire lad. There are no strings about the third place, though a "respectable public figure" is recommended by the articles. We can certainly swing you as that.'

'Constable? I thought he was a Cambridge man. Lancaster, surely?'

'Was. He got this professorship two years back, and he's now Vice-Chancellor for good measure. A bit of an old boot, but listens carefully to reasons.'

Peter nodded his approval and lit a cheroot.

'I'll have to think about it,' he said. 'One way and the other I've got rather a lot on.'

'Of course. Can you let me know by Monday evening? The Board meets on Tuesday.'

You'll do it, Somerset thought. Simply because you don't know much about business you'll conceive it your duty to learn. You'll come in the spirit, half respectful and half condescending, of an officer under instruction. And you'll help us more than you know, you and your great round face. It will be very useful to have our man from Westminster on the Board, even if he does turn out a party rebel.

'It's been very pleasant,' he said aloud, 'but I must be off.'

At the Hall Porter's desk somebody was cashing a cheque with the furtive air of one who would not care to explain what he wanted, so late at night, with ready money.

'Good evening, Carton,' Peter said. 'Carton Weir, Somerset Lloyd-James.'

'How de do. Just getting some cash for an early start in the morning.'

'I hope the fog won't delay you,' said Somerset gravely.

'I like the fog,' Weir giggled nervously. 'Nice for hiding in, don't you know.'

He turned back to the Hall Porter. 'No, *not* fivers,' Somerset heard him whisper urgently.

'Carton was to have come to dinner with us,' said Peter when they were on the steps outside: 'he is what you might call my deputy. But it seems he had an unexpected and urgent engagement.'

They smiled at one another, Peter tolerantly, Somerset with an air of being fully informed on this particular point.

'Give Helen my regards,' Somerset said. 'She's in London?'

'Just for the weekend. Then back to the boys at Whereham. You must help me pass my bachelor evenings. . . .'

How little I know of Somerset after all this time, thought Peter Morrison as he walked down Whitehall towards his big, placid wife in his big, placid flat: fourteen years, and I still never know what's going on behind those crocodile eyes. This seat on his Board: who's doing a favour to whom?

How lucky Peter is to be so comfortably married, thought Somerset Lloyd-James as he walked up the Charing Cross Road. If Maisie gets there before I do, I hope she has the sense not to ring the bell. If she's *very* good tonight I'll give her three pounds ten instead of three.

Ashley Dexterside, waiting in St. James's Square in Carton Weir's car, thought to himself that if the silly old bag didn't

buck up and cash that cheque all the best guardsmen would
have been booked before they even got to the party.

When Donald Salinger finally reached Vanessa Drew's flat
it had been in pitch darkness. Sitting down on the area steps,
Donald had begun quietly snivelling, when suddenly, miracu-
lously, a light went on inside and Vanessa's torso, in a high-
necked sweater, appeared stretching and yawning at the
window. Donald gambolled across the area and clawed at the
door, which was crossly opened by Vanessa who was wearing
nothing at all other than the high-necked sweater.

Donald's first reaction was one of almost insane lust, his
next, which in no way qualified the first, one of jealousy and
anger.

'Do you often open the door looking like that?'

'If someone knocks on it when I've just got up.'

'You mean . . . you let anyone . . . *see* you?'

'And much good may it do them.'

'Vanessa. I think you should understand that when I enter
on a relationship there are certain standards –'

'– For Christ's sake shut up and take off that ridiculous hat.'

Donald took off his bowler, unbuttoned his British Warm
and sat down on Vanessa's grubby sofa, pressing his umbrella
down into the carpet at a rigid right-angle between straddled
knees.

'Stop staring at me,' Vanessa said.

'I can't help it. If only you'd make yourself decent. . . .'

'. . . Dirty-minded, that's your trouble. Better get going.'

She flicked her rump at him and disappeared into her so-
called bathroom.

'The fog's terrible,' he called after her: 'I had to leave the
car at Chancery Lane. If you don't mind, we'd better drive
down in the morning.'

'Not much good if I do mind since you haven't brought the
car.'

'It was hard to know what to do for the best.'

A wet face and two tiny breasts were thrust round the bathroom door.

'All right then. Here's the programme. First of all we'll do it, to stop you looking like a dirty old man in the park. Then we'll pick up Jonathan Gamp and go out to dinner. And then –'

'. . . Why Jonathan Gamp?'

'Because he makes me laugh. Then we'll go back to his flat.' She looked at Donald wide-eyed. 'He's got a wonderful white rug.'

'Vanessa. I will not be treated in this way. If you had any sensitivity at all you'd realize that my feeling for you –'

'Calm down. I won't be a tick . . . I'm just stuffing my thing up.'

'Do you have to be so crude?'

'All right. With the assistance of the lever and the pre-scribed lubricant I am now inserting my contraceptive device. Having made sure it is in position, I am now coming, with a modest but proud and loving look, to join my partner, who should receive me with gratitude and tenderness.'

Vanessa crawled across the room on hands and knees and laid her head in Donald's lap, her chin resting against the poised umbrella.

'Come on, old thing,' she said kindly: 'get undressed.'

'Oh, Vanessa,' Donald said: 'I do love you so much. Why must you make fun of me?'

'I'm not . . . now.'

'But as soon as it's over you'll start again. And then dinner. . . . And Jonathan or whoever happens to be there. . . .'

'Donald' – still kindly – 'you don't own me, you know.'

'The thought of you opening the door . . . like *that* . . . to any-one that comes along. It makes me feel so hopeless.'

'First your coat. . . . *That's* right. Now your jacket. . . .'

'I want you to myself, Vanessa. All to myself.'

'You're a bit late in the day for that.'

'Never mind the past. If, for the future, you'd . . . promise me . . . then I'd . . . I'd . . .'

'You'd what, Donald?'

And so it had come about that when Vanessa and Donald at

last went out to dinner they drank champagne to celebrate their engagement. They did not call on Jonathan Gamp, either before or after, and about the time that Somerset left Peter Morrison outside the Infantry Club they were walking hand in hand along the King's Road towards Donald's house in Cheyne Row, there to spend the night before driving down to Chevenix Court.

Miss Beatty took the empty cocoa cups and the plate of digestive biscuits into the kitchenette and then returned to her mother, who was gazing into the television screen as if demanding from it the secrets of the next world.

'Bed time, mother.'

'When it stops.'

Miss Beatty flicked a switch.

'There. It's stopped.'

'Funny how it always stops when you say it's bed time.'

Miss Beatty made no comment but turned the wheel chair briskly (it was surprising how little her mother weighed these days) and propelled it through the curtain into the little alcove where Mrs. Beatty slept. It soon became apparent that Mrs. Brett, who lived above and was paid ten shillings a day during the week to keep an eye on mother, had neglected her main duty, which was to give mother a thorough wash before tea. Miss Beatty sighed and fetched a basin of warm water: Mrs. Brett, though a good sort, was unreliable, and soon even Mrs. Brett would be gone from the house, so then who would there be? The only person she had interviewed so far wanted a pound a day to come in from nine to five; and even if she could afford the money the hours were too short. It needed someone in the same house, who could look in every half hour or so; but Mrs. Brett's little flat was going to a young man, a journalist or something, who would be out all day, and there was no one else she could think of. . . . There was only one thing for it, Miss Beatty decided, pulling the bed clothes over mother's flannelled form: mother would have to go into a government home. She knew her duty, she'd held out and kept mother with her as long as possible, no one could deny that, but now at last the position was hopeless and there was no good beating about the bush. She'd start inquiries on Monday; perhaps Mr. Holbrook would help. And with the flat to herself, and a little more money to spend . . . who could tell? Miss Beatty straddled luxuriously in front of the gas fire and let the heat work up her thighs. After all, mother hardly knew her any more, she would be well taken care of where she was going – that was why one paid all those taxes to have a welfare state – it was really the kindest thing. And with the flat to herself. . . .

'Why not come up to my place,' she heard herself saying incongruously, 'for a last little drink?'

'Whaaah?' from behind the curtains.

'Nothing, mother,' said Miss Beatty, thighs glowing, 'you go to sleep.'

'So what,' said Angela Tuck as the third bottle of champagne arrived, 'had you thought for tomorrow?'

Jude Holbrook pursed his lips.

'Anything you like in the evening,' he said, 'and anything all day Sunday. But tomorrow afternoon –'

'– *What* tomorrow afternoon?'

Under the blonde hair the sulky face became wary, the ingrown sexuality stiffened to possessive spite.

'Dance?' said Holbrook.

'*What* tomorrow afternoon?' she repeated.

'It seems I promised Donny, days ago, to take him to the Round Pond and sail his boat.'

Angela's face relaxed.

'Well, if it's only that. . . . You can just ring up and say you're busy.'

'No. I rang up this evening to tell them I'd be away for the weekend. Donny spoke to me. He was so disappointed I promised that I'd go there for lunch and take him after all.'

The mistrust and spite returned to the light blue eyes.

'I see. So because of a spoilt child my weekend's to be bitched up.'

'It's my weekend as well. For Christ's sake, Angela, it's only for an hour or two.'

'It means we can't get out of London.'

'Who wants to in this fog?'

'Who wants to sail toy boats in this fog?'

'Donny does. And it's not so much the sailing. He wants to feel that I take an interest, want to *be* with him.'

'All right. Here's what you do. Tomorrow morning you go to Hamley's and buy him a bigger and better yacht, take it round and give it to him, explain the fog's much too thick to sail anything so beautiful and expensive and you can't wait to take him on the first fine day. Then we get going in the Mercedes –'

'– No, Angela. One doesn't buy children off, one simply keeps one's promises. Tomorrow I said and tomorrow it is.'

'Tomorrow's what you said to me too. A whole wonderful weekend, you said, Friday night to Monday morning.'

'A few hours to make a child happy, that's all I ask.'

'Oh, very good, very good indeed. Jude Holbrook the dutiful, loving father' - she mimicked him stridently – 'bringing happiness to the dear little kiddies.'

'Look, Angela.' Holbrook took one of her wrists and dug his thumb nail into it. 'I'm already married to one greedy bitch and I don't propose to put up with another. So watch your step. Because, my dear, your time's running out and you'd better make the most of what's left . . . if you want anything more than a pile of empty brandy bottles to show at the end of it.'

Slowly he eased his thumb away. Angela, looking down at the red weal, noticed how the skin round it seemed to have wrinkled and coarsened, though only that evening she had spent ten minutes rubbing cream into her wrists. For a moment it seemed to her that Holbrook's fingers carried a blight, a blight which must surely be eating further into her body every time he touched or embraced any part of it, her breasts, her thighs, her belly, to make her shrivelled and obscene. Then she remembered that she was well past her thirty-first birthday and had led a demanding life. Gathering her wits and trying to shake off fear, she smiled at Jude with

submission and invitation, trying to convey, for she knew it
would please and excite him, that his assertion of power had
roused her sex.

'Naughty Somerset,' said plump, good-natured Maisie;
'Nannie will have to smack.'

'No, no,' said Somerset. 'You must get the words exactly
right.'

'Naughty Somerset,' said Maisie resignedly. 'Nannie saw
him playing with it. Nannie will have to smack.'

'I wasn't playing with it,' Somerset lisped.

'Then Nannie must look and see. . . . *There*. Naughty,
naughty Somerset. And what must Somerset do now?'

'Somerset must pull down his panties,' pouted Somerset, 'so
that Nannie can smack.'

3

'I want you,' said Jude Holbrook to Miss Beatty, 'to send a telegram. Mrs. Holbrook, The Ferns, Peddars' Way, Whitstable. ARRIVING TONIGHT MONDAY SEVEN LOVE JUDE.'

'Wouldn't it be better if I phoned, Mr. Holbrook?'

'My mother refuses to have a telephone. She has some curiously old-fashioned ideas.'

Miss Beatty lingered.

'Well.'

'It's about *my* mother, sir, if you could spare a moment. She's got so old, so difficult to manage, I was thinking that it would be kinder really to send her . . . to one of those places.'

'I'm sorry,' said Holbrook. 'But where do I come in?'

'I was thinking you might be able to help me go about it. I'm not sure –'

'– Neither am I,' said Holbrook crisply, 'but you can soon find out. I've an idea that the authorities aren't too keen, not if there's still an able-bodied relative about. The theory is that the old folks are happier with their own people.'

'And a bloody nuisance,' Miss Beatty blurted out.

Holbrook regarded her with careful interest.

'That's just what you must *not* say, my dear Miss Beatty, unless you want every welfare worker in London to faint with horror. But since you have paid me the compliment of being so honest, I am going to help you. No questions asked and the sooner the better, right?'

'Right, Mr. Holbrook,' said Miss Beatty, feeling delightfully worldly and wicked.

'Well, I have a friend, a certain Doctor La Soeur, who specializes in old people's illnesses. Apart from a large private practice, he does a lot of work and research in an Old People's Home of Rest thirty miles south of London – lovely grounds, first-rate care, etcetera, etcetera.'

Miss Beatty nodded avidly.

'Now,' Holbrook went on, 'if my chum were to say that your mother had some interesting illness which he wanted to observe, they'd let her in tomorrow – and no fuss with forms and officials.'

'It sounds lovely, Mr. Holbrook. But I don't think there's anything special wrong with mother. Just old age.'

'Then it's up to La Soeur to invent an impressive name for it. I've done him some good turns in the past.'

'You're too kind.'

'My dear Miss Beatty, a pleasure.'

This was quite true. In the first place, it might one day prove very useful to have Miss Beatty under an enforceable obligation (do as I say or mother comes home). And secondly, if there was one thing Holbrook resented it was old people, like his father, who sat around using up good money and getting in everybody's way. By off-loading Miss Beatty's mother for her, he was striking a blow for a cause in which he believed on grounds both general and personal: he was fulfilling a duty and vicariously indulging a hatred.

'Oh, Mr. Holbrook, I don't know how –'

'– Then please don't. Just go and send that wire to my mother, then ring up Doctor La Soeur – number in the book – and put him on to me.'

Ashley Dexterside, steering a life-sized drawing of the tooth-paste cutie and her bubs down the stairs, met Donald Salinger, who appeared to be skipping, yes skipping, up them.

'Good morning, Ashley.'

'Good morning, Donald.'

'What's that?'

'Marjoram's tooth-paste.'

'Very nice too.' Then coyly, 'Ashley?'

'Yes, Donald?'

'You must congratulate me. I'm engaged to Vanessa Drew.'

Before Ashley could think what to say, Donald had skipped on his way upstairs.

'Mind the ceiling with those horns, dear,' muttered Ashley to himself at last, and propelled the dentifrice dolly viciously down the last flight.

'You don't seem very pleased,' said Donald to Holbrook.

'I'm a little surprised.'

'You knew I'd been seeing Vanessa lately.'

'To be candid, Donald, so have a lot of other people.'

'Yes,' said Donald sadly, 'I was afraid you'd mention that. It's all going to change . . . now. Vanessa and I have an excellent understanding.'

'I see. Of course I'm pleased for you, Donald, but this means a certain readjustment. Anything that affects you must affect me.'

'This will make no difference to the firm, if that's what you mean. Except that you'll be in sole charge during our honeymoon next spring.'

He had thought to please Holbrook with this announcement and was surprised at the bitterness of the reply.

'I suppose I can preside over the morgue,' his partner said, 'while you gallivant down the Côte d'Azur.'

'Morgue, Jude?'

'Unless you give me a free hand to take decisions.'

'I hadn't quite thought of that, certainly. But we needn't settle it straight away.'

'One thing we can settle straight away. *Strix*.'

'I've told you. If you raise fifteen thou –'

'– You won't go back on it? You won't say you want your share for new carpets at Chevenix Court?'

'What an extraordinary mood you're in. I've given you my word.'

It's really too much, Holbrook thought. Why won't he see it? If he marries a slut, the firm can suffer. Salinger's cracking up, they'll all say: judgment going. No need to worry – yet – but we'd best keep an eye on Salinger & Holbrook: plenty of money, oh yes, but with a woman like that in the house you never know what's going to happen next. And this on top of everything else – of Donny's ugly grizzling because there had been no wind to blow his boat along, another scene with Angela on Saturday night, a row with Penelope about some money she wanted (probably to take her new lover to Paris), and the impending interview with his parents that very evening. He wished Miss Beatty had a hundred ageing mothers on whom he might be revenged. But this was no time for a showdown with his partner.

'Forgive me, Donald,' he said with graceful mastery of his irritation. 'It's been a difficult weekend. I hope you and Vanessa will be very happy, and I look forward to greeting her as your wife.'

Carton Weir, refreshed after his weekend, typed a brief memorandum to send to Peter Morrison.

'One matter about which we shall need to be more precise,' the memorandum said, 'is our attitude towards our own (and Labour) members who have substantial business holdings. As you know, I share your mistrust of the tribe; but there can be no doubt that many of them are reputable men whose activities, while profitable to themselves, can also be seen as beneficial to the public welfare. In short, it is no good skirmishing on a broad front. We must formulate a critical apparatus to predict probable weaknesses in their position, check our predictions against informed intelligence, and then attack in strength where they are most vulnerable.'

Peter, reflected Carton Weir, was always fond of military metaphors.

Despite the promise of more fog, Holbrook decided to drive down to his parents' house, thus ensuring for himself an immediate means of retreat if things became too unpleasant. To this end a car was essential: for since 'The Ferns' was well outside Whitstable, tucked away by the sea shore at the end of a road too modest to appear in the A.A. Book, you might as easily have summoned a taxi to the House of Usher.

The door was opened by Holbrook's mother.

'Where's Tilly?' said Holbrook.

'Having her holidays. She always goes in November. I'm surprised you didn't think of that, laddie, before honouring us with one of your rare visits.'

'I shan't need much.'

'You won't get much. Take your case upstairs, and then go and talk to your father while I dish up the supper.'

Holbrook shuddered slightly and did as he was told. When he entered the drawing room, he found his father hunched over the whisky decanter and muttering, no doubt for his son's express benefit, into the *Financial Times*. The old man did not get up but offered a paw which contrived to be both scaly and clammy at the same time.

'A fortnight ago,' croaked Holbrook père without further ado, 'Selby told me to get rid of my Tobacco and buy Oil. Tobacco has now risen and Oil has dropped. Can you explain that, eh? Can you explain why whatever I do, with the best advice, always goes wrong?'

'Yes,' said Holbrook, who had had this conversation before. 'It's because Selby is using you in order to oblige larger clients.'

Knowing that he would not be asked, he helped himself liberally to whisky.

'If this goes on,' said his father menacingly, 'there won't be many more bottles of whisky in the house. There may not even be a house. So help yourself while you can, but please don't forget me when I'm in the gutter.'

'Nonsense,' said Holbrook. 'Everything will be all right as soon as you give up Selby and find an honest broker.'

'I suppose *you'd* like to handle it?'

'I couldn't do worse than Selby.'

Any minute now the whisky would be confiscated by his mother and not reissued until nine-thirty, half an hour before his father's bed time. There would not be wine with supper, there was unlikely even to be beer. Holbrook drained his tumbler and filled it seven-eighths full of neat whisky; by a judicious process of dilution he could now keep it going for half an hour or so.

'You turning into a soak?' his father said.

'I'm tired. It's been a long day.'

'I've been sitting here worrying all day. But I wouldn't fill my glass like that. Greedy, I call it.'

Mrs. Holbrook appeared with a trolley on which were three plates of watery scrambled egg, a dish of thinly cut luncheon roll, and a flagon of Cydrax. She picked up the whisky decanter, checked the contents, and carried it out of the room at arm's length, like a hospital nurse with a bed-pan. Her tall, thin frame and protruding buttocks reminded Holbrook of Donald. When she came back, she said objectively and without rebuke:

'A lot of whisky drunk this evening.'

'That was your son, madam.'

'Well,' she conceded, 'it's a long drive. Now eat this, both of you, before the goodness goes out of it.'

Each of them being provided with a small side-table, the repast began. Holbrook, who had drunk quicker than he meant to on sight of the trolley and its contents, watered and drained the last of his whisky and reached for the Cydrax.

'We've taken to eating in here,' said his mother, pursing her lips, 'to save heating the dining room.'

'I can't think why you stay here at all in the winter. You'd find it much cheaper and warmer abroad.'

'This is our house, laddie. We are not birds on the wing.'

'And I like to be in close touch with Selby,' grouched Holbrook senior.

'If you hadn't been, you might still have had those Tobacco shares.'

'There's the currency,' said Mrs. Holbrook.

'That can always be fixed,' said Holbrook brashly.

'In defiance of the law?'

'Health reasons. You could say father needed the sun.'

'That's what's wrong with this country. Too many of your sort fixing things,' said Mr. Holbrook; 'grab, grab, grab, and no sense of duty. No wonder the shares are never steady from one day to the next.'

When they had finished, Holbrook helped his mother out with the trolley.

'I must talk to you alone.'

'When he goes to bed,' she said, unsurprised. 'I'll put one of his pills in his tea now, to make him feel sleepy.' She smiled at her son, grateful that he had brought about this complicity, and patted the bun at the back of her head. 'Go along, laddie. And humour the poor old wretch as best you can.'

How had she ever come to marry him, Holbrook asked himself for the thousandth time. She's a dour woman and strict, but generous and warm beneath it. Intelligent, too, and well read. As he entered the drawing room he looked at the rich and solid contents of the shelves: Jebb's Sophocles, Jowett's Plato, Bailey's Lucretius, all the better known ancients in the Loëb edition; the English classics and sub-classics, poetry and prose, from Chaucer to Virginia Woolf; philosophy, mathematical theory, chess; Proust, and in French at that. And they were *used*: from any and all of these books, not one of which his father had looked at in thirty years, his mother, he knew, read variously and with attention for three or four hours by day and often, after his father had gone to bed, far into the night. Perhaps that was why she kept so serene in this horrible, dreary household; perhaps that was why she did not care to leave it, even in winter, for a milder climate: because it held her books. But the important question was still unanswered: how had a woman of such taste (if only it had stretched to food and drink as well) come to accept the greedy, bullying, philistine little man who was now dragging his life out on the sofa? Perhaps he had been different once, though his son had never known him so. Perhaps, long ago, there had been youth's brightness, some physical beauty or power, which had worked on the shy Scottish girl from the Professor's house in the Durham Close. Perhaps there had been a few years of . . . what? . . . lust? passion? romance? Whatever there had been, it had died at his birth or before. What a pity he could not have been the son his mother must have longed for, such a son, caring for written words and their truth, as might have upheld the tradition which she herself had inherited and would have wished, so dearly, to pass on. Not that she had ever said as much; for although she did not recognize his ambitions, she had never forced her own upon him, had said no word of bitterness when he left Oxford with his bare fourth class degree. But it must have been one more sorrow; he could only trust that her wisdom extended, as surely it must, to an understanding of human diversity: it was not his fault that his life must lie in action, action of a kind she despised, and not in the printed page.

'What are you brooding about?' said his father. 'See you once in a blue moon and nothing to say for yourself. How's Penelope and the boy? I was just asking him,' he shouted at his wife, who now entered with the tea tray, 'about that wife of his and the boy. Good girl, Penelope.' He chuckled, leered, dribbled slightly. 'Cuddly.'

'I've hopes of little Donny,' murmured Mrs. Holbrook, pouring the tea.

'We went sailing on Saturday,' said Holbrook, and suddenly saw his way. Education. Donny's education. If there was one thing his mother would support joyfully, it was a scheme which might make of Donny what she had never had in himself.

'So you've got a yacht now?' his father said.

'Of course not. Donny's toy boat.'

'Is he mechanically minded?' said Mrs. Holbrook.

'No,' said Holbrook carefully. 'Curious . . . mentally adventurous. This was a sailing boat, you see, and he was keen to experiment with different combinations of sail.'

'Scientific then?'

'He certainly likes to know reasons. But he's the same with his story books. How could Red Riding Hood possibly have fallen for it?' he improvised glibly: 'or why had Robin Hood been outlawed in the first place? Sensible questions which go to the root.'

His mother considered this; then nodded with cautious pleasure. His father set down his tea and yawned.

'Bed for me, if all you're going to talk about is children's books.'

'No whisky?'

'Too tired. It must be the strain of thinking about those shares.'

The old man rose, nodded spitefully at both of them in turn, and shambled out of the room.

'How's he been?' asked Holbrook.

'As well as can be expected for a man with no affections and no interests.'

'And all this fuss about the money?'

'The same as ever it was. If he listens to Selby, it's bad advice he gets. If he decides for himself, he's either too greedy or too timid. Either way he loses about a thousand pounds of capital a year.'

'I didn't think you took such a detailed interest, mother.'

'I can't help knowing when he talks of nothing else.'

Mrs. Holbrook left the room and returned with the whisky.

'You'll like some of this, I dare say, before you talk.'

Holbrook took a long drink and plunged.

'I want him to hand over some money, mother.'

'He'll not do that,' Mrs. Holbrook said indifferently.

'You could persuade him.'

'And why should I trouble?' Her indifference now verged – no more – on hostility. 'You spend your days running after money. Why should you want more?'

Holbrook drank again and played his trump.

'It's for Donny, mother. It's high time arrangements were made for his education.'

'What had you in mind?' Wary, but prepared to listen.

'Fifteen thousand pounds,' he said quietly.

'A tidy sum, laddie.'

'I intend that Donny should have something much better than the usual trek through the boarding schools. I think he should start going abroad as soon as possible in order to learn languages – and later spend most of his holidays that way. I think he should attend at least one continental university after Oxford or Cambridge. And I think he should have a little money to call on so that he needn't rush into anything . . .

money to help him' – he dangled the carrot carefully – 'in case he should have some vocation which didn't bring in very much.'

'If he had a true vocation he wouldn't want very much. You're not thinking,' she said with scorn, 'of the Church?'

'I very much hope not. Though I wouldn't stop him if that's what he wanted.'

Mrs. Holbrook nodded approval of this liberal sentiment.

'I'll not say I don't like your ideas,' she said (high praise from one whose habit of mind forbade her to commend save in negatives). 'But why do you want the money all at once? It'd be easier for me to get it from your father as it was wanted from time to time.'

'My way might save death duties. It would certainly save us both worrying lest he should turn up nasty and refuse later on. And it would enable me to make immediate arrangements to have some of the money put in trust for Donny.'

'And the rest of it?' Contemptuous of profit and loss, she insisted on rigorous accuracy as to disbursement.

'There are several reputable companies who in exchange for a comparatively small sum paid down will undertake to foot all or most of the school bills later on. The earlier you take up a policy the less you pay. If I act now, I can probably save a third and more of Donny's total fees.'

'And if something happens to Donny?'

'The money will be the least of our sorrows.'

He helped himself to more whisky. She's willing, he thought; but will she put the money where I want it – *in my hand*? Typically, it had not even occurred to his mother to suggest that he himself should pay for this elaborate scheme; but she was as shrewd as she was generous, as tight-fisted as she was large-minded, and he was now about to concern herself with the exact sums needed, the details, the methods of payment, far more closely than suited him. Although he had anticipated this, he had been relying on his knowledge of financial procedures to find plausible reasons why things should be arranged his way. He had forgotten, living as he did in a world where money-talk was governed by certain almost academic conventions, how devastating plain common sense could be when applied to the topic.

'Now then,' his mother was saying, 'how much did you think for the trust?'

'Enough to give him three hundred a year of his own from the age of eighteen on. Say six thousand invested now.'

'And what about the down payment for the school fees?'

Damn the woman. These matters were for him to settle: she had acknowledged the excellence of the project, so why couldn't she just produce the money and leave him to manage the rest?

'Take the fees as six hundred a year for ten years. A down payment of four thousand now should do the trick.'

'That's ten thousand,' his mother persisted; 'what do you propose for the other five?'

'Clothes, travel, extra tuition. . . .'

'Very well. I'll answer for it that your father will pay a cheque, to whatever reputable solicitor you name, of ten thousand pounds; six thousand to found a trust for Donny and four thousand for a policy to meet his school fees. As for the rest, you must ask me from time to time or send on the bills. How will that serve?'

Not at all.

'I'm most grateful, mother,' he said hesitantly.

'I never was one to grudge money in a good cause. No expense was spared for your own education nor should be for Donny's. Your father didn't like it then and he won't like it now; but pay he shall – I promise you that.'

'Mother. It will be much easier if the money is paid all at once. And to me.'

Mrs. Holbrook did not remark, as most people would have that her offer was by any standard munificent and that gratitude had been scant. This was not her way. She was now interested in one thing, in the efficient promotion of a scheme for Donny's education, and if Jude had anything within reason to say on the matter she was prepared to listen.

'Why will it be easier?' she said.

Holbrook swallowed hard at his whisky.

'If it were to become known . . . as sooner or later it would if the money went to a third party . . . that I had been forced to go to my father for fifteen thousand pounds, people would start looking askance at my credit – at the standing of my firm. Here's Jude Holbrook, they'd say, half-owner of Salinger & Holbrook, and he can't raise a few thousand pounds off his own bat.'

'And can't you?'

'No. The money's tied up. It's all right, but it's tied up.'

'They'd realize this as well as you do.'

'Yes, but they'd say I ought to have been able to raise a loan from the bank on the strength of it.'

'I don't know much about these things,' his mother said, 'but if you're so keen to save your face you could say the money was a gift. That your father volunteered it.'

'In which case it should come first to me.'

Mrs. Holbrook was more than equal to this sophistry.

'The gift is to Donny, not to you. What more appropriate than that a solicitor should administer it for him?'

On this point, Holbrook saw, she would never yield. Very well; he must cheat yet again.

'You're quite right, mother,' he said convincingly; 'I was being foolish. To a solicitor then. But I'd be grateful if it could be the full fifteen thousand. We could then form another fund of five thousand to take care of Donny's extras, and if we invested it sensibly it would go much further.'

This Mrs. Holbrook was prepared to accept. The more money spent on Donny's education, the better. By agreeing that it should be put in immediate charge of a solicitor Jude had established his good faith, and she was now ready to meet any reasonable request.

'Very well,' she said. 'It will take about ten days, I suppose, to arrange.'

'Fair enough.'

'And to whom shall I send the cheque?'

'John Groves, of Groves & Groves, Lincoln's Inn.'

It would be difficult to talk young Groves round, he reflected, but not *too* difficult. After all, he could remind him gently that he knew, having himself provided Doctor La Soeur's address, all about the abortion which Groves had arranged three years ago for Vanessa Drew. If, on the other hand, his mother should check up on Groves, she would find that they were generally held to be a most efficient and respectable firm.

'I'm glad that's fixed,' he said. 'Thank you, mother.'

Elated by the success of his diplomacy, slightly drunk with the whisky, he bent over his mother and kissed her tenderly.

'It will be a great thing for Donny,' he said.

'I hope so. At least we shall have done what we can ... I'm surprised and delighted that you take the matter so seriously.'

'I had your example ... I want to ask you something, mother.'

'Well?'

'How did a woman of your ... quality ... ever marry a man like father?'

The question was prompted partly by curiosity, partly by drink, and partly by a feeling of well-being and relief which made him genuinely disposed to understand and to sympathize with the mother whom seconds before he had deceived without scruple.

'Your father,' said Mrs. Holbrook, 'was a good-looking man. Also pathetic, like a poor little dog waiting for its dinner. The combination was irresistible. But when he finally got his dinner – when he inherited money from his father – he became peevish and arrogant instead. As though the money conferred a personal merit which I was too perverse to acknowledge.'

'Then why did you stay?'

'Because of you. Because of an old-fashioned notion I had, even though I am not a Christian, that marriage should be for life. But principally,' she said coolly, 'because I had nowhere else to go. *My* father left no money, as you know.'

'And now?'

'I have long since come to terms with life. Quite good terms, as they go.'

'Why not let him drink himself to death and be done with it?'

'I should miss him. You see,' said Mrs. Holbrook, 'he personifies the folly and meanness of the human race. Since I tend to live on rather a remote level of my own, it is salutary to be daily reminded of the sort of man by whom and for whom the world is mostly run. If ever I am in danger of thinking the truth lies *there*' – she indicated the books around them – 'I can always take a look at your father. Nasty, grovelling, greedy – *he* is the truth about the world, Jude, and it does not do to forget it.'

In Holland Park Angela Tuck mixed herself a final brandy and soda and climbed into bed. No money from Tuck for over three months now, she thought. What's the good of a Court Order when he could be anywhere in the world? If one considered the circumstances of the divorce, she had, it was true, been lucky to receive any award from the Court at all. The fact remained that she had received it, and it was really too bad of Tuck not to pay up. If this went on she would have to ask Jude, and that he would hate. Worse; he might go for good. Since her plan was that he should stay for good and make an honest woman out of her to boot, the thought was not easily tolerable, so she got up again and mixed herself another final brandy and soda.

'This is your last chance, my girl,' she said to the battered, sexy face in the mirror; 'so beg, borrow or sell yourself, but don't take a penny from Jude.'

In Russell Square, Somerset Lloyd-James put his teeth into a glass of water and knelt to say his prayers. As always, these took the form of a recapitulation of the day's events for God's benefit and a rehearsal, under pretence of asking guidance, of tactics for use on the morrow.

'. . . Peter Morrison rang up at tea time,' Somerset mumbled. 'He'd talked it over with Helen, who approved, and he'd also had a reminder from Carton Weir (to whose sinful soul be merciful, O Lord) that they must now work out their precise policy about the money men in the House. With these things in mind, he has decided to join our Board.

'It now remains, Father, to persuade the Board, which meets tomorrow, that Peter is the right man for the vacancy. Dilkes won't make trouble but Robert Constable might – he's very left wing and may not like Peter's politics. If he does object, I shall tell him that Peter is well known for his integrity and that politics, unless they are extreme, are not for our consideration.

'I have made a provisional engagement with Maisie for Thursday evening. I hope, Lord, that You will forgive this indulgence, which I regard as necessary for my physical health. Amen.

'One more thing. I am worried about Carton Weir, who is Peter's lieutenant and an important figure in the group. Now, I have only met him once and that briefly, but if all they say of his private life is true he could run into bad trouble any day – which would do the Young Englanders no good at all. Although Peter must be aware of this, he seems wholly unconcerned. This is typical of Peter, whose aristocratic indifference about such matters really will not do at all in this censorious age. I think, Lord, that I must give him timely warning, and I trust that You will lend my plea eloquence. In nomine Patris et Filii et Spiritus Sancti. Amen.'

'I've arranged,' Miss Beatty said, 'for you to go on a little holiday in the country. Starting next weekend.'

'Will *it* be there?' said Mrs. Beatty, pointing feebly at the television screen.

'Lots and lots of them, bigger and better than ever,' said Miss Beatty skittishly.

Two large tears rolled down her mother's cheeks.

'But I like *it*,' she said, still pointing; 'ours'.

Miss Beatty clicked her tongue, switched off the set, and wheeled her mother into the alcove. Nasty, smelly old woman, she thought, I wonder I've put up with it so long. But now, thanks to *him*. . . .

'Stop crying at once, mother,' she said. 'It's for your own good.'

'When can I come home again?'

'As soon as you've got the benefit.'

'How soon will that be?'

'That's for doctor to decide.'

The word 'doctor' sent Mrs. Beatty positively howling.

'For Christ's *sake*, mother. A lot of people have gone to a lot of trouble to make you well and happy. I never saw such ingratitude in my life.'

Words like 'home' and 'all these years' and even, Miss Beatty thought she heard, 'institution' came sputtering out amid the sobs. Miss Beatty could bear no more.

'You're a wicked, selfish old woman,' she screamed. 'It's nothing to you that I've used up the best of my life on you, that I've never even had the smell of a man. Well, it may not be too late even now. So you're going down to the country, whether you like it or not, and there you'll stay.'

All of a sudden Mrs. Beatty stopped crying and looked at her daughter out of her old eyes, usually so stupid, with the malign authority of a Sybil.

'God will punish you for this,' Mrs. Beatty said clearly, 'you'll see.'

'An April wedding,' said Donald, 'then away till the middle of May. And in June we'll give a ball at Chevenix Court, to tell the world that I've brought home my bride.'

'Very nice,' Vanessa said. And it would certainly be nice not having to worry about money any more. On the other hand, this thing of Donald's about fidelity was such a bore. Why couldn't he be like everyone else she knew? Realize how little it mattered? Still, Donald would be up in London most of the week, so it oughtn't to be difficult to arrange some bucolic amusement. Meanwhile, until they were married, she'd better be careful or he might not marry her after all. So what she'd do was this: she wouldn't do it in her own flat, where he might catch her, or with anyone he knew; only with Jimmy and his pals, in one of their pads. It was a pity Jimmy used up so much of his energy renting himself to queers, but one couldn't have it all one's own way at a tricky time in one's life like this.

Tom Llewyllyn rang up Jonathan Gamp.

'Jonathan. I've run out of cash.'

'Have you, darling?'

'I wish you wouldn't call me "darling".'

'If you come round to Hereford Square, darling, we might be able to arrange something.'

'I need rather a lot.'

'Then we'll just have to see what we can do, darling,' said Jonathan huskily.

Tom winced. Although his frequent borrowings from Jonathan Gamp, who was a generous man and appreciated Tom's quality, were entirely straightforward, Jonathan always managed to imply that they were contaminated beyond belief. It was only his way of amusing himself, Tom acknowledged, of getting *some* return for his money; but even so it was uncalled for.

'Have you heard about Donald?' Jonathan was saying. 'He's engaged to Vanessa Drew.'

'How very odd of him. Look, Jonathan. I shall need at least thirty pounds. I've got a hundred coming at the end of the month and –'

'– You don't seem very concerned about Donald.'

'He's old enough to suit himself. About this loan –'

'– But you *know* Vanessa, darling. Now, do admit –'

'– Jonathan. This thirty pounds –'

'– Just come along to Hereford Square, darling, and *then* we'll see.'

Tom put down the receiver and started unhappily for Hereford Square. He had not been to his constituency over the weekend and he had not done any work on his book. He must pull himself together. He would use whatever he got from Jonathan as eating money only and would work steadily for the

rest of the month. But perhaps he had just better give ten of it
to Norma for that cheque which was going to bounce . . . or
should he use the cash for another go with her before the
cheque came back and she got baity? But that would mean
another evening in the Tin Tack, and then all the eating
money he got from Jonathan would be gone and he'd be back
in square one. Life was really very difficult. Why was it he only
liked women if he'd paid for them? There was Vanessa Drew,
she'd fancied him well enough, but it was just no good. It must
be his Welsh conscience, he decided; he was conceding, in
the crudest possible way, that one must always pay for one's
pleasures.

4

The Board assembled at half past two of the clock. Present were Henry, Arthur Dilkes, B.Sc., Secretary to the Institute of Political and Economic Studies; Robert Reculver Constable, M.A., Vice-Chancellor of, and Professor of Economics in, the University of Salop; and Somerset Lloyd-James, M.A., Editor.

'Professor Constable, being invited by the other two members present to preside over the meeting, remarked with regret the absence of Lord Philby in America but reminded the Board that three members constituted a quorum. They might therefore proceed to business.

'The first matter for consideration was the financial position of the journal. Mr. Attwood, as Head of the Accounts Department, was called in to address the Board. He was able to reveal that circulation for the month of October had reached a weekly average of 55,000, this representing a weekly increase of 7,000 over the previous month. Still more satisfactory was an eleven per cent increase in advertising revenue, as reckoned against. . . .

'The third item before the Board was a proposal to commission Professor R. F. Kahn, of King's College, Cambridge, to write an article about the ethical problems posed by institutional dealing on the stock market. Mr. Dilkes was against the proposal on the ground that it gave undue prominence to a minority problem of moral rather than financial interest. Mr. Lloyd-James questioned the term "minority". The problem, he pointed out, was not confined to colleges in the older universities; there were many institutions up and down the country with funds presently available for investment, and most of them were holding back only because of doubts as to the propriety of dealing in the open market. It was important that they should receive informed guidance in the matter.

Professor Constable agreed, in principle, with Mr. Lloyd-James; and observed that even had the problem been of moral interest exclusively, it was surely to just such questions that *Strix* should give a generous allowance of its space. It was accordingly decided to approach Professor Kahn.

'The fifth subject for discussion was the many letters of complaint received by the Editor and other members of the Board in consequence of an article published in October. The article in question was a three hundred word review by Mr. Thomas Llewyllyn of a recently published biography of Horatio Bottomley. Asked by Professor Constable why such a book had been reviewed in the pages of *Strix*, Mr. Lloyd-James said that the article was intended as a piece of light relief; and not wholly light; for after all, he observed, Bottomley had been a phenomenon of some interest, and the early success of his ventures might be a comparison with some recent *coups* of a similarly questionable nature. Mr. Dilkes was disposed to grant the point, but regretted the "aggressive frivolity" with which Mr. Llewyllyn had deposed that "most entrepreneurs and many so called financiers were Bottomleys at bottom".' 'Their method,' Mr. Llewyllyn had written, 'is to borrow or scrounge small coins all round and shove them in the one-armed bandit, in the hope that the jack-pot will come up quickly. If it does, then they repay their creditors (if they must), buy a knighthood, and are left with a cosy balance. If it doesn't, they play on till the patience of their backers is exhausted, and then go bankrupt.' It was this passage, Mr. Dilkes said, which had particularly offended correspondents.

'After some deliberation, during which Professor Constable referred more than once to Mr. Llewyllyn's talent as a writer, it was decided that he should still be invited to review books but that Mr. Lloyd-James as Editor. . . .

'Sixth and last came the election of a new member to fill the place at the Board vacated by General Sir Reresby Peterson. Mr. Lloyd-James immediately proposed the name of Mr. Peter Morrison, Member of Parliament for Whereham and District. Mr. Morrison, he submitted, was a young man of unimpeachable public character who had before him a Parliamentary future of an unusual and interesting kind. While the scope of his interests was wide, he had hitherto had little acquaintance with the realms of finance or industry; this meant that he would bring a fresh and unprejudiced mind to the problems which confronted the Board. Mr. Morrison derived his income from his Norfolk estate; he habitually used his surplus profits for the development of his land and the welfare of his employees; he had no financial interests which might influence his judgements or recommendations as a member of the Board of *Strix*.

'Mr. Dilkes was fully prepared to accept Mr. Morrison as a colleague on the Board.

'Professor Constable said that while he himself was a supporter of the Labour Party, he did not choose to quarrel with Mr. Morrison on account of his politics. On the other hand, he must point out that Mr. Morrison was a close friend of Mr. Lloyd-James's, and had been at the same school. He himself (Professor Constable) had also attended this school, albeit some years before Mr. Morrison and Mr. Lloyd-James. Would it not create a peculiar impression, in informed circles, that three members of a Board of five should be wearing the same old school tie.'

'Mr. Lloyd-James: I never wear it myself. It is like a Neapolitan ice-cream.

'Mr. Dilkes: Three out of five. Not much worse than the proportion of old Etonians in the Cabinet.

'Professor Constable: I suggest we stick to the point.

'Mr. L-J: So do I. The point is whether Mr. Morrison is a good man for the job, not which school he went to.

'Mr. D: I must agree with that.

'Prof. C: It is important that *Strix*, at this early stage in its development, should not prejudice its public image by tactless alignments, on or off the Board.

'Mr. L-J: Public image? You yourself said that only *"Informed circles"*—

'Prof. C: Please don't quibble, Lloyd-James.

'Mr. L-J: And in any case there is no alignment. You and Morrison and myself, we are three widely different people of widely varying views.

'Prof. C: I know that. But all outsiders will consider is the superficial fact.

'Mr. L-J: The irrelevant fact. And suppose they do? Our school was substantial, reliable, in no way flashy, turning out modest and industrious men who do us credit in all professional and commercial fields. What could be a better advertisement for *Strix* than to have three such on the Board? Old Etonians might have provoked envy, old Harrovians suspicion, old Wykhamists mistrust of· their supposed cleverness, old Rugbeians a great yawn of boredom, but our lot—

'Prof. C: Will provoke use of the one word: clique.

'Mr. D: Suppose you'd all three been in the same regiment – in the Rifle Brigade, say – instead of the same school. You wouldn't let *that* make any difference.

'Prof. C: The comparison is false. In a regiment one serves. In a school one is *moulded*.

'Mr. L-J: I was never "moulded" and it doesn't strike me that you were.

'Prof. C: I *know*. What worries me is the immediate impression we shall make.

'Mr. L-J: You disappoint me, Vice-Chancellor. I did not think you were a man to worry over anything so trivial and misleading.

PAUSE

'Mr. D: Two against one, Prof.

'Prof. C: I am aware of that, and of course I shall yield. But I wish it to go on record that while I know nothing but good of Mr. Morrison, and while I shall feel myself honoured to welcome him here, I still think his election to be ill advised.

'Mr. L-J: How would you suggest your reasons for this be recorded?

'Prof. C: Let us say . . . that it could lay us easily open to imputations of conspiracy.

    'Mr. D: Conspiracy! That'll be the day.

    'Prof. C: Let us sincerely hope it will not.'

5

Ten days later Jude Holbrook walked over to see his solicitor, 'young' John Groves of Groves & Groves in Lincoln's Inn.

'So the cheque's here,' Holbrook said. 'What came with it?'

'A letter from your mother. It says the money is to be used, in consultation with yourself, to make provision for Donny's education.'

'Young' John Groves was a ponderous forty. He had broken veins high on both cheeks, and three extra chins. He was skilful at tuning his fruity voice to suit any occasion: he could be unctuous, reproving, exhortatory or insinuating at will. Just now he was being a cautious blend of all four.

'It is just like my mother,' Holbrook said coolly, 'to give no details.'

'She did say something about trust funds and a down payment to cover all the fees.'

'Basically,' said Holbrook, 'the idea is this. Invest the money soundly so that it appreciates over the next four years. Then, when Donny goes off to school, fees and expenses can be met for some time from interest already accumulated and interest still coming in. Sooner or later, of course, we shall have to break into the principal; but there should still be a nice bit left over for Donny when he goes to university.'

'Your mother implies a slightly different system.'

'My mother has no head for business.'

'She seems to be thinking in terms of specific trusts and policies, to be set up straight away.'

'What odds does it make? The important thing is that the money should start yielding. We can do all the pastry work later.'

'Perhaps,' said young Groves, 'I should write to your mother and ask her to be plainer.'

'And perhaps,' said Holbrook affably, 'you had better not. She hates being bothered about this kind of thing. She said, surely, that you were to consult with me?'

'Yes.'

'Then this is what we shall do. We shall invest the money in Salinger & Holbrook. The way things are going now, it could well increase to twenty thousand over the next four years. Time enough then to talk about trust funds and so on.'

'Jude,' said young Groves, all four chins wagging. 'You know as well as I do that your mother does not have speculative investment in mind. Never mind the details, if you like, but anything as . . . unethical as what you propose –'

'– Let's not talk about complicated subjects like ethics, John. Let's talk about simple, everyday things, like Donald's engagement to Vanessa Drew. You've heard about it, of course?'

Groves gobbled miserably.

'Jude dear.' He was doing something which was rare for him: he was pleading. 'If your mother ever called for an account, do you know what would happen to me?'

'You would just have to send her one. A simple statement would keep her happy. As I told you, she has no business head.'

'We have accountants, secretaries. . . . They'd all see there was something wrong.'

'Then it is best that the money should not pass through your account. Has anyone seen the cheque yet? And my mother's letter?'

'No,' said young Groves, who was no longer thinking very quickly. 'My secretary's ill. I opened it myself.'

'How very fortunate. Then you can endorse the cheque, so that I can have it credited to Salinger & Holbrook. You can write to my mother, on office paper but without anyone else knowing, and tell her that the money has been laid out in accordance with the spirit of her instructions. And you can send to her from time to time assuring her that all is well. She'll not bother you, I promise.'

'Malversion. Nothing more or less.'

'Only technical. The money will go where my mother intends . . . eventually.'

For a moment Groves looked as though he were about to have a seizure. His cheeks and chins, which were grey and dripping with sweat, swelled like a child's balloon; his mouth and nose seemed to disappear entirely in the encircling blubber. Then he expelled a long breath to let himself down again and said in a whining voice:

'What about my fee? I'd have got quite a lot for setting up those funds.'

'I'll send a hundred and fifty,' said Holbrook, rising, 'to your private account. The rest you must set against gratitude for services rendered. After all, John, it was a very narrow thing about Vanessa.'

Since Donald had to be out of London that night Vanessa went to The Cavalier, where she knew she'd find Jimmy and his friends. She was able to 'lend' them all a little money from what Donald had 'lent' her before catching his train; so after a few drinks they called at an off-licence and took a taxi to Jimmy's drum in the Elephant, where they had a lovely time with some students from Zanzibar who had just moved in below. What Vanessa didn't know was that Jimmy had recently made the acquaintance of Jonathan Gamp, who later on had no difficulty at all, though Jimmy named no names, in putting two and two together and adding them up to Vanessa.

When Donald returned to London the next afternoon, he went straight to the office in Chancery Lane. There wasn't very much in his In Basket (there never was) except for a memorandum from Jude Holbrook which informed him that Holbrook had that morning paid £15,000 into the firm's banking account. Half annoyed and half curious, Donald rang up the bank manager, who said yes indeed, a cheque for that amount had been paid in, a cheque drawn by a certain Anthony J. Holbrook in favour of Groves & Groves, solicitors, and endorsed, on behalf of Groves & Groves, by John Groves, partner. It was a little unusual, the manager said, but appeared to be in order; since the cheque was drawn on a country bank it would take three days to clear, unless of course Mr. Salinger wished him to effect special clearance. No, Mr. Salinger did not and a very good afternoon.

After this conversation Donald, who did not want to be held to his promise about *Strix* and had never seriously thought that he would be, wrote to Anthony J. Holbrook to ask if he knew what was going on and to suggest that if he didn't he should instantly cancel the cheque – a proceeding for which there was time enough as it would not reach his bank in Whitstable until the day after next. (It was typical of Donald to choose the cheapest means of communication; for although there was plenty of time, a prudent man would have sent a telegram – a method which Donald eschewed, to do him justice, not only out of meanness but also out of a distaste for fuss.) Since he did not wish anyone to know about this letter, he wrote it in his own hand, sealed the envelope and addressed it; but finding that he had no stamps, he left it in his Out Basket with a piece of paper clipped on which said 'For Dispatch'. (This too was typical of his incapacity for taking pains.) Then he went home to Cheyne Row because he was longing to see Vanessa.

Later that afternoon Miss Beatty found the letter in Donald's Out Basket. It was not her business to ask questions, indeed it might cost her her job, and normally she would have dispatched the letter as instructed; after all, both partners quite often sent private letters from the office in this way. But in this case Miss Beatty was worried by the address; there was something fishy going on, she decided; and since she was still light-headed with gratitude for the removal of mother, she unclipped the bit of paper saying 'For Dispatch' and accidentally dropped the letter face up in front of Jude Holbrook when he rang for her a few minutes later.

'I'm so sorry, sir. . . . That one's Mr. Salinger's, for mailing.'

Holbrook, who had already read the address, smiled his fallen angel smile so marvellously that Miss Beatty nearly fell on the carpet.

'Let me save you the trouble,' he said gallantly, and put the letter away in his pocket.

Jonathan Gamp was perhaps Donald's oldest friend and regarded Donald as an inexhaustible source of amusement. When he heard about Vanessa's goings-on at the Elephant, he was amused, certainly, but also, he told himself, indignant on his friend's behalf. The truth was that like all bachelors he resented marriages and was only too glad of the chance to throw a stink bomb at this one. Casting about for ways of achieving maximum entertainment and interference value without at the same time alienating Donald, he invited Holbrook to lunch on the pretence of seeking his advice about investments; and having listened to it carefully for some time (it was, as he knew it would be, good advice but not the best), he ordered two large brandies and said, *à propos* of nothing, that he hoped Donald wasn't being rash. Since Holbrook proved responsive to this remark, Jonathan elaborated a little on the company to be found at The Cavalier and left his guest to draw his own conclusions.

As far as Holbrook was concerned, the news that Vanessa was still up to her old tricks was very welcome; quite apart from the casual pleasure that might be available, there was now going to be a good chance of dissuading Donald from a marriage which might damage both himself and the firm. Meanwhile, there was a more immediate matter to hand. Having called at the firm's bank to make sure that his father's cheque had been duly cleared, Holbrook proceeded to Gower Street and an appointment with Somerset Lloyd-James.

'So,' said Somerset as soon as he was in the room, 'you have a proposition to put on behalf of Donald and yourself. Might one ask why Donald is not here too?'

'He did not wish you to think that he was in any way trading on your friendship.'

'And yet he is associating his name with the proposition?'

'Most unwillingly. The original idea was mine. In order to

keep me quiet, Donald said he'd come in with me *provided* I found a capital sum which he thought to be out of my reach.'

'But you found it?'

'Yes.'

'So now Donald is committed?'

'Hardly,' said Holbrook. 'He will try everything possible, I should hazard, to discourage negotiation.'

'Why?'

'Because he is lazy; he is without aspiration.'

'and to what would you have him aspire?'

'The proprietorship of *Strix*.'

Somerset blinked in deprecation, then wiped his palms with a grey and crumpled handkerchief.

'It isn't mine to sell,' he said at length.

'But it *is* Philby's to sell?'

'Lord Philby owns a 70 per cent interest in this journal. If he wishes to dispose of this interest, he must first obtain the consent of three out of the four other people who sit with him on the Board.'

'One of whom is yourself?'

Somerset inclined his head.

'And would such consent be forthcoming?' said Holbrook smoothly.

'That would depend entirely on the character and motives of the would-be purchaser. There are . . . rules, which it is the duty of the Board to uphold.'

'The Board is . . . flexible?'

'At present rather the reverse.'

'Faces changes quickly?'

'No. Myself, as Editor, must leave the Board should I be dismissed – which could only be done, by vote of the Proprietor and two other members, at not less than six months notice. Of my colleagues, two are *ex officio*, remaining at the Board so long as they hold their present appointments outside. The third can resign if he wishes, but cannot be expelled unless he is sent to prison, committed as a lunatic, or posted as a bankrupt. Lord Philby, of course, is inviolable as long as he wishes to retain ownership.'

'And how much,' said Holbrook, changing his tack, 'would Philby's share be worth?'

Somerset shrugged.

'He'd ask as high as he dared . . . and take something over sixty thousand, I dare say. As to that, the rest of the Board is indifferent. You see, however much the new Proprietor paid, he would still have a 70 per cent. interest in the profits and *he would still only have one vote in five on the Board*.'

Holbrook pursed his lips angrily at the emphasis on this remark, which to his mind indicated lack of due deference to money. Seeing this, Somerset smiled with a kind of discreet insolence and continued:

'You see, my dear Holbrook, although a small profit is always pleasing and useful, this journal does not exist to make money but to render a serious service to an intelligent public.'

'A growing public.'

'It can't grow enough, given the nature of the journal, to make the sort of profit you'd be interested in.'

'There could always be change.'

'The Board and the Articles by which it acts are there to prevent that.'

Once again, Holbrook scowled. There was something in Somerset Lloyd-James of the obstructive indifference which he had recently observed in Donald; worse, there was contempt. Lloyd-James despised him, not so much because he was anxious to make money, as because he let his anxiety show. He was allowing himself to be baited; still, he told himself as he fought back temper, I want this man's help, and to let him have a little pleasure at my expense will do no harm.

'Donald and I,' he said carefully, 'would value your assistance. You would be sure of our . . . confidence and esteem . . . both now and later.'

'You can speak so far for him? When he is against the whole scheme?'

'*You* are perhaps its only aspect of which he approves.'

Somerset bowed his head.

'Then we may hope for your support?' Holbrook pursued.

'I am prepared,' said Somerset, 'to give you, impartially, such information about this journal and its constitution as you may require.'

Holbrook hesitated, then rose. He had done as much, for the present, as he could.

'Very well. You'll be hearing from us as time goes on.'

'I look forward to doing so.'

Somerset in turn rose but did not accompany Holbrook to the door. When his visitor was gone, he drew a sheet of paper towards him and began writing in a clear and careful script.

'1) It seems that money is available to make a substantial offer to Philby. Since Holbrook has found his share, Donald, however reluctantly, will have to keep his word (he always does) and allow the scheme to proceed.

'2) As practising men of business, Salinger & Holbrook are virtually debarred from ownership by our Articles. Holbrook probably knows this; what he requires from me, then, is my good offices with the Board, in return for which he offers "confidence and esteem", i.e., I suppose, a continuing tenure of the Editorship at a higher salary. What he cannot seem to understand is that even if S & H should become Co-Proprietors (with only one vote between them) they can do nothing about my Editorship or anything else without the consent of two more members of the Board. They can therefore make no guarantees. But it is always possible, of course, that H is hinting at a straight bribe. . . .

'3) Although H did not repudiate a profit motive, his smart little mind is almost certainly looking more to the advance of his own ends through *Strix*'s prestige than to any dramatic increase in its actual revenue. If this is so, then once again he cannot have reckoned with the power of the Board. He can hardly hope to put pressure on such men as Constable and Morrison (whose appointment he must know of, as it was made public some days ago). Perhaps he hopes to infiltrate a man of his own into the *non-ex officio* seat instead of Peter. In which case, with my vote and his own as Proprietor he might hope to achieve a good deal, particularly if he managed to soften up Dilkes as well. Would he try to change the Articles? N.B.: consult these carefully to see if the Board is in fact empowered to revise them – I fancy not.

'4) Whatever he hopes to do, he cannot move, either now or later, without my assistance. Am I disposed to give it?

'5) Even if H gained control of the Board, Donald as his Co-Proprietor would be a brake on him – if, for example, he tried to double-cross myself. Provisionally, then, I could consider myself safe under the new ownership. But is there anything positive to be gained? Rather the reverse. H, if he could, would dictate to me in matters of policy; and his exploitation of *Strix*'s prestige would inevitably lead to the loss of that prestige.

'6) I conclude: things had best stay as they are, and I shall see to it that they do – unless concrete and very considerable inducement is offered. For the time being, then, I shall be polite but distant with S & H, giving them, as I have undertaken, any information they require but no active help . . . A.M.D.G.'

Somerset put down his pen, read carefully through what he had written, filed away each point in his mind for future reference, then tore his appreciation into very small pieces and flushed it down the torrential office jakes.

Part Two

Part Two

6

Now that Holbrook had made all his preliminary dispositions in the *Strix* campaign he decided to let the affair rest a few weeks. This went against his temperament, but for the moment there was not much else to be done. For since Philby was still in America and likely to remain there, he understood, for some time, it was impossible to confront him in a satisfactory manner; and until this had been done and his reactions were definitely known, there was no point in going to further trouble and expense.

However, there was one matter which still needed putting to rights in his own camp: the hostility of Donald Salinger. If it would be too much to expect enthusiasm from Donald, at least he must be persuaded, before the project reached a crucial stage, to show a little friendly co-operation – this for the sake of comfort as well as efficiency. Turning the problem over, Holbrook decided that a valuable ally was to be had in Vanessa Drew. It had been his original intention to use what he had heard from Jonathan Gamp of her recent behaviour in order to estrange Donald from her, in hopes of wrecking or at least delaying their undesirable marriage: he now decided on a less crude and more creative diplomacy. Following Jonathan's hint, he spent several evenings and a lot of money in The Cavalier, made pertinent inquiries about Vanessa and her habits, and took care to go there again on the next occasion he knew Donald was to be away for the night.

Vanessa, who arrived in a mood of cheerful and colourful anticipation, was not at all pleased to see him.

'Christ, Jude. What are you doing here?'

'Hoping to see you.'

'If you think –'

'– No, dear. I know you're keeping yourself for Donald these days.'

'I'm glad you've got that straight.'

'Not quite straight. There are, it seems, discreet exceptions to the rule.'

He gestured towards the bar, where Jimmy and associates were drinking with their backs turned, guiltily aware that Vanessa was in trouble and that they were somehow responsible.

'I see,' said Vanessa harshly. 'And I suppose you're now going to tell Donald. Unless I do what you want.'

'You were always quick on the up-take. But you'll be surprised when you know what it is.'

'Rotten sod.'

'Language, sweetheart. All you've got to do is to persuade Donald about something. Something in his own interest.'

'Money?'

'Not really. We're buying a magazine, Donald and I. He's told you?'

'A bit. He's not keen.'

'That's just what's worrying me. I want you to make him keen. Or at least helpful. It's no fun having him sulking.'

'And how do I do that?'

'You've got influence with him.'

'Not over that kind of thing.'

'Look, dear,' Jude Holbrook said. 'You're looking forward to wearing the family diamonds and being the lady of the manor, and we're all very happy for you. But you know as well as I do that Donald's a jealous little boy and would be very cross if he heard that Jimmy and Co. had been at his honey-pot. So there'll be no diamonds and no manor house for you, darling, unless you do what I say. Which is to use your well known charms to sweeten up Donald about this magazine. I don't expect him to shout with joy about it, but I do expect him to show a little interest. Right?'

The day before Christmas Eve Donald took Vanessa to a party, given by Max de Freville the gambler, where he won three thousand, five hundred pounds. When they arrived back at Cheyne Row at five in the morning (as often as not Vanessa spent the night there instead of in her basement), Donald said:

'You certainly brought me luck. With you sitting beside me I knew I had to win. But if ever you moved away, even for a few moments, the cards turned against me. Oh, Vanessa,' he said, mildly hysterical after his splendid *coup*, 'don't ever move away from me for long.'

'I won't.'

'What,' said Donald, pulling himself together, 'would you like for a *special* Christmas present?'

Vanessa thought of all the expensive things she could do with, but decided to leave them until later. Here was an opportunity, too good to miss, for getting from Donald the promise which she needed.

'There's something. . . .'

'Yes?'

'You say I bring you luck. So if there was something I badly wanted you to do, you'd be lucky at it?'

'I hope so,' said Donald, puzzled.

'Donald . . . I want you to be more serious over this magazine you were telling me about. For my sake.'

'*Strix?* For *your* sake?'

'You see, I don't want you to be just a business man. I don't want to be married to someone who's just a business man. It's not that I despise business –'

'– I should hope not –'

'– But I feel you've got it in you to do other things, bigger things, as well.'

'What's so big about *Strix?*'

'It's an opening,' said Vanessa stroking his hair, 'into another kind of world.' She licked his ear in the way he particularly loved. 'Important, worthwhile journalism. It's a contribution to culture, perhaps even to history. Don't you see?' She licked his ear again, put her tongue into it, and then leaned away from him. 'It would make you an influence. The voice, and the conscience, of commerce.'

As Vanessa laid his head in her lap and started to massage his scalp, Donald imagined himself as the voice and the conscience of commerce. The prospect was not displeasing. A contribution to culture, Vanessa said: *that* would surely make up for his wretched third at Oxford. An influence? 'Your car is waiting, Lord Salinger. You ought to leave now, if you are to be in good time to receive your honorary doctorate. . . . The P.M.'s private secretary telephoned to convey congratulations and best wishes.' Clad in scarlet gown and tudor cap, Lord Salinger, Honorary Doctor of Letters, O.M. (why not?), G.C.M.G. (for good measure), stood at the top of the steps while the bells rang in his honour and the undergraduates cheered themselves hoarse below. Doffing his cap gracefully, pausing to make one of the quick witticism for which he was famous to the Chancellor at his side, he moved slowly down the steps and into sleep.

In the end, Vanessa's 'special' Christmas present took the form of a slap-up Christmas holiday in Venice, her favourite place. But her appeal about *Strix* was not forgotten, except in the sense that Donald no longer regarded it as her appeal but as the timely voice of his own enlightened ambition.

'Now then,' said Donald, back from Venice on the first morning of the New Year, '*Strix*.'

'What about *Strix*?' said Holbrook crossly. He was still trying to work out how much it had cost him to see the New Year in with Angela Tuck.

'Action. Time we got things moving.'

So Vanessa had done her stuff.

'There's not much to be done till Philby gets back from America.'

'Nonsense. We can get word to him that we wish to make an offer. And has everything possible been done this end? There is no time to be lost.'

Perhaps Vanessa had overdone it. The last thing Holbrook wanted was a pyrotechnic exhibition of officiousness by

Donald, who was quite capable of letting all London know what they were up to between lunch and tea. While Donald must not be discouraged, he must not be allowed to beat the drum.

'Your chum Somerset Lloyd-James has been sounded. He implied that the Board might not be too keen.'

'He'll help us?'

'He'll hold the ring. But I fancy,' said Holbrook warily, 'that he'll need . . . an inducement, rather a strong inducement . . . before he declares himself for us.'

Donald looked unhappy. He did not like being crossed once he had made up his mind; still less did he like the prospect, however tactfully uncovered by Holbrook, of illicit dealing. Although capable of underhand actions in a virtuous context (as when he had tried to tip off Holbrook père about what had happened to his cheque) Donald could never be a conscious party to corruption: at bottom a cautious, even a timorous man, he had inherited a middle-class concern for respectability, which he decorated with the name of honour.

'Look, Donald,' said his partner gently, 'why not let me handle this? Lloyd-James is your friend; it would all be most embarrassing for you. And on this particular level, I think I understand him better than you do.'

Donald beamed with restored good humour. He was, he told himself, a man of the world. Great objects were never achieved without – well – machinations. And if someone else were prepared to undertake this, without keeping him too specifically informed. . . . 'Lord Salinger,' said a tiny, distant voice, 'your car is waiting.'

'I think,' Holbrook was saying, 'that we should wait until Philby returns and get his reaction. If he is willing, I will have another little talk with Somerset Lloyd-James.'

'No,' said Donald. His renewed optimism required instant progress. ('Lord Salinger,' whispered the tiny voice, 'Lord Salinger.') 'I think that we should approach Somerset straight away. I think we should make sure of his friendship, and get him to pass discreet word to Philby in America – it will prepare him and may even bring him back sooner.'

'I see,' said Holbrook agreeably. He was disposed to let his partner have his way to a very considerable extent provided only that Donald kept quiet and left the negotiations to himself. 'Then I suggest,' he went on, falling smoothly into Donald's idiom of equivocation, 'that I should go to Lloyd-James and express our sincere appreciation of his excellent work. I shall say that we wish to be more closely associated with this work, and I shall ask him to convey this sentiment, in a flattering form, to his absent employer. Finally, I shall tell him that when our association is established we shall, of course, be even more appreciative of his merits than we are now.'

'That's it,' said Donald; 'splendid.'

'There is only one thing, Donald. Acts of cultural patronage, which is what we are extending to Lloyd-James, are expensive. You will bear this in mind, now and later?'

Donald nodded, the seigniorial nod of a patron of culture, and went happily out to lunch at the Mirabelle.

'Two thousand down,' Holbrook said: 'three thousand the day we take over.'

'Three thousand down,' corrected Somerset Lloyd-James, 'and five thousand the day the Board gives its consent.'

Holbrook pursed his lips and picked at the skin round his thumb-nail.

'You must not make the business man's usual and vulgar mistake,' said Somerset affably, 'of expecting cultural services to come cheap.'

'Why don't we go up to my place,' Miss Beatty said, 'for a last drink?'

'Suits me,' the man said. He was a large, clean, well preserved man of about fifty-five, with the small curly moustache and close-cropped hair of a regimental sergeant-major.

Together they left the pub and walked towards Miss Beatty's place. Since this was the first time Miss Beatty had taken such dramatic advantage of her mother's absence, she was feeling rather nervous. But not unduly so; she had met this man in the pub several times before tonight, he had always been polite if withdrawn, and Miss Beatty, who had only started going there ten days ago, assumed that he was a regular in the place.

'Light ale?' Miss Beatty said when they were in her flat: 'I'm afraid that's all there is.'

'Suits me,' said the man.

'Make yourself comfy then.'

She switched on the television and went into the kitchenette. When she came out again with the tray of drinks, the man was gazing into the television screen with a blank absorption which reminded her uncomfortably of mother. Although he took his glass when she handed it, he neither noticed nor thanked her; nor did he respond in any way when Miss Beatty sat down beside him on the sofa.

An easy guest but a dull one, Miss Beatty thought.

Side by side they sat there, watching television; until at last, during the final bars of God save the Queen, the man drained his hitherto untouched beer in one and rose slowly to his feet.

My dear Philby, (Somerset wrote)

I think you should know that a certain party is prepared to make you a handsome cash offer for the Proprietorship. If such an offer would interest you, then perhaps you would care to consider the following points.

1) It is advisable that you should signify as soon as possible that you are prepared, in principle, to negotiate.

2) Do not, on the other hand, hasten your return home or otherwise show undue enthusiasm. *Strix* is gaining ground every week: the longer you wait (within reason), the higher the price.

3) Although the interested party is in most ways both responsible and respectable, there are circumstances which may incline the Board to make difficulties. I think I can deal with these, but not without trouble and perhaps expense. So when you write confirming your willingness to sell, would you also confirm that I may expect reimbursement in respect of

any services which I may have to render on your behalf?

Yours sincerely,

Somerset Lloyd-James.

That should do the trick, thought Somerset as he carefully sealed the envelope and put it into his pocket to post later. To judge from what a banking acquaintance had told him the previous evening, young Philby would be feeling the breeze badly by the end of March – must have started to feel it already. In which case, he would be glad to receive Somerset's letter and disposed to do the right thing by Somerset.

Where the devil is Miss Beatty today?'

'She must be ill, Mr. Holbrook.'

'Not like her. Hasn't she rung up or anything?'

'I'm afraid not, sir. She isn't on the telephone.'

'Well, never mind her. I want you to take some letters.'

'But don't you think, sir . . . I mean, Miss Beatty lives alone now, so perhaps we ought –'

'– Miss Beatty,' said Holbrook, 'is old enough to take care of herself.'

'. . . The fifth item for the Board's consideration was Mr. Peter Morrison's proposal that Mr. Thomas Llewyllyn should be invited to write original essays for the journal as well as book reviews. Mr. Morrison said that he had always admired the robust good sense of Mr. Llewyllyn's work and could wish to see its author allowed greater scope in the journal. Professor Constable agreed, but Mr. Dilkes reminded the Board of the offence which Mr. Llewyllyn had given to readers in the past. It was resolved, not withstanding, that Mr. Llewyllyn should be asked to submit possible ideas and subjects to the Editor, who might commission, at his discretion, up to three long essays from this writer.

'The sixth and last matter for discussion was the request of the Editor that members address their minds to what he described as "a delicate question of policy". They were all aware, Mr. Lloyd-James observed, that the Proprietor, Lord Philby, was a young man of various enthusiasms and that he might, in consequence, find it expedient to dispose of the Proprietorship in order to further other ends. The problem then facing them would be the correct interpretation of the Articles which dealt with this contingency.

'Professor Constable said that the purport of the Articles was so obvious that there could be no problem: no person with financial interests for which he might procure propaganda in the journal could be admitted to its Proprietorship.

'Mr. Lloyd-James: But are we to take this as ruling out anyone who has any financial interests whatever? If so, it means that no one in a position to make an offer can ever be acceptable.

'Professor Constable: The Articles certainly require us to be stringent. It is at least possible that the late Lord Philby did not wish the Proprietorship to pass out of his family – that he meant no offer to be acceptable.

'Mr. L-J: In that case why did he not say so? If he troubled to regulate the conditions of sale, he must have envisaged its possibility.

'Mr. Morrison: Can we not examine the clauses in question?

'Mr. L-J: I have the Articles here. . . . "In case of Lord Philby, his heirs or successors, wishing to dispose of the Proprietorship otherwise than by death, e.g., by gifts or sale, this shall be permissible provided that three out of the four remaining members of the Board are satisfied that the Proprietorship is not passing to a person or persons who might attempt to exploit or pervert the editorial section of the journal for the furtherance of their own financial, industrial or commercial interest.

"In case of the Proprietor's death . . . et cetera, et cetera."

'Prof. C: Just as I said.

'Mr. L-J: Not quite, Vice-Chancellor. It does not say that we are to reject *anyone who has financial interests*, but *the type of person who might abuse the paper for the promotion of such interests*. We are required to exercise our knowledge of human character and commercial probity.

'Prof. C: I must disagree. It simply says, ". . . person or persons who might attempt to exploit or pervert . . ." i.e. person or persons who have a motive to exploit or pervert, i.e. person or persons who have industrial or business interests.

'Mr. L-J: Surely not. It is the Latin construction of the relative with the subjunctive implying a qualitative judgement. "Who might attempt" equals *qui conetur* equals the *sort of person* who attempts.

'Prof. C: Or a person who has a motive to attempt.

'Mr. M: I feel that syntactical haggling will cast little light on the matter. Should we not leave the question until there is a practical need to answer it?

'Mr. Dilkes: Just so. I am surprised that it has been raised at all. There is no reason at present to supposed that Lord Philby is contemplating sale.

'Mr. L-J: *Qui contempletur*. He is *the sort of person* who contemplates sale. I merely raised the point so that members might be warned: the precise meaning of the clause is arguable, and it is as well that we should give our minds to it against a possible need for its clarification.

'Prof. C: Well, you know my view.

'Mr. D: I incline to the pragmatic school. I shall pay more attention to the character and reputation of the applicant, should there ever be one, than to the close interpretation of clauses.

'Mr. M: That makes good sense. After all, we know what the late Lord Philby stood for, and if we could say of an applicant, "The founder would have approved of him", we should probably be acting in the spirit of the Articles.

'Prof. C: We must first have regard to the letter.

'Mr. L-J: And if the letter is ambiguous?

'Prof. C: It is not ambiguous to me.'

'Policeman to see you, Mr. Salinger.'

'Oh well. Send him in . . . Oh dear, officer. Parking again?'

'Chief Inspectors don't deal with parking offences, Mr. Salinger.'

'I'm so sorry. I didn't notice all those pretty silver things on your shoulders. Please sit down. Now then?'

'You employ a certain Miss Beatty?'

'What on earth's Beatty been up to? Come to think of it, I haven't seen her today. Or yesterday, for the matter of that.'

'That is not altogether surprising, Mr. Salinger. Miss Beatty was found in her flat this morning. Or rather, most of her was.'

7

Somerset Lloyd-James passed Tom Llewyllyn an open cheque for £100.

'That's for February, Tom. Only March to go now. So how's the book?'

'Not too bad. I finally got it in a fortnight ago. Stern seems rather pleased.'

'But you'll be needing money until it comes out?'

'I always need money,' Tom said.

'Then listen. The Board has agreed that I can commission three long essays from you. Peter Morrison's suggestion.'

'Nice of him.'

'He admires your work. Three pieces of 4,000 words each, I thought: fifty guineas a piece and an advance if you want it. In principle, you submit a selection of subjects and I take my pick. But for the first of them I want you to do a specific job for me.'

'We aim to please.'

'I want a piece urging that in the rapidly changing conditions of today we cannot always stick fast to codes and regulations drawn up by dead men who had no idea of what we must now contend with.'

'I'm not quite there.'

'Take the question of Trusts. Permission has recently been given, in view of certain exigences unforeseeable by those who drew them up, for several important Trusts to be broken. To meet taxes or death duties, or even because the investment pattern enforced would clearly prove deleterious.'

'And so?'

'It is a principle which needs to be applied more widely. You have schools, institutions, corporations – even newspapers, bound hand and foot by articles which no longer make sense.'

'So what do you want done about it? Those Trust cases are

very few and very special. And they had the hell of a job breaking them.'

'I want you to advocate . . . flexibility . . . on the part of
Trustees and so on. Flexibility of interpretation.'

'A lot of people won't like it.'

'So long as I like it,' said Somerset. 'And of course Peter
Morrison, who so kindly put your name up. He likes brisk good
sense, which I rely on you to give him.'

'Bring him round, eh?'

'What do you mean?'

Tom grinned in a friendly way.

'I saw an old friend at a party the other day, an old friend
who's now Donald Salinger's fiancée. She seemed to think that
Salinger & Holbrook are keen to extend their interests. What
Vanessa doesn't know is that not everyone will be in favour.
Eh, Somerset?'

'Are you?' said Somerset mildly.

'I'm just a poor old mercenary, love. So long as I get my hire.
. . . Which I think – don't you? – should be just that little extra
on this occasion. A hundred and fifty, shall we say, for this very
important piece?'

'A hundred.'

'And twenty-five.'

'Done,' said Somerset. 'And you'll be discreet about what
you've heard? You'll find people grateful later on.'

'Certainly. But I can't answer for Vanessa.'

'I'll get Donald to talk to her. You know, contrary to the
usual opinion, married or engaged men are far worse security
risks than casual lechers or prowling homosexuals.
Promiscuous people are only interested in getting sex; but
when a man takes a woman seriously enough to marry her,
God knows what he won't go and tell her.'

'Anything of interest on the *Strix* front?' said Carton Weir to
Peter Morrison.

'Not in the sense you mean.'

They turned about, each turning in toward the other, and

walked back down the terrace with the firm but unhurried tread of officers waiting to be called on parade. A tug-boat wailed and the river lapped flaccidly below them. I wish, thought Carton Weir, that Peter had not got this ridiculous thing about fresh air.

'It is all a question,' Peter was saying, 'of who shall guard the guardians. *Strix* sets itself up as a moral referee for the business and industrial communities. But if you ask me there's something fishy going on in Gower Street itself.'

'What makes you think so?'

'Somerset Lloyd-James has a look in his eye. I've seen that look before, and it meant no good at all. Somerset thinks he's got a poker face, but when he's bluffing his eyes have a kind of glaze, as though he were afraid lest you might look through them and see the plot hatching inside his head.'

'Anything more substantial?' said Weir as they turned about once more.

'Yes. At the Board meeting in February, and again at the beginning of this month, Somerset provoked apparently theoretical discussions about the conditions of ownership. While these discussions were going on, the glaze was almost blinding, if you see what I mean.'

'What line did he take?'

'That we ought not to be too conservative in our reading of the Articles. He's even got Tom Llewyllyn to write a long essay about it – in general terms, of course.'

'A very good essay, I thought.'

'So did I,' said Peter. 'But if I know my Somerset it's part of a build-up. He wants everyone to agree that we mustn't be too stuffy about rules and regulations – and then, hey presto, we shall find the devil himself sitting at the head of the Board with Somerset at his right hand.'

'So what shall you do?'

'Take a long spoon with me when I go to Gower Street from now on. . . . There was something else, Carton. Somerset took me out to dinner, which is a rare treat coming from him, and started on about . . . well . . . about. . . .'

Peter broke off and looked almost guiltily at Weir's squat profile. 'Started on again about rules and regulations?' Weir suggested. 'No. He started on about you. He's been collecting stories about the company you keep.'

'Oh?' said Weir, annoyed and wary.

'I'm not one to moralize, Carton. Your private life is your own affair; unless it becomes public.'

'I know how to be discreet.'

'Others, it appears, do not.'

'So you're worried in case I let the side down?'

'No,' said Peter calmly: 'that's Somerset's worry. Mine is on behalf of a friend.'

Captain Detterling walked across the terrace to join them; he fell in by their side and the formal passagio continued.

'You look glum, my captain,' said Carton Weir, having quickly thrown off the outward signs of his irritation.

'It's Susan,' said Detterling apologetically, 'Susan Grange. I asked her to marry me, and do you know what she did?'

'I hope she didn't say "yes",' said Weir bluntly.

'She walked straight out in the middle of dinner. "It is foul bad manners," she said, "to propose at meal times, and anyhow you're after my money." And before I could explain that I've got five times as much money as she has, she was gone.'

'Where to?'

'I believe she has formed an attachment to a queen called Jonathan Gamp.'

'They deserve each other,' said Weir. 'I always thought she might turn into a queens' moll.'

'But that,' said Detterling, 'is not what I came to tell you both. I have had some disquieting news from my man in Washington.'

'Your man in Washington?'

'Ivan Blessington, formerly of my regiment. He has a plain, honest, stupid face, so people tell him secrets to relieve their tension. They think, you see, that he won't understand what he is told and will in any case forget it the next minute. They're right about him not understanding things very well, but what they don't know is that he has a tape-recorder memory. He sends me a weekly transcript for which I pay him quite a lot of money.'

'And what is his news?' said Peter, who looked as if he did not care much for this mode of receiving it.

'Not to go into detail, it looks as though the Yanks are getting ready to do the dirty on Nasser over the money for that dam of his.'

With one accord they stopped walking and made a quick huddled group, like football players crowding in to screen a companion who has lost his shorts.

'Which means trouble over the Canal,' said Weir, 'which in turn means trouble with every Blimp in the House and in the country. Ex-corporal Blimp as well as the colonel.'

'When?' said Peter. 'When are they likely to announce their decision?'

'It's not a decision yet,' Captain Detterling said. 'But it soon will be if Nasser gets many more of those interesting crates marked "Knitting needles" from Mother Russia.'

'Bitch,' said Holbrook; 'foul, dirty bitch. You love it, don't you? You know how filthy it is, yet you wallow in it like an animal. Admit it then: tell me you're a foul, dirty bitch.'

Eyes glistening with pleasure, he waited for Angela's answer.

'Yes, yes,' she moaned, 'it's filthy, vile, disgusting, but I love it, oh, I love it, and no one does it like you. Go on,' she panted, 'more, more, more. . . .'

A little later Angela said calmly,

'So how's Penelope? And Donny?'

'Donny's all right. Penelope's in Paris again.'

You want me to say it, he thought. You want me to say that I'm finally going to get rid of her and marry you. Well, that I may do, but I'm going to keep you waiting for a while yet. Nobody makes me feel so good, nobody lets me do what you let me do, nobody is in my power so much as you. Which is another reason for keeping you waiting; it won't do for you to start feeling too secure. Besides, there's a lot to see to in the near future – no time for fiddling about with divorces just now. Philby will be back in a few days, and then we can get this deal moving. We must get *Strix*; it will be the turning point, the beginning of the big time, the big money, the big talk, the big 'I-say-so-and-to-hell-with-you' for the whole cretinous and flabby lot.

No good pressing him, Angela thought. Provided I go on letting him do what he's just done, thinking that I like it, thinking that he has me grovelling at his mercy, sooner or later he'll come round. Just now he's obsessed; obsessed with how to get more money, more people to kick. It doesn't do to disturb a man while he's obsessed. Let him enjoy his dreams in peace, the little brute, and sooner or later, when he's badly in need of a woman to kick, he'll think of me and he'll come round. Why do I want him at all? Well, he's available, for a start, and then there's the money, and he could be an important man some day; but perhaps part of me really did like what he did, really did take pleasure in grovelling and moaning on the bed.

Ashley Dexterside kept himself to himself and unlike most of his kind was not much interested in trading cliquey gossip. He had, for example, heard all about Vanessa's antics in The Cavalier even before Jonathan Gamp, but it had never occurred to him to pass the information on, let alone use it to make trouble. If Donald wanted to marry a slut, that, thought Ashley now as ever, was Donald's funeral. On the other hand, Ashley did not lack interest in his fellow human beings, and what he did concern himself about, with curiosity and understanding, was the progress of current affairs and the personalities involved in them. On three evenings out of four, while most of his acquaintance were fluting away over their gin glasses about who was bedding with whom, Ashley was to be found at home in his neat little flat with *The New Statesman* and *The Spectator*, an assortment of news letters to which he subscribed, the latest ministerial autobiography, *The Economist*, *The Financial Times* (etc., etc.), and these days, of course, *Strix*. The information thus acquired was later spiced, supplemented and often seriously qualified by the copious inside items to which he was treated by his old friend, Carton Weir. At least twice a week they would dine together; and although as the evening went on their activities sometimes became dubious (Weir could not, of course, go to places like The Cavalier but was a great one for sniffing out private parties), dinner itself, a model of propriety and good food, was always devoted to the political and cultural events of the day.

On this particular evening in March they were dining, as they often did, in Ashley's flat, for Ashley was a talented cook and liked to make his own contribution to these occasions in exchange for the privileged confidences which he received. Carton, who seemed unusually short of material, had been going on for some time about the sensational failure of the Queen Mother's horse, Devon Loch, in the Grand National and speculating, rather thinly, as to the effect this would have on the popularity of the royal family. Ashley, bored with this topic, tired by the effort of cooking, piqued by his employers' continued prevarication over his rise in salary, and wishing, for all his usual reticence, to impress Carton (who was behaving rather smugly), suddenly said:

'I think I know something which will interest you.'

Since it was inconceivable that Ashley could know anything which he didn't, Carton smiled indulgently and went on talking about the amount of money which punters up and down the country had lost on Devon Loch.

'For Christ's sake stop being so silly,' Ashley said.

'Hoity-toity,' said Carton Weir.

'All right. I shan't tell you.'

'I don't want to know.'

'Never fear, madam: you won't.'

'Better draw the lace curtains or I might see in and guess.'

But when Carton saw that Ashley was vexed almost to tears, and when he thought to himself what a delicious meal his old friend had cooked for him after a long and bloody day at his office, he leant over, touched Ashley gently on the arm, and said,

'I'm sorry, old thing. It was too bad of me. Please tell.'

Ashley blinked a bit; then they both smiled at their own silliness and helped themselves to quadruple measures of Marc.

'You remember,' Ashley said, 'that day you first heard about the loan for the Aswan dam – how the Americans were thinking of withdrawing?'

'Yes. . . . There's been nothing more about that, by the way. I think Detterling's man must have goofed. After all, it would be about as tactless a thing as –'

But since Ashley was beginning to look impatient all over again, Carton broke off and allowed his friend to continue.

'*Well*,' said Ashley firmly, 'you told me about something else which happened the same day, only it seemed so unimportant by comparison that I'd almost forgotten. You said that your chum Peter Morrison thought that something was up at *Strix*.'

'Yes, dear,' said Carton, trying to look interested; 'but there didn't seem to be much in it.'

'You'd be surprised, dear. My bosses are in it – up to their dirty necks. You see, they always talk in front of me as if I wasn't there. I'm like an old family retainer; a piece of mobile furniture which neither hears nor talks. And yesterday, while I was in there checking specimen designs, out it all came. They're making a bid for *Strix*, and they're rather worried that your chum Morrison, if no one else, is going to get in their way.'

'Oh,' said Carton Weir, very thoughtfully indeed.

'One of the reasons I'm telling you,' said Ashley truthfully, 'is because I think Morrison should be warned. From what I can make out, he's a thoroughly good sort, and you say he's on *our* side about these stupid laws.'

'He wants consenting adults left alone, certainly.'

'Don't we all, dear? Now, I know this sounds a bit far-fetched, but what you should tell Morrison is that Jude Holbrook at any rate can get very nasty indeed when he's not having his own way. I've been with him since they started and believe me, I know. You read about that poor woman who was murdered in Wandsworth the other day? Well, she was our head secretary and –'

'Don't tell me Holbrook cut her up?'

'He's capable of it. But the point was that he just couldn't be bothered to come to the funeral. Donald and I had to make all the arrangements, go and see her idiotic old mother in a home, and God knows what. It was awful. You know what the idiot mum did when we told her? She sat there and screamed with laughter, until they had to take her away.'

That night was to be an early one, so Ashley did not accompany Carton when the latter left the flat at half past ten. Once by himself, Carton pondered what had been said about *Strix*. At first it seemed that he should indeed warn Peter Morrison as Ashley had suggested. Then it occurred to him that the struggle would be more amusing, from a spectator's point of view, if Morrison were not warned; for that way there would be a more searching and sudden test of Morrison's acumen, and it would be instructive, later on, to check Morrison's version of what happened against the information which Ashley had promised from Chancery Lane. If this attitude of Carton's was partly the result of spite (for Morrison's warning about his private life was rankling yet), it was still more the product of an oblique intellect which rejoiced in complexities for their own sake. Carton Weir was not really a man of ill will; but he liked life to be devious as he was then one of the few people clever enough to understand it, and he had no intention of spoiling his own pleasure in order to lighten the difficulties of Peter Morrison. Morrison, Carton told himself, was for ever trying to over-simplify things in the name of common decency or common sense; it was high time that he was called upon to cope with complication.

A few days later Lord Philby, newly back in London from America, made it privately known to Salinger & Holbrook that he was prepared to sell the Proprietorship of *Strix* for the sum of £75,000. After some discussion the figure was reduced to £65,000. In consideration of £5,000 down, Lord Philby recognized that Salinger & Holbrook now had the sole option on purchase for the next nine months, which it was hoped would give them ample time to make all the necessary arrangements and overcome any difficulties that might be raised by the Board.

After the April meeting of the Board, over which Lord Philby had deigned to preside, Somerset Lloyd-James took Peter Morrison up to his office.

'Philby wants to sell,' said Somerset bluntly.

'Why didn't he tell us this afternoon?'

'Negotiations are at an early stage. He wants to know his ground better before he shows himself on it. Reasonable, wouldn't you say?'

Peter did not answer. Clearly, Somerset had a purpose in this conversation: let him now go ahead and declare it. Whenever Somerset had a difficult request to make, he preferred to approach it by an intricate process of dialectic, which twisted this way and that until eventually and wholly unawares the victim said something that implied assent to the proposition with which Somerset, now and not before, would confront him. Peter, having no intention of being caught in this trap, sat tight and held his tongue. After a while Somerset smiled thinly and said:

'Do you want to hear about it?'

'Not much. No doubt Philby will tell the Board in his own good time.'

'I think,' said Somerset, carefully disguising his chagrin, 'that I had better tell you all the same.'

'If you insist.'

Since Peter was declining to co-operate in his own confusion, Somerset settled for his second best tactic: a brief statement so angled that no right-minded man could disagree with it.

'The potential purchaser,' Somerset said, 'is a respectable firm called Salinger & Holbrook. I am in their favour. Dilkes, with whom I have spoken, is also in their favour. Only Professor Constable, with his pedantic obsession with the letter of the Articles, will be against them.'

'How do you know that I will not be against them?'

But this, as Peter realized too late, was to play Somerset's game.

'Because,' said Somerset smugly, 'whenever the Board has discussed the clause which covers this situation you have appeared, generally speaking, to side with Dilkes.'

Peter drew a slow breath.

'Generally speaking, yes. But this is a particular issue. I shall need to know a great deal more about Salinger & Holbrook – the firm and the people – before committing myself either way.'

'Donald Salinger,' said Somerset easily, 'is an old friend of mine, the son of a dear friend of my mother's. He has money, taste and wide general interests, though he has always been too easy-going to look very deeply into anything. He is tolerant and well mannered, excellent company, inclined to be vague but a man of his word. I think you'd like him.'

Peter nodded.

'I've heard of him,' he said; 'he turns out for the Foresters from time to time. And what about Holbrook?'

'Jude Holbrook,' said Somerset, 'is the more efficient of the two. He is a man of enterprise and a first-rate executive. He is considerably poorer than his partner, but he has a grasp of organization and method which is just as important to the firm as Donald Salinger's capital. Personally he is not amiable, though attractive, I am told, to women.'

'What do they *do* – with this firm of theirs?'

'They print and distribute high quality advertising material.'

There was no way out of this; sooner or later Peter had to know. Oddly enough, however, the mention of advertising did not seem to upset him. He murmured something about responsible advertising being an important public service and rose to go.

'You'll consider it then?' said Somerset.

'Yes, I'll consider it. But I'll want details about the firm, and I'll have to meet both these partners.'

So far, thought Somerset as he accompanied Peter to the door, so good; but I shall have a quiet word with Holbrook before letting them meet. Returning to his desk, he thought with pleasure of the 5 per cent which Philby had agreed to pay him in the event of the sale going through. Which reminded him; Philby owed him £250 – 5 per cent of the option money already received – and had not sent a cheque. I'll give him two or three days, Somerset decided, and then pay a friendly call.

'The day after tomorrow,' Vanessa said. 'I can hardly believe it.'

'Nor can I. Mr. and Mrs. Salinger. . . . Nothing very grand after the Register Office,' Donald said; 'just a drink and a bite with a few friends before we get the 'plane. The real celebration will be the Ball in June. Lunch tomorrow?'

'I've got a doctor's appointment,' said Vanessa, coyly and untruthfully, 'at two.'

'Anyway, perhaps better not,' Donald conceded. 'I've got a big conference with Jude – putting him straight about what's to happen while I'm away.'

I've got something to put straight too, Vanessa thought, and only just managed not to giggle.

My dear Somerset, (Peter had written)

Although I shall postpone my final decision about Salinger & Holbrook until I've actually met them, I should tell you that my inquiries so far have made me rather doubtful.

In the first place, it appears that they do not discriminate as to the kind of advertising they handle. I think you misled me about this. 'High quality' their stuff may be, but the phrase refers to the printing and presentation, and not, I gather, to the goods advertised or the methods used to advertise them. Have you seen the new posters for Marjoram's tooth-paste? Very stimulating to look at, but. . . .

Secondly, I'm told that Holbrook is a thruster. No one has anything concrete against him, but he would not appear noted for scruple.

And third, a small thing, I suppose, but indicative. One of my colleagues has a friend who works for S & H. It seems that this friend, after years of good service, has not been given a promised rise in salary and that whenever he applies Holbrook fobs him off. (Nor can there be a financial reason for this: I am told the firm is definitely prosperous, as it would in any case have to be to put in a bid for *Strix*.) I have also heard from the same source that Holbrook 'just couldn't be bothered', the other day, to attend the funeral of an employee of long standing.

Though all of this may be merely trivial, I can't say it makes a good impression. Still, it would be premature and immoral to form judgement on hearsay, and, as I say, I shall reserve my opinion until I have met these gentlemen personally.

    Yours ever

    Peter

'You see,' said Somerset to the two partners, and put down the letter.

They were having the final conference before Donald's honeymoon started the next day. Somerset was attending by request in order that they might all discuss the state of play about *Strix*.

'Peter Morrison,' Somerset went on, 'is crucial. I shall vote in your favour and so will Harry Dilkes. Constable will vote against you if he hangs for it. We need three votes out of four, so we must have Peter's.'

'What do you suggest?' said Donald.

'I suggest that we leave him alone until after you get back in May. It will then be up to you, Donald, to work on him. From now on, now that things are reaching a public level, you're going to be our front man. Because, if Jude will forgive me for saying so, you've got the right sort of charm and he hasn't. Morrison is a good case in point: he is disposed, I know, to like you from what he's heard of you, and he is not disposed to like Jude. He'll have to meet Jude, of course, but you're the one who must get him to revise his bad impression.'

'I'd like,' said Holbrook tightly, 'to get things moving a bit quicker. Now we know where we stand with Philby. . . .'

'You've got a nine months' option. No need to rush.'

'Hanging about makes me nervous.'

'Look,' said Somerset. 'I know Peter Morrison. He is a good-natured man but he can be obstinate. If we try to rush him, we'll get his back up. So put yourself on your best behaviour for a month. Give this chap who's been complaining the rise you promised him. Start doing a few enlightened actions round the place – I'll see he gets to hear of them. But above all, don't show impatience about *Strix*. Morrison's a placid chap, a countryman born and bred, and he mistrusts impatience. Or enthusiasm, for the matter of that.'

'Yes, yes, yes,' said Holbrook, snapping his fingers: 'what shall you tell him?'

'That Donald's away and nothing needs to be decided until he gets back. That you're not as bad as you're painted – that your efficiency and success have made people jealous.'

'And this business of meeting him?'

'I'll give a bachelor dinner party,' Somerset said, 'at the end of May, and send the bill on to you. Nothing need be said about *Strix*; just a friendly evening. And then it might be a nice attention if Donald were to ask him to this Ball of his in June.'

'Won't he think I'm trying to soften him up?' said Donald.

'No. That would be far too obvious. He'll take it as a friendly act, as meaning that you won't bear hard feelings either way and want to know him better; that you're both gentlemen who can get on very well privately whatever differences you may have professionally.'

'The amateur touch,' sneered Holbrook.

'Yes,' said Somerset evenly; 'it often helps you to what you want, and even if it doesn't it prevents nastiness. And while we're on the subject of your Ball, Donald, could you ask Tom Llewyllyn? You know him, I think?'

'Not well,' said Donald hesitantly; 'and he's rather apt to make scenes.'

'I'll keep an eye on him. The point is that Morrison admires

Tom's work and might be pleasantly impressed if he saw him there.'

'And where does all this get us?' said Holbrook.

'It gets us to the end of June. At which time Morrison can be sounded, and if all's well the matter can go straight to the Board.'

'And if all isn't well?'

'Then we shall have six months left before the option expires.'

'I still don't like all this delay,' Holbrook said.

'Neither do I,' said Donald, 'but Somerset's quite right. Since we're dealing with a gentleman for once, we have no choice but to deal in his terms.'

'I wonder,' Holbrook said.

Nevertheless, he agreed to Somerset's schedule.

'Well, that's that, I'm afraid,' said Vanessa, fastening a suspender with a snap. 'Anyway till I get back next month.'

'I'm going to miss you, Nessa,' said Jimmy. 'We all are.'

'It's been fun, hasn't it?'

'All the fun in the world. . . . Lend us a fiver, Nessa. For old times' sake.'

'What a foul little tart you are,' said Vanessa, and kissed him fondly on his curly black hair.

The next morning at eleven o'clock Vanessa and Donald were married at Caxton Hall. After a few drinks and a buffet lunch in a private room at the Ritz, they left by air for Rome, where they were to spend ten days before going to Athens, Beirut, Alexandria and Tangier.

'Bless the darlings,' said Jonathan Gamp as he waved them away in the car: 'I hope they both remember what I taught them.'

Part Three

8

A month after Donald and Vanessa Salinger returned from their honeymoon they gave their mid-summer ball to proclaim, *urbi et orbi*, their installation as gentry.

For now that Donald had taken to himself a wife, Chevenix Court, promoted from an 'amusing' venue for occasional drunken weekends, was to become his home and more: it was to be at once the symbol of his establishment as a citizen of substance and the vehicle for furthering his social ambitions. It would be difficult to say by which conception of himself he was now more infatuated – that of Donald the rising man of business, of Donald the responsible family man, or Donald the country host. All three *personae*, which in another man would have been merely boring, achieved a certain piquancy in Donald's case when considered in the light of his past. His business, after all, had begun seven years before as little more than an accident, something which he had got up only because he had nothing else to do and Jude Holbrook had jostled him into it – something, in any case, for which he tended to apologize to his more cultivated friends. His pretensions as a husband, which sprang as much from self-regard as from love of Vanessa, could only be ludicrous to those who remembered Jonathan Gamp's story (one of many) of the Moroccan brothel in which Donald, having lost his glasses, was fobbed off with the oldest and ugliest whore at top prices. And as for his desire to play host, why should a man who had entertained some of the most brilliant names – or at least fringe-names – both in London and Paris be so proud of collecting for Sunday luncheon two commuting stock-jobbers and a decayed second baron?

But the new situation derived its charm less from the contrast which it made with the old than from the absurd self-satisfaction with which Donald regarded it. He remained, despite everything, an amiable source of amusement because now as ever he had got the whole thing wrong. He was glee-fully fumbling the old whore, society, without his spectacles. Because the stockbrokers ran small farms (at a deliberate loss to offset taxes) they had become, to Donald, country gentle-men with city interests. The second baron passed muster because he had recently been M.F.H. (as hunting country this was some of the most contemptible in England) and because Donald had somehow persuaded himself that although the peerage, a Lloyd George job, was new, the family was old and had 'always lived in the country' – as indeed it had for the last century, sanding the sugar in a scabby local grocery. Such errors and ineptnesses, as Tom Llewyllyn remarked to Somerset Lloyd-James on the drive down to the ball, were typical in Donald and endearing; and indeed it was just this blend of inaccurate snobbishness, personal self-importance and subtly misconceived formality that was to inform the cel-ebration ahead.

Tom and Somerset had carefully excused themselves from attending one of the numerous local dinners, which Donald had persuaded his new friends to organize, on the ground of prior commitments; by which they meant that they wanted to dine in peace. This they did about twenty miles out of London in a surviving country inn which Tom had looked up in the Good Food Guide, then at an early and erratic stage of its development. Peace they certainly had but appalling food with it ('Sound English cooking, vouched for by R.H.T.M., D.H.E., W. M-O, etc.'), so that during the final approach to Chevenix Court Tom, with a quart of sour claret inside him, was now less disposed to find Donald's antics 'endearing' and was clearly getting ready to take viciously against the whole occasion. His driving was as jerky and truculent as his mood; and as the car scraped spitefully against Donald's new heraldic gate Somerset reflected, not for the first time, that it had been unwise to accept a lift from a known drinker simply in order to save a fare of 7/6d. third class. He must cast about for a more reliable ride home. Come to that, it had been a mistake not to arrange to spend the night locally, even if it meant paying a hotel bill or being polite to one of Donald's frightful neighbours. But too late now. Beginning to feel, like Tom, that the auspices were against him, Somerset appraised the pretty little park in the late dusk and remarked peevishly:

'A proper house is built on a road or a river. Typical of a parvenu to buy a house called a "court" in a park. A contradiction in terms.'

'Jealous?' said Tom, clashing the gears.

'No,' said Somerset (truthfully, for his father's house in Devon was small but genuine in its kind); 'and I hope very much, Tom, that you'll be careful what you drink.'

'Tomorrow's Sunday,' said Tom; and then, imitating Somerset, 'typical of a parvenu to give a party on a Saturday night. Convenient though.'

'We still have to get back to London.'

Tom grunted. An R.A.C. man with a torch flashed them into a meadow. When Tom had succeeded, after four abortive attempts, in backing the car into the space indicated, they walked the last two hundred yards of the drive to Donald's front door, which was standing open with a powdered flunkey on either side within.

'You see?' said Somerset, waving at the unbroken front of what was little more than an elaborate farmhouse: 'how can it be a court if there are no wings? A court must have at least two sides.'

'Perhaps the others are at the back.'

'Invitations, please,' said the left-hand footman brusquely.

Somerset produced his.

'I've left mine at home,' said Tom savagely, and marched forward into two liveried arms which stretched from either side to encircle him.

'It's our instructions,' said the second footman insolently: 'no invitations, no admittance.'

'Another parvenu arrangement,' said Tom, taking two or three steps carefully backwards like a long-jumper measuring his run. 'Donald will have cut 10 per cent on the drink to fill the house with clowns like these.'

'*Gate*-crashing, my dear?' said Jonathan Gamp, swaying out of the dusk behind them with Susan Grange. Her face was a bright shade of orange and her hands were dirty: carefully Somerset filed away the information that Sue was back on the pills.

'Sir, miss. . . . Your invitations?'

'We didn't trouble to bring them,' said Jonathan crossly, 'but this is Lady Susan Grange and my name –'

'– Our instructions are plain. No invitation, no ad –'

'– Christ, what a silly bitch Vanessa is,' said Jonathan, whose particular type of social insight immediately hit on the truth which had eluded Tom.

'It does say, "Please bring this invitation",' said Somerset, showing his.

Quite a long queue was now building up in the drive.

'I don't care what it says, never before have I –'

'– If you please, sir, you're keeping the other guests waiting.'

Jonathan turned to address the queue.

'How many of you delicious people have brought your invitations?'

There was a low murmur of negation. Apart from a bald man with a strident wife, both local, no one, it appeared, had even thought of it.

'Sir, madam,' said the first flunkey, admitting this unappetizing pair; then, 'You, sir?' to Somerset.

'I think I'll stay and see what happens,' Somerset said.

The flunkeys closed ranks again.

'Look here,' said Jonathan, 'can't you see that at this rate there won't *be* a ball?'

'No affair of ours if there isn't.'

At this instant Tom, who had been quivering like a baited bull, made a swift but clumsy assault on the left flank. The left-hand footman turned and punched him hard on the chest; Tom reeled back and sat down in a puddle; and there was a gasp of well-bred dismay from the assembled crowd – for crowd it indeed now was.

'This won't do at all,' said a bland voice. Somerset recognized Detterling, who now stepped out of the dusk, complete with cloak and silk hat, like André Chenier about to burst into an aria of revolutionary protest. Instead of which, he quietly instructed Somerset to take himself and his invitation within and fetch Vanessa Salinger to sort things out. Somerset, having taken five paces into the stone-flagged hall, was mildly surprised to see Vanessa, who was standing to one side in a receiving posture and clearly cognizant of what was passing at the front door. Since neither of the footmen had announced him he was compelled to introduce himself; Vanessa extended a long brown arm, at the end of which a white glove dangled so limply that it seemed questionable whether there was a hand inside it.

'Donald has spoken of you,' she said dismissively; 'if you go down that passage, you'll come to the marquees.'

'Thank you,' said Somerset. 'You might like to know that about fifty of your guests are being refused admission by your servants.'

'One can't be too careful about gate-crashers. All sorts of journalists and riff-raff would like to get in if they could.'

As though spellbound by her own conceit she made no attempt to move and did not even look towards the door. What was her eventual intention Somerset never discovered, for at this moment Jude Holbrook, flourishing his invitation, stamped angrily across the floor.

'I hope you realize,' he said, 'that you're keeping about ten thousand pounds' worth of advertising waiting on your doorstep.'

The mention of a five-figure sum conjured Donald out of nowhere. One moment there was no sign of him, the next he had scurried across the hall, giving a furtive look at his wife as he passed, and was performing with both arms a semaphore message of such violence that one expected him to take off over the footmen's heads and go zooming out over the crowd. The footmen looked at him with concentration, as though taking time to decipher the signal, and then, gracelessly and

reluctantly, bowed themselves out of the doorway. The pent-up
mass of guests, with Tom in the van brandishing a mud-
stained handkerchief like the colours of a famous regiment,
swept screeching into the hall and there proceeded to jump,
writhe, snap, twist and flounder in a mêlée that reminded
Somerset of a net-full of newly caught dogfish. Leaving
Vanessa to deal with a predicament which she thoroughly
deserved, he went down the corridor which she had indicated
to him, out on to a terrace, and down three broad steps on to a
large lawn.

The scene which he now faced was a magnificent testament
to Donald's visual flair. On the left were two floodlit marquees,
the larger, from which came the strains of Gold and Silver,
being at least fifty yards square and connected by a tented pas-
sage-way with a smaller one which Somerset correctly guessed
to contain drink. Directly to his front two ranks of burning
torches, held aloft by bronze figures of naked boys, marked a
broad walk, which led down the lawn between rose beds and
ended at the foot of a raised and floodlit group of statuary representing Pan and three wood nymphs in the last stages of
heavy and communal petting. To the right a long wall, parallel
with the lines of torch-bearers, was festooned with fairy lights
which were so arranged as to draw the eye to a low door. Here,
at last, somebody's taste had lapsed; for over the door was a
neon sign which announced not only 'Buffet' but also
'Swimming Pool' and surely supererogatory intelligence –
'Tennis Court'. Of human beings there was no visible trace,
except for the bald man and his strident wife, who were checking up, in close and silent concentration, on the detailed ver-
satility of Pan's behaviour.

The low door was inviting. Passing through into a small
orchard, Somerset came first to a barbecue pit. Beside the as
yet unattended apparatus lay a pile of sausages, while a few
feet away was a single trestle table which held an unimagina-
tive cold spread. Tom had clearly been right: Donald's concern
with appearances, with flunkeys and decor, had led to footling
and marginal parsimonies over the refreshments. This,

reflected Somerset, was characteristic: for the sake of saving perhaps 1 per cent of his overall outlay, Donald was running the risk of sending his guests away hungry and disenchanted into the dawn. But then this, of course, was in line with his known theory of hospitality, which he held to consist in dispensing a sense of privilege and smartness rather than honest food and drink. For every coronet in the company, Somerset surmised, he would have ordered a dozen less of champagne, conceiving that blue blood was a compensatory stimulant.

Having decided to take the swimming pool and the tennis court on faith, Somerset returned to the lawn, which was now becoming animated.

'Been to see Donald's new toys?' said Jonathan Gamp as he came through the door. 'My dear, Vanessa put him up to them. After all, she said, if the place is called Chevenix Court, you must have a court of *some* kind. You should just see Donald playing. Hairy little, *thin* little legs, my dear, coming out of his panties like a *spider's*.'

'Where's Susan?'

'Can you keep a secret? But of course you can. She's playing a little *jape*.'

'Jape?'

'She's going round all the loos fixing the ball-cocks so that they won't flush. It's to pay Vanessa out for being so snooty. And to annoy all these local chums of Donald's.'

'Why them?'

'Do admit, dear. Donald's country neighbours – and it's really just a rather posh suburb now – are the bitter, bitter end.'

There was something in that, Somerset thought. And already it was clear, as he walked towards the drink tent with Jonathan, that the guests were dividing into two distinct and hostile factions: Donald's old friends, from wherever they might come, as opposed to his new and 'county' confederates. The former, to speak broadly, were younger, poorer, prettier, better bred (or altogether declassé), and already more or less drunk; whereas the latter were looking sullen and even vengeful, as though the invaders with their light-hearted behaviour were somehow insulting the countryside, and with it the persons and vested interests (albeit these lay largely in London) of the resident squirearchy. As Donald's motive had clearly been to enhance his prestige with both groups by showing them off to each other, his blunder was manifest. But not surprising; for what lay at the root of the schism was this – that whereas the locals took Donald seriously as one of their own kind, his earlier friends had never taken him seriously in any kind. Since Donald, in whose scheme of things no one with more than £100,000 could conceivably be ranked, even by his friends, as a figure of fun, was incapable of appreciating this invidious divergence, he had likewise been incapable of foreseeing its result, and was now agitating himself this way and that, like a neurotic goldfish, worried, puzzled and hurt.

The drink tent was the focal point of strife. At one end of the bar several of Donald's Oxford friends were happily drinking brandy, having left their women to sweat it out on or near the dancing floor. At the other end four season ticket holders and their wives were sipping champagne (at a ball, of course, one *only* drank champagne) and discussing agricultural prospects. Each party pretended to ignore the other while putting on a voluble act for its benefit. To Jonathan and Somerset, who joined neither group, the effect was of antistrophic boastfulness, the blasé answered by the rancorous.

'. . . Like the time Ian was sick in the guest-room reserved for the bishop. . . .'

'. . . I hear Gerry Lambton's buying Black Acre from George. . . .'

'. . . But there's a much better story in *that* line. When John Dorsetshire – he was still called Troubridge then. . . .'

'. . . It'll be a good ten years before Charlie gets his money back from that herd – if he wants it back, that is. . . .'

'. . . Chosen as page of honour for the Royal Visit. Of course the old coll. put on a slap up lunch. . . .'

'. . . *Make* the Government realize that whatever those damned civil servants say it's *our* money we're ploughing in. . . .'

'. . . You see, they'd built an entirely new loo in the Warden's lodge specially for *her*. Mauve plush on the seat and that kind of thing. Well, when she tried the door, it was locked. . . .'

'. . . Hard money earned the hard way, I don't mind telling you. There's fifty thou, I said to Harry, fifty thou says you're on to a good thing, provided. . . .'

'. . . So there *she* was, waiting outside like someone in the corridor of a train, and at last out comes John Dorsetshire looking *green*. . . .'

'. . . A six-figure contract from the marketing board. . . .'

'. . . Pulled himself together and said, "I'm exceedingly sorry, Ma'am, but I've just been inspecting your accommodation and I fear that through some oversight it is in a deleterious condition. If you will kindly follow me. . . .'

'. . . Irresponsible rubbish. . . .'

'. . . Cost the Warden his knighthood. . . .'

'. . . Degenerate, I'd say, all of them. Talking like that about the Royal Family. Degenerate parasites.'

'Nasty, loud-mouthed, money-grubbing toads.'

By this time the two sides were drawn up facing each other, like expensive chessmen.

'. . . Rotten, like all of them. If you want to know what's wrong with the country, look at the universities.'

'. . . The one on the left, with a face like a peevish truffling pig. He's got more truffles than any of the other pigs, mind you, but he's discontented because he hasn't got them all.'

'. . . Never pay their bills, never do *proper* work, make jokes out of everything important or sacred. . . .'

'. . . And as for his wife, she reminds me of that line of Donne's, "Get with child a mandrake root". Or perhaps it'd be more like having a cactus.'

'. . . Pansies. . . .'

'. . . Greedy, pompous trouts. . . .'

'. . . Think they're clever. . . .'

'. . . *Shop-keepers*. . . .'

'My angels,' came a voice fluting through the din, 'which of you is going to do me a cheque for a hundred? Just over the week-end?'

At this the Oxonians dispersed hurriedly, while the country turned in on one another and started muttering about next August at Juan Les Pins. Somerset and Jonathan were left to face the negotiator, a beautiful but ravaged young man with wavy black hair and abominable breath.

'Jonathan dear –'

'– It's no good, Mark.'

'Just let me explain. My Trust has been delayed for another three months –'

'– It's two years late already –'

'– So Felicity is making me over five thousand until then. But she can't do it till she's seen her broker on Monday, so she's given me this cheque for a hundred to be going on with, but by mistake she's dated it Wednesday. So if *I* give *you* Felicity's cheque, *you* can give *me* one of yours dated today.'

'Why can't Felicity just alter it?'

'She's pissed. I've had to put her in the back of the car to sleep it off.'

'Tomorrow then?' said Jonathan patiently.

'I was hoping to cash it tonight. Donald must have some money round the house.'

'The only trouble is,' said Jonathan, 'that since you've spent all Felicity's money her cheques are no good any more.'

'How *can* you say such a thing? There's her flat in Rome, and two Dali's, and –'

'– No, Mark. I already have in my permanent possession three of your cheques and two of Felicity's. I'm not going to do anything about them, but I simply don't, my dear, want to add, my dear, to the collection.'

'All right. Be bloody. But don't expect anything from me when my Trust comes in.'

'Who was that?' asked Somerset, as Adonis, having downed half a tumbler of whisky in one, went in search of other takers.

'Mark Lewson, my dear. I thought you'd have known him. He's *famous* for cheques.'

'And Felicity?'

'His wife. An Italian countess by birth, brought up in

England – and fifteen years older than he is. They are now known as the Con and the Contessa. In actual fact, she did have quite a tidy bit of money, but Mark got through it all in two years, sold the paintings, and then had to invent this story of a Trust. We all believed it at first – Mark can be very plausible – but it wasn't long before the bubble was pricked. So the Contessa, who despite everything was still wildly in love with him, offered to help out with the racket. Hence the little charade you saw just now. Oddly enough, she's now a much happier woman: because instead of just being Mark's money box she's been promoted to full confidence and partnership, so to speak. You know how silly women can get – and here's Susan to prove it.'

Susan Grange, looking even more orange in the face and even more dirty round the finger nails, came prancing towards them.

'I've fixed them all,' she said. 'It's going to be super.'

'Clever slut . . . Drinkie?'

Somerset, surprised and relieved that Tom had not been in the bar but thinking, nevertheless, that it was time to check up on his activities, excused himself and made for the ballroom. A tango was in progress, for the most part being danced, in the approved upper-class style, as a clumsy foxtrot. One pair, however, displayed a certain expertise: Jude Holbrook, moving with a disciplined arrogance which complemented the rhythm of the music, was partnered by a strong, lithe woman whose features, battered in complexion but immature in cut, lent her the appeal of a raddled schoolgirl. As he paused to watch this exhibition, Somerset discovered something familiar here: the spiteful sexuality of the woman's movements, the sulky droop of the long blonde hair. . . . Yes. There could be no doubt. It was Angela, Angela Tuck, eleven years older and eleven long years, by the look of her, at that, but still viciously attractive. Remembering a summer evening by the sea, Somerset was brushed for a moment by the ghost of dead lechery, and then by another ghost, that of the boy who had first introduced him to Angela, a school friend who had long since disappeared into the marches of banishment. With a curt shake of his head Somerset dismissed these importunate spirits and walked over to where Tom was talking, rather too energetically, to Peter Morrison and his enormous wife.

'The trouble with your gang,' Tom was saying, 'is that you haven't got a single concrete policy. You say – you're always saying – that you stand for honourable dealing in politics at large and no truckling to constituents, but when, I want to know, are we going to see all this translated into action?'

Somerset saw with misgivings that Tom was at the man-to-man stage. On brandy nights this was generally succeeded by the heckling stage and this in turn by the condemnatory, the destructive and the lachrymose. If, however, Tom had been drinking whisky, man-to-man was usually followed by man-to-woman ('only you understand me') and the damage was seldom serious. Which had Tom been on that evening and where? Both questions were quickly answered. As Peter and his wife smiled a greeting at Somerset, Tom took a flat half-bottle of Hennessey from his hip pocket, helped himself to a liberal glug, and proceeded, without bothering to acknowledge Somerset's arrival, with his discourse.

'Action. Honourable dealing, all right, but when are we going to hear the terms of the deal? Just one actual deal, that's all I ask. Or again. No nonsense, you say, from constituents or the local party boys. Admirable. But when are you going to give them a good kick in the arse?'

Helen Morrison gave the bland smile with which she always reassured herself against the approach of danger. Peter attempted a soothing reply.

'It's early days, Tom. We're junior men and we've got to feel our way. And just because we're not dripping with reverence for the prejudices of backwoods and constituents, it doesn't mean we deliberately want to get their hackles up.'

'So it's going to be the old story. A lot of big talk, but as soon as a tricky issue does come up you'll trot in after the whips with your tales wagging.'

'When we've got a tricky issue – the right sort of tricky issue

– we'll see. . . . How are you getting on with that constituency they've given you to nurse?'

'A perfect bloody treat. You ought to see me, every second Wednesday, addressing all my thirteen supporters.'

'They'll give you something more promising when you've had more experience,' Helen Morrison said hopefully.

This was tactless in the circumstances, but none of them expected what followed.

'Thank you for that, my dear, Mrs. Morrison. Thank you for allowing me a chance some time, because I know I'm only a poor intellectual and I must be grateful for any crumb I can get. Now if I'd been really suitable, like this sanctimonious husband of yours, if I'd had a *proper* school and a fucking great dollop of Daddy's estate behind me, of course it would be different. A dozen willing hands would lift me up by both cheeks of my arse and set me down softly in the first empty seat they could find – even if I couldn't spell cunt.'

Peter nodded, smiled at Somerset, put his hand in his wife's arm, and led her away to an empty table in the corner of the tent.

'That for them,' said Tom, jerking two fingers in a V-sign.

'Yes, yes,' said Somerset soothingly, 'don't let it upset you.'

The problem now was what to do before an even more disastrous phase of the brandy cycle set in. He had promised Donald to keep an eye on Tom; and then Tom's name was associated with *Strix* and therefore with himself, and if discredit rose beyond a certain point, some of it was bound to slop over on to him. Before he could devise a plan, however, Somerset was confronted by Holbrook and Angela Tuck.

'Old friend of yours,' said Holbrook thinly; 'wants to meet you again.'

'I recognized you dancing . . . Excuse me a moment. . . .'

But when Somerset turned Tom had already disappeared.

'What's the matter?' said Angela. 'Do I make you nervous after all this time?'

'I've a drunk friend. . . .'

'Come to think of it,' Angela said, 'there was a lot of drink about when we last met.'

'Your twenty-first birthday. . . .'

'And that pretty friend of yours with the funny name. Is he here?'

'Fielding Gray,'murmured Somerset. 'I haven't seen him for a long time. There was some trouble. . . . He ended up in the army.'

'Pity,' Angela said; 'he might have grown up well.' She paused briefly as if considering a mental picture. Then, 'It seems we may be seeing something of one another from now on.'

'Oh?'

Holbrook continued silent but picked irritably at the skin round his finger nails.

'You have some scheme with Jude, don't you? Something to do with a magazine?'

'There may prove to be . . . an interest in common.'

Somerset glanced at Holbrook, inviting him to confirm this and at the same time trying to deduce from his face exactly how much he had told Angela. Holbrook nodded noncommittally, picking fast and furious at his nails. He's told her too much, Somerset thought. Aloud he said,

'And Jude's interests, I take it, are yours too?'

'We're going to be married. As soon as he gets his divorce.'

She took Holbrook's hand in hers, a gesture less of possession than of connivance.

'I congratulate you both. Mrs. Holbrook will make it all easy, I hope?'

'She's going to be a bitch about the money,' Holbrook said. 'Otherwise easy enough. She doesn't even want the brat.'

'So you'll keep him?'

'I rather want to,' said Holbrook, with something like affection in his grating voice. 'Nice little chap.'

There was a sudden spurt of rage in Angela Tuck's light blue pupils. Then a muscle began to work high in either cheek, as though she were willing her eyes to soften before turning them on Holbrook to smile. You're a tough little cookie,

Somerset told himself, but your time's running out and you know it, and you've got to toe the line. I wonder what happened to Tuck.

By this time Angela had clearly finished with Somerset. Indeed, his impression was that she had been anxious, not to meet him again, but in some way to check up on him. She now knew whatever she wanted to, or thought she did, and that, for the time, was enough.

'Dance, darling,' she said to Holbrook. 'See you around, little Somerset.'

Clever girl, thought Somerset as he left the marquee to look for Tom: toeing the line, yes, but keeping Holbrook lively by scratching at the surface of his jealousy, not enough to hurt but just enough to cause a pleasant little itch. 'Little Somerset': a tickling hint of dead intrigue. Effective on himself too; but the ghost of desire, once again briefly conjured, was again dismissed. Where was Tom?

There was no sign of him in the drink tent, on the lawn, in the orchard or near the swimming pool (where Susan Grange was now having a naked bathe, applauded by Jonathan Gamp). Fearing the worst, Somerset went into the house itself, to have his fears immediately confirmed by the sight of a long queue of women stretching down the corridor from the garden and terminating in front of a door, from behind which came a medley of pants, groans, sobs and grunts. As Somerset appeared, a prominent and bulky lady novelist, whose hair was dyed somewhere between mauve and magenta, started to knock indignantly.

'You've been in there ten minutes, whoever you are,' she called. 'How can you be so insensitive? It's hopeless,' she added gruffly to Somerset: 'the two upstairs ones are blocked up, and now there's some drunk locked in here having a fit.'

A wail of desperation ran down the corridor and back again.

'You're a man,' said the lady novelist aggressively: 'do something. Knock the door down.'

Instead Somerset listened carefully, gauging the noises within.

'Tom,' he said casually. 'Susan Grange is bathing naked in the swimming pool. If you don't come out, you'll miss it.'

Although lust did not play an important part in the brandy cycle, this gamble paid off. There was a final and gigantic eructation, a great rustling of paper, then into the corridor shot Tom, eyes huge, jacket over arm, shirt out.

'Pull the plug,' said the lady novelist.

'It won't.'

While Somerset drew Tom apart and reorganized him, the lady novelist stood in the open door, self-appointed Horatius of hygiene, stemming the squawking mob.

'No, Violet, I won't hear of it. . . . Ursula, find one of the servants and explain. Find Donald Salinger if you can. . . . Ah, *Vanessa darling*, you may be able to help us. Please come and look at this.'

Their hostess, who looked as if she had been drinking alcohol out of a wireless battery, swayed into the loo like a crazed tragedy queen and slammed the door on her suppliants.

'Come along,' muttered Somerset, 'or someone will be torn to pieces.'

With a hop, skip and a jump Tom was down the passage and on to the terrace.

'I want to tell you something,' he said, turning enormous watery eyes on to Somerset, 'something important.'

'Don't you want to see Susan?'

'No. I came out to talk to you. I was thinking it over in there, and I thought, "By God, I'll have those bloody Morrisons looking down their noses at me. I'll tell Somerset all about it." Then you called and –'

'– *Tell Somerset all about what?*'

'Ah,' said Tom, with a sudden access of cunning. And then, 'Would Jude Holbrook give me money, do you think?'

'*Money for what?*'

'For a true story about Peter Morrison, M.P.'

For ten seconds only, but for all of those ten seconds, Somerset hesitated. In his world, facts were power. If there were unpleasant facts to be known about a public man, then he must know them. What to do about them could be decided later; but he must know. On the other hand, Peter Morrison was an old friend, and it was not desirable that Tom's disclosures should be made to a man like Holbrook until he, Somerset, had vetted them first.

'Never mind Holbrook,' he said when the ten seconds were up; 'tell me.'

'No,' said Tom, and gave a wriggle of childish obstinacy. 'I'm going to play a bloody trick, I know it's a bloody trick, so I might as well be paid. I haven't got any money, the last cheque I gave Tessie's going to bounce on Monday, and if Holbrook wants valuable secrets, he can bloody well pay. You yourself as good as told me they're bothered about Morrison, so it ought to be worth a packet.'

'Tell me, Tom. *Me*. I'll tell you what it might be worth to Holbrook.'

'Sell it yourself more likely, you scrofulous cow.'

Tom's moods were now changing so rapidly that any minute, Somerset thought, he might decide to dry up altogether – or indeed fall down unconscious. His information might turn out to be useful and it might not, but it would be foolish to take chances.

'Right,' Somerset said. 'You go and wait behind that statue of Pan and his girl-friends. I'll find Holbrook.'

Tom trotted obediently off down the lawn in a slight but not perilous zig-zag. Somerset went into the dancing tent, could not see Holbrook, overheard the lady novelist complaining to a fashionable poet of the people about Vanessa and the lavatories, longed to hear how the incident had ended but dared not linger, proceeded to the bar, and found Angela Tuck tucking into neat brandy with Burke Lawrence of Millennium P. R., the promising young director of advertising films. It appeared that Angela was not considering a career in this medium for herself but was checking up on Penelope Holbrook's.

'Fabulous in the Nubile Nighties series,' Burke Lawrence was saying, 'not so hot in Prue's Blue Shampoo. A nice little talent though – I give her two years.'

'Excuse me,' Somerset said to Angela, 'but where can I find Jude?'

'Just outside. Brooding.'

She gave this as a plain statement of fact, displaying neither censure nor apprehension. Somerset, who knew how nasty, not to say dangerous, Holbrook could be in his moods, remarked her coolness on the subject and determined to revise, later and at leisure, his notion of Angela as 'toeing the line'. For the present, here was another complication: Holbrook brooding was often impervious to all considerations, even those of profit. A quick look at him, however, revealed that he was not in one of his black states but was indulging what he fancied to be the 'poetic' side of his nature – standing with hands clasped in front of his crutch and staring up at the moon. This manner, which he reserved for opera or old buildings, indicated that his preoccupation, while creditable, was of low priority and could be discarded the moment, so to speak, that the telephone rang.

'You'd better come quickly,' Somerset said. 'Tom Llewyllyn's got some story about Peter Morrison. If he hasn't passed out.'

As if by instinct, Holbrook started to stride towards the polyerotic ensemble at the end of the lawn.

'Angela all right in there?' he said without turning his head.

'Talking to Burke Lawrence.'

'Plausible bastard. He was one of the first with Penelope, you know. Not *the* first, of course. He waited – trust him – till others had cleared the path.'

They approached the statue from the flank, undiscovered by the light of the torches.

'Tom wants money,' Somerset said.

'But Lawrence would never,' said Holbrook, apparently ignoring Somerset's remark, 'make a set at Angela, because no girl's any good to him unless he's got something to do with her promotion or production. Interesting that. He's completely impotent unless he's in some way the boss-man. And even when he is, it's no good taking them home. Has to lay them in his office.'

Behind the statue Tom sat on a tree stump smoking a cigar. He looked dishevelled but competent.

'How much?' said Holbrook.

'Two hundred.'

'How do I know it's any good?'

'It's a killer. I promise you that.'

Holbrook looked down at him and pursed his lips.

'A hundred down,' he said at length. 'Another if the story stands up.'

'First hundred in cash.'

'You don't trust me?'

'I need cash.'

Holbrook passed over a thick wad of pound notes.

'It was meant for Le Touquet tomorrow,' he said, 'so you'd better make it good.'

Tom put the money carefully away in an inside breast pocket. Then his manner changed. He was no longer a man with something to sell: he was a drunk being indiscreet. What he said made sense; but it was rambling and repetitious, jokey, boozy, anecdotal: far from a crisp item of intelligence, it was a diffusion of scandal over the port. Holbrook appeared to understand that this method of relation was necessary to Tom, that it was the only way possible for him to preserve some self-respect; he listened, in any event, without impatience or interruption, only taking his comb from his pocket from time to time to pass it through his hair.

'In Norfolk,' Tom said, 'there is a village called Luffham some five miles from the market town of Whereham. And in the village of Luffham there lives a sober married woman of twenty-six summers, called Mrs. Vincent, whose husband works hard in the fields all day to feed their four children, two-year-old Daphne, four-year-old Bernard, five-year-old Liza, and Peter, who is rising eleven. What does that suggest? You have it, of course, in one. Peter was born when Mrs. Vincent was fifteen – before, indeed, she was Mrs. Vincent at all. Hey day. Some had carnal knowledge of her when she was only fourteen, and little Peter was the issue of her fall.

'About two years after Peter's birth, back from his soldiering came Jake Vincent and married the wench, bastard and all. Local deduction: the brat was Vincent's, misbegotten during some rollicking wartime leave, and Vincent, a decent sort if slow, was now marrying to make amends. Some blame attached to him; worse irregularities than his were common in the country, and Betty Vincent had been, as everyone remembered, a well formed lass. So as the years pass the scandal, such as it ever was, is forgotten, and Peter achieves a courtesy title to legitimacy.

'1952. See Tom Llewyllyn, having spent all his money on drink, faced with a Long Vacation of despair and want.' There now followed a digression about Tom's predicament at this time and the activities which had led to it. 'So see, I say, Tom Llewyllyn, at the end of a summer of odd jobs and casual labour, helping with the harvest on 'Squire Morrison's land, which lies between Luffham and Whereham. The 'Squire, a young man of modesty and sense, has recently been elected Tory M.P. for the district, but is not above lending a hand in his own fields. All, including Tom Llewyllyn, are much taken with his affable condescension: only Jake Vincent, one of his regular employees, speaks of his master with a certain coolness. Yet Jake is a loyal soul, by nature hard-working and fore-lock-pulling as the rest: whence his disaffection?'

Another digression, on the feudal attitudes obtaining in East Anglia.

'So on the night of harvest-home the tenants and the peasants gather, strong beer flows, and St. George for merry England. Jake Vincent, unaccustomed to more than the occasional mild-and-bitter, longing to confide his secret yet still too prudent to reveal it to the fellow-ceorls with whom he must pass the rest of his life, seeks out the sympathetic and soft-spoken stranger, Tom Llewyllyn, whom he knows will be gone by tomorrow noon, and relieves his simple soul by disclosing his shame.

'Or rather, another's shame. Gesturing obscenely at the Esquire Morrison, as he mingles graciously with his humble guest, Jake Vincent recalls the old 'Squire's time, when the young master was still a shambling schoolboy of seventeen and he himself was away fighting for his King. According to Jake, who had his honest wife's word for it, the young master met Jake's Betty one sultry evening in 1944, and her not six months past fourteen, and down they tumbled into the bushes, by the young master's wish and not by Betty's; but she was ever mindful of her Ma and of the cottage which old Morrison had given them when Betty's daddy died, and she dared not oppose herself to the wicked lusts of her patron's son.

'The next June Betty's child was born; she named him Peter, after his father, and took her baby and her story to old 'Squire Morrison, who, being satisfied there was no other man and remembering, not without a sigh, his own lusty youth, offered handsome maintenance for the child and his mother – on condition of silence. This maintenance young master Morrison continued after his father died a little later and he became 'Squire in his turn, continued even when, in 1947, Jake and Betty were wed. For Jake, the returning soldier, forgave his lass and loved her still and let the village have it that it was himself deflowered her; but all the while he carried the truth in his heart, and every week, when the money arrived in a registered envelope, he trembled so much that he had to lay himself on his bed. At seven years old, Jake told me, young Peter was the spit of his father; and what made it worse was that whether or not she had been forced, it was Peter his mother loved the most.'

'So,' said Holbrook at last, 'you say that four years ago this man Vincent, drunk, told you that five years before that his wife had said that three years before that she had been raped by Peter Morrison and had later borne his child. Rather . . . tenuous?'

'There's the maintenance money,' mumbled Tom, exhausted by his own eloquence, 'and the child looking like Morrison.'

'So like Morrison that no one else in the village has guessed?'

'Perhaps only to someone who knows,' Tom muttered. 'I believed Jake. He's the sort of man you do.'

'You, of course, were you drunk too?' Holbrook pursued.

'Only on beer. . . .'

Reminded of superior consolations, Tom fumbled for his brandy bottle. This was empty. He shook it hopelessly, dropped it, and slid off his tree stump on to the damp grass, where he fell instantly asleep.

'What do you think?' said Holbrook, as he walked away with Somerset.

'I was at school with Peter Morrison at the time it happened. *If* it happened. Peter was full-blooded . . . but this story is not in character – no more then than now.'

'I agree. But life is full of amusing surprises. Seventeen and a half Morrison must have been. Quite old enough to know better. No question of a charge now, of course; but a nasty scandal. Particularly with everyone so sensitive about that kind of thing.'

'What are you going to do?' asked Somerset.

'Investigate discreetly and see what emerges. One thing I'm not going to do, and nor must you, is breathe a word of it to Donald. He might not approve such methods. He has curiously old-fashioned ideas.'

'So have I.'

'But you are more flexible in interpreting them, dear Somerset. Like all Roman Catholics, you are adept at finding a moral motive for a self-interested action – however mean. You'll excuse me . . . I must go back to Angela. Do you find her much changed?'

'Physically, yes. But I had no trouble recognizing her. Her essential personality is very durable.'

Holbrook scowled, but at the same time nodded, as if despite himself, in assent, and then walked away over the lawn. Somerset strolled slowly along the avenue of torch-bearers and towards the terrace under the house, considering the implications of what had just passed.

In the fifteen odd years since he had first met Peter

Morrison, he had never known him do a cruel or shameful thing. His average mark for Conduct, as one might say, was really too good to be true; something was bound to come up sooner or later to reduce it; and since Peter had never been a prig, was indeed notably tolerant in his attitude to moral failings, Somerset had been fully prepared to hear from Tom of some modest lapse from grace which, while unremarkable in a private man, might be dangerous for a public one. A modest lapse, juvenile or even contemporary, yes: *this*, no. It was altogether too violent, too extreme. The notion of Peter using a position of power in order to compel was utterly alien and perverse.

There remained two possibilities. Either the story was wholly untrue, or it had some substance but had been wrongly angled (the girl was that much older, perhaps, had welcomed Peter's advances or even made the running herself). If the former, then Tom, who sometimes romanced but did not maliciously invent, must have been misled, and this Holbrook's 'investigation' would presently reveal. If the latter, if there were *something* in it, then so much the worse for Peter, because whether or not he had committed statutory rape, the fact that he had been sexually involved with a *dependant* was going to stir up a nasty smell. Bastard, after all, was still an ugly word.

Of these two possibilities, Somerset, after weighing Tom's shrewdness against his wildness, his essential truthfulness against his love of drama, was inclined to plump for the second. Peter was going to be threatened, not with disgrace, but with discredit – though whether serious enough to give Holbrook the weapon he might need remained to be seen. Examining himself for personal reactions, Somerset decided that (leave aside the money he stood to collect) the predominant one was interest: how would the game go? Fond as he was of Peter, he could not feel really sorry for him. Peter's career to date had been privileged and smooth: even the dangerous affair in India nine years before had been straightforward in its issues and had ended in a round of applause. It was time Peter learnt a little more about life; and the dirty piece of in-fighting which now promised would be a valuable and toughening exercise for him, teaching him to protect himself below the belt and perhaps to aim a few blows there himself.

As he approached the terrace through the half-light of dawn, Somerset saw that seated round a garden table with a magnum of champagne were Detterling and a military-looking stranger accompanied, rather surprisingly, by Burke Lawrence.

'Very thoughtful, Somerset,' said Lawrence. 'Thinking about your poor old mag.? You know these two?'

The military-looking stranger rose with stylish courtesy.

'I don't think. . . .' he said.

'Somerset Lloyd-James, the well known editor,' said Lawrence brashly: 'Max de Freville, the well known gambler.'

De Freville winced but smiled politely at Somerset.

'We were talking,' said Lawrence, 'of the ideals of our lost youth. You might not think that either of these two had any, but you'd be surprised.'

'And what were yours, Burke?'

'Cinema as an art form,' said Lawrence, and gave a belch of contempt which dismissed both himself and the cinema; 'and if you think that's odd, just listen to Max.'

'I don't know that there was anything odd about my ambitions,' said de Freville shyly and thoughtfully. 'They were just unrealizable. You see, I wanted to be a pure mathematician. There was something so beautiful about all those elaborate pages of symbols, something positively romantic about those series which stretched away to infinity, or doubled back on themselves to get nearer and nearer to zero without ever quite making it. The only trouble was that I had no gift for mathematics . . . the concept of zero never meant anything to me except as a thirty-five to one shot on the roulette wheel which imprisoned the even chances. I ended my mathematical career by pretending to faint during my finals so that I could get to a race meeting on time.'

'At least you acquired a certain ability for *ad hoc* calculation,' said Somerset, who remembered hearing that de Freville was reputed to have made a quarter of a million over the last five years.

'Of the most childish kind,' said de Freville. 'It is not difficult to work out a 5 per cent caignotte. To run a gambling game you need only be neat with your hands and keep a good line of patter rolling off your tongue. Like a conjuror at a children's party.'

'You also need a conjuror's presence of mind. A banker must assess his risks.'

'But I never *am* a banker. I'd think more of myself if I were; because a banker pits his own money and his own wits against the money and wits of the punters, which is more or less a fair contest. Whereas I just set the game up and take a percentage of the turn-over. Nothing very heroic in that.'

'As organizer,' said Detterling, 'you are responsible for making up bad money?'

'Yes . . . But these days we inquire much too carefully to get caught like that. Before a man plays at my table, he's been guaranteed as thoroughly as any member of your syndicate in Lloyd's. It's become a *business* – a business in which I exploit, with almost no risk to myself, one of the most sterile and destructive of human follies. I'm not a gambler but a glorified caterer.'

'But when you started, surely, you used to gamble yourself?'

'Yes. In those days there was at least a certain bravado, for one was struggling, with youthful gaiety, against the odds. But I soon realized that it could never pay – enough mathematics lingered to make that clear. So then I changed sides, so to speak, and there was an end of youth.'

De Freville drained his glass. He looked bored to tears.

'One might say,' said Burke Lawrence, 'that you fulfil a social need. . . . Honest Max runs a smooth game. . . .'

De Freville set down his glass and looked at him, as though to say that here was one man who would certainly not be allowed at his gaming table were he to be guaranteed worth a million. All at once Somerset was aware that it was no longer dawn but day. Birds were singing and the fairy lights along the wall were irrelevant in the gathering sun.

'It seems to me,' said Detterling, 'that we have only ourselves to blame for our disappointments. We expect too much
. . . fail to use common sense. When I was first commissioned
in 1937 I chose a cavalry regiment which still had its horses. It
wasn't only that I liked horses and liked the expensive sort of
life we had. I really did feel that as a soldier on horseback I was
the heir to a tradition of chivalry which stretched back to the
middle ages and beyond. Although I might not amount to
much on the battlefield any more, I was worth my weight, I told
myself, as a symbol. But of course the last thing they wanted
just then was a symbol, and by 1939 I was being made to dirty
my hands and bark my shins on a tank. For me, all the joy and
pride had gone out of the Army and never really came back.
But it was my fault. I just did not have the common sense, even
as late as 1937, to see that I could not go on sitting on my horse
in a pretty uniform. Or rather, I wouldn't let myself see it. You,
Max, must have *known* that you were a phoney mathematician,
just as I must have *known* I was a phoney knight. But somehow
we contrived to deceive ourselves –'

'– Just as I deceived myself,' said Burke Lawrence, anxious
to proclaim himself of the company after de Freville's snub,
'into thinking that a slick production of a May Week musical
qualified me to direct great films. What was your dream,
Somerset?'

Before Somerset could hit on a suitable equivocation, the
morning was rent asunder by a howl of pain from the other end
of the lawn. Up the avenue came Tom, scampering from one
side to the other, seizing and hurling down the bronze boys
with their torches.

'Proper light now,' he screamed.

From the marquee came the sound of the national anthem.
The few people on or near the lawn gazed incuriously at Tom,
as at another drunken exhibition of a familiar and boring kind.

'Proper light,' yelled Tom. He looked up at the sky; then
snatched with both hands at the bronze figure nearest him,
seemed for a few moments actually to wrestle with it, as
though he were meeting resistance, but at last flung it into a

rose bed and hurtled across the avenue to the one opposite. Somerset could now see that his face was wet with tears.

'Judas, Judas,' screamed Tom, high above the national anthem, and down went another torch-bearer to drink the dew.

'Do you suppose he'll do any damage?' Detterling said.

'The damage has apparently been done,' replied Max de Freville.

Suddenly people seemed to converge on the terrace from all directions. Tom blundered up from the lawn, to stand trembling and panting by Somerset. From the door into the orchard came Jonathan Gamp with his arm round a dishevelled and shivering Susan. A stream of figures was approaching from the marquee. And lastly came Donald from the house itself, with Vanessa trotting behind him, pale but sober, and apparently trying to dissuade him, by plucking at his arm, from something he was about to do. Donald pushed at her with one arm, like a fretful child spurning its nanny, and raised the other for silence.

'Someone,' he said, 'has broken into my desk in my study and stolen seventy-five pounds. I should be grateful for any information which might help me recover them.'

There was a dissatisfied murmur. As host on such an occasion, the feeling was, Donald should have suffered his loss in silence. Instead he persisted.

'Someone,' he said, 'must surely have noticed something . . . gate-crashers perhaps.'

Jonathan Gamp, who had been carefully scanning the crowd, walked across the terrace and whispered in Donald's ear.

'Mark Lewson,' Somerset heard Donald mutter; 'the devil he did.'

'Perhaps he left the cheque behind in payment,' said Jonathan cheerfully.

'This is no joking matter. You're sure he's gone?'

'No sign of him.'

'For Christ's sake,' said Tom, lurching forward: 'if a few

miserable pounds mean so bloody much to you, have this. I've
no right to it.'

He jerked out the wad of notes which Holbrook had given
him and skimmed it through the air. It rapped Donald lightly
on the chest, disintegrated, fluttered to the ground to make a
loose pile over his feet. Tom shouted with laughter.

'Pity there's not enough to bury you up to the neck,' he said.
'Because that's what you are. Just a clacking face on top of a
heap of money.'

Still laughing wildly he shambled away into the house.

'Where did he get this?' said Donald. 'He didn't–?'

'No,' said Somerset firmly. 'It's his own. I can answer for
that.'

'Then he must have it back. He'll need it.'

Blinking back tears, Donald stooped to gather up the
money. His guests filed past him into the corridor.

'Tom shouldn't have said that,' Donald said, his eyes still
blinking rapidly behind his glasses. 'It was unkind of him. And
I had so hoped. . . .'

He broke off and handed the money to Somerset.

'He didn't know what he was saying, Donald. He was full of
brandy.'

'Then where's he gone? Ought he to drive? Oh dear,' said
Donald, sitting heavily down next to Detterling. 'I wish my
party hadn't ended like this. The whole thing's been a mistake.'

'Nonsense,' said Max de Freville; 'I've enjoyed myself very
much.' He poured the last of the magnum into his glass and
pushed it across to Donald. 'Have some of your own excellent
champagne.'

Absently, Donald lifted, sipped, then lowered the wine.

'Vanessa?' he said weakly, as though calling back to his aid
the nanny he had rebuffed.

'She's seeing everyone off, Donald.'

'Should I help her?'

'No,' said Detterling, 'you sit here. You've earned a rest.'

There was a long silence, during which Donald's face

gradually relaxed into a peevish yet stoic acceptance.

'You'll see Tom gets his money, Somerset?' he said at length.

'Yes . . . I must be off.' By now, Somerset thought, Tom would have gone, a swift and thoughtless departure being the final stage of the brandy cycle: he himself could look round for a lift without risk of embarrassment. 'Thank you, Donald. A memorable evening.'

Walking along the corridor he met Jonathan, who was waiting outside the lavatory.

'Susan,' said Jonathan, nodding at the door.

'Is she all right?'

'Tearful. Like to help me get her home? She needs someone to keep her warm in the back.'

'Very well,' said Somerset with the air of conferring a privilege. The door opened and Susan emerged, her face, which had been washed of make-up by her swim, was shrivelled and streaked with tears.

'I can't get the plug to pull,' she said hopelessly.

'Never mind, dear. Home now.'

When they were safely in Jonathan's car, with Somerset in the back condescendingly comforting Susan, Jonathan said:

'I'll say this for Vanessa. She waved us off like a royal duchess.'

'Why was she in such a state . . . about half past two?'

'Couldn't say, dear. Susan was having her swim just then. But it sounds as if she caught the party spirit all right. Positively penitential. Which is as it should be. The best parties have a spiritual function – they bring a salutary sense of degradation.'

9

At lunch in Le Touquet the day after Donald's midsummer Ball, Angela Tuck said:

'There's something about Somerset Lloyd-James which you ought to know.'

'Yes?' said Jude Holbrook greedily.

'If he's the same as he was ten years ago, and he certainly looks it, he'll be hedging his bets.'

'He stands to win handsomely when we get the Proprietorship.'

'He will also be making allowances in case you don't.'

'Not much harm in that.'

'It depends what sort of allowances.'

'I'm not really with you,' Holbrook said.

Although Holbrook did not know it, the relationship between himself and Angela was rapidly being reversed. The truth was that Angela, by feigning subservience, had made him totally dependent on her. He would never find another woman to be his creature in the way he thought Angela was; and if she had cared to stand up straight and announce that she was not his creature after all, the blow to his pride might have been mortal. As it was, she had no mind to disillusion him, only to get what she wanted in return for her services. Her problem was how to do this without stepping out of her role; for to exercise her influence was to run the risk of showing that she had it, whereas the convention between them demanded that she should be a mere humble and grateful concubine. Eventually she had decided that she might achieve her ends by intensifying her worship; she would pretend to regard Holbrook almost as a god to be prayed to: show me your power, she would say in effect, by answering my prayer, and I shall be even more your creature than I am already.

In this way she had finally got him to propose marriage. 'I know there are difficulties about Penelope,' her line had been; 'but there are no difficulties which cannot be overcome by you.' The formula had worked; but now there was another problem which required a different formula. Angela was anxious that Holbrook should become a man of importance (quite apart from anything else, he would otherwise be intolerable to live with). In a condescending way he had taken her into his confidence about *Strix*, with the result that she saw two things clearly: that *Strix* might indeed bring Holbrook the importance which she desired for him; and also that the brashness in his make-up, the tendency to overplay his hand, the clumsiness and impatience which offset his natural guile, might at any minute ruin the negotiations. The problem now, therefore, was to give advice (as distinct from praying for a favour) without appearing presumptive; and in order to do this she had determined very slightly to qualify her role: she remained a slave, yes, but a privileged and intimate one, the sort of slave to whom a Roman would have entrusted his correspondence and accounts. She could still be flogged or fed to the fishes at a moment's notice, but meanwhile she had access to her master's ear.

'No, I'm not really with you,' Holbrook said again.

'I'm explaining badly,' she said. 'But please try to be patient because it could be important.'

'Well?' Imperial permission to proceed.

'What I mean is that Somerset will have provisions. Although he may be anxious for you to get *Strix* and give him money, circumstances could arise in which, money or no money, he would prefer you to be kept out.'

'What circumstances?'

'I've noticed,' she said humbly, as if entreating his pardon for saying anything so obvious, 'that *Strix* has always had a lot of kind things to say about Peter Morrison and his "Young England" set.'

'Morrison's on the Board.'

'And whose idea might that have been in the first place?'

'What you're saying,' said Holbrook with irritation, 'is that

Somerset has reasons for being nice to Morrison – reasons which have nothing to do with bringing him round to this sale.'

Angela looked at him with admiration.

'Yes,' she said demurely. 'Somerset wants something which he thinks Morrison can give him. So he won't like it if anyone starts getting too rough . . . in the use, for example, of this story of Tom Llewyllyn's.'

'But it was Somerset himself who made me listen to Llewyllyn.'

'It is one of Somerset's favourite tricks,' said Angela, 'to appear loyal and helpful just when he's getting ready for the big double-cross.'

'You seem to know a lot about him.'

'I only knew him very briefly ten years ago. But it was long enough to watch him make someone else look very foolish indeed. He was lucky – he's the sort that always is – but he made expert use of his luck. Which reminds me,' she went on, judging that enough had been said for the time, 'did you give Tom Llewyllyn all your money or have we enough for roulette?'

In Russell Square, Somerset Lloyd-James was thinking along much the same lines as Angela Tuck.

'Last night,' he wrote on a sheet of foolscap, 'I decided that it would be interesting and prudent to stay outside the ring and just watch Peter fighting it out on his own. This morning I am not so sure. If Peter were badly discredited, he could no longer help with my parliamentary candidature when the time comes. If, on the other hand, he manages to ride through it all, he'll be bound to associate *Strix* and therefore myself with inconvenience and unpleasantness, and so to become disaffected for the future. Unsatisfactory either way.

'Of course, it may turn out that Peter is willing to vote our way after all, or that this whole story of Tom's is simply untrue. But if Peter *is* going to be obstinate, and if Holbrook really *has* got something he can use against him, I now realize that I cannot remain neutral as I had hoped. I shall have to plump for one side if I am not to lose my standing with both. Either I can support Peter and discourage Holbrook, thus retaining Peter's good will but sacrificing a lot of money; or I can join in putting pressure on Peter, collect my money when Holbrook wins (as he almost certainly would), and look around for another patron in the Palace of Westminster – where someone or other would surely be grateful if I thought it my duty to pass on this new intelligence about Peter by way of an inside warning.

'Expedience dictates the second course. But I should be sorry, after all these years, to see Peter distressed, and again, were it not for Donald's interest in the matter, I should be glad to see Holbrook get his come-uppance. The ideal solution would be one whereby the magazine is sold to S & H, I get my money, Holbrook somehow disappears from the picture leaving me with Donald as my Proprietor, and Peter is left untroubled throughout. Altogether too much to hope for. If only I had known this offer was coming *before* I invited Peter to join the Board, a lot of trouble would have been saved.

'However, this is a time for action and not regret. I imagine, though, that a few days must pass before anything serious can happen, as Holbrook must first check on Tom's story (?? Private detective). So I can defer decision for just a little longer . . . long enough, perhaps, to get a clearer notion of the odds. In the meantime, I shall approach Peter according to the original plan and find out where he now stands *vis à vis* S & H.

'I shall also pray hard for guidance. A.M.D.G.'

Downstairs the telephone rang.

'Mr. Lloyd-Ja-ames,' the Landlady called.

'Hullo, Somerset love,' said the warm voice of Susan Grange. 'I've just woken up. I thought you might like to come to lunch. Then I could say thank you for being so sweet in Jonathan's car.'

Somerset was not aware of having been particularly sweet in the car, only of having sat there stiffly while Susan sobbed into his shirt; he was, moreover, mistrustful of women, especially women who took pills; but it was not in his nature to pass up a free lunch, and the most strong-willed of men would have been flattered by a personal invitation from Lady Susan Grange. So he accepted gracefully, and then returned to his room to read through the notes which he had just made. Well, well, he thought on the stairs: I wonder what *she* wants.

In bed at Chevenix Court Vanessa tossed uneasily in the noon-day heat. She knew quite well why she had been so suddenly ill the previous evening. For a month now, although she had tried to tell herself that it was a freak miss, she had more than suspected what was coming, and there could no longer be any doubt. She was pregnant, two months pregnant, almost certainly by Donald (who wanted a child and refused to let her take precautions) but perhaps, just perhaps, as a result of one of those jolly afternoons just before her marriage with Jimmy in the Elephant. Donald would be delighted and could have no cause for suspicion; the only trouble was that on one of those afternoons in Jimmy's pad his student chums from Zanzibar had been invited to join in, and on that occasion, overcome by a frenzy of excitement, Vanessa had not been quite as careful as she should. Although the odds were still well in her favour (or rather, in Donald's favour or Jimmy's), she could not afford to lay them, for a mulatto baby would not be viewed propitiously as the heir to Chevenix Court; and she was now trying desperately, as she tossed in the stifling bedroom, to remember the name of the doctor to whom she had been sent after that dismal affair with 'young' John Groves.

Lady Susan Grange was a jaded young woman who had reached a stage at which, like Oscar Wilde's young man, she was bored with good wines and inclined to experiment with bad. It had occurred to her, in Jonathan Gamp's car, that one could hardly find a worse wine than Somerset, whom it would be interesting and novel to sample. Accordingly, as soon as lunch was over she proposed to Somerset in so many words that they should go to bed; and Somerset, with reciprocal candour, explained his own harmless but eccentric taste. Susan was highly delighted with this, so they spent a long afternoon playing nurseries, in the course of which Susan invented several amusing variations to the game. When they parted at six o'clock, however, Susan had had enough of Somerset to last her quite some time, while Somerset, delighted that so notable an afternoon should have cost nothing, was well on the way to being hooked.

'You look very chipper with yourself,' said Peter Morrison the next afternoon.

'It's been an exhilarating weekend,' Somerset said.

'Can't say I enjoyed it much myself. The fact that Tom Llewyllyn's a first-rate writer does not entitle him to make appalling scenes and insult my wife.'

'Tom wasn't himself.'

'Then perhaps he'd like to apologize. . . . And perhaps you'd like to tell me, Somerset, why you've asked me to tea at the Ritz.'

'I've discovered a gratifying way of saving money,' said Somerset, 'so I can afford to be generous for once. Though I must confess that I have a question to ask.'

'Fire away.'

'Have you come to any decision about Salinger & Holbrook's offer for *Strix*?'

'If it were just Donald Salinger,' said Peter, 'I'd be for accepting. Without enthusiasm, but still for accepting. Donald's a self-satisfied ass, but a nice ass and well meaning. Holbrook, on the other hand, is a killer. He is insolent and ruthless, and he is also a spiteful little coward. I watched him when we all had that dinner last month, and I watched him with that fancy piece of his last weekend – she's another killer, by the way – and nothing will now persuade me to let him near any enterprise in which I bear a part.'

'So you see,' said Somerset to the two partners: 'deadlock. I must say, though I thought Peter might make difficulties, I had not expected him to be quite so firm.'

'This is most disheartening,' said Donald peevishly. 'We set out to be particularly nice to Morrison, only to find ourselves turned down on personal grounds.'

'I told you he didn't like Jude.'

'If he's a man of such integrity,' Holbrook said, 'he should be above personal animosity.'

'It's not personal animosity,' said Somerset patiently: 'he merely thinks that you're unsuitable. He thinks, and of course he's right, that you would use *Strix* to exert undesirable pressures.'

'Whose side are you on?' said Holbrook, ripping a strip of skin from beside his thumbnail to reveal the raw flesh beneath.

'I was simply telling you his motives. If anything is to be done, it is important that we should first understand them.'

'It's all very disappointing,' said Donald. He removed his glasses and blinked with self-pity. 'After all these weeks of waiting . . . I don't know how I'm going to tell Vanessa.'

Vanessa had lately been irritable and preoccupied; so that he was particularly anxious to bring her good news about the project by which she set such store.

'I rely on you, Somerset,' Donald went on, 'I rely on you to think of something. We've got six months before the option expires, which I really think is time enough to convince Morrison that Jude here isn't some sort of criminal maniac, as he appears to think.'

'Of course,' said Somerset, 'if you cared to set up a separate company, in your own name only, and then repeat the offer. . . .'

Holbrook clenched both fists. Donald looked harassed and tempted, but replied:

'That would be very unfair. It was Jude's idea in the first place.'

'He could still be in on it. It's just that everything would be done in your name.'

'Morrison would see through it,' rasped Holbrook: 'in any case, no one's going to force me to hide behind Donald's skirts.'

Donald winced at the image and rose to go.

'Vanessa's expecting me,' he said sourly; 'let me know what you decide.'

'You see?' said Holbrook. 'Off he goes, head in air, and leaves it all to us.'

'That was exactly my point, only of course I couldn't say so. Even if the paper was in Donald's name only, you would have effective control. Far more effective, probably, than if you were known to have it.'

'I *want* to be known to have it.'

Vanity, thought Somerset, vanity and pique. Not content with the substance of power, he wants the public title.

'And besides,' Holbrook spluttered, 'what sort of time would I have operating through Donald – with Morrison still on the Board? Donald couldn't stand up to him for five seconds.' He paused to rip yet another strip of skin from his bleeding thumb. 'No,' he said; 'what we want is to bring Morrison to heel. Or get rid of him altogether.'

Somerset, who had been waiting for him to say this, at first pretended not to understand.

'He's not one to turn his back. And he has plenty of money of his own.'

'He has a good name to protect,' said Holbrook, 'and a wife and children whom he adores. I don't think – do you? – that he'd want them hurt. I shan't be unreasonable: if he doesn't want to vote against his conscience, let him just resign from the Board and get out of our way.'

'I told you,' said Somerset, still affecting not to understand: 'he's not a man to turn his back.'

'Stop pussy-footing. You know perfectly well what we've got on Morrison.'

'Oh, that,' said Somerset lightly. 'It all happened a long time ago and Tom may well have got the details muddled. Hadn't you better leave that till you've checked?'

Holbrook smiled like a fallen angel who had just received Lucifer's personal commendation.

'I have checked,' he said; 'it's all quite true.'

Somerset, who despite his elaborate marshalling of factors had hitherto regarded the problem of Tom's story as little more than theoretical, suddenly felt more dismayed than he would have thought possible. He flushed and lowered his eyes.

'Already?'

'I thought that might surprise you. But it wasn't very difficult. I sent a good man, one I've used before, down to Whereham, and he got hold of this man, Vincent, who, as Tom told us, is not used to strong drink. Vincent repeated, almost to the syllable, what he'd told Tom. He married the woman, took on her bastard and allowed it to pass as his own, but knew, from what his wife had told him, that it was fathered by young master Peter, who had used his feudal position to persuade a reluctant maiden who was substantially under age. Not a pretty story.'

'Second best evidence. You need the woman herself.'

'I rather think that it's good enough to be going on with.'

'All right,' said Somerset, swallowing back a mouthful of phlegm; 'but let me put it to Peter.'

'No,' said Holbrook. 'There's been enough pat-ball. It's time Peter Morrison learnt a few facts of life, and after what he's said about myself I'm going to enjoy teaching him.'

At last Vanessa had remembered the name of the Doctor to whom John Groves had sent her: Doctor La Soeur. He was delighted to hear from an old patient and suggested a date early in July. Since Donald had given her a handsome wedding present, there would be no difficulty about money; all she had to do was arrive, with the cash, at a converted country house, one small wing of which Dr. La Soeur had hired for the accommodation of his private patients. She remembered the place from the last time; it was very pretty and in charming grounds, but a little depressing, because most of the building was used by the authorities as an Old People's Home of Rest.

Despite his earlier resolution to take firm action, Somerset was now reduced to sitting, indeed dithering, on the fence. He could not, he finally realized, bring himself to outright support of Holbrook; something – was it the residual precept of family, or the remembered schoolboy summers? was it, indeed, the divine guidance for which he had prayed? – something, at any rate, inexorably forbade him so foul an alliance. On the other hand, he excused himself, to warn Peter or to invoke the aid of Donald's conscience, would be to expose the equivocal part he had already played and yet to achieve nothing. If Tom's story was true, as now appeared, Peter would be no better off for a warning; and as for Donald, though he would want no part in dirty work, he would simply close his ears if one tried to tell him of someone else's. For whatever reason, Donald was no longer lethargic and wanted *Strix* almost as much as Holbrook did; and Donald, while basically decent, was also badly spoiled and apt to let frustration warp his moral perspective if denied his own way. Words like 'bargaining' and 'diplomacy' would comfortably obscure any misgivings of Donald's about what Holbrook might be plotting.

The truth was that things had moved too quickly for Somerset; he had been denied the time which, like the chess player he was, he regarded as his due. Given time, he could have rationalized away that debilitating motive (his genuine if faintly derisive affection for Peter) which he had so stupidly allowed to obtrude itself. He must be growing old; ten years ago . . . but never mind that now. For now, he thought, loathing his own futility, there was only one thing for it; he must wait, after all, until the struggle was over and then present himself to the best possible advantage in the new circumstances. Meanwhile, needing light relief, he rang up Susan Grange to propose dinner. (Could *she* have anything to do with this new 'softness in his attitudes?' Love, he knew, could be dangerously subversive of purpose.) Susan was engaged for the evening; and only when pressed did she agree, with evident irritation, to dine with Somerset the following week. Altogether, it was a discouraging end to a bad day; so Somerset went to bed early, having first said an extra long lot of prayers.

Holbrook looked round the lobby of the House of Commons with distaste. Who did all these dreary little people think they were to come pestering their betters? For that matter, who did their betters think they were to walk so smugly and condescendingly about the place? He could have brought most of them up twice over. And here was Morrison now; true, he did not look smug or condescending, but there was a certain consciousness of personal merit about him which made

Holbrook's toes curl angrily in his socks.

He had decided to see Morrison himself rather than leave it to Somerset, first because Somerset's ponderous and leisurely methods were driving him mad with impatience, secondly because of what Angela had said at Le Touquet. Somerset, he felt, was getting ready to equivocate his way out of the whole business, whereas what was now needed was a direct challenge. There came a time, in every game, to put the chips down on the table, and that time had now come. People had been talking politely and doing nothing for months. So now I'm going to crack the whip under those big feet of yours, he silently addressed the approaching figure, and see how high you can jump.

'Would you care for some tea?' said Morrison courteously.

'Just to talk for a few minutes.'

'The terrace will do as well as anywhere. It's nice out there now.'

Terraces, thought Holbrook bitterly as he followed Morrison; privilege, style, charm. All we need is a small room with a closed door. They came out into the sun; Morrison crossed to the balustrade and stood smiling down at the river.

'Well?' he said.

'*Strix*,' said Holbrook. 'As you know, Donald and I have made an offer. Which way will you vote when it is discussed by the Board?'

Morrison looked at him calmly, smiled down at the river once more, then turned to face Holbrook square.

'I don't have to answer you but I will. I shall say that in my opinion Salinger & Holbrook, though evidently a respectable firm, is not suited to take over the Proprietorship of *Strix*.'

'Why shall you say that?'

'Because I believe it to be the truth.'

'On what ground?'

'Let us say that Salinger & Holbrook is concerned, as such a firm must be, with profit. *Strix* is not concerned with profit. There is a divergence of interest.'

'We could afford to run *Strix* as a non-profitable side-line.'

'Possibly; but you wouldn't.'

'What makes you think that?'

Morrison paused, then smiled.

'You make me think that,' he said softly. 'You're the sort of man who always takes something, and you'd take it from *Strix*. I don't say you'd take it in money; but the other way would be even worse. I hope I make myself plain.'

'Plain enough,' said Holbrook. 'But I'm going to be even plainer.'

In short, crisp sentences he started to tell the other exactly what he knew about him and how he came to know it. Morrison listened silently and politely, turning every now and again to look down at the river or the buildings beyond. When Holbrook was about half done, Captain Detterling approached.

'Excuse me just one moment,' Morrison said.

There followed an exchange of whispers. Holbrook caught the words 'my man in Washington' and a little later saw Morrison's face go very grave. Then Detterling was gone and Morrison was facing Holbrook once more.

'I'm sorry about that,' he said; 'please go on.'

Holbrook went on. But during the interruption he had lost his rhythm, so that his conclusion did not have quite the impact he would have wished. Morrison nodded sympathetically, as though aware that the performance had been spoiled and anxious that Holbrook should not feel too badly about it.

'So that's what you wanted to see me about,' he said with an air of mild interest. Holbrook reddened.

'You don't deny it?' he said aggressively.

'Of course not. You've been into it much too carefully.'

'And it's not a story you'd want to get round.' Holbrook gestured down the terrace. 'Round here for example?'

'Certainly not,' said Morrison reasonably.

'It's the story that will get round. If you vote against our offer.'

'So I supposed.'

'Well?'

'What do *you* suggest?'

'You could resign from the Board before the question comes up.'

'I wouldn't want to do that,' said Morrison. 'It might offend Somerset. Besides, I'm finding it very interesting and I'm learning a great deal. More than I expected to,' he added thoughtfully.

'Then why not stay on the Board and vote in our favour?'

'Why not indeed? You really leave me no choice.'

'So that's what you'll do?'

'I've told you,' Morrison said: 'you really leave me no choice.'

Holbrook telephoned *Strix*.

'I've fixed Morrison,' he said to Somerset Lloyd-James. 'When's the next meeting?'

'Next week. Tuesday.'

'You can settle the whole thing then.'

'Very well,' said Somerset. 'Tell me, how did Peter take it?'

'He saw sense. As he himself said, he didn't have much choice.'

'Wasn't he angry? or embarrassed?'

'He played it strictly upper class,' said Holbrook. 'You know, level voice, no scenes please, remember we're gentlemen.'

'Or that one of us is.'

'What's that?'

'Nothing. So Peter has come quietly to heel?'

'As quietly as a lamb,' Holbrook said.

Well, thought Somerset, perhaps it's all for the best. I shall get my money, rather a lot of money, and I dare say I shall be able to explain to Peter that it wasn't really my fault. How was I to know what Tom would come out with? And Peter could hardly expect that sort of thing to remain a secret for ever. As for Holbrook, even when he's Co-Proprietor there should be enough of us to cope with him.

Somerset's dinner date with Susan Grange was for the evening before the July meeting of the Board.

'Let's go to the Mirabelle,' Susan said.

Somerset swallowed hard, because he knew that the accounts department of *Strix* would never pass a dinner at the Mirabelle, not if he'd been treating the Chancellor of the Exchequer; but since this was the first time he'd taken Susan out, he could hardly refuse. As for Susan, she had proposed it by way of a test. She hadn't yet made up her mind about Somerset. At first, after their luncheon, she had inclined to think that she didn't want to see any more of him, a feeling which had persisted up to and after the day on which Somerset had telephoned to invite her. More recently, however, she had had second thoughts: Somerset knew a lot of inside gossip, he could be funny in his pompous way, and this sex angle of his might be amusing as an occasional change. So she had decided to put Somerset on probation as her second-string lover for July. One essential qualification for this post was routine generosity in the matter of meals and entertainments (to presents she was oddly indifferent), and she was therefore anxious to see both how he would take her suggestion of the Mirabelle and how he would comport himself when they got there. Although he had not, she thought, received the suggestion with notable composure, at least he had not demurred.

As the evening went on, her opinion of him steadily rose. Once committed to an expensive restaurant, Somerset knew that to skimp would be to get the worst of both worlds: the more you spent, in places like the Mirabelle, the better value you had for your money. He therefore seized the menu and did something which almost nobody did these days and which Susan always longed for: he worked out and ordered an elaborate but well balanced dinner for both of them, only pausing to inquire whether she had any spectacular fads. To her delight and astonishment, she saw that here was a rare man who shared her passion for food and her knowledge of it. When she reviewed all the young men who had champed through smoked salmon and grilled steaks, or who, at the other extreme, had insisted that everything should be buried in truffles and flared in brandy at the table she told herself that she had good reason for gratitude. Dear Somerset. It was a pity about those frightful spots, yet in a way they were part of his charm.

Another thing which impressed her was Somerset's
behaviour when Jonathan Gamp came in with a not very suitable friend. For although Susan was not self-conscious she was
bored by Jonathan's flamboyant posturing in public places and
had decided, soon after Donald's Ball, that from now on
Jonathan was 'out'; so that she regarded his arrival at first with
aggravation and then, as he squirmed towards her table arm in
arm with his teetering, fish-faced boy friend, with fury. But
Somerset had risen to the occasion: apparently aware of her distress, he had smiled, waved, and lowered his face back into his
food in a fashion which would have made it plain to a rhinoceros
that, while there were no hard feelings, it was to proceed on its
way at the double. The clever thing was, Susan thought, that
Somerset had managed to pose as the injured party, whereas
the boot was, if anything, on the other foot, and to pose so effectively that Jonathan Gamp had shrivelled with guilt under their
eyes and had been led away by a waiter who, sensing his discomfiture, had given him the worst table in the room.

Taking all this into account, and having drunk two large and
exquisite brandies, Susan decided to declare her terms. As
second-string lover, Somerset was to dine her twice a week
(but never from now on at weekends), to go home to bed with
her afterwards (but not to stay later than three a.m.), and to
vary the routine, when required, by taking her to a theatre and
then to a late dinner at a place where there was dancing – not,
she added hastily, that she expected him to dance. There was
to be no jealousy of the first-string lover (a place which had
been vacant since Detterling's time, Jonathan Gamp having
not really counted, but was now about to be filled), no scenes
unless she started them, or emotional demands, no proposals
of marriage, and no complaints when she didn't feel like it.
When she did feel like it, on the other hand, he could suggest
anything he liked provided he would respect her right of veto.

Somerset bowed his assent. The expense, he knew, would be
immoderate (how could he ever have grudged Maisie her £3?),
but there was a cachet to being Susan's lover, even her second-

string lover and even though she was now on the decline. Besides, Somerset was strongly sexed, and the thought of going home that night and many nights with this beautiful randy, twisted girl was irresistible. He had felt unhappy and disillusioned when she was so chilly on the telephone the other day: now, though he took care not to show it, he was restored to a rapture of infatuation. God had really been very good, arranging for so much money to be in view just when it would be needed. He had, as he remembered even in his rosy daze of lust, five thousand to come from Salinger & Holbrook after the Board had approved their offer tomorrow; and Lord Philby would owe him 5 per cent of £60,000, i.e. £3,000, as soon as the sale was completed. This amounted to a lot of money, even with Lady Susan Grange on the budget. There could be no doubt about it: it paid to take God into one's confidence.

'After the minutes of the previous meeting had been read and approved, the Board was invited to consider Lord Philby's wish to sell the Proprietorship to Messrs. Salinger & Holbrook, of Chancery Lane, W.C.2. Lord Philby retired during the discussion which ensued.

'Mr. Lloyd-James: As you know, gentlemen, three out of four of us must be in favour before this sale can be allowed to proceed. On several occasions past we have examined the proper meaning of the Article which covers conditions of sale, and I think each of us has made it quite clear to the others how he interprets this. However, before we put the matter to the vote, has anyone anything further to say – either about the Article in question or its application to the proposed sale? Mr. Dilkes?

'Mr. Dilkes: I can't help wishing members had been given slightly longer to investigate the standing of Salinger & Holbrook. However, I have been able to establish, to my own satisfaction, that the firm is financially sound, progressively administered, and respected for the high quality and prompt distribution of its product.

'Professor Constable: Advertising matter. But let us look no further from the focal point, which is the Article governing sale. You all know my views on that; and I must now insist that the financial security and business efficiency of the firm which has made the offer are entirely irrelevant.

'Mr. L-J: Mr. Morrison?

'Mr. Morrison: I can only repeat what I said earlier this year. These days we cannot afford to worry too much about the literal interpretation of regulations – the times are moving too fast. I think we shall be acting in the spirit required of us if we consider whether or not our founder could have approved of the applicants. I do not see that the connection of Salinger & Holbrook with the advertising trade – they only print the material, remember, they do not invent it – need disqualify the firm from becoming Proprietor of *Strix*.

'Mr. L-J: Let us then put the matter to the vote. The question is, gentlemen, whether this Board approves the proposed sale of the Proprietorship to Messrs. Salinger & Holbrook, of Chancery Lane, W.C.2. Professor Constable?

'Prof. C: No. I entirely disapprove of the proposed sale.

'Mr. L-J: Mr. Dilkes?

'Mr. D: If Philby wishes to sell, I shall not oppose him.

'Prof. C: You do not actually approve then?

'Mr. D: I'm not voting against the sale, if that's what you mean.

'Prof. C: Your vote was cast in terms too cool to indicate approval.

'Mr. L-J: Please, gentlemen. I think Mr. Dilkes has made himself clear. He is prepared to allow sale.

'Mr. D: Thank you.

'Mr. L-J: That is one vote either way. Mr. Morrison?

'Mr. M: I am totally opposed to this sale.

'Mr. L-J: What?

'Mr. M: I said, I am totally opposed to this sale.

'Prof. C: Good man.

'Mr. L-J: Well . . . er . . . in that case there is no need for me to vote. The two votes already cast against the sale mean, of course, that it may not be proceeded with. Perhaps we should now call for Lord Philby?'

Part Four

10

Holbrook heard the news about *Strix* at tea-time from Lord
Philby who had come hot foot from the meeting. After talking
to Philby for twenty minutes, he took a taxi and drove to
Lord's, where Donald was watching cricket from the Pavilion.
Since Holbrook himself was not a member of the M.C.C., he
was stopped at the rear entrance of the Pavilion by a deferential but firm official, and since he would not take the trouble to
explain himself politely, the official became markedly less deferential and more firm.

'Damn it man, it's an urgent matter of business,' Holbrook
said.

'This Pavilion is not normally used for business purposes.'

'Then get Mr. Salinger down here.'

'I'm afraid I can't leave this door,' said the official smugly,
'or anybody at all might walk in.'

'A good job, if they did,' shouted Holbrook. 'The whole place
needs shaking up.'

'That's not for me to say.'

'Then I'll say it. This is the Twentieth Century,' said
Holbrook, and ground his teeth, 'the Twentieth Century, and
life moves too quickly' – his voice rose again to a shout – 'for a
lot of senile idiots to sit on their arses watching this bloody
ridiculous game.'

At this stage the official beckoned. Two policemen appeared
and escorted Holbrook from the ground, to the quiet satisfaction of the official, who knew Warriors well and could have told
Holbrook, had he asked nicely, that his partner was in fact
watching Royal Tennis in the public gallery of the court just
opposite. Quivering with hate, Holbrook found another taxi
and drove to Angela's flat in Holland Park. By the time he
arrived there he had calmed down a little and was looking

forward to the relief of telling Angela what had happened and asking her advice. Angela was out and rage remounted. He still had sufficient self-control, however, to remember that he must telephone the office with an urgent message for Ashley Dexterside which he had forgotten to pass on before he left for Lord's. The taxi-driver took nearly ten minutes to find a telephone box, which was occupied by an adolescent lout with sideburns. After some minutes more, Holbrook realized that the boy was not actually using the telephone but just leaning over it. After a nasty exchange during which it emerged that the youth was waiting for his girl to ring and who did Holbrook think he was anyway, Holbrook solicited the aid of the taxi-driver, who suggested, with indifferent scorn, that money might do the trick. Only when he saw the look of spiteful glee in the boy's face did Holbrook realize that he had been conned, and by then he had already parted with his ten shillings. Twice his number was engaged (though Salinger & Holbrook had five lines) and when at last he did get through he was told that Mr. Dexterside left half an hour before — had obviously, thought Holbrook, taken deliberate advantage of his own absence to do so. Since the message referred to some urgent preparations which must be made that very evening, he tried Ashley's private number; the first burr-burr had that sullen flatness which warns one straight away that nobody is listening, but he let the telephone ring thirty times before slamming the receiver down, in doing which he sliced his knuckles on a screw that protruded from the wall. Pouring with blood, dabbing painfully with his dirty handkerchief at the raw flesh, writhing and mouthing in hatred of the whole human race, Holbrook was reduced to a state of diminished responsibility which may perhaps explain the mindless violence of what was now to follow.

The price of Holbrook's silence was Peter's support; this price Peter had promised but had now failed to pay. A child, thought Somerset, could have solved this equation: 'x' equals trouble. And not only for Peter. It was really too bad of him, when everything had been so comfortably settled, to turn subversive at the last minute.

Whatever was going to happen now, some immediate personal insurance was required. First of all, he rang up Salinger & Holbrook, to be told that Donald was out: did he wish to speak with Mr. Holbrook? For a variety of reasons he did not, but before he could say so the telephonist corrected herself: she was so sorry but Mr. Holbrook was in closed conference — with Lord Philby, she added, her voice plummy with snobbish pleasure. Having drawn his own conclusions from this, Somerset telephoned Captain Detterling's chambers in Albany and was informed, by a manservant, that his master was at Lord's. Since Somerset elected to go there by Underground, he arrived ten minutes too late to witness the ejection of Holbrook and so missed a great deal of enjoyment. However, he was not much in the mood for enjoyment that afternoon, and indeed his application to the doorman of the Pavilion, although more civil than Holbrook's, had the same kind of nervous anxiety and awakened the same kind of response in the official, who, having tasted blood and liked it, was quick to scent another possible victim.

But before the man could get his fangs properly bared, Somerset was saved by Detterling, who now emerged from the Tennis Court opposite accompanied by Donald Salinger. Somerset took one look and made his decision: here was a chance to clear himself, perhaps even to do himself a lot of good, on two fronts at the same time. For if anything really unpleasant was threatening, Donald would be as grateful for a warning on behalf of his firm's good name as Detterling would be on behalf of the Young Englanders. Both men were clearly surprised, even displeased, to see Somerset, so as he stepped forward, in order to confront them out of the door-keeper's hearing, he put on all the dramatic urgency of a Shakespearean herald in justification of his presence.

'Something perfectly appalling has happened,' Somerset said.

At this Donald blinked resentfully (how could anything appalling happen on a summer afternoon at Lord's?), while

Detterling, who liked a little excitement now and then, looked fractionally less bored and disdainful than usual. Somewhere in the background a bell tinkled to summon the players back on to the field; a large man with an Eton Ramblers' tie and an expensive face walked past explaining to a friend that someone or other was a goodish fast bowler but a perfect sod; and a champagne cork popped loudly from the Clock Tower. Meanwhile, Somerset, Donald and Detterling just stood and looked at each other. Somerset's announcement seemed to have paralysed the three of them, to have created a state of affairs comparable to that depicted on Keats' Grecian Vase, where any number of interesting events are permanently arrested just before they can take place. Unless someone broke the spell, Donald would blink, Detterling would look mildly speculative and Somerset would pause with his news on the tip of his tongue for ever and ever more. Typically, it was Detterling who finally freed them.

'I must have a crap,' he said. 'Join you out here in three minutes.'

When Detterling had had his crap, the three of them walked round to the Nursery, where they stood at a discreet distance from the nets while Somerset told his tale – omitting his own part in bringing Tom Llewyllyn and Holbrook together at the Ball and minimizing his knowledge of Holbrook's subsequent activities. When he had finished Detterling said:

'So what do you expect to happen now?'

'That will depend on Jude Holbrook.'

'But this is ghastly,' Donald blustered: 'he can't go round behaving like this. Why wasn't I told before?'

'Because you didn't want to know,' said Somerset rather nastily. 'Now you do know, and you'd better stop him before he does anything worse.'

'But why should he?' said Detterling. 'If he actually lets the story out his ammunition's gone. He'd have no way left of bringing Peter round.'

'If he lets the story out,' Somerset said, 'he'd at least be getting rid of a dangerous opponent. Peter would have to resign from the Board – and from a lot of other things. That's why I wanted *you* to know about this.'

'You've left it a little late in the day,' said Detterling. He smiled equably at Somerset. 'Too late for anyone to be very grateful.'

'I've only just realized the full implications of what's been going on.' As always when he was lying Somerset's lisp was pronounced.

'This is all very well,' said Donald peevishly; 'but I've been looking forward to this cricket match for weeks, and what happens but you come along and spoil all my pleasure?'

'That's not quite the point,' said Somerset. 'The point is that if you don't want your partner trampling round London like a rogue elephant, and if *you*' – he turned to Detterling – 'don't want an ugly scandal on your hands in the House, you'd both better take charge of Holbrook, and take charge now. Because Holbrook, as Donald will agree, has a very nasty temper and is capable of anything if crossed.'

'And what are you going to do?' said Detterling, looking wistfully up at Father Time on his weather vane. 'After all, Peter's an old friend of yours.'

'I,' said Somerset, 'shall have a disagreeable evening placating my employer, who is now going to be badly short of ready cash.'

'The odd thing is,' Detterling remarked, 'that *no one* stands to benefit from this. I mean, usually when something unpleasant happens *somebody* is going to be better off. But Peter seems to have buggered up absolutely everybody, including himself. What damage honest men do. But you know,' he went on, looking up at Father Time once more, 'I think we shall find, if we look very closely, that there's a prize in it all somewhere. There always is, in the end. I only wonder who's winning it. . . .'

'No good standing around being clever,' said Donald, who would normally have enjoyed this piece of theorizing but was now much too put out: 'we must find Jude at once. He was at the office, you say?'

'He *was*,' said Somerset, 'and Philby with him. So he'll

already have known the worst for nearly an hour. . . .'

Ashley Dexterside rang up Carton Weir.

'The balloon's gone up,' he said.

'How high and in what direction?'

'I can't really say, dear. Philby arrived with a face like Good Friday and was closeted with Jude. They wouldn't let anyone near them so I don't know the details. What I *do* know is that Jude then left the office in such a hurry that he forgot to give me some very important instructions. Most unusual for him.'

'What was he going to do?'

'He didn't confide in me, dear,' said Ashley, 'but nothing nice, I fancy. He was doing his imitation of Count Dracula.'

'How will he go about it?' said Helen Morrison.

'It will be interesting to see,' replied her husband, who was struggling sweatily with his evening tie.

'Let me, dear . . . Peter darling, is there any way I can help?'

'I want you to go down to Whereham and stay with the boys for the next few days. Things may be rather unpleasant, and I'd sooner you were at home.'

'I can put up with a little unpleasantness.'

'That's just it. I want you to be down there with the boys in case there's talk. It might frighten them if they heard something nasty and neither of us was there.'

'Of course you're right,' said Helen Morrison, and kissed him in the middle of his enormous, sweaty forehead: 'I'll take the ten twenty-five tomorrow morning.'

'Bloody nuisance, the whole thing,' said Lord Philby to Somerset. He snapped his finger at the head waiter. 'Two more large brandies,' he said.

'Right away, my Lord.'

Philby smirked as he always did when called 'my lord' and doused his cigarette in his coffee cup.

'What will this chap Holbrook *do*?' he asked.

'That's what a lot of people would like to know. He left his office just after you saw him there this afternoon and hasn't been seen or heard of since.'

'And the sale?'

Somerset shrugged. 'I'm afraid we shall have to wait until things have been sorted out.'

'Bloody nuisance. My trustees won't give me a penny over income and I badly need the cash. I don't mind telling you why. I've taken up with a grand girl, but she's hellish expensive. Real guinea a minute piece of work. Dare say you've heard of her: Lady Susan Grange.'

Holbrook's actions, the subject of so much speculation, were in fact as follows. First of all, he drove in his taxi from the telephone box to a nearby chemist, by whom he had his hand sterilized and dressed. Then he drove on to Chancery Lane, paid off the taxi and under-tipped the driver, let himself into the now deserted offices, and sat down behind the late Miss Beatty's typewriter. After some thought and a little rough work with a pencil, he typed, with two fingers, a letter which began:

Dear Sir,

It is in the public interest that the following facts should be made known to you.

The letter went on to give a succinct account, complete with names, dates and sources, of Peter Morrison's youthful misdemeanour and its results, and stressed the fact that generous hush-money was still being paid. It concluded without compliments but with the written signature, 'Jude Holbrook'.

The letter completed, Holbrook examined it, approved it, found some carbon paper, and made nine copies of it in three batches of three. The original he put in his pocket: the nine copies he signed and placed in separate envelopes, which he addressed respectively to the speaker of the House of Commons, the Chief Whip of the Conservative Party, the Chief Whip of the Labour Party, the Chairman of the Whereham and District Conservative Association, the Editors of one morning, one evening and one Sunday newspaper (all of them philistine and raucous), Somerset Lloyd-James, Esqre., Editor of *Strix*, and Mrs. Peter Morrison. He sealed and stamped the envelopes (not forgetting to make a note in the postage book as he was using office stamps), wrote 'Highly Confidential' in the top left-hand corner of each one, and slotted the whole pile at Chancery Lane Post office in time to catch the eight p.m. post.

Meanwhile, it had not of course occurred either to Donald or Detterling, who were by this time tired, hungry and exceedingly disagreeable, to look for him in Chancery Lane; for does not everybody know that the City is always deserted, except by cats and caretakers, after six?

'Why?' said Angela Tuck later that night. 'What can you possibly hope to have achieved?'

'The removal of Mr. Morrison.'

'The next man may be just the same.'

'Then I shall get rid of him too. And the next, and the next.' Holbrook's hands were twitching and his voice was shrill. 'They'll know now that no one tries to make a fool out of me and gets away with it. That smug bastard, Morrison. A very parfait gentil knight he thought he was, putting the upstart in his place.' He ripped savagely at the dressing on his hand. 'The Wellington touch – "Publish and be damned". He didn't think I'd have the nerve. He'll think different by this time tomorrow.'

It was, thought Somerset Lloyd-James, simply too bad. Captain Detterling had been right: there seemed to be no advantage in this for anybody at all. There certainly wasn't for Somerset: he had missed making a lot of money; he was on the way to losing two old friends – and with one of them any influence he possessed in political circles; and to top it all, though this could hardly be blamed on the *affaire Strix*, he had lost most of his pleasure in his new mistress, Susan Grange. For while it had been easy enough to accept the *theory* of a first-string lover who would take precedence over him, it had been a very different thing to hear Philby's casual announcement over the brandy last night that the post was in fact his.

'Mail, Mr. Lloyd-James,' his secretary said. 'One marked "High Confidential", so I've left it for you to open.'

As Somerset read what Holbrook had written, his buttocks began to sweat. When he came to a pencilled P.S., which explained to whom other copies had gone, he leant back in his chair, put his hands over his face, and moaned aloud with horror. That Holbrook might do something unpleasant he had been the first to anticipate; but for all the drama he had made of it at Lord's he had not expected anything as explosively destructive as this. The civilized structure of his world was tottering; the best he could hope for was to escape from the debris alive.

Vanessa Salinger, on her way to catch a train to the Old People's Home where she was to spend the next thirty-six hours in the care of Dr. La Soeur, saw a newspaper poster which read:

AMERICANS WITHDRAW AID
Nasser Speaks.

When Helen Morrison, just as she was about to leave for Whereham, received her copy of Holbrook's letter, she read it carefully and passed it to her husband without comment.

'Well,' Peter said; 'as good a way as any of getting people interested. It only remains for them to check up for themselves. . . . You'd better hurry if you're going to get your train. Give my love to the boys.'

'Here's a fine mess,' said Carton Weir to Captain Detterling.

'I told you it would happen. My man in Washington has been harping on it for weeks.'

'Never mind that bloody dam,' said Carton: 'I mean this business of Peter Morrison. There's been a letter.'

'A letter?'

Carton Weir explained.

'Lord love a duck,' Captain Detterling said: 'whatever next?'

'I simply don't know what to say to you,' said Donald Salinger to Jude Holbrook. 'I must have time to think.'

'It's very simple. Morrison has been stringing me along and now he's going to pay for it. He's going to squirm.'

'No he's not,' said Donald, getting to his feet. 'Whatever happens, Morrison won't squirm. They can crush him into the ground and he still won't squirm. You don't understand him.'

'I know him as well as you do.'

'You've met him as often, but you didn't understand. *You* couldn't understand, not in a thousand years. Morrison is a decent man, naturally decent, one of the very few. Anyone – even you – can behave decently when things are normal; the test comes when things are very good or very bad. And just as Morrison's kind don't gloat when they're on top, neither do they whine when they're brought down. They don't whine and they don't squirm, they lie still and take what's coming to them. And more often than you'd think they have enough strength to get up again when it's over.'

Breathing heavily, Donald made for the door.

'Where are you going?' Holbrook asked.

'I've got an appointment.'

'With whom, might I ask?'

'For what business it is of yours, my appointment has to do with a dependant of ours whom you've probably forgotten. A certain old lady called Mrs. Beatty. I've been thinking of a few simple arrangements to make her dotage a little more pleasant, and this afternoon I must go down and see the Matron in charge of her Home. After what we've been discussing, it is, I assure you, a relief to be so wholesomely employed.'

The first indication Tom Llewyllyn had that something was up was Tessie Buttock banging on his door at noon.

'Got to get up dearie. Man from the newspapers.'

'Tell him to go to hell,' said Tom, who had just had one of his nights at the Tin Tack on the strength of Jude Holbrook's hundred pounds (which he had guiltily allowed Somerset to restore to him a few days after the Ball).

'He says it's a vital matter of public interest.'

'He can stuff the public interest.'

The door opened and a little round man waddled in wearing a wide hat. He closed the door carefully but could not exclude a sense of Tessie Buttock listening heavily behind it.

'No need to disturb yourself, Mr. Llewyllyn. Just a few questions.'

'Piss off.'

The little round man took Tom's clothes off a chair, placed them daintily on a sofa, then drew up the chair by Tom's bed as if he had been a doctor come to examine him.

'Alfie Schroeder of the Billingsgate Press,' he announced, lifting and replacing his hat.

'How many times do I have to tell you to get out?'

'I wouldn't take that tune, Mr. Llewyllyn, if I was you. Let's see now . . . your book's due out in three weeks or is it only two?'

'What's that to do with you?'

'You wouldn't want to upset the Billingsgate Press just before it's published.'

There was something in this. The Billingsgate reviewers, tedious hacks who spent most of their time complaining that this or that author had violated the sanctity of the home, could be disregarded; but the possibility, cherished by Stern, that a Billingsgate paper would print long extracts from Tom's book at a high price, could not.

'Would you mind,' said Tom wearily, 'getting me a glass of Alka-Seltzer? Things over there. And as for you, you old cow,' he shouted at the door, 'rumble off and whip up some coffee.'

Having paid his rent for some weeks in advance out of Holbrook's money, Tom felt entitled to service from Tessie. Pleased with the aristocratic way in which he had asserted himself, he accepted his Alka-Seltzer with a condescending nod, drained it, belched, re-arranged his pillows, and leaned back to give audience to Alfie Schroeder.

'I suppose it's too much to hope,' he said, 'that it's my book you've come to ask about?'

''Fraid not,' said Mr. Schroeder.

'Well?'

'You know a Mr. Peter Morrison? M.P.?'

Tom stiffened and shook his head.

'By sight. Little more.'

'Know of him, perhaps?'

Tom said nothing.

'You see,' said Mr. Schroeder, 'we've had a very rum tip-off about this Mr. Morrison. We're not quite sure what we can make of it, and first of all we've got to check that we're not just being had on. You'd be surprised,' he said pathetically, 'how many people try to have us on.'

'Serves you right for shit-stirring.'

'Be that as it may,' the little man went on, 'you have been named by our informant as one of the people who can vouch for the authenticity of this information.' He now recited a swift and accurate precis of Holbrook's letter. 'So what we want to know, Mr. Llewyllyn,' he concluded, 'is what you've got to say about that.'

'What I've got to say,' said Tom, 'is that Peter Morrison is a good man who ought to be left alone.'

'He comes it a bit too high and mighty for the taste of the Billingsgate Press.'

'For my taste too. But that's not saying you're entitled to rake up scandal from ten years back.'

'We know what we're entitled to, Mr. Llewyllyn. So there is a scandal?'

'It's all hearsay.'

'We can soon get closer.'

'Then go away and get closer.'

'We shall. But it's always nice to have a colourful figure like yourself somewhere in on the act. Mr. Tom Llewyllyn, the well known writer and parliamentary candidate, said . . . Journalist too, aren't you? Just like me.'

'*Not* just like you,' Tom said; 'and I haven't said a thing.'

'You did this to Jude Holbrook.'

'I was drunk.'

'You know the old saying. Very colourful now, that bit is. Drunk at a ball, it seems, and spouting away as the sun came up.'

'I was asleep when the sun came up.'

'Mere detail. Makes a love scene either way. "While the noble and wealthy guests at the Summer Ball danced towards the dawn, the shadows outside were whispering with the secrets of the past. . . ."'

'For Christ's sake.'

'You may despise that kind of thing, Mr. Llewyllyn, but it's our policy to dish it out that way. It gives the dirt a bit of gilding, so to speak, makes it not quite real: as though the Babes in the Wood came on and started having a poke. All very thrilling and shocking for our readers, but it happened in another world, we tell them, so not to worry.'

'But they do worry,' said Tom, interested despite himself. 'That's just the trouble. You're always telling us how indignant they are, how they want inquiries, punishments, examples. . . .'

'Just part of the same old pantomime. Like with that executioner in *The Mikado*. A lot of talk, but you never see a head chopped off. Our function,' said the little man wryly, 'is to provide the proletariat with sublimation. Keep 'em happy in a dream world so they don't start asking for real heads.'

'They get one from time to time.'

'Only by courtesy of the Billingsgate Press. Special treat, sort of.'

'Peter Morrison?' asked Tom.

'That'd be telling. But since you're a journalist too, I don't have to remind you that Lord Billingsgate doesn't care much for young men who say snooty things about Commerce. And another thing, if there's going to be trouble with Nasser and his wogs, it's pretty certain that Morrison and his gang won't start singing "Rule Britannia." They're more Tory than the Tories in some ways, but they're finished with the Empire bit and they don't mind who knows it. So one way and the other, his lordship's feelings being what they are, I think Mr. Peter Morrison, M.P., had better watch out.'

'Ought you to be telling me this?'

'No,' said Alfie Schroeder disarmingly, 'but it's been a pleasure to talk to someone sympathetic for once. I'm Labour too, you know.'

He rose, lifted and replaced his enormous hat, steered his way past Tessie and the coffee in the doorway, and was gone.

'Get any money from him, dear?' said Tessie, plonking the tray down on Alfie Schroeder's chair and herself down on the bed.

'Only bad news. Tessie, I must get dressed at once.'

'Don't mind me, dear, I've had brothers. What sort of bad news?'

'They're gunning for a good man, Tessie, and it's my fault.'

'Go on! So what's to do?'

'I must go to him, Tessie. I must go to him, beg his pardon on my knees, and offer him my help.'

*

Donald, driving down to the Old People's Home of Rest to make the special arrangements for Mrs. Beatty, was badly held up in the traffic. This was a nuisance, because since Vanessa was to be away that night (visiting an invalid aunt in the country) he had made plans to dine and go to the theatre with Jonathan Gamp. At this rate he would be hard put to it to meet Jonathan on time, let alone to drop in at Cheyne Row, as he had planned, to bathe and change first.

So he drew up with an angry crunch outside the front door of the Home, surveyed the human flotsam on the lawn with conscientiously suppressed distaste, and plunged into the building. Having been there once before, just after Miss Beatty's death, he felt confident that he could find the way to Matron's office; and being already an hour late he was not minded to hang about until someone came to show him. In any case, the whole place seemed deserted – not surprising on a beautiful summer afternoon: no doubt all the nurses were supervising their unsavoury charges (now, now, Donald, their poor old patients, you mean) out in the open air.

He ran up the wide staircase which he remembered very clearly, turned left past a suit of armour and a bust of Alcibiades ('Get you, madam,' Ashley Dexterside had said to the bust on their previous visit), and then paused at a complicated junction of corridors, which resembled Piccadilly Circus in miniature. Surely . . . yes . . . half right, that was the way they had gone before, and very soon now one came to a green baize door marked 'Private', beyond which was Matron's suite and adjoining office.

Here, at any rate, was the green baize door: Matron's door, he remembered, was about a cricket pitch farther along on the right, unlabelled but easily distinguished by a door knob in the shape of a lion's head. Yes, this must be it; funny though, he had a distinct mental picture of a lion's head and this was a tiger's. He must be getting middle-aged: several times lately words and names which he knew as well as his own had slipped away from him just as he was about to give them tongue. Perhaps he was developing a block: would a psychiatrist help?

or a course of Pelmanism, which had done such wonders for old
Lady Evers? No time to worry now, already sixty-five minutes
late. No answer to the knock; better go in.

Inside, on a large pillow on a large bed, was a sleeping profile. Oh God: Matron's bedroom? But it was a youthful profile,
it was in fact Vanessa's. For a moment he felt mildly surprised,
as one does when meeting an acquaintance, with whom one
has not corresponded for some years, at the same Chemmy
table in Cannes. Indignation succeeded surprise and alarm
indignation; for on drawing closer, he saw the eyes open to recognize him, the whole face stiffen with terror, and the head
then slump, after a brief gasp, into an attitude which he knew
from countless films to be an indication of death.

'So that's it,' said Tom Llewyllyn to Peter Morrison. 'That's
how it happened, and I'm truly sorry.'

'I see.' Peter gazed sadly down at the river. What dismal
associations were now accruing round this terrace, upon which
he had walked with such pride and pleasure until a few days
ago. . . . Not that Tom's part in his betrayal came as any news
to him, for Holbrook had been explicit about that; it was
simply that Tom's account of what had passed at the Ball was
the first to make clear beyond dispute the deliberate and
treacherous role played by Somerset Lloyd-James.

'You mustn't blame Somerset too much,' said Tom, as if
reading his thoughts: 'he wanted me just to tell the story to
him. It was I who insisted on finding Holbrook.'

Peter nodded without conviction.

'At any rate,' he said, 'you can now collect the rest of your
fee. Another hundred, wasn't it, on confirmation that you'd
told the truth? It seems to have been confirmed to Holbrook's
satisfaction.'

'I'm not interested in the money. I never really was.'

'You may as well have it as not . . . I *want* you to have it.'

'I only want to help you.'

'You'll be helping me,' said Peter, 'by taking Holbrook's
money. That will annoy him. Which is a start.'

'All right. And then?'

'And then? What can you or anyone do then?'

'The man from the Billingsgate Press,' said Tom hesitantly; 'Schroeder, he was called. He seemed . . . sympathetic. He might be stopped even now.'

'There'll be others.'

'But for Christ's sake. You can't just sit on your bottom and do nothing. Inside there' – Tom gestured up at the Palace of Westminster – 'inside there they'll already be wondering and whispering and tip-toeing from room to room. Just as soon as Schroeder files the least little hint with his paper they're going to turn on you like the pack of mangy jackals they are. They're going to have a real field-day with you, Peter Morrison. All those city gents you've been so snooty about – they're going to hitch up their striped trousers and sharpen their expensive false teeth and have themselves the biggest meal ever.'

'What do you suggest?' said Peter wearily.

'Is there no way of upsetting the story?'

'You should know. You started it.'

'But you can deny it. After all, it was a long time ago, it's based on hearsay, it'd be your word against –'

Peter waved him silent.

'I can't deny it,' he said. 'If you are my friend – and despite all that has happened I believe you are – then the best service you can do me is to collect your money from Holbrook and forget the matter. It was bound to come out some time; these things always do. And as it is, at least one person – you – will be better off for it. By two hundred pounds.'

'Good-bye then.' And seeming that nothing more was to be achieved here, Tom turned to go.

'Tom.'

Tom turned back to see Peter's hand stretched towards him.

'Thank you,' Peter said as they shook hands; 'but there is nothing you can do.'

A few minutes after Tom had gone, Carton Weir crossed the terrace to Peter.

'Complicated day,' he said with satisfaction. 'It looks as if the Canal will be seized at any moment. Which is the least of your worries just now, I suppose.'

Peter gave a noncommittal nod.

'I'm sorry,' said Carton with one part genuine sympathy and three parts pleasurable anticipation of this new feast of intrigue. 'As far as I can make out,' he went on, waving up at the building behind them much as Tom had done, 'they're not quite certain what to do. They haven't enough to go on. So they're going to wait and see what the press comes up with and take their cue from that.'

'One of Billingsgate's men has already gone down to Whereham,' Peter volunteered.

'What shall you do?'

'Exactly the same as "they" will do. See what the press comes up with and take my cue from that.'

'There's nothing to worry about,' said Dr. La Soeur. 'It was just shock at waking up to see you there.'

'And now,' said Donald, 'perhaps you'd care to explain.'

'You'd better get your wife to do that. Until you showed up, I'd no idea she was married.'

La Soeur was a big man, blonde and calm. There was, his manner implied, no point to argue, and even if there were, he would get best. In any case, Donald was too relieved to quarrel. After the way Vanessa's head had slumped. . . .

'She's quite all right then?' said Donald after a pause. 'She can still have children?'

'If she wants them. But I don't think she much cares for the idea. Otherwise she wouldn't be here.'

Of course that was it, thought Donald, still half-hysterical with relief, as he went back down the corridor to Vanessa's room. He had selfishly forced her towards motherhood, she had been too dutiful, too loving, to object, but all the time she had been afraid, and then, when faced with an actual pregnancy, she couldn't stand it any longer, had come creeping down here, pathetic and alone. . . . What a heartless brute he had been: could he ever persuade her to forgive him?

'Vanessa,' he pleaded, lurching towards the bed, 'darling Vanessa, can you ever forgive me?'

'It's my fault,' Vanessa, still rather weak but taking her cue with characteristic aplomb: 'I should have been honest with you from the start. But I knew you wanted a child, and so I tried. . . . But I couldn't, Donald, I was so afraid. Not just the thought of the pain. Supposing there's something wrong with it, I kept saying to myself, supposing it's unworthy of Donald, supposing –'

'– Oh, my darling,' Donald said, removing his glasses and bending to kiss the wan face on the pillow, 'and for a moment I thought you were dead.'

'It's not as bad as that,' said Vanessa, a trifle huffily: 'but I must say I could do with a nice change now it's all over.'

'And you shall have one, my love. We'll go away again – a second honeymoon. Your favourite Venice, then Istanbul perhaps, Persia, India, Japan.'

'Not India; they're difficult about drink.'

'Wherever you say, my own love,' and he stooped to kiss her once more.

In the end, Donald left the Home in a daze of happiness, overwhelmed with gratitude that he still retained what for one agonizing minute he had thought was lost. This was lucky for old Mrs. Beatty, because Donald doubled the allowance which he was going to make her and ordered her a special television set of her very own.

Tom Llewyllyn knew a lot about guilt, in the sense that he knew just what it felt like to stand exposed before others, a fate which had frequently befallen him. Even when he had made allowance for Peter Morrison's superior address and deportment, his instinct and experience told him that something here was odd. A man who had been what Peter had been and was now in Peter's disastrous position should look . . . well . . . different. Not necessarily hang-dog, not necessarily chastened or ashamed, but uneasily and perhaps aggressively aware of

the unpleasant things which would shortly be said. Peter, on
the other hand, seemed tired and disillusioned but nevertheless poised. His behaviour was that of a chess-master whom
Tom had once watched when it was his opponent's turn to play:
the master had been, as he had to be, inactive for the time, but
also reflective and alert, pondering what he knew must come
and, while waiting for it, glancing occasionally and gravely at
the clock. Such attitudes, the attitudes of strength sorted ill
with Peter Morrison's predicament. There was an inconsis-
tency here; and whereas Tom had previously been inspired by
a blind wish to help, he was now prompted by curiosity to a
calmer and more rational approach. He returned thoughtfully
to Buttock's Hotel, packed a few things in a grip, and warned
Tessie Buttock that he would be away for one night and possibly two.

12

To Alfie Schroeder of the Billingsgate Press one thing was clear: unless he could get Mrs. Vincent herself to talk there could be no story; there could be hints leading as far, perhaps as unofficial inquiries in high places, but no story and no bonus for Alfie. For himself he wished Morrison no harm, but since Morrison would be in trouble anyway there might just as well be a story and a bonus for Alfie, which would be most appreciated by Alfie's wife and three growing kids. All of which added up to finding Mrs. Vincent and getting the dirt where the dirt ought to come from – from the horse's arse.

So much was obvious; but by the time his train reached Ely, where he must change for Whereham, something else was obvious too. The private detective, whom Holbrook had sent down a few days before, must have reasoned on much the same lines. None the less, he had contented himself with talking only to the husband, Jake, and sending in a report based on hearsay. (So much, while not explicitly stated, was plain from the terms of Holbrook's letter.) Either, then, Mrs. Vincent was not available, or she was unwilling to talk, or she was for some reason an unsatisfactory witness.

Having forty-five minutes to wait for his connection, Alfie, who was not one to miss a good thing, climbed the hill to have himself an eyeful of Ely Cathedral. The Isle of Ely, he remembered hearing, had once been styled a county Palatine, had been ruled by its princely bishops without reference to the royal jurisdiction. This proposition reminded him, in a devious way, of Peter Morrison, M.P. Here was a man who was taking an independent line, who was operating under his own jurisdiction: an island of probity in the fenland slough of politics. But now the central powers were going to take their chance (as the Tudors had with Ely) to crush this inconvenient stronghold until its splendour and independence affronted them no more. Rather a pity, thought Alfie as he waddled down the aisle; bonus or no bonus, rather a pity. But then (bonus or no bonus) he had his job to do for Lord Billingsgate, a job on which he and his family were dependent now and for ever, and that was that. He wandered into a side chapel and found himself reading the epitaph of someone called Bishop Alcock. 'He allè was a cock who so did crow . . .'; like Lord Billingsgate, Alfie thought. But even Lord Billingsgate, preening himself on his dunghill, had to respect the rules of evidence; and he would be the first to agree with Alfie that 'best evidence' here was Mrs. Vincent and that without it one might not proceed, or not very far. Back in square one: why had that private detective, who was known to Alfie by repute, not got on to Mrs. Vincent? And why had Alfie not thought of asking the man this question before leaving London? Getting old, he supposed; too interested in expounding his theories of journalism to young Tom Llewyllyn instead of getting on with the job. Well, there was still time to check up. Having taken a last regretful look round, Alfie passed out of the cool Cathedral and into the brooding afternoon.

Somewhere, surely, there must be a telephone box? Panting slightly Alfie started down the hill. Only when he came to a telephone box did he realize that he had not enough small change to telephone London. Shop opposite; blinds down; early closing day; try the station. But one of his endearing and unprofessional characteristics was that he did not carry a watch; and when he reached the station he found that he must have spent longer in the Cathedral than he realized and that his train was just about to leave. Dear God, thought Alfie, I really am getting past it. With a final pant he heaved himself into a compartment; the mystery of Mrs. Vincent must wait.

Tom Llewyllyn drove from London to Newmarket to Brandon to Whereham, where he arrived at six o'clock in the evening, booked himself in at a hotel, had a bath and then what passed for dinner. After this he drove, with rueful memories of his bucolic summer, to the village of Luffham and went into the public bar of the Townshend Arms, where, not altogether to his surprise, he saw Alfie Schroeder, who was despondently drinking gin.

'Waiting for Jake Vincent?' said Tim. 'He used to come in at about nine. They work late this time of the year.'

'I was waiting for Vincent,' said Alfie; 'but I don't think I shall bother now.'

'Don't mind me. I could introduce you.'

'I don't mind you. And I don't need an introduction.'

'I could help you in other ways. I know the country.'

'You can't help me in any way at all,' Alfie said. And then, not wishing to be unfriendly, 'Have a drink?'

'Whisky, if Billingsgate's paying.'

'He's paying. You can drink Vincent's ration.'

'It has occurred to me,' said Tom as he poured water into his whisky, 'that there is more in all this than meets the eye.'

'You weren't to know it, sonny,' said Alfie, 'but you never spoke a truer word.'

'So there's a mystery. So why are you leaving?'

'Because I know everything and nothing. Because there's no story and never can be.'

'Which makes it all right for Peter?'

'And no real let-off for him either. There's simply a nasty smell which no one will be able to track down and which will go on hanging about for ever.'

'Care to tell me?'

Alfie glanced across at the landlord.

'Where are you staying?' he asked Tom.

'The Earl Marshal in Whereham.'

'All right?'

'Just.'

'Got a car?'

'Sort of.'

'Then drive me to the Earl Marshal,' said Alfie, 'where I will rest my aching head this night. And as we go I will a tale unfold.'

*

For the ninetieth time, Angela Tuck read through the letter which she had received that morning. It was a letter from her ex-husband's solicitors, which began by apologizing for their failure to remit any maintenance money to her during the last few months but went on to explain that this was because they had temporarily lost touch with their client. Contact (of a kind) was now re-established: Mr. Tuck had returned to the United Kingdom the previous week, paid them the arrears of maintenance (a cheque for which they begged to enclose), deposited share certificates and bearer bonds worth a considerable sum with his banker, and had been run over by a removal van (he had been rather drunk, the bank manager said) as he left. Since Mr. Tuck died intestate and was known not to have any living relatives, his fortune would pass to herself. Payment of death duties and demonstration of probate would take some time, as most of the bonds, etc., while indisputably genuine, were of foreign issue. Meanwhile however, Mrs. Tuck might call upon them to arrange for the advance of any reasonable sum.

So, thought Angela; after all these years he finally hit the jackpot. I wonder how. He was often close to it but something always went wrong. That tea-planting swindle just after the war – a few hours earlier and the cheque would have been cleared; and then the white slaving in Naples, the brothel in Havana, the gambling club in Brighton, another brothel (of the most advanced kind) in London – something always went wrong just as he was about to scoop the kitty and run. And now that at last he's made it, he had to get pissed and fall under a truck. Unlucky to the end.

But lucky for some. Well, she would take up the solicitors' offer of an advance and go away for a little hol. God knew she needed one after this last year. And before she went she'd settle Jude Holbrook's hash; because if one thing was more certain than the next, she wasn't going to need him now.

'One little question,' said Alfie Schroeder as they rattled back to Whereham; 'one little teeny question that nobody bothered to ask. Or if they did, they kept the answer quiet, because it didn't suit their book. So let me ask you, sonny: when you were here that summer, did you ever meet *Mrs*. Jake Vincent? Betty?'

'No. These people are very close about their homes. But I gathered that she was a pretty woman and, once granted her little mishap, a good wife and mother.'

'Yes,' said Alfie: 'she's all of that.'

'Have you met her then?'

'No.'

'Then how do you know so much?'

'I asked the landlord of that pub. "Do you know a lady," I said, "called Mrs. Betty Vincent?" "Aah," he says; "Jake Vincent's Betty?" "Yes," I said, and bought him a brandy and ginger. Mind you I wasn't expecting much, because we know the village accepts Jake's story that it was himself first pushed Betty down in the grass. All I was hoping for was a rough preliminary sketch of our heroine. And that was all I got.'

'Then why all the excitement?'

'Because Betty Vincent, a model wife and mother, an excellent plain cook, an immaculate housekeeper, a comely and modest woman without an enemy in the world – this same Betty Vincent, as a result, very likely, of centuries of inbreeding, was stone blind with a cataract from the age of ten to the age of sixteen. In fact, it is only because of the goodness of the Morrison family, who paid for her to have an operation based on some new technique discovered during the war, that she can see now.'

The implications of this were so multifarious and appalling that for a long time Tom said nothing.

'More than meets the eye, you said,' remarked Alfie eventually: more than ever met Betty Vincent's eye. It'd have been her word against his in any case. What chance would she have now?

'Blind people are very sensitive in other ways. . . . Hearing, touch, smell. . . .'

'To get this thing on the road, I need evidence which would

stand up from a witness in a court of law. And with a witness in a court of law, seeing's believing.'

'But if he spoke to her. . . .'

Peter, it seemed, might be acquitted, but first every possible objection must be raised.

'Big boys who play with blind girls of fourteen keep their mouths shut.'

'Then how was she so sure?'

'We've only her husband's word she was sure. And it's no good asking her,' said Alfie, 'because whatever she says, *no one* can ever really know. "I heard a man coming towards me"' he improvised; '"he started playing with my little charlies and it smelt like the young master." "And how many times, Mrs. Vincent, had you smelt the young master at close quarters?" "He danced with me at the tenants' Christmas party." "I see. Eight months before." It could be as true as hell, sonny, and a lot of people could believe it too, but it would never quite stick. And I'll tell you something else. Even if she swore blind – sorry, no joking – that it *wasn't* the young master, no one could ever be sure about that either.'

'So no story,' said Tom, negotiating the entrance to the yard of the Earl Marshal; and then, seeing the full and dismal purport of Alfie's speech, 'and no proper clearance for Peter. Just a nasty smell, as you said.'

'A classical verdict of "not proven" – and those leave the worst smell of all.'

They got out of the car and moved, without needing to consult one another, into the Hotel bar. After a bit, Tom said:

'There are so many questions to be asked – on both sides. Was this eye operation a bribe or just kindness? What about the maintenance money for the child? What was a blind girl *doing out alone*? Why did Jake not tell me she was blind in the first place? There's every kind of loose end.'

'Well, you can start tying them up, chum,' said Alfie Schroeder, 'because there's nothing in it for Alfie, and so I shall tell his nibs.'

But there must be something else, Tom thought; something

to account for the expectation on Peter's face, the poise and gravity with which he had been waiting for the next move. He could never have looked like that if all that was to come was this mockery of an acquittal which only made the crime more vile. There was something more – something else which hadn't yet met the eye - and it would be his business to find it out.

At about the same time as Tom and Alfie arrived at the Earl Marshal, Susan Grange joined Somerset in the Rivoli Bar of the Ritz.

'You look dreadful,' Susan said, and ordered a triple dry martini.

'I feel dreadful.'

'I'm sorry about that, because I've got some news you may not care for. Your boss, George Philby, has asked me to marry him. And I think I'm going to say yes.'

Somerset nodded dumbly. It was not his day.

'And that,' Susan said, 'will mean an end to our little ménage. I'm not a good girl, but I've an old-fashioned belief in the sanctity of marriage. I mean, if one's going to do it at all. . . .' She broke off and looked at Somerset's miserable face. 'Oh, hell,' she said, 'it's the same for every girl. White dresses and orange blossom – it makes us all howl to think of it.'

'Still,' said Somerset, 'if you haven't actually answered yet. . . . Perhaps the new régime needn't start until you do.'

Susan laughed. 'What a dirty-minded little casuist you are. No, Somerset. I mean to start as I'm going to go on.'

'Why Philby?'

'For one thing, he's enormously rich.'

'It's all tied up. He's badly pushed for ready money.'

'He won't be when he announces his engagement. His trust provides for the release of a hundred and fifty thousand when he gets married. And it's comforting to know that he can't drink or gamble with the rest.'

Somerset listened to his last hope going down the drain with a gurgle. With a hundred and fifty thousand pounds to come Philby would now lose all interest in selling *Strix* even if it should later prove possible. Everything gone: an almost certain £8,000 dissolved like dream money on waking; his new and delicious mistress whisked away with a golden hook; Donald furious; Peter alienated; no seat in Parliament; Holbrook apparently off his head; Tom (or so Tessie Buttock said) vanished into the country and up to God alone knew what. Except that God probably didn't know; God, as He had shown several times that day, was altogether too Incompetent.

'And there's another thing,' Susan was saying. 'George Philby is like me – coarse-grained. We are very compatible.'

'He hasn't a quarter your intelligence.'

'Who wants a clever husband? Showing off all the time.'

'Lady Philby,' said Somerset, 'is a poor exchange for Lady Susan Grange.' At this stage it was the best he could do.

'Well,' she said. 'Dinner here? Or somewhere else?'

'Here,' said Somerset between his teeth. At least he would save on the taxi.

While they were drinking their fifth large whiskies, Tom said,

'You know, if you care to come along with me tomorrow morning, you might be interested.'

'I've told you. There's nothing in it for Alfie any more.'

'Nothing in it for the Billingsgate Press. But for Alfie the student of human affairs?'

'I'm thinking of Alfie the bread-winner.'

'He could surely afford one more day.'

'What are you going to do?'

'Consult a source which can't lie. About the *dramatis personae*. I've remembered something just about as obvious as the steeple on Luffham Church.'

'So I've made up my mind,' said Donald to Holbrook the next morning: 'Vanessa and I are going on a long trip, probably to the Far East. In view of what has happened, I shall withdraw the offer for *Strix*, and I shall engage a general manager to look after the firm in my absence. To look after the entire firm, you understand. Because I am going to buy your interest from you and delete the name of Holbrook from the books.'

'And if I don't accept.'

'It will be a fair offer, if only for old times' sake. If I were you, I should take it and get out. You may not realize it yet, but after what you've done your name is going to stink so high that no one will come near this firm until you're out of it. Better take good money now than sit here while the place crumbles over your head. At the moment there are only rumours going around, but people are already ringing me up and making inquiries in peculiar voices. So I've told them that you are threatened with a nervous breakdown through overwork and are resigning your partnership forthwith.'

Holbrook said nothing but picked incessantly at his thumb.

'I must know,' said Donald. 'What in God's name did you think you were doing? Were you mad?'

And then, for the first time, he realized what had somehow escaped him ever since he had first met Holbrook at Oxford nine years before. He saw Holbrook's eyes staring at him, huge, cold, furious, unwinking in the small ratty face; he saw the fingers clawing, each like a separate being in its own right, at the raw, shredded thumb; and at last, beyond all possible doubt, he realized the truth. I'm going to destroy you, the eyes said, I'm going to destroy the world. I want to kill and go on killing, the fingers said; I want to tear the universe apart. Donald shivered and turned away.

'I'll take the money,' said Holbrook very quietly, 'and I'll go. But one thing you can't prevent, Donald. You can't stop me crushing Morrison. It's too late now. A decent man, you said, naturally decent, one of the very few. But by the time they've finished what I've begun the decency will have been crushed out of him like slime, along with the mucus and the blood.'

At breakfast in the Earl Marshal Alfie was badly hung.

'Not up to the juice any more,' he muttered. He stabbed with his knife, and a large piece of brittle fried bread sailed across the room to hit the window with a clank.

'Oh God,' said Alfie, and gave up the struggle.

'Eat up,' said Tom; 'long day ahead.'

'I can't think what I'm staying for,' Alfie grumbled.

However, after burning his hand badly on the pot, Alfie managed a cup of coffee and felt brighter.

'All right,' he said, 'so you've remembered something. You told me last night but I wasn't hearing too well.'

'It didn't mean anything much until we knew about Betty Vincent being blind when the child was conceived. But now. . . .'

'Well?'

'Well, in 1945 Betty has her bastard. In 1947 Jake Vincent finishes his Army service, comes home, acknowledges the child as his own, and marries her. Which leaves two years during which the villagers have in their midst an unmarried mother, who was made pregnant when blind and under age, and yet not one of them turns a hair. Nobody worries about who the father was, nobody is remotely shocked, nobody tries to fix the blame or kick up a fuss.'

'Why should they? Bastards are quite common in places like this.'

'Certainly. That's why I didn't think too much about it at first. But a *blind* girl's bastard, Alfie? And again, even in run of the mill cases, people make it their business to know who's responsible; at the very least, they speculate. Yet here was this rather sensational case and no one, if we are to believe Jake Vincent's account, gives it the least little thought, except to approve vaguely when Jake finally came home to own up and make amends.'

'He was away, remember, during the two years. Perhaps there was more fuss than he knew.'

'He'd have heard. Even in Luffham people write letters to soldiers. No. For two solid years no one was at all bothered about poor Betty, except perhaps for the old 'Squire, who paid her a handsome allowance not to tell anyone that the child was, as she claimed, Peter's. And that too is peculiar. Why should the old man take her word – a blind girl's word – so easily? Why did no one find out that she was getting money and where it came from? In a village the size of Luffham?'

'Obvious answer: Vincent's story is one big lie.'

'No, Alfie. You haven't met Jake Vincent. He doesn't tell lies.'

'Then Betty told *him* lies.'

'Perhaps; but then why is Peter Morrison sitting down under it? Doing nothing to clear himself?'

'Search me,' Alfie said. 'The whole thing's a proper foul-up.'

'Right. A proper foul-up, with which everyone in Luffham was so thoroughly contented that absolutely nothing was said or done about it.'

'What are you going to say or do about it?'

'I told you last night. Consult a source which can't lie. We're going to see the Rector, first of all, and ask to have a look at his Parish records. And I've a rough idea,' Tom said happily, 'what we're going to find.'

What they didn't find was the Rector. Mr. Purchase had gone, his wife said, to spend a day doing archaeological research at 'Vane's Vaults', a notable group of prehistoric flint mines not far from the Whereham Ride. Could they see the Parish records? No, they couldn't, as her husband kept them locked up and himself retained the key.

'Fresh air and sight-seeing,' said Tom, 'will do you the world of good.'

In Tom's car they lurched down the Whereham Ride, turned sharp left about a mile out of Luffham, and drove through the pine trees, first down a secondary road and then along a sandy track, until they came to a crude car park beyond which was a small hut. Inside the hut was a despondent old gentleman in the uniform of the Ministry of Works, who took sixpence from each of them and offered them, without much hope, a pamphlet about the Vaults. Alfie paid threepence for this, and Tom inquired whether there was a clerical gentleman on the site. Yes; working in the big central mine; they couldn't miss it because of a large notice next to it about litter.

Alfie and Tom trudged through the heather. Vane's Vaults

was not a spectacular spot, indeed there seemed to be nothing in view at all.

'It says here that these mines provided the flint for the earliest hunting weapons in Britain.'

'I shan't try to refute it,' Tom said.

'You might join in a bit more,' said Alfie, who was beginning to enjoy his day out.

'Sorry. What else does it say?'

'That the flint was also used for barter . . . that the Romans thought this must be some kind of sacred place and treated it with respect. . . .

'I'm beginning to see the point.'

To the left and the right the pine trees whispered in the morning breeze; otherwise there was silence. But it was not the silence of desolation. Vane's Vaults, it now appeared, had more than met the eye: a power reigned here, a residual and malignant power which combined fear, pain and cunning into brute determination to survive. Here was the birthplace of the first man, no innocent Adam in a beautiful garden but a cold, hungry beast who must slink and kill. Here was the human spirit in its raw and primordial essence, as it was when it stirred for the first time and awoke to tear its crimson path down the millennia. Small wonder that the Romans had been circumspect.

They came to the litter notice. Just beyond it was a low mound, some ten feet in diameter and three feet high at its apex; in the mound, facing them, was a square aperture, from which, when they came closer, they could see that a steel ladder descended into the pit beneath. Far below an oil lamp was burning and a shadow was kneeling near a wall.

'Mr. Purchase?' called Tom.

There was a long pause.

'The same,' said a deep voice, coiling up out of the pit.

'Can we speak with you?'

'About what?'

'It's a little difficult. . . .'

'Come down the ladder.'

Tom went first. He climbed down for perhaps ten yards, to find himself in a circular chamber with a gravelled floor, empty except for the oil-lamp and a black clerical raincoat folded over a small grip. Out of the chalk walls several small caves, about a yard high and a yard deep, had been excavated at floor level. The air was damp, the feeling of malignance yet more pronounced; here was the womb of the first man's gestation. And here, one almost felt, was the first man; for the Reverend Mr. Purchase, in contrast to his deep and beautiful voice, was a lean and shrivelled little creature with restless, hungry eyes.

Alfie stepped off the ladder panting. 'What do you do down here?' he asked.

'I investigate,' said Mr. Purchase coldly, 'the probable methods used to extract the flint. What can I do for you?'

'We want to ask you some questions about your Parish records. Your wife said you were here. . . .'

'Well?'

Although obviously annoyed by their intrusion, he did not seem to find it odd: his manner was that of a man dealing with servants who had interrupted him in his study rather than with strangers who had pursued him into the deep places of the earth.

'Well?' he repeated.

'What is recorded,' said Tom flatly, 'of the illegitimate male child whom Betty Vincent bore in 1945?'

Still Mr. Purchase seemed irritated rather than surprised.

'That it was duly Christened,' he said.

'When?'

'In July of 1945.'

'And its paternity?'

'Why do you want to know all this?' The Rector's voice was soft, but his eyes shifted quickly and uneasily round the chamber.

'Because something important may turn on it. The child's paternity?'

'Jake Vincent, who subsequently married the child's mother.'

'And this was so recorded at the time of Christening?'

The Rector hesitated.

'No,' he said. 'An entry was made at the time of Christening. This entry was later deleted and emended when Vincent acknowledged the child.'

'And the original entry?'

The Rector opened and shut his mouth two or three times. There was a light clatter. Alfie, having inadvertently caught his shoe in a fold of the clerical mackintosh, had dragged it away from the grip and at the same time jerked across the floor a small crucifix of black wood. All three of them looked down at the crucifix, the Rector's gaze being now for the first time concentrated on one point.

'A digging implement?' said Tom. 'Or a protection against the ghosts?'

The Rector seemed if anything relieved at the interruption. 'This place is impure,' he said. 'I do what I can.'

It took a little while for this to sink in. At length Alfie said: 'Exorcism?'

'If you like to call it that.'

'And the ghosts are too tough?' said Tom. 'So you have to keep coming back?'

'Not exactly that,' said the Rector, who seemed almost amused now. 'Not exactly that.'

Meanwhile Alfie, remembering some press cutting of long ago about a similar site in Cornwall, had lifted the oil-lamp and was walking round examining the walls.

'Don't tell me these are prehistoric,' he said.

Tom joined him. Just to the left of the ladder, at head height and occupying a rectangle of approximately two feet high by four feet long, was a series of vigorous and by no means untalented representations of obscene tableaux. The figures had been cut into the wall, in some cases so deeply as to resemble carvings in relief.

'These mines,' the Rector said, adopting the tones of a guide, 'were discovered, or rather rediscovered, by a gentleman called Vane in the seventeenth century. He thought they were tombs of some kind.' He gestured at one of the little caves which opened off the wall. 'But of course none of these niches is long enough to accommodate a corpse, and it was subsequently established that they were examples of a crude mining technique. Meanwhile, whatever the Vaults might or might not be in origin, certain local elements found them very useful for their own noxious purposes. You knew, of course, that this part of the country was once notorious for witchcraft?'

Alfie pushed back his wide hat and nodded.

'I'll buy it,' he said.

'The covens used to meet here,' said the Rector. And then, meditatively, 'Tradition dies hard in the East country. These people are . . . atavistic in taste. Highly secretive as well.'

'You don't mean that covens still do meet here?'

'No. No, not as bad as that. But sometimes young people, prompted by an inbred instinct or by local hearsay . . . knowing this to be a fine and private place . . . in pairs or in groups . . . their elders too . . . I don't know on what principle is – er – organized. But sometimes, on a summer's night, I see little parties bicycling off down Whereham Ride, or drifting away through the bracken in the direction of Vane's Vaults.' The scene thus conjured affected him with no small degree of prurient pleasure. His eyes glittered in the lamplight and his mouth was set in a fierce grin.

'You follow them?'

'No. What could one do against many?'

He's lying, thought Tom as he watched the glittering little eyes; he comes and listens; he lies by the opening at the top of the ladder, and he listens; looks, too, if they have light.

'No,' said the Rector; 'but I come afterwards to purify the place of the evil it has known. And to ask God to forgive them. May God forgive them all,' he intoned in his deep voice, and the words went ringing round the chamber and up into the light.

'The caretaker?' said Alfie.

'He goes home at night.'

'All very interesting,' said Tom. 'And now, what about this

child of Betty Vincent's? You were going to tell us about the original entry you made.'

The Rector started, as if suddenly recalled to duty.

'I don't see that it's your concern,' he said.

'What have you to hide?'

'Betty Vincent's secret is, so to speak, held in trust.'

But there was on the man's face a lubricious desire to talk. Clearly, all that was inhibiting him was a fear lest if he did so he would be in some way compromised.

'Look,' said Alfie. 'Young Peter Morrison, your squire or whatever you call him, is in trouble. It seems that what you say will settle it one way or the other. So get on and say it. We've enjoyed your little tale of rural fandangoes, but now we want to hear what we came for.'

Although Alfie was a short man, he was taller than the Rector and altogether more substantial. As he waddled across the chamber in the light of the oil-lamp, his ridiculous hat pushed back like a cowboy's, he was a figure of menace. The Rector shrank back against the wall.

'All right,' the Record said: 'but you will be . . . discreet?'

The other two nodded.

'Jake Vincent,' the Rector began, 'was on leave in the late July of 1944. So he could just have been the father of Betty's first child. But he wasn't; because Jake was a good, honest boy, and all he'd done with Betty was to swear to her, young as she was and blind as she was, that he'd marry her when he finally came home. It was, you see, true love.'

The Rector had sounded rather bored by this necessary prolegomenon of virtue; now he warmed to his task.

'But Jake's mother had other ideas. Jake was the apple of her jealous old eye, and anyhow she wanted something better for her son than a blind girl who lived in a charity cottage. So even before Jake went back to his regiment she had made her plan.

'During the war, with many husbands away, the wickedness at the Vaults waxed stronger than ever. So one evening in August old Mrs. Vincent, who knew what nights were favoured, took Betty for a walk, treated her kindly as her daughter to be, and left her, for a few minutes, on the pretext that she wanted to gather some herbs. Under the moon the boys came by, on their way to the monstrous trysting place, and seeing blind Betty sitting by the path carried her along with them. Betty, who had been thinking of her Jake, struggled and shouted, but there was no one to hear. And her ravishers had nothing to fear from her, provided they did not betray themselves by their voices.

'Meanwhile old Mrs. Vincent, anxious to establish her innocence, was off to the 'Squire and his son Peter, pouring out a tale of how Betty had been snatched away from her by shadowy figures in the gloaming. The old 'Squire normally let ill alone where Vane's Vaults were concerned, but he knew of Betty and Jake's romance, as who did not, and set out with his son to save her. They came with torches and hunting whips; they came when the revels were at their height and they came, as Mrs. Vincent had intended, too late. The 'Squire and Master Peter broke up the orgy all right – and at no small risk to themselves – but not before any one of ten youths might have been the father of Betty's child.

'But Mrs. Vincent's scheme did not work. She had reckoned without her son's good faith. Jake was angry when he heard of the child – his mother gave no details, save that Betty had been ruined – and stayed away with the Army longer than he had need. But in the end his mother died, and he came home for good and kept his word. As for Betty, her last memory before losing consciousness was of being held in Peter Morrison's arms and hearing his soothing voice, and she woke in a state of shock which was succeeded only by the dimmest recollection of what had happened; so she was ever after convinced that Peter was the father of her child. For all the men who had held her, Peter was the only one she could name; and a woman will settle such questions as suits her wish and not the truth. Little by little she unconsciously edited her already slender memories of the evening until only a vague impression of struggle followed by a tender moment with Peter remained. So that by the time Jake Vincent returned she had this tale to tell him; and Jake Vincent, who loved her, believed.'

'And hence the lack of curiosity in the village about Betty's child? Almost every family, or so one may suppose, had good reason for keeping quiet.'

'That is correct. As a man of charity, the old 'Squire pretended to accept Betty's tale and paid her money he knew she would need. Later on he also arranged an operation on her eyes. . . . So there was, as mortal matters go, a happy ending. Jake and Betty had each other, they had useful extra provision. Neither of them realized the true horror of little Peter's parentage; and no one else was going to tell them or question any arrangements the 'Squire made. As for the secret which Jake and Betty imagined they were paid to keep it had its romantic side, even for Jake, who thought he was bringing up a little prince in his humble cottage. And the Morrisons . . . well, they were content so long as their dependants were content. Even if Jake or Betty did let their "secret" out, it could do no harm in Luffham, where the guilty truth was known.'

'But it could and had done harm elsewhere. Tell me, Rector, how do you know all this?'

'Old Mrs. Vincent on her death bed.'

'A good start. But the rest? All happened here?'

'I was here,' said the Rector, and grinned ferociously. 'I was here, silent as I must be among so many, but praying for their immortal souls, for God to turn their hearts from their lewdness. It is a mark of my own unworthiness that my prayers should have had so little effect.'

13

'I don't suppose,' said Tom as he drove Alfie towards London, 'that the Reverend Mr. Purchase would be keen to swear an affidavit. But it may be necessary to arrange something of the kind.'

'A broad statement of the circumstances should do the trick,' said Alfie. 'No need to go into detail. An assurance, from the parish priest, that Peter Morrison was in no way responsible for Betty Vincent's child and has behaved impeccably – and bravely, come to that – over the whole affair.'

'Bravely?'

'Going with his father to rescue her.'

'It struck me more as comic. Like a scene from Fielding: the 'Squire and his son laying about with whips while the peasantry pulled their breeches up. But I suppose you're right. And of course it explains why Peter has been behaving so complacently. Here was a story which did him and his family great credit but which could never, in all decency, be told, for fear of upsetting Jake and Betty Vincent's precarious happiness . . . which his father had been at such pains to assist. *Noblesse oblige*. But once scandal threatened and the news-hounds were on the job . . . he must have known it was only a matter of time before one of you discovered the truth. And now you've discovered it, what are you going to do about it?'

'I've been thinking about that,' said Alfie. 'It seems cruel to disturb the Vincents after all this time, and to publish the story would mean just that. But if it were quietly killed . . . Morrison could still have his name cleared in circles where it mattered to him most.'

'What about Lord Billingsgate?'

'He won't want to publish anything to Morrison's credit.'

'And if someone else gets the story?'

'They must do as they think fit,' Alfie said. 'I can't stop them. I only know that I'm not going to spoil two people's happiness . . . such as it is.'

'You're in the wrong job, Alfie.'

'Too late to think about that. Tell me, Tom: what did you hope to find in the Parish records?'

'More or less what Purchase said. An entry in some way suspicious or fudged. As I told you, the only possible explanation there could be of the lack of local curiosity about the child was that its origins were perfectly well known. There would, I thought, have been some reference to this. In view of what we now know, I dare say it was some tactful formula corresponding to the Tahitian phrase, "child of the dance". And then, when Jake Vincent claimed parentage, the original entry – whatever shape it took – would have been altered accordingly. One way or the other I expected something with which I could confront the Rector and so insist on an explanation.'

'What made you think of it?'

'I was merely following the first principle of scholarship: consult the soundest source. Your journalists don't seem to work like that. Most of you only talk to people who are likely to tell you what you want to hear – the acceptable version.'

'If you worked for Lord Billingsgate,' said Alfie, 'you'd know why. . . . Who are you going to tell about this? How are you going to set about clearing Morrison?'

'I shall go to him,' said Tom, 'tell him what we know and can, if necessary, prove, and ask him what he wants done. Mind you, the more I think about it, the less I care for the smug look he had on his face when I last saw it. But I owe him this debt and I am going to pay.'

In London, Angela said to Holbrook:

'I'm off tomorrow.'

'What can you mean?'

'What I say.'

'When shall you be back?' said Holbrook, who still did not understand.

'As far as you're concerned, buddy boy, never. Never in this world.'

'But you can't. . . . The divorce, the money I'm spending . . .'

'That hurts, doesn't it? Tell me,' she taunted him, 'which hurts worse? That you can't hold me with your cock? Or that you can't hold me with your money? You've got plenty of cock and plenty of money, but there's one thing without which neither of them's the least bit of good, and that one thing, lover, is what you haven't got. Do you want to know what it is?'

Holbrook said nothing.

'It's called humanity,' Angela said. 'It doesn't matter how wicked people are, how greedy or even how cruel, provided they know they belong to the human race; because if they know this you can get through to them in the end. Sometime or other, sooner or later, if they only know this, you can get through. But no one can get through to you. Anybody you see, you either want to own it or kill it, and "it", in your case, is what I mean. We're all "it" to you; as far as you're concerned, we're all blind and deaf and dumb; heated up corpses that can walk; so many pounds of flesh.'

But Angela was wrong. There was one person who could get through to Holbrook: his son. It was of Donny that Holbrook now thought as he drove away from Holland Park. In return for a generous settlement Penelope, who did not want the boy but knew his face value as a counter for bargaining, was prepared to let Holbrook have care of him. So perhaps, Holbrook thought, life will not be too bad: there will be all the money for my share of the firm; and with that we can manage very well together, my son and I, and he can be educated as his grandmother would wish.

That shrewd young publisher, Mr. Gregory Stern, knew another shrewd publisher, called Mr. Gene Emanuel, in New York. They had always been agreed in principle that Tom Llewyllyn's book about Communist expansion (*The Bear's Embrace*) promised well. Certain events in Egypt, middle-Europe and even in Cuba now led them to think that the book

promised even better than they had hoped: in a few months or
even weeks its subject would be highly topical, while many of
its forecasts, among them some of the more speculative, were
already on the way to being proved correct. This being the
case, Mr. Stern in London doubled his printing order and
decided to bring publication forward by two weeks, thus ensuring that the public should have ample chance to read Tom's
predictions before the first of them was fulfilled; and Mr.
Emanuel in New York, terrified of competition, was at last persuaded to pay for the American rights the very considerable
sum for which shrewd Mr. Stern had for months been holding
out.

And so it came about that Tom, on his way to meet Peter
Morrison by appointment at the Infantry Club, was surprised
and delighted to see that one window of Hatchard's bookshop
was occupied entirely by copies of *The Bear's Embrace* and an
enormous photograph of himself. However, he was too late to
stop and investigate the phenomenon now; he turned down an
arcade and as he neared Pall Mall tried to forget his pleasure
at what he had seen and concentrate his thoughts on the forthcoming interview.

What he had to say to Peter Morrison was presumably what
Peter, to judge from the expectant look he had worn when last
seen, was waiting for someone to say: 'I have found out the
creditable truth which lies behind Holbrook's attack.' But
what use would Peter want made of this? Debarred hitherto
from revealing the story himself, to what extent, now that
force of circumstance had revealed it, would he wish it to be
broadcast? It must obviously be told to his Parliamentary colleagues lest his standing in the house should continue to suffer. But beyond that? Would he, for example, initiate legal
proceedings against Holbrook? Or engineer some release to
the Press? Or would he remain true to the spirit in which, all
these years, he and his family had protected the Vincents by
their silence, and forbid use of the tale beyond what was
strictly necessary to ensure the continuation of his career?

The latter course was the one which Tom would have wished

him to take. It was also the one most consonant with all that was known of his character. Why then, thought Tom, am I now so doubtful as to the issue? Once again, he thought of the expression Peter had worn as he stood looking over the river. The expression had been in part reflective, in part alert, in part self-satisfied, as if to say, 'I know what must come and I am well content with my preparations.' In this there was nothing to which Tom could take exception; but there had been something more in Peter's face, something which went beyond the wariness permissible in a man so situated: there had been, Tom now decided, cunning, cold and deliberate cunning, which, by no means confined to the uses of self-defence, was already feeling its way to aggression and gain. It was the sort of cunning which would be quick to justify its actions by special pleading and sophistical excuse: 'I never wanted this to happen,' it would meekly declare, 'but since it has happened, since the story has at last been told, then surely I can be pardoned for using it to good effect.'

Or had he, Tom asked himself, imagined this? For although Peter, who was now greeting him in the hall of the club, seemed untroubled and even self-confident, he gave no sign that he contemplated profit or power.

'We'll go into the library,' Peter said: 'there will be no one there.'

Tom then told him, in the low tones which even a deserted library enjoins, of his visit to Whereham and what had transpired.

'I thought I told you,' said Peter when Tom had finished, 'to leave it all alone.'

'Yes, but others would have gone. You needed a friend there.'

'It was for me to judge of that.'

'Then forgive me,' said Tom with an edge to his voice, 'for my intrusion. It was my impression that you were in trouble, in trouble through my own fault, so I wished to help. And I cannot but feel that I have. I am now in a position to prove to those concerned that Holbrook's story depends on a misunderstanding of certain events which you yourself could not in good faith disclose and which do you nothing but credit.'

'Dear Tom,' said Peter. 'For a clever man you talk too much in absolute terms. "Proof", "truth", "right", "wrong". Has no one told you that everything in this universe is relative?'

'Beyond the galaxies or within the atom, perhaps. But on the human scale we can still have definition. This man, we can say, did this thing at this time.'

'We can say that. But who is to say that the act was good or bad? Its causes go back, as its results must go forward, to infinity. So much good and evil preceded it, so much of both will stem from it, that to call the one act itself good or evil is meaningless. I played my part with Betty Vincent and others played theirs. And that is all that can be said.'

'Even if your philosophy is sound,' said Tom, 'your colleagues won't share it. In their immediate and practical view, you have committed a scandalous act which requires them to repudiate you. Either you clear yourself or you are in trouble.'

'I am in trouble,' said Peter quietly. 'I am in trouble, I shall stay in trouble, and nobody can clear me; but there will be no need of repudiation as I shall repudiate myself.'

'For Christ's sake,' said Tom crossly: 'has Somerset been talking to you about original sin?'

'No. I am now back with you on a practical level. And on that level I tell you this. It no longer matters a jot what anyone thinks or says about this story of Holbrook's. As it happens your version is true – more or less. But to sue Holbrook would be like suing a mad dog for biting one, and it would probably mean upsetting Jake and Betty Vincent. So would any newspaper publicity – as well as being ridiculous and degrading.'

'I quite see that, but when it comes to your good name in the House –'

'– I've told you. It makes no difference what *anyone* now thinks. Because in any case at all I'm going to resign.'

'*For God's sake, why?*'

Peter sat down, opened his brief-case which he had brought with him into the library, and took out a book.

'Recognize this?' he said.

It was *The Bear's Embrace*, by Tom Llewyllyn, published by Gregory Stern at 25s.

'I can't think,' said Tom stupidly, 'why it's already out.'

'I wouldn't know about that. But as an admirer of yours I bought a copy yesterday afternoon and spent much of the night reading it. I congratulate you, Tom,' said Peter kindly and sincerely, 'on a remarkable and very readable piece of work.'

'Thank you. But what's my book got to do with your resignation?'

'Strictly speaking, nothing. I've known for some time what I must do. But it so happens that a passage you've written here confirms me in thinking that I've made the right decision.'

So that, Tom thought, was one part of what he had seen in Peter's face on the terrace: the intent awareness of one who knew his duty and how he must do it. But what about the rest? The smugness and the cunning?

'I'm glad we agree about something,' Tom said. 'What is this passage?'

'Towards the end, you are discussing Communist activities in Egypt since Nasser's rise to power. You predict, parenthetically, that sooner or later Nasser will bait the West by taking over the Canal. Which at any moment, from what I hear, will be true.'

'Nothing very remarkable in that.'

'But you also say,' Peter went on, 'that he'll succeed in making complete fools out of us. You suggest that tempers will be lost to such an extent that even armed intervention is not improbable. "The Suez Canal"' – Peter started to read – '"was brought into being by European science and European capital to facilitate the passage East of European trade and European guns. The Egyptians, since the Canal was to traverse their territory, were graciously allowed the privileges of digging it out of the desert and keeping it clean when dug; beyond that it was to be no affair – how should it be? – of theirs. There is a sense in which the Canal, that great artery of Empire, still stands for Empire's departed glories, as the Via Aurelia still stands for the majesty of the Caesars' Rome. On the day when a man of the Egyptians (the race which the British despise perhaps most of all the races they have subdued), a man with a hooked nose and fuzzy hair, claims that he owns and can himself control this master-mechanism of the West, the last and most vicious insult will have been uttered, an insult that calls for blood."'

'And so?' said Tom.

'And so you were right. At least I think so. Already, though only in whispers as yet, they are asking for blood. You know my friend, Captain Detterling?'

'By reputation.'

'Already, before Nasser has even moved, he has been unofficially notified that his old regiment will require his services.'

'But if this is so,' said Tom, 'it is the great chance which you and your group have been waiting for. You've always been quite plain – it's one of the things I've admired you for – that what's left of the Empire has got to go. Whatever the rights and wrongs, you've said, it is just not practicable to keep it. You know as well as I do what will happen if they mount an expedition to fight for the Canal. Leave aside any question of morality, it would be one of the most insane acts in the whole of British history.'

'It would be an anachronism,' said Peter, 'to which no man of reason could lend his support.'

'Well then?'

'It would also be a national undertaking which no true Englishman could publicly oppose.'

Tom opened his mouth and shut it.

'You're joking,' he said at last.

'I was never more serious. If the British Army marches, that Army in which I myself have served as a commissioned officer, I cannot stand up in Westminster and condemn its mission from behind its back. I can make it privately known to friends that I think the whole thing is a ghastly mistake; but to say so publicly, to organize Parliamentary protest, would be an act of treachery. It would be to undermine the confidence and reduce the loyalty of the men in the field – men who are there because they must be and are entitled, as faithful subjects of the Queen, to the respect and gratitude of their fellow country-men. To impugn their purpose would be to impugn their service.'

'But always before,' said Tom, 'you've stuck to your policy, even when the Army was involved. You've always insisted, for example, that Kenya must become independent. You didn't think *that* was treachery to the soldiers who were out there fighting the Mau Mau.'

'Nor was it. To say that Kenya must, in due season, be given independence is not to criticize an Army whose role is to pre-serve good order in the meantime. On the contrary, I've always been at pains to point out that the Army *must* suppress terror-ism before Kenya – or any other colony – can enjoy healthy independence.'

'What you're saying,' said Tom, 'is that you will never criti-cize a military action for fear of hurting the Army's feelings. I think the Army has a thicker skin than you suppose.'

'No. I was in India during the riots of '46 and '47. We took necessary action to restore order and were severely criticized in consequence both by politicians and the press. You cannot know, unless you yourself have experienced it, how bitter that was to us. We felt betrayed.'

'But in India the Army was acting with good cause. If there were to be an expedition to the Canal –'

'– It would still be impossible for me to criticize the action of obedient men under orders. And there is one more thing, Tom. It was summed up for me by something Detterling said. I asked him how he would feel about being recalled to the Colours. "That's just it, old man," he said. "Recalled to the Colours. When that happens you have to go. Right or wrong, like it or lump it, when you're called to the Colours you go. Not," he said, "that we have Colours in the Cavalry. But you see what I mean.'

'Sheer atavism,' Tom said.

'I should prefer to say that there is a duty. A duty to the

authority of the past. Detterling is the Queen's man. When the trumpet sounds, Detterling saddles his horse. So how can I, his friend, get up in Parliament and tell the nation that he is riding on a fool's errand?'

'Then why not keep quiet? Don't resign, we can't afford to lose men like you. Stay in the House and keep quiet.'

'If I stayed in the House it would be my duty to protest. For the reasons which I have given I could not protest. Therefore I must resign.'

'Rather extreme – for a man who believes that right and wrong are merely relative?'

'This is personal. Something of my own, the one thing of which I can be certain. You will forgive the word: my honour.'

'All right; but don't do anything just yet. Wait and see.'

'If I wait until something happens – and we both know it must happen – my resignation will in itself be seen as a protest. I have a certain position and my action would be publicized. But if I resign now . . . *without troubling to refute this accusation of Holbrook's* . . . gradually the news will get around that I resigned for rather discreditable private reasons, and that will be that. Detterling and the others will ride on their way, and no one will take my name to taunt them.'

'So that's why you looked so pleased with yourself the other day,' said Tom slowly. 'That's why you told me to take Holbrook's money and mind my own business. You wanted an excuse to resign. You didn't want to be cleared.'

'That's about it,' Peter Morrison said. 'I hoped and believed that no one would find the real truth, that Holbrook's story would stand. I hardly supposed Purchase would talk – his own part in the affair was far too dubious. Why did he tell you, do you suppose?'

'It excited him. There's something about those Vaults . . . something disturbing. He wasn't quite himself.'

'I suppose not,' murmured Peter. 'As you say, the place has an odd effect on one. When I found Betty there that night . . . if my father hadn't been with me . . . who knows?'

He shook his head, as if to clear it, then went on,

'You say the journalist will keep quiet?'

'Yes. The story's probably no use to Billingsgate anyway. But there may be other journalists.'

'I doubt if Purchase will tell the tale a second time . . . And you yourself will keep my secret?'

'If you wish.'

'Then take this book,' said Peter Morrison, passing over his copy of *The Bear's Embrace*, 'and write in it for me: "To Peter Morrison from Tom Llewyllyn, his good friend."'

14

Early in August Max de Freville gave a gambling party, the last
he would be giving before everyone left London for the rest of
the summer. Max himself, poker-faced and precise, was acting
as croupier. On his right sat Lord Philby and just behind him
his fiancée, Lady Susan Grange: both of them looked fit and
animated, and they were happily explaining, even to those who
did not inquire, that they were to be married in September and
would spend the winter in South America. Donald and Vanessa
Salinger, who were sitting opposite Philby, were a less radiant
pair but seemed content and in good understanding with one
another: they were leaving in a day or two for a tour round the
world, they said, and would be back for Christmas, which they
proposed to celebrate with a house party at Chevenix Court.
Donald was in luck and had won steadily; but if ever Vanessa
moved away, to find a drink or talk to a friend, he became
uneasy and would hardly bet at all until she returned.

Another player, a very cautious one, who was there for the
first time and had been sponsored by Lord Philby, was
Somerset Lloyd-James. He had now got over his disappointment about Lady Susan, and other disappointments as well, in
consequence of the sensational success of Tom Llewyllyn's
book. This had had the splendid press it deserved and had
early achieved solid sales – sales which had rocketed late in
July, when Nasser took over the Suez Canal and confirmed the
first of Tom's predictions, and which were to rocket still
higher, though no one on that August evening could know it,
as a result of events, also predicted by Tom, in Hungary the following October. In pursuance of their agreement, Tom had
already paid Somerset £2,000, which was half his share of the
sum received by Stern for the American rights, and it would
not be long now before English and American royalties, not to

mention serial, paper-back and translation rights, came pouring in to augment this. Good-natured Tom did not at all resent the high price he was paying for Somerset's loan; as Tom saw it, Somerset had made a shrewd gamble and good luck to him - and anyhow there was plenty of money for them both. It did not, of course, occur to him that sooner or later he would have to pay swingeing taxes, whereas Somerset would not.

Also present, though not at the moment playing, were Captain Detterling and Jonathan Gamp. Jonathan was leaving for Cannes the next day and Detterling was leaving for Catterick the day after: for the trumpet had now sounded and Detterling must answer the call. Both of them were discussing, with Carton Weir, the qualities of their ex-mistress, Susan Grange. Although Carton was bored with the conversation, he was listening politely as he wished to retain Detterling's goodwill for the young England group, of which Carton had become leader after Peter Morrison's sad resignation from the House a month before. He was also hoping that if Detterling's regiment later went to Egypt Detterling would send him special reports which could be used to embarrass the Government, a hope which only goes to show how foolish a clever man can be.

'The thing about Susan,' Jonathan was saying, 'is that basically she's serious about sex. That's why she used to take those pills – she was guilty about sleeping around. Vanessa, now, could never be serious about sex: she simply finds it fun.'

'Vanessa seems to have settled down,' Detterling said, 'to judge from the look of her tonight.'

'She doesn't want trouble with Donald, that's all, because the money's too good; so she's careful to camouflage his horns. Susan, on the other hand, is going to take her marriage seriously. She believes in love, though God alone knows what she sees in Philby. She believes on the traditional female lines: marriage, home, family. A crude matter of biology; the urge to have a nest and fill it with young. Simple enough, you might think; after all, it happens every day; but in every case women have to pretend that it's important, that it's somehow unique. Hence all this silly fuss about the "sacred mystery" of love and sex.'

'That's the boring thing about women,' Carton Weir remarked. 'If you just say, "Let's have a bit of fun," they looked shocked. But if you say something portentous, like "Darling, I'm so unhappy," they'll drop flat on the nearest bed. Your unhappiness makes the whole thing *serious*, you see, not as serious as marriage would, of course, but at least it removes any suspicion of levity, and levity outrages their female conceit. The result is that if one wants a woman one has to go moaning round pretending to be unhappy. Too tedious. Which is why,' he concluded brazenly, 'I prefer boys.'

Parliamentary success and continued evasion of the law were beginning to go to Carton Weir's head. Detterling thought: I shall think twice, I shall think ten times, before enlisting under you when I get home.

'That's why Vanessa is so valuable,' Jonathan Gamp was saying. 'She's one of the very few women who just enjoy it for its own sake. If only women would realize that by trying to make themselves significant they simply make themselves commonplace. . . . An honest to goodness slut is the rarest thing in the world.'

The *parti* had now finished and there was an interval in the play. Donald and Somerset (the latter looking rather furtive) joined Detterling's group.

'What have you done,' said Jonathan, hurriedly changing the subject, 'with that partner of yours? I haven't seen him in weeks.'

'Jude Holbrook has gone away,' said Donald. 'He was on the verge of a nervous breakdown through overwork, and then his little son died suddenly of meningitis, so he just gave up altogether.'

Donny's death, though tragic, had proved very useful for explaining Holbrook away.

'I never cared for the sound of Jude Holbrook,' said Detterling; 'but I wouldn't have wished him that.'

'He was my godson, the little boy,' said Donald. 'He was a sweet child. I wonder how he would have grown up.'

'A credit to his father, I dare say,' said Vanessa, brandishing

an immense pot of caviar. 'Do admit, Max certainly does one
well.'

'He can afford it on those 5 per cents, dear.'

Somerset drew Detterling on one side.

'Peter Morrison,' he said, 'has resigned from the Board of
Strix as well as from everything else.'

'And so?'

'There's a vacant place,' said Somerset with a faint air of
pleading.

'You know what I should do?' said Detterling. 'I should offer
it to Carton Weir. You'll get on well with him.'

'Carton's a brilliant man. But unsound. I was hoping . . . that
perhaps you yourself. . . .'

'I have other work to do,' said Detterling, and turned on his
heel.

Somerset edged back like a crab towards the central group.
After all, he thought, it would be amusing to work with Weir.
If only he would be more tactful about his private life . . . find
some steady and discreet equivalent of Somerset's own invaluable Maisie.

'You know,' Donald was saying, 'little Donny *was* a sweet
child. With two parents like that, I sometimes wonder why.'

'Genes are funny things, dear,' Jonathan Gamp said. 'Aren't
they, Vanessa poppet?'

But this question was to remain unanswered; for Max de
Freville, having shuffled and re-boxed the cards, now summoned his guests back to the serious business of play.

'Take your seats, ladies and gentlemen,' he intoned, his
voice honey-sweet with invitation, his eyes glazed with the *acid-
ité* of his calling: 'take your seats, if you please. *Maintenant le jeu
recommence*. The game begins once more.'

Deal. Autumn, 1963; Spring, 1964.

FRIENDS IN
LOW PLACES

I

A GAME OF CHANCE

"JESUS CHRIST," said Mark Lewson: "what a bloody boring place this is."

"You don't have to stay," said Angela Tuck.

They were sitting on the promenade at Menton, drinking champagne cocktails at half past noon on a Sunday in the April of 1959.

"I like being with *you*, dear. It's so suitable. We can console each other in our grief."

"Tuck was killed nearly three years ago," said Angela Tuck. "Néither then nor later have I needed consolation."

"You're heartless, that's your trouble. *I* need consoling. It's only a few weeks since my beloved wife passed away to the happy land, leaving me desolate in more senses than one."

"How did she die, Mark? You've been a little vague."

"Drink, dear. Even the coffin smelt of gin. It caused a great scandal among her dreary relations."

"They came all the way to England for the funeral?"

"The two sisters. To see if there was any money left."

"Which there wasn't?"

"There never had been very much. When the old Count Monteverdi died, having spent most of his life in England, he left about a hundred thou. in the funds, as they say, a few valuable paintings, and a little property in Rome. Felicity's share after duties was twenty-odd thou., one small Sisley and three Dalis, and a flat in the Piazza Navona."

"Enough to be going on with," Angela said.

"As it happened, not." Mark giggled. "The two sisters went home to Tivoli and interested themselves in pious works. Felicity stayed in England and interested herself in me. She was fifteen years older, of course, but I thought, what the hell, she's a good-natured cow and they say she's got a lot of cash. As usual, 'they' had exaggerated. We'd barely finished with the honeymoon before she announced that the crinkle had run out."

"Twenty thousand?"

"I'd bought a small yacht. You see, no one," Mark said petulantly, "had told me that twenty thou. was all there was."

"She must have been mad."

"Right, dear. Mad about me."

I'm not surprised, Angela thought. She surveyed the cherubic face with the weak, vicious chin; the dark wavy hair; the torso, thin but tough under the flowery shirt; the Botticelli legs under the white flannel shorts. She surveyed all these, and thought of other things, and decided that a woman fifteen years his senior might well have been mad about Mark Lewson, so mad as to spend her entire fortune buying him a yacht. But I, she thought, am not fifteen years his senior, only five; he'll get little enough out of me and what he gets he'll earn. In fact, I'm not sure that he hasn't already had his ration.

"What happened to the yacht?" she said.

"Sold at a loss when things began to get difficult."

"Rotten luck."

You mean sow, Mark Lewson thought. *I* know all this chat about Felicity's money is just a way of telling me that I'll get none from you. You'd hang on to the little bit Tuck left you if they tried to drag it out of you on the rack. And you'd better hang on, dear, because there's not going to be much left of *you* in another five years. You're all crows' feet and flab as it is, and teeth awash in cheap brandy nine nights out of ten. You're jolly lucky to get me, simply because I'm having a bad patch, for bed, board and pin money. But I'm only passing through. Something will turn up, it always does, and then it's toodle-ooh to you, Angela Tuck, you and your sagging tits.

Meanwhile, however, make the best of the bed and board. "Let's have another drink," he said.

"You've already had three."

"I'll do my stuff after lunch, if that's what's worrying you."

The narrow eyes glinted and the weak chin twitched with simulated lust. The Botticelli legs straddled. Sweating with the sudden excitement of it, Angela decided that she was not yet quite finished with him after all.

"All right," she said, as Lewson beckoned a waiter and gestured at the empty glasses, "but only one. They're expensive." She passed him two notes over the table, each for a thousand old francs. "What happened," she said, "after you sold the yacht?"

"We got along for a while. Then the Dalis went. Then the Sisley. Finally the flat. After that, we'd only got her family name and the title. *Née* Monteverdi. Contessa—or contessina for sentimental old men. This was a help in cashing cheques."

"Not for long, I bet."

"Longer than you'd think. We kept moving."

"And in the end?"

"In the end she died."

"Just when she'd ceased to be useful."

Mark grinned.

"She died of drink, dear. Drink and the English winter."

"I'll buy it . . . as you've been so frank about the rest."

"I wouldn't try it on with you, dear. You're up to everything."

The compliment was sincere. Mark Lewson was telling the truth, and finding it a great relief to be free, just for once, from the Jacobean complexities of his own invention. Not that he was consciously seeking relief in this unaccustomed candour; it was just that Angela—he felt it in his bones—would neither believe his lies, brilliant as they often were, nor, if she did believe, be impressed. This was still not to say that he told her the truth out of respect: there was just no point in telling her anything else.

"You're up to everything," he repeated. "You've got a kind of genius for being a slut."

And after three and a half champagne cocktails, he thought, you don't look too bad at that. So he leaned over to whisper in her ear, and she squirmed with pleasure in her seat.

"After lunch," she said with an effort. "So she left you with nothing?"

"Except a bad name in half the hotels in Europe."

"So what are you going to do now?" she asked him, not unkindly.

"Have some lunch and a lot of fun after it."

"And then?"

"Sufficient unto the day. . . ."

"But not unto the morrow."

"Since you ask me," he said, "I need an *angle*. Something I can *work*, like I worked the Contessa's name for cheques. Something to go on. That's why I get so fed up with Menton. There's nothing here, never could be."

"There's peace. And economy."

"Not what I need."

"We'll have to see what we can find for you," Angela said.

Angela had enjoyed her last fortnight with Mark Lewson and, other things being strictly equal, she wished him well. But with Mark other things, so far from being equal, were not even commensurate; and despite the manifest and mounting excitement of the present moment Angela knew, for she was an experienced woman, that in a few days time at most she must get him out of the way. He represented menace: to her, to her money, to her little house in the town. So rid of him she must be; but if she could only do him a service at the same time, so much better for both of them, as they could part in kindness and no harm done. She wouldn't, couldn't pay him off in cash; she must find him what he called his "angle". She might think, for a start, about that story she had heard from Max. . . . Angle, not Angela, she said to herself, and giggled.

"What's so funny then?"

"I'll maybe tell you later. Lunch."

Behind the closed shutters the bedroom, which faced north, was cool and reassuring. Angela, fed and pleasured, slept, pinching the nipple of her left breast between the first two fingers of her right hand, for all the world like a Rubens goddess about to squirt milk into the open mouth of a cherub. Mark Lewson's mouth was open, but not in expectation of Angela's milk: he always gaped when he was thoughtful. He was thoughtful just now because he was wondering whether he could open Angela's bag on the dressing table, remove two of the four ten thousand franc notes which he had seen in it before lunch, and then get out of the bedroom and out of the house without waking Angela, who, however well pleasured, was a light sleeper. Although this plan, which would conclude with a visit to the afternoon session in the Casino, offered action of a kind, something to offset the stagnation of Sunday in Menton, it had several disadvantages. First, Mark did not care for gambling and usually lost; and secondly, even if he returned the money later, Angela would almost certainly find out that it had been taken. She would turn nasty, she would probably turn him out. This danger, however, was the less deterrent as it had become increasingly plain, from Angela's demeanour over the last few days, that she was going to turn him out in any case. Before marrying the Contessa, Mark had had much experience of this kind of sojourn: he could read the signs as a poacher can read the weather, and they heralded the rapidly approaching end of this particular idyll. So what the hell, he thought: nothing to lose.

Stage one: to ease himself off the bed, inch by inch, so that it did not give out a tell-tale creak. This was easier said than done, for the bed, a huge and ancient *letto matrimonale* from over the border, was much given to creaks, and indeed

making love on it to Angela always sounded like being in the
bowels of a wind-jammer which was running before a gale.
But Mark was an agile mover and had devoted much of his
life to studying such skills; after a few discreet wriggles of his
delicate buttocks, he had both feet hanging over the side of
the bed, and with a final slow roll of his upper body he was
safely and silently off. Angela, still posed as some goddess of
peace and plenty, slept on.

Stage two : to open bag and take the money. While he was
about it he might as well take the lot. (Nothing to lose.)

Stage three : to open the door, which was almost as
rackety an apparatus as the bed. Here luck was with him :
Angela, frantic with post-prandial lust, had left it ajar.

Stage four : to creep to the dressing-room down the little
passage and get suitably togged up. (The Casino, while small
and friendly, did not encourage informality of *tenu.*) Thank
God he didn't keep his clothes in the bedroom. Now then :
the light grey suit, pink shirt, old Etonian tie (a falsity which
he had sported for so long that he now almost believed that
he had been at Eton), and the dark suède shoes. Hair : eau
de cologne : mouth wash. (Since one of the troubles about
this kind of life was that one was never in the same place long
enough to take a proper course with a dentist, his teeth and
gums were bad and he had, as he well knew, atrocious
breath.) Cigarettes. Passport. And that (with Angela's forty
thousand francs) was the lot.

Stage five : to go back past the bedroom, down the stairs
and out. She could hardly stop him now, but he might as well
keep up the charade. After all, if he could get out, make a
profit, return the forty thousand, all without her knowing,
so much the better. He might be able to hang on here as long
as another week. He tip-toed past the bedroom, was pleased
to hear a gross snore, slid down the short banister, opened
the front door, left the latch up in order to re-admit himself
(Angela refused to allow him a key), and emerged into the
blue and sticky afternoon.

*   *   *

Angela Tuck dreamt that she was back in India again, up in the hills near Oute, that day they came to arrest her father nearly fifteen years ago. They were sitting, she and her father, drinking gin before lunch. Since she had been playing golf and was very thirsty, she was having hers with lime juice and a lot of soda. Just as she was about to drink, her father said:

"Make the best of it, girlie. There may not be many more where that came from."

She raised her glass again but now it was empty, except for a small cube of ice which slid along the tilted tumbler to burn her lips.

"All gone," her father said, in the tones he had once used in the nursery. He leaned forward and started tickling her, a favourite game when she was little. But then there was a curt, loud knock on the door of the bungalow; her father's hands fell away from her; and in the moment before she awoke Angela knew that at long last they had found him out and had come to take him away.

As indeed they had, she thought to herself, sweaty, dry-mouthed, wide awake. Cooking the Pay Rolls; a wonder he'd got away with it for so long. But never mind him, dead and unlamented in his Hongkong grave. That knock on the door. The empty half of the bed.

"Mark?" she called.

It was obvious what had happened. He had slipped out and woken her as he left. She rose from the bed to check her handbag. Forty thousand, the little rat. But never mind: if he'd gone for good, forty thousand was not too disastrous a price; and if he came back and tried to brazen it out, she'd have a good excuse for giving him notice to quit. Thinking of him without rancour she returned, with the handbag, to bed, lit a cigarette, crushed it out, thought of her father in Oute again, thought wistfully of the pretty race meetings and the green fairways on the golf course, and fell into a light doze from which she awoke without difficulty when, ten minutes later, the door bell rang downstairs.

*　　*　　*

The patrons of the Casino at Menton have always been a predictable bunch. Since the stakes are low and the furnishings shabby, since the croupiers are for the most part ageing and kindly men who, too wise to aspire higher, too honest to sink lower, have spent a placid lifetime here, the place has acquired a "family" atmosphere in which even the Casino detective behaves with prim geniality, like nanny supervising a tea party of well conducted children. These latter are the regulars, expatriate ladies and gentlemen of the English upper-middle class with an addition of tight-faced French women of the indigenous commercial bourgeoisie, all of whom, English or French, are as well known to each other as they are to the management and staff.

If we leave aside the ethnical division, the regulars fall into two groups: those who come when the Casino opens at two in the afternoon and those, more resourceful, who do not arrive until after an early dinner. Both groups, as soon as they enter, seat themselves at the double-ended roulette table and stay there until it closes down at two in the morning, those who have exhausted the funds set aside for the day being quite happy to sit and watch, and not dreaming of giving up their seats to any more serious players who may (even in Menton) occasionally appear.

"Routine", then, is the Casino motto, and right loyally both staff and clients live up to it. The only variation is itself routine: every Sunday afternoon both groups, instead of arriving at two and eight-thirty respectively, arrive at half past four to take tea and anticipate the grand treat of the week—a two hour game of chemin-de-fer which runs from five till seven and is never prolonged, no matter how earnestly the players may implore, for fear, no doubt, of over-exciting the children and disturbing the wholesome discipline which must rule the remainder of the week. But from the given hours of five to seven something near anarchy is permitted: some six of the regulars, who are rich enough to afford the higher stakes, will be joined at the Chemmy table by two or three outsiders (a sensitive Italian, perhaps, sickened by the noise and crowding in the rooms at San Remo, and a local embezzler or two, anxious to risk their loot in the most discreet *venue* available); while the rest of the regulars, enjoying brief freedom from the tyrannous wheel, will stand round and *kibbitz,* occasionally soliciting a good-natured banker to take bets of a few hundred francs from the floor.

It was just as this weekly period of licence was about to begin that Mark Lewson entered the Salon. The *chef du parti,* who was, as tradition prescribed, the most benign and atrophied of all the croupiers, retained enough professional instinct to sniff money in Mark's demeanour; and since there was still one vacant seat, he smiled and beckoned, with both coquetry and command, like a worldly uncle who is just about to put one on to "a good thing"—a quicker cure for clap or advance intelligence of a new issue of stock. Mark, while he was not impressed by this *bonhomie,* recognised the convenience of the empty chair and the necessity of starting at once if he was to have any chance of getting back before Angela awoke. He grinned like a juvenile vampire, passed Angela's forty thousand to the croupier, received plaques and counters in exchange, ordered himself a bottle of champagne from a rusty waiter, lit a cheroot, and sat.

The empty place which he had filled was place five, dead opposite the croupier. To his left was an ample French woman who had crumbs of icing in her moustache; to his right an ageing and *distingué* Englishman (writer? poet? don?) with long and obscenely youthful hair, Marlborough suit buttoned high, wing collar and bow. The French woman looked at him as though judging, objectively, whether or not he might be edible; the Englishman smiled, very sweetly, and murmured something about the spring weather. The game begin. The first three bankers lost at the first *coup,* and the shoe was with the French woman, who put down an opening bank of ten thousand francs—rather more than this table normally ran to.

"*Banco,*" said Mark, and lost to a natural eight.

"*Banco,*" he said again, and again lost to a natural eight.

"Bad luck, dear boy," said the writer-don, sentimentally patting Mark's hair. "If you're not going to follow again, I'll take it myself."

Mark was not going to follow again. He had already lost three quarters of his capital and must use his remaining 10,000 with care if he was to survive at all.

"You're more than welcome," he said.

"Banco," chirped his neighbour, dewlaps foaming over the wing collar.

The French woman emitted four words, like a sharp burst of bren-gun fire aimed straight at the croupier's false teeth. No, he replied, Madame could not garage any of her winnings, under the house rules, until after the third *coup* of her bank. Madame, who knew this as well as she knew her married name, announced that it was "*effroyable*" and that the bank would nevertheless continue.

"Banco," repeated the Marlborough suit, and eventually won with a two to Madame's baccarat.

The bank now passed to Mark, who put down the minimum starter of 2,000, immediately lost it with a natural eight to the Marlborough suit's natural nine, and received another pat of sympathy on the hair. He was about to retaliate with the burning end of his cheroot, when he remembered that he now had only 8,000 francs left and had better preserve good relations. In return for the right to pat away for the rest of the session, wing collar might perhaps "do" him a small loan or a cheque. This question became pressingly pertinent after the bank had passed rapidly round the table, arrived at Mark once more, and cost him immediately the 5,000 francs which he rashly put up for it. Only 3,000 to go (and the champagne to be paid for).

Wing collar's frail hand now pushed 5,000 forward to start his new bank. The old idiot was in luck : cash in on it.

"Can I come in with you?" asked Mark. "Half shares?"

Hopefully he proffered 2,500, leaving himself only a miserable lozenge, of what looked like hotel soap, worth 500.

"Couldn't do that, dearest boy. Never play with other people's money. Makes for nasty quarrels, don't you know."

The Marlborough suit then won ten times running and received, when he finally went down, the better part of 200,000 francs from the croupier. If the old Yid had let me share, thought Mark viciously, I'd have been up, off and clear. And now the old bugger's got the cheek to pat my hair again.

"I've got my cheque book here," he began casually: "as one Englishman to another. . . ."

The hand was unhurriedly removed from Mark's head.

"Try the Caisse." The dewlaps wobbled like two buttocks parted by a crack in the chin. "They know all about that. Classical man myself—get confused by figures."

Deftly the pale hands sorted and counted the glittering *bijoux* delivered by the croupier's rake. Mark began to sweat in the crutch. Only 3,000 left. Stuck. Back to Angela? *Peccavi*? God, you look so sexy I can't wait? How bored he was with being tied to that bloody woman; if she wasn't so mean, none of this would have happened.

Meanwhile, another large bank was running. The hair-patter's right-hand neighbour, as often happens, was repeating his predecessor's luck. After his sixth win the new banker consulted with the croupier; a large pile of chips was placed to one side, a second, even larger, left in the middle.

"Cent milles pour la banque."

"Banco," said Mark on impulse. They *might* let him play without seeing the money; in which case the penalty for loss would probably be gaol. That was what it said in one of Fleming's novels, but of course they might just turn him out and leave it at that. In any case this was *action*.

"Banco," he said again.

The kibbitzers muttered blithely: banco on 100,000 was a rare treat. The hair-patter looked bland, the female cake-eater sceptical, the rest of the players expectant. The atrophied croupier's mind began to click over. The residual instinct which had led him to beckon Mark to the table had

told him that the young man was worth perhaps 60,000.
Not more. But the champagne, the carelessness over what he
had lost. . . .? On the other hand, the rather worn suit, the
placatory whispering to the English professor. . . . What was
one to think? No, he decided, one must see the money first.

"*M'sieur . . . l'argent?*"

"Up to your old tricks, Lewson?" said a soft voice in
Mark's ear. "I'll stand you this one, provided you give me
your seat when it's over. Win or lose."

A chunk of mauve plastic proclaiming 100,000 francs
landed by Mark's right hand. The professor smiled genially.
The cake-woman fingered her moustache with the practised
effrontery of a colonel of dragoons. Two cards were passed
to Mark: a ten and a king—makes nought. "*Carte, s'il vous
plait.*" The banker turned up his own to reveal a seven and a
knave, and flicked Mark an eight. "*Je reste.*" "*Sept pour
la banque et*"—turning over Mark's two openers—"*huit
pour m'sieur.*" All over. Mark received a second mauve
plaque for his winnings and turned to his benefactor.

Even though he had only met him once, three years ago
and briefly, he could not have failed to recognise, from the
numerous photographs which had since appeared in the press,
the gambling impresario, Max de Freville. The furrows
arching down from the base of the nose were quite unmistakable. But what was de Freville doing at a seedy little game
in Menton? De Freville, who was worth half a million (so
they said), who no longer gambled himself, who merely
organised discreet games 'for the big money and took his cut
on the turnover?

"De Freville?"

"I'll have the stake money back, if you don't mind. And
my seat."

Mark rose, passed one mauve plaque to de Freville and
put the other in his pocket. Clear, out and up—by 60,000.
Time to get back to Angela, replace the money he had
borrowed. But curiosity held him. It wasn't every Sunday
afternoon that one encountered as notable a figure as Max

de Freville, whose presence here certainly needed explanation. Furthermore, he was impressed that de Freville should have remembered so clearly his own name and reputation although they had done no more than pass in (literally) the night. Having waited until de Freville lost his bank on the second *coup*, Mark ventured :

"Haven't seen you in three years odd. Not since that dance of Donald Salinger's. What are you doing in Menton of all places?"

"I come here when I can. There's a smell of middle-class mortality which I find pleasing. And of course there's some good stuff to be seen inland."

He gestured out of the Casino and over the hills, away into Provence.

"They said you'd given up playing."

"I have." The voice was slightly blurred, as though coming from a great distance, from under many layers, formed by the inexorable years, of ennui and regret. "I'm only sitting here to keep you out of trouble and give them a sporting chance to get their money back. My professional conscience. I can't allow a seat to be vacated without warning. But we'll leave when the shoe's over. I don't think they can reasonably ask more."

"You came here because of me?"

"Because of Angela. I dropped in just now and I've been hearing about you. *Banco*. It seems she wants you out of the way, and so, since I'm to be here a few days, do I. She thought you might have gone for good, but I said, not you, your type never go until they've squeezed the last drop. So I volunteered to take a look round. And since you are still here—"

"—You know what to do about it."

"*Carte*. . . . I've already done it. You can cash in that mauve plaque, give Angie her 40,000 and keep the balance. For the rest, if it were up to me, I'd kick you out and leave it at that." He pushed over a pile of chips which he had just lost. "But Angie reckons she owes you a bit more for her good time. She wants to see you in business, as she puts it. Luckily we can give you a start."

"In your organisation?" said Mark eagerly.

"I wouldn't employ you, Lewson, to clean my lavatory floors. No. Last time I was here I heard an interesting story which may add up to occupation for you. If I give you the right introduction."

The tin rattled out of the shoe. De Freville rose, bowed to the French woman, and nodded to the Marlborough suit on his right.

"Come on," he said to Mark: "cash that plaque, pay for your fizz, and back to Angie's."

While Mark and de Freville walked back to Angela's villa, she was preparing with love and happiness an enormous English tea—this meal, as she knew, being de Freville's favourite.

The relationship between Angela and de Freville, now of two years' duration, was curious. It had started with a chance meeting on the promenade of Menton, when Angela had tripped over an Algerian carpet on display at the side of the pavement. She had fallen full length, badly grazed both her knees, suffered minor shock and major humiliation, and had been very relieved when a tall, taciturn and tactful Englishman had picked her up, brushed her down and settled her in a chair for a drink. Unsettled by the childish nature of her performance and slightly loosened by alcohol, she had treated him, as a kind of smoke-screen for her embarrassment, to an account of her recent widowhood and of the motives (love of peace induced by a rackety and uncertain youth, together with the residual need to know that racket was still readily available in her neighbourhood) which had brought her to harbour in Menton. Since de Freville's motives for frequenting the place were similar, a provisional sympathy had immediately grown between them. Later they had walked, dined, talked of local and domestic life, discussed the price of fish and the insolence of cashiers in French banks, danced together closely but without excitement, and had finally, sympathy being by this time absolute, gone to bed together without passion and without any attempt at consummation.

For although de Freville shared Angela's *letto matrimonale* for companionship, their relations remained entirely platonic. The one thing of which each had always been deprived and which each now found in the other was tranquillity—the placid expectation of an unhurried, unworried and common progress from day's beginning through day's triviality to day's end, when they would retire to lie side by side, just touching, as innocent and easily lulled as two children to whom the morrow could only bring sound nourishment and loving care. After five days of this, when de Freville had to return to his affairs, they both resumed their normal manner of life: de Freville the restless and ever more tedious supervision of his gambling tables in London, Angela the daily search for the nightly master of her flesh. Both knew what the other would do in his absence; both pitied and acquiesced; both waited eagerly, but without amendment of life, until they could meet again in Menton and once more be together and at peace. Although they had friends in villas up and down the coast, they visited them seldom, for the spell only worked, it seemed, in Menton, and a journey of even a few miles made them wary of each other and ill at ease. By the same token there could be no question of marriage, of a continuous life together wherever fortune might take them: their association could be no more than a periodic rest-cure, therapy which could be taken quite often but could not be indulged in permanently without abdication from life itself.

De Freville's unexpected arrival during the Lewson regime did not cause embarrassment either to himself or to Angela: it simply meant that Lewson must go straight away in order to make place. Since such an outcome was in any case desirable, and since de Freville could now lend assistance should Mark prove obdurate, the arrival of the former was doubly opportune. Indeed trebly so; for de Freville knew much more than Angela did about the bit of "business" which she was hoping to put in Mark's way to ease his predicament when he departed. So now, she thought, as she stood at her kitchen window watching them approach, we can discuss the whole matter sensibly and pack him off before night. I wonder where Max found him. . . .

When this had been explained to her and her 40,000 francs had been returned, they all sat down to tea.

"Right," said Angela. "Owing to Max's help you've got 60,000 francs in your pocket, so from now on you're on your own. But there's one more thing we can do for you. Tell him, Max."

She busied herself conscientiously about the teapot, with the air of a housemaster's wife giving a farewell tea to a boy who was leaving suddenly because his father had gone bankrupt to prison. Max, cast for the part of the housemaster, leaned forward, took his tea with a grave nod of thanks, and began to speak carefully and even sympathetically of his plan for Mark's future.

"I have a friend," Max said, "a Greek gambler called Stratis Lykiadopoulos, who is much in demand, because of his cool head and dignified presence, to play as banker for the big baccarat syndicates. With everything else, he is also supposed to be lucky, and the big money boys are nothing if not superstitious."

"Like Napoleon with his Marshals?"

"Something of the kind. But like even the luckiest of the Marshals, Lykiadopoulos is not immune from errors of judgment. Two years ago he accepted, in the course of play, a cheque for three million old francs from a Frenchman called Jacques des Moulins. By the time the cheque bounced, des Moulins was far away; and my friend, since he had acted on his own responsibility, had to make up the three million for the syndicate—which, however, allowed him the use of its extensive agencies in an effort to trace the defaulter. Des Moulins was finally run to ground, in a pretty bad way, in

Beirut. Although there was clearly no question of getting money from him, Lykiadopoulos, who is an amateur of human vagaries, went to see the man and enquired into his story. It seemed that he had been a professional diplomat of some promise, but had been dismissed the service, or rather, eased out of it, as the result of seducing the seventeen year old son of a certain Minister, to whom he had been acting as what we would call Private Secretary. Deprived both of livelihood and occupation, he had commenced gambler, run through his savings, and had then tried the *coup de dishoneur* on Lykiadopoulos in a final attempt to restore his position. When that failed, all had failed, and the poor wretch had fled East to hide his disgrace in the classical manner of his forefathers."

"Why didn't he join the Legion?" Mark said facetiously.

"For the same reason as you don't. Because he was too lazy. And less concerned to redeem his past than simply to live safe from its consequences. He had managed to blackmail an aunt into sending him just enough money every month to drag out a miserable living in the brothel quarter near the Place des Cannons, where he was attended by an idiot Arab boy, of hideous appearance, to whom he was passionately devoted and who returned his devotion. Indeed, as Lykiadopoulos remarked to me later, here was an important lesson about human love : it is not directed towards a particular person, it is *projected* out of circumstance or need and will embrace the first attainable object in its path. The Titania story, you see."

He glanced quickly at Angela to see whether she had drawn the inference. If she had, she ignored it, placidly pouring and distributing fresh cups of tea.

"It so happened," Max went on, "that Lykiadopoulos was detained in Beirut for several weeks, there being some delicate negotiation about foreign currencies with which his syndicate had charged him. One of the more amusing results of this intrigue was that Beirut was swamped with Egyptian pounds going at one and sixpence each, but that need not

concern us now. What you should know is that Lykiadopoulos, part from kindness and part from interest, went
two or three times more to see des Moulins in his hovel and
was able to .do him several small kindnesses. And when
Lykiadopoulos came for the last time to say good-bye, des
Moulins did his best to show his gratitude. In settlement of
the debt of three million, he handed him the only thing of
value that he had : a letter. A letter which was the property of
the French Minister he had served before his dismissal and
which he had stolen on impulse when he left the Minister's
house for the last time."

"If the letter was valuable, why didn't des Moulins cash
in on it himself?"

"He had kept it as a last resort, but when the time came
to use it he had given up hope. He no longer had either the
energy or the desire to change what he now regarded as his
fate. When he called his bet of three million against Lykiadopoulos and supported it with a worthless cheque, he was
asking God to tell him whether he should continue to live
in the old way or resign himself, virtually, to death. God
decided for the latter course and des Moulins accepted the
decision. He would bury himself in Beirut with his pittance
of income and his idiot boy until God disposed of him altogether. He was not unhappy, just numb; and he had, after
all, someone even lower than himself to care for. As for the
letter, it was no longer of any significance within his scheme
of things : let Lykiadopoulos turn it into money if he could—
for himself, he would stay at peace, lying down for ever in
the dirt and darkness to his beloved idiot's embrace."

"I see," said Mark. "And what was in the letter?"

"The letter," said Max, in a bored, objective tone which
he might have used to recite figures from an account book,
"was from an Israeli businessman of German birth, now
called Yahel. It had been entrusted to the Minister's son—
the one des Moulins later seduced—when he was on holiday
in Israel with a school party in 1956. Indeed, there is reason
to suppose that the whole expedition to Israel was arranged

simply and solely so that a secret message might be delivered back to the Minister in France."

"Rather cumbrous?"

"It is only in spy stories that things can be arranged slickly. In real life the wheels are all jagged and rusty from long exposure, and the grooves are invariably the wrong gauge ... Cumbrous or not, the scheme worked. As soon as the boy returned, in mid-Septemper of '56, he delivered the letter to his father, and what it said was this. One: the Israeli Army had prepared a plan for the invasion of Egypt which could be implemented at twenty-four hours' notice. Two: the feeling of Ben Gurion's Cabinet was definitely in favour of 'close understanding' with France as to common motives and 'compatible lines of action'; the moment the French gave the least indication that they were prepared for discussion, the Israelis would meet them in a spirit of 'total co-operation'."

"Nothing much more than is already known or suspected."

"Ah. Yahel's third point was this. He had been in touch, through his agents in London, with a senior member of the British Cabinet, who had been charged by certain of his colleagues with the top secret conveyance of their—top secret —policy. Names, I should add, are firmly named. From what Yahel then says, it is absolutely plain, not only that a section of the British Cabinet was ready and eager to join in the fun, but that the whole idea of tri-partite collusion—Britain, France, Israel—had originated in London and was the brainchild of the senior Cabinet Minister aforesaid. No question of just drifting in through force of circumstance, of tagging on to the column at the last minute. The guilt for the whole affair lies with one man, who deliberately and at an early date conceived the course of action, canvassed it among chosen friends, and conspired with foreign agents to promote all the necessary preliminaries. It was only after, *and because,* Israel had received the green light from London that the Israelis, speaking through Yahel, thought fit to approach the French."

"In other words," said Mark slowly, "the whole crisis was

engineered by a handful of Cabinet Ministers—regardless, one imagines, of the wishes of the rest of the Cabinet."

"And *without the knowledge* of the rest of the Cabinet. Which explains why some departments, notably those responsible for the armed forces, were so badly caught out when the balloon went up. Nobody had warned the warlords."

"But surely . . . the guilty Ministers would have made the perfect scapegoats when the whole thing turned out such a disastrous flop?"

"Not on your life. Could the Prime Minister get up and say that unknown to himself and most of his advisers a small body of men had successfully conspired to bring the country into what might have been total war? No. The whole affair had to be explained away as a well-meant response to a difficult situation, or excused as the dutiful support of a misguided ally, or even admitted as downright muddle—*anything you like* rather than revealed as a pre-concerted plan. And this involved keeping quiet about the guilty ministers . . . most of whom, I grant you, have since been edged out of the way. But three at least are too talented, too necessary, to be got rid of, and are riding high at this very moment. That letter, Lewson, not only discredits some leading members of today's government, it could destroy the country's confidence, for many years to come, in the entire image of Conservative rule."

"Valuable, as you say."

"Worth more than three million francs. Especially in an election year."

"And Lykiadopoulos?"

"Simply does not know what to do. Out of his sphere, he says. He doesn't want trouble, he says: he has an inbred Balkan fear that he'll be knifed or blown up the minute he comes within a hundred miles of politics. Unfair, he says, to the French Minister's son: to be compromised at the beginning of his career for having acted as go-between when still an innocent boy."

"So he is a sentimental man."

"All gamblers are. A compensation for their way of life. But the real trouble with Lykiadopoulos is that he is being inept. He is so conditioned to dealing with short-term issues at the gaming table that he cannot think straight through when it comes to the longer distance. He cannot even distinguish clearly between the two kinds of market: between buyers who would pay for the letter in order to cry scandal and those who would pay, even more heavily perhaps, in order to ensure silence. He will not understand that a sale on the latter terms would guarantee, among other things, that there could never again be any risk of anyone getting at that wretched boy."

"Greeks don't think in such terms. They are inured to a tradition of regurgitating personal honour, of vendetta, which ensures that no issue ever dies. Take the fortunes of the House of Atreus. . . ."

"Retribution inspired by a primitive religion," said Max crossly. "There is no reason why this letter should cause any unpleasantness at all. All he has to do is negotiate its sale, for a large sum of money, into safety and oblivion."

"For a treasury cheque, you think?"

"There are special funds for this kind of thing."

"Why not leave Lykiadopoulos to do as he likes? It's his letter."

Angela collected the tea things on to a tray.

"Since Lykiadopoulos has no use for the letter," she said demurely, "I . . . we . . . thought it might come in handy for you."

"I see. I just march up to him and ask for it."

"Listen to Max," she said, as if encouraging a petulant child to pay attention to paternal homily.

Max grunted and heaved himself out of his chair to hold the door open. Angela passed out with the tray.

"You can finish your little talk while I do the washing up," she said. "Then we might all go for a nice walk."

Really, thought Mark, if I see much more of this "little

woman" pose, I shall scream. Aloud he said.

"Well? How do I get hold of it?"

"You don't sound grateful."

"I'll be grateful all right . . . if you've got any kind of feasible suggestion."

"It's very simple," said Max. "I'll give you a note of introduction. As I've told you, he's a sentimental man. So you then take advantage of your opportunities to find out where the letter is and steal it."

"Very simple, I'm sure."

"You can't expect the whole thing on a plate."

"Supposing I'm not his type?"

"Anybody as young as you is his type."

"Suppose there's someone else?"

"He's not one to refuse a little extra."

"Where is he then?"

"In Venice. Hotel Danieli. He's to run a big bank out on the Lido in about ten days' time. You'd better do your stuff before it starts—he'll be rather pre-occupied when it does."

"Just tell me this," said Mark: "why are you so keen to have your own chum robbed?"

"I'm keen, or rather Angie's keen, to get rid of you on fair terms. As for my chum, the letter's not doing him any good. Last and by no means least, I shall be interested to hear what you do with it."

"I'm not quite with you."

"Corruption in high places," said Max patiently, "is a hobby of mine. I don't exploit it, because I've already got my own little corner in human weakness, but I enjoy collecting instances. I told you just now that gamblers were sentimental. They are also desperately in need of reassurance. I'm not a gambler any more, but I live through gambling, and I too require constant reassurance."

"Reassurance about what, for Christ's sake?"

"I like to be reminded that the world is run, even at the highest level, by petty-minded and venal men. It makes me feel more secure—that I'm inside the regular pattern, that

I'm conforming with an important human norm. You let me know how you dispose of that letter, what people say, what they want it for, and I assure you you'll find me generous. Just a straight-forward account of the facts, that's all. And don't amuse yourself with sending me lies, Lewson. Because sooner or later I'd find out, and then God help you."

"And what will you do with this information?"

"Hoard it like a miser's gold. Take it out, during the long winter nights, and gloat over it. Compare it with the pompous speeches, the unctuous voices on television, then laugh myself silly and go contented to bed."

Angela came in.

"I've done your packing," she said to Mark meekly. "There's a train at six. You can be in Milan by mid-night and go on to Venice tomorrow."

"And we can all come down to the station," said Max happily, "to see you off."

"Don't worry. I shan't hang around."

"My dear chap, a pleasure. I shall enjoy the walk, and Angie's a great one for stations."

"Stations are such fun," she murmured.

So a little while later they all left the house and walked down the road, Mark Lewson carrying the single grip that contained all his movables, Max and Angela arm in arm like a married couple of long standing.

2

A GAME OF CHESS

ABOUT THE same time as Mark Lewson was taking his seat at the chemin-de-fer table in Menton, two elderly gentlemen sat down on a terrace in Somersetshire. Although a chess board was set ready for play on a table between them, and although they went through the formality of moving the pieces, their attention to the game was cursory; which was not surprising, as they had both played much the same match together, down to the last tactic and almost to the last move, many times before. For the most part they looked neither at the board nor at each other, but gazed over the lawn beneath the terrace and the valley beneath the lawn and then away to the distant line of the Quantock Hills. When they spoke, it was as though they were taking part in a play and were addressing their words, quietly but firmly, to an audience on the grass below.

"One of these days," said Alastair Dixon, his bald head gleaming in the April sun, "I shall work out a new opening."

"It would make a change," said Rupert Percival, who was slightly the older of the two but still had a full head of glossy hair : "and of course you will have plenty of time for the game in your retirement."

"I'm not so sure. Remember my *magnum opus: Forty Years in the House of Commons.*"

"I should have thought," said Percival, "that it would have been enough to live through them without spending the rest of your life writing about it."

"The House is an addiction. Once it gets into your system

you never get it out again. I shall need my book as a
substitute."

"What it is to have a vocation." Percival shifted a knight
to complete the first stage of his own laborious version of the
King's Indian defence. "When I give up practice, I shall feel
nothing but relief."

"You've virtually given up practice already. How many
times a week do you go to that office of yours?"

"I keep an eye on things. The young men handle the wills
and the tax-returns. I reserve anything juicy for myself."

"*Juicy?*" said Dixon. "In Bishop's Cross?"

"You don't know your constituents. We've had two
divorces this last winter. And an amusing row with a headmaster about allegedly wrongful expulsion, which the headmaster quite rightly won. And a venomous to-do about the
rough shooting rights at Thyme. So you see, I'm kept quite
busy. And what with the Hunt and the Conservative
Association. . . ."

"That reminds me," Dixon said. He took Percival's knight
with his bishop and then, to save his friend the trouble, took
his own bishop with Percival's pawn.

"How do you know I want to do that? There's such a
thing as refusing an exchange."

"Not at your level there isn't."

"I suppose not. . . . *What* reminds you?"

"The Conservative Association. What are you doing about
my replacement in the House this autumn?"

"Ah," said Percival, leaning back and taking out his snuff
box, "I wondered when you'd get interested in that."

"Edwin Turbot wants to know."

"I don't see that it's his business. He'd better employed
paying proper attention to his Ministry."

"He sees himself not only as a Minister but as a kind of
Grand Vizier to the Party. And since the old man plays along
with him, he has to be humoured."

"All the same, you might remind him that local associations
are strictly independent."

"He only wants to know what's going on," said Dixon rather huffily: "after all, this is the safest seat in Wessex."

"The less need for Edwin Turbot to bother himself."

"He's interested in what he calls the Party's Overall Image for the General Election."

"Well," said Percival between prodigious sniffs of snuff, "there's an official short list of five names. But all you need to worry about is my personal short list, on which there are only two: Somerset Lloyd-James, whose father, you'll remember, lives just over the border in Devonshire, and—"

"—Shagger Lloyd-James? Roman Catholic?"

"That's right. Distinguished recusant family. Well, Shagger's son, Somerset, edits that beastly paper, *Strix*. You know, a sort of heavy journal of commerce which invents plausible reasons for money-grubbers to think themselves high-minded. But the boy's got his head screwed right down to his neck, and he does know a great deal about money. Practice as well as theory."

"That will please Edwin. Modern commercial image with no intellectual frills."

"On the contrary. Somerset Lloyd-James is bristling with intellectual frills. He won the Lauderdale at Cambridge in '48. But he knows when they're not needed."

"I never met an intellectual who knew that," said Dixon patronisingly. "And the other horse?"

"Peter Morrison. . . . Formerly member for Whereham."

Alastair Dixon castled on the queen's side, took out his cigar case, lit a cigar with avid concentration, and at last said:

"So they're bringing him back already?"

"*We* in Bishop's Cross," said Percival firmly, "are *considering* whether to adopt him as *our* candidate. One of the reasons being that he has a wife and two children, which goes down well with the women."

"Central Office had nothing to say about it?"

"Certainly not. He's on their list of course—they kept his

name there when he resigned in case he might want to come back. I gather, despite appearances at the time, that his resignation was entirely to his credit?"

"Yes," said Dixon. "There was some sort of family scandal, but he only used that as a smoke-screen. His real reason seems to have been that he didn't want any part of Suez."

"Then why didn't he say so? That Young England Group which he started—they've always been against antics like Suez and pretty plain about it."

"It seems," said Dixon, with a mixture of admiration and bewilderment, "that this Mr Morrison has a very nice sense of honour. He felt that to speak against Suez, as was his duty if he stayed in the House, would be to stab the Army in the back. And to resign, giving Suez as a pretext, would have been just as bad. So since there was a story going about just then that he'd got some girl in trouble, he let it be known that he was resigning because of that."

"*That* won't go down well with the women."

"There was never anything in it. . . . But I'm surprised he's coming back quite so soon."

"He came to see me about that," Percival said. "He told me—entirely off the record of course—that several of his friends in the Young England Group are anxious to have him back because they don't much care for Carton Weir, who's running it at present."

"I like Carton Weir," said Dixon. "He's a very civil . . . and civilised young man."

"You're not in the Young England Group. They want Morrison, who, come to that, could have Whereham back by lifting his little finger."

Underneath the table Dixon's short legs frisked in irritation.

"Then why has he come here?" he said.

"He doesn't want to unseat the chap who took over Whereham in '56. Unfair, he says. And since we've got a vacancy. . . . Whose turn is it to win this game?"

"Mine," said Dixon, untruthfully. "You might as well

resign anyway. . . . And which of the two do you really want? Lloyd-James or Morrison?"

"That," said Percival, po-faced, "will be for the selection committee to decide."

"Suppose they pick one of the other three on the official short list?"

"For someone who has spent forty years in the House, and boasts about it, you understand very little of politics."

"I understand enough to know that Edwin Turbot's not going to be keen about Morrison, whatever your committee decides. He's respected, Morrison, but he's apt to be a nuisance. The Young Englanders have settled down nicely, under Weir, as a harmless prestige group. No one wants Morrison stirring them up again."

"Apparently *they* do," said Percival. "And Sir Edwin can hardly complain about that."

"He won't. He'll just say that it's too soon after the scandal for Morrison to come back."

"You said there was nothing in the scandal."

"Who's being naïve about politics now? Check mate," said Dixon, spitefully plonking down his queen.

"Don't thump the pieces about," said Percival placidly. "They're expensive. Whatever Edwin Turbot may think or feel, Minister or not, Grand Vizier or not, there's no way he can bully a local association."

"Isn't there just?" said Alastair Dixon. "You wait and see."

On this same April evening, some three miles from the East Anglian market town of Whereham, Peter Morrison was bowling to his eight-year-old son in a net which he had put up on his abundant lawn.

"One more over, Nickie," he called. "This one will be well up and outside the off stump. Left foot well over now. . . ."

Six foot two inches tall, broad both at chest and waist but

giving no impression of overweight, carrying his huge round head thrown back like a guardsman's, he lumbered easily to the bowling crease and placed the ball just where he had told his son, who hit it back hard over his head and laughed aloud with pleasure.

"Not bad, but your foot wasn't there. That one should have gone through the covers, not straight back. After it, Jeremy."

Five-year-old Jeremy, younger brother and ball-boy, scampered down the lawn and returned his father a chest-high catch.

"Nice throw, my dear. . . . Now then, Nickie. Good length outside the leg stump. Don't hit too hard and aim at mid-wicket."

From a central door in the long, low house of stone, stepping (like a goddess) just a little larger than life, came Helen Morrison. She stood quietly behind Nickie, appraised his next stroke, murmured something through the netting, then moved to her husband and took the ball from his hand.

"Telephone call from the West country," she said.

"Hell. . . . Give him four balls, darling. Then pack it in."

"And Jeremy?"

"His turn tomorrow. Younger sons must learn their place early."

Leaving his wife to work out for herself how seriously she should take this remark (his tone had been light but without irony), Peter ambled away towards the house, like a comfortable monk strolling in a cloister. Never, in his sons' presence, would he betray any sense of urgency. For two pins, he told himself, he would have finished the over; but that might have smacked of discourtesy to his caller. As he stepped off the lawn and through the door, he heard with satisfaction the level tones of his wife:

". . . No, just some old friend of Daddy's he hasn't heard from for a time. . . ."

Later that evening, Peter said to Helen (who had not enquired):

"That telephone call was about the seat for Bishop's Cross."

"So I imagined."

"I gather my closest rival for the candidature will be Somerset Lloyd-James, of all people."

"Will that embarrass you? After that business three years ago?"

"No . . . though of course he'll need watching. Somerset's devious by nature, that's all. It's no good blaming him. He's always been like that, and in other ways he's a lot of fun. I remember when he stayed here once, just after the war. . . ."

He fell into a silence which Helen did not attempt to break.

"There's another slight worry," Peter said at length. "Rupert Percival said that Alastair Dixon, the retiring member, reckons Edwin Turbot won't like me coming forward just now."

"There's nothing he can do to stop you."

"Officially, no. Although Edwin Turbot's a kind of Provost Marshal inside the Party he still can't dictate to local branches. Not openly, that is; but he can make himself felt in other ways."

"What sort of man is Rupert Percival?"

"A strong man and an honest one."

"Then there is nothing to worry about."

"I don't know. Percival may be strong, but he is not one for superfluous exhibitions of strength. Somerset is in every way as proper a candidate as I am, and if Percival understood that senior men, in Central Office perhaps, had good reason for preferring him, he might just accept this and follow suit. His honesty would not be compromised. He is under no moral obligation to support me."

"But suppose," said Helen, "that Central Office's reason for preferring Somerset Lloyd-James are *not* good? Did Percival say what they might be?"

"No. He didn't even mention Central Office. He just said that *Turbot* might not want *me*."

"And Turbot's reasons?"

"Percival could only go on what Alastair Dixon had said, which was all conjecture anyhow, and he was kind enough to indicate that he didn't think much of it. But one thing you can be quite sure of : if Turbot has reasons, good or bad, for wanting me out of the way, they will be framed and presented as speciously as the Sermon on the Mount."

The next morning just before ten a.m. Somerset Lloyd-James shuffled into Gower Street from his lodging in Russell Square, paused to examine the weekly bill outside the offices of the *Spectator* ("Levin on Working-Class Fascism"), leered knowingly, and slouched on up the street to Philby House (so called since 1958) from which he edited *Strix*. Since only three out of the four electric fires in his office were switched on, he rang for his secretary to require an explanation, was reminded of a directive issued by Lord Philby, the Proprietor, who enjoined economy in such matters (it was, after all a delicious April morning), personally switched on the fourth electric fire and the second bars of the other three, and called for the mail.

"There is a gentleman," his secretary said, "waiting to see you."

"A gentleman?"

"I use the term advisedly. He has been here since half past nine, and claims to be an old friend of yours."

"Name?"

"Major Gray. A retired rank, I gather."

"*De profundis,*" said Somerset, mildly shaken. "Bring in the mail, and then, in exactly five minutes, bring in Major Gray."

When his secretary had set the mail on his desk, Somerset, having established in thirty seconds that what was not routine was merely trivial, selected from the pile of letters the one typed on the most imposing note-paper and placed it dead in front of him, side by side with a sheet of blank foolscap. On the latter he wrote carefully as follows :

FIELDING GRAY.

Left school Autumn 1945.

Father (died '45) well off; but (??) something odd thought to have happened to the money.

Anyhow, F.G. in smart cavalry regiment from '46 onward.

Last heard of in '55, when seen by Peter Morrison, who was on Parliamentary tour, on small island off Malta. At that time responsibly employed (? Officer Commanding a Squadron on detachment) and apparently resigned to his lot, though still bitter (in theory, so to speak, rather than practice).

Questions:

(1) Why has he left the Army?

(2) What does he want of me?

(3) Am I under any enforceable obligation to him?

Answers:

(1 and 2): To be presently resolved.

(3) No. But prudence directs that his claim of friendship, since he sees fit to call it so, be honoured, and any reasonable request considered.

Under these notes, which took up about a third of the page, he ruled two lines in red ink; the rest of the page could now be used for recording further information, under the pretext of drafting an answer to the important letter before him at the same time as he was conducting the interview. A corny technique, which seldom failed to unnerve his visitors. Since his secretary was now twenty seconds late in producing Gray, he reached forward with irritation to press the buzzer; but before his finger reached it the side door opened from the secretary's office and he found himself rigid in his chair, his hand arrested two inches short of the button, his every muscle paralysed by the horror of what he now saw.

Fielding Gray had been, when Somerset last saw him, a lithe and beautiful boy of seventeen. From Peter Morrison's description, given four years back, Somerset gathered that he had thickened somewhat, and that drink was already beginning to show in his cheeks, but that he still/retained poise and even distinction. As indeed he did now. His figure, correctly adorned as for an officer on leave in London (well cut dark suit with waistcoat, white shirt with stiff collar and regimental tie, bowler hat and gloves carried in the left hand), did him no discredit for a man in the early thirties, while his movements were easy and precise. The only trouble was his face. It was impossible to tell now whether Peter had been right or wrong about the burst veins in the cheeks, because the cheeks, like everything else except a thin, twisted line of mouth and one red, bald, tiny eye, were coated with a mottled surface of shining pink like icing clumsily spread upon a cake.

Gray moved calmly up to Somerset's desk, as though about to report to his Commanding Officer on a semi-formal occasion. A foot from the desk he halted and then, looking Somerset straight in the face with his one little eye, held out his hand.

"It is kind of you to see me," he said.

The voice was normal but the mouth writhed with every syllable. Somerset, who was already so far in control of himself as to have recovered his powers of motion, rose to shake hands. A prompt enough answer to question (1), he thought.

"Fielding," he said, his voice soft yet grating, like a mixture of powered ash and clinkers being raked from a dead hearth, "what a long time it has been."

He gestured to a chair, then sat down again himself; he took up a pen, glanced down at the letter and the sheet of notes in front of him. No, he thought, you can't do it, not now, not with him. *Yes,* he answered himself, you must; you must do everything as you always do—the more pitiable Fielding, the more steadfast your routine. Slowly he retrieved and straightened the two sheets of paper, which he had already begun to brush to one side.

"Well, my dear?" he said, and the words whispered back down the years, with echo upon tiny echo, so that it seemed nearly a minute before there was silence between them once more.

"As you see," said Gray in matter-of-fact tones, "I've been badly injured and have left the Army. An explosion in Cyprus," he added, almost apologetically, in answer to the question that glinted behind Somerset's thick lenses. "A local truce had been declared, you see, but the Cypriots neither understand nor respect the nature of contract. Any form of treaty with them will be meaningless. . . . But I don't suppose you need my opinions about that."

He glanced up at a shelf which held the bound volumes of *Strix,* as though to imply, if not without polite irony, that all knowledge and all wisdom reposed between their covers.

"I'm very sorry—"

Gray held up his hand.

"No need to be. It was time I had a change in my life. You may remember that I once had ambitions . . . of a non-military kind."

Somerset twitched slightly in assent. Answer to question (2) coming up.

"Well," proceeded Gray, "I have a pension and a gratuity which between them will keep me fed and watered. But little more. I could probably apply for a University Grant, but it's a little late in the day for that. I must do as best I can with what I know already."

"The Army . . . ?"

"The Army. Most of Europe and the Near East. East Africa. Hongkong. Extensive reading for the last thirteen years—soldiers have a lot of leisure, you see. It all adds up to a body of knowledge."

"Certainly," said Somerset; and then, amiably, "unspecialised knowledge."

"If you like. Wide but unspecialised knowledge of men, places and events. Not to mention books. The equipment of a general commentator."

Gray's tone was still steady, but Somerset could detect a thin, ghostly plea for encouragement, for one word to show that he understood and might approve. Well, perhaps he would give that word. But not yet.

"And so?" he said.

For the first time since Gray had been in the room Somerset now started adding to his notes. "Not broke," he wrote: "wants work and is convinced that he can do it. (?Ambitious?) But uncertain whether he can get anyone to share his faith in himself."

"I hope I'm not interrupting you in anything important," said Gray politely when Somerset raised his head again.

"Not really. . . . Just a point to be made in a letter. I didn't want to forget it. I find my memory slips more and more as I grow older."

"I know what you mean. Life is so complex. There are so many threads to be sorted and kept straight. That is why I have tried to keep my hand in all these years."

"Keep your hand in?"

"As a writer. You may remember that my little efforts were well regarded when we were still at school. But of course everything was very simple then; every day was either wet or fine, so to speak. It has grown more complicated since; so I have tried to develop my talent—such as it is—accordingly. To use it to sort the threads and keep them straight. For my own satisfaction . . . for my own mental safety."

Somerset considered this.

"By which you mean you've kept a journal," he asserted at last.

"Yes. Dating right back to the time when things first started to get complicated. To that last summer at school. You remember, Somerset?"

Somerset remembered. On the foolscap sheet in front of him he sketched a Maltese cross, his personal symbol for danger.

"But of course," said Gray indifferently, "I've no intention of trying to publish it. The journal was for myself, so that I might understand who I was. What I had hoped," and now the faint note of supplication was back in his voice again, "was that I might be able do something about publishing a couple of novels which I have also written."

"Based on the journal?" said Somerset heavily.

"No," said Gray. His mouth flickered briefly in what might have been either a smile or a sneer; there was no way of telling. "The journal is an attempt to analyse the characters and explain the actions of myself and people I have known well—you among them. The novels are also analytic, but of situations rather than people. They deal with technical problems, not moral ones. The first of them turns on a vexed point of military law; the other on the necessity to make a starving tribe eat food forbidden by its faith."

"A moral problem, surely."

"Perhaps, but in no sense individual and therefore not concerned with subtleties of human character. As you may see from the solution, which is merely administrative: you deceive them into thinking that the forbidden food is in fact something else, veal, say, and not pork."

All this he offered poker-faced. Somerset drew a small fish, which meant "danger passed", but qualified it with two question marks.

"Let the dead bury their dead," said Gray, as though reading his thoughts; "it was all too long ago. Things are as they are; and as they are, Somerset, I want your help."

Somerset excised the question marks. Before looking up he wrote: "A curious example of God's Grace. By his own endeavours alone, apparently by the simple effort of keeping a journal, Fielding has come to understanding and forgiveness. Even so, he could be troublesome if he chose. Therefore help him; but also make difficulties, so that the help may appear the more valuable. A.M.D.G."

"I'm sorry," he said, and pushed the papers away from him: "I just wanted to get that finally out of the way. I'm all yours, Fielding."

"I have come to you because you are the only person I know in this line. You presumably know a bit about publishers, and of papers, like this one, which might be prepared to give me a trial."

Gray had tried to speak bravely but there was in what he said the pathetic eagerness of a small boy on the beach claiming his turn to bat.

"This kind of work is sought after," Somerset said. "It is held to carry prestige."

His hair, he thought, is still as beautiful as ever. Ample, auburn, with the same gentle wave. Above such a face it is incongruous, obscene.

"But," Somerset said, "I can certainly offer you something. This paper deals mainly with economics and industry, but in the review section we often take on books which are on the margin of these subjects. Well documented travel books, for example. They should be within your compass. Or books on military organisation and supply—logistics, I think you call it."

Gray nodded enthusiastically.

"I'll give you two books to do during the next month," Somerset went on. "If I like what you write, I'll give you more, and perhaps commission a straight essay from you. If your work for *Strix* is any good, you'll find you get enquiries from other quarters soon enough."

Gray's one eye blinked. He's moved, Somerset thought he's moved because after all these years I'm going to help him. He was always a sentimental boy. . . . But this train of thought was interrupted by his secretary, whose voice now crackled at him from his desk.

"Tom Llewyllyn here to see you."

"Ask him to wait a few—No," said Somerset, "send him straight in. Tom Llewyllyn's publisher," he said to Gray, "has a reputation for helping new writers. Even aspirant novelists, God help him."

"Gregory Stern."

"You keep abreast."

"I told you. Soldiers have a lot of leisure. Particularly wounded ones."

Yes, thought Somerset, a great part of whose motive for

admitting Llewyllyn so promptly was to see how he reacted
to Gray's disfigurement.

"I want you to meet an old friend of mine," he said as
Llewyllyn came through the side door; "Major Fielding
Gray."

Gray rose and confronted Llewyllyn, who merely held out
his hand and nodded with visible annoyance, for he had been
hoping to find Somerset alone.

"Fielding's just going," Somerset said, reading Llewyllyn's
mind at once and reflecting that had the devil himself been
present Tom's only reaction would have been to indicate his
superfluity. Not that Tom was insensitive to other people;
but when he had something on his mind, as clearly he had
now, his anxiety to discharge it precluded any other emotion,
whether of sympathy, curiosity or fear.

"Fielding," said Somerset, "should meet your publisher.
He has written some novels."

"So have five thousand other people," said Tom grumpily.
But then he seemed to remember something, and looked
Gray straight in the face with candid interest. "I heard about
you," he said, "after that wretched business in Cyprus. Your
regiment . . . didn't a Captain Detterling belong to it? The
M.P.?"

"Yes. He retired a long time ago, but he rejoined us from
the reserve for Suez. As it happens it was Detterling, back
in '45, who persuaded me to become a regular."

"He is an interesting man," said Tom, "of a type I cannot
approve. Nor do I approve of the old boy net. But I'm going
to let you in on it now. . . . Christ, it's hot in here," he said,
and switched off the nearest electric fire.

Success, reflected Somerset as he switched the fire on again,
had given Tom the habit of airing rather pompous ethical
judgments—without, however, affecting the essential kindness of his heart. Although Tom might moralise adversely for
an hour together, it did not in the least detract from his
practical good-will.

"That thing is," Tom was saying, "that my publisher,

Gregory Stern, wants to expand, so he has been looking
about for partners who will bring some cash with them. One
day this chap Detterling turned up and offered ten thousand
in exchange for a nominal directorship, a proportionate share
in the profits, and the right to interest himself, anywhere
short of actual interference, in what went on. Stern liked
the look of him—he said he reminded him of a Trollope
character called Dolly Longstaffe—and jumped at him. Come
to that, I like him myself."

"Then why do you disapprove?" asked Somerset.

"He's too blatant a member of the old gang. He not only
takes his privileges for granted—White's, M.C.C., chambers
in Albany—but he expects everything to operate in that
particular medium. It's to his advantage, you see, that it
should. Because although he's a shrewd man, his shrewdness
doesn't extend beyond his own world. For example, when
Peter Morrison left Parliament three years back"—Tom
glanced furtively at Somerset—"Detterling dropped out of
the Young England Group simply because he couldn't understand the new leader Carton Weir—who's built on a more
contemporary pattern."

"I thought," said Somerset, "that he just *disliked* Carton."

"Same thing. Detterling disliked Carton because he was
incapable of understanding him in Detterling's terms."

Major Gray was beginning to fidget.

"Sorry," said Tom, turning back to him abruptly. "What
I was thinking was this. If you know Detterling, he should be
able to help you with Gregory Stern. As I say, he doesn't
interfere, but if he makes a suggestion, Gregory will
listen."

"Odd," said Gray: "that Detterling should take to publishing. And with this sort of firm."

"You mean a firm owned by a Jew?" said Tom sharply.

"No," said Gray unperturbed. "Detterling always admired
Jews. He used to say that Jewish blood gave a spice to personality, though like all spices it was perhaps better ...
diffused. What surprises me is that he should have chosen

a small firm of recent origin. Something outside what you just called his 'medium'."

"Gregory Stern," volunteered Somerset, "is very much of Detterling's medium. Eton and the House; his father the first Jew ever to serve as an officer in the Household Brigade; a massive merchant bank in the background. Cream of the establishment—with Jewish blood to lend spice, as you say."

Somerset seemed about to add something more, but then sat back in silence. The question was closed; so was Fielding Gray's interview.

"Thank you both," said the latter as he rose. "You've been very kind." And then, with his earlier hint of boyish eagerness, "You'll send those books, Somerset? Care of the Cavalry Club, until I'm settled."

Somerset nodded and rose. Tom Llewyllyn smiled and waved his hand but did not rise. Major Gray turned about smartly and marched out.

"Now," said Tom, the smile fading from his face, "what's the game?"

"Fielding's an old friend—"

"—Never mind Major Gray. Bishop's Cross, Somerset. I hear you've offered yourself for the seat."

"And why not?"

"Well. . . . Let's say that I thought you had your hands full already."

"I can always resign this editorship."

"Somerset. You are, in your own terms, a good editor. In no terms will you be a good politician. You have what the Americans call an unfortunate personality—for public life, that is."

"That is why," said Somerset, "I have chosen Bishop's Cross. The Tory candidate there cannot fail, not even if they adopt a barbary ape."

"You think they will adopt you?"

"To be candid," said Somerset, "no. I think they will adopt Peter Morrison. But there's just a chance, and it's worth taking. Why are you so keen to stop me?"

As someone had once observed of Somerset, he derived much of his massive self-confidence from a poker-face which he thought he possessed but didn't. When Somerset was bluffing his eyes glazed over, and they were rapidly glazing over now. It was clear, Tom thought, that Somerset's genial and modest disclaimer was not sincere: he had reasons for thinking he had a very good chance, and if Somerset had reasons they would be sound. Meanwhile, his attitude must be accepted, for the purposes of discussion, at face value.

"I wonder you bother, that's all," Tom said. "Years ago you told me to stick to what I was good at. It turned out to be excellent advice. Now I'm offering it back."

"Let me refer you," said Somerset, "to your own work." He went to a bookcase and took out a copious volume, the mauve cover of which proclaimed *An Analysis of Practical Politics,* by Tom Llewyllyn (Gregory Stern, 35s.). "Page 113. I quote. 'As with literature, so with politics: if a Party these days is determined to sell a policy, or a man, the merit of the man or the policy is a secondary consideration. The sale can be effected by high pressure methods which ignore or obscure the real issues and insist on others which, while irrelevant, are plausible and attractive. This has always been true, but never so true as now, when techniques of publicity are quicker and slicker than ever before. Just as a book may be made into a best seller by the announcement, at the right time and in the right tone, that the author keeps a canary or lost a leg at Anzio, so a hack politician, however disagreeable or discredited, my be transformed overnight into a potential Prime Minister—if only his sponsors can hit on the right image.' In other words," said Somerset, "there's hope for all of us. Once we get a footing, that is."

"For God's sake," said Tom. "You are now a successful, even a powerful man, who need depend only on his own undoubted abilities. What can you possibly want in Parliament? Your abilities will go for nothing there. You'll have to spend your odd time grovelling for the good-will of second-rate men and learning confidence tricks from television interviewers."

"But it is of our age. The power of the written word is declining, Tom. What counts is the personal appeal, the appearance on the silver screen."

"All I can say," said Tom, "is that it will take one hell of an image to make you acceptable on the silver screen."

"I am an ugly man," said Somerset calmly, "bald, liable to acne, prematurely aged, and long since deprived of my own teeth. I am, in fact, the very symbol of under-privileged humanity. To look at, I am the archetypal underdog in an era of underdogs. So my appeal to a large section of our industrialised and physically degraded community will be immense."

"Until you open your mouth and start in with your posh, clever talk."

"I shall affect the simplicity of Socrates—who was also, you will remember, an ugly man."

"Ugly or not, Socrates had charm."

"So have I."

This was undeniably true. Leave aside his ability to amuse and interest other men, Somerset had a distinct if possibly perverse appeal to women. This he seldom exploited, as he held that women made irrational demands on one's time and purse. But Tom could remember at least one notable conquest : Lady Susan Grange, now Lady Philby and wife of Somerset's Proprietor. It was whispered that Lady Philby still had a kindness for Somerset and was not above indulging it during Philby's frequent business trips. From his knowledge of Lady P's character, Tom doubted this; but the very existence of the story paid its own tribute to Somerset.

"So," said Tom, "you see yourself as a sort of . . . anti-celebrity. But first you've got to reach Parliament."

"Hence my application to Bishop's Cross."

"Where you nevertheless think they will prefer Peter Morrison."

"It'll be experience," said Somerset smoothly. "Local

associations, selection committees, chairmen. . . . It'll be useful practice for next time."

His eyes were glazed to the point of opacity. I wonder whether he can see out of them, Tom thought.

"What does Alastair Dixon say?" he enquired. "As retiring member he'll be listened to, I suppose?"

"Alastair Dixon likes Carton Weir, and Carton Weir wants me. Again: Carton leads the Young England Group—which has behaved discreetly under his leadership but which will cease to be so obliging should Peter return to take over. In sum: Alastair Dixon has a personal reason for wanting me to come in, and a political reason, which he shares with the rest of the Party, for wanting Peter to stay out."

This was the strongest point in Somerset's favour, and he saw no reason to conceal it from Tom, who was certainly shrewd enough to have hit on it for himself.

"Fair enough," muttered Tom. But this was not the whole story, he thought. There was something else behind those glazed irises. Something only embryonic as yet, a mere seed, perhaps not even a fertilised one. But a seed there was, needing only some chance spermatozoon to quicken it, to set the foetus swelling. Which must be as may be, Tom thought; there was nothing more to be discovered just now.

"Why are you so concerned in this?" Somerset was saying. "You'll forgive me, Tom, but a Labour sympathiser has enough . . . interfering to do . . . on his own side of the fence."

"My interest is personal. A Tory will sit for Bishop's Cross whatever happens. My hope is—you'll forgive me, Somerset —that it will be a decent Tory. Not, as you yourself put it, a barbary ape, but someone like Peter Morrison. . . . I've brought you the copy you asked for." He slapped an envelope down on the desk. "Don't try to underpay me like last time, Somerset. Three guineas a hundred is the rate we agreed."

"That was a try-on by Accounts. Mistaken zeal after Philby's call for economy."

"Just put them right then, dear."

Tom shook his curls reprovingly at Somerset and skipped

to the outer door, where he paused to perform a brief tap-dance.

"I shall be following what happens at Bishop's Cross, dear," he said. "You know how interested I am in everything you do."

When Fielding Gray left Gower Street, he took a taxi to the Regent's Park and sat down on a seat by the lake.

So Somerset would try him, it seemed; and Captain Detterling, one time comrade in arms, might be approached to help over the publication of his books. At least he should be able to ensure that they were properly read, not just tossed on one side and returned without comment six months later. And since Fielding knew that he had had something real if limited to say, and since he was confident that in his two novels he had said it with style and precision, he could reasonably hope for a fair outcome.

But what then? Suppose his work found favour with Somerset and his novels were published by Gregory Stern, suppose, even, that they achieved some measure of public esteem, what was to follow? Would there be anything more to say? Could he face the prospect of carrying on indefinitely with such a career? For did not even the two existing manuscripts pose the question, "While this is quite well done, was there ever, in truth, any real reason for doing it?" Works of supererogation . . . and of course that was how ninety-nine writers in a hundred made a living: producing work, conscientious in its kind, modestly saleable, worthy of some small critical attention, but work which, in the end of all, added not one jot to the human experience. Was consciousness of this essential sterility made bearable, he wondered, by the photographs, the occasional notoriety, the literary luncheons? Was it obliterated altogether, perhaps, by the women who wished to sleep, not indeed with the man, but with his books? (Would anyone wish to sleep with *his* books?) Or did authors suffer torment, in the reaches of the night, when faced with the inexorable fact that an entire *oeuvre* was little more than an elaborate tautology?

But then again, an author's occupation, by comparison with those of most citizens, could hardly be called sterile. At least he gave pleasure (a condition of earning his bread), did not spend his days persuading fools to buy rubbish or twisting regulations so that crooked little men might ride with their whores in Bentleys. The writer's avocation was decent, civilised. . . . Yes; but this was not why he had chosen it. He had chosen it because it was work he could do (or thought he could), work which might bring him reputation and money, and work—one of the very few kinds—the bare notion of which did not fill him with boredom or snobbish contempt. In other words, he was in it for the *cachet;* which brought him round again to the question with which he had started : would his proposed career be founded, so to speak, *in the truth,* or would it be one long vanity and vexation of spirit?

But of course, he reminded himself, he was taking much too much for granted. He had not so much as started on this career : time enough to pose superior moral questions when he was properly established in it. The error of equating aspiration with fulfilment was a dangerous one which had taken toll of him before now; this time there must be no dream before there was substance. There were, he told himself, only two things he had to do for the present : to get on with his work with as much professional competence as he could muster; and to come to terms with his deformity.

Or rather, to persuade other people to come to terms. Physical terms. For the most part, as he had already found, his appearance, after giving rise to brief shock as it had in Somerset that morning, was merely ignored. A very few seconds sufficed to reconcile people to his presence. But what, if anything, would suffice to reconcile people to his touch, to his bodily love? Since he required no one to kiss his hideous face, and since the rest of his body was wholesome enough for anybody's kisses, in logic there should be no difficulty.

But in the eye of the beholder, he knew, the part would infect the whole : because his face was an obscenity, his body would be deemed untouchable; and Fielding, now as ever, required urgently and often to be touched.

He rose to leave the park. Nothing would be achieved by sitting here brooding; he would go and check through his novels, and that afternoon, perhaps, he would walk down Curzon Street and see if one of the girls would take him for ready cash. That would be a start. . . . There was a small, choking cry, and a little girl landed almost at his feet. Since no one came to her aid, Fielding knelt, helped her up, and started to wipe the dirt from her bleeding knees while she blubbered quietly into his shoulder. Eventually she drew back her face and regarded him with care.

"One eye?" she said, with curiosity but without censure.

"I mislaid the other."

The child accepted this explanation without further comment and allowed him to proceed with her knee. She at any rate did not resent his touch.

"Where's your mother?" Fielding said.

The child pointed to a bench a hundred yards away, where a large sluttish woman was talking with animation to a small wizened one.

"Run back to her, then, and ask her to bandage you up."

But the child lingered, then leered into his face.

"Pink," she said, "lovely and pink."

Her hands came towards him in order to feel.

"Nice, nice," she cried, as her fingers passed over the smooth surface of his cheeks. "Not rough, like Dadda. Nice."

Fielding rose unsteadily to his full height and gave the child a gentle shove in the direction of her mother. Then he walked away trembling violently in every muscle, as he had not trembled since they brought him a looking glass for the first time.

When Tom Llewyllyn left Gower Street he took the Underground to South Kensington, whence he walked to Buttock's Private Hotel in the Cromwell Road. In the hall was Tessie Buttock, who was busy gluing up letters she had just steamed open and placing them in the letter rack.

"Censoring the mail now?" said Tom.

"Only the old ones, dear. They've been hanging about for weeks, waiting for people who haven't come."

"Then why are you putting them in the rack?"

"Makes a bit of a show, dear. Which is about all they're good for. It's been a dull old morning I've had reading them."

Albert Edward, Tessie's terrier, lifted his leg against the grandfather clock. Really, thought Tom, it was high time for a change. And a change there was now to be. But what should he tell Tessie? After all these years.

"Tessie," he said hesitantly, "I'm going away for a couple of nights. Down to the country."

"Very nice too, dear. . . . It's not that Albert Edward doesn't know better, but he never cared for that clock. Woozums, woozums," she intoned; "woozums widdle on horrid clock."

"Tessie. . . ."

"Yes, dear?"

"I'm engaged. You'll see it tomorrow in *The Times*. That's why I'm going to the country, to stay with my fiancée's parents. . . . She'll be there too, of course."

"Well, don't go overdoing it, dearie," said Tessie, as if he were going round the corner for a drink. "Leave a little something to look forward to. That's what I always told Buttock."

"And did he?"

"Not so's you'd have noticed, no. Real horny, Buttock was. Until he went on the booze, and even then he could do as well for himself as most men between here and Highgate Hill. I remember one Sunday afternoon, just before the war—"

"—Tessie," said Tom, sadly but firmly. "When I get married I'll have to leave you."

"So I supposed, dear. Though you can have one of the back rooms for two quid a week. *Pied-à-terre*, if you take my meaning."

"Tessie. I am very much in love with my future wife."

"Of course you are, dear. But it never did no harm to have a *pied-à-terre*. You can come and do your writing when she starts throwing the pots about."

"She's a lady, Tessie."

"Go on? Starts breaking up the mirrors, then, since she's a *lady*." Tessie paused to quiz him with something as near affection as her bleak and greedy eyes could convey. "You've really come on these last few years, haven't you, love? Those books and all, and now this. What's she called?"

"Patricia. . . . Patricia Turbot."

"Turbot. . . . Anything to do with that bossing minister man? The one that's always telling us to work harder and save our money."

"Daughter," said Tom reluctantly. "Oldest daughter."

"My, my. You *have* come on. But all the same, dear," Tessie said, scooping up Albert Edward and tickling his groin, "I should think hard about that *pied-à-terre* if I was you."

"Like to look at some pictures, dear?" said plump, kind Maisie to Fielding Gray.

"I don't think that will be ncessary."

"No," said Maisie, looking down at him rather apprehensively, "I can see that. But they're rather fun all the same. There's this photograph of two girl guides and a scoutmaster, and—"

"—No pictures, thank you. . . . What did you say your name was?"

"Maisie."

"Well then, Maisie. Like this. . . ."

About thirty seconds later, Maisie said,

"Don't go away at once, love. Stay and talk a little."

"I thought . . . you'd want to go out again."

"No, love. I don't usually go out in the afternoon. Or at all, for the matter of that."

"Then why were you out this afternoon?" said Fielding peevishly.

"Lovely spring day. A girl gets restless. But what I really do, dear, is to have regular gentlemen. They come here for appointments, or I go to them. Lucky for me, really, now this new law's going to come."

"Regular gentlemen?"

"Ones who want something special. Or ones like you who might find it awkward getting a girl of their own."

It was so easily and pleasantly said that it was impossible to take offence.

"You see," Maisie went on, "even the girls on the line might not be too keen. They're an ignorant lot, and some of them think that an injured face means—well—an injured mind."

"They could be right."

"Not with you, dear. Not yet, anyway. I spotted that quick enough when I saw you coming along just now—it was the easy way you walked. You'll be all right if you have someone regular, someone who understands. . . ."

"You think you understand?"

"Not everything, love. But quite a lot. For instance, I know why you were so quick just now."

"It's been a long time."

"Not only that," Maisie said. "You wanted to get it over quick for my sake . . . and for yours, in case I said anything."

There was so much in this now he came to think of it, that Fielding, who had been on the point of leaving, sat down again on Maisie's bed.

"That's right," she said. "Now we can relax. Spend the afternoon, if you like. It'll only be another five quid if you're going to visit regular. And you may as well look at these pictures, now we know each other. They're all good for a laugh."

When Fielding left Maisie at half past five that evening,

they had arranged regular appointments for two afternoons
a week until further notice on either side.

Ever since Tom Llewyllyn had left his office that morning,
Somerset Lloyd-James had entertained vague feelings of unrest and dissatisfaction. The unrest he attributed to the surprise, by no means unpleasant but still unnerving, of seeing
Fielding Gray again. The dissatisfaction he blamed on Tom.
Why was Tom interesting himself in the Bishop's Cross
candidature? To what extent would he, could he, interfere?

If Somerset had known about Tom's engagement to
Patricia Turbot and his consequent visit to Sir Edwin in the
country, he would have been very put out indeed. Even as it
was, past experience told him that Tom, if so minded, could
do a lot of damage. For Tom, despite tendencies to dissipation,
combined energy, integrity and intelligence; as he had shown
more than once, if he undertook something he saw it through.
It was plain from what had passed that morning that he
wished Peter Morrison, whom he had always admired, back
in Parliament, and that for this reason among others he
resented Somerset's application to Bishop's Cross. If Tom
had nothing much else on for the summer, thought Somerset
crossly, he would make every difficulty he could.

But what difficulties could he make? Tom was a "heavy"
journalist of some reputation, and he had also published three
books: an early and striking political novel, then, in 1956,
a brilliant assessment of Russian cold-war strategy since 1945,
and finally, in the Autumn of 1958, his *Analysis of Practical
Politics,* which had enjoyed even greater critical esteem than
its much acclaimed predecessors. All this added up to
authority, to waxing authority at that; as things now stood,
Tom might request and receive space from almost any
prestige journal in the kingdom; the question was, how much
of it would he care to devote to so trivial a matter as the
candidature at Bishop's Cross?

Very little, Somerset decided. Editors wouldn't like it; the

Bishop's Cross selectors wouldn't heed it; and in any case the only really damaging material Tom had against him was quite unprintable. It followed that Tom's activities must take another form, that of personal intrigue or canvass; and while Tom, as he acknowledged, was a tried performer in *that* genre, Somerset was no novice himself. It would be a fair match, one to which in other circumstances he would have looked forward with some relish. The trouble was that he would have so much else to do this summer that he was not anxious to open up a special new front for Tom.

But that, he thought, must be as it may be. Leave Tom aside for the moment, and how did things look? *Pro* : his family had a good name in the country round Bishop's Cross; Alastair Dixon was on his side; Carton Weir, a rising M.P. who was privileged to whisper in important ears, would whisper in his favour; and last, least but not negligible, his own brand of conservatism was less flexible than Morrison's and might therefore find the more favour with Bishop's Cross. So far, so good. But . . . *Contra* : Rupert Percival, the local chairman, did not like him; Carton Weir's support was only valid in the House itself and might at any moment be rendered useless and even dangerous by grave scandal, for Carton persisted in playing with private fire of a kind liable to cause public conflagration; Morrison was, quite simply, a more attractive man and—what would undoubtedly operate to his advantage—a far less able one; and to top everything, Somerset's long association with *Strix,* though it would commend him in many quarters, would arouse distaste in the leaders of a rural and agricultural community—who would instantly recognise in Morrison the farmer a kindred spirit, albeit from a distant land.

All in all, the odds were unpromising, and there was no reason why Somerset should not have been speaking the truth when he told Tom that he did not give a lot for his chance. But he was not speaking the truth, as Tom had perceived, and he *did* give a lot for his chance. He gave a lot for his chance because (as Tom had also more or less per-

ceived) he had one impalpable but very powerful advantage:
he was prepared, indeed determined, to fight dirty if he saw
his way. He had yet to see it (here too Tom was right); but
his spies were posted and his aircraft hovered, and any day
now he might hope for the intelligence he needed to mount
his subtle and treacherous campaign.

Meanwhile it was important, with all that lay before him,
that he should not neglect his health; so he had made an
appointment with Maisie for half past six. Maisie, so lust-
making yet always (any time these four years) so soothing
and understanding; Maisie, mistress and mother, aphrodisiac
yet anodyne, the prostitute-priestess who incited frenzy and
then extended pity. Our Lady of the Red Lamp. (Steady
now: God be merciful to me a sinner.) And tonight, she had
promised him, a new consignment of photographs would
be in: a brilliant series of permutations of boy scouts with
girl guides. With any luck, this should help them to construct
a whole new fantasy, for the present one was wearing rather
thin. Maisie could be a cub-mistress and he would be a wolf
cub, who had wetted his camp bed . . . Jubilantly Somerset
lurched down Gower Street, barely restrained himself from
the expense of a taxi, and stuck his tongue out at the *Spectator*
bill ("Gilmour on God") as he passed.

3
CUPID AND PSYCHE

"TELL ME," said Patricia Turbot: "who else?"

"No one of importance," Tom said.

"Nevertheless I must know."

Patricia Turbot was a girl of spirit in more senses than one. To start with, as her father never tired of saying, she had a lot of spunk, and she was also endowed with a high moral and spiritual sense. It was her habit to employ the "spunk" in the propagation of the morality; and now, as she walked across the Wiltshire Downs with Tom, she was conducting an inquisition into his past. Her spiritual sense, to say nothing of female possessiveness, had told her that such an enquiry ought really to be conducted before they became engaged; but she had been afraid lest this might deter Tom from proposing at all, and had restrained both conscience and curiosity until he was safely in the bag. Since in the bag he certainly now was, with all the authority of that morning's *Times* to prove it, she felt safe at last to obey her spiritual promptings and was more than making up for the delay.

"It's a question of truth," she was saying. "I quite see that you may have had adventures—Daddy says most men do—and I promise I won't be angry. But I must know, in order. . . . How can I put it? . . . In order to exorcise the past."

"The past," said Tom, "is not exorcisable."

"All evil can be exorcised."

"So you assume my past *was* evil?"

Patricia flushed. Although she was eager to go into things,

she did not want to be caught out, just yet, making overt judgments.

"Well," Tom went on, "in your terms you are quite right. Though perhaps sinful would be a better word. But there is nothing to be done about it now. One can exorcise ghosts, I dare say, but not the actions or events in which one joined with them. Past actions are immutable; the only thing to do about them, if they are inconvenient, is to forget."

"You can atone," Patricia said. "You can ask forgiveness."

"Why should I? Many of my worst actions have in the end proved mentally—even morally—enriching."

Patricia pondered this remark with peevishness and anxiety. Truth to tell, she was out of her depth. Brought up in confinement, her only close companions a younger sister and a faithful but stupid nurse, she had been able to take her intellectual pre-eminence for granted ever since she could remember. There had been no possible rival: her mother had bolted when her sister was ten months old; while her father, a stern and able man before the world, yet encouraged and indulged Patricia in a manner which implied that even he had nothing to teach her. Apart from outlining the basic rules of social practice, he had abrogated his role as tutor and deferred to what he called "the inborn feminine wisdom" of his daughter to the extent that she firmly believed this quality to be equivalent, if not superior, to intellect. Since she had been confirmed in this fallacy by the doting of her foolish nurse, by the subservience of her young sister, and by the Platonic attentions of an evangelical governess, Patricia Turbot had grown up a prim, priggish, spoiled, ignorant and not unkindly girl, whose substantial intelligence was badly stunted from lack of the need to exert it and whose assumption of superiority had yet to meet its check.

And now here was Tom, the man to whom she was to give herself, questioning her edicts, disputing the moral and religious truths on which they were based, and, worst of all, advancing propositions which she could neither understand nor confute. It was not to be borne.

"You're evading the issue," she told him. "I have to know about the other women, and you have to tell me, so that we can start fresh. With everything clear between us."

"There are no fresh starts in life," said Tom, who was enjoying teasing her, "and you can never get anything clear. But I'll tell you about my sex life, since that's what you want, provided you'll tell me about yours."

"I've had no sex life," said Patricia smugly.

"What? No crushes on the girls at school? But of course, you had a governess. . . . Odd of your father, that."

"Daddy doesn't believe in boarding-schools for girls."

"He sent your sister to one."

"She was getting out of hand. And when she went, it was more important than ever that I should stay at home to be with him."

"So no sex life. No games of doctor with visiting cousins? No hot, straying little hands during the Christmas game of Sardines? And what about that governess? From what you say, she was rather keen."

"No gentleman would talk like that."

She really meant it too, thought Tom. But she'd started it all and she could jolly well take what was coming to her. It would be useful practice for marriage.

"Who's evading the issue now?" he said cheerfully. "I'm going to tell you something, my sweet. One of the conditions of marriage, or of any relationship between two people, is that neither must try to see too much. You can look as hard as you like at what is shown you; don't ask to see what isn't."

"But two people in love should share everything."

"Only what they both understand. If you are shown what you don't understand, you will resent it, and there will be the first breach in love. That's where the Greeks were so sensible. They did not consult their women on important matters because they knew that lack of understanding would result in jealousy."

"We were talking of something quite different," she snapped.

"Of my sexual past. It is rather squalid, though no worse than a lot of other people's, and you would not understand it. You may be able to when you are older, in which case I will tell you about it. Meanwhile, you must take my word for it that nothing which happened was important or need in any way call in question my love for you."

He turned towards her and kissed her on the forehead, then on the eyes, then on the mouth. Although she made no response, she pulled him back when he began to draw away.

"Tell me why you love me," she said.

"Because you are beautiful and good. . . . Another Greek speciality. Because you are true. And because you will be worth teaching."

"What must I learn?"

"Almost everything. When I first saw you at that party in London, I said, 'There is the beautiful princess, sleeping the sleep of ignorance. When the prince comes to wake her, kissing won't be enough : she'll need a damned good shake.' "

"She had one this afternoon."

"I know and I'm sorry. But there will be kisses too."

They walked over a meadow towards a sloping croquet lawn and a large, smug, square red house beyond it. Tom opened a door in a brick wall and stood aside for Patricia to pass. As they stepped on to the lawn, they saw Isobel Turbot, Patricia's eighteen-year-old sister, come dancing out of the shrubbery towards them, her big breasts flapping, her thin legs (so unlike Patricia's strongly fleshed ones) back-heeling sexily under her bottom, on the verge of a Charleston.

"Lovely day for snogging," she yelled.

Her respect for her elder sister had declined since nursery days; low cunning and a boarding school education had supplied her with some dubious mental acquirements, on the strength of which she had set up as the sophisticated member of the household.

"Heavy petting," she said, giggling wildly, and Charlestoned off towards the stables which adjoined the east side of the house.

"I can't think," said Patricia, "where she gets her frivolity."

"I can," said Tom, remembering mama the bolter.

"I hope there's not to be trouble," Patricia said.

"She'll sober up."

"Some of the young men she sees in London. . . . The ones that take her to those cellar places. . . .'

"She also has some more suitable friends," said Tom dryly. "That guardee she produced the other day—"

"I'm so afraid she leads them on. And the way she keeps running off to the stables to see Wilkes. . . ."

There was in her eye a fierce, prurient look, combining acute distaste with speculation and even with yearning. Quite what it boded Tom did not know, and would not until their wedding night : because this time, he had told himself, he was going to wait; it might not be wise, but it would be a novel experiment—and not the only one which he proposed. For he had noticed with interest that he was still capable of such detachment, of loving Patricia with all his heart and yet of making cynical evaluations, about how to get the best value out of her, on the side.

"Do you think she—?"

"Forget it," Tom interrupted her; "Isobel won't come to any harm. She's indestructible."

Although he could not be sure, he fancied he caught a gleam in her eye which hinted at a wish for a very different answer : she wants me to cry lechery, he thought, because her conventions forbid her to give tongue herself; there's strong magic bottled up there, and I'm the one that's fated to remove the cork and release the djinn. This prospect he found exciting, yet also remote, unreal, like the dreams he sometimes had of being in bed with the Queen.

They moved into the drawing-room for tea.

Sir Edwin Turbot placed his buttocks before the fire and then stuck them insolently out at it. He held one crumpet in the flat of his left hand while he used his right to feed another into his mouth. He did not take separate bites; he placed it between his teeth and then slowly absorbed it, like a snake with its prey. When the first crumpet had been engulfed, he surveyed the second cannily, as though he half thought it might try to escape, and said:

"Bad business about Bishop's Cross. Why does Morrison want to stick his nose in?"

"I gather," said Tom, "that he has quite a following at Bishop's Cross. Enough to put him on the short list."

"Rupert Percival should never have allowed it," said the Minister peevishly. He looked sharply at his crumpet, then whisked it to his mouth with a glint of revenge.

"They say that Percival rather likes Morrison."

Sir Edwin, mouth full, acknowledged this by raising the toe of his left' shoe and rapping smartly on the stone hearth. Patricia, who knew this indicated a sense of deprivation, poured her father an out-size cup of tea with seven lumps of sugar and proffered it with both hands.

"April," said Sir Edwin with contempt, and sucked down the last of his crumpet with a kind of inverted belch. "No more crumpets in a day or two, I suppose?" He took his tea from Patricia with a courteous nod. "April. Spring. I've always hated it. Brings nothing but trouble. And where's Isobel?" he demanded, the connection of ideas being ominously plain.

"Gone for a walk to the village, Daddy," said Patricia smoothly.

Sir Edwin decided to let this pass; but being determined to be put upon one way or the other, for he derived much pleasure from grievance, he reverted to the intrusiveness of Morrison.

"Trouble," he said with relish, as though it were the name of a family estate. "We knew just the sort of man we wanted in Alastair Dixon's place for Bishop's Cross. And when they took up this chap Somerset Lloyd-James, it couldn't have been better. People knew his father, Shagger Lloyd-James"

—for a moment he looked a bit dubious—"and they also knew that the boy was clever about money. Just what we wanted : someone to help keep the money straight. Because," he said, fixing his future son-in-law with a look that mingled irritation with respect, "even you left-wing fellows will admit that there isn't an unlimited supply. And what there is is getting jolly wonky, believe me."

Tom believed him.

"So everything was fixed up for Shagger's boy," continued the Minister in the smug tones of rational complaint, "and then what happens? Along comes the spring, and along comes trouble with it, in the shape of Mr Peter Morrison pushing himself in where he isn't wanted. Rocking the boat. Alastair Dixon says that's all he'll ever do; rock the boat. It's all he did last time he was in the House—him and that Young England Group. The fellow's just a confounded prig. Prig," he repeated delightedly, as though he himself had just invented the word.

"At least one can trust him, Minister," said Tom quietly, "which is more than can be said for Shagger's boy Somerset."

"Oh," said Sir Edwin, who, unlike many other important men, was always prepared to listen to what he didn't want to hear. "You know Lloyd-James well enough to say so?"

"For several years now I've done a lot of work for his paper. He is a brilliant editor and an amusing companion. He has a very shrewd grasp of practical economics, which is well supported by knowledge of relevant theory, both mathematical and political. He is a stylist. Despite a deplorable physique and bad utterance, he can charm. He is socially adept. He knows how to order a well-balanced and imaginative dinner, and he can cut a dash at the card table without getting himself into trouble. To know Somerset Lloyd-James is a first-rate education and at times an exquisite pleasure. But," said Tom, slapping both hands down on his thighs, "he is a killer. He is as mean as hell with money and there's nothing he won't do to get it. He is also, when it suits his book, a betrayer. He has the authentic Judas touch."

Patricia sat goggling at this insight into the world and its wickedness. Sir Edwin, who disapproved of Tom to the point of obsession but was sharp enough to know when he was on to a good thing, gave him the look of commendation which he reserved for upper servants, and remarked:

"Something of the kind used to be said about Shagger. A lot of people pooh-poohed it, but he was always regarded with caution."

"It has something to do," said Tom, "with the special morality of Roman Catholics. They have always been adept at adjusting moral issues to suit their own circumstances . . . at claiming for themselves, as adherents to the original faith, a sort of divine licence for obliquity. And in England, where their faith has been actively persecuted, they have an even stronger excuse."

Sir Edwin snorted. This was mere speculation—not what the fellow was paid for. More and more Sir Edwin found himself thinking of Tom as the hired secretary or adviser he devoutly wished Tom was—someone to be ejected with a month's notice if he got out of hand, not a permanent addition to the family. When first told of the engagement, Sir Edwin had been dumbfounded; but the habit of letting Patricia have her way had become so much a matter of course over the years that it was unthinkable that her intention should be thwarted or her wisdom questioned. For had it not been he himself who had always fostered and underwritten her pretensions? Too late to impugn them now. And so, conscious of his weakness and studying to compensate for it by craft, he had devised, in self-defence, a fiction whereby he accepted Tom as a disagreeable but talented assistant, whose personal shortcomings (the long curly hair, the sexual knowingness, the left-wing attitudes) were none of his affair provided only the young man did his job. Quite how he was going to adapt this system of deceiving himself when Tom and Patricia were actually married, he had not yet thought. Meanwhile, however, he contrived to tolerate Tom as a general tolerates a conceited but able aide-de-camp. Which did not mean, he now told himself crossly, that he had to listen to the fellow's theories about the psychology of Papists.

"I should prefer a more concrete and factual assessment," he said pompously. "Somerset Lloyd-James: in what respects has he *shown* he is not to be trusted? Never mind his religion."

"I mind it very much," said Tom: "without it he'd just be another amusing rogue. But his religion lends him a conviction of righteousness which makes him pitiless. Nobody's safe: not friend, lover, servant . . . dog."

"Please to be specific."

"Very well. Usury—at fantastic rates."

"It takes two to agree the rates."

"Granted. What about bribery?"

"Give me an instance."

"He once offered me three times the normal fee," said Tom blandly, "to fudge the facts for an article he wanted written."

"Editorial privilege," rasped Sir Edwin. "They're allowed to be selective."

"Attempted blackmail then?"

This time Sir Edwin turned thoughtful.

"For money?"

"There was money in it. But mainly for power."

"*That*," the Minister said, "is certainly something. You can vouch for it?"

"I was cat's paw . . . I didn't realise till too late."

"You seem to have been much . . . involved . . . with Somerset Lloyd-James."

"One can't help it if one lives in certain circles. He haunts them like a ghoul."

"But *now* . . . ?" put in Patricia hopefully.

"*Now*," said Tom, "I am by way of being an expert on him. But I still have to look sharp. It's like dealing with Proteus: you don't know what shape he's going to take from one second to the next."

"Hmm," mused the Minister. "Not the sort of chap one

puts up for one's club."

"He'd get in just the same if he set his mind on it."

"But for all this," said the Minister, "I don't care for the idea of Bishop's Cross adopting Morrison. He'll stir up that Young England Group again, for a start. And damn it all, it's not three years since he resigned because of that scandal."

"Nobody believes in the scandal."

"Some of the public will. The public memory is as long as it's inaccurate . . . for any kind of dirt, that is. It's just too *soon* for Morrison, and that's all about it. His name should never have been kept on the list at Central Office."

"From what I hear," said Tom, teasing faintly, "there was a number of very important people who took great care that it should be."

This reminder that Sir Edwin's disciplinary hold on the Conservative Party was not as absolute as he would have wished produced, at last, a sense of injury too strong to be merely pleasurable. The Minister put his cup down with a crack and strode to the door.

"Black tie for dinner," he said, as though proclaiming an interdict. "Eight for half past. The Canteloupes are coming with the dowager and a house guest. Chap called Detterling, who says he knows you and that Jew publisher of yours." For a moment Sir Edwin looked as if he had been about to institute a progrom but had thought better of it at the last minute. Instead, "Please not to pass the port too freely," he enjoined with gloomy rancour: "Canteloupe's head does not improve."

"So when," asked Lady Canteloupe with a saccharine smile, "is the wedding to be?"

"Time enough to think about that," Sir Edwin said, "when we're through with the general election."

"The wedding's to be at mid-summer," said Patricia firmly.

Sir Edwin turned up his eyes and stuck his spoon into the

middle of his peach melba, with the air of a soldier planting a sabre to mark a fallen comrade's newly filled grave.

"I'm going to be chief bride's maid," said Isobel. Even the ice-cream running down her chin seemed somehow to have sexual significance. "Patty and I have fixed on the dearest little short green dresses."

"Flowers?" said the Dowager Marchioness Canteloupe, mopping up the last of her melba juice with a stray piece of toast.

"Carnations."

"*Green* carnations?" said Lord Canteloupe, who affected to think that all young men with long curly hair and left-wing opinions must of necessity be sodomites.

"Yes," said Tom; "we've already arranged to have them dyed."

Lord Canteloupe laughed generously. He liked young men with spirit, whatever their social provenance, nor did he give a tinker's fart, as he himself might have put it, whether Tom was a sodomite or not.

"Hear that, mother?" he shouted—quite gratuitously, for the old lady's hearing was perfect. "They're having them specially dyed."

"*Very* expensive," said the dowager, looking maliciously at Sir Edwin.

"What nonsense," the Minister mumbled from the head of the table.

"Don't be such an old stick, Edwin," said the Marquis. "You can perfectly well afford it. Now, suppose you were like me, with the Lord Lieutenancy hanging over you. . . . *That's* going to be like having a wedding every week."

The Marquis Canteloupe would never be Lord Lieutenant, because he drank too much and his flushed bruiser's face frightened the ladies. In sober daylight, he knew this very well and did not resent it. He had the consolation of being an immensely rich man who was daily growing richer, this from the exhibition of his house and gardens, which he directed with a kind of stunted genius: for since he combined considerable native shrewdness with the tastes of a retarded adolescent, he knew just what would appeal to other adolescents, and arranged rallies and spectacles which drew them in tens of thousands from all over Wessex. But although the money and notoriety thus accruing more than compensated him for lack of official place, there came a stage every evening (after about three whiskies and two thirds of a bottle of wine) when he suddenly conceived that as the senior nobleman in the area he *ought* to be offered the Lord Lieutenancy, and from this it was a short step to claiming that he very soon would be. Thus far the illusion was harmless; unfortunately, however, brandy in any quantity would then lead him to reflect that the long postponement of the honour was a deliberate slight to his order; a grudge that issued in a spiteful peevishness, which he would express by accusing his host of conspiring to keep him short of drink. Since the accusation was often well founded, it was hard to rebut save by making him free of the decanter; and since such indulgence only inspired him to comment the more cuttingly on the antecedent stinginess, the problem was considered insoluble throughout the county.

The Turbots' answer to the dilemma was to invite the Canteloupes as seldom as possible, old friends though they were; but as Canteloupe had recently threatened, in a fit of boyish mischief, to take himself and his strawberry leaves over to the Labour benches of the Lords, Sir Edwin had felt obliged to undertake a series of entertainments to flatter and dissuade him. The best time to do this was over the port—while Canteloupe was still good-humouredly convinced that he would soon be Lord Lieutenant and before later doses of brandy had turned the conviction to rancour. When, therefore, the dowager had finally finished dunking at her melba, Sir Edwin gestured at Patricia, who rose and led off the ladies. The Minister now turned briskly to the reclamation of Canteloupe's political loyalty, leaving Tom to talk to the Canteloupes' house guest, Captain Detterling (M.P.), with whom he had been vaguely acquainted for some years and had recently come to know more closely as the new colleague of his publisher.

"I suppose I ought to congratulate you on this engagement," Detterling said, "but the very notion of people getting married irritates me beyond endurance. Nothing personal, you understand. It's just that the best of couples behave so smugly—as though they thought they'd done something original."

"I entirely agree," said Tom: "but as the years go on I feel the need for a little smugness in my life. I promise you I'll not pretend that I'm doing anything original."

"You won't be able to help it," said Detterling morosely. "It's a necessary condition of bringing yourself to get married at all. And another thing: all married couples—even working class ones—seem to think that the mere fact of marriage confers status . . . privilege. I put up with a lot of it in the Army. Quite junior men, subalterns, would ring up to say that they couldn't do this or that—whether it was playing squash or going on a night exercise—because it didn't suit their wives. Seemed to think that was the last word to be said."

"So what did you do?"

"Told 'em not to be so damned silly and be there on time, *or else*. . . . It made me quite unpopular."

"The theory is," said Tom, "that bachelors lead a pleasant and carefree existence, and ought to make allowances for those who are rearing the new generation."

"Nobody asked them to," said Detterling, his voice brittle with irritation: "in fact before long people will be begging them not to. The country's too full already; a man can hardly *move*. But still these bloody women sit about breeding like mice, and then expect to be told they've done something clever."

"It *is* rather onerous," said Tom: "they must be given some comfort."

"Why? It's not compulsory. People just don't think straight. Old friend of mine turned up at the club the other day with a face as long as a riding boot. Wife expecting third child, he told us: got to give up the club, give up his cricket tour in the summer, even give up his occasional round of golf. Why? I said. Money, he said, and went into a long spiel about education policies and the Lord knows what. But the thing was, he thought he was being dutiful, that everyone ought to say what a splendid fellow he was. In fact he was just one more bloody fool, and so I told him. You didn't have to get married in the first place, I told him, and even if you did you don't have to spawn like a frog. He was quite put out, I can tell you."

"Have you no crumb of consolation for me?" Tom said mildly.

"Yes," shouted Canteloupe, who had been trying to engage their attention from the far end of the table: "whenever you sleep with another woman it'll be adultery and not fornication. Sounds more stylish, don't you think? Now *pass the port.*"

Detterling made a long arm and passed it. Sir Edwin gave a persecuted look, seized the decanter as soon as Canteloupe had filled from it, and impounded it in the crook of his arm with the officiousness of an excise man.

"Drink runs in the Canteloupe family," Detterling explained softly to Tom. "Canteloupe isn't too bad, but his brothers and sisters are in and out of the bin like cuckoos on a clock."

"You seem to know a lot about them."

"I'm a second cousin. Canteloupe asked me down to look at some memoirs his father wrote. Although he's as rich as Midas he's always sniffing round for a little extra, so he reckons I can get Gregory Stern to publish them."

"And will you?"

Detterling turned his eyes up.

"I'll see they're read."

"Someone else," said Tom, "is shortly going to ask the same favour. I'm afraid I put him on to you. Major Fielding Gray."

This time Detterling did not turn his eyes up. He narrowed them into a look which conveyed a shrewd interest rather oddly mixed with remorse.

"I heard what happened," he muttered. "He should never have been in the Army. Not as a regular."

"Will his books be any good?"

"Could be," said Detterling non-committally, having quickly reverted to his normal manner. "He was a clever chap. Something had gone wrong—I never quite knew what."

"But you'll help him?"

"Of course. We served together. Pass the port," he called sharply to his host.

"Yes," boomed Canteloupe; "before we all die of thirst."

"The ladies. . . ." began the Minister.

"Can wait. Port," said Canteloupe. The decanter passed round. Canteloupe filled, drained, filled again, and then clasped both hands round the decanter, like a rich child who refuses to part with his toy to a poorer one. Sir Edwin, blinking with self-pity, resumed his blandishments.

"We'll have to get him out soon," murmured Detterling to Tom; "but one can't sit with an empty glass all night just because there's a drunk in the party. I'll tip Molly the wink to have the car called early." He looked meditatively at Tom. "And since there's something I want to tell you before I go," he said, "I'd best tell you now. You know Max de Freville? The man who runs the big chemmy game?"

"I've seen him occasionally."

"He's by way of being a chum of mine. The thing is that lately he's developed a very odd sort of hobby. A new game, you might say."

"I should have thought," said Tom, puzzled, "that he'd had enough of games."

"That's just it. He's bored and needs distraction, and this is new and different. It's a kind of power game. He collects information. He doesn't use it, he just collects it, so that he can feel he's got to the bottom of things and that if he *did* want to interfere. . . . You see what I mean?"

"Roughly."

"Well," said Detterling. "He's already got a lot of sources and he's busy getting more. He shows me a lot of the stuff, you see. And I thought you should know that he's got an informant in this house. I mean, if you're going to marry into the family. . . ."

"Not . . . not the Minister?" said Tom with a giggle.

"No. Isobel."

"Isobel?"

"It seems she got into one of his gaming parties with a boy friend one night. The boy friend guaranteed her, so although she was obviously under age Max let her play. She lost a thousand odd, couldn't pay of course, and didn't want Max to make her look silly by coming down on the boy friend for it. So they did a deal. Max would cancel the debt and Isobel would send in regular bulletins about the Minister's home life."

"I can't think that amounts to much."

"I don't know. Dinner parties like this. Canteloupe's a name, to say nothing of Llewyllyn. And as Max says, the most boring information very often contains the essential clue to something really big . . . the missing number in the combination. . . ."

"Isobel's a perfect little madam," Tom said. "Any day now she'll get herself knocked up by an errand boy."

"Max thinks she's cleverer than people know. So I thought I'd give you the tip."

"But you say de Freville doesn't actually use what he's told."

"He could turn dangerous later. He's vain, bitter, obsessed. . . . So if I were you, I'd keep clear of Isobel."

Detterling rose as if he himself had been host.

"Come on, cousin Canteloupe," he said. "You can't sit there sozzling the whole evening."

"No," said cousin Canteloupe. "I'm sick of port anyhow. I need a little brandy." He pushed the port decanter peevishly away. "A lot of brandy," he emended.

In the drawing-room the four women were discussing hymns for the wedding. Isobel had just contributed "Perverse and foolish oft I strayed," when the men entered in some disorder which had been occasioned by Canteloupe's neglect to button his fly after going to the loo. When reminded, he had simply opened it wider and announced that these days there was never anything worth seeing. Sir Edwin, who was more put out by this than anyone else, had constituted himself a movable screen between Canteloupe and the public, and was now bobbing uneasily from side to side in order to sustain the role. Fortunately or otherwise, he did not have to do so long; for Canteloupe turned his back on the company as soon as he entered the room and made a rush for the sideboard, where he announced his intention of trying every single bottle. After signing to Lady C., who nodded wanly, Detterling went to the telephone to order the car up from the village; while the dowager sat back happily, long since inured, like a member of a Greek chorus, to any form of disaster—and indeed rather grateful to it for passing the time. Desultory conversation continued in front of the fire. Patricia took up some sewing and attacked it with moral fibre. There was an occasional slurp from the sideboard.

"Kent has a good chance in the County Championship this year," said Detterling as he re-entered.

Sir Edwin, who had been interrupted in the middle of his favourite story about Lord Curzon, looked like an affronted guinea hen. What he didn't realise was that Detterling's remark was a special code for warning Lady Canteloupe that the car was on the way without letting her husband know; for if he twigged that he was being taken home early he used to hide or lock himself in the lavatory, and had once even pretended to have a fit, in the hope that a particularly parsimonious host would come across with more brandy. This evening all went well. On receipt of a second code-message, "I wonder why Colin Cowdrey's bottom is so huge," ("*What?*" said Sir Edwin), Lady Canteloupe and the dowager moved into the hall to put on their coats. After another two minutes Lady C.'s head came round the door, to indicate that the car had arrived and the dowager was safely inside it. This was the testing moment: the essential thing was to get Canteloupe out of the house and into the car before he realised what was happening and could start a scene. Expedients ranging from cries of "Fire" to promises of naked ladies on the lawn had all been used and superannuated in their time; and it was getting difficult to think of anything effective. Oddly enough, however, on this occasion Lord Canteloupe, without a word being said to him, suddenly muttered, "Car's here, I suppose," and moved from the sideboard towards the door with no attempt at protest.

"I'm going quietly," he said, "so nobody need worry." He struck a match and carried it shakily to his half-smoked cigar; the flame never came within six inches of its target, but he seemed satisfied with his effort and sucked contentedly on the dead tube. "And I'll tell you why I'm going quietly," he continued between sucks: "my car's not the only one out there. If you look through the window by the sideboard, you'll see that you are about to be visited by three car-loads of police. The fun—such as it ever was—is over for tonight."

Canteloupe had exaggerated. There were only two cars, and only one of them connected with the police. His lordship was further mistaken in supposing that he could slip away quietly, as it was himself who was wanted.

"Quite a rumpus the other night" (as Isobel was later to write to Max de Freville). "Canteloupe dined here with Lady C. and the old woman, and by ten o'clock he was absolutely squiffed. Just as they were all going home about a million cars came up the drive brimming with policemen. Lord C. is scared stiff of the police, rather odd for someone in his position, but apparently they were beastly to him on Boat Race night years ago. Anyway, there he was scowling away on the front steps with his trousers open from top to bottom and just about to lunge into his Rolls, when out of one of the cars which *wasn't* a police car steps a squat, queeny little chap in one of those joke dinner jackets which look like all cuffs and collar.

" 'Ah, Lord Canteloupe,' says this nance; 'I thought we'd never find you. These country lanes . . . like a labyrinth, my dear . . . my dear Lord Canteloupe, that is.'

"So Canteloupe stands there with his underpants streaming in the breeze and says nothing, then out comes Daddy in a frightful bait, takes one look at the siss in the D.J., and says :

" 'Oh, it's you, Weir. What the devil's all this ?'

"So then lovey-dovey, who turns out to be an M.P. called Carton Weir, explains that he couldn't find the way and had to get this brigade of bobbies to guide him. It seems that he's by way of being the Downing Street go-between and he's got an important message. So then Daddy preens himself up, thinking it's for him, but it isn't at all, it's for poor old pissy Canteloupe. So then the policemen salute like crazy and we all go inside again, having first dredged Lady C. and the other old cow out of the Rolls, and Lady C. tells C. to do up his trouser buttons, and C. as good as thumbs his nose at her, and Daddy looks ready to shit with temper because *he's* not the centre of attention, and C. looks so full of juice that it's clear he can't understand a single thing that's being said to him. He's funny when he's sozzled, he can talk more or less like he was sober but he can't take anything in. Anyway, the end of it is that Daddy and Canteloupe and the faggot go off to Daddy's study, and Patty and me and Patty's boy Tom are left to make polite noises at Lady C., the dowager, and some chum of C.'s called Captain Detterling who they brought along to din-din . . . rather a poppet this one, a bit long in the tooth but with that *distinguished* hair, he must have done his captain bit about ten generations ago. Both the captain and Tom know all about the poovy man in the tux, and the dowager, who's as sharp as the razor she shaves with, asks about a trillion questions, while Lady C. looks as sour as goosegogs because she's afraid her old man is in no

shape to rise to the occasion. . . . Which it turns out about
three hours later is quite some occasion, because Lord C. is
being made a kind of mini-minister, a Parliamentary Secretary
I think they call it. All drop dead."

"Parliamentary Secretary for the Development of British
Recreational Resources," said Sir Edwin to Tom when the
guests had at last departed. "It seems that this is an
experimental appointment to give the Party a . . . new look,
as they call it . . . for the election."

"You yourself were consulted?"

"Of course," said Sir Edwin. He went to the sideboard
and mixed himself a very stiff whisky. "And I must tell you
straight away that I was violently opposed to it. It appears
that my wishes have been disregarded."

Sir Edwin was in many ways an honest man. Although he
often found it expedient not to form an opinion, he was
jealous and eager for those which he did hold, and he was,
moreover, prepared to own to their consequences. In admitting that he had been snubbed he was paying Tom no special
compliment : he had done and said what he felt was right, and
anyone who enquired into the matter should be told so.

"It's not even," Sir Edwin continued, "as if he was a reliable member of the Party. He treats the Lords as 'a jolly
good laugh'—his own expression. As you know, he's so lacking in responsibility that he was even threatening to change
sides."

"For a jolly good laugh, presumably. Perhaps that's why
they've made the appointment. To keep him loyal."

"That's not Party discipline as I was taught it."

"True. But these stately home impresarios are right in the
public eye. They are considered to be modern, progressive,
with it. Canteloupe's defection would have been *noticed*. . . .
Though for the life of me I can't think why Carton Weir had
to drive down here in the middle of the night."

"Likes a bit of drama. He was charged, he told me, to

acquaint Canteloupe with the P.M.'s intention as soon as possible and persuade him to accept as a matter of vital urgency. Said he thought it might be easier if the man was mellow. As if there was any doubt of Canteloupe accepting."

"Did he know *what* he was accepting?"

"He affected to think that he was being made Lord Lieutenant . . . but he'll get it straight when he wakes up with Weir in the house. I gather Weir's to represent him in the Commons."

"That's shrewd. With Weir to shore him up he can't go far wrong."

"All the same," said Sir Edwin clenching both fists, "it won't do. It's too bad and it won't do. This isn't the eighteenth century, and you can't appoint clowns like Canteloupe to govern. If he wouldn't do as Lord Lieutenant of the County, he won't do as a Parliamentary Secretary."

"With respect," said Tom slowly, "I think the P.M. has been rather subtle. The fact is that Canteloupe has shown a conspicuous talent for entertaining the young. He knows the kind of rubbish they want and he gives it to them in just the right package. Given enough scope, he can lay the same sort of thing on for the young of the whole nation . . . for all those who are just old enough to vote, or soon will be. And this in a so called age of leisure. It could help to give your crowd just the look they want—attractive, forward-looking, the party of progress and pleasure. An illusion of course, but it'll take everyone some time to twig that, and by then there'll be some other bright bubble to gawp at."

"None of which is government as I was taught it."

"Well, there you are," said Tom. "If you will support people like Somerset Lloyd-James and keep out honest men like Morrison, you must expect this kind of thing."

"Hrrmmph," said the Minister, and stumped off to bed.

4
PAN AND SILENUS

Mark Lewson wrote to Max de Freville from Venice. "What a dear little chap Lykiadopoulos is. Like the Michelin man and as bald as a balloon, a life-size toy for rich children to play with. Not a cold fish either, as you'd expect a Baccarat banker to be, but warm and frothy. I suppose that's what fools the punters. 'We *can't* lose money,' I can hear them all say, 'playing against a sweet little man like that', and in they go laughing; and even after they have lost, it must seem more like giving it to a good cause, as though Lykiadopoulos were an orphan or something, so they feel all warm inside and hurry back to lose more. He really is a poppet.

"But of course you know all about that. So down to work. I arrived in Venice the day after I left you and booked in at the Cavaletto, not quite the luxiest thing going, but I'm afraid the Contessa and I got ourselves a bad name in most of the bigger ones. The next morning betimes I rang up Lykiadopoulos at the Danieli and begged leave to present your note of introduction. The telephone nearly cracked with excitement, because it seems the poor old thing is very much alone in Venice as the police are so severe that he has to be horribly careful. He didn't say so in so many words, of course; but I gathered that the idea of a nice, clean tourist chum with a British passport was very *bien vu*.

"So we met for a delicious lunch in Harry's and got on together like a kibbutz on fire. But then the trouble started. Lykiadopoulos (call me Lyki) wanted me to move in on the Danieli, and that was all right with me—had I not known that the minute I set foot in the place the manager would storm out with a load of the Contessa's duds drawn on the Banco di Spirito Santo, which would really be v. shaming in front of a new friend. So what to do? Well, clearly I'd got to get the entrée to the Danieli sooner or later, because if the letter was anywhere it was probably there, so I made a sort of semi-clean breast. There had, I simpered, been a little misunderstanding some years ago, when the currency regulations were still very fierce. . . . The dear, tactful, generous fellow took that at face value and volunteered to square the management. Quite what he did, I don't know; if they produced the Contessa's stumers, he never mentioned it then or later; but the upshot was that within three quarters of an hour I found myself installed in a suite at the Danieli, with everyone from the manager to the lift boy fawning on me like the Pope. My bag came over from the Cavaletto on a sort of magic carpet, the bill there was fixed with a flick of someone's finger, and I was to regard myself, it seemed, as the guest of "Signor Lyki" at the Danieli Royal Excelsior Hotel until (and here, despite the tooth-flashing, there was *precision*) the Signore moved out to the Lido to be nice and handy for running his bank.

"Well, a suite with a drawing-room amounts, in hotel convention, to a built-in chaperon, so you'll have guessed the rest. Hardly had I unpacked before there was the pitter-patter of Signor Lyki's little feet. *Son cosas de la vida*. And really life is quite pleasant. There are delicious meals and amusing trips to look at churches, both in Venice and on the islands, about which Lyki is remarkably informative. His speciality is the Ghetto—did you know the Venetians claim to have invented the system?—where we have just spent a very long morning. Lyki is so energetic about his sight-seeing, to say nothing of his other amusements, that unless I find the letter and get out I shall soon be a total wreck.

"And what about the letter? you'll ask. Nothing doing so far. For a start, he always comes to *my* room; and so far, if you can believe this, I haven't even been able to find out where or which his is. If I ask at the desk, they just ring through ("*Camera di Signor Lyki*—never a number) and tell him I want him, whereupon he either joins me straight away or fixes a meeting place over the buzzer—never, although I constantly suggest it, his own room. Very odd. The other tack I've tried is drawing him out about his gambling career, in the hope we'll get on to des Moulins and the letter. No luck. He's told me stories—v. good ones—about every trick in the game, but nothing about des Moulins and his *coup de dishonneur*.

"So I'll just have to keep trying. I've been in the Danieli for three days now, which gives me another six, I make it, before he moves out to the hotel on the Lido. He might take me with him but I doubt it. I gather that while the bank's running he leads a dedicated life, and anyhow I don't know that I could stand up to the wear and tear. Six days then: I'll do my best but I guarantee nothing. And incidentally, if you meant what you said about making it worth my while to keep you informed, a little on account would not come amiss. I have to make *some* pretence of paying for the odd luncheon. By telegraph to the American Express is quickest— or so the Contessa always said. And that's it for now. We're just off out to the Lido to have din-dins and go to the Casino a preliminary reconnaissance, I gather, to see what nick the place is in. . . ."

Max de Freville, just back from Menton, made a note on a desk-diary to send Lewson £50 by wire the following morning. Although the information was thin, Lewson had at least got inside the castle if not yet inside the keep. If he had spoken the truth about his efforts to date, he deserved a refresher now: if he had been lying, he would get his deserts later.

"Not bad," said the Marquis Canteloupe, surveying a hundred square yards of thickly carpeted office complete with cocktail cabinet and day bed, "not bad at all. So what's to do now, eh?"

"I dare say the civil servants will have something to say about that," said Carton Weir; "but as far as *we're* concerned, we want a bigger and brighter image of government-sponsored public recreation."

"More opera?" said Canteloupe dubiously. "That kind of thing?"

"No," said Weir : "*not* that kind of thing."

"And where do the civil servants come in?"

"Advice. Ways, means, money. Legal difficulties. There are a lot of laws against entertainment, you'll find."

"Let's get them repealed then."

"Oh dear me, no. Although the public demands to be entertained, it would be most upset if it thought the government approved of pleasure. The public must be entertained in spite of itself : in spite of the opposition which it will feel in duty bound to put up."

"But you just said it *demands* to be entertained."

"So it does. But in the teeth of its own puritanical traditions. So first of all it wants to be reassured. You've got to convince it that entertainment is somehow a social right, almost a duty, like having its kiddies educated. That will make it all respectable. But pleasure for the sake of pleasure . . . oh dear me, no."

"I'd thought," said Canteloupe, shyly, "of government brothels."

"*No,*" said Weir.

"But all this talk of teenagers riddled with clap. *My* brothels would be medically vetted."

"NO."

"I see. . . . State Casinos?"

"In six or seven years, perhaps. Provided you charge a 50 per cent tax on winnings and only allow hard seats."

"Ah," said Canteloupe, "I'm beginning to get the idea. Now what about this? Government-sponsored caravan sites for holidays. Make a filthy mess of some well known beauty

spot—they'll love that—and then publish a lot of balls about
The People enjoying Its Rights in the Countryside, that kind
of blab. Jam the bloody caravans as close together as
possible—you know how they love being crowded—make a
song and a dance about being good neighbours, give a prize
for the best behaved family, and perhaps throw in compulsory P.T."

"That's it," said Carton Weir: "that's just the ticket."

"Further to my last," wrote Mark Lewson from Venice,
"we're a little warmer now though hardly hot.

"After I signed off the other evening, we duly set sail in
Lyki's motor-boat to take a butchers at the Casino. The only
plan I had, and a pretty poor one, was to wait till we got back
to the Danieli and then follow Lyki to his room, so that at
least I'd know where it was. If he caught me, I was going to
pretend to be tight and say I'd lost my way; so the first thing
I had to do was to prop myself against the Casino bar and
consume, or appear to consume, an immense number of
drinkies.

"The end of it was that I really did get tight. Lyki, who
disapproves of drinking in casinos, had gone prowling off on
a tour of inspection, and I was enjoying an interval in my
dipso act, when in came Burke Lawrence, the advertising
man. Now, believe it or not, Burke is one of the few people
on earth who might be said to owe *me* money, because the
Contessa, who was a nutty old cineast, once put up a few
hundred quid for some amateur film he was trying to make.
Whenever we meet he always buys me champagne to stop
me going on about what happened to the money, and this
time was no exception. In fact he called for a magnum. Very
pleased with himself was Burke. It seems that he's in Venice
to help organise some festival to do with advertising films—
I believe the Venetians would throw a Festival of Plumbing
if anyone suggested it—and he regards this as professional
recognition of a high order. The only trouble, apparently,

is that he's lumbered with an out of date model called Penelope Holbrook, who was once his mistress and now follows him around wherever he goes making scenes and whining for work. Not that she needs it, as her ex-husband pays her a handsome alimony, but she's anxious to make a come-back. This evening, however, he reckons he's safe, because one of the other geniuses to do with the festival has made a pass at her and she's busy goosing him up in high hope of an offer.

"So there we were, tucking happily into Burke Lawrence's magnum of fizz and talking about the dear old days, when a sort of frisson goes over the entire room and we see an agitated crowd forming round the top roulette table at the far end. And guess what's going on. Lyki, looking like a man in a fever, is plastering the table with maximum bets all round the number 20. 50,000 lire *en plain*, 100,000 for each of the *chevaux*, and so on through the *carré* bets and the *transversals* right out to the even chances—*noir, pair, passe*—on each of which he places one and three quarter million. God alone knows what's got into him. As soon as the chef sees what he's up to, he suggests to Lyki that he should call the bet and deposit the total sum needed with the croupier, thus leaving room on the cloth for someone else to play; but Lyki's beyond listening and just goes on wanging down plaques as though they were dominoes until he's made the entire spiel. You never saw such a sight. The table piled high with plastic of every colour in the spectrum, Lyki's eyes glaring through the smoke like fog lamps, the croupiers all sweating buckets, and the spectators squawking and yakking like a parrot house. Only the chef kept calm; he was a chap with a pan like Tiresias who'd obviously seen the lot in his day and was beyond being impressed by anything. Which was just as well, because otherwise they'd still be sitting there; he had to flick his fingers three times before he could get the croupier responsible to pick up the ball and throw for the coup, and even then the poor fellow bungled it and had to stop the wheel and start all over again.

"But eventually we were off. Wheel turning, ball whirring round the grove at the top of the bowl, dead silence now, Lyki's whole body trembling like a witch-doctor throwing a seizure, ball begins to drop, bounces on one of the diamonds, rides for a second on the rim of the wheel, and then *clunk*.

" '*Uno*,' calls the croupier; '*le premier*.'

"So that was that, it seemed. But as you of all people will know, one lies next to twenty on the wheel; and when the wretch looked again, his face turned a rich green and started sort of oozing. Whereupon the chef took over.

" '*Venti*,' he called after a stern inspection of the wheel, '*vingt, zwanzig*, twenty. *Noir, pair, passe*.'

"After this they led Lyki away to the manager's office to make him out a cheque. He re-emerged, rather flushed, about twenty minutes later, came over to Burke and me, ordered more champagne, and started lapping it up like a figure of farce. And he didn't forget his chums. Pretty soon we're all floating in the stuff, and what with the brandy I've already put down in order to pass my drunk act off on Lyki, and what with the gamblers pressing round to gawk at him and touch him for luck, I'm beginning to feel mildly hysterical.

" 'The first time,' Lyki was saying, 'the first time I have ever drunk wine in the Rooms. And you know why? It is not the money, though that is pleasant. It is that I have now fulfilled one great ambition: to make the *Grand Coup de la Table*, to back the winning number in every possible way, all seventeen bets, and to do it at the maximum. Roulette is a miserable game, a game for old women and children, but this I have always wished to do, as some men wish to climb a mountain or sail alone across great oceans.'

" 'An expensive hobby,' Burke suggested.

" 'Yes. But this evening I was certain. It was as though a little devil was standing on the number and beckoning me. . . . I was always lucky.'

"At this stage our pleasant evening was sharply interrupted. A tall scowling woman, with a low forehead and mean, prying nostrils, marched up to Burke and demanded to know what the hell he thought he was doing. This was the passée model, Penelope Holbrook; it seemed her escort for the evening had ditched her soon after dinner and had not been at all helpful about her career. Bad temper and disappointment had turned her very ugly, and the wonder was, from where I sat, that she'd ever made it as a model at all. Why Burke has anything to do with such a frightful bitch I can't imagine; he was clearly irritated by her arrival, as he'd taken a fancy to Lyki and *vice v.*, but he treated her with considerable courtesy all the same, got her a chair, introduced her all round, and never once batted an eyelid though she was pumping pure poison at him without stopping to draw breath.

" 'My whole career at stake,' she was saying, 'and you have to sneak off here without telling me.'

" 'But my dear,' said Burke meekly, 'you said you wouldn't need me.'

" 'You should have let me know where you were. So that I could get you if I wanted you.'

" 'I did try to tell you. But you were so absorbed in the prospect of your dinner with Perry—'

" '—Perry,' she snorted. 'Another dried up queen. No wonder it's so hard for a girl to get proper recognition.'

"She was one of those women who've got homosexuals on the brain. You know the sort of thing : anyone who doesn't fawn round *them* all day long is automatically a criminal pervert and ought to be put in chains.

" 'Get me a coke,' was her next contribution.

"Lyki offered her champagne, but no, she'd got some idea that Coca-Cola was the smart thing, she'd read that story about the top model who'd insisted on drinking it at Maxim's and afterwards married a Viscount, so *she* was going to have Coca-Cola too. Brother, what a woman. You could just hear her tiny little brain clicking over as she wondered what was the surest way of making herself the centre of attention and spoiling everyone's evening at the same time. Eventually she thought up a real winner.

" 'Since we're here,' she said, 'we may as well gamble.

Give me some money.'

"So Burke passed over 10,000 lire.

" 'I said money.'

"Burke gave her 10,000 more, whereupon she sniffed at Lyki and me as though we were samples of inferior cocaine and stalked off to one of the chemmy tables, with Burke trotting after her like a page boy.

" 'We should see this,' Lyki said. 'It will be interesting. That woman lives in her fantasies, and her present fantasy is that she is an ex-king's mistress losing a spectacular sum in full view of all at Monte Carlo.'

"How right he was. As soon as she got to the table she called 'banco' to 60,000, lost, handed over the 20,000 Burke had given her and 40,000 more which he reluctantly produced, and then called 'suivi'.

" 'No, dear,' Burke whispered, 'I haven't got it.'

" 'You'll just have to find it, won't you?'

"God knows what sort of hold she'd got on him. It was certainly a great deal stronger than that of a former mistress. Whatever the answer, Burke went quite haggard; his face drooped in despair and anguish just because he hadn't got 120,000 lire on him for this ghastly woman to toss away at chemmy. Not that she was taking the slightest notice of what he said. She'd already picked up her cards and asked for another—which she didn't get because the bank held a natural. So far from being put out, she was obviously delighted, and stood there triumphantly flicking her fingers at Burke for the money, for all the world (as Lyki had foretold) like a royal courtesan.

"But Burke just hadn't got it. Flick, flick, flick went her fingers, while he looked miserably at her and shrugged, terrified at what was coming. After a bit even she got the message; at first she looked at him like Medusa, then she stuck her nose in the air, started to walk away from the table —and was stopped by two polite men in dinner jackets. Burke stood there trembling and moaning; and finally it was Lyki who moved in to mend matters.

" 'You have no money?' he said.

" 'No.'

" 'At your hotel?'

"She was ready to spit with rage. If there's one thing a woman like that can't stand, it's being made to pay her own losses.

" 'Ask him,' she said, pointing at Burke.

" 'No,' said Burke, shuddering. 'I've enough, just enough, to pay the hotel when I leave. You had 60,000,' he said piteously : 'I did tell you there wasn't any more.'

" 'You see?' said Lyki. 'Either you must pay yourself or you will be charged by the police. In this country it is a criminal offence.'

" 'All right,' she said, snarling like a vampire in one of those films : 'I'll send the money in the morning.'

" 'One of these gentlemen,' corrected Lyki, 'will probably choose to accompany you now.'

"So that was the end of her. Off she went with one of the casino officials, while poor Burke scurried and fussed about behind them. God help *him*, I thought; and I should add that I'll be very interested to find out, if ever I can, just what's between that pair.

"Well, you'll have been wondering what all this has to do with the letter. Simple. What with the excitement of his coup and all the champagne and the pleasure of putting down Madame Holbrook, Lyki was disposed to be garrulous; and since the Holbrook incident had set his mind working that way he started up about similar cases of default. Now, the significant thing was that though he told me about several of these, involving sums of anywhere between ten pounds and ten thousand, he never once mentioned des Moulins. Unhelpful, you say? Certainly; but at least I now knew that he regarded the matter so warily that even in his unwonted cups he wasn't going to tell the story. Conclusion : he was nervous. Further conclusion (tentative) : other people had found out about the letter and were after it. Perhaps he even suspected me. Final conclusion :—no good pussy-footing round playing at Raffles in the Royal Danieli. If he was being so cagey, the letter was probably locked up somewhere very safe; perhaps his bank. There was only one thing to do: come right out with what I knew, watch his reaction, and play it by ear from there.

" 'You know, sweetheart,' I said, 'you've left something out. I know you were taken for a big ride by a frog called des Moulins—and I know how he paid you off.'

"I'm not sure quite what I'd expected. Shock, suspicion, anger. Fear, perhaps, or just curiosity. But he showed none of these. He just looked terribly, terribly sad.

" 'Poor des Moulins,' he said. 'He was a truly religious man. That's what ruined him.'

" 'Religious?'

" 'He was for ever trying to ascertain the will of God. You don't read Dante? No, none of the young do now. "In His Will is our Peace." Since des Moulins thinks it was God's will that he should be totally destroyed, he has accepted his degradation almost with rapture.'

" 'And it was God's will that you should be given the letter?'

" 'You are interested in the letter?'

"He seemed resigned and faintly amused.

" 'Everyone is who knows of it.'

" 'Yes,' he said; 'that letter. It could do much harm . . . not least to innocent people. There is a boy, a youth, the one who carried it . . he would be crushed. It is a burden. I wish I could so dispose of it that it no longer had power to hurt.'

" 'Why not destroy it?'

" 'It was a gift, my dear. It is evidence of a most important historical truth. One must not destroy such things. There is little enough truth left in history.'

" 'Then have it locked up.'

" 'Then I die suddenly and it is discovered.'

" 'Sooner or later it must be.'

" 'Later is my hope. When everyone concerned is dead.'

"Meanwhile, it appeared, I was not the first to show interest. When the minister from whom des Moulins stole the letter had discovered the theft, he had known who must be guilty and made enquiries. These had started talk in certain circles, des Moulins had been approached in Beirut, his hovel and himself turned upside down without result. Then, since something was known by the seekers of des Moulins' former involvement with Lykiadopoulos, he in turn had been approached.

" 'They will never find it,' he said.

" 'They might turn nasty.'

" 'They already have. And they may turn nastier yet.'

" 'Then you must destroy it. Historical evidence or not.'

" 'They would not believe me when I told them. To such men it is unthinkable that a document which could bring money or power could be wilfully destroyed.'

" 'Then you must get rid of it. Give it away. Sell it.'

" 'These men—the ones who have been pestering me— offered me a high price. But I do not need money, Mark, and I must protect that boy. What I really wish is to forget the whole thing. That is why I do not tell the story of des Moulins. Anyway, it does not belong among a gambler's anecdotes.'

"So there we were going round and round in circles. I've reported all this at some length to let you know, in case you didn't realise already, what a very odd bird your chum is. Rather fascinating. These scruples of his, about not destroying historical evidence on the one hand and yet not incriminating that French boy on the other, indicate a moral conscience one would not expect to find in a professional gambler (beg pardon, my dear, but you know what I mean). And again, in many ways he's so subtle but in others so crass. It's just as you said. He's taken no trouble to find out whether these people who are after him want to publish the letter or to suppress it, or what sort of agreements they might be prepared to come to if he let them have it. He's as short-sighted as he's devious. Or is he? What he really wants is for scholars to find the letter in 100 years' time; and I suppose his hiding place has been chosen with that in view. Which is *something*

to go on. At least I now know that the letter still exists and
what processes of thought have dictated the method of concealment. 'They'll never find it.' That surely indicates, for a
start, that it's not in this mysterious hotel room of his; so for
the time being at least I've decided not to risk annoying him
by trying to track it down. Nor could it be on his person, as
they say. Positive conclusions are harder to come by, and
you'll agree that the odds are unpromising. But I'll keep at
it like the Trojan I am and I'll keep you posted. *Arrivederci*.
Mark.

"P.S. This has been a long and painstaking account, you
will agree. Pray let this be borne in mind when pay day comes
round once more. Which can hardly be too soon. M."

Max de Freville, though amused by Mark's second despatch, was by no means as pleased with it as he had been
with the first. While he had always realised that for Mark to
put his hands on the Greek's letter would be difficult, he had
yet assumed, such was his confidence in the instinct which
had led him to assign the task, that the thing would
somehow be done. Now it seemed likely that the thing
could not be done. A substantial disappointment; for although
he did not want the letter for his own use, he had looked
forward with keen enjoyment to following Mark's machinations for its profitable disposal. Powerful and pompous men,
once confronted with such a document, could have been
made to cut some humiliating capers; and to Max in his role
of political voyeur the spectacle would have been choice. This
pleasure, as it now seemed, he must make up his mind to
forego. But there were consolations: there was other folly
doing in the world for him to relish. Spring had brought with
it the usual rich crop of sexual antics and disasters in
important circles; a prominent trust lawyer, whose name was
a byword of integrity, was about to be apprehended (so he
was informed from a reliable source) for embezzlement in
the sum of half a million pounds; and there was a heartening

promise of low comedy in Lord Canteloupe's sudden promotion.

One of the first people to call on the new Parliamentary Secretary was Somerset Lloyd-James. The interview, which ostensibly had to do with the economic problems which faced Canteloupe, had been set up by Carton Weir, who opined that the Marquis might now constitute a politico-social ally of some prestige. Aware of the threat posed to his leadership of the Young England Group by Peter Morrison's possible return to Parliament, Weir, who would in any case have supported Lloyd-James in return for favours past, was now doubly assiduous in his cause.

"There's nothing direct the old fool can do for you," as he remarked to Somerset the day before the meeting; "but it will do you no harm at all to be well in with him. *To be known* to be well in with him."

And so Somerset had called on the Lord Canteloupe—in correct morning dress, a courtesy which he rightly surmised would both flatter the patrician ego and appeal to the patrician sense of style.

"*Strix*?" said Canteloupe dubiously. "Never had much time for reading, I'm afraid. Not what you'd call cultured. That," he added with characteristic insight, "is why they've asked me to do this job."

"*Strix*," said Somerset smoothly, "has nothing to do with culture. We're interested in money."

"Ah," said Canteloupe with undisguised warmth.

"The thing is," Somerset pursued, "do you see your way to running this show at a financial profit for the exchequer?"

"Any damn fool can run at a profit. Find out what they want and make 'em pay a proper price for it."

"Exactly," said Somerset; "but how does one find out. what they want? Impresarios, P.R.O.s, film magnates, men who are accounted experts in interpreting the public taste, are constantly getting it wrong and losing millions."

"Because they don't keep in touch. If a thing works once it'll probably work twice; the mistake they make is to think that it'll work for ever."

"But won't it?" said Somerset. "Basically, what they want stays the same. Sex, flattery, and a spot of mystery to keep them curious."

"Right," said Canteloupe. "But you've got to shift the emphasis from time to time. It's a matter of suiting presentation to the public mood. You take that period just after the war. People were frustrated because they'd won a great victory, or so they were told, and they hadn't got a damn thing to show for it—not even enough to eat. They felt cheated. So what to do with them? Simple. Invite them to revenge themselves on those who are cheating them (i.e. the authorities) by cheating back. That's why the spiv was the most popular character in the late forties—the fellow who got whatever he wanted despite all the regulations saying he mustn't have it, and got it, what's more, for nothing. That gave me the clue: let them think, I told myself, that whatever I'm offering them or showing them in my house is somehow illicit, that they're getting what they're not allowed."

"Rather difficult in the stately home business?"

"Not at all. Emphasise the luxury, the social injustice, the immorality of it all—and then invite them to join in. Encourage them to feel like lords and ladies living in the lap and grinding the faces of the poor. There wasn't much they could actually *do*, of course, except feel each other in my park, but I made them *think* they were being awfully wicked by getting everything up to look naughty. Horny paintings, the third marquis's silver jerry for pissing in under the table while the port went round, the odd man trap in the cellars, the authentic bed where they caught Lady Kitty rogering her black page. That sort of thing."

"And how shall you apply this formula to public recreation?"

"I shan't. That was just after the war, and the mood's changed since then. Many times. We've had romantic moods and aggressive moods and so called creative moods and teenage moods and hands off the Empire moods—we've had the lot. Just now the mood is one of aspiration and high ethical principle. Everyone's got everything he wants and more—except a purpose. So civic virtue, respectability, married love, moral rearmament—that's the line now."

And Lord Canteloupe went on to enlarge on his scheme for caravan parks and to explain how their ugliness and regimentation would appeal to the contemporary taste for moral endeavour. Somerset, impressed by Canteloupe's theory and wondering why the man was commonly written off as a moron, reflected that if his premise about a prevailing passion for virtue were correct, the Conservative Party might be well advised to change its pre-electoral policy of plugging material benefits and introduce a more spiritual tone.

"But don't you worry," said Canteloupe, as though reading his mind: "if anyone was to take this morality line so far as actually to suggest people could do without a few things, could lower their own standard of living to help feed a few of their black brothers, they'd lynch him. They want it both ways: they want to live wealthy and feel worthy."

"Moral seriousness is a prerogative of full bellies?"

"Something like that," said Canteloupe, who mistrusted other men's epigrams. "They'll come and play at austerity and moral seriousness in my caravan parks, like Marie Antoinette played at being a dairy maid. But when the chips are really down, when they've got to vote about their future, it'll be cars, cookers and fancy cans, and up yours I'm laughing."

"You wouldn't mind if I wrote an article for *Strix* about these caravan parks? Illustrating your theory of the economics of entertainment?"

"Is it a theory?" said Canteloupe, pleased. "I thought it was plain common sense."

"It'll look like a theory by the time I've finished with it," Somerset promised.

"Good of you to take the trouble."

"Not at all. It's my business to go into these things—not only as editor of *Strix* but as a prospective Parliamentary candidate."

Somerset lowered his eyes demurely and allowed this to sink in.

"I see," said Canteloupe. And then, "From what I can make out we need a few more chaps like you. Chaps who know a good thing when it's under their nose. Who look into matters first and make their theories afterwards. It's usually the other way round."

The interview ended a few minutes later, when Somerset undertook to complete the first draft of his article within five days and invited Canteloupe to dinner on the sixth so that he might read it and give his comments.

Both parties were highly satisfied with their meeting. Somerset considered that he had found a useful supporter who, while his political influence was as yet small, was destined for higher circles of government as time went on. Clearly, in this instance someone (the Prime Minister?) had at last decided to revert to the sound pragmatic principle of giving jobs to men who understood what was needed and how to provide it. In a generation which was increasingly concerned with fighting off boredom during its ample leisure, opportunities for Canteloupe to practise his proven expertise, and so to magnify the power of his office, could only multiply. True, the probable outcome was such as to make a civilised man shake in his shoes, but that was not the point. The point was that Canteloupe, despite his rank and background, was of the age and understood it. This transformed his rank and background from liabilities into assets and opened up for him all save the very highest places in the kingdom, and possibly even those. His diagnosis, that what was currently required was something ugly and uncomfortable, was a minor stroke of genius, Somerset considered. Here was a new and bright star in the mid-century firmament, and Somerset proposed to hitch his wagon to it . . . at a discreet distance, of course.

For his part, Canteloupe was much impressed with Somerset. Here was a fellow who knew how to dress and behave, who was (as Carton Weir had made plain) soundly connected, who understood and appreciated what Canteloupe was trying to do, and who was prepared to give it a boost in his mag. Canteloupe knew nothing about *Strix* (though he was to learn a great deal in the months which followed) but he knew a gentleman when he saw one and he recognised intelligence. In short, Somerset Lloyd-James would do. That he was manifestly not only a gentleman but also a howling shit did not deter Canteloupe one iota : for one thing, as he reflected, he was a shit himself, and for another he preferred working with them. For the great thing about shits was that they got on with it (provided the price was right) and didn't ask damn silly questions.

Max de Freville, setting out for a meeting with his accountant, was handed a telegram :

SUCCESS SUCCESS CATCHING FIRST POSSIBLE PLANE EXPLANATIONS LATER MARK.

5
SOMETHING OF VALUE

RUPERT PERCIVAL and Alastair Dixon sat on Percival's terrace and gazed towards the Quantocks. The cards on the table between them were ready for Piquet, but Dixon, restless and fretful despite an excellent luncheon, had twice refused to begin.

"It's no good sulking," Percival said, "just because you can't have it all your own way. You're old enough to know that."

"I'll have it my way yet. But I don't at all care for it when men like Edwin Turbot prove unreliable."

"He's got his own troubles. They appointed Canteloupe against his considered advice. One in the wind-pipe for his *amour propre*."

"That's no reason," said Dixon, "why he should vacillate over other matters. Some time ago, as you'll remember, he asked me to enquire what was doing down here. When I told him what you told me, he was quite plain : he supported Lloyd-James for the candidature—"

"—Which, by the way, has nothing to do with him—"

"—And he didn't want Morrison at any price. And now what? He's not exactly howling with enthusiasm for Morrison, but he's indicated very firmly that he would prefer him to Lloyd-James. Why the change?"

"You're nearer these things than I am," said Percival smugly, "but as I understand the story, his future son-in-law has been giving him a few straight tips."

"But he doesn't like young Llewyllyn, so why does he

listen? It's common knowledge he was against the engagement."

"But he's letting it go on. Wedding in June, they tell me. And whether he likes Llewyllyn or not, he knows a clever man when he sees one."

"Llewyllyn's just a common scribbler."

"Or a distinguished contemporary writer. It depends how you look at it. But why," said Percival, picking up a pack and shuffling it for the twentieth time, "are you so put out? What does it matter to you which of 'em gets in?"

"I want my seat to go to the man I want it to go to," said Dixon mulishly. "Lloyd-James is a gentleman. He's in the correct tradition for this part of the world."

"Apparently others are beginning to doubt that. Anyway, Morrison's a gentleman too."

"Damned trouble-maker. Barrack-room lawyer."

"Well," said Percival, "as I've told you before, we in Bishop's Cross don't take orders from Edwin Turbot. So you needn't be afraid that his change of mind will affect Lloyd-James's chances. Such as they are."

"And as I've told *you* before," said Dixon with rising petulance, "Edwin Turbot has more ways of putting the screw on you and your selection committee than you might think. You just wait and see. . . . Which reminds me: when does the committee make its final choice?"

"End of July," said Percival, "before everyone disappears. Which leaves plenty of time, I grant you, for Edwin Turbot to try his hand for what it's worth. Or anyone else who fancies his cards."

He nodded courteously towards the blue, familiar Quantocks, then turned his eyes on his old friend and began to deal.

"So there I was," said Mark Lewson to Max de Freville, "getting nowhere at all really, when Lyki picked up a morning paper and read about a bomb outrage in Paris. Algerian job."

"And so?"

"And so there was a list of people whom the bomb had done for. And right at the top was the son of the Minister from whom des Moulins stole the letter. You know, the boy who carried it back from Israel and whom Lyki was so anxious to protect."

"So now one of his strongest reasons for hanging on to it was gone."

"Right."

So Stratis Lykiadopoulos had taken Mark Lewson up to his mysterious room, from which he had debarred him hitherto because it contained a miniature shrine, complete with cross and eikons, and was not to be profaned by the activities associated with Mark. Now, however, the shrine had been dismantled for carriage over to the Lido and in any case the business on hand did not amount to desecration. It was the business of making a seemly farewell.

"He told me, in the nicest possible way, that since he was moving to the Lido in a day or so to start his bank, it was time to hand me my cards. He was wondering what to give me as a parting present, he said, and he'd decided that as I seemed so interested in it he'd give me des Moulins' letter. It was a gift which would suit my character and the character of our friendship. Now that the Minister's son was dead he could dispose of it with a good conscience; and in many ways he'd be relieved to get rid of it. He added a word of warning: if people continued to pester him about it, he'd tell them who had it, and in the event of his being believed I could look out for trouble. In sum, he was telling me politely, 'You're a crook, and you've been paid off, and to hell with you.'"

"No more talk of the letter being a historical document?"

"No. But you know what I think? I think he reckons I'm in such a hurry to cash in that the whole thing will explode into headlines. Which would now suit his book very well: the boy's dead, everyone else deserves anything that's coming to him, the letter itself would be preserved and appreciated at its proper value, and all the cloak and dagger boys would leave him in peace. He's using me as a kind of bomb disposal outfit. Cunning old Lyki. . . . But *cunning*. You just guess where he'd hidden that bloody letter."

Max shrugged.

"In one of the eikons? Or the cross?"

"Not bad, but not up to his standard. It worked like this. . . ."

For the last time, Lykiadopoulos and Mark had set out for the Gaming Rooms on the Lido. There Lykiadopoulos had gone to the Caisse and signed a cheque for five plaques, each of them worth 5,000,000 lire.

"He explained to me that there were only these five worth that amount kept in the place. They weren't used often— only for big games in the high season—and naturally enough they were always cashed in immediately after use. People might leave the Casino with the odd chip for five or ten thousand, but no one was going to lug one of these great bastards off with him. . . ."

So there were the five plaques, always in the safest of keeping, always available, save possibly for an hour or so during an unusually high game, on demand and payment. On this occasion Lykiadopoulos had retired with Mark to his private speed boat, where he used a small screwdriver to unfasten tiny screws at the four corners of each of the plaques. When this was done, the plaques split open into two sections, so moulded that when fastened together they left a hollow space between them of ten inches long by four inches wide by one-sixteenth of an inch high—just room enough to contain one of the five folded sheets which comprised the purloined letter.

"So he removed the five sheets and passed them over, then screwed the plaques together again, took them to the Caisse and got his cheque back, and that was it. Rather neat, don't you think?"

"Typical Greek elaboration, and not even foolproof. They might have decided on a new issue of counters and scrapped the old lot without his knowing."

"But they hadn't, had they?"

"You've got the letter with you?"

Mark tapped his breast pocket.

"Documentary dynamite. Any use to you?"

"No. I told you. I want *you* to handle it. I'm only interested in what happens next. . . . But I'd like to check it through."

"Touching costs extra, darling," Mark lisped.

Max nodded assent and Mark passed him the letter. When he had read it through, Max said:

"Much as I thought. It's all there."

"Isn't it though? So now you're satisfied, dearie, it's time for a little arithmetic."

"Very simple arithmetic. You were sent fifty when you first reached Venice. For reports since then, plus the privilege of reading this letter, I'll pay you another seventy-five."

"Very *detailed* reports. I was rather hoping for a hundred. Remember all those little extra bits . . . like that scene with Burke Lawrence and the model girl."

"What's that to me?"

But nevertheless there was hunger in his eyes.

"Nothing just yet," said Mark carefully, noting the hungry look and drawing his own conclusions. "But unless I'm mistaken there's something very odd going on there."

"Burke Lawrence," mused Max. "Conceited little man in advertising, with pretensions to know about cinema. Right?"

"Right. And Penelope Holbrook, the girl he was with, she was married to Jude Holbrook, who let her divorce him about the time he disappeared, something over two years ago. Jude wanted to marry our nice chum in Menton, Angela Tuck, but she walked out on him at the last minute."

"So she's told me," said Max stiffly. "I gather there was good reason."

"The very best. Jude was always a nasty little man, and just about then he was busy blackmailing half London to help with some shifty business deal he wanted to put through. When all this blew up, it was too much for old Angie. She'd just inherited some money, so she told Jude his fortune and pulled out."

"You seem very well informed. What happened to Jude Holbrook?"

"No one really knows. On top of everything else his little son died suddenly of meningitis, so his business partner, Donald Salinger, gave out that Jude had had a nervous breakdown and gone on a long holiday. After a bit 'Salinger & Holbrook', their printing firm, quietly became plain 'Salinger', and no one's heard of Jude from that day to this. It's thought that Donald bought him out, in which case he won't be short of money."

"And this slut he was married to. You say she gets alimony?"

"Paid through lawyers, Burke said. She's heard no more from Jude than anyone else."

"And what about her modelling?"

"She was quite near the top," Mark said, "about five years ago. But too many late nights out and about put an end to that. So now, as I told you, she just tags around with Burke, nagging him to find her work she doesn't need and for which she's no longer suited."

"You also said she used to be his mistress."

"That was way back, before she got her divorce. Not any longer, as far as I could tell. But she's got some hold on him which amounts to considerably more. That's what interests me. Those two have something in common far more . . . *serieux* . . . than bogus festivals in Venice."

"All right," said Max. "You find out what it is and you won't be the loser. I'd be glad to hear something of Jude Holbrook, too. From what Angela says, he was a thrusting little chap, and I can't think we've seen the last of him."

He went over to a desk, unlocked a drawer, and took out a sheaf of five pound notes.

"Now," he said, "back to more immediate concerns. There's a hundred pounds here. Let's say seventy-five for services rendered, and the extra pony to see you on your way to dispose of that letter."

"But what am I to do with it?"

"Find out who's willing to pay what for it and why, and let me know. That was the plan from the start."

"I know. But when it comes to it . . . I mean, I can't just waltz up to No. 10 and say, 'Prime Minister, dear, I've got something here which might amuse you.' "

"You'll find a way," said Max, "because you stand to make money. And don't just flog it for the first offer. Interest as many people as possible and let them compete in the bidding."

"I'm beginning to feel like Lyki. I don't want to wind up on a slab."

"Then you should choose more conventional ways of getting your bread. One hint I will give you. If there's one man in England who'll be interested in suppressing that letter, both for his own sake and the government's, it'll be that egregious major-domo of the conservative party, Sir Edwin Turbot. It so happens that I'm in correspondence with his younger daughter, Isobel. You'll find her co-operative . . . in more ways than one, very likely. You could make a start there."

"What about the press?"

"That would be wasteful. With the press everything— even this—is here today and dead tomorrow. The highest bids will come from people whose interest is *abiding*. People like Sir Edwin, who want the letter to suppress it. Or those who want it to apply pressure by threat. Find someone like that, and you could make yourself comfortable, very comfortable indeed, Mark, for the rest of your natural life."

"What little was left of it, dear," said Mark, "but thank you for the tip."

When Mark left Max de Freville, he had already made three decisions.

First, he would certainly go to see Isobel Turbot, because

Max made her sound amusing, something might come of it, and the whole Turbot set-up, so English and rural, seemed reassuringly tame. The contents of the letter revealed that Sir Edwin had that to answer for which, whatever his motives, would cause many to call him archfiend; but one thing you could be sure of—he wouldn't stick a knife in your ribs while you were his guest, or even while you weren't.

Secondly, however, before he went to see Isobel Turbot or anyone else, he would seek advice from his old friend, Jonathan Gamp. For while Mark was a scoundrel of some experience, this experience was all hand to mouth, superficial. He was, truth to tell, little more than a second-rate con-man, and an amateur one at that. To get perspective in depth in the present affair he must consult someone of more powerful and objective insights into grand chicanery, and who better than Jonathan, who was both connoisseur and scholar in this field?

Thirdly, most firm decision of all, he was not going to stick his neck out for the amusement of Max de Freville. It would be silly to let his property go for a song, and it would certainly be sensible, as Max had suggested, to stir up a little competitive interest; but the first' offer that was "anything like" he was going to grab with both hands, and then clear off for a well earned rest on the loot.

When Max de Freville was left alone, he too had already come to three decisions, or perhaps "judgments" would be an apter word:

First, that Mark, despite his undoubted luck in winning the letter, was a moderate performer now batting right out of his league.

Secondly, however, that this was a good thing, as it might lend the subsequent intrigues that kind of ineptness and even absurdity which gave scandal its true relish. That highly placed people should be detected in evil was much to Max; that they should be laid open to ridicule at the same time was much more.

And thirdly, almost as an afterthought, he blessed the

moment when he had thought of bringing Mark together
with Isobel Turbot. In that combination lay endless
possibilities both dangerous and comic.

What Max failed to take account of was that Mark had
an acute sense of self-preservation (an attribute which is
often very strong in second-rate performers and does much
to explain their mediocrity) and that this, when it came to
making a settlement, would more than outweigh his vanity
and greed. What Max also failed to take account of, and what
had been obvious to Mark, was that the former was not far
removed from insanity ("barking", as Mark later expressed
it to Jonathan Gamp). For what had at first been an
amusing interest, to counteract his boredom and disgust at
making easy money from fools, had now become an obsession.
Max had reached the stage at which he must know more and
ever more, when information, about small people now as well
as great, was the staple of his existence, when he yearned to be
privy to the secrets of the entire human race. Max, in short,
was playing God. Had he been able, he would have constructed
his own little universe, that he might sit and brood on every
movement of his creatures. As it was, omniscience of this
world was his end, and his resources, even his resources, were
feeling the strain. His accountant, the day before, had had
some cautionary things to say to him. His reserves were de-
pleted, some of the oldest of the clients at his chemmy tables
were taking shameless advantage of the long credit he allowed
them, the payments to his many informants now amounted
to several thousand a month. 'What do you pay them for,
Mr. de Freville?' 'Assistance.' 'All I can say, sir, is that you
must do with less.' But how could he? For Max de Freville
was hooked; he had allowed a whimsical pastime to grow
into an imperious necessity which was devouring both his
substance and his soul.

In Menton, Angela Tuck mixed herself a stiff brandy and
soda, looked at the American sailor slumped on the bed, and

wondered how to get him back to Nice before he was missed from his ship.

In Venice, Burke Lawrence said to Penelope Holbrook:

"I think we've done all we can here for the time being. May as well blow tomorrow."

"*Blow?*"

"Army slang for shove off."

"I never knew you were in the Army."

"Everyone my age was. How quickly people forget."

"The money," said Penelope. "Has Salvadori paid you the money?"

"I've arranged for it to be credited in London. In case you get another of your gambling yens before we leave."

"That wasn't a gambling yen. It was temper."

"It worked out just as expensive."

"And what about the festival?" she said. "That's what you're meant to be here for."

"That's in good shape. They can manage without me."

"And the next . . . the next assignment?"

"Salvadori will let me know. Stockholm, he thinks. In a month or six weeks."

"As long as that?"

"Sales technique, love," Burke Lawrence said: "in this trade it pays to keep the customer waiting."

Two days later, in her flat off Curzon Street, Maisie opened the parcel which Burke Lawrence had just delivered. Carefully she counted the little tins, then locked them up in a drawer. She didn't understand it very well, but it was wonderful the difference a sniff or two made to some of her customers. Apparently it made what usually took ten seconds go on—or seem to go on—for more than a minute. Very odd. Perhaps Fielding . . . when he came that afternoon? No, she decided: he was a thoroughly nice boy and she didn't want him getting nasty habits. Besides, it was very expensive, and Fielding ought to be saving as much as he could just now. Strange boy; keen enough, yet always so gentle and polite; such a pity about his face.

She looked at her watch and decided there was just time for a toasted tea-cake and a cup of Earl Grey.

In his room at the Cavalry Club, Fielding Gray finished the first book review (of the memoirs of a retired West End locksmith) which he had been asked to do by Somerset Lloyd-James. The book had no literary merit whatever, but he supposed the economics of the lock trade must be of interest to Somerset's readers. In any case, it was no business of his to quarrel with such work as he was given, and he had done his best in his short piece to ensure that Somerset would be satisfied and give him more. In other ways as well his new career had got off to quite a promising start; for Gregory Stern, who had read his two novels surprisingly fast, had asked him to come in next week and discuss them.

For all that, he thought, he could not go on living in the Cavalry Club much longer. Quite apart from the expense, the setting, however agreeable, was wrong for a man of letters and encouraged him in certain modes of thought and behaviour which he felt he must now eschew; for an instinct told him that they were incompatible with humility, and that humility, a disposition to expect only the worst, was essential in an aspirant artist of any kind. This led to the question of whether or not the humility would be genuine in his case, and how far, if it were merely assumed (to deceive the gods, so to speak) it could still be efficacious; but this question he deferred for later thought. The immediate point was that he must find suitable and economic digs for a bachelor called to his new station in life. Perhaps Somerset, who had always had a turn for economy, would be able to help.

And now, he thought with a quick lift of the blood, it was

time to visit Maisie. (He had considered economy here too, but without sincerity.) With hands that shook slightly he folded his review; he could post it on the way. But no; he must make *sure* it got there. He would deliver it to *Strix* himself. Since he was already pressed for time if he was to be punctual at Maisie's, he took a taxi from the Cavalry Club to the far end of Gower Street and then round and down to Berkeley Square. Not really a very economic performance, he supposed; but after all, this was his debut as a professional literateur, an occasion unsuited to parsimony.

"The Board of *Strix* assembled at half past two of the clock on the twenty-second day of April, 1959. Present were the Right Honourable the Lord Philby, Proprietor; Henry Arthur Dilkes, B.Sc., Secretary to the Institute of Political and Economic Studies; Robert Reculver Constable, M.A., Professor of Economics in the University of Salop and Provost Elect of Lancaster College, Cambridge; Carton Weir, M.A., Member of Parliament for Chirt and Wedderburn Regis; and Somerset Lloyd-James, M.A., Editor.

"Lord Philby having taken the Chair, he proposed a motion of congratulation to Professor Constable on his recent election as Provost of Lancaster College. The motion was seconded by Mr. Dilkes and warmly received by all present.

"Mr. Lloyd-James: May one ask, Professor, when you take up residence at Lancaster?

"Professor Constable: In September, in time for the new academic year.

"Mr. L-J: Your new appointment. . . . It may perhaps affect your attendance at this Board?

"Prof. C: Why should it?

"Mr. L-J: I was wondering, among other things, whether the Council of Lancaster would approve of your association with a journal well known to be conservative in tone.

"Prof. C: Since it has been my constant concern to make it less so, I have no reason for embarrassment before the

Council of Lancaster.

"Mr. Dilkes: Anyway, they're not as red as all that. I'm told that several of the younger dons are starting a new fashion in Toryism. They'll be delighted you're on this Board.

"Prof C: Their approval is of no moment to me.

"Mr. Weir: I wouldn't be too sure of that. Take Jacquiz Helmut, the historian. You wouldn't want *him* for an enemy. As rich as a money-lender—come to think of it, his father *was* a money-lender—friend of royalty, blue-eyed boy of the Billingsgate Press—

"Prof. C: Inside Lancaster College, Mr. Helmut is Assistant Tutor and a member of the College Council. As such he has one vote, no less and no more.

"Mr. W: Don't you believe it. Half of them vote as he tells them because they hope he'll get them asked to Buck House.

"Lord Philby: All very interesting, gentlemen. But, with respect to the new Provost of Lancaster, we're here to discuss the affairs of *Strix*.

"Prof. C: I entirely concur.

"Mr. L-J: So we were in a way. I was hoping Professor Constable would take the hint, but as it is I must now remind him that his place at this Board is *ex officio,* deriving from his position as Professor of Economics at Salop. Since his appointment to Lancaster will necessitate his resignation from the Professorship, it follows that he must also resign from the Board.

SILENCE.

"Mr. D: Surely not. I too might be described as an *ex officio* member of the Board, in as much as I was asked to join it because of my position at the Institute. But as I understand it, it was not part of our founder's intention to displace sitting members. When, in the fullness of years, Professor Constable sees fit to withdraw his services from *Strix,* then of course his place here will revert to whoever is then Professor of Economics at Salop. But just because he himself is now honourably relinquishing that office—

"Mr. W:—There is surely no need of speculation. Our founder, the first Lord Philby, will have made his intentions quite plain in the Articles of this journal.

"Prof. C: I must say, I have always considered the matter in much the same light as Mr. Dilkes.

"Mr. L-J: In the past, Professor, on several occasions, you have insisted that we follow the Articles to the letter. I take it you are still of the same mind?

"Prof. C: Er . . . yes, of course.

"Mr. L-J: Then let me quote you the relevant clause . . . 'Two seats at the Board shall be reserved, respectively, for the Secretary of the Institute of Political and Economic Studies, and for the incumbent of the Chair of Economics at the University of Salop.'

"Mr. D: Nothing about resigning.

"Prof. C: But the meaning is clear. The clause refers to the 'incumbent' and can only mean the actual and present holder of the chair. Your point is taken, Mr. Lloyd-James, and I shall act accordingly.

"Ld. P: We shall be sorry to lose your services.

"Prof. C: Such as they are, sir, you will have the benefit of them for some months to come. My resignation from the Chair at Salop will not be effective until August first of this year. It follows that until that time I shall continue to do my duty at this Board. . . ."

"Neat work," said Carton Weir to Somerset after the meeting. "It'll be a relief when Professor Constable removes his dreary face from the table."

"It was only a question of following the Articles . . . which may not suit our book so well when it comes to filling the empty place."

"Automatic, surely. The next Professor of Economics at Salop."

"Suppose we wanted someone else.?"

"Have you anyone in mind?"

"I had thought . . . . perhaps Canteloupe."

"You were impressed by your meeting?"

"With reservations, yes. I hope you're seeing to it that he doesn't drink too much."

"Hardly my job. He spends a lot of his time in White's, of which I'm not a member," said Carton Weir resentfully.

"Do your best to keep him out of mischief. I'm giving him a bit of a build-up in this journal. These camping sites of his."

"Good on you."

"I might even do a second piece later on . . . if he comes up with anything else."

"Don't go overdoing him, Somerset."

"I told you. I have my reservations. But the image is dead right. Morality with profit."

"If he can hold on to it. . . . Change of subject, Somerset. There's something you ought to know. As far as I can make out, Edwin Turbot's going to back Morrison for Bishop's Cross. We all thought he'd be behind you, but now. . . ."

So Tom's been busy already, Somerset thought. Well, it was only to be expected. Aloud he said,

"What can Turbot do? Will they listen to him at Bishop's Cross?"

"He's a persuasive man."

"I dare say something will turn up. They tell me the Selection Committee at Bishop's Cross won't decide till late July. That leaves three months . . . for me to bustle in."

"And for others to bustle in."

"Morrison won't bustle."

"There are those that'll bustle for him."

"And for me," said Somerset, scraping a blackhead out of his ear with a jagged finger-nail.

6

BUYERS AND SELLERS

"I THOUGHT YOU'D like to know," Captain Detterling said. Peter Morrison finished his coffee and said nothing. Helen Morrison put her head round the study door.

"The boys are waiting for you," she said. "It *is* Nickie's last day before school. . . ."

"Tell them we'll be right out. You're strong enough," said Morrison to his guest, "to bowl a few overs at the nets?"

"It'll do me good. So Nickie's off to school already?"

"Eight and a half. I thought it'd be jollier for him to start in the summer."

"Yes, the summer was always the best. . . . That reminds me, Peter, though I can't quite think why. Fielding Gray's back."

"Back?"

"Out of the Army. You knew about the accident in Cyprus? What happened to his face?"

"I'd heard something. Poor Fielding. Nothing ever went right."

"I hope it will now. He's been writing books, and I've got Gregory Stern to take an interest."

"Good," said Peter non-committally, and rose to his feet. "What you were saying just now," he said, "before Helen came in. . . . That's all?"

"All I can tell you so far. Edwin Turbot is now on your side. It's thought that Tom Llewyllyn has been talking to him—as the future son of the house."

The two men walked through a door and on to the lawn,

at the far end of which Nicholas Morrison stood ready in pads while Jeremy tended gloves like a squire at a tournament.

"Tom," said Morrison, "is like a poltergeist. A well meaning one, but apt to create confusion."

"I think you will find that he's more discriminating these days. He's certainly done a good job on Sir Edwin. But even so, Peter—"

"—Come along, Daddy," called Jeremy: "Nickie's waiting."

"—Even so," persisted Detterling, "it's time you took the field yourself."

"What could I do at this stage?"

"Show yourself at Bishop's Cross. Get to know the Selection Committee. And start keeping a very sharp eye on Somerset Lloyd-James."

"Come *along*, Daddy."

"I can't compete with Somerset at his game. You know that."

"We want you back, Peter."

"Very nice of you, but you must let me get back in my own way."

"*Daddy.*"

"Your way," Detterling said, "is much too easy-going . . . much too fair for these days."

"I don't know," said Morrison, and caught the ball which Jeremy had thrown him. "It is possible to bowl fairly according to the rules and yet to be deceitful and aggressive. Come along. We'll try some elementary tricks on Nickie."

"I quite agree with you, dear," said Jonathan Gamp to Mark Lewson. "You're way out of your class. Way out of mine too, for the matter of that."

They were talking in the dainty drawing-room of Jonathan's house in Hereford Square.

"What do you suggest?" said Mark.

"We'll have to think, darling. The great thing is to keep the game going. Poor Max may be going off his rocker but he's still good for lots of lovely lolly. So you must keep finding *amusing* things to tell him, mustn't you?"

"It's a strain. I'd like to cash in and be done."

"Of course you would, darling, but it's not that easy. People like you are always dreaming of lump sums, when in fact their best hope is to go on drawing small ones. Lazy and greedy, that's your trouble; always butchering the poor goose because it won't lay more than one golden eggie at a time."

"Well, what *do* you suggest?"

"As for that letter, we'll talk about it in a minute. A little frivolity first, dear. You did say you'd got Max interested in that ghastly Burke Lawrence and his trollop?"

"If she is his trollop."

"Well then, dear."

Jonathan unlocked a drawer, produced a small tin and took out a cylindrical capsule with rounded ends and about an inch in length. This he snapped in two; then he held the broken ends just under Mark's nose.

"Not very appetising."

"No?" Jonathan threw the remains of the capsule on to the fire. "But expensive. And in certain circumstances—believe me—effective. An oriental recipe for prolonging natural pleasures. Ever seen one of those Japanese pictures of a woman holding a saucer under a man's nose? Well, that"—he gestured at the fire—"is what the man's inhaling. And *that* is what Burke Lawrence is peddling round the place."

"Where does he get it?"

"He's not saying, dear. And those little jobs aren't the only things he's got for sale. He's got goodies much more dangerous and more expensive—though I don't touch them myself."

"I see . . . and Penelope?"

"It's only a guess, sweetie, but I'd say she was helping with transport. She still calls herself a model, right?"

"Right."

"Well, models can haul trunk loads of kit round the place without making anyone suspicious."

"Someone'd jolly soon get suspicious if he opened one and found it full of little tins."

"*Darling*. . . . Pills and packets can be sown into dresses. Stuffed into hollow heels of shoes. An ordinary make-up case—all those pots and things—can conceal enough junk to keep half London high for a month. Though mind you, it's only a guess."

"It would certainly explain why he was so polite to her in Venice."

"And it'll make a nice little tale for Uncle Max."

"Indeed," said Mark, "though it's pity we don't know where the stuff comes from . . . who's behind it all."

"I think, dear, that that is one of the things it is better *not* to know. Anyway, you mustn't be so demanding."

"Sorry. . . . Now, what about this letter?"

"I think Max is right, dear. Approach Edwin Turbot through Isobel, let him see a copy, and then promise to suppress the jolly news for so much a month. On the other hand, you could do worse than try that old crook, Somerset Loyd-James. It's right up his street."

"He'd print it in *Strix*?"

"Not him. Like Max said, sweetie, it's far more valuable for threatening, and Somerset will love that."

"Which of them would pay best?"

"Hard to tell, darling," Jonathan said; "Sir Edwin will have more in the bankie, but Somerset's very resourceful. So why not try a little chat with both parties, and see who's most forthcoming? Your main trouble will be to get them to believe that the original letter's authentic without actually letting them get hold of it. If you're called upon to give a demonstration, you can't reasonably refuse, but don't let it out of your hot little hand for a moment."

*   *   *

"I'll make no bones about it," Gregory Stern said to Fielding Gray. "I'm interested in those two novels of yours, but they won't quite do as they stand."

Gregory Stern was a tall, elegant man with a long lugubrious face. He had fussy hands which moved constantly over the buttons on his dark check suit, testing and re-testing for weaknesses and thereby effecting them. His voice, in contrast to his physiognomy, was light and girlish; his eyes candid and intelligent; his teeth much metalled and wired.

"And another thing," Stern went on. "Although I hope to publish these novels—provided we agree the alterations—I shall be doing so less for their own sake than for their promise. You see, they're lacking something . . . something which you've deliberately withheld. Detterling here agrees with me on that."

He nodded towards Detterling, who was examining a bookcase which contained all Stern publications to date.

"It is felt," said Detterling, "that your work could do with more . . . of yourself."

"These two novels you've read," said Fielding: "there is no place in them for more of myself."

"I don't question that," Stern told him. "As far as they're concerned, it's just that they're both a little too short and too compressed. Some of the technicalities need expansion."

"I'll gladly provide it."

"Then you can have a contract this morning. But," said Stern, his voice fluting slightly, "that contract will bind you to let us publish the next three books you write; and in these we shall look for more . . . well more. . . ."

"Of myself. In what respect?"

"More emotion rooted in experience . . . which has affected your—well—psyche. These two"—his fingers slid nervously over the typescripts on his desk—"are merely theoretical. Like riders in geometry, which end in a pat solution but offer no . . . human . . . comment."

Fielding pointed to his single eye.

"This?" he said.

"If you like."

A telephone rang, Stern started angrily, tested the buttons on either cuff while he recovered himself, and lifted the receiver.

"Send him up," he said after listening briefly. "Tom Llewyllyn," he announced to the room at large. And then quietly to Fielding, "You don't mind him being in on this?"

"I'll be glad to meet him again."

"Good. . . . The thing is this, Mr. . . . er . . . Major Gray. I like to publish good books which make money. I don't expect all that much money and sometimes I'm prepared to make none at all, but in your case I think we've got the makings of a minor prestige novelist with a broader appeal than most such. Which means both cachet and cash." He giggled rather wildly. "Forgive my little joke; I have an old-fashioned taste for puns. Well then . . . I think you write good English in the traditional manner and I think, though you have yet to show it, that you have a highly individual approach to— er—the human predicament. The combination promises well . . . if I am right. But where is the evidence for this individual approach? Not in these." He fingered the typescripts. "And yet it *is* in these—in the strong feeling I get from them of deliberate omission. Now, have you written anything from which you have not omitted . . . what has been omitted . . . here?"

He drummed on the typescripts, then sat back and clawed at his Old Etonian tie. Tom Llewyllyn entered without knocking, gestured to Stern to ignore him, and went straight on to join Detterling by the bookcase.

"I've written a journal," Fielding said at last.

"Ah?"

"It's unprintable as it stands, but it contains . . . the kind of reactions . . . which seem to interest you."

"It could be turned into fiction?" said Detterling, without turning from the bookcase.

"Yes. . . . A lot of people might recognise themselves. Including you."

"I promise not to sue. Others might be less amenable."

"We could sort all that out," said Stern, fluttering his hands. "It's what we pay John Groves for. Is there a theme to this journal? Something to provide a basic plot?"

"You might call it a love story. A vision of . . . of the true and the beautiful. I need hardly tell you that it has an unhappy ending."

"Through whose fault?" asked Tom Llewyllyn.

"Mine. With a bit of exterior malice thrown in. Jealousy, deliberate misunderstanding."

"Right," said Stern, who seldom asked for details once he was satisfied as to competence. "I'll take your two novels for an advance of £200 each, on the understanding that you'll loosen them up in the way I've suggested. Our editor has details."

He pressed a buzzer on his desk.

"You'll be given a cheque now," he said, "and you can fix an appointment with our editor for tomorrow. We'll do our best to publish the first of them—the Court-Martial one—in October. *But*"—his fingers flew over his coat buttons and then up to test his lower teeth—"what I'm really interested in is what you can do with that journal. I'm commissioning you to make a novel of it in the sum of £100 down, a further £100 on delivery, and yet a further £100 on the day of publication—all this, of course, being an advance against royalties on the usual scale."

"This is generous," said Fielding Gray, who was resisting a strong impulse to cry.

"Let us say that I am prepared to . . . er . . . back my beliefs with hard money. So many publishers are not. With the result that in the end they lose both money and author."

"Was that altogether wise?" said Tom Llewyllyn after Fielding had gone.

"Yes," said Stern. He tapped the typescripts on the desk. "There's quality here. And if he can find a little something else as well . . . which I hope is in that journal . . . a love story, he said . . ."

"I think I know what it's about," said Detterling. "Among other things, the boyhood of our friend, Somerset Lloyd-James."

"Don't tell me Gray was in love with Somerset," said Tom.

"Perhaps it was the other way about."

"And where do you come in?"

"Peripherally, I should imagine. When things went wrong with Fielding, I had a lot to do with finding him a place in the Army."

"What did go wrong?" asked Stern.

"Better wait for his version," Captain Detterling said. "After all, you've just offered him 300 quid for it."

As for Fielding Gray, for him it had been a morning of triumph. In his pocket was Stern's cheque, which not only represented a substantial sum of money but acknowledged him as a proper and practising novelist. On top of this, when he returned to the Cavalry Club, he found a note from Somerset Lloyd-James, who was very pleased with his first little piece and was now prepared to offer him a basic fee of £300 a year to write reviews and articles for *Strix;* subject, the note said, to giving *Strix* "first refusal" of all his journalistic work, but this did not seem an unreasonable condition. For a moment Fielding thought uneasily of Somerset's probable displeasure when his third novel should appear (for Detterling's surmise about its matter was largely correct); but it had all happened, he told himself, over ten years ago, he would try to be tactful in his treatment, and in any case the novel's completion, leave alone its appearance, was many moons away. So he turned with satisfaction to consider his third piece of good luck: in answer to an enquiry in Stern's office, Tom Llewyllyn had advised him that the cheap and suitable digs he had been wanting were to be had in a place called Buttock's Hotel. Indeed, Tom had said, he would arrange for Fielding to inherit his own quarters there, for these he must shortly vacate against his bridal day, which was not long. . . . Sweet Thames run softly, Fielding mused, until I end my song. A vision of the true and the beautiful, he had told Gregory Stern : if others would only see it too, through his eyes, then everything would have been worth while.

In the event, Somerset sent a copy of his article to Canteloupe two days before they were to dine so that he might be fully prepared for its discussion.

"I notice," said Canteloupe over the lobster soufflé, "that you call them 'camping sites'. Nothing about caravans."

"Caravans imply something cosy and casual—even anarchic : gipsies and so on. 'Camping' is more stern, bringing to mind campaigns, expeditions . . . heroism on Everest."

"I see . . . I was thinking; perhaps it won't do to be *too* stern at first. After all, I've got to attract people to these places."

"The sort of people you hope to attract won't read my article in *Strix*. We're interested in building you up as a politician who combines practical good sense with high moral ideals. You'll prove your practical good sense by making a profit—and we shan't enquire too closely how you do it : you can run your sites like Butlin's for all we care. But in order to put across your moral ideals we've got to . . . *let it be understood* . . . that campers are leading a life of self-denial, dedicated physical effort and so forth. You understand? Like Edinburgh's Outward Bound rubbish, only a family version."

"In your view then," said Canteloupe, "I'll end up providing the working class with the usual candy floss and slot machines, while the readers of *Strix,* who won't bother to come and see, think that everyone's sweating up mountains and practising first aid."

"That's about it," said Somerset, as the duck press was wheeled up. "Of course, there must be a certain attention to appearances in case someone should investigate. You might hire a few Army throwouts to hang around; call them 'camp leaders', 'fitness guides', that sort of thing. And give the sites impressive names : 'Hilary', 'Wingate', 'Montgomery'. You might even get Edinburgh to open one. Which reminds me: what actual progress have you made? When will the first site be ready?"

"Late June," said Canteloupe. "But don't you think it might be safer not to hurry? I mean, people can get all this moral uplift and so on just by reading about these camps: need we risk actually having one?"

"There's a lot," said Somerset, "in what you say. But I think you should have *one* in existence, if only to get the publicity of the opening ceremony. You could always close it quietly down afterwards. This one that'll be ready in June . . . where is it?"

"Somerset. No, not you—the Quantocks."

"Splendid. We'll give it some sensible west country name . . . 'Drake', perhaps—"

"—Wasn't he a Devon man?—"

"—No need to be pedantic. A bracing west country name, a royal opening on television, and presto, in moves the first lot of campers—"

"—Wearing lederhosen—"

"—Singing Jerusalem—"

"—Men and women hand in hand, but peeling off emphatically to separate quarters—"

"—Except for the family parties with bright-eyed children to prove it—"

"—A service of dedication—"

"—Taken by Donald Soper—"

"—Accompanied by a skiffle group—"

"—And I've got just the name. Westward Ho!"

"But how," said Canteloupe as the crêpes flamed skyward beside him, "can I be sure of getting suitable campers for the occasion?"

"Out of work repertory actors. You can hire them by the gross. Tell me," Somerset said, "now we've got all this buttoned up, have you got any more projects in mind? I'd like to do another piece for *Strix* in about a month."

"Well," said Canteloupe, "Carton Weir suggested that we

ought to do something for the popular arts. More recognition for band leaders, and so on—why should the Shakespeare boys hog all the honours? All right as far as it goes, though no money in it, but it gave me a better idea. Government recognition of popular pastimes. Bingo, for example. It's all the rage just now, and why shouldn't H.M.G. cash in? Publicly owned Bingo Palaces, that kind of a thing?"

"But the moral line? Not very elevating."

"Ah. Leave aside our profit, a big proportion of the prizes would be awarded in special bonds, which in theory at least would be financing medical research into incurable conditions. 'Win Bingo Bonds to Beat Disease.' Make it a moral duty, you see. And you know how sentimental the English are about health; so the bonds could carry bugger all in the way of interest, and even so no one would ever dare cash them in. Imagine going to the Post Office and selling a bond with 'Paralytic Old Folk' or 'Spastic Kiddies' written all over it. You'd feel like a murderer."

"Go on," said Somerset; "this is fascinating. . . ."

Mark Lewson, though undeniably second-rate in his chosen profession, was subject to flashes of inspiration. He was, and always had been, hampered by incompetence, fecklessness, captious changes of plan and negligence in their execution; but he was seldom short of good ideas. In the case of des Moulins' letter, it occurred to him that if he could get more than one party to bid for it he might also get more than one party to pay for it; and with this firmly in mind he paid a call on Somerset Lloyd-James, taking with him a photostat copy of the original document.

To Somerset the letter was just what he had been waiting for, the answer to his most fervent prayers, in Westminster Cathedral, the Brompton Oratory, Farm Street, and on his knees by his own little bed, for the last month. Here was matter to compromise several leading members of the Cabinet and in particular the party's Dean of Discipline, Sir Edwin

Turbot. With this letter in his possession he could demand anything he wanted short of a dukedom, and Sir Edwin, pastmaster of ways and means, would be compelled to devise a formula to see that he got it. There could be no question now of Sir Edwin refusing his support over the candidature for Bishop's Cross; and that was only the beginning.

But clearly there were dangers and difficulties: for a start, was the original document genuine? The photostat was impressive; the contents of the letter were consistent with everything he knew or suspected about the Suez affair; but even so, it was not beyond Mark Lewson to have got the whole thing up himself. What was it Jonathan Gamp had once said? "My dear, he's *famous* for cheques." Just so; if cheques, why not letters?

"You know Max de Freville?" Mark said.

"I've played at his parties."

"He put me on to this. Why not ring up and check with him?"

"He can't *know* it's genuine any more than I can."

But Somerset, clammy with excitement, was anxious to believe, and on re-examining the text he found something which convinced him, if not that the original was beyond suspicion, at least that here was a gamble worth making. For the letter purported to be written by a cosmopolitan Israeli of German birth; it was in English; and in two respects the English, otherwise excellent, betrayed a weakness common among those to whom German is their native tongue. In the first place, there was a pedantic tendency to write 'shall' where 'will' would have sounded more natural: 'I shall not claim to understand quite why, but it seems that the Cabinet Minister, Sir Edwin Turbot. . . .' Secondly, and far more convincing, was a confusion of subjunctives: 'If the Prime Minister would go' for 'if he were to go' (or 'went'); and 'If your Government would wish (wished) to provide such co-operation, it could swiftly make this plain.' It was of course possible that these errors had been deliberately planted by Lewson, but Somerset doubted this: had the thing been a forgery, the fake errors would have been cruder.

All right, thought Somerset, so I accept the document as genuine. But the original will be very expensive. Can I do without it, can I work with a copy? The answer to this, in the long run, was 'no'. To bring pressure to bear effectively he must be in a position, not only to print the letter, but to adduce the original when he was challenged. A threat to print when he was supported only by a photostat would scare nobody. *Ergo,* he must first make sure that the original still existed and then he himself must possess it.

"The thing is," said Mark, who had a fair notion what Somerset was thinking, "that a lot of people will be feeling the same. I wonder whether you can afford it?"

"Afford what?"

"Let's say . . . twenty thousand."

Somerset retched.

"After all, it's the scoop of the century, so I should have thought *Strix* could pay that much. Or were you perhaps thinking of going into business on your own account?"

"I'll give you five thouthand down," Somerset lisped.

"Darling," said Mark, pretending to be Jonathan Gamp. "Theven."

"Now look, thweetheart," said Mark, "let's get one thing straight. Are you bidding for *Strix* or for Somerset Lloyd-James?"

"For the latter," said Somerset, gagging.

"So I thought. But you can't pay enough, can you? On the other hand, you have got what is sadly lacking in little me—application and expertise. So listen carefully, darling, and I'll tell you what we're going to do."

It had all come to Mark as he entered Somerset's office. Here was a Headquarters; here was authority and organisation; here was a man able and ready to pay attention to the tedious details, which he himself could never abide. The answer was obvious: in return for a substantial but not impossible payment, he would admit Somerset into partnership, thus obtaining a nice sum of ready and a competent excutive who would assist him in further extortions, Blithely he now declared his terms. For seven thousand pounds he would entrust the original letter into Somerset's keeping. Somerset could use this as he saw fit; but it must not be resold or published without Mark's agreement. Further, Somerset must be prepared to produce the letter whenever required to do so for Mark's purposes, and must be prepared, moreover, to advise Mark on the furtherance of these.

"So long as it doesn't go out of my sight," said Somerset. The idea of being in a syndicate with Mark Lewson gave him little pleasure, but he was in no position just now to argue. Later on perhaps. . . .

"And don't go getting ideas about double-crossing me," said Mark; "because I've got Max de Freville behind me and he might turn nasty."

On this Somerset made no comment.

"If I'm to help you," he said, "I must know what you have in mind."

What Mark had in mind, he explained, was a visit to Sir Edwin Turbot, whom he proposed, in accordance with Max's advice, to make his first victim; one point being that Max's connection with Isobel would smooth the way.

"We'll go together," Somerset said.

"How friendly. If you'll undertake to manage the old boy, we'll split down the middle."

Mark Lewson was an open-handed man by nature, particularly to those who relieved him of bother. As for Somerset, he did not trouble to explain that his own price would not be reckoned in pounds sterling.

"This," said Tom Llewyllyn to Tessie Buttock, "is Mr. Fielding Gray. Or should I say 'Major'?"

" 'Mister' will serve from now on."

Tessie, warned by Tom about Fielding's appearance, nevertheless examined him with the frankest attention, and finally shook her head, as though to say, "That's what comes of playing with dirty children."

"Well dear," she said: "naughty Tom tells me you want to move into his room when he leaves next week?"

"If I may."

"You may, dear. Any friend of Tom's. Did he tell you the rules?"

"No."

"Only two, dear. Weekly payment in advance, and no dragging back."

"Dragging back?"

"No rubbish off the street. They nick things and spread crabs all over the house."

"I see."

"Not that I'm a prude. If you've got a *nice* girl, you know, a lady, bring her in and welcome. But try to pop her out again before the maids get here in the morning."

"I'll remember."

"Now dear," said Tessie turning to Tom, "that little back room I thought you might like as a *pied à terre*. You're sure you don't want it?"

"'Fraid not, Tessie."

"Because I've had another offer. Funny little chap came in here yesterday, common voice but dressed like a gentleman, wants a room for a few weeks, he said. Kept picking at his fingers, which I didn't care for, and Albert Edward didn't like him—did 'oo, woozums?—but I thought, if Tom doesn't want it, and if he pays as sharp as he looks—"

"Kept picking at his fingers?" said Tom with interest. "What was his name?"

"Holford, Holworthy, something like that."

"Holbrook?"

"That's it, dear. He's coming again today. Know him, do you?"

"Yes."

"All right?"

"No," said Tom, "very much not all right. But as far as you're concerned, he'll pay weekly in advance and I don't think there'll be any dragging back."

Later on, when Tom and Fielding were walking together in Hyde Park, Tom said :

"I think I'll move out even sooner than I told Tessie. I don't want to see more of her new guest than I can help."

"Holbrook? What's the matter with him?"

"He reminds me of what I'd sooner forget."

"Most people have that effect on me," Fielding said.

"I know what you mean. But Holbrook's a special case. My very own personal plague rat."

"Where will you go?"

A spring breeze skimmed the Serpentine and the trees rustled with the familiar invitations.

"Off into the blue. A walking tour. I always planned it, to nerve myself before getting married." Tom hesitated. "You . . . wouldn't like to come with me? There's a lot we might talk about."

"There's nothing I'd like better," said Fielding, obscurely moved by this suggestion. "But I must get down to work. Stern's been very good, and if I'm to—"

"—You're quite right," said Tom, flicking his fingers. "That's where I nearly came unstuck when I started—kept delaying. You get down to work and stay down. But you'll take a day off for my wedding?"

"With the greatest pleasure."

"Patricia's family are rather grand, you see. I'll need a few friendly faces on my side of the church."

Fielding shuddered slightly and Tom looked him straight in the eye.

"I meant exactly what I said, Fielding. To me, your face is now that of a friend. And so, however disfigured, it is a friendly face . . . a face to call up love."

Max de Freville was spending a week in Menton with Angela Tuck. On his fourth day there he received a letter from Mark :

". . . So as soon as Somerset's cheque went through, I got out the jolly old letter and off we pranced to Wiltshire to talk turkey with Edwin Turbot. I was in favour of having a word with Isobel first, but Somerset said no, we'd announce ourselves as the editor of *Strix*, and that would get us straight in. He'd already rung up from London, it seemed.

"In the hall was a galumphing lass with a lot of jerseys and a po face.

" 'You must be Miss Patricia Turbot,' Somerset said. 'I'd like to congratulate you on your engagement to Tom Llewyllyn.'

"She thawed out a bit at that, though she still seemed suspicious. I don't know Tom well, but it's funny he should chose a kind of female gladiator after all these years of dainty ladies from the chorus at the Tin Tack Club. Wants a change, I suppose, and he'll certainly get it : like going to bed with that statue of Nurse Cavell. Anyway, this Patricia just stood there simpering and blocking up the doorway, till Somerset reminded her we'd got an appointment with her old man. At this she let us in and strode along in front at heavy infantry pace on the way to what she called 'the study'. But before we got there, she suddenly stopped, did a parade ground turn, and said to Somerset,

" 'Do you know where Tom is?'

" 'He's on a walking tour,' said Somerset. 'Didn't he tell you?'

" 'Yes. But I'd like to know where.'

" 'He didn't know where he was going. He told me he was just going to start and see where his feet took him.'

" 'How childish,' she said. 'And what about his work for your paper?'

" 'No more now till after the honeymoon.'

"At this she went a deep, sweaty scarlet, not only bashful, if you ask me, but ripe and randy, so perhaps Tom has picked well after all. But it seems that she doesn't approve of Tom wandering away over the countryside like his namesake Jones, and though she gave permission she's now thought better of it (wildly jealous of possible picaresque adventures) and wants to get her great big capable paws on him again. If Tom had seen the look of greed in her face, he'd start sending back the wedding presents tomorrow.

"Well, Somerset couldn't help her, so she clanked off to her own quarters, and we went in to see Sir Edwin, who was busy stuffing himself with digestive biscuits and spraying the crumbs all over *The Times*.

" '*Strix*,' he said, 'of course. I suppose you've come to ask my views on the forthcoming election?'

" 'No, we haven't,' says Somerset, as sharp and nasty as a rusty bayonet, 'we've come to do business with you. We have proof positive that you and other ministers conspired with Israeli agents to force a crisis over Suez. We're here to tell you how you can make amends.'

"One in the teeth for Sir Edwin. But he took it like a real trooper. You've got to hand it to the old gang—they've a monopoly in sheer brass neck.

" 'Llewyllyn told me about you,' Sir Edwin said. 'What he didn't tell me was that you were foolish as well as unscrupulous. What sort of storyteller's rubbish is this?'

"For answer, Somerset held the letter under his nose. Sir E. was just about to take it, when Somerset withdrew it and gave him a photostat.

" 'You read this,' Somerset said, 'and then you tell me what sort of storyteller's rubbish it is.'

"You could almost see the poor old chap shrinking as he read it. But when he'd done, he stood up with his back to the wall (Steady the Buffs), reinflated himself, and took a steady return aim.

" 'It's a fake,' he said.

" 'There are those that can prove otherwise.'

" 'What it says is untrue.'

" 'That will be for others to judge. They might think it fitted in rather well with what they already know.'

" 'You publish a word of this, and I'll sue you through every court in Christendom.'

" 'Even if you won, you'd still be finished after what was said.'

" 'And to think,' Sir Edwin said, 'that originally I was going to back you for Bishop's Cross. I'm glad I changed my mind.'

" 'Won't you have to change it back again?'

" 'Very probably. But at least I've the satisfaction of knowing that I reached the right decision . . . even if circumstances now prevent me acting on it.'

"For of course he was too old an operator not to know when he was beaten. But once again, you've got to hand it to him : there was a kind of offhand dignity about his surrender which implied that although he was having a bad run just now, he was still in the game and ready to wait for his own turn. It was very well done. Somerset had hoped to have him grovelling, instead of which he was a model of self-possession and turned out, when they came on to the terms of treaty, to be much the cooler and more accurate of the two.

" 'Very well.' he said : 'so you're asking for my support at Bishop's Cross?'

" 'I'm asking to be assured of selection as conservative candidate there.'

" 'I can't assure you of any such thing.'

" 'They'll listen to you.'

" 'No doubt. But I can't make them do more.'

" 'Then somewhere else?'

" 'Look,' Sir Edwin said; 'the truth is, and a lot of people are beginning to know it, that you're not fit to represent Bishop's Cross or anywhere else. So I can't promise. You must see that.'

" 'And you must see that I've got enough here to blow you to fragments.'

" 'After which I wouldn't be able to help you at all.'

"This elementary piece of logic went home. While Somerset chewed away on it, Sir E. started on me.

" 'And what do *you* want?'

" 'Money.'

" 'Thank God for that. I can cope with your sort. But him'—he pointed at sulky Somerset—'he'll want a ministry before I can turn round.'

" 'I can't see,' huffed Somerset, 'that there's anything ridiculous in that.'

" 'Except that for some years now these things have been rather difficult to arrange. How's your father?' he shot at Somerset, then turned away without waiting for an answer, went to a desk, and came back with a cheque book.

" 'His father's called Shagger,' he told me as he started to write. 'You know why? He had a reputation for bedding half the shop girls in Cambridge. Put about by himself, of course. If you ask me, he just stayed in his room and had dirty thoughts. Like his son, I wouldn't wonder. Here's £500 to be going on with. You can have another £1,000 in September, and the same after Christmas. All right?'

" 'All right,' I said. 'But after that?'

" 'We'll have a little talk about a regular arrangement. That's if smarty-boots here hasn't opened his spotty mouth.'

" 'Look here,' said Somerset, who was looking positively sorry for himself, 'there's no need for all this personal talk. All I'm asking is your assistance and good report.'

" 'You shall have both. The question is, who's going to believe me?'

" 'There's only one person need believe you. Rupert Percival. He can answer for the Selection Committee at Bishop's Cross.'

" 'Granted. But what makes you think he'll like the cut of your jib?'

" 'That's up to you,' Somerset said.

" 'Well, I don't really know the chap,' said Sir Edwin, as easily as if we'd been talking about the local cricket club,' 'but I'll ask myself over there and see what's to do. And now, in order to keep up the domestic fiction that you are welcome visitors, you'd better come and meet my daughters over lunch.' "

*   *   *

"Tell me," said Angela to Max de Freville in Menton, "is anything the matter?"

"What should be?"

"You've been odd. And all that time you spend brooding over those letters."

"That's my business," snapped Max: "don't interfere."

"Darling, I don't want to. I was only asking. . . ."

"There's not enough to tell, not yet. One day I'll know it all, and then I'll tell you. One day I'll have the key, and then—"

He broke off when he saw how strangely she was looking at him.

"Just don't interfere," he muttered. "You wouldn't really understand."

"Gloomy old faces," Isobel had written to Max, "at luncheon today. Daddy had two guests, a scabby old journalist thing called Lloyd-James, and a younger man, raddled but devastating, who told me on the side that he's a chum of yours. The silly thing was that everyone was meant to be all palsy, but I could tell that underneath Daddy was ready to widdle with fuss, while the Lloyd-James creature, though he behaved smoothly enough, was quite rancid with frustration about something. He was like a little boy who finds that his new toy isn't nearly as big and as blissy as he thought it would be from the picture, but still has to go on being grateful in order not to annoy mummy. On top of all this, Patty was in a rare old bait because she still hasn't heard from Tom on his walking tour and she suspects him of having it off with every other woman he meets. All nerves of course. Tom's now as staid as an old cow in a field, whatever he may have been like once; but nothing's going to stop her worrying till she's got him locked up in a glass case on the mantelpiece. I wouldn't wonder if she comes out in shingles—and *that'll* be nice on the honeymoon.

"Anyway, what with one thing and another, the only

people there who were enjoying life were me and this celestial Mark Lewson. We played a bit of footy under the table, and then a bit of kneesy, and after lunch I managed to get him to himself, because Daddy went off for his nap and Patty was conducting an inquisition on the Lloyd-James monster about Tom, though Mark said she'd already had one go that morning. It was now Mark told me he knew you, so then I realised there was more in all this than an interview for L-J's dreary paper and I asked Mark what was frying.

" 'Your old daddikins, dear,' he said.

"Then he told me all about the Suez do-da and Daddy being so naughty, and how L-J wanted a seat in Parliament, and how galling this was for Daddy because of L-J being such a piece of sparrow-crap, and so on and so forth. And I said, was it wise of him to be telling me, and he said he didn't suppose I'd want to land my old pater in the manure, and that anyway he'd done quite well out of it all by now and didn't really care if the news did get out.

" 'It'd annoy Somerset,' he said, 'and Somerset's a prick. And as for making more money, I've thought of another scheme to take care of my old age. Much less risky and much more fun.'

"And then he kissed me in a way that hasn't happened before, and even though his mouth tasted foul he thrilled me into little bits, so that he could have had the whole caboodle there and then (which no one else really has, I'm not such a tart as I look) only Patty and Lloyd-J. came in, both of them looking like empty slabs in a morgue, and Lloyd-J. said it was going time.

"So that was that. But I'm seeing lovely Mark in London again next week."

For Fielding Gray in Buttock's Hotel the days passed quickly. First of all he altered his two novels along the lines suggested by Gregory Stern and the firm's editor. Then he took out his journal, sorrowed briefly over the memories which it revived, and began to calculate how it could be cast as a work of fiction.

From time to time, in hall or corridor, he passed a small, tense man, of about thirty-five years old, who moved as though he were always on his way to take an urgent part in great events. This, as he had heard from Tessie Buttock, was the new resident, Jude Holbrook. He found it difficult to understand why Tom Llewyllyn's aversion was so pronounced; for Holbrook, while shifty and tight-lipped, had in his manner a lack of co-ordination, a spasmodic nervous jerk, which, taken with his size, gave him the appearance of a marionette: a villain, possibly, but a villain on a stage of puppets.

For Tom Llewyllyn too the days went swiftly by.

One afternoon, walking through the Quantocks, he breasted a rise and found himself on a small wooded plateau lying along a spur which jutted from the range to the north of it. To the south the county unrolled itself like a great patterned eiderdown : green pastures sprawled at leisure, woods nestled, and orchards lay tidy and demure.

The plateau itself, with its groves of lady birch, would have been enchanting—were it not that gangs of men and machines were clearing away the woodland at a rate of ten yards a minute, and that a large space already cleared was occupied by closely packed caravan-trailers of identical design with a perimeter of prefabricated stalls and huts. There were two large notices : one carried the name of a contractor; the other proclaimed,

WESTWARD HO!
First of the Government-sponsored
Canteloupe Country Culture Camps
**FITNESS FAMILY
FAITH.**

As he walked downhill towards the south, Tom wondered whether he should telephone Patricia that evening. He decided not. In his good time he would move east again to Wiltshire, where he would be with her, as promised, some seven days before the wedding in order to settle any last minute arrangements. Meanwhile, she must do without further reassurance; she had already had plenty, and she must learn to put up with his long withdrawals which, for one reason or another, would be bound to continue during their married life, probably to the great benefit of them both. So let the days pass in silence and soon enough they would bring him to his bride.

Two meetings with Isobel in London confirmed Mark in the idea which had come to him in Wiltshire. A regular arrangement, Sir Edwin had said. Very well; let him hand over his younger daughter and a suitable dowry, and Mark would abandon any further claim upon him. In this way he would have achieved security and social status (for both of which he had always had a secret longing), to say nothing of an amusing, vivacious, appetising wife. He wanted a bit of peace and permanence; he was fed up, worn out with the constant struggle for petty cash and the endless antics in strange beds. All ways round, Isobel would do very nicely: she was his Sophy Western, waiting with arms wide open at the end of the turbulent road.

But there were two formidable obstacles. First, Sir Edwin, who was already somewhat put out by the imminence of one dubious marriage, might be reluctant to hand over his remaining daughter to a penniless adventurer. And secondly, although his objections might be overcome by reference to the letter, he would surely want this to be given up to him, as confirmation that he had now paid the final price. Since the letter was in Somerset's possession, and since Somerset had no intention of giving it up to anybody, Mark was in no position to close the deal . . . even on the assumption that

Sir Edwin would consent to make one.

But as the days went by and the grass grew fat and rank in the Royal Parks, he conceived a plan. A bold, roystering plan, full worthy of his gay Sophy Western.

Sir Edwin Turbot consulted warily with Alastair Dixon in London. After all, he said, he had decided that Somerset Lloyd-James was the better choice for Bishop's Cross: would Dixon, as outgoing member and mutual friend, do his best to convince Rupert Percival? Dixon would, but wanted to know what part Sir Edwin himself proposed to bear in the matter. The trouble was, Sir Edwin said, that while he would much prefer to make a discreet and personal approach, he was but little acquainted with Percival. Dixon, who knew that the old country lawyer would resent and resist any pressure exerted through hierarchy but might perhaps yield to personal suasion, approved Sir Edwin's choice of method and suggested that Percival should be asked to the wedding, where their acquaintance might be renewed as a preliminary to further negotiation. Dixon himself would be staying with Percival the night before the wedding, so Percival's invitation would appear quite natural: it would be seen as a graceful if not mandatory way of recognising that his house was harbouring one of the more prominent wedding guests. Sir Edwin opined it a pity, since time was passing, that their movements should be quite so stately; but Alastair Dixon pointed out that any sign of fuss or urgency would put Percival against them for good.

"We've been asked to Tom Llewyllyn's wedding in Wiltshire," said Peter Morrison to Helen.

"It seems a long way. . . . And I've hardly ever met Tom. Except for that awful time when he was so drunk at Chevenix Court."

"He's changed a good deal. I think we'll go, if you can bear it. There'll be several people there who'll be in the know

about Bishop's Cross. And if Turbot really is going to back
me, as Detterling says, it'll do no harm to be polite to him."

"Will Somerset Lloyd-James be there?"

"I expect so—Tom's editor, you see." Peter chuckled. "I
wouldn't mind seeing his deceitful old face again. I might
even ask him what he's up to. You never know, he might
tell me; he's got a peculiar sense of humour—like all Papists."

"You're much too kind about him."

"He's got a bit of a kink, that's all. I expect someone
dropped him on his head when he was one."

He looked along his lawn, and then beyond it to his fields,
which were already well forward.

"Not bad for early June," he said; "and the old men say
we're in for a hot summer." He gripped his wife's arm just
above the elbow. "I think—don't you?—that we can afford
to be kind about Somerset Lloyd-James."

And so the days lengthened and drew on towards mid-
summer; days bringing Fielding Gray to slow fulfilment and
Canteloupe's first caravan camp to punctual completion;
bringing Burk Lawrence and Penelope Holbrook to their
engagement in Stockholm and Jude Holbrook ever closer to
the information which he sought; bringing Somerset Lloyd-
James and Peter Morrison nearer to the time when one of
them must be chosen; bringing Mark to Isobel but little comfort to Max de Freville; and bringing Tom Llewyllyn back
from his wanderings to his affianced wife.

Neither Patricia nor anyone else learnt much of where he
had been. Something indeed he told of the men and machines
which were making hideous the little spur of the Quantocks;
but nothing at all of the middle-aged woman whom he had
visited in her cottage by the Severn, a woman whom Tom
called 'mother' but who would not be in the church to see
him wed. For it had always suited Tom to come from nowhere; and of those that would gather to drink at his
marriage feast, he and his bride alone would bear his name.

7

MIDSUMMER WEDDING

'GROOM, DEAR," said Jonathan Gamp, winking saucily at the usher, and trolled himself up the aisle to find a place next Somerset Lloyd-James. From the bride's side a block of country faces regarded him incuriously; they had been warned what to expect. In the front row, Canteloupe fidgeted thirstily while his lady and the dowager eyed him with contempt. Carton Weir, who had not been invited but had come, on Somerset's suggestion, in the capacity of Canteloupe's *aide*, passed his master a copy of the order of service in the hope of keeping him amused. Just like a bloody great Christmas card, Canteloupe thought, only no pictures, worse luck. What was this on the front?

> With that I saw two Swans of goodly hue
> Come softly swimming down along the Lee;
> Two fairer birds I yet did never see :
> The Snow which doth the top of Pindus strew
> Did never whiter show. . . .

Great God, Canteloupe thought, so that old fraud Edwin Turbot's taken to writing poetry.

"Overdoing it rather," said Jonathan to Somerset. "Two geese if ever there were. But I must say, Tom looks rather sweet."

Tom, hair disciplined, shoes gleaming, his hired morning coat only a size or so too large, looked unprecedentedly respectable as he waited for his bride. The audience on the groom's side averred to one another that this must be the

work of Gregory Stern, who stood beside him conducting
a furious last minute test of his waistcoat buttons.

"He looks all right to me," said Rupert Percival to Alastair
Dixon : "why was Turbot so put out about it ?"

"No one knows who he is. He just turned up at the 'Varsity
one Michaelmas with a scholarship and went on from there."

"I should have thought it was perfectly clear who he is. A
writer with three rather distinguished books to his credit and
a prominent by-line as a political journalist."

"No one knows who he was, then."

"Does that matter these days ?"

"His . . . er . . . morals. . . ." Dixon deposed with vague
deprecation.

"Is that anything new ?"

"It's all right if you *know* about people. But if you don't
you have to be careful."

> So purely white they were (read Helen Morrison)
> That even the gentle stream, the which them bare,
> Seemed foul to them. . . .

A man with a badly disfigured face and only one good eye
sat down next to her. Poor thing, Helen thought, as her
husband leaned across her.

"Fielding," he said softly.

The disfigured face tormented itself into what was presumably a smile.

"Peter. Peter Morrison."

"You've never met my wife? Darling, you've heard me
talk of Fielding Gray."

The one eye looked at her suspiciously. The head inclined
in formal salute.

"Mrs. Morrison."

"I've heard. . . . That is, Peter has. . . . Please call me
Helen."

"When I know you better."

Blinking slightly, Helen read on while the two men
whispered across her.

> . . . Seem'd foul to them, and bade his billows spare
> To wet their silken feathers, lest they might
> Soil their fair plumes with water not so fair
> And mar their beauties bright. . . .

Stone the crows, thought little Alfie Schroeder of the Billingsgate Press, waddling in the wake of a phalanx of Parliamentarians, Tom's really hit the jackpot with this crowd.

"Press?" said an usher, looking at Alfie's shining Sunday suit.

"No," said Alfie with spirit. "For the bridegroom."

For Tom Llewyllyn had not forgotten his old companion.

"Pardon me," said Alfie, as he trod first on Captain Detterling's beautifully polished Mess Wellingtons and then on Mrs. Donald Salinger's pointed patents.

"My bloody bunions," Mrs. Salinger said.

"Funny friends Tom has," said Salinger to Detterling.

"The lot on the other side look just as odd to me. Look at old mother Canteloupe."

And indeed, while Carton Weir squirmed, Lord Canteloupe scowled, and Lady Canteloupe looked faintly unhappy, the dowager was munching with gusto an egg sandwich which she had brought along in her handbag. What her party didn't know was that she also had several slices of garlic sausage stored up against the sermon.

"Already five minutes late," said Percival to Dixon.

"I hope nothing goes wrong for him now," Alfie Schroeder prayed.

"There's something so *naïve* about country churches," remarked Jonathan Gamp.

"I had to get special dispensation from His Eminence," Somerset Lloyd-James replied.

"Seven minutes late," the county faces murmured without anxiety.

"Stern's looking a bit fussed," said Captain Detterling.

"They say his father's still orthodox," mused Mrs. Salinger.

"No, his grandfather," corrected her husband.

"They always said Turbot didn't like it," mumbled the Parliamentarians. "Do you suppose. . . . ?"

"Please, madam," Carton Weir entreated the dowager; "they should be here at any moment."

"It's no good," said Canteloupe. "Much better ignore her."

The Dowager Marchioness dropped a bit of egg on the seat and bent happily to pick it up again.

"I'll tell you what little I know after the service," Fielding was whispering to Peter across Helen Morrison: "but it's not much. As far as I'm concerned, Somerset's only my editor these days."

     And mar their beauties bright, (read Helen Morrison on the third time through)
     That shone as Heaven's light,
     Against their Bridal day, which was not long:
     Sweet Thames, run softly, till I end my song.

And now at last, with a peal of triumph from the organ, came Patricia Turbot on her father's arm, confounding the malicious, making glad the heart of every female, stepping strong as a sentry on his beat. A kilted page, fussed over by the radiant Isobel, bore the train, and six more bridesmaids, in swanky short green dresses, pressed on behind, urging the virgin sacrifice to Hymen's altar. Tom's face lit up like a winter's sun breaking through mist and he held out both his hands to greet her.

"Mistress Isobel looks very pleased with herself," mused Somerset.

Gregory Stern bowed a tall and noble bow. Sir Edwin drew back.

"Here in the sight of God, and in the face of this congregation. . . ."

Helen Morrison grasped Peter's hand.

". . . First it was ordained for the procreation of children. . . . A remedy against sin. . . ."

"There's something definitely queer about Isobel's demeanour."

A strapping wench, thought Alfie; I hope he can manage her.

". . . Such persons as have not the gift of continency. . . ."

"I'm sure I heard it was his *father* who's Orthodox."

"Nonsense, Vanessa. His father served in the Brigade."

"Let him now speak, or else hereafter for ever hold his peace."

Peter Morrison disengaged his hand from Helen's; she always got so sticky at weddings. I don't suppose Fielding can help about Somerset, he thought, so I'll have a word with the old crook myself. Odd about Fielding. He's a wreck, yet there's a . . . a serenity there which I don't remember— even if he was a bit sharp just now with Helen. Guiltily, reluctantly, he repossessed himself of his wife's sweaty palm. The big ones always have a lot of juices, he thought; that great hoyden of Tom's will be just as bad.

"Wilt thou have this woman to they wedded wife, to live together after God's ordinance in the holy estate of Matrimony?"

"I will," Tom said in tones which rang round the church.

Edwin Turbot looks rather down, thought Somerset: perhaps he's not finding my little affair too easy. Later on I'll have a word with him. What to do about Peter? Just be polite—he's not one to bear a grudge.

"To have and to hold from this day forward, for better for worse, for richer for poorer. . . ."

I wonder about this Morrison woman, Fielding thought; capable, I dare say. I wish I hadn't come; I wish I'd stayed in London and got on with my book. *My book*.

". . . in sickness and in health, to love and to cherish. . . ."

God, make them be happy, Alfie Schroeder thought.

God, make me be happy, Isobel Turbot thought.

Something . . . queer . . . about Isobel today.

God, I could use a drink, Lord Canteloupe thought.

God, this revolting hag and her sandwiches, Carton Weir

thought; and tomorrow we've got to inspect that bloody caravan park.

Oh God, I don't know, Captain Detterling thought; it was never for me, all this cherishing and so on. Though there's a nice bit in Homer which the old man used to read us at school. About a man and his wife, a great joy to their friends and a grief to their enemies. But the old man was a bachelor himself.

". . . till death do us part, according to God's holy ordinance; and thereto I plight thee my troth."

And now what had at first been a mild snivelling, then a repressed sobbing, then a barely controlled bodily heaving, became an open and impassioned bawling, full-throated and lusty, the tribute of a tried but generous heart. It was Tessie Buttock weeping, part in happiness and part in sorrow, for her lost favourite, naughty Tom.

For as long as possible, Sir Edwin Turbot had postponed considering what attitude he should adopt to Tom once he was fairly married to Patricia. Until just before the wedding he had coped with his aversion by regarding Tom as a talented nuisance, as an irritating employee who must be tolerated for his undoubted ability. Plainly this view of the matter would serve no longer. The wretched fellow was now his son-in-law and must be admitted to full family privilege: the question was, how should this be done without imposing too much of a strain on Sir Edwin's *amour propre*.

But now, as Sir Edwin surveyed the long queue which was waiting to pay compliments to the newly married couple, and as he reflected that neither here nor anywhere else in the house was a single relative of Tom's to be found, the answer came to him. Tom, so to speak, was the scholarship boy with no background; while he, Sir Edwin, was the traditional but farseeing headmaster, making concessions to a new age. Tom would be accepted forthwith as absolutely "one of us", indeed as one likely to do "us" great credit in the long run, but also as one who had not had quite our advantages : a fact which we would never mention but would always keep at the back of our minds, to excuse ourselves (and Tom) in case he should make some fatal blunder— which would otherwise have disgraced us wholly but could now be promptly attributed to an upbringing deficient because unknown. Patronage, that was the word, Sir Edwin thought : he was the eternal patrician braving and taming the eternal parvenu, he was the enlightened head of house welcoming the young F. E. Smith to Oxford, or even the King of France summoning Cellini to his court. Sir Edwin glowed with pleasure at his new *imago*. A pity, of course, that Patty hadn't let him enquire more closely into the young chap's past, but it was all settled now, with a good get-out clause in case of nasty accidents, so *noblesse oblige* and he'd better go round encouraging people to make free with these beastly refreshments, which looked as if they'd been specially dyed for the occasion.

"My dear old boy," he said, punching Tom in the back as he passed behind him and Patricia. Make the chap feel at home, eh—how was that for a start?

But Tom, who was facing an even more brutal attack from the front, hardly noticed.

"Oh, Tom," Tessie was saying; "and is this your lovely bride? Oh Gawd, I feel quite faint."

She kissed Patricia greedily but not without all restraint; Tom she might have swallowed whole, had not Fielding Gray prodded her from behind to indicate that it was time to desist.

"There's rather a long queue," he said.

So Tessie unclamped herself and waddled off, and Fielding took her place.

"Major Gray, darling," said Tom before he could stop himself. Somehow the formality seemed appropriate today.

"Your servant, madam," Fielding said, with about eighty per cent. irony. He bent to kiss her hand and was gone. Next came Peter and Helen Morrison. While the two women eyed each other warily, Tom whispered to Peter,

"Have a word with old Edwin. I've done what I could."

"So I heard, and thank you."

"But," said Tom, "he's been very shifty these past few days. I don't know anything for certain, but there's beginning to be a familiar smell in the air. Half sulphur and half stale sweat, if you see what I mean."

"A smell one associates with an office in Gower Street?"

Tom nodded and then inclined himself towards Helen, remembering their last meeting three years before.

"I'm sober today," he said. "Kiss and be friends?"

"Kiss and be friends."

"What—?" began Patricia sharply as the Morrisons moved off.

"—A squalid lapse," said Tom airily, and deliberately left her guessing. "Ah, here comes Somerset," he said.

Further down the queue, back in the ante-room, Jonathan Gamp complained,

"I don't believe there's an ash-try in the entire house." He held up quarter of an inch of cigarette between two finger nails. "It must be a special torture which that prim Patricia's thought up."

"Throw it into the fire-place," said Captain Detterling, and turned away crossly because he hated social ineptness: in Detterling's view, if there were no ash-trays provided in a room one refrained from smoking there.

So Jonathan threw his butt towards the fire-place and didn't bother to see where it landed, which was a good two yards short and on a thick carpet. This was noticed by Carton Weir, who thought it would be amusing to say nothing and see what happened. Carton Weir liked to complicate situations because he was quick-witted and could appear to advantage.

They filed on into the next room.

"*Darling,*" said Jonathan to Tom several times, while the county faces pretended not to notice.

Meanwhile Somerset, having said something polite to

Alastair Dixon and having received a cool but courteous nod
from Rupert Percival, passed through the crowd to Sir Edwin,
who was wondering where Isobel had got to and, still delighted with his new role as aristocratic patron, was drinking
quite a lot of champagne, despite its palpable acidity.

"Ah," he said to Somerset, "I suppose you'd better have
some champagne."

Somerset sipped and winced.

"I don't wish to appear importunate," he said, "but how
are things going?"

"Things?" said Sir Edwin, knowing what he meant.

"Bishop's Cross."

"Mills of God, dear boy. I've got Percival here to fix up a
proper discussion."

Somerset looked dissatisfied.

"More urgency—," he began.

The Minister waved him down like a policeman.

"It's like stalking deer," he said. He took a large gulp of
champagne and decided to expand the simile. "You've got
to get downwind of them. And even then, the slightest noise
and they're off. If Percival suspects. . . . You'll excuse me."
His glass was empty and he wanted more. "Other guests. . . ."

"Please don't forget what's at stake," said Somerset, smiling
urbanely to reassure a covey of M.P.s who were scratching
their way towards his host.

"My dear fellow, I'm a professional."

Cut off from the bar, Sir Edwin marched up to the covey
of M.P.s with the determination of a beater and sent them
fluttering in all directions. Politeness could wait; he wanted
more champagne. "Oh Patricia," he thought, "all these
years I've guarded and loved you like a mother, how could
you?" But this would never do. All that, he reminded himself,
had been settled once and for all : he wasn't losing a daughter,
he was gaining a scholarship boy. A protegé. Rumpff. Playful
stuff, this champagne. He reached the bar and poured himself
a tumbler of it. "Oh Patricia—" *No.*

"Sir Edwin?"

Young Morrison. What did *he* want?

"This is my wife, Helen. You never met. . . ."

"How de do?"

Strong, reliable sort. But you never could tell. He would have sworn before God and man that his own Diana . . . And then, as soon as Isobel had been born. . . . Rumpff.

"So sorry," he said to the surprised Helen. "Trying sort of occasion, you know. No, we never met. And it must be nearly three years," he said to Peter, "since I've seen you."

"I hope that will be different after this autumn. You may have heard—"

"—I've heard." Sir Edwin reflected. Finally he said,

"Always tricky, this sort of thing. Wish you the best of luck, of course."

Not the voice, thought Peter, of a firm supporter. Tom was right : there was a smell of sulphur here.

"Won't be a moment, darling—excuse me, sir," he said on impulse, and screwed his way through the crowd to where he could see Somerset, who was standing alone at one corner of a large table which held the wedding presents.

"What did you send . . . you old crook?"

"That," said Somerset, pointing to a florid edition of Saint Augustine's *Confessions*. "Rather appropriate if one considers Tom's younger days."

"Proselytising, Somerset?"

"It is a duty enjoined upon us. How are you, Peter?"

"Pleased to see you, in a dreadful sort of way. And curious."

"Curious, my dear?"

"Bishop's Cross, Somerset. What's going on?"

"Naturally I'm very anxious to be chosen. It's high time I got started."

"I'm anxious too. I want to get back. But you haven't answered my question. What's going on?"

"You know very well," Somerset told him, "that you can't expect a direct answer to a crude question like that. What makes you think that anything's going on?"

"The way certain people are behaving. And the glazed

look in your eye. It always used to come when you were up to something."

"Oh dear," sighed Somerset, "I hoped I'd got over that."

"I find it rather endearing. A reminder of our childhood."

"When all the best prizes went to you," said Somerset with sudden and naked resentment. "Well, Bishop's Cross is one prize that isn't coming to you. That much I will tell you. And if you want to save time and trouble for yourself and everybody else, you'll withdraw your name. Because just this once the clean-limbed hero of the school is going to be put down by the school swot, and it might look better if he resigned gracefully first."

"I wonder," Helen Morrison was saying to Sir Edwin, "what my husband is saying to Mr. Lloyd-James. They look rather flushed."

"I could tell you why," said the Minister as he refilled his tumbler, "but I'd much sooner not. I'll tell you something else instead. You remind me of my wife."

Helen looked distressed.

"She left me, you know, when my younger daughter was a baby. I wonder," he said, looking vaguely round the room, "where Isobel is?" For a moment his eyes misted, then focused again on Helen. "As I was saying, she left me very suddenly and no one ever found out why. There wasn't even another man, not a proper one, just someone who—Well. So I had to look after the girls, and I've done my best, but sometimes, today of all times, I wonder whether— Oh dear. I don't know why I'm telling you all this. I expect because you look like—"

"—Please," Helen said: "Patricia is a very fine young woman," she instructed him stoutly, "and Tom Llewyllyn is—" She tried to say a "fine young man" but for all the world she couldn't manage it. "—Very clever and distinguished," she concluded.

"Rumpff," went Sir Edwin. "Sorry, dear lady. A trying occasion. Have some more champagne."

He gestured with vigour but made no attempt to get it

for her, then, seeing Peter on his way back to them, excused himself hurriedly and made across the room towards Dixon and Percival, for it was time, his instinct told him, to start throwing a bit of charm about in that quarter.

"Something's up with Somerset," whispered Peter as he rejoined Helen; "but I'm blessed if I know what."

"Something's up," whispered Alfie Schroeder to Tom on the other side of the room.

Alfie had waited at the end of the queue so that he might have a better chance to make his point. Patricia had now strayed a few yards away to talk to some of the bridesmaids, and Alfie was urgent.

"There's something up," he said.

"On the job, Alfie?"

"I came here as a friend, laddie, you know that, so I'm telling you. Get that girl of yours and get out—before something happens to stop you leaving. I wouldn't want to see your honeymoon spoilt. It was about the one good thing that ever happened to me—but never mind that. You get going at once. That's my advice, and it's the best wedding gift you've had so far."

"But Alfie. There are going to be speeches and a cake and God knows what." He glanced at Patricia; but she was safely occupied, it seemed. Even so he moved Alfie further away. "What on earth's the matter?" he said.

"Never you mind. It's just that there's going to be a nasty shock round here before the day's out, and I'd like to see you well away from it."

"But Alfie. . . . How can you know?"

"Let's just say I looked in the woodshed. Or the stables, to be more precise."

"Whatever you saw, we can't just push off."

"You would have done three years ago."

"Things change. There must be speeches, Alfie. It must all be done properly. For Patricia's sake."

"I suppose so," said Alfie miserably. "Try to get a move on, that's all."

But the proceedings, Tom reflected, would take their own time. There were too many rules and too many people; nothing he could do. In any case, Alfie had roused curiosity in him rather than apprehension. If something was going to break, Tom wanted to be in on it. As a writer, he could not afford to miss a good scene; and he was—always would be—a writer before he was a husband. No, he thought; let things take their course : the wedding trip was to last six weeks, and he could well afford a day or two's delay if there was anything to show for it. Absent-mindedly he took a glass of champagne from a tray, then realised this was the first drink he had had time for and drained it in one.

"*Christ,*" he nearly shouted, as the malignant fluid rasped down through his chest.

"*Christ,*" Vanessa Salinger was complaining to her husband Donald. "They must have made it themselves."

"Champagne's always like that at weddings," Donald said; "it's the occasion that counts, remember."

"Stop being so smug."

Donald pouted.

"We ought to have a word with Lord and Lady Canteloupe," he said.

"Why?"

"Good manners require it."

"For Christ's sake, Donald. We don't even know them."

"That's just the point. We ought to. The firm's printing the stuff for the advertising campaign about Canteloupe's Country Culture Camps."

Deferentially Donald stalked Lord Canteloupe, who was standing, glumly and with an empty glass, between Lady Canteloupe and Carton Weir. (The dowager was busy gathering a representative selection from the buffet to take home in her handbag.) Since the Salingers knew Weir slightly, having met him over de Freville's chemmy table from time to time, Donald signed to him for assistance; but Weir, preoccupied with the sight of Sir Edwin courting Rupert Percival, did not respond.

"Lord Canteloupe, I'm—er—Donald Salinger," Donald evenually said.

"Who?" said Canteloupe savagely.

Carton Weir, his attention recalled by this exchange, whispered in the Secretary's ear.

"Of course," boomed Canteloupe. "Delighted to meet you. Doing a great job with the printing. Be a good chap," he said to Weir regally, "and get me some more of this poisonous stuff."

Refusal being tactless in present company, Weir took the empty glass and moved off towards the bar.

"And this," Donald Salinger began, "is my—"

But Vanessa, anxious for a little light relief, had followed Weir.

"Shall I tell you something amusing?" she said.

"I could do with it. Trailing round with that lot isn't very joy-making."

"Well then. Sir Edwin Turbot's pissed."

She nodded towards where the Minister was talking, red with effort, to Percival and Dixon.

"What of it? So would Canteloupe be if I gave him half a chance."

He poured an ungenerous glass of champagne and started back with it.

"Sir Edwin's pissed," Vanessa said, "because he doesn't like this marriage."

"We always knew that. He doesn't care for Tom Llewyllyn."

Deftly, Carton Weir forged a passage between a jowly M.P. and a shapeless county lady, Scylla and Charybdis.

"You haven't seen the point," Vanessa said. "It's not that he doesn't care for Tom. He's *jealous.*"

"Old Oedipus again? Quite normal."

Vanessa put up her hand to detain him while they were still out of earshot of Donald and the Canteloupes.

"When a girl hasn't got a mother," she said, "she sometimes has a very special thing with the father. And *vice versa.*

Far more than the usual father-daughter thing. I had a girl friend once . . . it was much the same story as this, important family, almost as much money. Just before the couple went off from the wedding breakfast in their car, her father went beserk. He raged round the car cursing at the top of his voice, and started cutting all the old shoes and things off the back bumper with a pair of garden shears. Then he ran into the house again snapping the shears at the guests—dangerously, not just pretend—and wouldn't leave his bedroom for a week."

"Why are you telling me this?"

"Helpful hints, sweetie, for a young politician on the make. Afterwards, my friend's father was a changed man. Within a year of the wedding he was caught with his hand in the till. Embezzling clients' money. Only a few hundred quid—which he didn't begin to need. You see what I mean?"

"Edwin Turbot's made of sterner stuff."

"I wouldn't be too sure, sweetie. Change of life, you see."

"*Please,* darling."

"Men can have it as well as women—particularly if they've been doing a woman's job, standing in for mummy like Sir Edwin here. Now, most women have their change at just about the same time as their children are growing up and leaving them, so if Sir Edwin's going to have one, it'll happen now. Elder daughter getting married—just the time when her mother would have been going funny and having all those operations. As surrogate mother, he must do it instead."

"*Angel,*" said Carton, who was getting rather restless and was not at all sure how seriously Vanessa's theory should be taken.

"And if you throw in a dose of jealousy to help unsettle him—"

"—Are you suggesting he'll go potty like your friend's papa?"

"Not potty. Odd. It can take a number of forms—like this boozing today. One thing which happens at the change of life is they start taking to the bottle."

Carton Weir dilated his eyeballs at her, then led on firmly
to the Canteloupe group, which had now been rejoined by the
dowager. Canteloupe, who was panting slightly, snatched at
the glass of champagne. Donald flashed vicious annoyance
at Vanessa and went on being ponderously bonhomous to the
marchioness. The dowager offered wedding canapés all round
out of her handbag and then, taking an immediate fancy
to Vanessa and having an instinct for likely informants,
propelled her on to one side to ask questions about Tom
Llewyllyn's private life. Carton Weir, keeping a careful eye
on Canteloupe, considered Vanessa's theory about Sir Edwin.
It was, of course, preposterous; but there was no doubt that
the Minister had been soaking up champagne—out of a
tumbler at that. Smaller things than this had been known
to herald important changes in important men. . . .

"So that's fixed," Sir Edwin was saying to Rupert
Percival.

"What is?" said Percival, who was being wary.

"That I'll drive over and talk to you on Monday. Before
I go up to London."

Suddenly Sir Edwin felt exhausted. If only they'd all go
away; Patricia, Tom, Dixon, Percival, the lot. Go away and
leave him in peace. Never mind Lloyd-James and his threats,
never mind squaring this smug provincial solicitor, never
mind this abominable wedding and the concomitant follies:
sleep, that was the thing, sleep. . . . Come, come, this wouldn't
do. In a minute or two he must make a speech, he must pull
himself together, life must go on to the last, what he needed
was more champagne.

"Alastair," he said to Dixon in a brittle voice, "please get
me something to drink."

Dixon, accustomed by years of political life to fagging
and bootlicking, took the empty tumbler and moved away.
Percival, who had long since sensed an ulterior motive behind
the Minister's attentions and regarded Dixon's despatch as
the preliminary to a private assault, bristled and made ready.

"Yes?" he said sharply.

"Yes what?" sighed Sir Edwin.

"Your proposal—to visit me on Monday—is a little sudden. I'm not very clear as to its purpose."

"Exchange of ideas. It's always a good thing for those of us at the centre of the party to hear what you're thinking down in the constituencies."

"It's a long time since anyone of your . . . eminence . . . has shown such an interest."

"Too long perhaps," muttered the Minister. Where was Dixon with that drink?

"We aren't fools," Percival said. "We know that this kind of interest . . . this condescension . . . is only the preface to some demand. Why can't you leave us in peace?"

"I sympathise with your attitude, believe me."

"Then why not leave us in peace?"

"Because something has come up . . . to disturb the peace."

"Ah. So there is something you want."

Dixon returned with the Minister's champagne. In a wine glass, Sir Edwin regretfully noticed : what had he done with that commodious tumbler? And then, Percival's not giving much away, he thought : how will he react? After all he's no catch-penny moralist, he's one of us, one of the old guard, he should be able to take it. But with these country chappies one could never tell; they might turn out to be the most colossal prudes, or they might develop some kind of feudal mania and start asking for earldoms. Not, he gathered, that Percival was the type who asked for things . . . and so much the worse. But he was really too tired to consider the details now. He would give the fellow some idea and leave the rest till Monday. Sir Edwin drank off his champagne and for a moment felt slightly better.

"We need your help," he said in a level voice : "don't we, Alastair?"

Dixon, as yet unconscious of the real issues at stake, assented with a practised air of conviction.

"In what respect?" said Percival.

"Over your choice of a successor to Alastair here."

"Indeed," said Percival, his eyes rippling with hostility: "not a topic for a wedding breakfast."

"No," said Sir Edwin suavely: "for Monday."

Trained to achieve the last word (and thus to leave every contest, if not victorious, at least for the time undefeated), he turned before Percival could answer and moved off to arrange for the speeches to start. As he went he passed Peter Morrison, who was talking, he noticed, to that odd chap with one eye. Still euphoric from the last glass of champagne, he smiled genially, forgetting that Morrison was now an obstacle which must, at any cost, be shifted.

"Well, well," said Peter to Fielding. "Earlier on he hardly knew me. What's all this you were trying to tell me in the church? About Somerset?"

"That he'll be a tricky opponent."

"Not news, Fielding."

"I dare say not. But there's one thing more." Fielding lowered his head slightly. His good eye was both amused and shifty. "Mind you," he said, "Somerset's been kind to me since I've been back. But it seems to me from what I've heard . . . from what Llewyllyn and others have been saying . . . that it would be better if you were given the seat at Bishop's Cross."

"Better?"

"Yes. The House of Commons may no longer enjoy much esteem, but there are limits, and they don't include Somerset. So for old times' sake I've something to tell you."

Peter said nothing but turned his enormous face full on to Fielding.

"Something," Fielding went on, "about yourself rather than Somerset. Something which your supporters are too close to you to see. Or perhaps too respectful to mention."

"Well?"

"Just this. Your trouble is that you're such a frightful bloody prig. Oh, I know what you're going to say," he continued steadily as Peter opened his mouth to speak; "you're going to say that I've hardly seen you in fourteen years, so what can I know about it? Well, I've always followed your career, more recently I've listened to friends of yours in London, and just now I've spent the afternoon watching you and your wife. So I'll say it again, Peter. You're a pompous, self-satisfied prig. All this prate about duty and honour and loyalty, and not a row of beans to show for it. Nothing : except for this resignation three years ago—just when things were beginning to look difficult. You're so infatuated with your own vision of yourself that you think it's beneath you to make an effort, to do something concrete. You won't lift a finger—in case you spoil your pose. Say what you like about Somerset, at least he joins in. He's not afraid to get his hands blistered."

"Or dirty. I thought you were on my side," said Peter, sweaty and flushed.

"I am. That's why I'm telling you that it's no good just sitting on your arse and expecting to be wafted back into Parliament on clouds of virtue like a baroque picture of God."

"Decency imposes certain rules."

"So does necessity. First you've got to get back. Then you can start talking about decency—and I grant you that a little's badly needed. But for God's sake stop being so self-righteous and get yourself moving. Otherwise Somerset's going to walk all over you."

"So he's just been telling me."

"There you go again. The retort courteous. It's no good any more. People don't want your unruffled gentleman act, all patronising and paternal, they want interference, action, indignation—even pettiness, so that they know you're one of them."

"At Bishop's Cross they're still rather old-fashioned."

"Not so old-fashioned that they want to send a stuffed dummy to Westminster."

"I think," said Peter, irritated but kind, "that you had better stick to what you know about. I liked your last piece in *Strix*."

"Don't change the subject. It's always the same with you people who inherit money when you're 'young, nobody contradicts you and you soon start thinking you're Christ Al—"

"—Isn't there some talk of a book?" persisted Peter, knowing just where and how close under the surface vanity would lie.

"Two books as it happens. But we're not talk—"

"—Who's publishing them?"

"Gregory Stern. And I'm writing another one for him," said Fielding, his face becoming fatuous with conceit, Peter's shortcomings now graciously dismissed. Capitulation, Peter thought: what is it about writers that makes them so naïve, as if they thought that writing books was the only worthwhile occupation and that the whole world talked of nothing else? Self-absorption, he presumed; their careers, to be fair, were so difficult and precarious that without their egotism to protect them they wouldn't survive a week.

"Stern's over there with Detterling," Peter said. "I thought he looked very well as best man. Let's go and have a word."

On their way over they were joined by Tessie Buttock, who felt that she now had certain proprietary rights in Fielding. Stern, who looked a little tense, nevertheless bowed to Tessie with princely elegance when she was introduced.

"So you're the guardian angel of my authors?" he said. "I've often heard about you from Tom."

But since mention of Tom seemed likely to reduce Tessie to tears again, the subject was changed.

"I've got to make a speech," Stern said. "I've been trying to think of an original joke."

"There are none," said Detterling: "not for this occasion." The topic foundered.

"I see," said Detterling after a pause, "that Donald Salinger is keen to ingratiate himself with Canteloupe."

"Business, dear," said Jonathan Gamp, who had suddenly appeared in their midst. "Donald's printing the posters about Canteloupe's caravans, and he's hoping there'll be more where that came from. He's been steadily losing business for the last three years . . . ever since he got rid of Jude Holbrook."

"Jude Holbrook?" said Fielding with a glance at Tessie.

Jonathan, who had never met Fielding, started a polite explanation.

"Jude was Donald's partner, you see. Until he put up a whopping great black. But the thing is, he really did understand business, so after he disappeared—and disappeared is the *mot juste*—poor old Donald started running downhill. Slowly, mind you. Donald's no fool, it's just that he hasn't got the thrust Jude had, won't ever take a risk."

"Would it amuse you," said Fielding, "to hear that Jude Holbrook's back in London?"

"It would not," said Detterling, "but it would interest me. I wonder what he's up to."

"He pays regular," Tessie put in; "and no dragging back."

"Need he be up to anything?" Fielding asked.

"Oh yes, dear," mewed Jonathan, wriggling his hips with pleasure. "Jude hasn't come to London for the bracing air, you may depend upon that. Tell us *more*."

"Nothing to tell. He's taken a room with Tessie here and keeps himself to himself."

"Never stops for a chat," Tessie said. "Hardly says good morning some days."

"I *wonder*," Jonathan said.

Helen came to stand by Peter.

"I've been talking to Patricia Llewyllyn," she told him, "and some of the bridesmaids. Patricia's worried stiff about something. I hadn't met her before, so I couldn't press—"

There was a loud rapping and a call for silence. Stern went white; though he always acquitted himself beautifully on these occasions, he suffered torments of nerves beforehand. Alfie Schroeder belched loudly. "SSSHHH," everybody went. Sir Edwin, standing on a chair, began to speak. His voice was without tone of any kind, without authority, without warmth, like the thin, level drone (Fielding thought) with which the ghostly heroes greeted Odysseus from the banks of hell.

"I have an announcement to make," Sir Edwin said. "The house is on fire. Those that wish may leave through the door on to the terrace."

He pointed to the exit in question, got down from the chair, and started talking, as if nothing at all had happened, to a lady in a vast yellow hat.

"There's a nice thing," Tessie said, "to happen on Tom's wedding day."

But neither she nor anyone else made any effort to move. Apart from the conversation being rather muted, while people tried to remember what they had been discussing and take it up again, everything went on as before. It seemed generally agreed that Sir Edwin's interruption could be ignored.

"Bonkers," Vanessa Salinger was saying to the dowager : "the house is no more on fire than I am. I knew he was going funny."

"There *is* rather a smell of burning," said the younger Lady Canteloupe.

"Only cigarette smoke," said Donald, who had a horror of fires and was looking slightly peculiar.

"Gamp's cigarette," said Weir, remembering.

He hurried away past the bar, peered into the inner room through which the queue had stretched, and returned grinning.

"The carpet's caught," he said, "and there's a large sofa smouldering."

"That doesn't mean the house is on fire," Vanessa sniffed : "sheer exaggeration."

"Ought it to be put out?"

"Turbot must have seen it, otherwise he wouldn't have made that speech. So I expect he's made arrangements. Told the servants or something."

"Then why did he ask us to leave?"

"He didn't. He only suggested."

"I think," said Vanessa, who had been watching Tom and his new bride talking together in one corner with anxious faces, "that there's more in all this than meets the eye."

Lord Canteloupe was taking advantage of this diversion among his attendants.

"Can you get me a drink?" he said to a passing waiter.

"Sorry, my lord."

"What do you mean, sorry."

"Been told to drop everything and look for Miss Isobel. Sharpish."

"Miss Isobel can take care of herself."

"But the house is on fire, my lord."

"It's nothing of the kind. Please get me a drink."

"I'm only a servant here, my lord. Which means I believe what Sir Edwin says and do what he tells me."

And indeed, as the waiter moved away (none too eagerly, Canteloupe noticed), smoke started wafting into the reception room and with it a faint uneasiness among the weaker-minded guests.

"Do you suppose he really meant it?" said Tessie.

"It can't be anything much," Jonathan Gamp assured her. "I expect someone's dropped a cigarette."

"I think," said Gregory Stern, "that everyone feels it would be bad form to show panic. So no one can be the first to move, and they'll all roast to death rather than commit a social solecism. Very English."

Alfie Schroeder, who was perfectly prepared to commit a social solecism, hovered near the glass door on to the terrace, where he was joined by Tessie.

"Quite right, love," Alfie said. "Much the safest place."

"But what *is* going on?" bleated Tessie.

"If you want my opinion," Detterling was saying to Stern, "the motivation is slightly different. Refusal, by members of a ruling caste, to acknowledge that *they* could be inconvenienced. Therefore they must behave as if the fire did not exist. There was an officer in my regiment who was once mortally offended because a soda-siphon ran out while he was using it.

He regarded it as a kind of insolence on the part of the siphon. That's what this fire is—a piece of insolence on the part of nature, to be pointedly ignored until it gets ashamed of itself and goes away."

Meanwhile the smoke grew thicker. Vanessa Salinger, who wasn't quite well enough bred to know that the fire mustn't be acknowledged, coughed and attracted pitying glances. The dowager selected from her handbag a canapé of a curious mauve and sat down to enjoy it.

"I think your theory is over-sophisticated," Fielding Gray was saying to Detterling. "I think this is more like a nasty smell in a car. You just drive on and hope for the best."

"Same thing," Detterling commented. "*My* car wouldn't *dare* break down. A member of the lower class, on the other hand, would get out to see what the matter was."

"Only," contributed Peter Morrison, "because he would know about engines and we don't."

They were joined by Somerset Lloyd-James.

"It reminds me of the time John Dorsetshire tried to kill himself," he remarked. "In full view of everyone at Newmarket, but they all thought it would be impolite to take any notice. They left him on the ground, I'm told, until after the result of the photo-finish was announced."

"That's because they were too interested in the photo-finish . . . unlike poor Dorsetshire. He knew where *his* horse had come in."

"They do say it was slowed down by one of the bookies . ."

At this stage Sir Edwin got up on the chair again. This time he was more animated.

"Ladies and gentlemen," he said, "I fully appreciate the delicacy of feeling which prompted you to ignore my first warning. But now, since the fire-brigade will be here at any moment, and since they will require space in which to manoeuvre. . . ."

As Sir Edwin's courteous speech droned on, Alfie and Tessie, standing by the glass door, witnessed the following sequence of events. Along the road, which was visible beyond some 300 yards of down-sloping meadow and which led to the entrance of Sir Edwin's drive, came a large black limousine, which Alfie correctly assumed to be the hired car that was to take the newly weds the fifteen miles to Salisbury station. Behind the limousine, clanging its bell but unable to pass because of the narrowness of the road, came a fire-engine of a design which Alfie had not seen since the blitz. When the limousine was still about a quarter of a mile from Sir Edwin's gate, there was a loud roar from the area of the stables on the other side of the house, and a few seconds later an open sports car of blue and white, rather like a giant co-respondent's shoe, could be seen by Alfie and Tessie shooting down the drive. At the wheel was a young man whom neither of them knew; next to him was a girl dressed in the striking shade of green affected for the occasion by the bridesmaids.

"That's the chief one," Tessie said, "the one who was taking care of the little boy in the kilt."

"I know," said Alfie with grim satisfaction.

As the sports car hurtled down the drive towards the gate, it was hidden from the limousine on the road by thickets of rhododendron, while its noise (Alfie presumed) was drowned by the clanging of the fire-engine. The chauffeur of the limousine was therefore quite unprepared for the emergence of the sports car, which, without any pause and doing about fifty miles an hour, shot out in a wide left-handed turn on to the limousine's side of the road and then made straight for it. True, the driver of the sports car was steering it back on to the proper side of the road, and succeeded in gaining this without hitting the limousine; but by that time the limousine had braked very sharply and the fire-engine had run into it from behind. The sports car—God knows how it squeezed through on the narrow road, Alfie thought—did not stop but roared away in the direction from which limousine and fire-engine had been approaching; a dazed chauffeur lurched out of the limousine and tottered to the rear; some men climbed off the fire-engine and began to inspect a twisted figure which seemed somehow to be impaled against the back of its open driving seat; and that, Alfie thought, is one poor bugger's one-way ticket home.

"And so," Sir Edwin was saying, "if you will kindly proceed on to the terrace. . . ."

I told Tom, Alfie thought, to get away before anything happened; and now this. Not that it was quite what I expected, but it will serve even more surely to delay him.

"Oughtn't we to tell someone?" Tessie said.

Alfie nodded. First things first, he thought. Get this absurd fire put out, and then tell them about the girl and the rest of it. He pushed his way through the crowd to where the Minister was still politely perorating from the chair. Since Alfie was short, his head hardly reached Sir Edwin's knees; so he tugged at one tail of his morning coat, and was brushed off like a fly.

"It will not, of course, be possible to have the usual speeches before we go outside," Sir Edwin was saying, "and there will be logistic difficulties about refreshment. But if you will take your glasses with you and congregate at the southeast corner of the lawn, we will contrive to drink a toast. Thank you."

Sir Edwin got down from the chair and was rather surprised to see Alfie get up in his place.

"Ladies and gentlemen," Alfie said. "The fire-engine has had an accident. It can't get here."

No one disputed this, and there was a buzz of tired interest.

"Why didn't you say so straight away?" said Sir Edwin. "I'll go and telephone for another."

But as Alfie had anticipated, there were those who favoured action more direct. The Minister's first speech had simply been a scientific proposition, but his more recent mention of the fire-engine had constituted social recognition (so to speak) of the fire, and it was now permissible to have dealings with it. While Tom escorted Patricia, who was still talking at him intently, to safety with Tessie by the glass door, Captain Detterling picked up two buckets of melted ice and marched through to the conflagration. Peter and Fielding did likewise. Somerset took the opportunity of going over to the Canteloupe group to tease Donald Salinger, who had been nervous about fires ever since his hair was set alight during a drunken party at Oxford. Detterling came back out of the inner room.

"It's taken quite a hold," he said : "find all the buckets you can."

Fielding came after him.

"The water's been cut off. I've been through to the kitchen. . . ."

"It often happens," said Sir Edwin conversationally. "about this time of the afternoon. They're laying new pipes."

"The stables?"

"It will be the same there."

"Only one thing for it, Edwin," said the dowager. "Use the champagne."

"The *champagne*?"

"*Not* a time for economy."

Canteloupe came to life.

"Champagne," he roared.

He ran behind the bar, had two bottles open within seconds, took a swig from each, then rushed through to the fire and started hosing it with a twin frothy stream.

"More," he called from within.

"Champagne," the cry went up.

With gay abandon bottles were opened and passed down an improvised chain gang to where Canteloupe, supported by Weir and the dowager, poured the amber fluid through clouds of steam on to the immense sofa and large areas of carpet.

"About all it's fit for," Canteloupe was saying, though treating himself to copious gulps.

"More . . . more," howled the dowager.

"Over there in the corner," Weir said : "there's something odd behind the writing desk. . . . I can't quite see. . . ."

"Nonsense. Finish the sofa first."

In the reception room Alfie took Tom on one side.

"The chief bridesmaid," he said: "it *was* your sister-in-law?"

"Yes. Patricia's very worried because she's been behaving oddly . . . disappeared somewhere after the service."

"She's disappeared in the rough direction of Bristol," Alfie said, "doing about ninety miles an hour in a sports car which is driven by a young man who'll have manslaughter to answer for."

Alfie explained.

"Isobel has peculiar friends," was all Tom could find to say.

"Have you seen my little boy," a harassed woman was asking them, "the page in the kilt? Isobel Turbot was taking care of him, but she seems—"

"—I should look in the garden," said Tom gently.

The woman hurried off.

"Upstairs?" said Alfie.

"Perhaps. 'Now, darling,'" Tom said in a clumsy parody of Isobel, "'Auntie Isobel's got to go. So you walk through there to find all the nice people. . . .'"

"But he couldn't have been—"

Tom set off down the champagne chain and into the smoke.

"Have you seen the page?" he shouted at Weir.

"The page," the cry went back along the chain, "the page."

"There's something behind the desk."

"Oh my God."

The smoke was thicker now. Tom blundered over to the desk.

"The champagne's run out." "Has anyone seen the page?" "There's some men at the door with a stretcher and—er—something on it." "A chauffeur, out of his wits with temper." ". . . The page. . . ."

Tom hauled out a small, dirty, blubbering figure in a kilt.

"What were you doing there, laddie? Why didn't you call for help?"

"The man told me to hide. Half an hour, he said, and if I didn't he'd find me one day and cut my head off."

On the lawn, after comfort had been administered by paternal Alfie and then by Mummy, the rest of the story came jerking out.

"This man. . . . Auntie Isobel's friend. . . . He said, here's five bob for you, duckie, and you go and hide, and don't tell anyone we've gone for a good half hour, that's what he said, or I'll find you one day and I'll—"

"—Yes, yes. What was he like?"

"He had a funny bottle he kept drinking from. And he smelt nasty when he talked."

But Auntie Isobel had liked him well enough, it seemed, and had been expecting him, because they'd gone specially to the stables to find him, and Auntie Isobel had put her arms round him straight away and gone umshlllppp all over his face. And then the man had had a drink from his funny bottle and had said something about leaving a letter or something, but Auntie Isobel said "No". So then the man had gone umshlllppp all over Auntie Isobel's face, and after that Auntie Isobel had gone all funny and hadn't said anything. So the man had given him the letter and also the five-shillings, and told him to hide, and he'd hidden, and then the smoke. . . .

Tom took the letter from the page and started to read it. A second fire-engine came clanging up the drive. An angry man in a chauffeur's hat stamped across the lawn.

"Who was it?" he shouted, shaking his fist at Alfie. "It was someone from here. Who was it?"

"Ask him," said Alfie pointing at Tom.

"Isobel and I are in love and are going to be married," Tom was reading. "We hope for your consent, and that everything will be pleasant about money and so on. When you agree to this, just put a line in the Personal Column of *The Times*, 'All is forgiven. T.', and we'll come back. Meanwhile we'll be living together as man and wife, so the sooner you agree the better. And of course there are other reasons for us all to be friendly, as you well know. So please don't turn nasty and try to follow us, or get some doddering judge to issue an injunction. Let's all be sensible and make the best of what we've got, which is quite a lot when all's said."

Yours sincerely,

Mark Lewson. Isobel sends love.

The chauffeur came at Tom from one side, Sir Edwin from the other. Firemen came round the house with hoses. Some men appeared on the terrace and put down a stretcher which bore a suggestive object wrapped in a dirty blanket. The page boy observed this and was led away howling. Sir Edwin took the letter from Tom—"Mine, if I'm not mistaken"—and started to read. The chauffeur shook his fist.

"Who was it? That's what I want to know."

"Apparently," said Tom, "it was a man called Le—"

"—We don't know," said Sir Edwin, looking coolly up from the letter. "A stranger. Not one of the guests."

"But '*e* was going to tell me." A nod at Tom.

"He's had a bad shock. His wedding's been ruined and he doesn't know what he's saying."

" 'E looks all right to me," the chauffeur said, and drew up to Sir Edwin with unmistakable menace.

"I am Sir Edwin Turbot, a minister of the Queen. If you lay hands on me, you'll go to prison for the longest sentence Her Majesty's Courts can award. You would be better employed summoning the police."

Sir Edwin turned and beckoned Tom to follow him. The chauffeur approached Alfie.

"Something odd going on, mate."

Alfie said nothing but looked anxiously after Tom.

"Why—?" Tom began.

"It must be kept quiet," Sir Edwin said.

"It can't be."

"Not about Isobel, I agree. But no one must know who's with her."

"Why not?"

Sir Edwin snuffled and shook his head without speaking.

"Why not?" persisted Tom. "He's a wanted man. Over there on the terrace there's a—"

"—Did anyone recognise the driver as Lewson?"

"No, but now we know it was him—"

"No, we don't," Sir Edwin said. "You just help clear up the mess and get everyone out of the place. And when the police come, send them straight to me."

Very soon, the fire was brought under control, the guests were dismissed ("My favourite wedding ever," said Jonathan Gamp), the police were received, witnesses questioned, and statements taken.

"Saw them driving off but didn't know him from Adam," said Alfie, who along with Tessie and the page had stayed behind to help the enquiries.

"A funny bottle," the kilted page repeated, "and a nasty smell."

"So *that's* plain enough," the Inspector said. "You run off to mummy." And to Tessie, "You saw him, madam?"

"First time in my life. No idea who he was."

"So he can't have been at the wedding. What about this letter the little lad talked about? Might tell us who the fellow was."

"The page dropped the letter in the fire—when he was rescued," Sir Edwin deposed.

Both Tom and Alfie opened their mouths. Then they shut them; Tom because Sir Edwin was now his father-in-law and must be given a chance to explain himself in private, Alfie because he trusted Tom and was prepared, for the time at least, to follow his lead.

"Well, it shouldn't take us long to find them," said the Inspector. "Mind you, it would be a help if we had the number. But a blue and white open sports car—conspicuous, I'd say."

That was what Sir Edwin was afraid of; but evening

yielded to night, night to morning, morning to afternoon again, and there was still no word. Meanwhile it was agreed that the start of the wedding tour should be postponed—"It seems there's one honeymoon in the family already," as Sir Edwin grimly remarked—and that Patricia and Tom should stay with Sir Edwin until the situation had been made plainer. On her wedding night, so long, so lovingly, so greedily awaited, Patricia turned away: "not now," she implored him: "not yet."

8

A BEAST IN VIEW

"RIGHT," SAID Lord Canteloupe to Carton Weir: "now for a little word with the staff."

They were in the Quantocks inspecting the completed caravan site, which was due for its ceremonial opening in three days' time. They had inspected the dance-hall-cum-gymnasium, the swimming pool ("Fed by Clear Mountain Waters"), the dinette, the nursery-crêche, the project and discussion centre, and the Maison Bingo. This latter had rather a contrived air, since it had been popped up at the last moment as a result of Canteloupe's recent decision that Bingo should be included in what he called his Country Culture; but all in all the camp's outer periphery, of which the Maison Bingo and the other amenities formed the greater part, was a credit to the Scheme, especially if one considered how quickly it had all been run up. The shock had come when they started inspecting the caravans and sanitary appointments in the central body of the camp, a shock in no way palliated by the attitudes of Camp Commandant Hookeby (an ex-lieutenant-colonel, once mildly celebrated as the laziest officer in the Royal Corps of Signals), who was showing them round.

The first thing that had been wrong was that half the caravans had no wheels and were supported by piles of oil cans and similar detritus.

"It's not as if they're ever going to move," said the Camp Commandant.

"Looks bloody awful," said Canteloupe. "Anyway, where

are the wheels?"

"The peasants stole them," said Hookeby, gesturing out over Somersetshire, "before I arrived to take over."

"Then get new ones and post a piquet."

Hookeby nodded wisely, then sealed one nostril with his forefinger and winked at Carton behind Canteloupe's back.

"My wife," Hookeby said, "maintains that you can't trust the natives."

Canteloupe snorted and climbed into a caravan. Then came the next disillusionment. At the second step inside his foot had gone straight through the floor.

"They don't season the wood these days," the Commandant explained. "Too impatient to get their money back on it. It's the same with cricket bats, I'm told."

Again he winked at Carton, who despite his official dignity started sniggering like a school-girl. He had not expected such a bonus of entertainment.

The next caravan which Canteloupe inspected had survived the ordeal but turned out to be concealing a large pile of decaying sandwiches in a clothes cupboard.

"Contractors' men," said Hookeby cheerfully: "filthy brutes."

"Get it cleaned up."

"The man's off ill."

"Then clean it up yourself."

By this time Weir had recovered his gravity. If something went wrong at the opening, Canteloupe would be in trouble and so would he. And so now, as they moved towards the showers and the rears, which were at the very centre of the site ("The heart of camp life," smirked Hookeby), he began to think about ways of dissociating himself from the department at short notice.

The first shower, when tested, had spat rusty water like a snake, shuddered, and gone dead. The second, on the other hand, performed with such crazed intensity that the spray had shot off the pipe and hit Carton hard on the knee; furthermore, it refused to be turned off.

" 'And here's the interesting bit,' " Hookeby quoted: " 'There was no way of stopping it. . . .' "

Canteloupe snorted at him and led the way to the toilets. As they entered someone slouched resentfully past them on his way out. This someone had a huge, yellow, drooping moustache, carried a pile of Sunday newspapers, was smoking a pipe and chewing something at the same time, was also buttoning his trousers, and made no attempt at greeting.

"Who in the name of God was that?"

"Sergeant-Major Cruxtable," said Hookeby: "physical fitness and so on. I think we caught him at what he calls his 'time'."

This had been the last straw. Canteloupe looked at the retreating Cruxtable, he looked at Hookeby, he looked down the long rows of partitions, turned away with a slight heave, and at last he looked, as if here at least he had hoped for sanity and support, at Carton Weir.

"Right," he said grimly and sadly: "now for a little word with the staff."

This was all too easily arranged. Since the refuse man was absent with what he termed "haemorrhoids" and the boiler man with varicose veins, since the cook and her two assistant sluts were not due until the next day and the Camp Matron was out to lunch with a colleague at the nearby mental home, they were left with Cruxtable, Mrs. Hookeby (a chinless, mem-sahibish woman whose role was not very clearly defined), and Hookeby himself. These being duly assembled in the project and discussion room, Canteloupe said:

"This place is a pig-sty. I have no alternative but to stay here myself until we open, in order to bring things into a condition befitting the honour which Her Royal Highness will pay us."

There was something rather magnificent about him as he said this, something which even Hookeby and Cruxtable seemed to sense. As for Carton, he was reminded that Canteloupe had organised the most famous and profitable "Stately Home" of them all, and now he saw one reason why. If no one else would do the job properly, Canteloupe would see to it himself. Repenting of the disloyal thoughts which he had entertained earlier in the afternoon, noticing that he had unconsciously come to attention during his chief's short speech, Carton inclined his head to hear his instructions.

"You'll be no good here," said Canteloupe dismissively, "so go back to London and handle things there. Call in at my place on your way and send the car back here with a camp bed and a dozen of burgundy. I suppose," he snapped at Hookeby, "you can feed me?"

"Sir," Hookeby said.

"Off with you then," said Canteloupe to Weir; to Hookeby, "Get me that contractor on the telephone—Sunday or no Sunday"; to Cruxtable, "Find a suit of overalls and report back in five minutes"; and to Mrs. Hookeby, "You too, madam—with a bucket and a mop."

Sir Edwin Turbot had originally opined that Mark Lewson would be easier to deal with, since all he wanted was money, than Somerset Lloyd-James. The situation had now changed. In the first place, it now appeared that Lewson was demanding his daughter as well as his gold, and Sir Edwin was disinclined to concede her. But in the second place, if the police found Isobel for him, they would also find Lewson, which would not do at all; for there was a strong chance that Lewson, desperate and illogical, would seek to distract attention from his crime by revealing his secret.

Another problem was what to tell his son-in-law. Tom had so far kept quiet, out of deference to himself, about the identity of the hit and run driver; but if this silence was to be maintained, Tom must have an explanation. Yet what could he be told? Certainly not the truth, or anything near it. There was really only one thing to do : he would have to appeal to Tom's loyalty as a member of the family, and on that basis ask for his trust. And his help, which would be badly needed. And if Tom showed signs of restlessness, then Patricia must be told off to deal with him. After all, she was his wife, his newly wedded wife, and Tom (to judge by his grave and loving demeanour in the church) would surely heed her.

With all this in mind, the Minister summoned both Tom and Patricia to his study.

"You've seen the morning's papers?" he began. "Rather hostile, I thought."

"Perhaps," said Tom, "you should have issued a fuller statement. They feel thwarted. The police have had the devil's own job keeping them out of here over the week-end."

Sir Edwin looked thoughtfully at the paper which lay nearest to hand:

MINISTER'S DAUGHTER BOLTS WITH MR. X
Hit and Run Elopement.

"They seem to have enough to be going on with," he said: "what else could I tell them?"

"Yes," said Patricia, protective. "What else could Daddy have told them?"

"The press is the self-appointed guardian of public morality. In such cases, it likes to assure its readers that steps are being taken to uphold that morality . . . that chastity and family honour are being defended."

"But what could Daddy have done?"

"He could have obtained an injunction against Isobel's abductor."

"But if we don't know who he is?"

Tom and Sir Edwin exchanged glances.

"We do know who he is," said Sir Edwin with a small sigh. "He's called Lewson." He did not remind her of Lewson's visit with Somerset Lloyd-James as he did not wish Tom to know of this. Nor, as it happened, did Patricia, who was conscious that she had cut a very foolish figure on that occasion.

"Then why haven't you told the police?" she said.

"Because I don't want him to be caught," said Sir Edwin flatly.

"Why not?"

"I must say, sir," said Tom: "we are entitled to know."

"It's a matter of tactics," said Sir Edwin, firm and glib. "Here I am, a senior Minister of the Crown. My younger daughter has run off with a man at present unknown who is wanted for drunken driving . . . worse, for manslaughter. If they are caught together, investigation and trial will take months and Isobel's name will become indissolubly associated with a vicious lout and a scandalous case in the criminal courts. My position would be intolerable and I should have to resign."

He snapped open a packet of chocolate biscuits. In his way he was enjoying himself.

"But if," he continued, "we can contrive quietly to bring her back without anyone's assistance . . . and if the young man disappears still unknown . . . then the whole affair will die down, Isobel will be seen as injured innocence, or at worst as folly repentant, the fatted calf can be killed with discreet advertisement, and no more need be said."

"And the dead man?" Patricia said.

"That wasn't Isobel's fault or ours. Nothing we can do will bring him back. Best concentrate on our own essential problem—which is to avoid any further fuss."

He's lying, Tom thought. All this is plausible enough in its way, but it's not the whole truth. With the means at his command, he could get Isobel accepted as "injured innocence" without protecting Mark Lewson. There's something else. But before he could voice this suspicion in suitably ambiguous terms, Sir Edwin had passed from exposition to appeal.

"So I'm asking you, Tom," he was saying, "to find them. Find them, see Lewson on his way, out of the country if that's still possible, and bring Isobel back here. Of course it's a damned shame about your honeymoon—"

"—What makes you think I can find him?"

"Because you've got to. For my sake . . . and Patricia's."

"How?"

"Put yourself in his place. Ask yourself what you'd have done in his position."

"If you'll play fair by me—" Tom began.

"Of course Daddy will play fair by you," said Patricia, not understanding the hidden query.

"I meant, if your father will. . . ."

He hesitated.

"Will what?"

"Undertake to deal . . . truthfully—"

"—What do you mean?" Patricia blazed. "Daddy's told us what the position is and what must be done. If you're the man I married two days ago, you'll not sit there hedging and hair-splitting, you'll get off your backside and see to it."

Tom looked at her, red and spluttering as she was, ashamed for her sister and anxious for her father, cruelly disappointed and shocked by this grotesque interruption to her happiness; and suddenly he felt pity enter into him, so sharply and brutally that it might have been a needle at the base of his spine. He had been, as it were, violated by compassion.

"Very well," he said. "I'll start at once. Come with me, love, and help me pack a case."

"One thing," the Minister called after him.

"Sir?"

"Your journalist friend, Schroeder. What does he know?"

"He knows we've suppressed that letter which was left with the page boy. So he'll be suspicious."

"What will he do about it?"

"Nothing," said Tom, "until I've spoken with him."

"What will you say?"

"I shall ring him up and ask him to join me in Salisbury or Bath."

"Join you?"

"To help me."

"But discretion," said Sir Edwin, taken aback: "the fewer people who are involved. . . ."

"Alfie's already involved," said Tom. "If I put it to him,

he'll probably be prepared to see it your way . . . if only for my sake. Provided, of course, he thinks you're on the level."

He took Patricia's hand and led her out. Well, Sir Edwin thought, I suppose I had it as much of my own way as I could reasonably expect. He took a handful of chocolate biscuits from the packet. Patty was rather a brick, he thought, cupping a biscuit securely into his hand and slapping it into his mouth; when the family's in trouble she forgets her silly moral fads and becomes a real Turbot. Should be a great help if things get tiresome later . . . if Llewyllyn and that journalist of his. . . .

But never mind all that now, he thought; I've done what I can. With the practised insouciance of his calling, he dismissed Isobel and Lewson altogether from his mind and turned to the next item on the agenda. In just two hours' time he would be seeing Rupert Percival: how best to win his backing for Lloyd-James?

Max de Freville received a letter from Isobel.

". . . Mark and I are writing this together, among other things to thank you for your part in bringing us together. We know it sounds silly, but if things come right, about money and so on, we're going to be the happiest people that ever lived. Mark is so—super. I can't say anything more about him because he is looking over my shoulder as I write and it makes me feel a fool. Proud, but a fool.

"You'll have read about what happened at the wedding and drawn your own conclusions. Mark had been drinking— nerves, he said, and of course one doesn't elope every day. But if was frightful—though we'd no idea, until we saw the papers, that that poor fireman had been killed. Rotten luck, really, for everyone: that road is usually empty for days at a time. Mark feels horrible about it; but we both agree that there's no point in giving himself up at this stage. It wouldn't help anyone and it might spoil everything for us.

Jolly lucky that according to the papers no one who saw us driving off knew who he was. And more luck: it seems no one had time to take the number of that car, so they can't trace us that way. But it's the sort of car which shows up rather, so Mark sold it for cash—no questions asked or answered—to a little man he knew of near Warminster, and took an old Morris shooting brake in part exchange. Mark says the little man will repaint it and anyhow keep it out of the way until the fuss dies down. What it is to know one's way around. But of course it might have been more sensible, for an elopement, to use a less prominent car in the first place. That's one of the things I love about Mark: he's awfully naïve in so many ways, innocent almost.

"But whichever way you look at it, we shall have to lie low for some time. We can't go abroad, though Mark seems to have lots of money with him, because Daddy keeps my passport locked in the safe and I couldn't get at it. But Mark's thinking up a plan for hiding, he's superly clever at that. You must blend naturally with the surroundings, he says. Never hide under a table, sit down at it and start eating, and then no one will take a second look.

"And later on? Well, what we're hoping is that Daddy will play along with us, that because of this peculiar letter he'll let us get married and give us some more money—Mark's won't last for ever, he says, even if he has done quite well just lately. I don't really see that Daddy can refuse, Mark knowing what he does and being able to prove it, and it's a good sign that he hasn't told the police who 'the hit and run driver' is, though he must know because of the note we left him. He daren't risk trouble, Mark says. So it really looks as if there may be a happy ending. If only the police don't find us. But of course it's *me* they're looking for, as they don't know who else, so we're going to be cunning about that—travelling separately and staying at different places, hardly meeting at all until Mark's hit on the ideal place to hide. So if they do find me, they still haven't found Mark, and what can they do then?

"We're writing this in a wood outside a dear little village near a place called Blandford. I'm going to take a bus later on, and Mark will follow in the Morris—we're not quite sure where, but that can be settled later. Because it is wonderful, being in this wood with Mark, on this beautiful summer day—hasn't it been a marvellous summer?—only the two of us in all the world who know where we are, and only mattering to each other. And that brings us to the last thing we've got to tell you. Dear old Max, you've been so kind to us in your way. I've had such fun writing to you all this time, and Mark's enjoyed it too, not only the money you've paid. But now, whatever happens, we've agreed it's got to finish. You see, Mark and I are now *private*. Can you understand? Whatever we may do, we shall be doing it so closely together that to tell you would be, I don't know. . . . Mark says exhibiting ourselves, like a circus act, and from now on it's not going to be like that any more. It was all right when we were separate, it would even be all right if we didn't love each other, but as it is. . . . We do hope you understand.

"Love from Isobel and Mark."

"Will he understand?" Isobel had said to Mark when she finished writing.

"I don't know. He's been very odd lately. I think perhaps . . . by the time he gets this . . . it won't matter to him."

"But we had to tell him," she said.

"Yes, we owed him that. If only all our debts could be so easily paid."

They both lay back. The mid-morning sun, penetrating a gap in the leaves, cast a small patch of light over Mark's eyes. He threw his arm across them, moaning slightly.

"You're still thinking of that man," she said. "You shouldn't. He died at once, the papers say."

She lifted his arm from his eyes and bent over him.

"But there must have been a moment, Isobel, a split second, when the pain. . . . That shaft, driving through his body, smashing through the flesh and the tissue. . . . So delicate, you see, and that brutal shaft, that was me, *driving* through. . . ."

"It's over now."

First to the left, then to the right, then back to the left again, she kissed his eyes until the horror left them.

About the same time as Isobel was kissing Mark in Dorsetshire, Somerset Lloyd-James received a telephone call in Gower Street.

"It's me, dear," said Maisie's voice, strained.

Although Maisie had instructions on no account to ring Somerset at his office, he did not waste time and make matters worse by reminding her of this. He simply said nothing, which conveyed his displeasure far more effectively.

"Can you hear me, dear?"

"Perfectly."

"I'm sorry. I know that you—Look," she said, and there was something desperate in her voice which pierced even Somerset's carapace of self-esteem. "You must come round. Please."

"This evening."

"Now."

Somerset had known Maisie for several years but he had never known her rattled or importunate. Now she was both. More; she was afraid and she was pleading. Trouble, thought Somerset: keep out of it. She's only a public whore, let her settle her own affairs, she's got no claim here: don't get involved.

"Can you hear me, Somerset?"

"This evening, I said."

"No, no, now."

If he rang off, she would only ring again. This was what came of being—well—distinguished. Sooner or later, however little you told them, people like Maisie saw your photograph in the paper, found out what you did, where you worked. You felt flattered, of course, but you told them not to take advantage, never to ring up, they agreed, and then—this. You should have changed your whore, he told himself, as soon as she found out who you were. Or had you yourself told her, late one night, boasting? He couldn't remember, it made no difference anyway, because,

"Somerset," shrilled the telephone, "*Somerset.*"

"I'm coming," he said.

Oh God, he prayed, as he walked down Gower Street searching for a taxi, if this is something the other side's thought up, some come back of Sir Edwin's (who could have told him about Maisie? Tom? but did Tom know? perhaps), then make me strong in cunning.

"Curzon Street. Near the cinema."

Presence of mind, O Lord, that's what I need. God damn the woman—sorry, Lord. Of course one should have foregone such childish pleasures long ago, but the flesh is weak, the member unruly, one had to think (Lord) of one's health. But if this turns out to be all right, a false alarm, just some bill she can't pay, then I promise that from now on—I'll get married, that's the best way. Whom shall I marry? He thought with mounting distaste of the three or four girls whom his father had from time to time recommended, tipped the driver twopence ("Thanks for sod all, Guv"), rang Maisie's bell, and lifted his brown bowler hat to Maisie.

"Please be brief," he said as she closed the door behind him; "I've got a long morning's work."

She nodded, smiled nervously, led the way through to her sitting-room. He had never been in her flat during the morning before. It felt all wrong, cold and exposed. And yet the electric fire was burning, imitation log and all (Maisie knew he felt the cold, even in summer), the curtains were drawn, the corners of the room were in shadow, it might just as well have been afternoon or evening, so why this discomfiture? It was no longer irritation at being disturbed, not even curiosity, but a feeling of being out of place, worse, of being in an element wholly alien. Not a hostile element, exactly, because hostility he understood and this atmosphere was

something which he could not understand, for all the cosy
curtains, the familiar fire. No, this was worse than hostile:
it was indifferent. It neither recognised him nor cared for
him nor hated him nor understood him, any more than he
understood it; but for some reason it had need of him. Was
this how whores were when one did not bring money to pay
for attention? Utterly indifferent, without sympathy or
understanding of any kind? And yet, Maisie had always
seemed a good-natured girl quite apart from the offices of
her trade; and after all, it was she that had summoned him,
apparently wanted his help, so she ought to make an effort
to put him at ease, to dispel this . . . this fog of anonymity
which flooded the room.

"Please be brief," he repeated.

"Gladly," said a man's voice.

Maisie smiled—weakly, guiltily, rather affectionately— and
left the room.

"Jude Holbrook," the voice went on. "You remember
me?"

"Yes."

But the name did nothing to restore normality. Even when
the squat, remembered figure moved out of the shadow and
stood in front of the electric fire, there was still total
indifference in the room, the same impossibility of communication.

"Not that it matters," Holbrook was saying, "whether you
remember me or not. What concerns us is . . . isolated.
Nothing to do with past or the future. Just something that
must happen . . . now."

"The sooner the better," said Somerset sincerely. "I'm a
busy man."

"I must have that letter," Holbrook said, in a bored,
courteous, reasonable voice.

"What letter?" said Somerset, bored, courteous and reasonable in his turn.

"The one you bought from Lewson."

Somerset looked carefully at Holbrook and did not bother

with denials or evasions.

"It isn't for sale," he said equably.

"I didn't suppose it was," said Holbrook in equable exchange. "All the same I must have it."

"What do you propose?"

"I propose that you hand it over to me. I don't want any . . . childishness."

"You've changed," said Somerset. "You are altogether less crude."

"The past is not at issue, as I've already told you. Such comparisons are irrelevant."

"Interesting though . . . if only one were at leisure. Good morning, Jude."

But the door was locked.

"You mustn't blame Maisie. I frightened her, you see."

He took a small bottle from his pocket.

"A little of this in her face and she'd be out of business," he said: "for good."

"My livelihood," said Somerset (Lord, give me strength), "is not so precarious."

Holbrook stepped softly up to Somerset, whipped his glasses off his face with the speed of a conjuror, and placed them carefully on the sofa behind him.

"I don't suppose you can see much now," he said casually: "your livelihood is more precarious than you think."

Somerset blinked and made a mild, deprecating movement with one hand.

"I suppose it's just possible," Holbrook was saying, "that a blind man might be elected to Parliament despite all the difficulties. But a blind editor. . . ."

He unscrewed a stopper from the little bottle, then, keeping the bottle vertical with the most delicate attention, raised it until it was just under Somerset's nose.

"How did you find out?" Somerset said.

"The usual way. I was given a strong scent and I used my nose to follow it. But let me repeat: we're not concerned with the past, only with what's happening now."

Now, Lord, now. Somerset lowered his head and butted. He felt a sickening pain in his bald scalp. He put both his hands over it, clasped them to make a helmet, butted again at nothing, and crashed to the floor.

"It will make a nasty blister on that pate of yours which will look very silly. And that was only a quick dab with the stopper. I did say I didn't want any childishness."

Somerset lay still.

"You can't cope with this sort of behaviour," said Holbrook affably. "You're clever enough and crooked enough to cope with almost anything—provided you can take plenty of time and proceed in your own way. The intellectual's way. But physical action . . . no. You don't understand it. You're not a coward—you've shown that. You're just incompetent."

He kicked Somerset carefully in the groin.

"That hurt," said Holbrook, "but not much, and it'll do no permanent damage. Any more than that blister on your bonce." He bent down and talked straight into Somerset's face. "It was much more difficult," he said, "just to raise a blister than to blind you. But I could do it because I have a talent. You have a talent too. You're as good at teasing, torturing, if necessary destroying, as I am—in your own abstract and cerebral way. But here, in this room, that way's no good. Mine's the way that counts."

He kicked Somerset with gentle precision at the base of the spine. Somerset's whole body stiffened as if in ecstasy. His hand shot out towards Holbrook's ankle.

"No, no, no," said Holbrook briskly.

He ground Somerset's hand with his heel.

"This just isn't your thing. As a rational man, you must see that."

He held the bottle over Somerset's face and began to tilt it.

"Very well," said Somerset, breathing heavily, "you shall have the letter. But I'd be interested to know what you want with it."

"That is for those who employ me to decide."

"If you say so. Pass me my glasses, if you would."

"With pleasure. Tell me, where is it hidden?"

"In my office. In the *Oxford Companion to Classical Literature*. Not a volume people refer to these days."

"Then let's be off. . . . You needn't be ashamed, you know," said Holbrook, solicitously dusting down Somerset's coat. "Only fanatics and morons are capable of resisting pain indefinitely, and if one's going to give in anyway, one may as well do so at once and save a lot of trouble."

They left together discussing this proposition in general terms. Some sort of relationship, after all, had been established by what had passed.

"Good of you to come," said Rupert Percival.

"Good of you to see me," smiled Sir Edwin, wearing his humility like an ill-fitting set of false teeth.

Percival led the way on to his terrace. As they sat down, the Minister hummed a few bars from Lilac Time, his favourite music when his spirits were low. For most of the time he kept them up very well without Novello's assistance; but the events of the last two days had been somewhat lowering, and the interview now in prospect was going to be the more difficult as he had no lever with which to prise Percival in the desired direction. Sir Edwin liked to have leverage. He liked to be in a position to propose a deal, or, failing that, he had no objection to having a deal proposed to him. What he did not care for was occasions, like this one, on which there was no proper basis for negotiation. He would have to *ask*, and of all things he hated asking. If only there had been something which Percival wanted for himself. . . . But Percival, as Dixon had told him, wanted nothing—a piece of intelligence borne out by the placid gaze with which he was now examining the Quantocks. He did not even seem curious to hear what Sir Edwin would say; at all events he made no effort to get him started.

"This election," said the Minister with all the resolution he could muster.

"Yes?"

"I gather you're not choosing your candidate until next month."

"The selection committee meets on July the thirtieth," Percival deposed. "Can I get you a drink?"

"No, thank you." He took a toffee from his pocket, unwrapped it and hustled it into his mouth. "What does Dixon think about it?" he said.

"He thinks," said Percival blandly, "that the committee will choose one of the five candidates on the short list."

"Five? But surely—?"

"—Five."

This was getting Sir Edwin nowhere. He had been told, of course, that theoretically there were five men for the Bishop's Cross committee to choose from; but as he understood the case, everyone in the know acknowledged that in truth the choice lay between Lloyd-James and Morrison. To be treated as if he were not in the know was aggravating. He fumbled in his pocket for another toffee.

"I am going to take you into my confidence," he said, seignorially unwrapping his sweet.

Percival inclined his head politely.

"We need more ability in the House. To be candid, we're a bit low on intelligence just now."

Once more, Percival inclined his head.

"When it comes to intelligence, of the applicants for the candidature here two stand out."

"That had occurred to me," Percival said.

"I," said Edwin, sucking hard, "that is to say we, that is to say . . . well, no doubt you know who I mean?"

"Roughly," Percival replied.

"Well. We . . . would find young Morrison . . . an embarrassment."

"Indeed?"

"Yes. Indeed. Some years back he made a lot of trouble

through that Young England Group of his, and we reckon he means to do it again. If he comes back."

"If he comes back."

"Well, will he? I'm asking you."

"That," said Percival, "is for the committee to decide."

Full stop. Percival turned his eyes back to the Quantocks.

"Look," Sir Edwin said. "At five o'clock this evening I have to attend a Cabinet Meeting, at which I must report on an important new proposal to do with the constitution of the Upper House. Instead of preparing what I shall say, I am sitting here talking to you. What does that suggest?"

"That you want something."

"*We* want something. To be precise, Somerset Lloyd-James returned at the General Election. And don't tell me it's for your committee to decide, because we both know better."

"Why do you want Lloyd-James?"

"I've told you. We want someone intelligent, and the only other intelligent chap you could choose is Morrison, and Morrison will be a bloody nuisance. I'm appealing to you for the good of the party."

The Minister sat back, fixing Percival with what he secretly thought of as his "Dunkirk" expression.

"Perhaps," said Percival, "it would be for the good of the party, in the wider view, to be made to accommodate a bloody nuisance."

"Not as bloody as this one," said the Minister between his teeth.

"I see." said Percival. And he did see. From the start he had thought it odd that a senior Minister should be paying him court in person; and now, watching Sir Edwin as he gritted his teeth and sucked the life out of a third toffee, he realised, very broadly, what was afoot. Quite accidentally, he had become involved in a big game; without knowing why or how, the quiet country solicitor had been set down in a seat at the Centre Table where there was no limit—none at all—to the stakes. For some reason, the Minister was trying to pretend that it was still an everyday, friendly affair, and the chips were only marked at a fraction of their real value—presumably to prevent him, Rupert Percival, from knowing the true amount of his winnings and claiming them in full. Alastair Dixon had been right when he said there was nothing which Percival wanted for himself; but this did not mean that Percival was prepared to sit back and be robbed. If they asked him to join their game, then, as a matter of equity, he must be told the real terms of reckoning and, as a matter of principle, he must be paid out in full. In short, the one thing which Rupert Percival did want was a proper degree of respect.

"Let's pretend we're starting again at the beginning," he said pleasantly, "and that when you say 'confidence' you mean it. Even we provincial lawyers have our pride."

The Minister smacked his lips as if relishing this rebuke. It seemed that Percival had a price after all : the truth. How very singular. Hoping for the best, he decided to go some way to meet it.

"Lloyd-James," he said, "is a crook. Therefore we would have settled for Morrison, nuisance value and all. But unfortunately Lloyd-James is too good a crook. He's got hold of something that could smash us to pieces, and he wants Bishop's Cross in return for holding his tongue."

"What has he got hold of?"

"Some regrettable facts about Suez. Which reflect on several gentlemen still in office."

"He can prove them?"

"On balance, yes."

This was enough for Rupert Percival. Although a lawyer's instinct is to ask for chapter and verse, Percival had always been a lax lawyer and preferred to deal in generalities. Again, by issuing a general confession of wrong-doing Sir Edwin had shown him sufficient regard; gentlemen need not concern themselves with details.

"The thing is quite simple," Percival said : "Lloyd-James must have his way."

"I was hoping you'd say that."

"Then why didn't you tell me the truth at the beginning?"

"I suppose I thought you'd be shocked."

"I," said Percival, "am a pragmatist. Like everyone else, I always suspected there was something fishy about Suez. But what is past is inevitable. Recrimination, retribution will not mend it. A good recovery has been made. Why ruin the party's prospects for a dead issue?"

"Some people would say it was still very much a live one."

"Moralists."

"So . . . Lloyd-James will be chosen?"

"Yes."

"Your . . . loyalty . . . will not go unnoticed."

Percival nodded. He did not particularly want his loyalty to be noticed, but it was only fitting that it should be.

"Don't let me detain you," he said rising. "You'll want to be starting for London. I hope you have a satisfactory Cabinet Meeting. And I should say how much I sympathise with you over this sad affair of your daughter."

"Like you," said Sir Edwin, who had been much heartened by the outcome of the discussion, "I take a pragmatic view. Once a thing has happened, one should regard it as inevitable. That way there is comfort both for heart and head."

When Somerset handed over the des Moulins letter, Holbrook said casually:

"Don't tell anyone that you've given it to me, will you? We don't want any more childishness."

By way of reminder, he struck Somerset in the small of the back with the edge of his open palm. Although the blow was light and the pain small, it seemed to Somerset to jar his very bowels, slyly hinting at an immensity of possible anguish.

"You see?"

"You needn't worry," Somerset gasped at him. Lord, can this be happening to me, your servant?

Holbrook nodded. "There's a good boy,", he said.

When Holbrook left Somerset, he returned to Maisie's flat

and used her telephone to put through a call to Venice. While the exchange made the connection, Maisie said :

"You realise you've just lost me one of my best clients?"

"Can't be helped. It was Salvadori's idea to use your flat. It was just bad luck that the chap we wanted was a customer of yours."

"You tell Salvadori to think of some other place for his dirty work."

"You tell him," said Holbrook, grinning.

"I've never met him. I've only—"

But at this point the exchange rang to say that Venice was on the line. Holbrook waved Maisie out of her sitting-room, and then listened for some minutes to the instructions, which were given him in a simple code, for his return.

After this he gave Maisie some money, which cheered her up a bit, and took a taxi to Buttock's Hotel, where he packed his two small suitcases. He had paid his bill in advance and had no mind to hang around saying good-byes; but as it happened he ran into Fielding Gray on his way out.

"Just off?"

It was the first time that either had spoken to the other.

"Yes, London is getting too hot."

"It's certainly been an exceptional summer," Fielding conceded. "Already the grass in the parks is drying up."

"Yes. High time to leave."

He walked urgently into the Cromwell Road and hailed a taxi.

"Ill-mannered tyke," said Tessie that evening : "going off without saying anything."

"Tom did warn you," Fielding reminded her, "that he wasn't much of a chap."

"Poor Tom," Tessie said. "Fancy that little madam choosing his wedding day to run off. It says in the paper that the honeymoon's been indefinitely postponed."

"I expect he's busy helping Sir Edwin clear up the mess."

"The more fool him. He was always too soft-hearted. If

he's not careful that Turbot lot 'll drink the life's blood out
of his body."

In Tiverton, two days later, Mark Lewson said good night
to Isobel, who would be sleeping in a youth hostel, walked
back to his hotel, and went into the bar for a drink.

"And now," said a cheery, unctuous voice from the television set, "Wessex Line-Up. Local news and views from
Salisbury to the Dart."

"My fiancé was on Wessex Line-Up once," said the
middle-aged barmaid to Mark: "he belonged to some funny
religious lot who thought the world was going to end."

"Oh?" said Mark politely, thinking of Isobel and the lonely
night ahead.

"Yes. So one day they all went up a hill, waiting for the
Son of Light to come and find them there, and the Telly got
to hear of it first. My fiancé broke it all off because I laughed
at him about it after, what a lot of right fools they all looked
praying away in their white nighties in front of this telly
camera, and nothing to show for it. It was bad of me really."
She snivelled. "I shouldn't have laughed like that. I shouldn't
have, should I?"

"Perhaps not."

Mark, judging that he had heard the more amusing portion
of this story, shut her off by turning to watch the television set.

". . . Her Royal Highness," the unctuous voice said, "had a
particular word for ex-Sergeant-Major Cruxtable, the Camp
Physical Fitness Officer."

Her Royal Highness appeared grinning toothily up the
nostrils of an obese but otherwise presentable man in a track
suit. The ex-Sergeant-Major seemed about to say something,
when Her Royal Highness was whisked smoothly away by a
determined-looking man with a bruiser's nose and a bowler
hat.

"The Marquis Canteloupe, Parliamentary Secretary for the
Development of British Recreational Resources, showed Her

Royal Highness round the rest of the Westward Ho! Caravan Site."

Lord Canteloupe and another man, identified by·the commentator as Camp Commandant Hookeby, helped H.R.H. into a gleaming caravan, from which she emerged two seconds later with gestures of enthusiasm.

"After the party had visited the nursery-crêche (picture of a fully accoutred but questionably sober matron recovering from a curtsey), the delightful modern-style dinette, the discussion room and the Maison Bingo, the Princess welcomed the first arrivals."

Two coaches came up atrack, and Lord Canteloupe stepped forward with Hookeby and Cruxtable to help the campers out. This went well, for Canteloupe showed undeniable panache and the picture of Cruxtable carrying a baby revealed only his top half, so that the viewers could not see him aim a vicious kick at a puppy. H.R.H. simpered and waved by the gate; some sturdy and wholesome family groups moved past her with cheerful deference; the Matron appeared, walking with commendable steadiness, to make a fuss of a pregnant woman; and a man in peaked hat and spotless white coat (the refuse man with the haemorrhoids, if only the audience had known) started to distribute ice-cream among the children.

"Aaaaaah," went the barmaid.

"Westward Ho!, first site of many planned, is in the unspoiled Quantock Hills, a holiday-makers' paradise. Let's hear what Lord Canteloupe had to say in his address of thanks to Her Royal Highness at the end of this proud and happy day."

Canteloupe appeared on the steps of the Maison Bingo; he looked strained but was plainly still well under control.

"Your Royal Highness's gracious presence at this opening" —gruffly, chivalrously, rather movingly the old scoundrel repeated what Carton Weir had written for him—"has, among so many other values, a symbolic one. Your youth and beauty (a quick shot of H.R.H.'s splendiferous teeth) remind us that this camp exists, above all, to bring the glow of health and happiness into the fair cheeks of our young. And not only the young in years but also the young in heart. ('That's modern English for senile,' Weir had explained. 'For Christ's sake don't leave it out. "The old folk" are all the rage just now.') Yes, for the young in spirit as well as for the young in strength there is an honest welcome here. Come one, come all . . . to Westward Ho!"

"That's what I like," the barmaid said: "not forgetting the old folk."

But Mark wasn't listening. He had had an idea: if Isobel and he hired separate caravans on Canteloupe's site, they would be together and yet seemingly apart. They could "meet" in the natural course of events without anyone's knowing of their prior connection. And what better hiding place than among a crowd of lower-class holiday-makers? They need wander no more: they would go to the Quantocks the very next day and there bide out time until Sir Edwin's surrender appeared in the Personal Columns of *The Times*.

It was Max de Freville's custom to hold a special gambling party in late July or early August every year in order to mark the end of the season. This year he had announced the party for much earlier, for the end of June.. When the guests arrived they found, instead of the usual sumptuous canapés of caviar and foie gras, slices of dry bread covered with cheddar cheese; instead of champagne, bottled beer; instead of a properly appointed Chemmy cloth, a plain kitchen table on which lay two packs of greasy cards. However, since Max's prestige was immense and since this evening he moved easily among them talking in his usual manner, they were reassured after a time and imagined that he was playing some kind of joke. Perhaps he had devised a transformation scene to amuse them: the cheese and beer would suddenly disappear through the floor, to be replaced by refreshments even more succulent than usual; the splintering surface of the kitchen table would somehow be metamorphosed, at the touch of a switch, into luscious green baize. . . .

And so, when Max announced, as he shuffled the greasy cards, that this evening they would be playing Slippery Sam for threepenny stakes, there was a good-humoured laugh all round.

"I mean it," he said.

This time the laugh was rather awkward.

"Threepenny stakes," he shouted. *"Cash."*

All his energy left him then. He let the cards fall to the table and sagged back into his chair.

At this stage his guests at last realised something of what had happened. With low murmurs of deprecation they moved off into the night: sooner or later, they told each other, the end had been bound to come; Max had had a sensational career, but it was over now, and they must look for someone else to fill his place. As Jonathan Gamp summed it up for them, "He made more money than was decent, my dears, and now God's being puritanical about it."

Of the guests, only Captain Detterling, who had watched Max rise all the way from scabby poker games and post-dated cheques to undisputed pre-eminence, remained behind to comfort him; and this he did more out of curiosity than affection, though there was affection too.

"What's all this about?" he said.

"An idea I cribbed from Shakespeare. 'Timon of Athens.'"

"Has everything gone?"

"Oh no," said Max lightly. "But things were beginning to break up. People weren't paying—they thought I had so much that it didn't matter. And besides, I was bored."

That makes sense, thought Detterling; but all the same there's something disastrously wrong. His eyes.

"So I've deposited a nice little sum," said Max, still speaking lightly but staring straight before him, "in France. Thank God Angela persuaded me in time. I shall go to her now and settle with her there in Menton."

"You always said she couldn't be a permanent thing."

"I can give it a try. Move on if it's no good."

Silence. Fascinated, Detterling watched the eyes bulge, as if they were about to explode out of their sockets.

"How much I achieved," Max suddenly shouted. "Nobody achieved as much as I did."

He put his head down on the bare wooden table and started to weep.

"You were the most famous gambler in Europe," said Detterling, soothing him.

Max raised his head and brushed the tears away. His eyes subsided, deflated and wizened balloons, back into his head.

"You don't understand," he choked. "It isn't that I'm proud of. It's the other thing. Given time, money," he blubbered, "my network would have encompassed the whole world . . . the *universe*."

"You did very well as it was."

"Yes, you could say that. There just wasn't enough money. Mind you," he said, with a temporary return to calm and rational discourse, "I'd been neglecting my business, letting the debts go, not bothering to attend the games myself. The accountant warned me but I wouldn't listen . . . because, you see, I was so absorbed in the other thing. Every day, letters, cables, phone calls, messages by hand . . . from all over Europe. I was really beginning to see the pattern behind it all. But it's useless now."

His eyes began to swell again. I must get him to a hospital, Detterling thought; he can't go off to France like this. But once again Max's eyes subsided.

"Where was I?" he said.

"You were neglecting your business interests . . . in favour of your very expensive private correspondence. So the money was running down?"

"So the money was running down. But there wouldn't have been enough anyway. There wasn't enough money in the whole kingdom to pay for all I wanted to know."

"How much did you know, Max?"

For hour after hour Max told him. He told of facts established, connections proved, of policies and plots uncovered; of men made wealthy overnight, of men who lay down in the fullness of power and woke with a prison cell for their only empire. Much of it was speculation, much fantasy and much sheer madness. But here and there Detterling recognised a fragment of probable truth; and one such fragment, explaining several odd things which had lately been brought to his notice, was the story of the des Moulins letter and its sale by Lewson to Somerset Lloyd-James.

For Max, this crazy outpouring of what he knew or thought he knew had acted as a kind of purgation. Despite the insanity of much of what he was saying, his manner was now consistently calm, his eyes no longer dilated at short intervals. Even so, Detterling judged that he should be given into medical custody; but before he could do anything about this, Max was gone. Perhaps he had anticipated Detterling's purpose. At all events, he had excused himself on the ground of wanting a pee; and when, fifteen minutes later, Detterling went to look for him, the house was empty and Max's car no longer parked in the square outside.

So Detterling shrugged his shoulders and walked home in the light blue dawn to his chambers in Albany, reflecting with some interest on what he had heard that night and on what might now be done to prevent Somerset Lloyd-James from using the new weapon which had come into his hand.

Although Alfie Schroeder had been prompt to respond to Tom's telegram, he had pleaded commitments for the next few days. In the end they met, on the day after Westward Ho! had opened, in Bath, which seemed as good a base as any for the search. The trouble was that there was nothing to go on. Isobel and her companion had driven off, as Alfie had put it at the wedding, "in the rough direction of Bristol." They might be anywhere in England by now. Tom's only hope was that suggested by Sir Edwin's briefing: he must put himself in Lewson's place. But before anything else was begun, Alfie must be brought up to date. So Tom had explained, as he drove Alfie from the station, that the hit and run driver was identifiable, by the letter he had left, as Mark Lewson; he then told Alfie what Lewson had said in the letter, what little more he himself knew about the man, and finally the reasons which Sir Edwin alleged for protecting him.

"So what it comes to," said Alfie, "is that you've to find Miss Isobel and bring her home to Daddy—having first swept this Lewson chappie safely under the mat."

"That's it."

"And why have you called me in?" said Alfie sourly.

"In case something nasty turns up."

"Something already has. A man's dead, if you remember."

"That's just it. A man's dead and my father-in-law is trying to protect the man that killed him. Why, Alfie?"

"Why ask me?" Alfie took off his enormous trilby and fanned himself. "Christ, this summer," he moaned. And then, "Why drag me in? Suppose there is something smelly in the closet. Do you think I want to be there when you find it? I'm your friend; I don't want to be the one to dish up the dirt about your father-in-law."

"Someone may have to."

The car stopped.

"Five star job, eh?" said Alfie, surveying the hotel. "You wouldn't have stayed at a place like this when I first knew you."

"I've come up in the world."

"You could still start sinking."

"Too true I could. For God's sake have a drink and stop grouching."

When Alfie had worked his way morosely through two large Tom Collinses, Tom began again.

"Alfie. . . . You must help me. Patricia and I—we'll have no peace, no honeymoon, nothing, till all this is cleared up.

You remember what you said about your honeymoon," Tom went on shamelessly, "how it was the one good thing that ever happened? I'm still waiting for mine to start, Alfie."

Alfie sighed, almost sentimentally.

"Same again, laddie," he said.

The drink came and Alfie fondled it thoughtfully.

"How are you supposed to start looking?" he said at last. Tom told him.

"Jesus Christ," Alfie said, "the ideas educated people get. Put yourself in the other chap's place! That's Dornford Yates, laddie, back in the nursery. Don't people like Sir Edwin ever grow up?"

"If you'll take time off from being so bloody superior, just what do you suggest?"

"Elementary. You say Lewson's letter instructed Sir Edwin to put an 'all is forgiven' notice in *The Times*?"

"What of it?"

"Most people who read *The Times* have a regular order. Casual buyers in the provinces are rare and therefore conspicuous. And they are often disappointed, in which case they get irritated and make themselves even more conspicuous. When they have recovered themselves, they ask to be directed to other newspaper shops; by which time," Alfie said, "they are positively memorable. Now then." He opened a Racing Diary at a road map of the West Country. "Let us assume, as we must to have any hope, that they are still in this part of the world. Small towns and villages are our best bet. Where do you think we should start?"

"So if you'll allow me to sum it all up," said Captain Detterling, crisp and authoritative, "the position is as follows."

They were all in Gregory Stern's office—Stern, Morrison, Fielding Gray, and Detterling who had summoned the convention. Of those present, Stern and Fielding Gray were both in doubt as to why they should have been asked, but Detterling had undertaken to explain that later.

"If we are to believe Max de Freville," Detterling said, "and I for one am prepared to, then we must conclude:

"One. Mark Lewson has got hold of a genuine document which incriminates Sir Edwin Turbot and other members of the Cabinet.

"Two. Lewson, in return for a sum of money, has passed the document to Somerset Lloyd-James. And three; both Lewson and Lloyd-James, as partners, are now using its existence to put pressure on Sir Edwin.

"Four. In Lloyd-James's case, he requires Sir Edwin to persuade Rupert Percival that Lloyd-James rather than Peter here should be adopted as conservative candidate for Bishop's Cross.

"And five. As for Lewson, he is the unknown man whom the police want for manslaughter and who eloped with Isobel Turbot. This is proved by the farewell letter which Isobel sent Max from Blandford. What Lewson wants from Sir Edwin is consent to a marriage and a comfortable dollop of cash to support it."

There was a thoughtful silence.

"Any questions?" said Detterling in the approved military manner.

"Yes," said Fielding. "Why are you telling *me* this?"

"And me?" said Stern.

"I was coming to that. Now, my object and Peter's is to see that Peter gets back into Parliament this autumn. This means some kind of show-down about this letter. In the course of the show-down almost anything might happen, including the letter's publication. This would bring total disgrace on Sir Edwin, cunning as he may be at finding ways out, and Tom Llewyllyn, as a member of his family, would be involved in this. So I wanted you, Fielding, and you, Gregory, to be here as friends of Tom's and representatives of his interests."

"You and Peter . . . you're Tom's friends too."

"But we have other interests. . . . which might well conflict with Tom's."

"I'm sure," said Stern, "that Tom would be the last person

to want anything covered up."

"Think again," said Detterling. "He might not care whether or not his father-in-law was exposed, but he'll want to protect his new wife. The shock would half kill her."

"She might be tougher than you think," said Fielding.

"Anyway, a sense of public duty—" Stern began.

"We'll let Tom decide about his duty," said Detterling. "You and Fielding are in on this to see he gets a proper chance."

"How are we to do that?" snapped Stern.

"By acting as umpires?" hazarded Fielding.

"Right."

"And by helping you," Fielding persisted, "to reach the right choice."

"Choice?" said Stern.

"Yes. The choice will be a very awkward one. Between destroying the letter for the sake of peace and making it public for the sake of purity."

"Nicely put," said Detterling.

"Is there not a third way?" said Peter Morrison, speaking for the first time.

Detterling gave him an odd, enquiring look.

"I mean ... perhaps we ourselves might undertake ... to hold it in trust."

"Why would we do that?" said Stern. The look in Peter's face at once gave him his answer; Stern flushed scarlet with shame for the human race and squeezed his Old Etonian tie into a knot the size of a garden pea.

"You all seem to forget," said Detterling, who was eyeing Peter with wary amusement, "that before we can choose what to do with the letter, we've got to get hold of it. That's what we're here to discuss."

"You can count me out of that," said Fielding. "I'll willingly hold Tom's hand when the time comes, but meanwhile I've got my work." He nodded at Stern, who nodded back. "Let me know when I'm wanted again," he said, and rose to go.

"Sit down," said Detterling, briskly but without heat. "You had the curiosity to come here, and now you can see it through."

"My work—"

"—Can wait a day or two." Detterling looked at him gravely. " '*Res unius, res omnium*'. Remember?"

Fielding winced and sat down.

"Well then," said Detterling blandly. "The letter. The document. We must and will possess it. How?"

"Lloyd-James has it, you say . . . according to de Freville's account."

"I've been to see Lloyd-James. He says not."

Detterling allowed this to sink in.

"You believe him?" said Morrison at length.

"I don't know. He says it's been stolen."

"Then we can forget it," said Morrison. "If he no longer has it, he can't use it."

"Perhaps not. But is he telling the truth? And if he is, someone else may pop up with it at any minute and start making a nuisance of himself. It is essential, one might almost say for the national good, that the document be finally found and disposed of one way or the other. In any case," Detterling went on, "according to Lloyd-James the thief must have been his partner, Lewson—because he was the only person who knew where it was hidden. Lloyd-James deposes that Lewson must have taken it before absconding with the wretched Isobel—he soon guessed *that* was Lewson's work—as a handy weapon in case papa proved difficult. If this is true, then the letter is still held by the Lewson/Lloyd-James combine, and Lloyd-James is still to be reckoned with. It all leaves us just where we were : we must find the letter."

"Well," said Stern, taking an analytical interest, "there are only two assumptions you can act on. Either Lewson's got it or Lloyd-James is lying and still has it himself. If anyone else has it, you might just as well go home."

"Precisely. Only two assumptions we can act on, so we

shall act on both. Two parties—one player, and one umpire, so to speak, in each. I know the West Country, so I thought Gregory and I might hunt for Lewson and see what he's got to say for himself, while you, Peter—"

"—But how will you search? It's hopeless," Morrison said. "After all, the police have been looking, and if they've got nowhere—"

"—The police only know one of the people they're looking for. We shall have a double target. Anyway, that's our worry. You and Fielding will have your own job to concentrate on here—keeping an eye on Lloyd-James."

"It doesn't sound a very positive line of action," Fielding said.

"No," said Detterling. And then, with the faintest hint of contempt,

"Peter doesn't care for positive lines of action. In any case there's none open. If Somerset *has* still got the letter, he'll have hidden it far too carefully for you to find. We'd have to . . . coax it out of him later on."

"And meanwhile?"

"Watch him, to see if he does anything out of the way. Like making strange contacts. Visiting unlikely places. Anything," Detterling said, "that may give us a line on what cards he's really holding in his hand."

But Somerset Lloyd-James made no strange contacts. He visited no unlikely places. He was acutely conscious that he now held no card at all in his hand. The best that he could do was to pretend that the card was currently held by his partner, Lewson; for while people still thought this, they would probably regard him with some respect. In no case at all, even to a trusted ally, did he wish to disclose how he had fared with Jude Holbrook; for, quite apart from anything else, he was humiliated by the memory, not of the speed with which he had surrendered, but of the gross outrage offered to his person.

However, it now seemed only a matter of time before someone found Lewson. Once this was done, a number of things
might happen, all of them to his disadvantage; because all
alike must end in the arrival of someone or other on his doorstep to demand the original document, and in his own confession, which could not be avoided for long, that he did not
have it. Whether he was compelled to make this confession
to a policeman or to Detterling, it would amount to the
same : the end of the power with which possession, or supposed possession, endowed him.

After much thought and some hours of prayer, Somerset
went to see his loyal supporter, Carton Weir and for the
first time made him privy to the summer's secrets. Weir, as
he had expected, was both pleased and amused by the tale
of the des Moulins letter. But, Somerset went on, the letter
had now been stolen; he did not know where it was; and
for the time being he was only holding his own by giving out
that it was with Lewson. This might be true, Somerset said,
or it might not; either way it was essential, if Somerset was
to be sure of Bishop's Cross, that they should find Lewson
before anybody else did. Since Weir desired Somerset's election, since he had the ideal excuse (Westward Ho!) for
taking time out of Parliament and visiting the West Country,
and since Somerset himself was exceedingly busy with his
editing, let Weir get on with the search—and the quicker the
better.

When Weir opened his mouth to protest against being
sent on this expedition, Somerset sharply reminded him to
whom he owed his place on the Board of *Strix*. When
Weir seemed unimpressed by this argument, Somerset
efficiently recited a few choice facts from Weir's private life
which Weir had supposed to be secret, and the discussion
closed.

So as June gave place to July and the grass in the Royal
Parks of London turned slowly to dust, three different parties
set out to hunt for Mark Lewson. Tom and Alfie, with a
family mission to fulfil, much uneasy curiosity to quieten, and

as yet ill-defined duties (to the nation? to the press?) beyond; Captain Detterling and Gregory Stern, searching, on behalf of a friend, for five sheets of paper which Lewson did not have; and the lone, reluctant Carton Weir, who was beginning to see that he had allowed Somerset to bluff him, and was now meditating a little scheme of his own.

9
THE CHASE

FOR SOME DAYS Tom and Alfie had no joy at all. No one in Bath, Trowbridge, Frome, Shepton Mallet or Glastonbury had any recollection that anyone out of the ordinary had tried to buy *The Times*. Alfie began to be restive. As a long-established and trusted employee of the Billingsgate Press, he was allowed some latitude as to where and how he spent his time, provided he gave assurance that there might be a story at the end of it. On this occasion he had given the usual assurance ("Line on the Turbot girl"), but he had done so with considerable misgiving as he knew that his friendship for Tom might require him to be less than candid about whatever might transpire. He had left London under false pretences, in fact; and even if his mission had been wholly genuine, it would not excuse his indefinite absence. Four days after he had arrived in Bath, as they were driving through a faultless summer morning to pursue their enquiries round Bridgwater, he put the difficulty to Tom.

"If we don't come up with something," he said, "I must leave tonight."

"Just two more days," Tom begged: "today and two more."

"Can't be done, laddie. They're already spitting down the 'phone."

"Alfie. . . . I can't manage this alone."

In Bridgwater, Taunton and Longport they discovered nothing at all.

"That settles it," Alfie said. "I'll take the night train."

"It's your system that's let us down," said Tom petulantly.

"Granted. But could you think of a better?"

"Alfie. . . . Two more days. Please."

"Sorry, son."

"There must be something else you could report on round here. Something . . . anything . . . to keep them happy in London."

"Sorry."

"Don't you understand, Alfie? I'm being played along . . . blackmailed in a sense . . . by my own wife. I can't cope and I need your help."

"We're all of us blackmailed by our wives."

"You've had time to get used to it. I was only married last week, Alfie. That's what makes it all so desperate."

"God, I hate it when you whine," said Alfie. "Stop the car."

"What—?"

"—Just do as I say. Now."

Tom stopped.

"Get out," said Alfie.

He led the way to a small public house. There was a little river, Tom noticed, and a bridge. Flat meadows, marsh and bat-willow; and beyond them, in the east, low, black clouds. Perhaps the weather was going to break at last.

"Get me a whisky."

Alfie went to a coin box in the corner of the bar. Tom bought two large whiskies and carried them over.

". . . Just till tomorrow night," Alfie was saying. "Yes, tomorrow. I don't think anything'll come of the Turbot business, but while I'm here there's something else I want to look at. . . . This new Caravan Camp in the Quantocks. There was something not quite right about the opening. . . . Yes, I know it was on television, that's what gave me the idea. There was something a bit fake. . . . Night train tomorrow. 'Bye."

He put down the receiver and took his drink without thanks.

"One more day," he said. "You know why? Because I can't bear to go away and remember you whining. I'll need a day to wipe out the memory. So for God's sake, when I go tomorrow, shout or foam at the mouth, but don't whine."

"All right. Do we really have to go to this caravan place?"

"Why not?" said Alfie. "It won't take a moment and we may as well look at that part of the country as anywhere else."

Captain Detterling was of sanguine disposition. Gregory Stern was not.

"A needle in a haystack," he said, irritated into cliché by the expense of time and trouble now in prospect.

"Two needles," Detterling remarked: "Sharp, bright needles at that. Bound to have pricked somebody's consciousness by now."

With this hope in mind, he carried Stern away to the west, where they would stay with his distant cousin, Lord Canteloupe, ostensibly in order to have a closer look, as potential publishers, at Canteloupe's father's memoirs.

"I saw them when I was there in the Spring," Detterling said to Stern, "And they're a complete dead loss. But they'll make a handy excuse now."

"I dare say. But they'll hardly help us find this Lewson creature."

Detterling, who was not only sanguine but sane, had given some thought to that. He had one undoubted advantage: he knew where to start. Max de Freville, on the night before he disappeared to join Angela Tuck, had told him that Isobel's last letter had referred to a village near Blandford; and Blandford was an easy drive from Canteloupe's pile in Wiltshire. Two days of enquiry, first in Blandford itself, then in villages around, then in Sherborne, Yeovil and Crewkerne, revealed a gradual progress to the north-west, not indeed of Lewson, but of someone who might well be Isobel. She had been travelling alone, apparently, in trains and buses; though someone had once seen her getting out of a grey Morris Traveller whose number plate bore the arresting letters—

hence his memory of the incident—YOB. The Morris had immediately driven off, it seemed, and Detterling's informant had not caught sight of the driver.

Detterling wondered how much of this was known to the police, but reminded himself once more that the police did not know where to start, indeed were probably active only in the Bristol area, towards which the infamous blue and white sports car had last been seen heading. There was, in any case, nothing he could do about that. From Crewkerne his enquiries had led him and Stern, who was still sceptical but was now taking an interest in what he termed "the theory of the human spoor", to Chard. There Isobel's trail was lost, but in answer to a lucky question at a garage they were told by a mechanic that a dark-haired and excitable young man in a grey Morris Traveller had asked to be put on the road to Tiverton some days before.

"Very careless," commented Stern in scholarly fashion, "for someone who lives by his wits."

And now, on a cloudy evening—the same evening on which Alfie rang up London from the lonely inn among the bat willows—Detterling and Stern were driving slowly along beneath the Quantocks, whither the scent had drawn them earlier that day.

"Tonight," said Detterling, "we won't go back to Wiltshire. We'll sleep somewhere round here and get an early start."

"No luggage," said Stern, who liked to do things in an orderly way.

"We can buy a toothbrush and a razor."

"I need a clean shirt."

"We can buy that too."

Stern, thinking of the neat pile of clean silk shirts which awaited him in his bedroom at Canteloupe's, gave a little mew of protest.

"Don't whine, Gregory," Detterling said.

"I don't see why we have to be so *Spartan* all of a sudden."

They passed a notice which said :

Two Hundred Yards Turn Left
For the First Canteloupe
Caravan Site and Country Culture Camp
WESTWARD HO!

"The next thing," Stern went moaning on, "you'll suggest we hire one of your cousin's beastly caravans for the night."

"That," said Captain Detterling, "would be going altogether too far."

"God, what a dump," Mark Lewson said; "but it's certainly handy for us."

"Home is where you find it," murmured Isobel, tickling his palm with her finger nail.

Every day the Caravan Site became dirtier and emptier. The morning after the opening the bulk of the "campers" had taken their fee for the television masquerade and left by special coach. The few genuine holiday-makers, puzzled and distressed by this desertion, had sniffed the air suspiciously but then, having paid in advance, had decided to give the place a fair trial. By the time Mark and Isobel arrived, however, few even of these were left. The almost total failure of the plumbing for two and half days; the indifference of Commandant Hookeby and the insolent manners of his wife; the vile language of Sergeant-Major Cruxtable; the two occasions on which the Matron had got crying drunk; the absence of the refuse man with a resurgent batch of "haemorrhoids": all this had made for a lack of refinement which members of the British proletariat were not prepared to tolerate.

But it suited Mark and Isobel down to the ground. Officially installed in separate trailers to maintain the impression that they had arrived independently of each other, they spent all of every night and most of every day together, and even while apart were enclosed in the same rainbow bubble of bliss. What was it to them that the Maison Bingo had closed

its doors, probably for ever, that the dinette had succumbed
to a plague of cockroaches, that Sergeant-Major Cruxtable
had ruptured himself in his brief and sole attempt to teach
three small children to play basket-ball? They had a bigger
and more thrilling gamble on hand than any which a Bingo
card could show them; for their meals they drove to a charming little hotel which they had discovered a few miles away;
and for their physical activities they did not need the
assistance of Sergeant-Major Cruxtable. A larger crowd, on
which Mark had originally relied, might have given them
more effective concealment; but as it was, their fellow-
campers were too preoccupied with their own miseries to give
anyone else a second thought. Nowhere is it easier to escape
remark, however conspicuous one might otherwise be, than in
a run-down city or a foundering ship : low morale inhibits
curiosity. Furthermore, there was something in the air of
desolation, they found, which was very nutritive of romance.

So Mark and Isobel were happy amid the growing piles
of filth and broken glass. To complain of these gave a zest
to love; as did the sullen clouds which were now gathering
in the evening sky, for the threat of storm when shelter is
near always stirs a delicious thrill of mock anxiety in the
stomach, and to lovers rain is one more hostile element that
gives greater value to the cosy, impregnable huddle into
which, at will, they may retreat.

"It's going to *pour*," said Isobel, with a shiver of pleasure.

"First time in weeks. What a wonderful summer it's been."

"It's not over yet," she said, and went on tickling his palm.

"It's going to rain," said Canteloupe, looking happily down
from his window at the Amusement Arcade which he had
lately erected in place of the formal rose garden. "And about
time," he added, thinking of the trippers who would now be
compelled to stop frigging about in the park and seek shelter
in the Arcade.

"Yes indeed," said Carton Weir politely. "And what do

you think about what I've just told you?"

He had arrived in Wiltshire to see his superior that afternoon and had spent most of it telling him everything that he
had recently learned from Somerset Lloyd-James. For Carton Weir had a new ambition. He was tired of being grateful
to Lloyd-James for his place on the Board of *Strix*, tired of
accepting Lloyd-James's suggestions as to his manipulation of
the Young England Group, tired of being dependent on
Lloyd-James for his continued leadership. There were now,
he told himself, fatter fish to fry: Lloyd-James's information
had put fame and power within his reach; all he had to do
was to initiate a public and sensational scourge among high
persons. He would fire the fuse to scandal and dance round
the flames, the acknowledged author of the conflagration. But
he felt the need of an ally; someone who carried weight with
the government and the country at large. There was one
such to hand: Canteloupe. True, until the preceding April
Canteloupe had been regarded, by serious people, as a mere
figure of fun; but the general public had not so seen him,
and now even serious people had reluctantly begun to revise
their estimate, not least because of the recently published
encomia of the man and his policies in *Strix*. Careerist and
patrician united, thought Carton Weir, he and Canteloupe
would make a mighty team; he would put up the brains,
Canteloupe would provide the credit; and tradition would
march hand in hand with progress, while the sword of purity
was brandished and the angry war cry—"Who shall guard
the guardians?"—rang against the battlements of Westminster Palace like the trumpets outside Jericho.

And if Somerset again tries to blackmail me, Weir thought,
into playing it his way, I've got the perfect comeback: he's
guilty of suppressing information which concerns the security
of the realm. And now what's the matter with Canteloupe?
Cat got his tongue?

"What do you think, sir," he said again, "about what I've
been saying?"

"I think," said Canteloupe, "what I always thought. Lloyd-

James is a shit." He gazed at the clouds and almost heard the coins as they tinkled into his new slot-machines. Could he get permission for penny roulette?

"Then you agree with me that the whole affair should be uncovered?"

"First," said Canteloupe carefully, "we must make sure of the truth and be able to prove it. Now, this man . . . Lewson . . . the one you're meant to be looking for . . ."

"He's very small beer. And he may not even have the letter. My idea was to confront Sir Edwin and the rest—"

"—First things first, boy." Penny roulette? Perhaps something like Boule would be better. "We don't want to rush round making fools of ourselves. This chap Lewson may or may not have the confounded letter, but he'll be able to tell us the story."

"Lloyd-James has already done that, sir. That's enough. With a man of your public eminence to take the lead—"

"—Drink?" asked Canteloupe curtly.

"Thank you."

Canteloupe poured two colossal whiskies.

"Public eminence, you say?"

He drank half his whisky in one swallow.

"I do, sir."

"Well, boy, I shouldn't count on it for too long. I've just had some very awkward reports about the new camp of ours out in the Quantocks. Unless something is done . . . quickly . . . they'll be howling for our heads. So we'd better put our own house in order before we go banging into somebody else's. You'll stay the night, if you please, and tomorrow we'll drive down to Westward Ho! and see what that infernal fellow Hookeby thinks he's up to."

Some days before all this was happening in Wiltshire and Somerset, Fielding Gray had consulted with Peter Morrison. As Fielding saw it, they had been left on duty in London in a supporting role: they were to watch for possible trouble from Lloyd-James while their allies made an active sortie into the west. Since the whole campaign had been undertaken for Peter's benefit, Fielding expected to find him helpfully disposed. Quite the contrary. Peter was vague, uninterested, had no idea what either of them should do, made it plain, between bouts of irritable shrugging, that he found any notion of positive action distasteful if not indecent.

"So you're not going to make any effort?" Fielding said at last.

"Not this kind of effort."

"You'll just leave it all to your friends?"

"It's to oblige them," said Peter complacently, "that I've consented to come back at all."

"You don't want to come back?"

"I want to meet their wishes . . . if they think it's the best thing for the party. But that's not saying I'm going to take part in a running fight with cheap crooks. Anyway, I'm not sure they're handling this right."

"Look," said Fielding. "What your friends are trying to do, as I understand it, is to get you this seat without causing too big a bust-up or letting things go altogether to pot. Correct me if I'm wrong, but it seems that you don't care if everything does go to pot so long as you get the seat."

"Not quite that. But I can't undertake to involve myself with the wilful crimes and follies of other people. These must take their course and reach their destined end."

"After which you come marching out through the corpses in a nice, clean uniform and volunteer to take everything over? 'I'm sorry about the mess,' you can say, 'but it wasn't my fault, and I'll make a good job of cleaning it up.' "

"Someone has to."

"And here and now? What do you mean to do about Lloyd-James?"

"Wait for him to become one of the corpses. He's carrying a powerful bomb about, and with any luck it'll go off in his face."

To hell with him, Fielding had thought. If that's the way

he wants to play it, if he's just going to stand clear until the shooting's done, then I'm damned if I'll do anything to help. I've enough work of my own. So let him skulk away behind the lines, and serve him right if he stops a stray bullet.

But despite this reaction, and despite his fascination with the task of converting his youthful journal into the sumptuous novel for which Stern hoped, Fielding could not altogether lose interest in the *affaire Lewson,* and this interest was quickened, several days after his talk with Morrison, by a chance revelation of Maisie's.

One evening, as he was just about to leave her, Maisie had beckoned him to the bedroom window.

"Have a look at this, love," she said. "That chap hanging about in the street. Something went a bit wrong one day, and he swore he'd never come back, but he's been sniffing round ever since. Wondering whether to sink his pride and ring the bell."

In the street, lurking guiltily, was Somerset.

"I know him," said Fielding, relaxed to the point of casual indiscretion.

"Then you'd better wait till he goes."

"He might ring the bell after all."

"I don't think so," said Maisie: "he was rather badly put off."

"Come, come, dear. Professional secrets and all that.'

"Nothing to do with me, love. I'd no idea what was going on. In fact, if you know him, perhaps you can tell me."

"I doubt it. What happened?"

"I've a correspondent . . . an Italian . . . who sends me little things from time to time. One day an agent of his turned up, one I hadn't seen before, and said he wanted to use my flat for a meeting. He was going to pay me well, and anyway there were . . . reasons . . . why I couldn't refuse, so I said yes. Then he said, would I ring the man he wanted to meet, because this man would recognise his voice and he wanted the meeting to be a surprise. So I said yes again, and the next thing I knew I found it was Somerset Lloyd-James I'd got to ring up, one of my oldest regulars, love, so was my face red."

"Maisie," said Fielding, grabbing her, "who was this agent and what did he want with Somerset?"

"The agent was called Holbrook," said Maisie, puzzled by Fielding's sudden excitement but anxious to please. "Bute or Jute Holbrook, something funny like that. I said to myself, how odd, what funny names these agents always have, because the usual one's called Burke Lawrence, which is pretty pec—"

"What did Holbrook want?"

"I couldn't hear very well. Some letter, I think."

"And Somerset agreed?"

"He agreed all right, love. This Jute or Bute was fair poison, I/can tell you."

"You don't need to."

"You know him too?"

"Yes. Maisie, I'll tell you the whole story, I promise you, when there's time. But just now you must tell me: who is this Italian who sent Holbrook?"

A look of fear and distress appeared on Maisie's face.

"Sorry, love," she whispered; "I'd like to please you, but not that. Please not that."

"All right, not that. Then what about this other agent you mentioned? The usual one, you said. Burke something. Where can I get hold of him?"

"You promise you won't say I told you? He's all right, Burke, but others might get to hear I'd sent you and then—"

"—I promise."

"Burke Lawrence, love. If he's in London, which he often isn't, you'll find him at the Infantry Club. Funny place to stay, but he says it's cheap. Thirty-five bob a night with your own bathroom."

"Angel. . . . Has Somerset gone?"

"He's gone, love. You'll take care?" said Maisie, who had become very fond of Fielding.

"Only having one eye," said Fielding, "makes a man very circumspect."

After Fielding left Maisie he had telephoned the Infantry Club. Yes, Mr. Lawrence was staying at the club but he was out. So Fielding had eaten a quiet dinner in a small Greek restaurant in Charlotte Street (he had a taste for Greek food which his sad experience in Cyprus had not diminished) and then gone to the Infantry Club in person. Yes, Mr. Lawrence was now in the club; the porter would let him know. After about fifteen minutes,

"Mr. Lawrence, sir," the porter said at last.

A young man of his own age, Fielding noted, watching a figure come unsteadily down the stairs: vulgar good looks, oiled hair, a frightened expression, which was briefly replaced, when the eyes focused on Fielding, by one of undisguised repulsion.

"I'm sorry to disturb you," Fielding said.

"Who are you?"

"I gave my name. Fielding Gray."

"Can you identify yourself?"

"Why should I?"

"Because I'm not going to answer any questions until you do."

Clearly there was a misapprehension here; equally clearly Lawrence was very drunk. In which case it might be easier to exploit his mistake than to explain it. Fielding showed him an ordinary Army Officers' Identity Card which, through oversight, had not been withdrawn when he was invalided out.

"Major Gray," muttered Lawrence. "So they're bringing the Army in." He gave a little cackle of laughter. "At least one's dealing with officers and gentlemen."

"Shall we go upstairs? Or outside?"

"Out."

Together they walked down Pall Mall, Lawrence staggering at every third or fourth step. Fielding took his arm and piloted him down the Duke of York's steps, across the Mall and to safe anchorage on a park bench.

"Well, Major Gray?"

"Does the name Holbrook mean anything to you?"

"Yes. I had a girl friend called that. Penelope."

"I'm enquiring after a man. Jude Holbrook."

"Her husband. Or was. They were divorced some time ago."

"And more recently?"

"He survived," said Lawrence.

"Where is he now?"

"In Venice. Or rather, getting out of it, I imagine, as fast as his bandy little legs will carry him. If they let him."

"They?"

"For Christ's sake. You've come to pick me up. Can't we cut out all the crap about Holbrook? The wops will deal with him."

Fielding said nothing. Lawrence leant over the back of the bench and emitted a spurt of vomit. Then he turned again and said confidentially,

"You know, I couldn't believe it. No warning. Nothing on the grape-vine. And then to read about it, just like that, in an inside column of the evening paper."

Fielding still said nothing.

"Salvadori arrested. And dozens more of them. After all this time. And so bloody silly. Beating up that nice little Greek gambler who never did anyone any harm. Sheer spite."

"Salvadori," said Fielding, carefully groping his way, "is a big man. Too big for that, one would have thought."

"Salvadori never beat up anyone," said Lawrence with the grave conviction of counsel for the defence. "It was Holbrook. Must have been—before he left Italy for this last trip here. He's a mean bastard, Holbrook. I can just see it. He went to Lykiadopoulos to ask him what he wanted to know, and Lyki made some difficulty, and so Holbrook got impatient. That'd be it."

"He always seemed a very patient man to me."

"Yes, but mean. If there's one thing he can't stand it's the sight of a happy man, and that little Lykiadopoulos was a happy man if ever I saw one. So then, when Lyki held out a bit, Holbrook got impatient, couldn't resist it. . . ."

"It all seems highly conjectural."

"He was beaten to pieces, poor little sod. If that's what you call conjectural. Acid used on him. Bloody near killed. And so then the wop police came in, and this and that and t'other, and the next thing is they've got back to Salvadori. After all this time."

"Tell me," said Fielding. "If Holbrook gets out of Venice ahead of the police, where will he go?"

"Dunno. Or do I? I hadn't seen him in years, and no more had Penelope. Then, only a few weeks ago, I was told that someone was coming to England, and I must meet him and give him any help he wants, and it turns out to be Holbrook. The old bad penny. We saw quite a lot of him, me and Penelope, because she was curious about her ex. Took rather a fancy to him again—you know how it is after a long interval. So perhaps," said Lawrence, his drunken logic rambling to its conclusion, "he'll shack up with her. She's been through a lot of men since him, so she might be ready for a second time round. And she's a good liar, if people like you come poking their noses in."

"You think he'd come back to England?"

"As safe as anywhere. He hasn't committed any crimes here —or nothing like that foul business with poor little Lyki-thing."

"Where do we find. . . . Mrs. Jude Holbrook?"

"Just round the corner. Victoria. Carlisle Mansions. What are you going to do about me?"

"You can come too. Can you make it to Trafalgar Square?"

"Get a taxi here."

"Taxis," said Fielding sententiously, "may not pick up fares in the Royal Parks."

If, he thought in the taxi, Holbrook has managed to leave Italy, and if he is coming back to England, he'll be here by now. Salvadori—whoever he may be, the boss presumably, the one Maisie's so scared of—Salvadori must have been apprehended this morning, since it was announced in the evening paper. So if Holbrook has escaped what sounds, from Lawrence's version of the news item, like a mass arrest, he must have left last night or early today.

"Look," he said to the slumped figure beside him: "when we're there just ring on the bell and ask. I'll keep out of sight."

"What are you going to do with me?"

"That's not for me to decide. But if you're helpful. . . ."

"I get it. But I can't promise anything. Jude may have done a Gauguin for all I know."

With a great effort Lawrence lurched forward to tap the glass behind the driver.

"Just here . . . on the right."

Lawrence, followed by Fielding, tottered through an entrance hall into a dignified lift, which carried them to the second floor. About thirty yards along a corridor, Lawrence stopped and thundered on a door. Fielding flattened himself against the wall.

"Christ, you're reeking," said a shrewish voice.

"Jude been here?"

"Yes. But I didn't ask him to stay and I'm not asking you. You lot can bloody well keep out of the way till the row's over. I don't know you, see?"

"You had your share," mumbled Lawrence.

"The party's over now. So we'll all get quietly into our own little beds and go to sleep."

"Where's Jude?"

"He's gone running to Mummy. And brother, is he in a nasty temper."

"What's he going to do now?"

"Ask him yourself. I had enough to do keeping him out of here. Now git."

The door slammed and Lawrence got.

"He's gone to his mother," Lawrence said as they went down in the lift.

"Where's that?"

"I don't know. But I know who will. His old partner, Donald Salinger."

"Jesus," said Vanessa Salinger when Fielding rung up, "how in hell should I know?"

"Perhaps your husband. . . ."

"He's in the Princess Margaret Rose Hospital for Gentlefolk," she said in a prinking voice. "He thinks he's got a duodenal. If you ask me, it was the champagne at a wedding we went to. Enough to burn a hole in a rhinoceros."

"Perhaps . . . in his address book?"

"You sound nice. Come round and we'll see what we can find."

"I don't look nice."

He rang off, then consulted the directory and dialled for the Princess Margaret Rose Hospital.

"I'm Major Gray of Special Investigations," he said, rather enjoying the role which Lawrence had thrust upon him. "Kindly find out from your patient, Mr. Donald Salinger, the address of the mother of his former partner, Mr. Jude Holbrook."

"Mr. Salinger cannot be disturbed at this time of night. He has a stomach condition."

"So have I, baby," Fielding said. "Now get that address before I blow an ulcer."

Too strong a flavour of television? But no. The voice said it would see. After all, what could be more authoritative, in the television age, than the television idiom? Fielding wondered why more people hadn't realised this. Would it work on head waiters? Or tax inspectors? What effect would it have on Tessie Buttock? Or Somerset Lloyd-James?

"Mrs. Anthony J. Holbrook," the voice said, "The Ferns, Peddars' Way, Whitstable."

"Thanks, doll," he said, feeling quite skittish with triumph.

"Your friend's gone," said the taxi-driver when he came out of the telephone box.

"We don't need him any more." Should he? Yes, surely this was the television way.

"Drive to Whitstable," he said.

"Sweet bleeding Jesus, Guv. It'll cost you at least a tenner."

"Then start earning it."

He sat back and lit a cheroot. For the first time in what seemed years it started to rain. Nice and cosy in here, he thought, still warmed by the wine he had drunk at dinner; and what's a little rain to Major Gray of Special Investigations?

But when, an hour and half later, he arrived in Whitstable, Fielding's enthusiasm for the expedition had waned with the wine and he was bitterly regretting the expense. Peddars' Way turned out to be a long cart track, or little better, and by the time the taxi reached The Ferns at the very end of it he was feeling both empty and sick. But here he was and he must see it through.

"Wait," he told the driver, "or I'll never get away again."

"Very true, Guv," said the driver looking happily at the meter. He muttered something about adding 30 per cent for all journeys over five miles, but Fielding, gathering himself for a last effort, hardly heard. He went through the pouring rain to a low front door in a porch, could not see a light, could not find a bell, seized a knocker shaped like a lion's head, and knocked as if to summon the dead.

Almost immediately, a light went on and a sad, intelligent looking lady in a dressing-gown, her head surmounted by a neat bun, appeared at the door.

"Mrs. Anthony J. Holbrook?"

The bun bobbed assent.

"I'm sorry to disturb you."

"I was only reading."

"Even so. . . ." Come, come. Politeness to elderly ladies was no part of the new role. "My name's Major Gray." He decided against specifying his branch. "I must see your son."

"He's in bed."

"Nevertheless—"

"—Please show me your credentials," she said, calmly and sensibly, one hand on the door ready to swing it shut.

Fielding produced his identity card again. Mrs. Holbrook examined it carefully and passed it back.

"I don't know much of these things, but as far as I can see it's just an ordinary Army identity card. And I am reluctantly bound to observe that the photograph is one of a young man with regular features which bear no resemblance to your own."

Very slight Scottish accent, he noticed; with the tone, the logic, the attitude, not of a shrilly protective mother, but of an intelligent man. Very well; treat her as such.

"Mrs. Holbrook. I can't make you admit me. But I should tell you that your son is in very bad trouble, and that it is probably in his interest, in so far as anything is, to hear what I have to say."

"Trouble?" said Mrs. Holbrook dispassionately.

"Trouble. Don't tell me you expected him here today. He's on the run."

"His visits are always sudden."

"Whenever he wants something, I suppose. Just now he wants refuge."

"And you? What do you want?"

"Simply to talk to him."

She looked at him quietly but sternly.

"Very well," she said, and drew aside to allow him to enter. "Please follow me."

She led him up a flight of stairs to a landing and knocked on a door.

"Jude. Someone to see you."

She gave Fielding another stern look and went down the stairs. Fielding opened the door. He found himself in a narrow bedroom decorated as a night nursery. Holbrook, fully dressed, lay smoking on a white bed. Above his head was a picture of a small, bright boy, who might have been himself at the age of five or, to judge from the modern style of clothes, his son.

"I didn't expect to see you," Holbrook said. "You're a long way from Buttock's Hotel."

"The letter," said Fielding. "Did you give it to someone in Venice or have you still got it?"

"What's that to you?"

"Friends of mine ... important friends ... are anxious to know where it is."

"Indeed." Thoughtfully, Holbrook picked a strip of skin from his thumb. "Well, I've no objection to their knowing. I've still got it, and as long as I'm left alone, no one will know what's in it. I suppose that's what they want?"

"Can I see it? I hate to appear mistrustful, but I must be able to give them proper assurance."

"Surely."

Holbrook opened a door in the little white cupboard by his bed. He took out some large folded sheets of paper and a small bottle.

"Now then," Holbrook said. "You can look at that letter for as long as you think necessary in order to assure yourself and your friends that it is the genuine article. While you look at it, I shall be holding this bottle." He unscrewed the stopper. "If you make the slightest suspicious movement, if you tear so much as half an inch of that paper, then you'll get a face full of acid." He gave the bottle a slight shake.

"Fair enough."

Holbrook passed the letter.

"Tell me," said Fielding as he looked over the first sheet, "why didn't you deliver it in Venice as planned?" Careful now. "To. . . . Salvadori?"

Make time.

"Salvadori was away, thank God. By the time he came back I knew there was something wrong. The police had been sniffing round ever since that little Greek was beaten up. . . ."

Make more time. How to get out of here with the letter and without receiving quarter of a pint of acid in the face?

"They tell me it was you that beat up the Greek. Not very prudent, surely?"

"Necessary. He wouldn't talk."

"Oh? I heard he was the sort of chap who'd be quite easy to persuade."

"He still wouldn't talk. I think he was going to. Then he stopped and gabbled something about protecting someone. It turned out later, when the job was almost done, that he didn't want to tell us about Lewson in case Lewson got hurt. He'd warned Lewson, when he gave him the letter, that sooner than get hurt himself he'd spill the beans right off, but when it came to the point. . . . Funny man, Lykiadopoulos; sentimental."

Although none of this meant much to Fielding, it was providing him with time during which means of escape might occur to him.

"But surely," he said, "it wasn't Lewson you took the letter from. It was Somerset Lloyd-James."

"Yes. But I'd never have got on to him if I hadn't known about Lewson first. Lewson very nearly *did* get hurt—the Greek was right about that—but fortunately for him I found out that he no longer had the letter and what he'd done with it."

"How?"

Time. *Time.*

"Logic. A little luck. Lewson had been to see Lloyd-James and come away with a lot of money to spend. The answer wasn't difficult."

"What would. . . . Salvadori have done with the letter if things had gone according to plan?"

TIME.

"I think he was going to use it to procure certain unofficial trading concessions for his own line of goods. He had legitimate interests as well, you know. Small arms. A word or two from one of the mandarins into an ear at the War Office might have been very helpful."

"But as it is. . . . I wonder," said Fielding slowly, "that you left it so late to leave Venice. You knew Salvadori's time was running out. Yours too."

"I had other business to finish up. I always know," said

Holbrook complacently, "just how long I've got. I'm the kind of man that always has a seat booked on the last train out. Have you finished with that letter?"

A bottle of acid. In the face. The face. *The face. Of course.* Why hadn't he thought of it before? Holbrook would very soon call the bluff, but even an extra second might make all the difference.

"I've finished reading it," he said. "I think I can assure my friends that it is genuine."

He folded the letter with care and moved closer to Holbrook, who held up the bottle.

"Careful," Holbrook said.

Fielding pointed to his face.

"Plastic surgery," he said, as he put the letter in his pocket. "I can't get any uglier and I shan't feel a thing."

Just for a moment Holbrook hesitated, and it was long enough.

"So the bottle was safely on the floor," Fielding told Peter Morrison in London two hours later, "and then there was a scuffle. He'd been well taught somewhere, but the dear old Army teaches you quite well too. Anyway, we hadn't been at it long before his mother came in and dressed us down like a couple of kids. Holbrook may be a killer but it seems he has a great respect for his mother. He just couldn't go on brawling while she was in the room. I fled . . . and that was it."

Peter crammed his hands fiercely into his dressing-gown pockets.

"Fielding," he said : "let me see that letter."

"I thought that you were not prepared to be involved in this kind of thing."

"If it comes to me . . . unsought. . . ."

Fielding laughed. He sounded as if he were whinnying.

"I'm just an umpire," he said. "Remember? At this stage in the game I must consult my colleague. As you know, both Detterling and he are staying with Lord Canteloupe in Wiltshire, and I propose to go there straight away. If you want to come too, you're welcome. You might like to drive us and so save an impoverished ex-officer his train-fare."

He went to the window. His haste to see Stern and Detterling was prompted, as was this visit in the small hours to Morrison, less by a sense of expediency than by desire for congratulation. He was delighted and astounded by his own performance.

"The weather's broken," he told Peter, "but it should be an interesting drive. We can discuss the old days ... and consider how both our characters have deteriorated since."

"They're not here," said Canteloupe. "Detterling rang up last night to say they were going to stay in some place near the Quantocks."

"Oh," said Fielding, heavy with fatigue and disappointment. "Where?"

"Didn't say. But I suppose they'll be back this evening. Spend the day here, if you like. There'll be some lunch. Stay the night if it's important."

Canteloupe, as always when action was in prospect, was in an expansive mood.

"Better still," he said. "Come with Weir and me. We're going to the Quantocks to put my bloody caravan site to rights. Might run across Detterling and his chum. Good day out anyway. If only the rain lets up."

"That would be interesting," said Peter. Other things being equal, he was always polite to men in office.

"I'd like to come," said Fielding; in his present mood, tired though he was, any activity was better than none.

"So that's settled. We'll have a spot of breakfast first, and we'll be at Westward Ho! by twelve."

"Right," said Alfie to Tom. "We should get to Westward Ho! about twelve. I'll have a quick look, and then we'll have the rest of the day to hunt for the love birds. And that's the end of it for Alfie. If we've found nothing by five this afternoon, I'm off to London. Understood?"

"Understood."

"What's on today?" said Stern. "Not that I mind. Anything to get out of this unspeakable hotel."

"Usual procedure," said Detterling. "I thought we'd try up in the hills for a start."

"We can't start too soon for me. Did you see that look the waitress just gave us? Let's go before we get poisoned."

"Dreary day," said Mark to Isobel, as he looked out of her caravan window. "What would you like to do?"

"Be with you."

"Easy. Let's drive down to Weston-super-Mare and giggle at the people. And if the rain doesn't stop, let's come back here after lunch, and then—"

"—Yes please," said Isobel. "I shall enjoy that very much."

And so at about ten o'clock that morning, within a few minutes of each other, all four parties set out.

10
THE KILL

CANTELOUPE'S CAR was the first to reach Westward Ho! By this time the rain, which had been falling intermittently since ten o'clock the previous night, had become a heavy, continuous, absolutely vertical downpour, from a sky that was like an immense slab of filthy cotton wool which was being slowly lowered to stifle the earth. Not surprisingly, the caravan site looked appalling; but Canteloupe was quick to distinguish between the damage done by the elements and that done by man, and to find the latter even more deleterious than he had expected.

"Bloody great puddles are one thing," he said: "but when you can see dead dogs floating about on them, it's time to take action."

"Dead dogs" was an exaggeration; there was in fact only one dead puppy, the one which Cruxtable had kicked on the day of the opening and which, having fallen into a decline in consequence, had been deserted by its owners when they left the site. But one puppy was quite enough to make Canteloupe's point, and he now strode off through the mire, Carton Weir bringing up miserably behind him, to confront the Camp Commandant. Fielding and Peter, there being nothing else for it, sat in Canteloupe's Rolls having drinks from the miniature cocktail cabinet. They were just about to pour themselves a second round, when they saw Tom Llewyllyn's 1935 Mercedes, which was giving off dense fumes of protest after its struggle with the muddy uphill track, skid to a halt by the gate.

"Company," said Fielding, who found himself oddly unsurprised by this apparition. "Let's invite them over."

Canteloupe's chauffeur was despatched through the rain with the invitation. Tom accepted this, but Alfie, who was conscientious about his reporting, felt bound to undertake a tour of inspection; so he was fixed up by the chauffeur with a golfing umbrella and some galoshes, which Canteloupe had been too angry to bother with, and trudged away gallantly into the wet. The other three exchanged desultory chat over their drinks for a while and then, overwhelmed by the desolate aspect of Westward Ho!, by the total lack of human activity and by the constant drumming of rain on the roof of the Rolls, abandoned further social effort. Tom picked his nails; Fielding prepared the account he would give to Detterling of how he had outwitted Jude Holbrook; Peter sulked; and in front the chauffeur, who had fallen asleep, gently but persistently snored.

Mark and Isobel, having found nothing in Weston-super-Mare to giggle at on such a morning, and being still nervous of the police, decided to return to Westward Ho! even earlier than they had planned. There was a tin of something which they could eat for lunch in Isobel's caravan, and they would go out to the little hotel they had found for a proper dinner in the evening.

"If we can still get out," said Mark as they drove away from the sea front.

"The site's on a hill, darling. All the rain will be drained off."

"If it goes on like this, we'll find ourselves on an island. Like Noah and Co. on Ararat."

"Delicious," Isobel said, and started tickling the inside of his left thigh.

After a while Mark said :

"I found a *Times* in Weston. Still nothing from your old man."

"I don't mind. I like it as we are."

"Something's got to be settled sooner or later."

Isobel started to cry.

"Darling heart . . . what is it?"

"I don't want it to end," she sobbed, "I want it to go on like this. Even if Daddy did put a message in *The Times,* what could we do? We couldn't come out in the open, not with the police still looking for you."

"Perhaps your father could make it all right for me."

"He'd never do that. He's so upright, so hard. He won't understand about us. Sometimes I think this time in the caravans is the only time we shall ever have. In our own little world, because if ever we leave it there'll be some curse to break the spell."

They were both too preoccupied to notice a cerise Rover which was parked in a lay-by. The two men in the Rover were also preoccupied, as they had been quarrelling about where to go for lunch, but one of them gave the grey Morris Traveller a quick glance as it passed.

"YOB," said Detterling: "remember?"

He started the engine and dawdled along behind the Morris.

"Try to see who's in it," he said.

"I can't see anything in this rain," grumbled Stern. "I think there are two of them."

"Could be. . . ."

"Could be the Queen and the Duke of Edinburgh. Just because Isobel Turbot was seen, days ago and miles away, getting out of a Morris numbered YOB. . . ."

"It's worth trying."

Stern twitched.

"I want my lunch," he said, "and I want to ring up London. I'm meant to be running a business. Remember?"

Detterling nodded, then settled the Rover at a steady thirty-five miles an hour and about a hundred yards behind the Morris. As they neared the Quantocks, the black sky moved lower and lower, as though it must surely engulf them at any second.

"Yes, yes, yes," Lord Canteloupe was saying to Commandant Hookeby, "I understand your difficulties. But what I want to know is why there've been no new arrivals. Until yesterday the weather was perfect. For every one who moved out there should have been ten moving in."

Hookeby muttered something about teething troubles.

"You'd have got over those—if there was an atom of morale in the place. But because you've let things slide, let all the campers drift away, the staff have lost any guts they ever had." Canteloupe banged the office table with his fist; a tray of pencils clattered on to the floor; Hookeby began resentfully to pick them up. "But for all that," Canteloupe went on, "I still can't understand why no one else is coming. We could make everything all right—even now—if only people would come here. And God knows, we've run a wide enough advertising campaign."

"Salinger's have been going downhill," Weir remarked.

"It's nothing to do with Salinger's. They only print the stuff. It was good stuff—I saw to that."

"There never *were* any visitors worth talking of," said Hookeby, still scooping up pencils. "That opening—we had to hire most of them. You know that."

"That was just to get things off the ground. Of course people weren't going to come straight off. The holiday season hadn't really started, for one thing. But now . . . with that splash on television . . . they ought to be pouring in."

"The locals," said Hookeby, "have a story about this place."

"Story?"

"Legend. It seems that there was a wood on this spur before it was all cleared away."

Hookeby paused. Like many lazy men, he had a taste for

local chatter, which he would absorb by the hour in the nearest pub. Uncritical by nature, he listened with placid interest to whatever he was told, little caring whether it was true or not; but it had now occurred to him that Lord Cante- loupe might make a less tolerant audience.

"It's nothing really," he said.

"Go on, man."

"Well, it was a great place for lovers, this wood. Always had been from right back. So far back that it wasn't quite a joke. There was supposed to be some kind of ... guardian, I suppose you'd say ... who was very fussy about who came up here. Only real lovers could be happy. The rest found they weren't—well—welcome. Not that this guardian was hostile, exactly, he just didn't make them welcome. So what I mean is, perhaps none of us are wanted ... if you get me."

Canteloupe did not. But he had no time to say so, because his chauffeur came into the room unannounced, dripping wet, and with a very funny look on his face.

"Please come at once, my lord," the chauffeur said.

Alfie Schroeder, sloshing round the caravan site, wondered whether there was a story in it. He'd seen the opening on television and he knew there had been something phoney about it; and now here was the camp, festering and derelict, looking for all the world as if it had been briefly occupied and then deserted by retreating troops—bored, unhappy, frightened men, who did not know where they were or where they were heading, only that they were passing through doomed wasteland in a foreign country, far from home. And yet ... surely the place had been beautiful once?

Alfie looked at the dead puppy dog, then away to the blank windows of the Maison Bingo. He walked a hundred yards to the swimming pool; the outlet had been blocked, and scummy water lapped over the edges towards a shuttered ice-cream stall. He turned in among the caravans. One at least was inhabited, for the door, which had been left un-

locked, swung open as he passed to reveal a gay little row
of summer shoes and a bright cape hanging above them.

"Is anyone in?" called Alfie.

No one answered, so Alfie poked his head round the
door. He saw the remains of breakfast for two, a lot of wine
bottles both empty and full, and, at the end of the room,
occupying the entire width of the caravan, a double bunk,
unmade but somehow jolly and inviting, as though it expected people to leap back into it at any moment. So someone's having fun, thought Alfie, and his spirits lifted a little.
But not for long. As he passed down the rows of lifeless
trailers, most of which were supported by rusty iron bars or
piles of brick, as he walked through the echoing toilets (his
soles scraping on the dank and gritty floor), as he turned back
again, through the obscenely dripping showers, out into the
rain (surely it was even heavier) and down another row of
soggy caravans, Alfie began to feel as low as he had ever felt
in his life. A story? What story? Official incompetence? It
seemed more like the wrath of Jehovah, who had apparently
decided, by contrast with the quick, clean end which he had
allotted Sodom, to destroy this place by gradual infection—to
let it be slowly rotted to pieces by the spreading poisons of
its own rain-diluted filth.

Well, thought Alfie, I'll tell them about it at Billingsgate
House and see if they want something made of it. It all
depends what line the old man's going to take on Canteloupe: the old man likes the idea of British Holiday Development, so he may want to give him a good, long chance; on
the other hand, he won't like the idea of its being mis-
handled, so he may want to crunch him straight away. These
galoshes are no sodding good and this umbrella weighs a
ton. Only another fifty yards, Alfie boy, then into that steam-
ing Rolls for a lovely goblet of fire-water.

But this was not to be. As Alfie emerged from the ranks of
trailers and into view of the gate in the outer perimeter, he
was greeted by an extraordinary spectacle. The door of the
Rolls was wide open and three heads—Gray's, Morrison's,

Tom's—were absurdly sticking out of it. The heads were all turned towards the gate, through which marched Captain Detterling, carrying a limp figure over his shoulders in a fireman's lift. Behind, twitching and gesticulating, stumbled Gregory Stern. And circling round them both, kicking up her heels behind her in a desperate, jerky trot, round and round and round, went Isobel Turbot, her mouth opening and shutting, like that of a ventriloquist's dummy, in a series of low howls which only just carried through the rain to Alfie:

"Eheu. Eheu. Eheu."

When Detterling was ten yards inside the gate he halted. Stern drew up to him and looked into his face, as if asking for instructions; while Isobel, whimpering, began to stroke the head which hung down by Detterling's left hip. From all sides people converged on this group : Alfie from the caravans; Canteloupe, Weir and the chauffeur from Hookeby's office; Tom, Peter and Fielding from the Rolls.

"I couldn't get the car up the hill," Detterling explained to no one in particular; "and she wouldn't let me leave him down there."

"What's wrong with him?"

One look at the dangling head which Isobel was caressing was enough to answer that.

"How . . . ?"

"For God's sake," said Canteloupe, "we must get out of this rain."

"Hookeby's office," Weir suggested.

"We'll leave Hookeby out of this."

Canteloupe looked round him, then walked straight through twenty yards of puddle and up the steps of the Maison Bingo. When the door wouldn't open, he put his shoulder to it and at the second heave sent it crashing inwards. One by one the rest trailed after him, except the chauffeur, who knew his place and went back to the Rolls.

Detterling took his burden to the far end of the Maison

Bingo and laid it on the low stage. He pressed a switch on
a panel in the wall, hoping to get some light, and got Harry
Belafonte singing "Mary's Boychild" instead. Isobel, who had
followed him to the stage, clapped her hands over her ears
and ran towards the entrance.

"It was my fault," she squealed above Belafonte; "we were
so happy and I knew it couldn't last, not after what he said,
and I twisted the wheel."

Everyone turned towards her as she stood in the door. She
looked back at them with hatred, opened her mouth as if to
curse them, then turned and disappeared into the rain. Fielding made to follow her.

"Leave her," Canteloupe said. "Let her cool off."

"Born on Christmas Day," sang Belafonte, "Born on
Christmas Day, Born on Christ—"

"—For Christ's sake turn that bloody thing off. What
happened?"

"We were some way behind," said Stern in a high voice;
"we couldn't see."

"Could it have been what she said?" asked Tom.

"I don't know," said Detterling. "They disappeared round
a sharp bend. When we came round it, their car had left the
road and run down an embankment . . . not very far. Could
have skidded. There was nothing the matter with her except
hysteria. He'd broken his neck."

"Who is he anyway?" said Canteloupe.

"Mark Lewson," said Tom.

They all turned towards the body on the stage, rather as
if Tom had uttered a summons and they expected to see the
body acknowledge it. Instead of this they saw Peter Morrison
with his hand in Lewson's breast pocket.

"What the hell are you doing?"

Detterling laughed. "He's taking action at last," he said.
"Looking for the letter."

"What letter?" said Tom and Alfie, like a well trained
chorus.

"No, I'm not," said Morrison, cringing slightly. "Fielding's got it. But I thought Lewson might have a copy, I thought it should be destroyed before anyone—"

"—*You've* got the letter?" said Detterling to Fielding.

"What letter?" repeated Tom and Alfie.

"I was right," said Peter. He held up some sheets of paper. "A photostat by the look of it."

"Let's have a look," said Weir soothingly.

"Give it to me," said Canteloupe.

Peter handed over the photostat copy. Canteloupe began to read.

"You see?" Weir kept prompting him.

Gregory Stern sat down on the floor, although there were at least twenty rows of chairs, and started to weep.

Tom, Detterling and Alfie crowded round Fielding, who shyly produced the original. He had been hoping to tell the full story of his ingenuity detail by detail, but this was not possible because of the incessant interruptions from Tom and Alfie. As Tom began to understand approximately what had happened and what was in the letter, his brow darkened and his eyes receded. He breathed deeply and muttered words like, "Treason . . . murderer . . . exposure." "Steady, laddie," Alfie kept saying, though he too looked quietly furious. Meanwhile, Fielding did his best to continue his tale of Holbrook to Detterling, who was not really listening as he was too busy instructing and observing Tom.

"So that was it," Alfie said at last. "Someone was putting pressure on the old man. Lewson."

"And Lloyd-James."

"But neither of them even had the bloody letter," said Tom. "That's good, that is."

"They did at first. Then Holbrook must have pinched it—"

"—And I," said Fielding fatuously, "got it back." He brandished it above his head. "For God's sake listen to me. . . . As I was saying, I found Burke Lawrence at the Infantry Club, and after I'd questioned him—he thought I was an authorised investigator, you see—after I'd quest—"

"—You shut up," said Lord Canteloupe, who was now

standing on the stage by Lewson's body as if about to make
a funeral oration, "and listen to me." He folded the photostat
copy and put it in his pocket. "Now then. There's enough
here"—he tapped his pocket—"to send several highly
respected public men to the Tower of London for life and
make a scandal to last a generation. If it's true. All I've seen
is this copy." He tapped his pocket again. "It could be a
fake, it could be a joke, it proves nothing at all—unless there's
an original which will stand up to every test in the book. You
apparently claim," he said to Fielding, "to have that original.
You will be so good as to hand it over to me."

Fielding did not move.

"You heard. Give it to Lord Canteloupe," said Weir
smugly.

"To the Leader of the Labour Party," said Tom.

"To the Director of Public Prosecutions," said Alfie.

"Keep it," said Peter Morrison. And then, when Detterling
laughed, "*We* found it."

"And you stop blubbering," shouted Canteloupe to Stern,
in order to have something to do while the squabble continued
in the body of the hall.

"There has been a death," said Stern. "Have you not eyes
to see and ears to hear?" He rocked slowly backwards and
forwards and began to wail more vigorously than ever.

"It's quite obvious," said Weir, "that either Lord Canteloupe, or myself as his representative in the Commons—"

"—Edwin Turbot must be publicly exposed—"

"—The nation has a right to the truth—"

"—We have a right to what we found," said Peter Morrison to Fielding. "We should take it into our own safe
keeping."

"What shall I do?" said Fielding to Captain Detterling.

"You're the umpire."

Fielding looked at Tom Llewyllyn, who was silly with
rancour; at Alfie Schroeder, who was bubbling with outrage;
at Peter Morrison, who smiled with open, honest, boyish
charm; at Lord Canteloupe, who stood splendid and pro-

consular upon the boards; and then he looked at Detterling, who shook his head.

So Fielding walked over to Gregory Stern, where he sat cross-legged upon the floor, and dropped the letter into his lap.

"You're the other umpire," he said. "You decide."

"There is nothing to decide," said Stern. "This man"— he pointed up to Canteloupe—"represents government here. He must have it."

He rose to his feet, walked to the stage and passed the letter up to Canteloupe, who received it with a bow and stood examining it with care. Carton Weir executed a little dance of triumph. Stern went out into the rain. Canteloupe looked up from the letter and glared at his audience.

"What is there left," he said, "at the end of the day? A piece of paper which proves a debt. But it is not a debt owed to any of us here. Let the dead do their own dunning—if they still want to collect."

He stepped down off the stage and stalked towards the door. Nobody said anything or tried to stop him, though Carton Weir, for one, was writhing with frustration. But like the rest of them he silently followed Canteloupe, into the rain, down the steps of the Maison Bingo, past the dinette and the discussion centre, until they came to the camp incinerator.

But the camp incinerator had ceased to burn.

Still nobody said anything. They all followed Canteloupe back past the discussion centre and the dinette and the Maison Bingo; down a long row of caravans; past the caravan inside which Gregory Stern was comforting Isobel Turbot; past more caravans; past the showers; and into the toilets, where Lord Canteloupe tore the des Moulins letter into tiny shreds and then, with a great clanking of hardware, flushed them for ever down the drain.

11
VERDICTS

"WELL?" SAID Tom to Alfie, as he drove him through the slowly brightening afternoon to pick up his luggage and catch his train.

"You've got your answer," said Alfie, "which is more than a lot of people get. You know what happened and why. So why not leave it at that?"

"You were as angry as I was."

"Certainly. But the proof's gone—half way up the Bristol Channel by now. No good being angry if there isn't any proof. Simply makes you look a fool. Not much good being angry even if you have got proof: you only get ulcers and die young. What is there left," he said, in passable imitation of Canteloupe, "at the end of the day?"

"But whatever Alfie says," said Tom to Patricia that night, "I should do something. There's a duty here. What Canteloupe did was a conjuring trick, sleight of hand. I know I should do something."

"What?"

"Find a copy. Swear I'd seen the original before it was destroyed. Expose your father."

"They wouldn't believe you," Patricia said.

"I should still try."

"Why? Make us all unhappy, ruin yourself very likely, for something that happened years ago."

"A woman's attitude."

"A woman who loves you."

"There were bullets, bombs. Men died."

"Scandal won't bring them back."

"Canteloupe said something of the kind. But I hadn't expected you to be so complacent."

"A woman's attitude. If once things are right with her. . . ."

"And are they?"

"Now," she said. "The night, after the wedding, I was shocked. Not by any particular thing which had happened, but by . . . the farce of it all. Everything seemed to lack dignity. It had been . . . a festival of clowning and bad taste. But now. . . ."

"Yes. Now?"

"I see how silly I was. None of it had anything to do with us. I should just have taken you in my arms and shut it all out. I think that's what Isobel was trying to do in her own disastrous way. . . . What will happen about Isobel?"

"Detterling and Stern are taking care of that. They'll quieten her down, and then she'll just tell the police that Lewson's car skidded on the corner. She probably imagined the other thing."

"I'm not sure. It's the sort of—"

"—Who's making trouble now? I wish I knew what to do . . . about your father. There's a duty."

"There's a duty owed to me," Patricia said. "Come to bed now." She came up behind him, put her arms round his neck, and kissed the curls at the back of his head. "I'm your first duty from now on. You can decide in the morning what to do about my father . . . my father and yours."

"I must say," said Sir Edwin the next morning, "everything seems to have fallen out very conveniently. Master Lewson was never any good. Poetic justice, you might say. And provided Isobel doesn't persist in saying his death was her fault. . . ."

"She was hysterical. Nobody else saw what happened. There was a sharp bend, a wet road. . . . I think you'll find Detterling and the police between them sort all that out without any trouble."

"Good. So. . . . I am to be grateful to you, Tom?"

"I told you what happened, sir. You'd better be grateful to Lord Canteloupe. And to Patricia."

"To Patricia?"

"She has had the last word over this. You see, sir, I want her to be as happy as possible. There will be a lot to make her unhappy as time goes on, because she cannot understand that a writer's first love will always be his writing. I can't and won't alter over that; but I love her so much that I must concede something. Let's say that I'm making Patricia a wedding present of my moral conscience . . . for what it's worth."

"In return for which she will take second place to your writing?"

"Yes . . . though she doesn't yet know it."

"A very fair compromise," said Sir Edwin. "But I wonder whether you've got your priorities right?"

"I don't think that you of all people are qualified to judge."

"I'm not judging. I'm just wondering. Have a piece of butterscotch?"

"No thank you, sir. If it's all right with you, Patricia and I will leave for our honeymoon tomorrow."

"My dear boy. . . But of course. And may all joy attend you."

"Thank you. Just one more thing," said Tom, "before I go."

"Yes?"

"Now that the letter is no longer a factor . . . now that there is no pressure . . . what will you do about Bishop's Cross?"

"You mean. . . . I'm now free to let them choose Morrison?"

"Yes."

Sir Edwin began to feel the funny new kind of excitement which had first come over him during the disastrous conclusion of the wedding and had reappeared several times since.

"Do you really mind which I choose?" he asked.

"As you know, I've always favoured Morrison," Tom said.

But then he frowned, remembering that Peter's behaviour at Westward Ho! had not been quite as he would have wished. There had been a degree of opportunism: Peter had made an oddly disaggreeable impression ... as of a man trying to sell places in the life-boat of a sinking ship? No, not quite that, because whatever Peter was up to, it had been in accordance with the rules. It was more as though Peter, given privileged notice of war or famine, had been quietly flying the country under pretence of a routine business trip.

"Well," said Sir Edwin, "I've been thinking about that. You know, it's not really for me to interfere. I shall leave Percival and his committee to get with their own job."

Sir Edwin had spoken the truth to Tom; from now on he was going to leave Percival alone. But he did not mean by this quite what Tom thought he meant. To Peter Morrison, who had solicited an interview with him in London, Sir Edwin was more explicit.

"I suppose, sir," said Peter politely, "that now there are no more complications, I can consider myself sure of your support."

"No, you can't," the Minister had said. "I'm leaving it all to Rupert Percival. As I always should have done."

"It comes to the same thing," said Peter. "Rupert Percival has always been behind me."

"He isn't now. Before these ... complications, as you call them, were finally dealt with, Percival had been instructed, and had agreed, to choose Lloyd-James. I don't propose to countermand the order."

Peter bit his lip.

"May one ask why not?"

"One may," said the Minister, feeling the thrill of excitement, of liberation, that had been affecting him more and more often over the past few days. "The answer is simply this: you're too damned wet. Lloyd-James is pretty foul, I grant you that. But he does things. He doesn't sit around moaning about his honour. He gets on with it."

Sir Edwin thought of what Lord Canteloupe had told him over dinner at White's the previous night. "I won't teach my grandmother to suck eggs," Canteloupe had said: "But remember this. When it comes down to brass tacks, one's better off working with shits. They'll kick you in the ghoulies as soon as look at you, but one knows that and can be ready for it. It's these chaps who have scruples that really kill you dead. They'll drop you in a sewer to drown when you least expect it, and then go round whining that it was their moral duty."

"It's the whining I can't stand," Sir Edwin now said to Morrison. "I've put up with so much of it for so long. Now I've come to a time of life when I won't put up with any more. I don't say I like Lloyd-James, but in one very important sense I know just where I stand with him: he's like Nature itself—he has few liberal sentiments and no moral ones. I find this singularly refreshing."

"He's a religious man," said Peter with insinuation, "a Roman Catholic."

"Exactly so. Of all religions, Catholicism is the least liberal and the least moral. I'm going to *enjoy* having Lloyd-James in the House. It'll be like having one of the Borgias. As for you Morrison," the Minister said, "you're a kind of social Bowdler. You take all the spice out of life. Give me that bald bastard from Gower Street any day of the week."

This last phrase was, of course, Canteloupe's, but Peter Morrison neither knew nor cared about that. Deeply hurt, he rose, bowed to Sir Edwin, and went off to spend the afternoon at Lord's. There he met Captain Detterling, who, when told what had happened, was less than sympathetic.

"You know your trouble?" Captain Detterling said. "You're like an officer in my regiment who could never have a crap when he was out in the field. You know why not?"

"No," said Peter miserably.

"Because he thought his men would cease to respect him if they found out he had an arsehole just like theirs."

"So it seems," said Somerset Lloyd-James to Carton Weir, "That everything's in order after all."

Carton Weir was not at all pleased with the way in which things had turned out. Canteloupe had thrown away a winning hand, and now he, Carton, was back in Square One—being, as ever, deferential to Lloyd-James. Still, things were as they were, and he had been in the game long enough to make the best of them with a good grace.

"If you ask me, my dear," he said, remembering what Vanessa Salinger had told him at the wedding, "Sir Edwin's going a bit funny. Change of life."

"Do you think that's why he's settled for me at Bishop's Cross? Out of sheer perversity?"

"One reason. And then Canteloupe's been pushing for you. Apparently he's very pleased with those bits you've written about him in *Strix*. He thinks you're the sort of man we need in Westminster these days. 'Someone who knows how to play it rough,' he told me: 'train us all up a bit to cope with the Ruskies.'"

"I'm obliged to Canteloupe for his good opinion. He doesn't exactly play pat ball himself. I keep wondering why he destroyed that letter. I should have expected him to make use of it."

Weir suppressed a spasm of ill temper.

"Very simple, dear," he said. "He told me later. 'I like a rough game,' he told me, 'and even a foul one, but I won't risk having the entire stadium blown up.'"

"A balanced view, on the whole. I think," said Somerset, "that when Professor Constable leaves the Board of *Strix* next month we might do a lot worse than Canteloupe. If we can square it with the Articles, of course."

"Come, come, sweetie," said Weir rather nastily: "you're **not going** to let those boring old Articles upset you? Why not take a lesson from Canteloupe and just tear them up?"

"I've told you before," said Somerset severely: "you will never attain to really responsible office until you suppress your taste for silly jokes."

"Cup of tea, love?"

"Thanks, Tessie," said Fielding Grey.

"Getting on well?"

"Not too bad. Stern's very pleased with what I've done so far."

"Is it true about Mr. Stern . . . that he's going to marry that Isobel Turbot?"

"Looks like it."

"Well, well. Next thing we'll have to find someone for you."

"I've got someone, Tessie."

He thought tenderly of Maisie. It now seemed certain, despite the Salvadori arrests, that she was going to be left alone. Maisie had been very marginal. As for Burke Lawrence and Jude Holbrook, God 'alone knew what had happened to them. . . .

"You know, love, you can always bring her here," Tessie was saying.

"I like going to her place, Tessie. I'm very happy here, but it makes a nice change to get out for a blow now and then."

"I suppose so, dear. What's her name?"

"Maisie."

"And her surname?"

"Do you know," said Fielding, "I've never thought to ask."

"So Mark Lewson's dead," said Angela Tuck to Max de Freville in Menton. "Killed in a car crash, it says here."

"*Requiescat*," said Max. "He wouldn't have been happy with that Turbot girl for long."

"I don't see why not."

"He was like me. He enjoyed being unstable. People like Mark and me, we get tired sometimes and think we want to settle, but after a bit we find security unbearable. That's why I enjoyed being a gambler in the old days but got fed up with being a big-time organiser . . . just sitting there and taking the five per cents. It was a bore not being able to lose."

"So in the end you just didn't bother to collect. . . . When are you going to get bored with me, Max?"

"Pretty soon, I'm afraid. You were splendid for time out. But as a regular thing . . . no."

"Swine."

"Sorry. As a matter of fact, I'm thinking of going to Venice for a few weeks. There's been one hell of a stink about a chap called Salvadori, and I want to see what I can find out. It was one of the things on which none of my highly paid informants ever got a proper grip. It seems poor old Lykiadopoulos was badly beaten up by one of the henchmen—perhaps he'll be able to give me a line."

"Can I come?"

"No. You're my rest cure. I'm well again now."

"When will you be back?" Angela said.

"When I need another cure."

"I might not still be here."

"Women like you are two a penny," Max said: "frustrated mothers."

"You know, there's one big difference," said Angela bitterly, "between you and Mark. He was a man; when you'd been to bed with him, you knew it."

"Heigh-ho," sighed Max de Freville: "as good an epitaph as any, I suppose."

THE SABRE
SQUADRON

Contents

PART I
IL PENSEROSO

"KAFFEE, bitte. Schwarz," said Daniel Mond.

The waiter bowed and shuffled off over the terrace. From a little lower down the hill a drowsy bugle called from the British occupied barracks. On the ridge above, the summer woods of rustling green and scented pine spread away to Daniel's right and swerved down as far as the formal park which skirted this side of the town. Then there were the suburbs, prettily ranked; and then Göttingen itself, like an eighteenth century pastiche of a medieval city, ordered, polite and yet perceptibly Gothic, its three towers flickering in the haze of high afternoon. A seemly place, thought Daniel as he looked down from the terrace on the hill; serene, civilised and seemly.

The waiter shuffled back along the terrace, set down the coffee, and, for an instant, gave Daniel that look, quick, guilty, aggressive, which he had seen in so many faces during the last three months and which, even now, stirred a light, chilly tremor in his gut. Ah well, he thought, reassuring himself for the thousandth time: we're already well into 1952, over seven years since it all stopped, very soon now they'll forget, they must forget. A brief glance must not be allowed to spoil an afternoon like this. In a few minutes he would start over the meadow and down the hill, would meet and follow the wall of the oddly elegant barracks which the Nazis had built in 1935 (nothing to fear now, surely), would veer away to the right through the cool woods; in half an hour he

would be back in Göttingen, would greet the statue of the
Goose Girl in her little courtyard and turn down the narrow
street, past the den where the Germans played *skat*, to his
lodgings in the house with the crooked white front. There he
would settle to the work which waited; he would trace the
manuscript pages of graceful symbols which must surely
reveal, before much longer, the truth which he sought, his
truth, pure, formal and ascetic, yet alive with the stuff of
romance and even fantasy, with mysteries which lay beyond
itself. Later, much later, exhausted and so for a few hours
appeased, he would stack his sheets, say good night to them
aloud, and walk out through the friendly alleys to dine.

A brilliant afternoon in late July, a gentle walk down hill
into a peaceful and pleasant little town, several hours ahead
of a congenial and absorbing search. No; not a prospect to be
easily spoiled by one glance from an elderly waiter still rancorous at his country's well earned shame. And yet that glance
reminded him of so much else that he would wish to forget.
It reminded him that this evening, as always lately, he would
dine alone; that for weeks now there had been something—
he could not quite say what—something sly, something
treacherous about the behaviour of the symbols and series
to which he would shortly return; that there was, too, something wrong in a wider sense, something which included his
loneliness and the threat posed by his symbols and yet
transcended these, something which, as he sat warm and well
fed on the sunny terrace above Göttingen, seemed suddenly
to settle all about him like air from a tomb.

Back in January, soon after Dirange, his research super-
visor, had first suggested that he should spend some months
in Göttingen, Daniel had discussed the matter with Robert
Constable, the College Tutor.

"Why Göttingen?" Constable had said.

"Dirange thinks there's some stuff there which will help

me. Unpublished dissertations, some manuscript papers . . ."

"I thought they were best known for physics at Göttingen. Max Planck, for example: Atomic Theory and so on. As I understand it, your research is concerned with the purest of pure mathematics."

"Physicists often develop new methods which are of interest to us. In the same way . . . regrettably . . . as our formulations often turn out to be useful to them."

"Regrettably?" said Constable, who, an economist himself, resented the airs and graces of "unapplied" men.

Daniel shrugged miserably. Of all things he hated the line of argument which he knew to be coming, the bellicose assertion of the benefits conferred by science, the patronizing reminder that, while the pure mathematician might indeed be "of value" in himself, he must not be too proud to assist in practical ventures. But he had brought it on himself by one careless word, and now, for what seemed the millionth time, he must see it through.

"I mean," he said carefully to the affronted Tutor, "that physicists aren't always very delicate in the use they make of our help. The Atom Bomb . . ."

"Perhaps. But doctors? I'm told that Bio-mathematics is proving a great help in developing new cures for diseases of the blood."

"By the application," said Daniel, "of elementary theories of Chance to the behaviour in motion of the corpuscles. A child could do it."

One of Daniel's troubles was that he so often, out of sheer nervousness, said either much more or much less than he meant. If the former, he was apt to sound petulant (rather than arrogant), if the latter, to appear as grovelling (rather than discreet). As things were just now, he had allowed himself to be irritated into a piece of peevish inaccuracy, and he awaited Constable's retort with horror. Fortunately, however, the telephone rang.

"Tutor, Lancaster College," Constable said, and listened

for three minutes with growing impatience. "I'll see him to-night," he snapped into the receiver : "if he doesn't pay in seven days, he can pack up and go home."

He turned back to Daniel, his eyes raw with distaste.

"Contemptible," he said. "He comes up here and pretends he's rich, champagne parties and hired cars, causes all kinds of resentment among the poorer undergraduates, and then won't pay his landlady."

Constable pronounced the word "resentment", Daniel noticed, as though it were a commendable and even ennobling quality of mind.

"He can either pay up or get out," Constable went on, his indignation at once cheapening and sharpening his idiom. "We're through with that sort of lark. I will not tolerate extravagance," he said, reverting to general issues as his anger began to subside, "even in those who can afford it. Where were we?"

"Dissertations and papers at the University of Göttingen," Daniel said. "In particular, Dirange thinks, the Dortmund papers."

"What's so special about them?"

"When he died in 1938, Dortmund was working on a new type of matrix. His idea was that the symbols should be arranged in a rectilinear framework, not just of two dimensions as before, but of three dimensions, thus greatly increasing the variety of relations between them."

"Like three-dimensional chess?"

"Quite a good comparison," said Daniel, trying not to sound condescending. "The trouble was, though, that it all had to be expressed on paper, so that he needed an entirely new notation—to put in the third dimension, so to speak."

"Couldn't he," said Constable, tense and admonitory, "have fixed up three-dimensional frameworks—modelled them in wire or something—and then used bits of cardboard with the symbols written on? Clipped them in place?"

"He could have. Perhaps he did. But that wouldn't have

been much good when he came to publish. I mean," said Daniel, feeling exceedingly silly, "he could hardly send little cages of wire all round the world with symbols dangling all over them. So he devised this new notation for representing what he wanted on the page. And died before he had explained it to anyone."

Constable said nothing, a sign of his qualified approval.

"His widow," continued Daniel, "gave all his papers to the University. The Nazis were curious at first, but when they were told that his work had no obvious scientific bearing they lost interest. The point really was, though, that no one at all could decipher the new symbols which Dortmund had invented. There were some good men at Göttingen, and they called some more in from outside, and still they couldn't crack the code . . . so to speak. But Dirange thinks," said Daniel, cringing like Uriah Heep, "that I might be able to . . . disentangle it all. This would mean that I could understand Dortmund's matrices, and these in turn might give me some help I'm looking for in my own line of investigation."

"*Might* give you *some* help," Constable insisted.

"Even if they didn't, the work would be worthwhile. Dortmund was never quite in the front rank but he was an important man. What he did in those last years ought to be understood and made available."

There was a long silence.

"So what it comes to," said Constable kindly but firmly, "is that you want the College Council to give you leave of absence to go to Göttingen, there to undertake an ambitious task which has defied senior men for years and which, even if accomplished, may take you no further in the line of research which you proposed to us when we awarded you your Grant."

"Dirange—"

"—Dirange may be a big man in the Faculty of Mathematics but he is not a member of this college, still less of the College Council. The council has to take an official

458   *The Sabre Squadron*

view. You were elected to a Post-graduate Studentship," said
Constable, his prim, boyish face knotted in conscientious
caution, "in July of last year—1951. This means we expect
the first draft of your Fellowship Thesis by Christmas 1952—
this Christmas. Supposing your work at Göttingen turns out
to be a side-track—no matter how interesting? You'd never
have time to get back on your proper course and turn in a
thesis by Christmas. This," said Constable, "the College
Council would find very displeasing. It is, after all, a matter
of contract."

"I'm ready," said Daniel snivelling, "to take the risk."

"You may be. But you are *our* investment. As I just said,
if senior men have failed with the problem ever since 1938—"

"—Then it's possible the problem needs a younger man
with a fresh approach. The whole point is," said Daniel,
beginning to honk, "that in pure mathematics you do your
best work, your creative work, as a *young* man. So if you
think you see your way—and it's bound to be a bit of
a gamble—you've got to follow it up at once. After you're
thirty there's nothing left for you except consolidation."

"And you are . . . how old?"

"Twenty-two."

"Leaving you eight more years." Constable looked en-
quiringly at Daniel, picked at some of the spots which marred
his cherubic complexion, and then let his face go absolutely
blank, a signal (to those, like Daniel, who understood him)
that he had reached a final decision. "Eight years. Not long,
really. So let us hope," said Constable, facetious and energetic, "that your summer in Göttingen will not be wasted.
For I shall recommend to the College Council that they
accede to your request, so I think you can take that as settled.
But there is surely," he said, "one other problem to be thought
of, Daniel?"

"I know," said Daniel: "I think of it all the time."

* * *

The "other" problem he had discussed a few days later with his contemporary, Jacquiz Helmut the historian.

"It's not as if the Germans can *do* anything to you," Helmut had said, looking placidly along the Backs from Lancaster bridge. "For the time being at least they've been tamed."

"But how would you feel about going there?"

"It's different for me." Helmut's eyebrows, which normally met in the middle, seemed to part for a moment in polite protest. "I'm the real thing, you see. You're only Jewish on your father's side, and therefore not a Jew at all by a strict reckoning."

"The Nazis took a different view."

"The Nazis have gone for good."

"No, they haven't," said Daniel; "that's just my point. The uniforms have gone, but the mass of the men that wore them are still there. In every shop, every restaurant, walking along the street . . ."

"They're too busy just now to bother with you," said Helmut, suave and dismissive. "They've got their living to make. A whole country to rebuild. I grant you, they're rebuilding it just a little too quickly for comfort, but there's work to keep them out of mischief for some time to come."

He turned from the balustrade of the bridge, clasped his hands together in front of his groin, and indicated to Daniel by a slight nod that it was now his pleasure to walk. They progressed in silence along the avenue and towards the Fellows' Garden, Daniel, as usual, being sadly embarrassed by the difficulty of matching his stubby legs to the august stride of his six-foot-six companion.

"For someone wholly Jewish," said Daniel crossly, "you've no business to be so tall."

"Among the Jews as elsewhere height is a sign of aristocratic descent."

It was not always easy to know whether Jacquiz Helmut's

remarks were intended seriously or not. Silent once more, they approached the gate of the Fellows' Garden. Helmut produced a key on a golden chain and let them in.

"No one's given me a key," said Daniel resentfully.

"You only have to ask at the Porters' Lodge. All resident graduates are entitled to one."

"I did ask. Mr Wilkes said they'd run out."

"That was what Wilkes said to me. I told him," said Helmut with a twitch of his cardinal's nose, "that unless I was given a key within twenty-four hours his slackness would be reported to the Bursar." He looked round the deserted garden with condescension. "Uninviting," he said, "but at least there is privacy. Now we can be serious about your little problem."

"You've just said that there is no problem."

"Superficially, none at all. To start with, you don't look particularly Jewish. Small and dark, yes, but without that distinguishing facial structure. You, my dear Daniel, could be anything. And even if the whole of Göttingen knew of your paternity, even if they discussed nothing else from morning to night, you are still under the protection of His Britannic Majesty, their conqueror, who will not allow them to whisk you off and turn you into soap."

Helmut paused in his walk and surveyed the Judas Tree with growing annoyance, as though it had been that kind of joke which, excellent at first hearing, turns out to have tactless and grating undertones.

"However," he continued, "there *is* a problem, if only because you feel there is."

Then he fell silent and began, with both hands, to stroke the fur collar of his overcoat. Although his manner was still composed, his eyes were uneasy and even furtive.

"There has recently been an elaborate and scholarly book," he said at last, "written by a Jewish historian with whom I am in occasional correspondence. It purports to prove, beyond any further question, that the Romans were exclusively responsible for the execution of Jesus Christ."

"Exclusively?"

"You have taken my point. Everyone knows that the Romans must bear a share, a substantial share, of the blame, but no one in his senses could pretend that the Jews were wholly innocent. And yet this is just what my correspondent, apparently a sane and erudite man, wishes to maintain. What does this suggest to you?"

"That we are a self-righteous people."

"And what else?"

"That we are a self-deluding people . . . in some matters at least."

"Come on, Daniel. More still."

Helmut's tone was now hectoring, like that of a rugger coach calling for greater effort.

"We are . . . a self-loving people?"

"All peoples are that. We are worse than self-loving, Daniel: we are self-obsessed."

His eyes cleared again. Delivery of this judgment had evidently restored his ironic good humour.

"Hence to your problem," he said. "You feel, to put it crudely, that in Germany you will be surrounded and contaminated by the murderers of your kin. Every time you show your ticket on a train—and on German trains one is *always* required to show one's ticket—you will imagine that same conductor herding thousands of Jews into cattle-trucks. In other words, you are thinking only in one set of terms: you are—or will become, if you are not careful—self-righteous, self-deluding, self-loving and self-obsessed."

"Self-deluding?" said Daniel after a long pause.

"Yes. You delude yourself into thinking that the Nazi massacre of the Jews is the only thing which counts, almost the only thing which ever happened, in the whole history of Germany. Try thinking of something else for a change. Try thinking of Arminius, Goethe, Theodoric or Dr Faustus . . . anything you like, but just forget for once in a way about Adolf Hitler."

"You think . . . we should just behave as if it never occurred? All that death . . . the deliberate planning . . ."

"Listen," said Helmut. He wagged a reproving finger at the Judas Tree and stalked on towards the summer house. "Listen to me, and you shall hear my very last word on this tedious topic. The crime you talk of can never be wiped out. But you are going to Göttingen of your own free will, and the work you have there is important. If you want to do it properly, I suggest you will find it easier to think of yourself as a mathematician first, as a visitor in a foreign but well ordered country second, and as a Jew, if at all, a long way third. After all, half of you's solid Anglo-Saxon."

"That's just the trouble. It would be nicer to be complete. One way or the other."

"Nonsense," Helmut said. "We're all very pleased with you as you are."

In the end Daniel had accepted and profited by Jacquiz Helmut's advice. He had insisted to himself that he was a scholar doing research work in a foreign university, nothing more and nothing less. True, this did not prevent him from noticing the sullen and suspicious looks which often came his way in public places, but he reminded himself that in a poor and defeated country any stranger, comfortably fed and dressed, must provoke resentment. Since the Germans, as a whole, were already well on the way back to prosperity, Daniel was not being strictly logical in this; but then his had never been a problem which could be solved (for all Jacquiz Helmut's calm good sense) by strict logic. It was necessary to cheat a little, and Daniel felt sure that the flexible Helmut would, on balance, have approved the slight shift from the letter of his instructions.

Despite the mild apprehensions he retained of anonymous Germans in the mass, Daniel found no difficulty whatever in his private dealings. His landlady, a huge, resigned woman who had seen better days and walked with a waddle, performed her duties punctually and unobtrusively; while the only other German on whom he must depend to any extent had treated him with a blend of professional courtesy and personal indifference which he found entirely reassuring. This was Doktor Aeneas von Bremke, to whom he was recommended by Dirange and whom he had visited promptly after his arrival in early April.

"The Herr Doktor Dirange has, of course, written to me," von Bremke said solemnly. "It is my pleasure and privilege to be of assistance. Will you care to come with me?"

He had led the way down a high, bleak corridor on the top floor of the building until they came to a door on which was a printed card:

HERR DOMINUS DANIEL MOND.

"Dominus," said von Bremke, his stern face becoming, for a moment, flaccid with satisfaction: "that is the correct title of an English Bachelor of Arts, is it not?"

"I suppose so . . . I mean, yes indeed," said Daniel, trying to look impressed.

"Very good. Then this room we have put aside for you to work. Most of the Dortmund papers, you understand, cannot leave this building. But the Herr Curator will be pleased to place them at your disposal in this room."

"You're very kind."

"Please . . ."

Von Bremke tested the desk-lamp and inspected a bust of Archimedes which stood on the window-sill.

"Naturally," he said, as though addressing Archimedes, "we are honoured that a learned and proficient young gentleman, from so ancient and remarkable a university, carrying the esteemed recommendation of the internationally regarded Herr Doktor Dirange, should be coming here to examine the Dortmund remainders. But please do not hope for too much. I too, some years ago—"

He broke off like a record from which the needle has been lifted without warning.

"There is dust on this filing cabinet," he said.

"Never mind, Herr Doktor."

"I do not mind. It should not be there, that is all." He took out a handkerchief of fine linen, dusted the top of the cabinet, and then dropped the handkerchief into the waste-paper basket. "I too, some years ago," von Bremke said, as though the gramophone needle had been suddenly replaced, "examined the Dortmund relics. Our national calamity interrupted my work, but I had already done enough to know that I could do no more. This is all that I am trying to tell you : do not assure yourself of success."

"I realise the difficulties."

"No, you do not." There was neither rudeness nor aggression in this, Daniel noticed; just a flat statement of fact. "You know, as we all know, that Professor Dortmund invented a novel notation. This notation, we say, was necessary in order to convert an ordinary matrical method into one much more complex, occupying three dimensions. This was the Professor's object, this must be our clue : relate the notation to its function and the way of its working must sooner or later become apparent. You agree?"

Daniel nodded.

"Then why has it not become apparent? Through nearly fifteen years?"

"Because so little is known about the function to which it must be related."

"Precisely, Herr Dominus. And then suppose that we knew even less. That Professor Dortmund was not always devising his novel notation for what we would be thinking but for something else. That he transferred himself, at some stage, from his three-dimensional matrices to a different, even more complicated field—related, very possibly, but *different*. What then, Herr Dominus?"

"We are agreed," said Daniel slowly, "that the nature of the

Professor's work in his first field—little as we know of this—could give us the clue to the notation. Perhaps the notation, in turn, could give us the clue to this later field...into which, as you say, he transferred himself."

"Perhaps," said von Bremke, turning a poker face on Archimedes. "But no one has yet accomplished even the first step. As for the second, when the Professor started to change his field, to work towards another object, in many ways he also changed the notation. So you have not only one notation to decipher, but also a later variant. And for what this was intended we have no possible—"

Again he stopped in mid-speech without warning.

"I should have wished," he said, "that my wife could receive you in our house. But she has been ill."

"I'm sorry."

"Do not concern yourself. We cannot receive you; that is all. At this time there are no compatriots of yours here—in the University, that is to say. But there are the British soldiers up on the hill."

"I don't know much about soldiers."

"You did not do—what is it you say?—your Government service?"

"I was excused National Service. As a child I suffered from—"

"—It does not matter. You need not excuse yourself to me. For the rest, there is an American, an Herr Earle Restarick, so he calls himself, who studies modern history. He has heard that you are coming and will make himself introduced. Is there anything more you wish to ask?"

"Yes," said Daniel, who had taken in very little of von Bremke's social information and was still considering what had been said about Dortmund. "This second step, this second field which you say Professor Dortmund strayed into—"

"—He never 'strayed' into anything, Herr Dominus. A most disciplined man."

"Progressed into, then. Surely you must know *something* about it. Or at least have made a few guesses."

On the face of a man less dignified, Herr Doktor von Bremke's expression would have been called a pout.

"No thing," he said, keeping the two words deliberately separate. "But you, Herr Dominus?" He now seemed anxious to shift the ball into Daniel's court. "What are you looking for in the end? Doktor Dirange tells me that if you solve the notation then Professor Dortmund's work may help you with your own. What is your own?"

"An Englishman called John Wallis," said Daniel, deliberately oblique, "wrote a book, nearly 300 years ago, called 'Arithmetica Infinitorum'. It is often said to have contained the germs of the Differential Calculus. I think it may have contained the germs of something even more surprising. Something exceedingly delicate, in working on which I shall need a very precise and sensitive method. Both Dirange and I were hoping that Professor Dortmund's matrices would provide that method."

"But first you must solve the notation," von Bremke said gently. "Allow me to wish you good fortune and to offer any assistance, of an administrative kind, that I can render."

He walked across the room to the door. There he hesitated, then turned.

"There is one more thing I should tell you," he said, suddenly and unexpectedly diffident in tone. "When Professor Dortmund died he had been ill for some time. A... *krebsbildung*... a cancer of the bowel. Whatever else those symbols stand for, they signify a man in pain. Please do not forget that. You must be ... worthy."

As Daniel opened his mouth to reply, Doktor von Bremke raised a hand to silence him, bowed elegantly and was gone.

Within two days Daniel found that the room prepared for him by von Bremke was unsuitable to work in. Quite why he could not have said, for the furniture and fittings were admirably if economically contrived: the drawers of the filing cabinet ran smoothly, the desk-lamp gave a generous light, his chair was exactly angled (or so the Curator from the Library told him) to ensure that he sat in a healthy posture. Even the view from his window (south-west over placid suburbs and rolling corn-fields) might have been arranged for its therapeutic qualities, relaxing and reassuring yet too dull to invite delay.

Perhaps this was why Daniel found the room so disagreeable: he had a sense of being bullied, of being compelled to sit in a healthy posture, forbidden to look at the view for more than five minutes in every hour. Although he was in many ways a methodical man, he resented discipline imposed, however discreetly, from without. If he was to work properly, there must be, as there always was at Cambridge, at least the possibility of self-indulgence and disruption, there must be some temptation to resist. But the only temptation in his room on the top floor was to break the smirking bust of Archimedes, and this was almost certainly made of some efficient German material which could withstand a steam-hammer. No, whichever way he looked at it the accommodation so courteously provided by von Bremke was intolerable; he would work in his lodgings instead, slumped in an arm chair as crookedly as he pleased, constantly delighted and distracted by the grotesque church tower with the phallus tip which bridled over his window as if about to violate it at any moment.

This decision led to difficulties over the Dortmund papers. As von Bremke had observed, many of them were not allowed to leave the building, and the Curator, a friendly little man in most ways, had a Teutonic relish for regulation. However, there was nothing to stop Daniel making copies; and he found that if he spent one hour a day doing this, usually in the early evening when his room on the precincts was least objectionable, he could take away enough material to occupy him over the next twenty-four hours, and at the same time ease his conscience with the reflection that he was, after all, making some use of the amenities which von Bremke had been at pains to proffer. There was also, he later found, a further advantage in this system: the act of copying Dortmund's manuscript required an attention to detail which not only made for a thorough introduction to the matter before him but also began to lend him a limited yet real insight into the working of the mysterious symbols, as though he had acquired by his devout imitation a certain affinity of spirit. On several occasions he found himself supplying the next term in a series before he had referred to the original; and although he was still ignorant of the meaning which lay behind the notation, it was no small encouragement that he was beginning to understand how to operate it.

One way and the other, then, he started to look forward to his evening hour in the otherwise detestable and antiseptic apartment over the Library. At this time of day Archimedes, his back turned to the sun as it declined over the cornfields, lost his smugness in the shadow which obscured all but his noble forehead; at this time of day there was a light, elusive whisper, which found its way even into these prim confines, of pleasures and excitements (albeit they were not for him) held in store by the coming night; and at this time of day, some two weeks after he had arrived in Göttingen, Earle Restarick the American had bowed himself into Daniel's life, a tall, silent figure, slipping through the door without knocking, confronting Daniel with a bland, seductive smile, as though he were about to remark that the pleasures hinted at by the vespertine whisper were readily available in the next street and that he would now take Daniel by the hand and lead him to them.

Instead,

"Herr Dominus Daniel Mond?" Earle Restarick had said, in a deep voice and entirely without irony.

"Yes . . . ?"

"Earle Restarick. They told me you were coming, but I've been out of town." He frowned as though he had been caught picking his nose. "Away from Göttingen," he emended, and again his mouth curved into the inviting and mysterious smile which seemed to promise so much but which, once more, heralded only the flabbiest piece of social commonplace.

"I called at your lodging," he said, "and the old lady said you might be here."

"I often work here for a little in the evening."

"You're sure I don't disturb you?"

Earle Restarick put his hands in his pockets and leaned companiably against the door. Americans, Daniel reflected, even educated ones, did not respect privacy. "You're sure I don't disturb you?" was not really a question but an affirmation, not only on Restarick's behalf but his own, of the American belief that no sane and moral man could prefer an intellectual occupation to human company, however dull or ordinary. Indeed, the more ordinary it was, the more a sane and moral man was expected to prefer it. If this new acquaintance was to be pursued, Daniel would have to find a way of establishing that meetings could take place by prior agreement only. But for this once, well, Restarick had taken trouble to seek him out, the least he could do was to show good will, and he was more relieved than he would have expected to find himself, after two weeks, talking to someone who approximated to a fellow countryman.

"Not at all," he said: "you don't know how glad I am to see you. Just let me finish this off."

He lowered his head to his page. Restarick raised an eyebrow and lounged over to the window.

"Nice view," he said, as if complimenting Daniel on a piece of personal property.

"I suppose so . . . I shan't be a moment."

"Nice piece of sculpture. They gave me Thucydides. That's because I'm an historian."

Dear God . . . "Sorry, but this bit's a little complicated."

"Nice cabinet," persisted Restarick. He opened and closed each drawer in turn, announcing aloud what he found each time, which was nothing.

"Nothing here either," he said, slamming the last drawer to and turning reproachful eyes on Daniel. "It's a shame not to keep something in such a nice cabinet."

"I keep my stuff at home . . . Just this last line."

"At home? But that can't be. Your home's in Brit— England."

"My lodgings," Daniel said and gritted his teeth. Perhaps he needn't trouble to be friendly after all? Perhaps he could say he suddenly felt ill? He looked up from his finished work to see Restarick smiling at him. After the inanity of everything the man had said, the smile still promised something well out of the ordinary. An invitation, as it were, to Xanadu, or a taste of the Golden Apples. Something, at any rate, which was certainly not to be rejected out of hand. You must come with me, the smile said, and see for yourself. Very well, thought Daniel: this once at least I will.

"Sorry to be so long," he said, surprised by the eagerness of his own voice; "it's all done now."

In the street outside, and blocking it, was a 1935 Mercedes, the sort of car in which German generals cavorted about (smoking cheroots and making cynical remarks to handsome aides-de-camp) in war films. A German policeman who was hovering looked hard at Restarick and then stalked resentfully away.

"Still an occupied country," Restarick had commented, "but only just. This time next year he'll want an apology, and the year after he'll try to make a charge. Peaked caps are reappearing, if you've noticed."

Both the car and the observation Daniel found indicative, the first of a stylish and individual taste, the second of an articulacy which Restarick had suppressed hitherto. There was, furthermore, something slightly sinister about his remark, an uncritical acceptance of authority, whether his own or that of the peak-capped policeman who must in time supplant him, which Daniel was still nervously trying to analyse when, five minutes later, they emerged from the last of the suburbs along a lumpy road to the south-east.

"Dinner," said Restarick : "we'll go to Bremke."

"Dinner with Doktor von Bremke? But has he asked us? He told me he couldn't receive people. His wife—"

"Not him . . . though I dare say there's a connexion. Bremke is a village about fifteen k's away. There's an inn which will give us a beautiful meal. Veal steaks stewed in milk. You're not Orthodox, I take it?"

"No. I'm not Orthodox."

"Lucky for you. These steaks are not to be missed. And first we might take look at the border—to give us an appetite. For I don't suppose," Earle Restarick said lazily, "that many people in East Germany will be having veal steaks stewed in milk for their dinner to-night."

"I didn't realise the border was quite so close."

"You climb a hill above this gasthaus of mine and there it is. Just over the next valley."

And so they had climbed the hill to see the border.

A dispiriting sight (as Daniel was to write to Robert Constable at Lancaster a day or two later), a high barbed-wire fence of several thicknesses with watch towers every quarter of a mile standing a short way back on the other side. It was evening when we saw it, so that the valley which lay between us and the ridge along which it ran was in deep shadow, while the fence itself was still visible in every detail and so appeared to be the only clear-cut reality in a world of shades. Not only that, but the sun, flashing along the strands of wire, gave the impression that the whole network was alive with some malignant current which would leap out and consume to ashes any living thing which came near.

Most depressing of all, however, was a small village which was a kilometre or so the other side. You see, at first sight it might almost have been the same village in which we had just left the car and ordered our dinner. The same grassland all round it, the same little hills above it, the same friendly houses with their off-white walls and red roofs, with their barns and stables and yards; and yet, because of some accident of war, because of a tactical decision taken seven or eight years ago and perhaps at a very junior level, the village on the other side was condemned and forsaken, and became a region beyond the Styx where *they*, the pale and bloodless ghosts, must drag out their weary days for ever. And indeed if there are still inhabitants in the village they can only be ghosts; for a second look reveals that it has long been deserted, presumably because it is too near the border for official comfort. The grassland is wild, the hills bare (trees give cover from watch towers), the red roofs pitted and gashed, the yards derelict.

"Cold comfort farm," said my American friend.

At first I thought this was one of his callous jokes, for he had already made two or three of them in the single hour he had known me; but when I looked at him I saw that he was very much affected, that his face was tense with outrage. This was a very understandable reaction, yet there was something about the jut of his chin which made me uneasy, suggesting that here was not so much sorrow or indignation, but contempt. However, I didn't think much of this at the time because I was trying to reassure myself, to tell myself and my battered left-wing conscience that it couldn't really be as bad as all that. Since the scene was peaceful and the brutal fence was getting harder to see in the dark, I had almost persuaded myself; no doubt they're really quite happy over there, I thought, all this about slavery and starvation is just propaganda, how foolish of me just now to think of them as damned.

"Look," I said to Restarick, fatuous with hope, "the lights are coming on over there. Just like everywhere else."

"The lights are coming on all right," he said : "in the watch towers."

And he pointed up at one of them from which a search-light suddenly stabbed out towards the ruined village and then swept back in a slow arc picking out, yard by yard, the eastern approaches to the wire.

Every day, Robert, East Germans in tens, scores, hundreds risk their lives to cross the border in this area. Refugee camps have been established; there is a large one not far from Göttingen to which Restarick has promised to take me one day soon. He says that they are already horribly overcrowded; it is easier to escape from an old life than to be admitted to a new. Yet still they pour in from the East, dodging beneath the cruel search-lights, ripping their flesh on the wire.

You must tell our friends this. There must be less of the facile pretence that everything over the border is (more or less) well. Socialist hypocrisy is even more vile than the right-wing kind, because we claim moral integrity, whereas they can always plead a pragmatic tradition ...

But for all the doubts and emotions raised by the barbed-wire fence the evening at Bremke had been a success. The food was as good as Restarick had promised, and there was a brisk red wine, served from a barrel in jugs, which was locally famous, Restarick said, for loosening both tongues and bowels. The service was casual yet prompt; and the room in which they dined was snug and friendly, disposing them to confidence. Although it was not Daniel's habit to say much about himself until he had known a person for some time, he found himself, over the third jug of wine, telling his companion something of those fears which so far he had discussed only with Jacquiz Helmut.

"My father's parents were Jews ... from Hannover. They

had the sense to get out early, in the late 'twenties. But you see, Earle, Germany is my country in a way . . . and also the country which has rejected me."

Resterick considered this.

"You know German?" he said.

"Only a few words from the phrase book. My grandparents both died when I was four, and my father refused to have the language spoken in his house. He gave away most of my grandfather's German books. The rest he burnt."

"If you don't speak German," Restarick said, "this isn't your country."

"Even so I have a sense of returning . . . returning to a place which has expelled me . . . so that I am more afraid of it than if I were simply coming here for the first time."

"But you are simply coming here for the first time," said Restarick doggedly. "However long your ancestors lived in Hannover or any other damned German place, you were born in England, you hold an English passport, and you have never in your life set foot in Germany until sixteen days ago. These people have nothing on you, nothing at all."

"They know different."

All the same he found this unsubtlety oddly comforting.

"The English," Restarick persisted, "they didn't intern your father in 1939?"

"No. They found him work in the Ministry of Information."

"And your mother—you say she wasn't German nor Jewish either?"

Had he said that? He couldn't remember, but it was true enough, so he supposed he must have. This wine was rather confusing.

"She was the daughter of an English schoolmaster. Strictly old style he was—a housemaster at a big public school. I never met him. My mother's parents didn't like the marriage, you see, and neither did my father's. They weren't strict, mind

you, but they kept the main Jewish festivals. I can just remember my grandfather standing at the head of a table and
saying, very gravely and sweetly, 'Next year in Jerusalem'.
He didn't mean it, of course, and in any case next year he
was dead. A little later my grandmother died ... and then
my mother."

"She must have been very young."

"An accident on the river. Near Staines, of all places. I
was never really told the details, and somehow I didn't like
to ask. Sometimes I wonder—"

"—You wonder too much. Your trouble is," said Earle
Restarick, "that you're too polite to ask straight questions,
so then you get to torturing yourself by making up your own
morbid answers."

Daniel was pleased with this diagnosis. So true, he told
himself; and indeed I've been sitting here all through dinner talking about myself without a single attempt to find out
about Earle Restarick.

"Tell me, Earle," he said; "what are you doing in
Göttingen?"

For a moment Restarick looked startled and even
affronted.

"You did suggest," said Daniel, "that I should start asking
questions."

"Sure I did. Only I thought you knew the answer to that
one. I'm an historian, like I said, a modern historian. You've
heard of a guy at Oxford called Trevor-Roper? An expert
on the top brass of the Nazi Party and what happened when
things started to break up? Well, I'm following up a few
little hints from him."

"Then you've been at Oxford?"

"No ... I came straight from Harvard. But I know this
Trever-Roper's work."

"But surely," said Daniel, much interested, "Göttingen is
hardly the place to go into all that. A peaceful academic
backwater."

"A lot of stuff drifts into backwaters," said Restarick sharply: "you never know what you'll find among the rubbish."

Daniel opened his mouth to comment on this proposition but Restarick was before him:

"Besides," he said, "there's a family connexion. An uncle of mine, he studied here back in 1910. Mother's side of the family—the Boston side."

He paused to see whether the significance of this remark had been taken. Daniel, who was not strong on American social distinctions, merely nodded non-committally.

"Father's people really come from Boston too," said Restarick with a frown, "but they moved to Connecticut some time back."

"How long have you been in Göttingen?" said Daniel, rather confused by all this topographical insistence.

Again Restarick looked startled and affronted.

"Since early this year . . ."

It was said almost furtively. But then Earle Restarick looked at Daniel and smiled his smile. After the wine it promised even more than before; it promised Helen of Troy, the Treasure of Minos, the Tree of Life.

"I've been very lonely, Daniel," he said. "I'm so glad you've come . . . a friend?"

It was both an appeal and an offer, modest, sincere, irresistible.

"Call for more wine," said Daniel: "the best."

For a month and more after that evening at Bremke Earle Restarick and Daniel Mond were together nearly every day, dining, walking, making excursions in the 1935 Mercedes. Daniel need not have feared that Earle would disrupt his work. On the contrary, his new friend was at great pains to discover exactly at what hour each day it would best suit Daniel to meet him or be picked up, and never once intruded on him before that time. So far from distracting Daniel,

Earle seemed to regard himself as responsible for rationing his amusements.

"I'm not sure that you ought to have the day off," he would remark, à propos of some projected expedition to Hannover or the Harz.

"But it's only for once in a way."

"That's just the kind of excuse which can become habit-forming . . . particularly with a weak character like yours."

For it was Earle's contention that Daniel had an all too malleable nature which must be both stiffened and protected. Daniel, who liked being mothered, enjoyed this concern for his welfare, the more so as it was little needed. For his work was going steadily and well; and indeed if anyone required to be kept up to the mark it was Earle himself, who had no routine and seldom seemed to settle to his research.

"What did you do today?" Daniel would ask at dinner.

"Messed about in the car . . . Read that novel of Anthony Powell's you lent me. I didn't realise you English could be so oblique."

"Don't you ever do any work, Earle?"

"It'll all come right in time, you'll see. Just now I'm waiting for a line. No good starting off until you know which way you're going."

"Surely it's up to you to decide that."

"In this case—no."

And then the topic would be changed.

They seldom tried to say anything of intimacy or intellectual depth to each other, remaining happy with light comment on whatever they were doing at the time. Daniel, whose mental energies were fully taken up by the increasing complications of the Dortmund papers, found this triviality of intercourse easy and restful : to Earle, on the other hand, it did not apparently occur that any other way was either possible or desirable. "No point going too far into it just now," he used to say whenever their conversation touched on some serious subject : "only find trouble." And although at another place or time Daniel might well have considered it his moral duty to "find trouble", it seemed that Earle's company acted on his conscience as an anodyne, persuading him to sink back in his seat and enjoy, for so long as the drug should last, the peace of mind which it bestowed. Perhaps, he sometimes thought, Earle was right about his character: it lay wide open to corruption of whatever kind.

If Earle eschewed profundity, he evinced, on one occasion at least, a disquieting turn of logic. This was on the day when the visited the refugee camp for East Germans. They had been introduced to a Professor of Art History recently fled from Dresden, a snowy and, despite his sleazy brown battle-dress, distinguished old gentleman, who was convinced that the only proper recompense for his sufferings was the im-mediate offer of a chair in England or America. Although Daniel thought the Professor was too shrill and presumptuous in this claim, he nevertheless felt that something handsome should be done for him by the scholarly fraternity of the free world, and later, as they walked past the seedy Nissen huts towards the Mercedes at the gate, he expressed this view forcibly to Earle.

"You know his record?" Earle said.

"Only that he's been at Dresden for many years."

"Too many years. He's been sitting there since 1930, and never once, before, during or after the war, has he been in the smallest trouble with authority of any branch or persua-sion. What do you deduce from that?"

"That you are remarkably well informed."

"It cuts across my subject, you might say. What do you deduce about the Professor?"

"That he is of amenable disposition."

"Too true."

Earle looked with displeasure at a family of gipsies who were brandishing rusty billy-cans on the steps of a cook-house.

"They make their way up from Greece," Earle said. "They

get everywhere. No money, no passports—and no stopping
them ... This Professor you're so steamed up about. He's
been sitting in Dresden being amenable, as you call it, for
over twenty years. He's all of sixty; so why does he stop
now?"

"He's finally seen too much."

"He never saw a thing he didn't want to see in this whole
life. And just suppose he *was* in trouble at last, or that something *had* happened to hurt that plasticine conscience of his,
he didn't have to come all the way to Göttingen to make his
crossing. It'd have been half the distance north to Berlin
or south to Coburg. He came to Göttingen, Danny boy, because Göttingen marks the beginning of the British Zone, and
it was therefore the nearest place he could be sure of being
interned by the British and not by the Americans or the
French."

"A compliment."

"In a back-handed way, yes. The French hate the Krauts so
much they'd have starved him to death, and the Americans
are so hot on security they'd have cracked his cover to pieces.
It's only you British who are soft enough to feed him and
believe him both. He's a plant, Danny; a good old-fashioned
plant ... Not that it's his fault. They just got fed to death
with him sitting there in Dresden as smug as a new banknote
in the middle of all that Art, and they said, 'Now, comrade,
your big chance to serve the cause has come at last. You get
off your arse and escape like hell to the British. And when
they've set you up in a nice big office in the British Museum,
our representative will call around to tell you what to do
next.'"

"Poor old chap. What will happen?"

"Our intelligence boys will tip off your lot. Your lot will
think it's all ungentlemanly American hysteria, but they
won't want to cause offence because of all those dollars you're
short of, so they'll just see that he stays where he is and rots.
And sooner him than me."

They both turned to look at the lines of Nissen huts. From the cook-house, which had now absorbed the gipsies, rose a column of yellow smoke. "Stays where he is and rots," thought Daniel.

"And if he's genuine?" he said.

"Too bad."

"You seem very sure of what you say."

"I'm a student of modern history," Earle replied, "and this is just what most of my subject's about."

Other excursions had been more cheerful. The weather, uncertain in April, had changed in early May and yielded a long succession of Arcadian days, warm and breezy, green against blue. They drove into the Harz Mountains, to Paderborn with its strange barn-like cathedral (ancient scene of God knew what theological excesses), to Osnabruck, to Hameln, to Minden, to the walled brothel quarter in Brunswick, to the sandy heath round Luneburg, and, one weekend, far to the south, where the pretty spa-towns had once more been taken out, so to speak, and dusted, like expensive toys which had lain packed away during the season of danger.

Of all their journeys Daniel most enjoyed this last, because it was the only one on which there had not been the constant sight of British Army uniforms. Since these were still a familiar enough spectacle even in England, it was hard to say why he found them so oppressive here. Explaining himself to Earle in their usual light terms (and therefore telling something less than the truth) he deposed that he was bored by the dowdy battle-dress, that if there must be soldiers round the place they might at least dress the part with style.

"Then you'd feel more inferior than ever," Earle said. "Because that's what you really mean. You resent the military because you've never been in the Army yourself."

"It's more than that . . . Those officers we saw dining in the Alte Krone the other night. It wouldn't have been so bad if they'd shouted or smashed the place up. What I couldn't bear was those quiet, level voices which assumed automatic obedience."

"They must have come from the barracks on the hill. The Wessex Fusiliers, I'm told. Know anything about them?"

"I know nothing about the Army."

"My informant said they were 'undistinguished'. In your Army, that apparently means an ordinary regiment of the line which has fought bravely in every action since Blenheim but only has middle-class officers."

Daniel considered this piece of expertise.

"Your . . . informant?" he said at last.

"American I met in Kassel. And that reminds me. Tuesday's out. I've got to go to Kassel then instead of Thursday."

Every Thursday Earle had what he called "my jaunt to Kassel". Daniel understood that there was an American centre there, of a vaguely cultural kind, and that Thursday was an "at home day" attended by the handful of American civilians in the area and sometimes by American Army officers from Bad Hersfeld and further south. In Göttingen there was a similar British institution, called Die . Brucke, which housed an English library, many pamphlets about the British Way of Life, and a pleasant Scottish Director who occasionally got up a play-reading or a debate. But Earle's centre in Kassel—he never told Daniel what it was called—seemed somehow more formidable; from the deference with which Earle referred to it and the absolute regularity with which he attended its Thursdays, Daniel had concluded that he was under an obligation to report himself, as though to some consular agent or to someone appointed by Harvard University to keep an eye on him. For Americans, Daniel knew, were always on a leash which stretched back to America. One thing at least was clear: if Earle had been summoned to Kassel next Tuesday Earle would go, and this was disappointing, as they had arranged to drive into Hannover for a concert.

"Why have they changed the day?" Daniel said morosely.

"Important visitor ... Don't get upset. There'll be other concerts; we've all summer."

But Daniel continued to sulk. Eventually Earle turned the car off the road and stopped on a track which led through a grove of fir-trees.

"Come on, Danny," he said: "it's too good an evening for that."

"I'm sorry. You're right, of course."

And indeed, Daniel thought, there could not be so many evenings like this in a life-time, evenings passed with a friend in a little wood under a darkening but kindly sky, still warm from the sun. A soft floor of pine-needles to walk on. A car to retreat to the moment the first chill of night crept through the trees, hinting deliciously at atavistic terrors, and gave warning that it was time to be gone. How many more such evenings? There was all summer, Earle had said. But Daniel belonged, if only in part, to a race too ancient and too wary to trust in any promises of future seasons.

And as it turned out there were to be no more evenings in pine-woods, no more journeys to the south. When Earle returned from his Tuesday jaunt to Kassel, he had changed. He was like a man who, assured of a great inheritance, is suddenly told that he has been discovered to be illegitimate and must content himself with a pittance, even that being given him only by charity of the true heirs. He was angry, disillusioned, trapped. At first Daniel assumed that he had at last been rebuked, by whatever authority dwelt in Kassel, for his laziness, had been told to amuse himself less and settle to his work; for this would explain why he no longer suggested drives or excursions, and indeed would only meet Daniel every third or fourth day. But it was soon obvious that something must have occurred far more serious than a mere telling-off. People told to work harder are still permitted to meet their friends and dine at leisure from time to time; but Earle would no longer dine with him at all, confining their meetings to a sparse half-hour at lunch time or to a brief afternoon walk. This Daniel would have been prepared to accept, on the ground that his friend had received a nasty shock and must have time to recover, had it not been for Earle's palpable hostility. This not only wounded him deeply, it was beyond any possible explanation : for while he could readily understand that some unlooked for reverse might make Restarick bad-tempered and inattentive, he could find no excuse for naked malignity directed straight at himself. Unless of course he, Daniel, was in some way to blame for whatever had happened; but how could this be?

After this state of affairs had continued for nearly three weeks, Daniel decided to ask Earle what was wrong. He was reluctant to do so because he sensed here something that it would be unwise to probe. But after all, it was Earle himself who had recommended, when they first met, the virtue of straight questions; and the fact that Earle still met him at all, however disagreeable he was while they were together, must mean that there was still something between them which could be rescued and preserved.

And so, as they walked silently along the city wall in the heat of the day, Daniel red and sweaty in his heavy sports jacket, Earle smooth and aloof in a suit of gaberdine, Daniel took his friend by the elbow and said :

"What's the matter, Earle? Have I done anything?"

Earle stopped, moved his arm slowly and deliberately from Daniel's grasp, and then walked on, keeping three or four paces ahead and talking straight in front of him.

"You just don't know, do you? You just don't know what you're doing. Every day you stick your face into a pile of papers which nobody up till now has understood, and you work six, seven, sometimes ten hours, hoping to find the answer. But what happens if you do? Have you thought of that?"

So that was it. Earle, who had always seemed so solicitous about Daniel's work, was in truth jealous of it.

"Of course I've thought about it," Daniel said to the blank expanse of gaberdine moving before him. "If I find the answer, I shall go back to Cambridge and make use of it, if I can, to help me finish my research. What else would I do? I'll be sorry to leave Göttingen, sorry to leave you, I shall miss those drives we have—used to have—"

"—You just don't know, that's what. You work away on those papers, trying to put life into symbols that have been dead fifteen years, and in the intervals you're happy because you've got a tame chauffeur to drive you around. But do you have any idea what those symbols may do if you call them up from the grave? Of course you don't. You don't even have any idea where your tame chauffeur's driving you. When he says, 'We're going to Bad Harzburg today,' you just sit back with a smug smile on your face and look forward to a nice, cosy ride. But for all you *know*, he might be planning to drive you straight to Hell."

"I don't understand you," said Daniel sadly to the gaberdine back. "I'm sorry, Earle, if I seemed to take you for granted, but I thought—"

"—Pardon me, that's just what you haven't done." Hitherto Earle's voice had been one of peevish anger: now it took the bleak tone of one who, though he has abandoned hope, nevertheless tries for the twentieth time to explain a simple proposition to a backward child. "You haven't thought at all," he said. "You've got your priorities all wrong. You're so full of imaginary fears that you don't see the real ones. You worry so much about whether or not to take an umbrella when you go out that you forget what you're going out for. Or take that socialism of yours: you fuss yourself sick about whether some bloody labourer should get another shilling a day, and meanwhile you don't notice that your whole country's going bankrupt . . . Or you're scared that everyone hates you because you're a Jew. They don't give a rap, most of them, what you do with your bacon; what bothers them is the way people like you parade your consciences round the world, yapping and squealing about morality and justice and making trouble where there was peace and quiet before."

"But with you . . . I've kept quiet about all that . . . because I knew you wouldn't care for it."

"It was there all the time in your face. Wherever we went, whatever we saw, there was that great oozing conscience of yours hanging out to dry."

Two large tears appeared at the inner corners of Daniel's eyes.

"If you felt like that, why didn't you say so before? Instead of letting me believe you liked me, wanted me with you. And why did it have to be so cruel? One day the same as ever, the next this horrible, silent hate."

At last Earle turned to face him.

"It isn't hate. It's fear. I'm afraid of you, Daniel."

"Afraid of *me*?"

"Afraid of what you might do . . . without meaning it, without knowing it even. I'm afraid of that patient, subtle mind of yours, caressing those dead symbols into life. Why can't you let them stay dead, Daniel?"

"But you . . . you always encouraged me."

Earle looked carefully round, as though to make sure they were unobserved. "Listen, Danny boy," he said, almost into Daniel's ear. "Leave Göttingen. Put those symbols back in the tomb where they belong, tell everyone in a loud, clear voice that you can't do anything with them, and then go home."

"Not now. I couldn't. I'm just beginning to understand—"

"—You understand nothing," Earle hissed at him. "You won't even listen when you're told." He touched Daniel in the crook of one arm. "Go home before it's too late," he hissed; "just go home."

And then he walked away very fast along the wall.

That had been in the middle of June, and Daniel had not seen him since. After that there had been only work.

This became daily more fascinating, and he thought that he was now near to an important breakthrough. If this were so, then the problem of the Dortmund notation, in its first stage, would soon be solved, and he would be able to understand at any rate the earlier matrices. His trouble would then lie, as von Bremke had warned him, with Dortmund's shift in usage, which seemed to correspond to a shift in purpose, or rather, to a more rigid definition of purpose. That problem was for the future, but Daniel had looked far enough ahead to form a general hypothesis. Dortmund, he considered, had at first developed the matrices, together with the notation through which they must be expressed, without any particular purpose in view; he was forging a mathematical instrument and that was all. However, at some late stage in the process it seemed to have struck Dortmund that this instrument would be very well suited, provided certain rather complex adjustments were made, to one definite form of investigation. This, of course, was very much what von Bremke had suggested, but in one respect Daniel had advanced further: he now had a shrewd idea what particular investigation Dortmund had decided on; and this, if he was right, was related more closely than he had dared to hope to the investigation which he himself wished ultimately to pursue.

So there had been work, on balance very good work; but work was not enough.

I can't tell you (he wrote with defensive suavity to Jacquiz Helmut) how dreary it is in Göttingen now. The German summer seems to scorch the life out of everything. I had never realised before what it meant to live on an island, never to be more than an hour or so from the sea.

My American chum has disappeared. He started to sulk in June, I never knew why, and finally blew himself up into a remarkable fit of pique and vanished for good. It was very odd. I thought at first that it was all caused by jealousy of the way I worked—for poor Earle never seemed to come to terms with his own work or even to know where to start. But thinking it over since I've decided that jealousy is not in character. I've an idea he was irritated because he thought I was wasting my time on something too difficult, and that even if I did solve the problem the answer would be no good to myself or anyone else . . . (This, thought Daniel, was something less than a candid assessment, but for the time being it was as much as he cared to tell Jacquiz) . . . Even so, it's hard to see why he behaved as he did; he went on at me as if I were practising black magic or hunting for the Philosopher's Stone. I'm sure there's some simple but entertaining quirk of trans-Atlantic psychology here which you will at once explain to me when we meet again.

I wish this could be soon as it would be pleasant to talk to someone. My landlady has been so well trained over the years to efface herself that there can be no communication there. Herr Doktor Aeneas von Bremke, whom in any case I have hardly seen since I presented my credentials, has withdrawn to a summer fastness up in the Harz. Even the Librarian, who used to tell me how he visited Lancaster before the war, has left for his annual month by Lake Konstanz; and his assistant is a sour, self-pitying youth with technicolour spots. To crown everything, my favourite restaurant has closed its doors for three weeks.

It would be nice if you could come here for a few days. I know what I've said in this letter can hardly be much inducement, but Göttingen is really an attractive little town, just what a university should be . . . if only it offered the sight (or even the hope) of a familiar face.

But I don't suppose for a moment that you can leave Cambridge just now. You must be working very hard on Garibaldi, and of course the Long Vacation is always right for work—the college half empty, just a few friends to ensure a little discreet gaiety when needed. In Göttingen there is no gaiety, so I think of you often, of what you might be doing at this hour or at that.

By now, I imagine, the Summer Festival is in full swing. In March the talk was that the Marlowe would do The Family Reunion in July, not my favourite play, though I like that bit about the clock stopping in the dark. Have you been to see it? If you have, do let me know if Toby had a part (he was very anxious, I remember) and how he got on; I always enjoy the way he gangles so shyly on to the set and then upstages everyone without meaning to.

I long so much to be back. But the work I have will take at least two months more, even if everything goes as well as possible, and it will be late in September before I can hope to be finished . . .

He thought of this letter now, as he sat with his coffee on the sunny terrace of the restaurant on the hill. He had written it two days ago, feeling at last that he must send some signal, to those who might care enough to read it right, that all was not well with him; but although he had told Jacquiz as much as he dared of his loneliness, he had told him nothing of his fear: the fear which now rose in him every time he sat down again to the Dortmund papers ("Put them back in the tomb where they belong"), and the other fear, even vaguer yet even more ugly . . . "go home before it's too late".

Daniel laid a note on the bill in front of him and added some coins from his purse. Then he walked to the edge of the terrace and looked carefully down at Göttingen. A seemly town and surely innocent : there could be nothing to fear except the oppression and the heat. Once again, a bugle sounded from the barracks below; he did not know what the call meant, but it spoke somehow of an afternoon far advanced. It was time to walk down the hill, to return to Dortmund's dead symbols that he might bring them life.

PART II
THE BAND NIGHT

ONCE across the meadow which lay beneath the Gast-haus where he had been lunching, Daniel followed a tall wire fence through bushes and scrub for two hundred yards and then emerged on to a road by the main gate and guard room of the barracks. The meadow he always enjoyed; but the barrack fence posed a disagreeable mystery and the barrack gate a positive threat, suggesting a Kafkaesque nightmare which tormented him every time he passed . . .

"*You there, come inside at once. Yes, you.*"

"*Me? There must be some mistake.*"

"*On the contrary. I have a warrant here with your name on it. 'Daniel Mond,' it says: 'posted for National Service'—and high time too.*"

"*I'm exempt.*"

"*So you keep telling everybody. But we know better, don't we?*"

"*I assure you—*"

"*—Sergeant-Major, have this man arrested and taken in-side. Cut his hair, burn his clothes, take his money, and just to be on the safe side give him a new identity. We don't want any of his left-wing friends making trouble . . .*"

"Hey, YOU. You there outside the gate."

A clatter of boots. And a roaring noise in the background. Keep calm, he can't possibly mean you.

"Not so fast."

A large man blocking his way. Two stripes on his arm. A corporal? (*Habeas corpus.*) A black band above the stripes with the red letters "R.P."

"Come with me . . . sir."

"Sir"? Ironic, obviously. *"Because you've got what is laughingly called a degree, Mister Mond, we're officially compelled to let you serve your time as an officer . . . in name only, of course . . ."*

"I'll do no such thing. Who do you think you are, shouting after people like that?"

The large man sighed and looked as if he were going to burst into tears.

"No harm intended," he said in the thick accents of the west country. "It's *'im.*"

He pointed back towards the gate. Daniel turned to see a plump freckled face hung round with earphones and supported by a torso which had been clumsily crammed, like a swollen cork, into the turret of what he took for a small tank.

"Daniel," said the face, splitting juicily in welcome.

" *'Im,*" insisted the large corporal, bending gently and lugubriously over the terrified Daniel.

The cork eased itself out of the turret with a plop to reveal a pair of bright pink thighs. At first Daniel assumed these must be naked (something to do with the heat inside the tank?), then he realised, as calves followed thighs into the open, that he was looking at a pair of elegant and unusual trousers. These, though intriguing, could not help him to identify their owner; but then the earphones were whisked off like a wig, and the raddled and receding fair hair above the young face suddenly recalled a score of happy and unedifying evenings.

"Julian . . . Oh Julian, is it really you?" Daniel called, while the large corporal melted with pleasure. "But I thought . . . You said when you went down that you were going to sell wine."

"National Service first. Didn't want to upset your sensitive feelings by telling you . . . Hat," said Julian to the side of the tank.

A hand appeared out of the turret holding a huge peaked hat of khaki felt which was fronted by a silver device of a grinning skull that wore an earl's coronet. Julian put on the hat with care and then trotted towards Daniel.

"Cornet J. James of the 49th. Earl Hamilton's Light dragoons," he said saluting smartly. "Thank you, corporal. Pray dismiss."

The corporal did several very noisy things with his hands and feet, and lumbered off.

"Sorry if he gave you a fright just now, Daniel. These west country boys are really as soft as butter but the Fusiliers will teach them to bang and shout."

"Fusiliers? I thought you said you were a Dragoon?"

"The barracks are occupied by the First Battalion of the Wessex Fusiliers. I belong to a squadron of armoured cars that's been sent here for special training with them. We only arrived last week. What about you?"

"I've been down at the university over three months."

"Lonely . . . after Lancaster." The assumption was immediate.

"Yes."

"Well, now you've got friends."

"I'm not sure that Dragoons are quite in my line."

"We're a very jolly lot, you'll find. The Fusiliers now, they're rather stiff and gloomy, but you needn't meet any of them. Dinner this evening?"

"Just you, Julian?"

" 'Fraid not. There's two of my crowd I've asked and the doctor. You'll like them, I promise."

Daniel hesitated.

"Come along, my dear. It's been over a year and I want all the Lancaster gossip."

"Your friends . . ."

". . . Will enjoy it as much as me. It is perfectly respectable,

Daniel, for an intellectual to mix with the military. Or have you forgotten Proust and Doncières?"

At first, as he set out for the restaurant Julian had named, Daniel was full of misgiving. After all, Julian was little more than a pleasant acquaintance, associated with frivolous dinners and summer afternoons in punts, never received (nor wishing to be received) into moral or intellectual confidence. Although he was intelligent (he had taken a good idle second in the Classics), he was light-minded, sceptical of aspiration, and politically unconcerned to the point of callousness. To Daniel, Julian was an agreeable reminder of good days rather than a man of value in himself; he was an acceptable bit-player "to swell a scene or two", peripheral and slightly suspect; so that a year in bad company might well have brought out displeasing tendencies towards philistinism and reaction which had always, Daniel thought, been lurking beneath the amiable neutrality of his Cambridge persona. And the possible corruption of Julian was only one of Daniel's worries. How was he to talk to his friends? "A jolly lot. . ." What did that imply? Fornicating redcoats from Farquhar? Bumperising and melodious Magyars? One thing it did not imply (thank God) was the even speaking and self-satisfied officers (presumably Wessex Fusiliers) whom he had seen dining some weeks ago and on whom he had commented to Earle. But would it not be even worse if Julian's companions turned out to be Regency rakes who expected him to introduce them to some prodigiously gilded brothel or stake his entire year's income on a single card at Faro?

The event was reassuring. Julian's guests were dressed in unpretentious civilian suits, had long if well cut hair (unlike the remembered officers of the Alte Krone, who had all been cropped), and spoke in mild, friendly voices. Much ot the talk was of what they hoped to eat, as it seemed that Julian had elaborated his expertise, already evident at Cambridge, as a gastronome; while for the rest the conversation consisted of informed and articulate gossip, which ranged from the current state of ante-post betting on the St Leger to the Earl Marshal's preparations for the coronation the following summer.

All present were so easy and unassuming that it took Daniel some time to sort out their official precedence and functions—a task to which, with typical perversity, he had at once addressed himself. In the end, it appeared that a quiet, shambling man, who looked like an over-nourished version of Douglas Fairbanks Junior, was called Major Giles Glastonbury and commanded Julian's squadron of armoured cars. Then there was a bright, nervous youth in his mid-twenties, who had a girlish but ravaged face and dazzling auburn hair; this was Captain Fielding Gray, second in command to Major Glastonbury. Daniel gathered that besides these two and Julian James there were two more officers in the squadron, both of them subalterns and both expected for some unspecified entertainment later on; but the only other guest at dinner was a certain Lieutenant Motley of the Medical Corps, who was doing his National Service as Battalion doctor to the Fusiliers and who spoke with a high-pitched Liverpool-Irish accent. Before Daniel could puzzle out what Motley was doing in this particular gallery Julian led them to table, where Daniel was placed on his host's right with Captain Gray to his own. A pattern of exchange was soon established: Julian was too concerned about the service of dinner to talk to anyone except waiters; Motley and Glastonbury settled to an expert discussion of National Hunt courses in the Midlands; and Daniel's entertainment was left entirely to Captain Gray. Perhaps this had been previously arranged; for Gray, as one about to try a prepared but perilous gambit, breathed deeply and said:

"I was interested to hear that you were at Lancaster with Julian. I was to have gone there myself."

"Was?"

"A squalid misunderstanding. Please tell me what I have missed."

"Where should I start?"

Gray smiled narrowly.

"What I should really like to be told is that I have missed nothing. If you could tell me that I would have been frustrated by second-rate pedants and sickened by callow undergraduates, it would be a great relief to me."

"Not everyone cares for it, certainly."

"But would *I* have done?"

"I don't know you well enough to say. In any case, the question is too theoretical to bother with. As things are, you have your own place"—Daniel gestured lightly over the table "and your own friends to share it."

"Not," said Gray intently, "the ones I would have had at Lancaster. The kind I used to have when I still thought I was going there. It is as though my ... rejection ... paralysed, or even killed, some faculty within me."

Daniel shuddered. Much given to self-pity himself, he was always revolted by its ugliness in others.

"Short run in," rumbled Glastonbury from the other side of the table, his face turned towards Motley but his eyes settled on Daniel and Gray.

"No worse than Uttoxeter, Giles," said Motley.

Glastonbury appeared to wink at Daniel, then switched his eyes back to the doctor.

"U'xeter," he said.

"Pay attention, chums"—this from Julian—"and for what you are about to receive may the Lord make you truly grateful. Lobster Lucullus. I particularly want you to notice the white truffles."

For a while there was general chat about the Lobster Lucullus. Then Captain Gray, who was clearly tenacious of his thread, leaned close to Daniel and said :

"I've told you what I have because it is my nature to worry a sore place until it is gangrenous."

"A dangerous habit."

"I know. But there's one more thing I must ask. Julian tells me you are the friend of a man called Robert Constable."

"Our Tutor."

"Your Tutor. It was Constable who was ultimately responsible for refusing my entry to Lancaster. What kind of man is he?"

Daniel studied a truffle.

"A just man," he said at length.

"A Christian?"

"No."

"So not a man of charity?"

"I suppose not. He angers easily. He's a powerful hater. He is kind to honest failure, but merciless to indifference."

Gray flinched.

"That explains a lot," he said wearily. "A committed man . . . He can't have had much time for Julian then?"

"Oddly enough, he rather liked him. He used to say that no pilgrimage was complete without Mr Worldly-Wise-Man. A rationalization, of course. Like the rest of us, he just enjoyed Julian's charm."

"You know," said Gray, who seemed unaccountably cheered by this remark, "Julian is an excellent officer. He encourages people to underrate him. He puffs and pants and simpers until his opponents are right off their guard, then he comes whipping back and ties them in knots before they know it."

"His opponents?" Daniel was glad of this opportunity for a decisive change of topic. Gray's obsession for conjuring the ghosts of a past which he had never had was making him increasingly uneasy. "Julian's opponents?" Daniel persisted. "Surely he's in a peace time Army and serving among friends?"

"He is a resourceful man," said Gray. "He thinks of short and easy ways of doing what tradition prescribes should be long and toilsome. This is never popular with senior men, who feel more secure when people are safely occupied. So they find Julian immoral and subversive."

"Major Glastonbury thinks that?"

"Major Glastonbury is a civilised man in a civilised regiment. He favours intelligence and good will. Most regiments still work the old way—blind obedience and bloody-mindedness. Our hosts, the Fusiliers, are an excellent example."

"I'm rather intrigued by this *animus* you all seem to have about the Fusiliers."

"The animus is more on their part. We," said Gray, not without irony, "are the 10th Sabre Squadron—old titles die hard—of Earl Hamilton's Light Dragoons. Our motto is *'Res Unius, Res Omnium'*, which implies more concern for private loyalties than the public service. We wear decorative trousers of a deep pink because Lord Hamilton was in his rose garden when he received his commission; and we call them 'cherry' out of deference to William IV, who had the story wrong and thought it was a cherry orchard. In the winter we wear riding cloaks lined with silk of the same colour and trimmed with collars of white fur, to buy one of which absorbs the whole of an officer's uniform allowance for about ten years. So you will not be surprised to hear that most of our officers, though not myself, have substantial private incomes, or that Giles Glastonbury, to take only one instance, has connexions which might be called princely. All this, as I think you will agree, adds up to amplitude."

"Whereas the Fusiliers"—where had he heard this?—"are middle-class and jealous?"

"Worse. The Fusiliers are not only tortured by lack of money and incessantly nagged by their discontented and snobbish wives: they are also so afraid of losing even what little they have that they allow themselves to be bullied hysterical by superiors who are in much the same case. From their Colonel down to the newest joined Second Lieutenant they are hag-ridden by precedent and precedence. They hardly dare let their wretched soldiers out of their sight for fear of what may go wrong. And here we have the most significant and injurous difference between us : we can afford to speak our minds and treat our men liberally, while the Fusiliers cannot."

"Then why have you been sent here . . . if it means such an uneasy alliance?"

"We were the only cavalry squadron available that was properly equipped for the role."

He was about to expand on the statement, Daniel thought, when they were distracted by noise from over the table.

"What you don't understand," Major Glastonbury was saying to Doctor Motley, in a voice far too loud to suit either his personality or the sentiments expressed, "is that steeple-chasing is not merely a public circus. There is a tradition; there are standards to be kept up. If you make the Grand National course easier, then the standards will drop with the height of the fences."

"And what you don't understand," said Motley, "is that these days the public—the paying public—insists on interfering. The public wants the fences lowered out of kindness to the horses."

"Kindness kills standards," remarked Julian with satisfaction. "To get a Strasbourg pie you must be cruel to the goose."

"That is why public opinion is against Strasbourg pies."

"No it's not. It's because the public can't afford them. Envy."

"Wrong," said Glastonbury. "It's because the public mistrusts perfection. To appreciate and deserve perfection, you need a trained palate, a trained eye, a trained mind—superior taste, in short. And this of course is an offence to popular notions of equality."

"It's not so much that," said Daniel, unhappy and conscientious. "The general feeling, to adapt Julian's image, is that starving children should be fed before trained palates are titillated with Strasbourg pies."

Glastonbury and Motley both nodded, at once sincerely

conceding the point and thanking God that Strasbourg pies were still smooth on the tongue.

"Pure mathematics," said Captain Gray, "is a Strasbourg pie if ever there was one. On your own showing, you ought to be advancing the general nutriment with technical inventions."

Julian grinned with affectionate malice and turned to harrass the waiters. Glastonbury nodded once more, as though indicating to some distant colleague that all danger had now passed, and resumed his quiet duologue with the doctor.

"You must excuse all that noise and smoke," said Gray to Daniel. "Giles interrupted because he thought I was about to be indiscreet."

"Indiscreet?"

"Tell you what we're doing here. It wouldn't do for every public busybody to know about it."

"I'm sorry if I've given that impression. I'm told I let my feelings show."

"On the contrary, you've reassured him. You entered your protest honourably but with civilised reluctance. With proper consideration for the company."

"I'm not sure I feel complimented."

"You can feel trusted," said Captain Gray. "That is much rarer."

Two almost indistinguishable young men, both of them having weak chins, jelly-fish eyes and braying voices, now greeted Julian and sat down at the end of the table. Daniel was introduced to Jack Lamprey and Piers Bungay. Both smiled limply; both turned to a hovering waiter to order coffee and cognac without reference to their host.

"Both Troop Commanders, like Julian," Gray explained. "A sabre squadron consists of three sabre troops, a Headquarters, and in our case a more than usually elaborate technical section."

He waited for Daniel to ask the obvious question; but

Daniel was considering Lamprey and Bungay, and wondering how it was conceivable that a bicycle, let alone a "sabre troop", should be entrusted to their care.

"The technical section," said Gray in a lecturing tone, "is because we must be self-supporting. Very important in our line of business. I must tell you about it," he insisted, "now that Giles has approved of you."

"I'm not very interested in all that. I prefer the social details."

"They become more piquant if you know the military ones. A few facts of life for you, Daniel."

"Don't patronise me, Captain Gray."

Gray's face sagged slightly.

"You misunderstood. I'm the one who's asking favours. You'll see why when you hear what I have to say."

"I'm still not sure I want to listen."

"Not now anyway . . ."

For now everyone was suddenly stirring. Julian was flipping through a pile of bills, signing some and waving others away. Glastonbury and Motley were ponderously gesturing each other towards the lavatory. The lately arrived subalterns were on their feet, draining their glasses and shooting their cuffs, in anticipation of immediate action.

"Tomorrow," continued Gray, "I'm up in the Harz for reconnaissance. You know the Jagdhof in Harzburg?"

"I think so."

"I'll meet you in the bar at twelve."

"I work in the mornings."

"Suit yourself. I'll look for you in case."

Gray followed Glastonbury and the doctor to the lavatory. The subalterns looked at Julian, fawning slightly like greedy dogs uncertain of their master's continued indulgence. Julian looked back, feigning indifference, finally and deliberately relenting.

"All right, boys," he said. "The Schwarzer Keller. Come along, Daniel."

"I don't think—"

"—We shall be very hurt if you leave us now. Shan't we, boys?"

The subalterns nodded eagerly.

"It was a lovely dinner, Julian, but I think I'd better go home."

Daniel became aware that Glastonbury and the doctor were standing on either side of him.

"Do come," said Glastonbury quietly and unrefusably; "we've hardly had a single word."

Nor did they have many in the Schwarzer Keller, which was dominated by the strains of a small cinema organ. But with the lack of conversation the evening achieved a shapeless but cosy gaiety of a kind new to Daniel. It was, he supposed, "the spirit of the Mess". Whatever it was, it promoted, after one and a half bottles per head of the best hock, a feeling of friendliness and solidarity (even with the chinless subalterns) which persuaded Daniel that all of them were somehow in league against an undefined but common enemy. The blaring organ became, as it were, the band behind which they marched; and later on, when it broke into selections from "The White Horse Inn", he found himself banging his glass in time on the table and bellowing out, with the rest, his intention to join the legion and face the foe.

Only Fielding Gray had not come on to the Schwarzer Keller.

"He goes home and reads," as Giles Glastonbury explained to Daniel, "reads and drinks."

"Unfriendly," said Doctor Motley (Mick), and downed a bumper of Rhenish.

"Oh no. He's friendly enough in his way. But he can't stand noise."

"Funny he should be in a tank regiment," Daniel opined.

"Armoured cars . . . I suppose so. He says it's human noise

he really can't bear because men have no excuse."

"I see his point," said Daniel, already rather ashamed of his contribution to the singing.

"I don't know. Not a bad thing to change the air in the old lungs from time to time."

A medical exposition in support of this thesis now followed from Mick Motley but was swamped by the organist. As he watched the doctor's mouth noiselessly open and shut, Daniel was reminded for a moment of Dortmund's symbols in their ordered yet still almost meaningless succession. This increased his guilt at the time he was wasting; until a grin from Julian, as he lifted a bottle from an ice bucket to refill Daniel's glass, once again restored the warmth of the occasion and drove out doubts as to its worthiness. It was so pleasant simply to be accepted, to belong, to be a christian name among christian names (Giles, Mick, Piers *et al.*). And then the mindlessness of it all was so reassuring. Undeniably "the spirit of the Mess" had something to recommend it : it shut out the questions which one did not wish to answer, it made one feel safe and loved; and this, he supposed, was the reward offered to soldiers in return for risking their necks. For even while they sat here drinking happily in Germany, were there not wars in the East which might claim them at any moment? Fighting men, he had read, were jealous in the bestowal of their company; he now began to realize why, and to count it a privilege, if not a wholly desirable one, that he should be so courteously admitted.

His great moment came when he was invited to help carry the unconscious Jack Lamprey out to Giles Glastonbury's car.

"I expect he'll be sick on the way up," Glastonbury confided, "but these little outings do them good. Good night, old chap. See you soon."

"Good night," echoed other voices all around him : "see you soon."

*　　*　　*

In the morning, Daniel was divided between pleasure in having been kindly received by the unfamiliar men and irritation at so easily allowing himself to feel flattered. A combination of drowsiness and light-headedness, which from second to second disrupted his work, at first made him nervous and even more irritable but at length resolved itself into a euphoric excitement which induced him to declare holiday. He would go to Harzburg and meet Fielding Gray. This decision was reached less from curiosity to learn what Gray wanted to tell him than from a novel and collective affection for the whole of the cavalry group, as a representative of which rather than as an individual Gray at this stage still appeared to him.

Finding the bus service incommodious, Daniel engaged a taxi and was still irresponsible enough, on arrival at the Jagdhof, to pay out ninety marks without noticing. Although the time was only ten minutes to twelve when he entered the bar, Gray was already waiting.

"You're early," said Daniel blithely.

"In the Army, to be punctual to the second is a punishable offence. One must be ready five minutes before the stated time of parade. A prudent man allows ten."

"Meeting me isn't a parade."

"It is an engagement which I have undertaken . . . I've got lunch for us both in my Land Rover, and I'm very glad you've come."

He looked at Daniel with gratitude, then led the way outside to a yellow Land Rover, the bonnet of which carried the regimental device, prominently executed in deep pink, of skull with coronet. A grinning soldier, whose acne flared as bright as the ensignia on the bonnet, was formally introduced to Daniel as Trooper Michael Lamb and then helped them both into the vehicle with warm, well chewed but very clean hands.

"Where to now?" the grinning soldier said.

"The Warlocks' Grotto."

"Righty."

"You know," said Gray as they drove off, "you made a very good impression last night. I had to hear about it when they all got back."

"I enjoyed myself."

"That's what pleased them. They thought you'd find them crude. Instead of which you joined in. The doctor said the same thing over and over again—'Nice chappie for a brain-box, worth bloody ten of you.' "

"How aggressive of him."

"Just drunk. The doctor's a devout Catholic but intelligent enough to know it's all a load of rubbish. The trouble is that family pressure's too strong to let him escape, so he drinks his way out every night and feels unworthy of the Virgin every morning. Then he has a good crying jag to make him better and gets nicely tanked up at lunch."

There was no attempt, Daniel noticed, to keep any of this from the driver. Gray simply spoke as if he wasn't there—or so it seemed, until suddenly he acknowledged the man's presence by inviting his opinion.

"You've met the doctor, Michael?"

Trooper Lamb screwed up his face in thought, not as one who wishes to be tactful but as a free agent whose view will be heeded and even valued. Daniel was reminded of his own feeling the previous night, that he had been admitted to fellowship on equal terms. "We band of brothers", he thought reluctantly: *res unius, res omnium.*

"I've met the doctor," Lamb said, "and liked him. It's true what you say about his drinking, but he's got a way with illness."

They turned off the main road along a track which climbed steeply uphill through pine-trees.

"Take Johnnie Burden," Lamb continued as he went smoothly down through his gears. "Captain Joyce back at the Regiment said he was just constipated and gave him a pill. But when he first gets here a few days back and goes sick to Mick Motley, he's in an ambulance in ten minutes and has his appendix out before dinner. Another few hours and it would have bust wide open—and Captain Joyce none the wiser, though he's a regular and all."

"I know," said Gray. "You'll find that Captain Joyce won't be there any longer when we get back to the Regiment."

The sentence was somehow the more sinister, Daniel thought, for being so vague. Trooper Lamb shook his head, regretting but acknowledging the mutability of human fortunes, and deftly changed the subject.

"And when shall we be getting back then?"

"Immediately after Apocalypse. It came through yesterday."

This apparently explained everything. Lamb nodded thanks for the information, took them in a quick spurt up a steep rise ahead, then slowed almost to a halt before nosing down a sandy bank.

"The Warlocks' Grotto, gentlemen."

The uphill track had ended on the rim of a perfect natural bowl which was entirely surrounded by pine-trees except for the narrow entrance through which they had driven in the Land Rover. The bowl itself was open to the sky, and all of it except for one small corner was flooded with sun. At its centre, which lay perhaps ten yards lower than the circumference, was a rectangular slab of grey rock, six feet long by two feet wide by one foot of visible depth, the rest being embedded in the soil. The surrounding pine-trees were very close along the rim; and behind them was circle upon circle, the trees in each of which, evenly spaced, guarded the gaps left by those in front, so that beyond a few yards their ranks were impenetrable by the eye and for all one knew might stretch away to the ends of the earth. It would not be wise to leave the sunny bowl for the forest.

"Who told you about this place?" said Daniel.

"We found it the other day. Lamb named it."

Lamb smiled modestly and started to unload a hamper from the back of the Land Rover.

"In the shade, Michael . . . You see," said Gray, "I've been up here a lot lately, planning a little exercise for the Squadron and the Fusiliers. I thought this grotto would make a good Rehabilitation Centre. Nice and remote."

"What have you to do with rehabilitation?"

Gray took Daniel by the arm and led him over to where Lamb was spreading the lunch: rough pâté, cold chicken and mayonnaise, a bottle of hock.

"Imagine," said Gray, "that the enemy is concentrating his forces in this area. Then imagine that you've fired an atomic shell to wipe the whole lot out."

"I didn't know," said Daniel turning cold, "that there was such a thing."

"There probably isn't. But there very soon will be, or something similar, so one fine summer morning you pull a lever—and crunch . . . The next thing you've got to do is move into the devastated area, take it over and tidy it up. That's what this exercise is about. The tenth Sabre Squadron and the first Battalion of Wessex Fusiliers are being sent in to practise tidying up. Food."

All three of them sat down together. Lamb took his share of the dainty provisions, including a glass of hock.

"So," Gray went on, "the cavalry arrive first in armoured cars, having first taken precautions against radio-active contamination. Everything is a complete shambles for miles. We burn the dead where they lie, along with their equipment. Then we see whether there are any survivors, soldier or civilian. These are suffering from obscene injuries caused by flash or blast, they are out of their minds with shock and horror, and they have absorbed massive doses of radiation; they will die very soon in any case, and can only be a nuisance until they do. Logically we should shoot them down and burn their bodies on the spot. But it has been decided that we must make a civilised gesture. Instead of killing the survivors straight away, we must herd them together and take them to a 'Rehabilitation Centre', where there will be a medical unit to make every effort on their behalf. In practice, Mick Motley tells me, 'every effort' can only amount to filling them up with morphine and, once more, burning the bodies as soon as possible. By this time the Fusiliers will have moved up on foot to join us, so that will probably be their job. We shall be too busy getting ready to go on to the next devastated area. Some chicken? More hock?"

"So this is your ... your role," Daniel said, accepting food and drink automatically. "This is what Major Glastonbury thought public busybodies shouldn't hear about."

"There's a lot more to it than Captain Gray's told you," said Lamb, who showed no doubt of his right to share in the dissertation. "We're responsible for mapping out the area— it'll need a new map, see—so that when the Fusiliers come up they can take over as guides for the main body of the Division."

"I should have thought," said Daniel, appalled but fascinated, "that the main body would have kept as far away as possible. Moved forward by another route."

"Ideally, yes," said Gray. "But we've got to prepare for a situation in which the whole length of the front has been contaminated in this way. In that case, a section must be cleared for the advance to proceed. So each division is to provide itself with what is called a Courier Team, which will consist of one highly mobile squadron of armoured cars and one battalion of infantry to bring up behind. Hence our connexion with the Fusiliers: between us we're atomic couriers to our division."

Daniel stared into the infinity of trees beyond the grotto. Up till now academic interest had outweighed repugnance. It was time for morality to reassert itself.

"And here," he said, "you're to have a Rehabilitation Centre for poisoning people to death."

"The most permanent and comfortable form of rehabilitation which the circumstances will permit ... In August," Gray continued in a firm expository voice, "there are to be two preliminary exercises, Broomstick I and Broomstick II, to practise us in our new function. We shall assume the devastation of the entire area between Bad Harzburg and Goslar inclusive. Broomstick I will concentrate on the procedures involved in re-mapping and re-planning the area: Broomstick II on ... administrative measures ... in the remains of towns and villages."

Daniel began to feel rather sick.

"And then in late September," Gray went on, like a museum guide running efficiently through his stale repertoire, "there will be a large-scale manoeuvre, code-name Apocalypse. 'This manoeuvre will comprise two British Divisions, two American Divisions, one French Division, one Belgian Brigade, and Dutch and Danish Units to be later specified. Present as observers will be general officers designate of the West German Army, currently re-forming. Apocalypse will presurmise an invasion of West Germany from the Communist occupied territory of Czechoslovakia; and will consist of a massive counter-attack delivered in a southerly direction against the flank of the invading army by the Allied Forces enumerated above. It will be posited that both sides have a limited number of tactical atomic weapons at their disposal; and the prior objects of the manoeuvre will be: (1) The Exercise of Senior Commanders in the use of such weapons; (2) The Exercise of All Ranks in the procedures peculiar to this type of warfare; and (3) The Exercise of the newly formed Atomic Courier Teams in clearing passages through areas of nuclear devastation.' You see," said Gray, offering the hock and reverting to his normal tone, "what is being cooked up?"

"Why did you want me to know?"

"Because I want you to understand our position. I'm telling you, before you can find out from elsewhere, just what

is going on, and asking you not to hold it against us ... not
to abandon us, Daniel, before you really know us."

Trooper Lamb looked anxiously at Daniel, associating himself with the appeal.

"It will only be exercises, Mr Mond," he said. 'Practice,
like. Not a hair of anyone's head will be hurt."

"And if the day comes when it's all real? This Rehabilitation Centre with the rest?"

Daniel looked slowly round the bowl in which they sat.

"It's just a little clearing in the woods," said Fielding Gray,
"like many others. The odds are a million to one that nothing
—nothing out of the way—will ever happen here." He
glanced at the central rock. "You know, you scholars are an
odd lot. There's so much you refuse to acknowledge. How
often, for example, does anyone admit that the famous
Athenian democracy was nothing of the kind? That it was
a minority assembly of superior citizens, who built their priceless civilisation on the bodies of aliens and slaves? Or take
yourself, an aspirant mathematician. How often do you care
to remember where the work of other mathematicians has
led? Which is straight to Broomstick and Apocalypse."

"I know that well enough. I aim to keep my own work
entirely pure."

"There's always someone," said Fielding Gray, "who comes
along and spoils things. However pure the intentions, there's
always someone—he used to be called the Devil—who finds
a way of perverting them. I wanted to be a scholar too,
Daniel. But the Devil caught up with me before I'd even
started. He took hold of my beautiful intentions and persuaded the world they were obscene, and there was an end
of that. He'll catch up with you in time, and then you'll
be doing the same as the rest of us. Looking through the
woods for quiet grottoes ... to rehabilitate people in."

There was a long silence.

"Funny," said Daniel at last. "Until a few weeks ago I
would have laughed at what you've just said. If I hadn't

been too indignant. But since I've been in Göttingen . . ."

"*What* since you've been in Göttingen?"

"One or two things have happened . . . never mind what . . . to make me suspect that you could—just *could*—be right."

For a moment both Gray and Lamb looked unmistakably relieved. Then,

"So that's settled," Gray said lightly. "Now you can get to know us better. The day after tomorrow there's a band night in the Mess. It's the Fusiliers' show, but we'll all be there and you can come as my guest. You've got a dinner jacket here?"

"No."

"Then you can borrow Bungay's. He's about your size and cut, and he'll be wearing uniform like the rest of us . . . Time to go."

Lamb busied himself with the remains of the picnic. Daniel and Gray walked across to the slab of rock.

"You think it's a good thing, that I should come to this . . . band night?"

"Yes. You'll see how we justify ourselves. Or rather, how the Fusiliers do, but it comes to much the same."

"I thought you were so different from the Fusiliers."

"In many ways. But at bottom we all suffer from the same guilt, so we use the same mechanics for self-deception . . . We'll drive you into Harzburg to pick up your car."

"I haven't got a car. I came by taxi."

"Did you now?" said Gray with a quick flush of pleasure. "Then it will be our privilege to take you home . . . if you can put up with a little of my reconnoitring first."

At six o'clock on the evening of the Band Night Trooper Lamb called at Daniel's lodgings with the Land Rover to take him up the hill to the barracks. The main body of these consisted of three rows, ranged one above the other, of white three-storey blocks, each row having a terraced parade ground just beneath it. The officers' mess was the furthest block of the bottom row, and thither, after some altercation with a sergeant at the barrack gate, Daniel was driven. Fielding was waiting for him outside.

"Fusilier Sergeant at the gate making trouble," said Trooper Lamb. "Said no civilians allowed in without proper authority."

"Mr Mond has my authority."

"I told him Major Glastonbury's to make it simpler."

"Well done."

"He said it should be in writing. He's going to report the matter to his C.O."

"You see?" said Fielding as he led Daniel on to a sloping lawn that lay beyond the officers' mess. "Fusilier pride. They're so convinced of their own importance they think you might try to spy on them."

"I'm sorry if it'll cause trouble."

"None at all. Giles will get a chit from their adjutant requesting an explanation. In order to annoy them he'll say you were a barber specially ordered from Göttingen to shave him, or something of the sort."

"His Jewish money-lender?"

"I beg your pardon."

"Just a pleasantry. Very impressive," said Daniel, surveying a large swimming pool at the bottom of the lawn: "for the common use?"

"The men have their own. And the Sergeants. And the Corporals."

As they approached the swimming pool, three scrawny women called their scrawny children out of the water and hurried them away into a line of tented cubicles.

"Fusilier officers' wives," commented Fielding. "They're in a bad temper this evening because their husbands will come home drunk after the band night."

"What exactly is a band night?"

"You're here to see for yourself. But I'll give you a hint. It's the military equivalent of Holy Communion."

It was said with irony.

"What are you doing in the Army, Fielding?"

"I like closed institutions. They protect one. They demand conformity, but in return they offer security and privilege. They impose a routine, which makes the days pass smoothly. Best of all, they leave no one in doubt as to his place."

"One could say the same of a college, I suppose."

"Precisely."

The three scrawny women, clutching their children fiercely by the hand, trailed away up the lawn giving Daniel and Fielding resentful backward glances. From somewhere not far off a French horn sounded a beautiful and melancholy phrase of music.

"Officers' Dress Call. I've got Piers' dinner jacket ready for you in my room."

"Why was it so sad . . . that call?"

"This is essentially," said Fielding, "a lugubrious occasion."

The force of this judgment was not at first apparent, for when Daniel entered the ante-room with Fielding half an hour later he found every colour in the spectrum deployed for his pleasure. The Fusiliers, to be sure, were nothing out of the way in their dark blue tunics and trousers; but the five Dragoons, who wore skin-tight cherry overall trousers, sky blue tunics with black bandoliers from left to right (each containing twelve live revolver cartridges), ornamental daggers slung on the outside of the left thigh, and highly polished mess boots with gilded spurs, made a very remarkable sight indeed. Daniel, who could neither approve of anything so insolent nor disapprove of anything so beautiful, resolved his difficulty by examining the other diners. Although there was no one among them as splendid as the Dragoons, there was much else to catch the eye: the gold order at the throat of a

General (the guest of honour); the scarlet mess jacket of his A.D.C.; chain mail on the shoulders of an Hussar (Giles Glastonbury's guest); and the elegant dark green of a small group identified by Fielding as visiting Riflemen. The Fusilier servants, far grander than their own officers in regimental liveries of deep yellow piped with purple, passed and repassed with chased silver trays on which were Victorian decanters of hideous yet massively opulent aspect; and the Colour Sergeant of the Sutlery (for such, Fielding said, was his title), when he marched in to announce dinner, carried a halberd which he thumped three times upon the floor:

"May it please Your Royal Highness to dine."

"You see," explained Fielding, "their Colonel in Chief is Prince Charles, and on Band Nights he is considered symbolically present."

Further comment was drowned by a blast of bugles just outside; all present made way for the Fusilier Colonel and his guest of honour; and as the two of them stepped out of the ante-room, there commenced a colossal roll of drums. When he followed a little later with Fielding, Daniel saw that the long corridor down to the dining-room was lined, on either side and at intervals of five yards, by scarlet-coated drummer-boys, who kept up their rapid beat until the last diner was standing behind his chair. The Colour Sergeant at the dining-room door then raised his halberd, and at the exact moment at which he brought it down on to the floor, with a crash that made the table quiver along its length, the now almost intolerable tattoo ceased, to be succeeded by absolute silence for twenty seconds clear.

"God grant that we may rise as many as we sit," an egg-shaped chaplain intoned.

"A reference to the plague in Hong Kong," said Fielding; "One night three of them fell dead at dinner,"

Once seated, Daniel started to absorb the strange spectacle around him. Tears, laughter, delight, denunciation—he did not know which was the most appropriate and was in turn inclined toward all four. At the top end of the dining-room ("hall" would have been a more apt description) the wall was decorated by a pair of crossed flags, banners or standards, as he supposed, beneath which hung a large photograph in colour of the infant Prince Charles, who was playing with a woolly ball. On the floor under the photograph was a kind of wigwam of piled drums; and huddled inside this, at the head of the table, sat an unimposing major in Fusilier blue, who, to judge from the periodical twitch which shook his entire frame, was responsible for the management of the affair. The table, which was without a cloth and polished jet black, stretched forty yards down the room and so gave ample space for the twenty-five odd officers on either side of it, these being served by liveried waiters under command of the Colour Sergeant, who directed them, from his station to the left of the wigwam, by a code of signals performed with his halberd.

All of this, though novel, did not grossly exceed Daniel's expectations: what moved him to something near hysteria, however, was the triple-ranked array of ornamental silver, which occupied every spare inch of the table from one end to the other. The middle rank, which made a kind of water-shed down the centre, consisted of the tallest and most contumacious pieces: six sets of candelabra in the form of casuarina trees, a minutely detailed reproduction, two feet square by four feet high, of the Edwardian keep in the Regimental Depot at Shepton Mallet (or so Fielding vouched), a model airship ("They shot one down with rifle bullets at Dover during the '14 war"), and, half way down the table and opposite the guest of honour, a silver mountain complete with woods, tracks, châlets and Fusiliers of the late eighteenth century stalking beaver-hatted Americans.

Parallel with the centre row and on either side of it were two lines of lesser offerings, such as loving cups, miniature howitzers, statuettes of horsemen and cricketers; and in addition to all these, each guest had a small object placed for his private admiration to the immediate right of his cover. Daniel's was a silver-gilt snuff-box of the early nineteenth century, perhaps the only piece in the whole display which approximated to seemliness but not enough by itself to remove the impression that he was in some nightmare of Freudian fantasy.

"Where on earth did they get hold of all this?" he asked Fielding when he had resumed control of himself.

"Mostly presentations from retiring officers. But some of it's loot. That snuff-box was pinched when they sacked the White House in 1812. And there's a silver-mounted bidet somewhere which an ensign lifted from Napoleon's bedroom for a bet when they were guarding him on Elba."

"This was the lot that let him escape?"

"Oh no. They were relieved long before that. Whatever the Wessex Fusiliers have in hand," said Fielding with grudging respect, "they do it thoroughly."

This observation was now borne out by the appearance, in a small minstrel's gallery at the bottom end of the hall, of a squad of Fusilier Bandsmen, who let fly with a selection of Italian arias. The effect, even more bloated than usual, which these produced when rendered by brass instruments, combined with the sheer expertise of the performance (for some score and a half of bandsmen were contriving to play in a gallery large enough for ten), nearly reduced Daniel to hysterics once more. To fight these off he distracted himself with a more careful survey than he had yet attempted of those present.

Moving in a clockwise direction from the harassed major under his canopy of drums, Daniel's gaze slipped over three elderly and wooden-faced Fusilier captains, all of whom were eating for dear life, to Giles Glastonbury, who was talking past his guest to Doctor Motley. The latter was sweating heavily, drinking water out of a tumbler and, as Daniel watched him, waving away a plate of roast beef; the fact that it was Friday, along with heaven knew what deposits of guilt and acid from the previous night's activities, might be held to account for this abstinence. Some four places down from Motley, to the right of the guest of honour, was Julian James. A vague facial resemblance between Julian and the General explained his proximity); but clearly blood was all they had in common, for the General, who was listening with strained politeness to an anecdote of Julian's, was also inspecting the latter's liberal paunch with disapproval, and winced hectically when a gay and gallic gesture from Julian concluded his story.

The fusilier Colonel, to whom the General now abruptly turned, was a long, lean gentleman with a long, lean face which, in repose, was blank to the point of imbecility. However, as soon as the General began to speak, which he did with a slight nod back at Julian and with obvious reference to the impropriety of his conversation, the Colonel's face came alive with an almost baroque anguish, this causing it to change colour and expand laterally, as though a limp and yellow sausage-balloon had suddenly been further inflated and become a big red round one. And filled with gas at that; for the Colonel's head bobbed furiously on his shoulders, as though in dynamic compensation for not being able to take off vertically, and eventually gave a fierce accusatory flip in the direction of Lieutenants Bungay and Lamprey. These were sitting some way down to his left and helping one another to a double magnum of champagne, which was clearly out of order as everyone else was being served with a fruity red burgundy by circling waiters. Daniel decided that the Colonel, inspired by complaints about Julian, was issuing a collective indictment of the Dragoons: an indictment which woefully miscarried; for a bald and white-tied German civilian on the Colonel's immediate left conceived that the latter's stare of rebuke was somehow intended for himself, and bridled like a sexually rejected gorilla. As Daniel watched this peculiar exhibition of temperament, it was unexpectedly accounted for by his own neighbour on the left, to whom he had not yet spoken.

"That Kraut is dead nervous," a dry, rather grinding, voice said to him : "as a young major he once commanded a train carrying political prisoners to a labour camp near Erfurt. He's terrified it'll be brought up against him and his new appointment cancelled."

Turning towards the voice, Daniel found two square feet of silver portcullis, through which, as through a grill, his informant continued to address him.

"He's to hold an important staff appointment in the new Kraut Army. He *says* that he thought the train was carrying voluntary workers. In which case why did it need a major and a whole company of troops to control it? Luckily for him the official records have disappeared."

"Who told you all this?"

"An uncle who has knowledgeable friends . . . My name's Percival, Leonard Percival."

Percival pushed the silver portcullis from between them. Daniel saw a young man of about twenty-four with a face like Mr Punch's, at first sight knowing rather than intelligent, the pointed nose of which seemed almost to meet the up-turned chin; scant dark hair emphasised the ascetic pallor of the forehead, while behind aggressively mounted spectacles were the eyes of a paranoiac scholar. Beneath this interesting ensemble was the dowdy blue tunic of the Fusiliers, decorated by a lieutenant's two pips on either shoulder and, on the left breast, by a single medal, which hung from a green and purple riband overlaid by a silver oak leaf.

"You're Julian James's mucker from Cambridge," Percival prompted, patient under surveillance.

"Sorry . . . Daniel Mond."

"Glad to know you. I'm flattered to sit next the only educated man in the party."

"Oh no," said Daniel, fatuous and disingenuous; "there's Julian . . . and what about Captain Gray?"

"I'm afraid I haven't seen enough of them to say. We tried to be friendly with the Cavalry boys, but they stood off from the start."

"I've been told that there are . . . differences of outlook."

"You've been told, I suppose, that they are men of taste who exercise a quiet, well-bred authority, and that we Fusiliers are a lot of squealing martinets."

"Something of the sort, yes."

"You could see it that way. Or you might find, if you looked closer, that they are selfish and lazy men who leave most of their work to cleverly selected N.C.O.'s."

"That I wouldn't know."

"Well, I would. I've watched them at it. 'Carry on, Sergeant-major'"—he mimicked the breathy neighing of Messrs Lamprey and Bungay—"'I'm off for luncheon now and I shan't be back this afternoon. Or tomorrow morning either.'"

"Perhaps," hazarded Daniel uneasily, "soldiers have more regard for their officers if they don't see too much of them."

"That's easily said. But it puts too much strain on the N.C.O.'s."

"If they're intelligently chosen, as you imply . . . ?"

"It's still wrong. I know what you're thinking," said Percival; "you're thinking that here's a busy little man who breathes down his soldiers' necks all day long, until he's become thoroughly worn out and unpopular and jealous of people who have a lighter touch."

"I wasn't thinking anything of the kind."

"Oh yes, you were. But understand this. That Sabre Squadron, as they so grotesquely call it, consists of eighty per cent regular soldiers, mature and reliable and intelligent men, because they only accept above-average entrants for armoured regiments. But the poor bloody infantry, who don't have glamorous clothes to show off in and have to walk everywhere on their flat feet—we have to take anything we're sent. Most of them are clod-hopping west country boys, under twenty and as sick as mud because they've been called up for National Service just when they'd found some silly slut to drag into the bushes every night."

"Country copulatives?"

"With a sprinkling of small-town delinquents. They can't even keep themselves clean, half of them, unless there's someone to stand over them sixteen hours in every twenty-four. Every time they go out of barracks, they get drunk on raw spirits or pick up a dose of clap from some old whore who's been here since Bismarck. What would you do with a crowd like that?"

"I should tell myself," said Daniel, "that they were very young and lonely men in a strange country."

"All right. But what would you *do*?"

"Try to educate them."

"The Army isn't a finishing school. We're short of men— even the kind they send us—and there's a lot to be done."

"This Atomic Courier Team?"

The moment the words were out of his mouth, Daniel realised that he had made a bad mistake. Percival's nose seemed to grow an inch and his spectacles flashed like morse lamps.

"Who told you about that?"

"I . . . I read about it."

"No, you didn't. It's still on the secret list. One of your cavalry friends has been opening his mouth, that's what it is. Flagrant breach of security—but of course they wouldn't understand that."

"Surely, everyone will know about it when they have this manoeuvre in September?"

"So you've heard about that too? You're a mathematician, Mond, or so they tell me. But you seem to need reminding that between now and the end of September is a good seven weeks. For obvious reasons, the Army Council is anxious that nothing should be known about Apocalypse until as late as possible."

"Afraid of public disapproval?"

"In a way. Afraid that public disapproval could be used in political circles to stop the exercise. This," said Percival, who now ceased to cark and assumed a manner cool yet earnest, "would be a grave pity. Because Apocalypse has been devised in response to certain known and concrete realities."

"Some of us think that a different response is needed. Protest. Your Apocalypse is a form of acceptance."

"Of preparation. That is our job. There are plenty of people left over to do the protesting."

"People whom you despise," said Daniel, angered by Percival's smug and quizzical expression. "Like those National Servicemen of yours. *You're* going to decide what's best for them and for all of us, whether we should be clean or dirty, whether we should be allowed out of barracks to risk getting clap, and *we're* not going to be consulted in case we make trouble. In case we get drunk and open our mouths and kick up such a rumpus in the whorehouse that the whole world gets to hear of it and puts a stop to this obscene game you propose to play in September. You couldn't bear that, because for all your talk of duty and preparation you relish the thought of playing at Atom Bombs with the whole of Europe for an arena. You'll be the big man then, the one who burns our bodies or hauls us off to Rehabilitation Centres to supervise our death. You'll be God, Percival, and you can trample all over the long-haired students and the smelly, malingering workers until there's nothing left of them but a vast desert of radio-active dust."

"You have a point," said Percival, blinking slightly behind his lenses, "but I don't think you're being very polite or very clever. You've been taken in, Mond; you've been had. When your nice friends in the Dragoons were so foolish as to tell you about all this, did you accuse *them* of wanting to play God? Of course you didn't. Because they put on their little act. Because they were apologetic and cosily confidential. But all that means is that if ever *they* had to fire an Atomic missile, they'd say it was work unfit for a civilised man—and make the corporal press the trigger. I'd have the guts to press the trigger myself, or I hope I would. You see, I don't believe in fudging issues and to you that apparently makes me a maniacal killer. I'm disappointed in you, Mond. You're a bigot."

And with this Percival pulled the silver grill back between them.

By this time the pudding plates had been removed and preparations were being made for desert. Space was found, not without difficulty, for several large bowls of oriental design and unexciting content (mostly apples and bananas), and before each diner were set three separate port glasses.

"One for the Queen," said Fielding, "one for Prince Charles, and one for later. The port, for a miracle, is quite decent: they've had a standing order with a firm in Lisbon ever since the Peninsular War."

"I'm afraid," said Daniel, "that I've been indiscreet. My neighbour strongly resents my knowing about your Courier Team. He says it's a breach of security."

"I told you. These Fusiliers are so pompous they think everything they do is top priority and top secret. Though Leonard Percival, from what little I've seen of him, is shrewd enough to know better."

"That's what I thought. Do you suppose he was putting on some kind of act?"

"Fusiliers don't put on acts."

"And he certainly seemed sincere . . ."

"I expect he's been indoctrinated like the rest of them. You have to be quite strong-minded to resist all this." Fielding gestured up the table towards the piled drums and the crossed colours. "And I understand that their speciality has still to come."

The port now made its appearance in five decanters, each placed on one of five trucks which were attached to a silver model of Stephenson's Rocket. This was driven by slow clock-work; and the trick, apparently, was to lift a decanter, fill your glass, and replace the decanter in the correct truck without stopping the train.

"You don't think that *this* is their speciality?"

"Heavens no. It'll be something altogether more alarming. Something to do with the toasts, I expect."

The Queen's toast at least was drunk without much elaboration—beyond the fact that they all had to remain standing, with glasses held high, while a pink-cheeked band-boy carolled three verses of "Here's a health unto Her Majesty". Nor did the toast to Prince Charles, as Colonel-in-Chief, produce anything sensational, although the convention that His Royal Highness was symbolically present involved everyone's bowing low in the direction of the wretched major at the head of the table, who twitched so much that he nearly dislodged a drum. After this, during a pause while the clock-work train went its round for the third time, Daniel felt expectation in the air; on his left beyond the grill Leonard Percival was smiling thinly but happily, rather as though he were about to pull a switch which would release naked ladies from under the floor-boards, and even the three wooden-faced Fusilier Captains at the top end of the room were giving off mild palpitations of excitement.

"It's coming now," he whispered to Fielding.

As indeed it was.

The Fusilier Colonel, his long face undulating like a tooth-paste tube that someone was squeezing from the bottom, rose to his feet; the Colour Sergeant's halberd crashed to the floor for silence; the electric lights were switched off; and a liveried corporal with a huge set of bellows passed down the table puffing out the candles on the six sets of candelabra. When the room was in total darkness,

"Absent friends," the Colonel croaked.

"Absent friends," came an answering murmur from round the table; and suddenly, to the right of the piled drums, a tall figure was seen, holding up a single candle and so casting a dim light on its uniform, which recalled to Daniel a long forgotten plate in his first history book.

"Captain Thomas Keyne," said Percival, in a soft but clear voice, obviously intended to be heard by all in the room : "in the Forlorn Hope at Minden. A sword-thrust through the heart."

"Captain Thomas Keyne," came the low murmur from the invisible diners.

For perhaps ten seconds the figure stood silent and motionless, while little noises of clinking and sucking down the table told Daniel that glasses were being raised to the dead Fusilier. Then the figure stirred and passed its candle, as it went, to another figure in uniform of a later date.

"Fusilier Joseph Sutton," said an Officer's voice from somewhere down the table, in the same tones as Percival had used : "to save a fallen comrade at Saratoga. A bullet in the throat."

Again the murmured toast. Again a change of figure and another voice.

"Sergeant John Upwood. In the rear-guard action at Corunna. Of mutiple sabre-cuts."

"Major Rupert Forsdyke. Leading the charge at Waterloo. A bullet in the brain."

"Ensign David Rory. Guarding the Colour at Balaclava. Trampled to death."

"Fusilier George Bates . . . Calcutta . . . Regimental Sergeant-Major Adam Roberts, Victoria Cross . . . a bayonet thrust . . . Mafeking . . . Mons . . . Ypres . . . Distinguished Service Order . . . a shell-splinter . . . gas . . . the Somme."

And now a figure in the battle-dress and beret of the 'forties.

"Second Lieutenant Conrad Stern, Victoria Cross, the Normandy Landing. Leading a detachment of—"

But his figure elected to speak for itself.

"Daniel Mond," intoned the figure in a low, sarcastic wail,

"what are you doing with the soldiers? Stay away from the soldiery . . . Jew Mond."

And that was all (as Daniel wrote to Jacquiz Helmut some days later), but quite enough to upset their little pageant. There was much scrabbling about and calling for lights, the band suddenly struck up with a march, and everyone shuffled off to the "ante-room" and started to drink a lot rather furtively. The colonel was full of apologies. It must have been, he said, some crude form of joke. He explained that the silent figures who appeared in fancy dress were all corporals or sergeants, among whom the office is held to be an honour, and that the brief epitaphs were spoken by selected officers. "Conrad Stern" had certainly been on the agenda : he was one of several Jews who held commissions in the Wessex Fusiliers during the last war (a brother, oddly enough, of your publishing chum Gregory) and was killed by a land-mine on the Normandy beaches. Appropriately, they'd found a young Jewish lance-corporal, who's doing his National Service, to impersonate Stern in the procession of *imagines*, but he'd been injured while on training that day, so they'd decided to leave Stern out. The epitaph-speaker had been duly notified, but when he saw "Stern" appear after all, he assumed all was well and started in with his piece—only to be interrupted as I've described. Obviously, the colonel said, someone had taken the lance-corporal's place, perpetrated this little "jape" (the colonel's word), and then disappeared in the confusion. The colonel seemed entirely satisfied with this version, despite all the questions it left unanswered, though a general who was there as a guest looked very put out indeed. I must say, it was a peculiar thing to happen.

And there was something else I thought distinctly curious, though by no means so bizarre. After all the apologies, Gray persuaded me to stay on for a while, in order, as he said, to show there was no ill will. Would I care to play a game called Chemin-de-Fer? Giles Glastonbury was getting up a table ... not without difficulty, as the Fusiliers disapproved of gambling and always celebrated these occasions with an extraordinary rite which consisted largely of forming themselves into rugger scrums and whooping. So while the Fusiliers, who were by now recovered from the Stern fiasco, capered round the Mess like red Indians, I settled down with the doctor, the five dragoons and a visiting hussar at Giles's gaming table, where for a full hour we played a childish and mechanical game dependent solely on counting the number of pips on one's cards. Upon my soul, I don't know which party was the more stupidly employed; and to make matters worse I was embarrassed by beginners' luck, winning a large sum mainly from the doctor, who had abandoned his earlier abstinence and was making up to the tune of one double brandy every ten minutes. Clearly, I should have to stay 'put until I lost at least some of it back; and what with the blinding tedium of the game, the cacophony still making all around us and indigestion brought on by the coarseness of the food and wine, I began to feel very unhappy. However, rescue came from an unexpected quarter, in the form of Lieutenant Percival, my neighbour at dinner, who now arrived as herald to the second oddity of the evening. Percival, who had taken no part in his companions' antics, suddenly appeared through a side door and asked Glastonbury to release me, as the colonel wanted to speak to me again. This request was ill received but unrefusable, so I was lead away by Percival, through the side door and into a narrow corridor.

"It's not the colonel, it's Pappenheim," said Percival, naming the German guest. "He's anxious to meet you."

Since I'd have been happy to talk to the Minotaur so long as it let me out of that dreary game of cards, I followed Percival down the corridor to a door which said P.M.C. and opened into a smelly little office. Inside it was Pappenheim, a pot of coffee and a bottle of brandy in front of him, sitting at a desk. He rose, shook hands, pointed to a chair and poured me brandy, as full of himself as if the whole place had been his own.

"Thank you, Herr Oberleutnant," he said to Percival, who bowed gravely and left the room.

"A very excellent regiment, the Wessex Fusiliers," the gratified Teuton proceeded; "I simply asked that young officer to introduce us, and he arranges all this."

"Perhaps he's ashamed of the spectacle outside."

Pappenheim gave this notion serious consideration.

"I think not," he said ponderously. "It is a tradition, no?"

"I'm a stranger in these circles."

"Of course, Herr Mond . . ."

He now started to look very self-conscious and silly, like a man about to propose to a girl thirty years younger, but after nearly three minutes of huffing and puffing and re-lighting his cigar, he managed to get under way.

"You have interesting work at the University?"

"Very."

"The Dortmund papers, I hear. How does your attempt proceed?"

Just then I had such a vicious spurt of indigestion that I hardly knew what he'd said, and all he got in reply was a smothered burp.

"Quite so . . . Herr Mond, if ever you are in difficulty . . . I cannot help you with your work, of course, but any other way. What I mean is—"

But at this juncture the door opened and a fat, neurotic officer, the one who'd been sitting at the head of table during the dinner, came reeling in.

"One's own office. I mean to say, a bit much. Strangers drinking one's brandy. A bit much."

With this he sat down in an armchair and instantly fell asleep. Pappenheim gobbled like an affronted hippo, but he was very quick to follow me out into the corridor, where he made as if to continue our discussion. By this time, however, I'd managed to realise that he was being shady or presumptuous or both, so I gave him a bleak look and went straight back to the ante-room. There I found that Percival had been "sitting in" for me and had already lost back all but a few pounds of my winnings.

"The game's automatic," he said, "so it makes no difference who plays your cards."

Although he was quite as insolent in his way as Pappenheim, I was too relieved to care. I was beyond thinking of anything except my stomach and how to get home . . . whither Percival, aware of my condition, now volunteered to drive me. Gray looked rather conscience-stricken, but it was clear that the game had a fascination for him, so I accepted Percival's offer gratefully enough.

"I suppose Pappenheim was inquisitive?" Percival said when we were nearly in Göttingen.

"Worse. Prying."

"That fits. I was inquisitive to find out whether *he* was inquisitive, which is why I set it all up. But to spare you too much annoyance, I arranged for old Archie to barge in."

He seemed to think that no further explanation was required, and that he had been both clever and thoughtful. For my part, I was too far gone to question this. All I remember after that is getting upstairs, being miserably but mercifully sick (a deep red colour) and collapsing into bed.

And so, my dear Jacquiz, ended a memorable if hardly a pleasant evening. At first I thought that the dragoons, whether from guilt or embarrassment, might hold off after what had happened, and I told myself that I didn't care if I never saw a soldier again. But in fact they've simply ignored the whole affair, I've been meeting some or other of them almost every day, and I must say I'm very glad of it. For while their company sometimes makes me uneasy, particularly when I think of this "Courier Team", it is also stimulating because totally unlike anything to which I am accustomed; and in any event it is *company,* so welcome after the dreadful loneliness which I was beginning to feel and the effects of which must have been all too apparent in my last letter. Thank God that's over now.

Oddly enough, though Julian introduced me, I've seen very little of him and much more of this Captain Fielding Gray, who is fast becoming my chief friend among them. A melancholy man, interesting in more ways than one. It seems that he had a scholarship to Lancaster some years back, but that Robert Constable was somehow instrumental in having him refused entry. From what I can make out, Fielding has been brooding about this ever since. If you could find out Robert's version of the story, I'd be glad to hear it . . .

The real if rather suspect happiness which his new friends brought to Daniel's leisure also had a beneficial effect on his work. In the second week of August he was able to submit to Dirange in Cambridge a series of specimen workings to demonstrate that he had solved the problem of Dortmund's first notation and could now manipulate the first type of matrix. Dirange wrote back that in his opinion the work which Daniel had sent him was sound, and that even if Daniel were to advance no further, he could congratulate himself on a substantial achievement. In time, Dirange observed, this would have to be written up and published; but meanwhile Daniel must proceed with the second stage of his enquiry and find out whether it would indeed give him the help which he hoped for in completing his Fellowship Thesis—which, in such case, promised to be a remarkable document. In all the circumstances, his advice to Daniel was to keep silence, for the time being, about what he had so far accomplished, lest enquiries and correspondence should distract him from making further progress. Academic etiquette, however, to say nothing of common courtesy, required that some indication of his success be given to Doktor Aeneas von Bremke, whose sponsorship of Daniel had made that success possible. In Dirange's view, and although von Bremke had a character for discretion, Daniel should be vague and tentative in his report, expressing qualified hopes and eschewing concrete definitions.

Since Daniel did not look forward to this exercise in evasion, he was relieved to reflect that von Bremke was still away in the Harz and that any such interview must wait till his return. However, it seemed that von Bremke had a sixth sense in such matters; for some two hours after Dirange's letter had arrived from Cambridge a note was delivered by hand to Daniel's lodgings to announce that von Bremke was in Göttingen and would like to see him that afternoon. This meant putting off a drive through the border villages with Julian and Fielding; but despite the brevity of notice Daniel felt bound to comply with von Bremke's request— if only to get a tiresome obligation quickly out of the way.

Were such a thing conceivable of such a man, Daniel would have said that von Bremke was agitated.

"Herr Dominus," he said as soon as Daniel was seated, "you have been in Göttingen, a most welcome and honoured guest, for four months. May I ask what you have achieved?"

"Some useful steps," said Daniel carefully, "towards solving the first stage of the problem."

"Useful enough for you to be calling for papers which bear explicitly on the *second* stage. Or so the Assistant Curator tells me."

So that was it. But why not? Von Bremke had a right to question his own subordinates.

"I've been calling for those," said Daniel, "ever since I arrived. I like to look ahead."

Von Bremke took a clean handkerchief from his sleeve and flapped it open more vigorously than necessary.

"Yes. But now you are calling almost exclusively for such documents. This says to me that for you the first stage is over. Why was I not told?"

"You were away."

"We have mails in Germany."

"I would have told you as soon as you were back."

"I am back now."

"I don't wish to be over-confident . . . premature."

"Then please to tell me, Herr Dominus Mond, what you *think* you have established. You speak in confidence; I shall make no claims on your behalf, or on the late Professor Dortmund's, until I am so authorised by you."

This was square dealing. Daniel could equivocate no more.

"Very well, Herr Doktor. I am virtually certain that I understand the earlier notation and the earlier matrices."

"And to what functions would these matrices lend themselves?"

"To the solution, among other things, of certain abstract problems of motion."

"You are interested in these problems?"

"No. They are relatively simple and have already been solved by other if more cumbrous methods."

"And so?"

"And so I am interested, now as ever, in discovering the second method which Professor Dortmund developed from the first."

"More matrices?"

"Yes. But of an even more elaborate and elusive kind."

"Elusive . . . or delusive?"

"I beg your pardon, Herr Doktor?"

"Dortmund, as I have told you, was a sick man towards the end. Sick men delude themselves. Sick men of genius— or something near it—could delude others."

Daniel frowned and remained silent. There was a heavy sweat on his brow which he now mopped at with a handkerchief that seemed very grey when compared with von Bremke's.

"Herr Dominus. Have you ever noticed, in the course of your work here, something . . . wrong . . . about the Dortmund papers? Something perverse. A deliberate rejection of normality, in the notation perhaps, where normality would have served very well."

"It's funny you should say that," said Daniel reluctantly. "At times I have felt something—something very like hostility in those symbols."

"Ah. Of course, it is a long time since I worked on them, and I did not have the success we hope you have had. But could not this perversity which we have both observed have sprung from the pains of illness?"

"Ill or not, perverse or not, Dortmund did sound work, at least as far as I have followed him."

"Yes. But later, when the pains of cancer became all but intolerable, perhaps the perversity, the torturing of symbols . . . for the mere sake of continuing to do *something* . . . was all that was left?"

"No . . . no."

"I said, perhaps. How far, Herr Mond, have you proceeded towards elucidating the second notation?"

"I have established what it has in common with the first."

"The easiest part of the task. Do you really think, after all the months you have already spent and with all the difficulties that still lie ahead, that it is wise to go on? When all you may find is the nightmare of a tormented mind?"

"Von Bremke's changed his tune," said Daniel to Fielding the next day.

Fielding was by now in Daniel's confidence, at least where day to day problems were concerned. Daniel had already found that his new friend had a valuable capacity for cross-examining him on general grounds and an intuitive understanding of the human factors involved in an intellectual quest.

"When I first came here," Daniel continued, "and on the few occasions when I saw him later, von Bremke took the line that while he would be surprised if I achieved anything he would also be gratified. He would like, he said, to have me do work worthy of the good man Dortmund was. But now, now that something has been achieved, he seems upset."

"The guardians of the Sphinx are very jealous of its secrets. There were a lot of angry faces, you may depend on it, the day Oedipus answered the riddle."

"He's certainly rattled, and I've only answered half the riddle, if that. I was given hollow congratulations and advised to drop the rest of it. Dortmund was very ill towards the end; probably, von Bremke said, he didn't know what he was doing."

"I disagree. If he had the will-power to go on doing it . . ."

"That's more or less what I think, but von Bremke does have a point. From the start there's been something odd about the way Dortmund set all this up. Perversity was von Bremke's word for it. And the further I go the more perverse I'm finding it. So it is at least possible that Dortmund just went to pieces."

"If you assume that," said Fielding reluctantly, "and go back to Cambridge now, would what you have done be enough to win you a Fellowship?"

"Perhaps. It's not what I promised, as they'll be quick to point out, but it's quite a lot and it's important. Dirange will make them see that. But the thing is, Fielding, I can't give up now. Because if we're right, you and I, in thinking that Dortmund's work was valid till the end, then there's something very much out of the ordinary still to come."

"What sort of something?"

Daniel hesitated. While he was glad to have someone to whom he could give a running report of immediate progress or setback, he was not at all sure that he wished to talk in longer terms. It might be imprudent, even impious, to discuss such mysteries as these before they were finally revealed. And yet, he needed so badly to talk to somebody whom he could trust, from whom he could ask sympathy, for his plans as well as his hopes.

"Well," he said at last, "what I've disentangled so far amounts to a new and neater way of accounting for motion in spatial fields of various types. All right?"

"You mean spatial fields of more than three dimensions? That sort of thing?"

"No. It's all of it three-dimensional space, but complicated by other factors. Curved or otherwise distorted. Subject to more or less rapid processes of expansion or contraction. And so on. Now, what's coming—as far as I can tell—is an adaptation of the method in order to deal with very *tiny* movements, the movements of almost infinitesimally small entities within an almost infinitesimally small compass."

"Electrons? Things like that?"

"No," said Daniel sharply. "Dortmund's entities, and the kinds of space in which they move, are theoretical . . . abstract."

"If you say so. But surely, if Dortmund has already established laws of motion in these different kinds of space, then those laws will hold even on the tiniest scale?"

"Not necessarily. Because as we move towards the infinite on the one hand or the infinitesimal on the other, the normal rules become less and less dependable."

"All right. I'll buy it."

"Well, in order to investigate what goes on at an extreme level of smallness, Dortmund, at the stage I've reached, is about to postulate a quantity called *zeta*, which is to be the *smallest possible existing quantity* which is not infinitesimal. A very powerful concept. More powerful than the infinitesimal itself, because it rubs against it, so to speak, yet remains real."

"Real?"

"In the mathematical sense."

"So what he's after is to see how these little zeta-things, moving on a zeta-scale, get on in various conditions . . . if, for example, the overall spatial field they're in were suddenly twisted or inflated or whatever?"

"That's about it . . . in crude terms."

"Hmm," mused Fielding. "You're sure that this is the sort of thing Dortmund was up to?"

"Not absolutely. Von Bremke could be right, and it could be a meaningless nightmare. Or . . . or he could be right about the nightmare, wrong about it's being meaningless. That is—"

He broke off abruptly and brushed the sweat from his upper lip.

"Yes, Danny?"

But when Daniel shook his head, Fielding pressed him no further. There was a long silence.

"How much time have you got?" Fielding said at last.

"I want to get back to Cambridge by the end of September. But I suppose I could take as long as I want, within reason. Unless there's interference."

"Constable may summon you back?"

"Pressure of some kind."

"There usually is. Pressure of hunger just now. Dinner, Daniel. Giles and the doctor will be waiting."

My dear Daniel (Jacquiz Helmut wrote from Cambridge),
    I'm sorry I left your first letter so long—I was away from here when it came, spending a week with the Stukeleys at Crowleigh. But to judge from your second the first has answered itself. I'm delighted you've found such nice friends to play with. Julian was always an amusing boy (albiet rather coarse) and just what you need to take you out of yourself. In every way your new gang seems entirely *comme il faut*. Giles Glastonbury is well worth attention;

he's a second cousin of John Dorsetshire's. Even this peculiar Fusilier, Leonard Percival, has interesting connections: he was brought up, if my memory serves me, by his uncle Rupert—a solicitor in Somerset who is not only a power in the county but also heard with respect in London.

But I don't suppose you see much of a mere Fusilier when you've got all those glamorous Dragoons running after you. Do remember, though, that it is the plain infantry regiments of the Line who *are* the British Army; Dragoons and so on are often merely top-dressing, or so my acquaintance with military history tells me, and not always a credit to the service. During the Peninsular War Earl Hamilton's Regiment was so cluttered up with officers' private baggage that it was known as Hamilton's Carnival: at least three of them "sold out" and returned to London in mid-campaign because conditions were not to their liking and Wellington refused to let them bring more than one mistress each. There's a long passage in Gronow about it; in his view the gentlemen in question should have been court-martialled at the drum-head and shot for desertion in the field. The Wessex Fusiliers, on the other hand, have never given an inch, except at Corunna and Dunkerque; and on both occasions they put up formidable rear-guard actions. After Waterloo the Duke said of them, "The dullest officers in Europe and the steadiest in the world."

"Which makes it all the more surprising that such a very odd incident as you describe should have occurred at one of their band nights. In such circles things just do *not* go wrong or get out of hand. So perhaps you should take it as a compliment that it was your persona which inspired this outburst. It seems very strange that no one should have traced the interloper. Conrad Stern, by the way, though one of those Jews who exult in anti-Jewish jokes, had a far more delicate sense of humour, so it certainly wasn't his ghost. But then even you can hardly have supposed that it was. In case you are inclined to hark back to your fears of persecution, let me advise you to regard the whole thing as a thoughtless and drunken prank—got up by an officer who fought in Israel perhaps? Forget it.

Jacquiz made no reference, Daniel noticed, to his subsequent interview with Pappenheim, an occurrence which he had since come to consider the more important as it was the more palpable. Perhaps Jacquiz felt that his indulgence had already been sufficiently stretched: that one oddity should have taken place during an evening out might be acknowledged, but two exceeded the limits of good taste.

As you requested (Jacquiz went on) I have asked Robert Constable about Fielding Gray. For the first time since I've known him, Robert was a good deal less than frank. It seems that there was some kind of scandal at Gray's school in the summer of 1945, that Robert, as an old boy of the school and a friend of the Headmaster's, was made *au fait* with it, and that on his representations the College Council decided to withdraw Gray's scholarship (in consequence of which Gray opted for the Regular Army). But just what the scandal was Robert refused to tell me; under mild pressure he grew more and more shifty, until eventually he mumbled something to the effect that the whole thing was perhaps a mistake. *What* was a mistake, I insisted: was there a scandal or wasn't there? Oh yes, said Robert, there was a scandal all right, a very nasty one, but it had later appeared that Gray's part in it had probably been misreported. Then why wasn't Gray reinstated? Well, the mistake—if such it was—had only come to light four or five years later, by that time Gray was established in his career, it would have been painful to a lot of other people to dig it all up again . . . and so on. Not at all Robert's usual precise and conscientious self.

Anyhow, he refuses, to tell me any more, so you'll have to have a go at him yourself.

Well, Daniel. I'm delighted you're in good fettle again. Don't spoil it all by drinking too much with your cavalry friends and then imagining things to brood about. I'm glad I'm no longer needed in Göttingen as I have a very full summer of country visiting ahead. Please remember me to Julian and also to Giles Glastonbury, whom I last met three years ago at Harewood.

That evening Fielding Gray said:

"Broomstick's been brought forward. We're off tomorrow."

"Oh . . . For long?"

"Two days for Broomstick I and another three for the second part. Then a debriefing conference at Divisional H.Q. About a week."

"I'll miss you."

"It's nice to be missed. I'll be in touch as soon as we're back."

"Suppose I came up to Harzburg one day. Would there be any chance of seeing you?"

"I wouldn't do that," said Fielding with a flicker of irritation; "not if I were you."

PART III
REAR-GUARD ACTION

WALKING down the Nikolaistrasse the next morning, Daniel saw the soldiery pull out for Exercise Broomstick. It was not an exciting scene. A few Land Rovers bearing the Fusilier crest, then some three ton trucks painted a drab green and full of men in denim overalls, then more Land Rovers, then more trucks. A wagon decorated with a red cross on a white background and containing a dazed Mick Motley in the co-driver's seat. More Land Rovers, more three ton trucks. A small saloon car, of the same drab green as everything else, and the Fusilier Colonel sitting very straight in the back. A few motor-bicycles chivvying. No horses, no band, no banners when a Courier Team went out to war. But where were the Dragoons and their armoured cars?

"Don't bother to wait for your cavalry friends," said Earle Restarick on the pavement beside him. "They've gone across country."

"Earle . . . How very nice."

"Let's hope so. Take me up to your room, Daniel. Now."

Five minutes later, when they reached Daniel's room (oddly unfamiliar in the morning light) at the top of the University building, Earle Restarick said :

"So it didn't work."

"What didn't ?"

"I told them it wouldn't. I told them they hadn't understood the English mind. A scene like that, I said, will simply draw them all closer together. A public insult to an Englishman's guest is the one thing to ensure that he'll make a friend of that guest, even if he hated him before, for life. But of course they wouldn't listen. You're only a go-between, they said; you leave this to us."

" 'They'?"

"Well, now they know I was right. Not that I'll get any credit."

"Earle. Where have you been all these weeks?"

"Waiting. Waiting for you to get so soft with loneliness that when I came back you'd flop at my feet and tell me all they wanted to know. But unfortunately for them you found yourself some new friends. So then they said, 'We must break this up. Before he gets happy and well balanced again. Otherwise he won't talk.' "

"So . . . 'they' . . . put on that act with Stern?"

"The idea was that you'd go off in a huff, and your new friends would say, 'What the hell, it's too difficult, we can't be bothered any more.' So then you'd be alone and vulnerable again, and *they* could proceed according to plan."

"That's why you've come back now? Because I've been left alone?"

"Alone, but only for a few days, and certainly not vulnerable. Because you now know where you can turn for comfort. *Their* little trick didn't work, and your friends will be back in the barracks in under a week, and so now *they're* trying something else. No more psychology, no more waiting around for loneliness to turn you to pulp : just a straight . . . request."

Earle pondered his silver gaberdine thighs with less than satisfaction.

"A straight request," he said, "with me as messenger boy. I'm very sorry, Daniel. When I made a friend of you I was only acting on instructions, but in a way it really did take. I got to liking you, for Christ's sake. That's why I'll never be much good in this game, but we won't go into that. I liked you and so I warned you : 'Go on home,' I said. But you wouldn't listen, and you're still here, and now it's too late."

"I can go tomorrow if I want," said Daniel with reflex indignation.

"But you don't want. Because now you're really on to something at last. And that's the reason *they* won't let you go."

"How would they stop me?"

"Never mind that. Just take my word for it. As long as you seemed to be getting nowhere, like all the rest that have tried, they wouldn't have bothered. They'd have kept on watching, but if you'd packed up and gone back to Cambridge, they wouldn't have lifted a finger. But *now*, Daniel, now that you're on to something . . ."

"I don't know that I am on to anything."

"They know better."

"Who told them? Von Bremke?"

"So they're right?"

Daniel shrugged.

"Let's be plain," he said. "Who are 'they', and what exactly do they want?"

"You don't need to know who they are, Danny. Better not. As for what they want, it's the pot of gold buried underneath the Dortmund papers."

"If you mean the final answer, I'm nowhere near it."

"Correction. You're getting warmer."

"What if I am? What possible good can it be to them? A batch of symbols conveying an abstract idea which will be properly appreciated by perhaps ten men in the whole of Europe."

"That's just it, Danny. Ten is too many. My employers want it all to themselves. Greedy of them, isn't it?"

"Pointless."

"That's for them to judge. What shall I tell them?"

"Tell them . . . that if I'm left in peace I may—just may—find the answer. And that if I do, it will be published in the Cambridge Journal of Pure Mathematics, the editors of which will be very glad of 'their' subscription. Enquiries c/o The University Press or Heffer's Bookshop, Petty Cury."

"I'll tell them, Danny. And I'll be back with their answer."

When Earle had gone, Daniel's first reaction was to observe his own lack of surprise. It was as if he had always known that Earle would turn up again bearing some such proposition, with the result that he was neither frightened nor angry nor even particularly curious—merely irritated, as though a policeman had called with a long expected summons for illicit parking.

His second reaction was more violent. Anger in one direction he certainly felt; anger with von Bremke. He left his room and strode down the corridor like a storm-trooper.

"Herr Doktor, why have you betrayed my trust?"

Von Bremke nodded to a chair.

"Explain please."

Hotly, Daniel explained. Some persons unknown had been told of his purpose and his arrival in Göttingen, and had been kept informed of his progress since. Though friends of his own had been in his confidence from time to time, no one had been continuously so for the last five months. Only von Bremke had been that; only von Bremke could be responsible for the leak.

A tinge of melancholy came into von Bremke's face.

"I was never in your confidence," he said.

"You knew I was coming and why. You knew how I proposed to set to work. You were told, the other day, when the first important stage was complete."

"Professor Dirange, he too knew of this."

"Dirange? Unthinkable."

"But thinkable—this treachery—for me? Of course. A stranger in a dishonoured country. It is quite natural."

"What else can I think?"

"What else indeed? No doubt you believe I was offered money?"

"I didn't say that."

"Money which I very much need. So perhaps I wish I had been offered money, Herr Mond." The irony came awkwardly from the stern, ponderous face. "Perhaps I would have taken it. We shall never know. Who are these inquisitive people?"

"I've told you, I've no idea. All I know is that the American, Restarick, is their agent. He must have been planted here when they knew I was coming."

"Certainly I disliked him. He claimed to be an American gentleman. But he was . . . *nicht geboren.*"

Daniel's mouth twisted in distaste.

"That's not the point."

"It is very much the point. He was a pretence, a fraud. If you had noticed that, perhaps you would not have trusted him."

"Perhaps you should have warned me."

"You would have ignored the warning. Because you despise me." Von Bremke smiled voraciously; for the first time since Daniel had known him, von Bremke thought something was funny. "You consider, like all Jews, that I am a pedantic German, coarse and unsubtle." Von Bremke began to laugh in great heaving bursts of merriment. "The Jews, who invented Jehovah, think *others* are coarse and unsubtle. The Jews, with their Talmud and their Torah, think others are pedantic. The Jews, the race of Judas, accuse others of treachery. Oh, Herr Dominus Mond, it is so long since I laugh like this."

He lowered his head into his hands, snorting and slobbering in his mirth. Mirth? At a certain stage it is not easy to tell between a gasp of laughter and a sob of pain. Daniel, affronted yet guilty, moved silently from the room.

For the next two days Daniel went on with his work, which was presenting neither more nor less difficulty than he had expected, as though nothing had happened. It was, he told himself, the only thing to do. He had no way of finding out who was behind Earle's threat or how seriously this should be taken. It was absurd to think that "they" could prevent him from leaving Göttingen if he wished; but in any case he had no intention of leaving. Too much had been done, too much was at stake, to give up now. Presumably Earle would reappear. When he did, the situation must be appraised in the light of whatever he had to say: perhaps "they" could be fed enough advance information—if indeed there was any—to satisfy them, or perhaps he would have to seek help. Either way, this was a free and friendly country in the West of Europe, and really a solution should not be hard to find.

On the third evening after his confrontations with Earle and von Bremke, Daniel was walking along the town wall when a sudden flash of light half blinded him for several seconds. He recovered himself to see that Leonard Percival, his heavy glasses glinting in the setting sun, was standing in his path at some twenty yards' distance. Percival, who had appeared from nowhere, was wearing a double-breasted blue blazer with large gilt buttons and grinning like Mephistopheles.

" 'If there were dreams to sell,' " Percival said, " 'What would you buy?' "

"I beg your pardon?"

" 'Some cost a passing bell,
Some a light sigh . . .'

"Thomas Lovell Beddoes. He lived in Göttingen for quite some time, you know. He is reputed to have held orgies here. Perhaps this is where he picked up his pox. For such a pretty little town it certainly has some nasty surprises."

"Why aren't you on Exercise Broomstick?"

" 'If there were dreams to sell,
Merry and sad to tell,
And the crier rung the bell,
What would you buy?' "

"Peace of mind. Why aren't you in the Harz with the rest of them?"

"Rear-guard. Someone has to take care of the barracks . . . An interesting case, Beddoes. He was a doctor but he couldn't cure his own syphilis, so in the end he did himself in. But I'm sure I don't have to spell out the moral to you."

"You seemed so dedicated to your task," Daniel said irritably, "and yet on the very first rehearsal they leave you behind."

"A good job for you that they did. Because now I can take you to see Pappenheim."

"I don't want to see Pappenheim."

"You do if you did but know it. He's got news for you." Percival pointed his nose accusingly at Daniel's forehead. "So I don't want any ingratitude or coyness. Just come along with your uncle Leonard and everything will be all right."

So saying, Percival linked his right arm with Daniel's left and propelled him gently but very firmly in the direction from which he had come.

"My car's in the Goetheallee," he explained. "I wonder why they don't name one after Beddoes."

Ten minutes later they were driving through the main gate of the barracks. A soldier standing outside the guard room gave them a shifty look, and Percival stopped the car.

"Come here and salute," he hissed.

"Sorry, sir. Didn't recognise you in civies."

"So you were going to let a stranger drive straight in?"

The soldier gave a hopeless shrug. Rather surprisingly, Percival ignored this and said quietly:

"Put the barrier down, Fusilier, and only raise it when you have recognised the people arriving. Low morale," he said to Daniel as they drove on. "They don't like being in an empty barracks."

And indeed a feeling of desertion crept off the ground like

a mist. The windows of the barrack-blocks were as blind as vacant eye-sockets. Already, one would have thought, there were weeds pushing up through the asphalt of the parade grounds. The two women and children, who were trailing away with their bathing towels as Percival drew up in front of the Mess, only made the emptiness more eerie: it was as though they were the last human beings who would be allowed to leave before the whole scene were petrified for ever.

"Pappenheim is upstairs," Percival said. "The Mess staff is much reduced but I don't manage too badly. I take it you could do with some dinner?"

Remembering the food he had last eaten here, Daniel shuddered violently, a reaction which Percival misunderstood.

"No silly jokes this time," he said, and led the way to the ante-room, where Pappenheim was morosely drinking beer in a far corner. He did not get up to greet them but flapped a limp hand and contrived to wrinkle the bald skin on his scalp, as if smiling with that instead of with his face.

"We dine alone," said Percival.

In the dining-room the great table was blank except for three places laid at the bottom end, which was lit by a single casuarina candelabrum. A trolley by the wall carried bottles of wine and a burner, over which Percival now busied himself with a chafing dish.

"My uncle taught me," he explained: "a man of many gifts. I shall be about ten minutes, so perhaps, Herr Pappenheim, you would like to entertain our friend."

Pappenheim swallowed hard and emitted a guttural noise as of getting into his bottom gear.

"I like so much the English understatement," he said. "Entertain. Ho, ho."

Another grinding from his throat, and now he was moving in second.

"You have had a disagreeable visitor," he announced to Daniel.

"Why should I discuss it with you?"

Pappenheim was not at all perturbed by the hostility in Daniel's voice.

"Because I can help you. Let me tell you," he said, "That when the new German Army shall be fully existing I shall be an important person in what you call its Intelligence."

Daniel received this in sulky silence.

"This means that I am already privileged to have much information. I can tell you of some matters which you are needing to know."

"The only thing I need is to be left in peace. By all of you."

"You'd better listen," said Percival from the trolley: "you really had."

"And where do you come in?"

"The Oberleutnant and I," said Pappenheim, "have discovered, since the night of the feast here, that we are of mutual assistance."

"What's that supposed to mean?"

"Let's say," said Percival, "that we have interests in common. Now sit quiet like a good boy and listen to what the kind German gentleman is telling you."

"Ja," said Pappenheim. "You have no doubt been told that when Professor Dortmund died the Nazi authorities were assured that no one could understand his work and that it had in any case no scientific application."

"Nor has it."

"You will know more than I do about that. Nevertheless, in 1944 a rumour started in some scientific circles that Dortmund's theories, if properly worked upon, might indeed have surprising practical results. So there come some high-ranking visitors to the University here; but once again the Professors said that there was nothing to be done with the Dortmund papers, and they repeated that Dortmund had been at the end very sick. And since this was 1944 and there were more urgent things to give worry, the matter was again put by."

"On what possible ground," said Daniel, "was it supposed

that Dortmund's theories might lead to 'practical results'?"

"That I cannot tell you. The fact remains that it was believed, and believed strongly enough for the rumour to stay alive, in some quarters, until this very day."

"Nobody reputable has ever suggested—"

"—I did not say the quarters were reputable. Quite the reverse. It was the Nazis who listened to the rumour in 1944, and the rumour is part of their legacy."

Pappenheim wrinkled his scalp into an expression of disapproval and sorrow.

"A legacy," he said, "which not everyone has renounced as thoroughly as we like the world to think."

Percival came over with the chafing dish and helped all three of them to slices of veal cooked in cream and mushrooms.

"You see," he said wistfully to Daniel, "why you are so sought after?"

He fetched two bottles of wine and started to pour.

"Eat it while it's hot," he said. "Otherwise it's apt to congeal."

It was so hot that it burned Daniel's tongue.

"Von Bremke?" he spluttered.

"Drink some wine . . . Not as far as we are aware. Von Bremke has always been a neutral figure—wouldn't you say, Herr Pappenheim?"

"The Herr Doktor was among those who urged, in 1944, that nothing was to be gained from further enquiry into the papers."

"He's been urging that lately," said Daniel. "Though when I first came he was more encouraging."

"Perhaps he was. But perhaps he now has some notion about the . . . outside interest . . . you have aroused, and is trying, in his discreet and neutral way, to give you warning."

"Against what, for Christ's sake?"

"Inquisitive men," said Percival, "who are liable to turn nasty if they don't get their way."

"But it's all so childish," Daniel whined. "There is nothing to turn nasty about. My results—if ever I'm left alone to get them—will be about as practical as Clarabelle Cow."

"Who is this Fraulein Cow?"

Percival said something in German.

"Ho, ho. Your English humour. But," said Pappenheim fiercely to Daniel, "it is not so funny after all. Listen. Because of some things which have happened in the war, I am not entirely trusted. Pappenheim, they say, he could be one of those who does not wish to forget. And so, to show them they are wrong, I am giving all my time, for five years now, to finding out about those people . . . who do not wish to forget. Who want back the Germany of 1939. Now, to want such a thing is to want, as you say, the moon, and to want the moon you must have faith. Crazy faith. Once you have that you will believe anything you wish to believe, and these people wish to believe that there is a secret in the Dortmund papers which can help to make them powerful once again. If you tell them there is no such secret, they will not listen. They will tear you into pieces to find it. I know these people. You must believe me, Herr Mond; you must trust me."

But Daniel saw a long line of cattle trucks rolling through the night to Erfurt, and Pappenheim, ten years younger, yapping orders through the door of a first class compartment to a faceless group with knee boots and sub-machine guns. He might or might not believe him; he would never trust him.

"You are thinking," said Pappenheim, "the same as all you English. 'He was one of them.' Yes, Herr Mond, I was one of them. I did not complain. I joined no conspiracies against them. I did whatever they told me because I was afraid of being shot dead. And so now that they are defeated and gone I do not want them back. I am just as sincere in my way, you see, as you are."

Daniel shook his head and pursed his mouth.

"These . . . recidivists," he said. "Who are they? Where are they?"

"They are Germans and they are everywhere in Germany. There are not yet many of them but they are widespread and determined. And if there is encouragement, others will join them. If they should make some success . . . if they should have something—like this secret—which would enable them to deal with our Government, with other Governments . . ."

"I've told you: there is no secret. Not in the way they mean."

"And I have told you: they will not choose to believe this."

Percival collected their plates and set down a dish of interesting cheeses.

"The truth is, Mond," he said, "that either way you're up the creek."

"But this is ludicrous. You can't tell me that this country, to say nothing of the occupying powers, is incapable of disciplining its lunatic fringes."

"Disciplining?" said Percival. "What naughty words you left-wingers use when you're upset."

"I'm not upset."

"Good. Because there's more to come. You see, a lot of people . . . Americans, for example . . . who have invested heavily in Europe and its recovery, are rather uneasy just now. About Communism and so forth."

"Reactionary elements."

"Let's just say worried. Even the dear old British Labour Party makes them nervous. So like all greedy capitalists they are keeping a careful eye on their investments . . . which is harmless and conventional enough. But within the large organisation necessary for this purpose there are bound to be shades of opinion, variations of policy and method; and since operations are secret, operators not always strictly accountable, it is not easy to control these."

"People can be disci— Dismissed."

"Not," said Percival, "if they have made themselves indispensable. Let us take a case in point. A highly skilled American director of agents, who has an impressive war-time record and an unrivalled knowledge of this country, who since 1945 has continued to do invaluable work . . . but who holds (alas) to rather embarrassing political theories. One of these has to do with what used to be called the Balance of Power: you know, if there's a giant strutting around in seven-league boots, then when no one's looking you lend the dwarf a banana skin. To cripple the giant and make him more appreciative of your investment." He flashed his glasses at Daniel. "Have some more brie."

"You're saying . . . that the American secret service here in West Germany is supporting neo-Fascism? To impede democratic progress?"

"That would be grossly overstating it. All I'm saying is that from time to time, illicitly but very discreetly, the resources of one American director and his branch are being used to equip malignant political dwarves with banana skins. And sometimes even with landmines. Herr Pappenheim is very anxious that you shouldn't tread on one."

"Earle Restarick?"

"Exactly so," said Pappenheim with a smug purr.

"The whole thing should be publicly exposed."

Both Percival and Pappenheim sighed deeply.

"First of all you'd have to prove it exists. You might as well try to net the old man of the sea."

"You almost seem," said Daniel, "to approve of it."

"Naturally one admires professional expertise. But we've told you where we stand. We want to help you—and you don't appear very grateful."

"Because I can't take it seriously. For the sake of argument, I'll grant what you say about these Nazi survivals and even about this American group which helps them sometimes. But why should the Americans interest themselves in anything so preposterous as this mythical secret? Why should they help these Fascists to pester me?"

"The director is a romantic, so perhaps he believes in the old rumour. He is also rather eccentric: he doesn't like Jews."

Daniel lowered his head. This at least he was ready to believe.

"So consider," said Percival. "On the one hand some fanatical Germans, supported, however unofficially, by American money and resources. On the other hand . . . you. Don't you think you should accept Herr Pappenheim's offer?"

"What is his offer?"

"The same," said Pappenheim, "as I would have made to you the other night—if you had been more patient. Protection. My department does not yet exist officially, but I can promise you that."

"Does nothing have official existence in your world?"

"That is its charm," Percival observed. "It's something the British are very bad at understanding—which is incidentally the reason why I myself can't offer you what Pappenheim can. British Intelligence over here is all on an official basis and therefore woefully clumsy. Men in bowler hats and policemen's boots. The Labour Administration dug up our war-time network. They said it was immoral."

"Good for them. And just who and what are you?"

"A junior officer serving in a battalion of infantry. What could be more official and above-board than that?" Percival wagged his chin. "Now I think—don't you?—that you should say thank you to Herr Pappenheim for being so kind."

"Herr Pappenheim," said Daniel slowly, "says he will protect me. This also means, I take it, that he would help me if I wanted to leave Germany and . . . the others . . . tried to stop me?"

"Very much what we had in mind. On one condition, of course."

Pappenheim gave Percival a warning look, but he shook his head.

"No, Herr Pappenheim. When Englishmen make an agreement, they like to get all the clauses straight from the start. It saves ill feeling or disappointment later on. On one condition," he said to Daniel: "that before you leave you tell us what you don't want to tell them."

Daniel jerked to his feet.

"*You* believe it too," he shouted; "*you* think there's something you can use."

He walked away along the black table.

"I might have known. Why else should you offer your help?"

Percival lifted the candelabrum from the table and followed Daniel.

"The lights are all out," he said; "if you'll allow me to show you the way . . ."

As they came to the top end of the table, the candles lit the crossed colours on the wall. Tonight they were furled and sheathed in tubes of black leather which were tipped with brass. Underneath them the infant Prince Charles played with his woolly ball.

"If you change your mind," Percival said, "you know where to find me."

But Daniel did not hear him. He was standing absolutely still, while the cold sweat started down his thighs from his crutch, and looking at the photograph of Prince Charles, at the ball with its strands of wool. Knitted, woven, somehow intermingled to form a central core and then to protrude, singly but very close together, at the surface; with the result that the surface looked continuous, until inspection revealed that it was made up of thousands of little woollen dots. The sweat poured down his calves to his ankles. Christ. Jesus Christ.

"Do you want to sit down again? Or shall I ring for a taxi? You don't look at all well?"

"That's because I've got a lot on my mind," said Daniel, the buttocks quivering beneath him: "I think I'd like to walk."

PART IV

THE OO-WOO STUBE

To celebrate their return from Exercise Broomstick, Giles Glastonbury decided to give his officers a party, to which he also bade Daniel and Doctor Motley, at the Oo-Woo Stube. This interesting establishment was in Hannover, and Giles accordingly booked rooms for the night in a large hotel near Hannover station, so that his guests might recuperate in comfort and return to Göttingen at their leisure.

At first Daniel was not at all keen to go. In so far as he could make sense of his situation and the new elements of which Percival and Pappenheim had (truthfully or untruthfully?) apprised him, it now seemed more than ever desirable that he should finish up and get out. There was no time for larking about in Hannover and limping home with a crapula. Besides, it could hardly be his kind of evening, since the staples of the Oo-Woo's entertainment (he understood) were tarts and gambling. But his affection for the friends whom he had hardly seen in ten days, his pride in being invited by their leader to their private celebration, overcame his objections: and after all, as Julian James pointed out, this would be the last "significant spree" for some time; for now that Broomstick was done, there must be intensive preparations, in the light of what they had learned or failed to learn from it, for Apocalypse, which was only just over three weeks away.

So late in the afternoon of September the first, Daniel

found himself waiting on Göttingen station for Fielding Gray. Julian was driving the other two subalterns to Hannover in his Citroen, Giles was taking Mick Motley in his Bentley. Although either car would have had ample room for Daniel and Fielding, it was apparently assumed that after the separation imposed by Broomstick they would sooner have the journey to themselves.

"He's had to stay behind at Divisional Headquarters," Giles had said, half apologetic and half conspiratorial, "but he'll meet you at the station here at 5.15. These German trains are really quite comfortable and you've probably got things to talk about."

Which was true enough, Daniel now reflected, as he watched Fielding march down the platform towards him in an arrogant brown felt hat. But how much can I tell him? How much do I want to tell him? Although Fielding, unlike Jacquiz Helmut, would not automatically incline to scepticism or scorn, Daniel had an unpleasant feeling that, should he seem to be asking for help, Fielding would quietly duck out. Where difficulties were theoretical, or where only advice was sought, Fielding was a shrewd counsellor; but if it came to action, inconvenience, commitment . . . ? Sadly, Daniel remembered Jacquiz' remarks about the Dragoon officers who had returned home in mid-campaign rather than tolerate discomfort.

"Broomstick," said Fielding briskly, "was a fiasco."

"Oh? Giles seemed content when I saw him."

"The Squadron did all right. But the Fusiliers just farted about."

"I thought they were so reliable."

"At doing things by numbers. But when a little flexibility, a little imagination is required . . . They spend the whole time saluting each other and forming themselves into three ranks."

"Suppose it had been real," Daniel said diffidently, "then the familiar discipline might have helped to keep them sane."

Fielding gave him a sharp look. The train came in.

"First class."

"I've taken a second class ticket," Daniel said.

"Then you can pay the difference."

"You seem rather prickly this afternoon."

Fielding flushed with annoyance.

"I'm *not* prickly. Just fed up with exhibitions of incompetence. Fusiliers who can't read their maps. People who buy the wrong tickets."

The train pulled out. The phallus-tipped tower in Daniel's street seemed to quiver for a moment, as if it were going to stretch out over the intervening roofs and yank him back to his duty. Remembering that Fielding had had a large part in preparing Exercise Broomstick, Daniel decided to forgive his ill temper and sit it out in silence.

"They haven't realised," Fielding grumbled, "that modern war is going to be a matter of small groups which must move very fast and act independently. That any man's got to be ready to set off on his own at a moment's notice. I asked one of their platoon commanders to send an N.C.O. and three men to set up a check point two miles away. The N.C.O., a senior corporal mark you, was scared out of his wits. The platoon commander took me on one side, said his men wouldn't be able to find their way there by themselves. All right, I said, Trooper Lamb would take them in the Land Rover. But, said the platoon commander, they won't be able to find their way back : the platoon will have moved by then. All right, Lamb could bring them back too. But, he said, my men will be unhappy away from their mates. As though they could all spend the entire exercise huddled together like sheep."

"What happened?"

"In the end I had to detail some of my own men, who were badly needed for something else, and tell the Fusiliers to get on with the only thing they *can* do—digging bunkers. We didn't want the bunkers but they had to do something, and they were all as happy as field-mice. Then their C.O. came along and said, 'Glad of some good men to do the spade work, eh? Can't see any of your chaps helping.' I could have shot him."

Daniel imagined the Fusilier Colonel's lugubrious head popping like a balloon in a shooting gallery and went into a cascade of giggles. This cheered Fielding up.

"Sorry I was bloody," he said. "How have you got on, Danny? You look rather tired."

"I've had several surprises. Disagreeable ones."

"Dortmund was off the rails after all?"

"No. It might have been better if he had been. It's more as though he'd suddenly switched on to an utterly unexpected branch line . . . which led away into a fairie country. You know that poem of Browning's about Childe Roland riding to the Dark Tower? You get a feeling that he's passed into a region which isn't shown on any map, that he'll never be able to return."

Fielding looked at him carefully.

"All you mean," he said, "is that things are not working out quite the way you thought."

"That's certainly true. But they're working out. Oh yes, they're working out." Daniel gave an awkward little laugh. "You see, the other night I had a kind of . . . revelation. There was a picture I was looking at, and all at once I knew, *knew*, what Dortmund was after, as though he himself had suddenly appeared with a diagram. Since then everything's fitted as closely as a jigsaw puzzle. It's only a matter of a few days now, checking and confirming and tying a loose end or two, and the whole thing should be finished."

"Then you ought to be very pleased."

"That's just it. It's all so very different from what I thought. Everything's changed, Fielding."

"Might one ask how?"

"It's not the material, it's the way of looking at it. If you set a particle in motion, it makes a definite path, a thread through space. At a given instant you can *either* say, as we usually do and as I have been doing, that we have such and such particles in such and such positions; *or* you can think of it in terms of these threads' having reached certain points in the course of their elongation."

"Like a plate of spaghetti?"

"Yes, except that each strand is growing all the time, and the truth at any given moment is not the entire mass of the spaghetti—that represents the past—but only the positions occupied by the end of each strand and the pattern which these points make up."

"Where will all this get you? Effectively you've still only got a set of particles in certain positions."

"You remember," said Daniel, "that Dortmund is concerned with very small quantities?"

" 'Zeta' you called it. Something which is as small as it can be without disappearing altogether."

"More or less. Well, I thought this 'zeta' was to express the entities he wanted to deal with. That wasn't quite right. 'Zeta' applies to these strands: it is the smallest possible amount by which a strand can be lengthened. It expresses the development of a strand from one instant to the next."

"A different way of looking at things, as you said. You'll forgive me, Daniel, but I don't see anything so very mysterious in all this."

Daniel swallowed hard.

"Suppose . . . suppose you followed a strand of spaghetti backwards. Retraced its path with your eye. For a time you'd be able to follow it all right, but then you'd lose it in the labyrinthine muddle made by the rest of the spaghetti. But if you retraced this path in the smallest possible segments— zeta by zeta, so to speak—you could never lose it. You could trace it right back to its origin."

"And so?"

"And so, Fielding, if I take a certain kind of space—any kind of space—and a particle which is moving in it, that particle has a previous path which I can explore back, zeta by zeta, as far as I wish. I can never lose it. And unlike a strand of spaghetti, that path won't just end somewhere on the bottom of a plate."

"Rather sinister, put like that . . ."

"There could be metaphysical implications. Dortmund never got round to these, or I don't think so. Neither have I. Yet."

"Don't look so depressed about it. Anyone would think you expected to find the Devil at the end of the thread."

"There's a sense in which somebody might. The kind of person who isn't interested in metaphysics."

"Daniel? I don't—"

"—Ten days to finish off," said Daniel, tense and abrupt, suddenly conscious that the comfort of companionship had beguiled him into going too far. "Two weeks at most. Then I shall go. The sooner the better."

Fielding's face flushed with pain.

"Just like that? You sound . . . *glad* to be rid of us."

The train stopped in Hannover station. They walked in silence along the platform and down into a tunnel-way crammed with summer flesh, brown and ripe beneath brief liederhosen. Zigarren. Dortmunder Bieren. Reisebüro. Stadtplan. Into the open. Ernst August on his horse, pale green in the evening sun, father of his folk.

"The Central-Hotel, Giles said. Look half-left from the equestrian statue, he said, and you can't miss it."

"There's something you haven't told me, Daniel. I always knew you'd be glad to get back to Cambridge, but now . . . you . . . sound . . . different. Feverish. There's more changed than you've said."

"Much more. There it is. Just over the street."

"Then tell me."

Fielding's voice was peevish, as it had been on Göttingen station.

"Funny thing," said Daniel, remembering this; "there was

no inspector on the train to check the tickets. Unusual in
Germany."

"Don't you trust me?"

"Yes. But I don't want to tell you. I'm sorry if I've roused
your curiosity, but it's for your good not to know. I wish to
God I didn't."

Fielding flushed again and bit his lip.

"You're quite sure it's as . . . serious . . . as you think?"

"Quite."

They crossed the tram-lines to the Central-Hotel.

The Oo-Woo Stube was something of a surprise. Daniel
had been led to believe that it boasted a bar for the sale of
drink and women and an inner room in which, roulette being forbidden in Hannover, some variant of Boule was
played; and he had wondered why Giles Glastonbury, who
took an educated interest in his pleasures, should have
thought such a place worth a special visit. He now found
out. Beyond the gambling room was another bar, champagne
only, and a tiny theatre, in which one could watch, at intervals
of half an hour and for a charge of fifty marks a time, a selection of ingenious and obscene cabaret acts. Giles, the perfect
host, had paid a lump sum and arranged that members of
his party should be admitted to the theatre as and when they
chose throughout the evening.

"It's a hangover," Giles explained to Daniel, "from the
gay days just after the war. They'll stop it any time now. Any
minute, I wouldn't wonder. I hope it's still going when Detterling passes through."

"Detterling?"

"Didn't anyone tell you? Captain Detterling the M.P., late
of our regiment. You'll like him. He's stopping off for a night
or two next week on his way to Baden Baden."

Music struck up and the curtains parted. There was a
whinnying noise from the champagne-only bar, where Messrs

Lamprey and Bungay were comfortably settled with three magnums.

"I want," said Giles, "to get into the front row. Just to see that nothing's faked. Coming?"

"I'm all right here, thanks."

Julian James and Fielding Gray had disappeared. Not wishing to hurt his host's feelings, Daniel waited until the spectacle on the stage (a Roman Senator being pleasured by four female slaves) was well under way, and then slipped through to the gambling room, where Mick Motley was sitting with a huge pile of counters in front of him.

"Wretched poor game this, but it's been going for me. I'll give it a rest and buy us a drink."

Daniel started reluctantly back towards the theatre.

"Not, if you don't mind, in there," Mick Motley said.

They walked into the ordinary bar.

"You may think I'm old-fashioned," Motley went on, "but I don't approve of that sort of thing. Besides, I hate champagne."

He ordered two brandies. When a woman sidled towards them, he jerked Daniel away to a far corner where there was an empty table with only two chairs.

"It's funny," he said. "When these cavalry chaps got here they just about saved my life. Do you know, the Fusiliers were too snooty to talk to me. Me and my Liverpool accent. Then along came these Dragoons, who were too grand to talk to the Fusiliers but seemed to have all the time in the world for me. How do you explain that?"

"A kindred spirit. Racing, gambling . . ."

"But that's just it. That's *all* we share. In other ways I can't follow them at all. You know where Julian and Fielding have gone?"

"No."

"To a sort of club where there are boys. I heard them talking about it at dinner."

"Only curiosity, I expect."

"Even so, it's disgusting. And that business through there. It's abuse of God's gift."

Earle Restarick came in, ordered a drink at the bar, drank it down in one, waved gaily to Daniel, and went out.

"Who's that?"

"One of my fellow students from Göttingen."

"Doesn't look your type to me. Too cocky."

"He's American."

"Ah . . . Where was I?"

"Abuse," said Daniel, "of God's gift."

"Yes. Well, you see it's not that I'm a prude. But I believe in doing things the natural way and doing them privately. A man can have all the fun he needs like that."

"And do you, Mick?"

"The Fusilier wives," said Motley with a hot look. "When they meet me in public, they're as snooty as their husbands. Worse. But they're always ringing up in the afternoon . . . 'Doctor, I've got such a terrible headache.' So along I pop with my little black bag, and there they are, all alone and hardly able to keep their hands out of my fly for ten seconds." Motley giggled. "And the other rank wives are just the same. But one has to be more careful there, of course."

"But this," said Daniel, "is adultery. Surely an abuse of God's gift?"

"Mortal sin, yes, but not *too* bad as long as you don't try to avoid the consequences. By doing unnatural things or using contraceptives."

"Now you *have* surprised me."

"I know. And it would surprise Giles and the rest of them too. That's why I can't think what they see in me."

"It could be," said Daniel, "that they simply find you likeable."

"Oh," said Motley: "do you think so?"

"Or," said Daniel, annoyed by this disingenuousness, 'perhaps they think it prudent, what with the lives they lead, to have a physician dancing attendance."

Motley considered this without taking offence. Julian and Fielding came in.

"Nothing but tram-conductors and middle-aged waiters," Julian said, while Fielding glanced spitefully at Daniel. "I shall stick to Giles's hospitality from now on. Do you suppose he'll stand me one of these women?"

"You can perfectly well afford one yourself," said Fielding.

"That's not the point. It's Giles's party."

Giles came in.

"Quite good, that first turn," he said. "And the next will be even better. Two niggers in a girls' school, the man promised. I *do* hope they don't close down before Detterling comes."

"A Member of Parliament watching that filth?" snorted Motley. "Unthinkable."

Everyone laughed at such naïveté.

"The trouble is," said Giles, "that we'll all be so busy in barracks by the time Detterling arrives. Perhaps you can bring him, Daniel?"

Daniel shrugged non-committally. Bungay and Lamprey came in.

"Very lust-making," they said.

"That reminds me," said Julian to Giles. "Does one have to pay for one's own women, or are you treating?"

But this question was never to be answered. Two tall, blond men, having moved silently from the bar, were now confronting the group round Daniel and Motley. One of the men inclined himself toward Daniel.

"Disgusting Jew," the man said softly.

Giles Glastonbury shivered and his face went mottled.

"You're talking to my guest."

"Who is nevertheless a disgusting Jew. But if you think him worth the trouble, you know what you can do about it." He clicked his heels. "Von Augsburg. My friend here will make the arrangements."

Von Augsburg went out. It had all happened so quickly

that it was only when the second German began to speak that any of them realised what was in train.

"In the bombed area along the Limmerstrasse," said the second man in a calm, reasonable tone, "there is a place which we often use. It was once a stable, but now—"

"—Stop this nonsense," said Fielding, who was the first really to grasp what was being said. "Either apologise for your friend or get out. But stop this childish talk."

"It doesn't matter," said Daniel. "For God's sake don't let's have any trouble."

"It is," said the tall blond, "for this gentleman to say."

He looked straight at Giles, who said nothing.

"I am waiting, sir."

"Five-thirty tomorrow morning," Giles said. "Send a man—"

"—Giles, for Christ's sake—"

"—Send a man to meet us outside the Central-Hotel, or we shan't find the way."

The blond bowed.

"Good. The weapon, sir, to be the sabre."

"Suits me. And no padding."

"Giles, please be sensible. Be your age."

"Excuse me, sir, but for many years in these affairs—"

"—If we're going to do this," said Giles, "we'll do it properly. Your man picked a fight and now he's got it. No neck guards and no padding. Bare buff. That's how we used to do it where I come from."

Daniel felt a ridiculous and tearful urge to cheer which he at once surpressed.

"Please, Giles," he said. "I really don't mind. Stop all this before it's too late."

"You may not mind," said Giles Glastonbury, "but by God, I do." And to the blond, "Five-thirty then."

"Very good, sir. We shall try to arrange a doctor."

"No need," said Mick Motley. "I'm one."

"You keep clear of this, Mick," said Giles. "It could land you in trouble."

"I wouldn't miss it for the world," Mick Motley said.

Shuffle, shuffle : beat. Beat . . . beat, and shuffle.

On three sides they were enclosed by damaged yet still substantial walls. On the fourth they were screened by two large piles of rubble, a gap between which revealed an apparently interminable prospect of desolation. Somewhere, only a few hundred yards from them, a city was waking to a new day; yet the intervening no man's land of broken bricks had insulated them totally. They might have been the last men on the last morning of the world.

Beat . . . beat, shuffle, beat. Shuffle, shuffle : beat.

At one end of the wrecked enclosure were Mick Motley, Fielding Gray, and Daniel; Giles had forbidden his subalterns to be present. At the other end, a sheaf of sabres under his arm, stood the German who had negotiated with them the previous evening and a tubby little man who had guided them here from the Central-Hotel. In between, stripped to the waist, the swordsmen danced.

Beat, shuffle; beat, shuffle; beat.

It was not the dance that Daniel expected. He had fatuously imagined the rapid thrust and parry, the nimble circling movements, of a Fairbanks Jnr encounter on the screen, and was surprised, rather disappointed, at the cumbrous exercise which he was now watching. For several seconds at a time the heavy sabres would stay crossed and still, except for a slight quiver which gave them an appearance of prying antennae. Then, as though some piece of essential intelligence had passed back down his blade and into his arm, one or other of the fencers would disengage and execute, almost in slow motion, it seemed, a ponderous lunge or cut; upon which his opponent, also in slow motion, would move his weapon to parry with an ugly clack, retiring his back foot and then his front over perhaps twelve inches of the gritty floor. They kept, Daniel noticed, always in the same axis: something (convention, honour, a mere limitation of technique?) disqualified lateral movements whether for evasion or attack.

Beat . . . beat . . . beat. Shuffle, shuffle : beat.

He had come, Daniel supposed, because he was the ultimate cause of what was doing. He was not responsible, he had tried to stop it, but he was the cause, and rightly or wrongly he felt that he should be present to see what passed and bear his champion what aid he might. Secretly and guiltily he was excited and flattered; nor had he properly considered, even yet, what nuisance or scandal such an affair might bring about. And what a story to tell Jacquiz! *"In the end, of course, it was all very childish and they stopped as soon as one of them was scratched. Still, Jacquiz, it's not every day that one is the subject of a duel." "I must say, Daniel . . . a privilege. The Glastonburys have always been noted as duellists—one of them called out Cumberland but Prinny put his foot down. And of course Giles fenced for the Army, so you had an exhibition of real style."*

Shuffle . . . shuffle . . . beat.

Who had told him that Giles fenced for the Army? Fielding, of course, as they were coming downstairs in the hotel. "So with any luck it'll be all right," Fielding had said. "He can play about with the German, then slice a millimetre off his hide and call it a day." Well, all Daniel could say was that if this was top-level fencing he didn't think much of it. It was beginning to be a bore; let Giles slice off his millimetre so that they could all go home to breakfast.

Shuffle. Beat.

The only trouble was, as even Daniel now began to notice, that Giles's movements were becoming slower, sweatier and clumsier with every exchange, whereas the German remained as cool and as deft—in so far as one could be deft with these clanking great weapons—as he had been at the start. Von

Augsburg was beginning to tease Giles, and Giles was losing his bate. A particularly loutish cut at the German's ribs was easily parried, and Giles was all but caught by a vicious riposte. Von Augsburg grinned; Giles, mottled and furious, dragged himself back two steps. The German pursued; Giles grunted and swept wildly at his head, leaving his whole body exposed; and although, once again, he was just in time to parry the riposte aimed at his stomach, the two further steps he now retreated were made with a shambling feebleness which showed that he was at the end of his strength. His knees were trembling, his sword-arm drooping, his chest heaving, his mouth dribbling. With a broad smile of anticipation, his tongue protruding slightly through his teeth, von Augsburg surveyed the plump, slimy torso before him, like a butcher's favoured customer at leisure to choose his cut. Giles made one last desperate thrust straight for the German's navel; and von Augsburg, with casual grace, rolled his wrist down for a simple parry—only to find Giles's blade, which had swerved up over his guard, sawing along the tendons of his neck.

"Oldest trick in the book," said Fielding to Daniel: "let them think you're beaten and wait for 'em to get careless."

But Mick Motley had seen more than Fielding had.

"Get an ambulance and fucking quick," he shouted as he ran for the staggering German.

Fielding moved off between the two piles of rubble. Motley busied himself with a small black bag which the tubby German produced. Daniel confronted Giles.

"It's not serious really?" Daniel said.

Giles did not answer.

"You didn't mean it?" Daniel persisted.

"He shouldn't have smiled like that," Giles Glastonbury said.

*   *   *

Some thirty hours after these events, Daniel was visited at his lodgings in Göttingen by a very large Englishman with a very small head.

"Tuck," announced the large Englishman : "Control Commission. Liaison Branch."

He produced an elaborate identity card to support this claim.

"My job," he explained importantly, "is to regulate the relations between British Military personnel and German civilians."

"I'm neither."

"You're involved with both. This business in Hannover."

"What about it?"

"You'll hear what in a moment," said Tuck in a bullying way, "but let me first advise you to change your tone. You may think, like a lot of people, that the Control Commission's finished with—"

"—It's nothing to me either way."

Tuck's shoulders heaved until his head almost disappeared between them.

"I have authority," he boomed, "equivalent to that of a lieutenant-colonel, and I am acting, in this instance, in concert with the consular service. Now then. There is a young German in a hospital at Hannover, and it's quite possible that he'll die there. Whether he does or not, grave embarrassment has been caused. It is thought that you are possessed of information which has bearing on the matter."

"I was there, if that's what you mean."

"Then you are to hold yourself in readiness to give evidence before a properly constituted board of enquiry."

"When?"

"That," said Tuck, "nobody knows." This pronouncement gave him a satisfaction which considerably softened his manner. "You see, five years ago, even with a German civilian involved, it would certainly have been a matter for Court Martial. Five years hence, God help us, we shall prob-

ably have to kow-tow to the German judiciary. But just now,"
he said, with profound relish for the type of confusion which,
throughout history, had brought him and his kind a fat
living, "just now things are *transitional*. So an enquiry is to
be held at which there will be German legal representatives,
British legal and military representatives, diplomatic representatives, liaison representatives, welfare representatives,
representatives, in short, of every conceivable interest involved.
They will establish what happened and the forensic implications thereof, decide what sort of trial there is to be, and
where. *When*, that is, we manage to get them all together."

"As far as I'm concerned they'd better be quick. I'm off
in a week or so."

"Oh no, you're not," said Tuck, reverting to the bully. "It
is essential that we show the Germans that we are acting in
good faith. So we have guaranteed that all British witnesses
will remain in Germany until the enquiry is convened."

"And if I just go?"

"You'll be detained at your port of egress by the German
police, and no British authority will interfere on your behalf.
All that's already arranged."

"I see," said Daniel, who suddenly felt a hundred and
seventy years old.

Tuck smiled. That is to say, a horizontal incision appeared
in his wizened little head.

"But of course," he said, "if you wish to claim that there
are special circumstances ... of a compassionate nature,
perhaps ..."

"I'm just anxious to be gone."

"Important business or professional commitments? I am
empowered to recognise those. Are they so important, I wonder, that you'd be prepared to ... er ... deposit five hundred
pounds with me as security?"

"I haven't got five hundred pounds."

"I thought not," said Tuck with a snap; "so you'd better
stay put, hadn't you? And a tiny word in your ear. If you

do try anything on, we'll not only back the German police but we'll impound your passport for the next five years. We've got important work to do," he said, blowing out his chest, "and we're not going to tolerate any nonsense from the likes, Mr Daniel bloody Mond, of you."

About half an hour after Tuck's departure, Earle Restarick arrived.

"You see?" he said. "I told you we wouldn't let you leave."

"You mean—?"

"—I mean that we fixed the whole thing. We planted those two Germans in the Oo-Woo Stube. Of course, there was no guarantee that your chum would rise to it. But there was nothing to lose if he didn't, and once he did ... Well, you've seen for yourself."

"You reckoned on a duel?"

"Or something similar. A big enough row—with you in the middle of it—to call for official action. My employers remembered what I'd always told them, that the British feel mightily obligated to their guests. Not that I'll have any credit."

"At least," said Daniel maliciously, "your man got more than he bargained for."

"More than he bargained for, perhaps, but not more than my employers did. They wanted quite a splash, you see. They knew Major Glastonbury was a fighter and they selected von Augsburg as just the man to bring him out at his fiercest."

"Funny," mused Daniel. "I should never have thought Giles had it in him. He always seemed so mild."

"He had a bad streak. They often do in those old families of yours, and anyway it was on the record. He shot one of his own men during the war. Found him asleep while he was meant to be on guard, and shot him just like that."

"I'm sure there was excellent military precedent for such a proceeding."

This blasé comment was not an affectation; the events of the last two days had so numbed Daniel, for the time, that he was beyond being shocked by anything.

"In extreme situations, yes. Which is why he's still serving. But you'll agree that it takes an unusual temperament to shoot a comrade while he sleeps."

"To say nothing of arranging for a comrade to be sliced up with a sabre. Ingenious, I grant you." Daniel's temporary numbness had brought not only moral atrophy but also freedom from fear. "But I don't suppose," he went on, "that you've come here to discuss the niceties of your profession. What is it you want?"

"Just to remind you that my employers have been as good as their word. They said they'd stop you leaving and they have. So hadn't you better tell them what they want to know?"

"I've nothing to tell."

"That's not what that nice Curator in the library thinks."

"Those librarians spend far too much time gossiping about things they don't understand. Between them," said Daniel gaily, "they've apparently been broadcasting daily statements about my progress round half the Electorate of Hannover. But they only know what documents I ask for. Supposing I couldn't make head or tail of them?"

"Then my employers," said Earle, "will be very disappointed. So disappointed that I really couldn't answer for their actions. On the other hand, Daniel, they're not unreasonable. They quite see that you must have a proper opportunity to check back over your work and write it all up in a fair round hand. So they'll be happy to wait until this enquiry convenes. As that man Tuck doubtless told you —he's quite genuine, by the way—this will probably be some time, so you can't say you're being hurried. But don't abuse my employers' patience, Danny. You know how—what was your word?—*ingenious* they can be when they try."

*　　　*　　　*

By the next day Daniel's blithe indifference had worn off, like the effect of a dentist's injection, and the nerves were starting to ache.

When Earle had left him, he had still regarded the Hannover episode as too unreal to have any consequences; even Tuck's official pronouncement on the subject had failed to convince him that it was more than a dream. It had happened in another country; or in a bubble of time, as it were, that had floated for an instant over the rubble, then burst and for ever ceased to exist. But the reality behind the dream started to make itself felt when Trooper Lamb arrived in the Land Rover with a note which excused Fielding from dinner that evening. He was now in charge of the Squadron, Fielding wrote, and up to his neck in work; Giles was in close arrest and relieved of his command indefinitely; they were all (he understood) to be brought before a board of enquiry; and he, Fielding, though for the time being he enjoyed the benefit of the doubt, might have some awkward questions to answer about his own role, which amounted to that of second and could be held to make him a guilty party.

At first this communication summoned up an almost laughable picture of Giles in a bare room contemplating a whisky bottle and a revolver; but when Daniel re-read it, he found that the use of phrases such as "close arrest", "indefinitely", "guilty party", was less dramatic than functional; a disagreeable situation was being soberly described. In so far as he still refused to believe in this situation, he was sharply set right the next morning, when a uniformed despatch rider presented him, in return for his signature, with an imposing document which amounted to a subpoena given under the authority of the British Occupation with the full recognition and consent of the German civilian power. Or *vice versa*. Either way, the word of Tuck was upheld and Daniel Mond was trapped.

When this was fully borne in on him, Daniel attempted, in mounting misery, to cut away all accretions of fantasy and emotion and to calculate exactly where he now stood. He had found the answer to the Dortmund papers; it was not the answer which he had expected and which would have had only abstract significance, but something which, he did not doubt, could open up whole new areas of scientific discovery and exploitation. The method which Dortmund had invented could be used to seek out ... what? He was still not absolutely certain, but after what had already been done either he himself, or another if made privy to his work, could find out in a matter of hours. It was, then, too late to turn back. Destroy everything he had written? It was written on his mind. Refuse to tell of it? But he was not strong enough, he knew, to endure pain, and pain, in one form or another, was what ... "they" ... held in store for him. So tell them false? They would not be deceived for very long.

Well then. Pappenheim and Percival had promised help. But on their terms. Presumably they represented what passed for decency, the Western Alliance, "our side", and certainly it were better the secret should go to them than to the others. Better, but still very bad; for if once it were known, by anyone, it could be used. No. If it was as momentous as he had reason to think, then he must never speak it. Never? They've got you where they want you, Danny boy: you're good and stuck.

Why was it that the low, the trivial, the greedy always turned out to be right? For years such people had scented something here to their purpose. For years himself and those like him had replied that there was nothing, that it was simply an unsolved problem of interest only to the mind. He had believed this, sincerely and passionately he had believed it, and he had set himself to find the solution with the dedication of a scholar who unravels a tongue long dead and unknown, that thereby knowledge may be increased and celebrated for its own sweet sake. But now the lovingly deciphered tablets had yielded a hideous rune to raise the powers of the deep; the scholar must creep away in shame, and the low men, the grinning and the greasy and the cunning, had come, once more, into their own. Was there nothing they could not turn to their ends? Only silence, and they had long since found instruments and acids to slice and burn their way through that.

"... And so, Herr Doktor, I want your help."

"What can *I* do, Herr Dominus?"

"Let me bring Restarick to you when he next comes. Then tell him that there's nothing here for those who've sent him, that there never has been, that there *can't* be."

"I have told others that before, Herr Dominus. They did not believe me, it seems."

"On your authority as one of the leading mathematicians in Germany ..."

"If that authority—such as it ever was—was not accepted before, why should it be now? The only thing you can do is to convince them that you have failed. Presumably they have a mathematician of their own whom they will trust. You must take this man through your work and show him where and how you have failed."

"Of course ..."

"Listen to me, Earle. You must believe that I've got nowhere with all this. I didn't do too badly at the start, but since then I've got nowhere at all. Tell these ... employers of yours ... to send a competent mathematician along with you, and I'll show him. I'll show him just what went wrong."

"Too easy, Danny boy. You could show him a thousand ways of getting it wrong as easy as spelling your name. We want to know what went right."

"I'll show him that too. I'll show him everything that went right early on, all the stuff I've sent to Dirange in Cambridge,

and then *he must believe me* when I explain how after that
I simply lost the track."

"You ever heard of Pascal's wager, Danny boy? You believe in God, see, and you go on believing, because you've
nothing to lose if He isn't there and everything to gain if He
is. Well, that's the way my employers feel about this
secret . . ."

He must know the worst. He must at least find out precisely
what power it was that he now had under his hand. After
all, it might, it just might, be comparatively harmless. He
had checked the Dortmund method through and through,
he knew exactly how to use it. Set a moving particle in space,
any kind of space . . . But this time it was going to be
different. Take a real particle in real space; there is
the thread, made by its path; follow it forward a little to
determine this and that; then turn and retrace the way you
have come, back to the point at which you started, and then
beyond, back and back and back . . .

". . . Officers' Mess? I want to speak to Lieutenant Percival . . . . Leonard. You know what's happened?"

"If you mean the case of the *beau sabreur*, the whole barracks is heaving with it."

"I mean the enquiry. I'm not allowed to leave."

"Tough titty."

"You said . . . Could you and Pappenheim still get me
out?"

"Yes. In return for what we asked."

"I'll give you all the stuff I've given Dirange. I'll show
you how well it all went up till there, and then I'll show you
when and how I stuck."

"We're not interested in failure, Mond."

"But failure's all there is."

"Then you tell that politely to Restarick, and perhaps they'll let you off the hook."

"That's just it. They refuse to believe me. Christ, Leonard, I must have help."

"Why not try your cavalry chum, Captain Gray?"

"What could he do?"

"Sweep you up into his saddle and carry you into the sunset."

The telephone went dead.

". . . Officers' Mess . . . . *Fielding*. When shall I see you?"

"Sorry, Daniel. All this work for Apocalypse. And I've been politely told that though I'm not under arrest like Giles, it would be tactful of me to stay in barracks."

"But I *must* talk to you."

"That's another thing. I think they think that we might cook something up between us to fox this enquiry."

"Not about Giles. Something else. Can I come up and see you?"

"No, Daniel. They wouldn't like it."

"But Fielding—"

"—*No*, for Christ's sake. Things are quite bad enough."

"FIELDING . . ."

But again the telephone went dead.

Daniel was in the forest near the Warlocks' Grotto, looking for Julian James. Since he couldn't see Fielding, he would find Julian instead, and Julian, he knew, was in the Grotto with Trooper Lamb. If only he could find his way through all these trees. But of course! He needn't go forward, he could turn back, trace his path back, become a thread through space, threading back to where he last saw Fielding, so that he could speak to him again. Daniel was a particle in space, and Daniel was also outside it, tracing its path back. Back and back and back. There were no trees now (yet surely they had stretched to world's end?), only emptiness and, very far away, a dull red sun. In the sun was Fielding, but he would never reach him now, because the particle that was Daniel had gone as far back as it could go. There was a blinding flash which had once, aeons before, been its birth, and then Daniel, the Daniel who was watching, was alone in no-space, before the universe and before time.

"Oh God," moaned Daniel as he woke, "what have you let me do?"

And then, the next morning, Trooper Lamb drove down the street in the Land Rover and out stepped a cool, confident customer (the word seemed appropriate) with an air that was two parts military to one part lackadaisical.

"Detterling," said the customer as soon as he was through Daniel's door.

"Captain Detterling? Er . . . M.P.?"

"The very same."

"You've been expected. Giles Glastonbury was worrying in case they closed the Oo-Woo Stube before you got here."

"I shan't have time for the Oo-Woo Stube, thank you all the same. I'm on my way to Baden Baden, and I was intending to spend two nights here visiting a unit of my old regiment. But what do I find? One of my oldest friends under house arrest, another friend confined to barracks like a common trooper, and a whole lot of gratified Fusiliers goggling and giggling like schoolboys at a public birching. A very nasty spot of trouble. Which is why I've come to see you. To get your account of the matter, and then explain to you the mildly modified version which I want you to give for the future."

"At the enquiry?"

"If necessary."

"Shan't I be on oath?"

"Please," said Captain Detterling, "do not make trivial difficulties. It is important that we get your story in line with the one the rest of them will tell. First of all, will you kindly tell me what you think happened?"

Daniel told him.

"Thank you," said Detterling. "Now this, in case anyone asks you, is what *really* happened. The business in the Oo-Woo Stube remains unchanged, except that the two Huns were far more aggressive and insulting. Von Augsburg, for example, called you a filthy, Jewish, homosexual pig."

"Rather overdoing it?"

"Courts of enquiry like everything in black and white ... Even then, Giles did not take up the challenge, until the second German called him a shit-swallowing coward in a voice that was heard all over the room. Later that night, Giles explained to you all that his sole intention in fighting this duel would be to make von Augsburg look ridiculous. He was hardly going to scratch him. Even so, he insisted that this Army doctor—what's his name?—"

"—Mick Motley—"

"—Motley should be on hand just in case, as the Germans had made no mention of medical assistance. As to the duel itself, it was quite obvious to you from the beginning that Giles was just playing with his man and waiting for the chance to inflict some quiet humiliation. It was most unfortunate that his front foot slipped on a patch of damp and turned a harmless feint into a full-bodied lunge."

"I see," said Daniel. "I don't think I need object to any of that. What about Fielding and the doctor?"

"Fielding will do whatever I tell him. The doctor is grateful to you all for what he calls 'a barrel-load of laughs' over the past few weeks. Being a Catholic, he can translate our motto, *Res Unius, Res Omnium,* and he is commendably clear as to its present application."

"So now we just sit and wait for the enquiry?" Daniel said.

"No. This will be my first visit to Baden Baden since 1936," said Detterling reproachfully, "but I am going to give up the first three days of it while I fly back to London *via* Berlin. In both cities I shall tell certain people the unsolicited story which you have just told me. That the duel was viciously provoked, its outcome quite accidental. I think they can be got to believe this and will agree with me that it would be a waste of time and money to bother with further enquiry. But there may have to be concessions to save Teutonic face, and people may come knocking on your door for a statement. So you're quite sure you've been telling me the truth? Particularly about that most unfortunate patch of damp?"

"Quite sure," said Daniel gleefully. "*Res Unius, Res Omnium*, as you say."

PART V
VENERY

FIVE DAYS after Captain Detterling's visit, Major Giles Glastonbury was released from arrest and posted instanter to staff duties in Hong Kong; Captain Fielding Gray was confirmed in command of the 10th Sabre Squadron (until such time as it should rejoin its parent regiment); and Daniel Mond was notified, by special despatch, that he might consider the injunction against his leaving Germany "indefinitely suspended". Which being so, he thought, let's go while the going is good.

For all the work which he could do on the Dortmund papers and their possible application was now done. He knew what he knew. What, if anything, he was going to do with his knowledge, he must decide later. Meanwhile, there was comfort in the thought that no one else could share it, not without his personal assistance every step of the way. Even if his enemies stole or photographed the hundreds of pages which he had written over the months and which were now packed away in his suitcase, they could make nothing of them without his aid; for all of this work was in the form of rough notes, untidy and often illegible, pitted with gaps and omissions, too compressed, even at their most lucid, for the most expert mathematician to unravel. He had deliberately avoided making a formal summary or any kind of fair copy. His secret would leave Germany with him. In his head. To-morrow. Only pain could prise it from him; and now he was free to leave the country where pain was threatened. Tomorrow. "You know how ingenious they can be when they try." Tonight.

Tonight? But before he went he must say good-bye to his friends on the hill. He had been much in their company; there was no knowing when they would meet again; he must do the proper thing, he must bid them to dinner and drink their health. Unwise to linger? Let it be that very evening, then, and after dinner he would catch the night train to Hamburg and the early morning flight on from there.

He telephoned Fielding Gray's office in the barracks, was told by his Sergeant-Major that Fielding was out, and tried Lieutenant Motley's Medical Inspection Centre. Yes, Mick would be delighted to "beat up the boys" for Daniel's farewell dinner, sad it was so sudden, what would they do without him, just one thing, old dear, this evening wouldn't be any good because there was a night training scheme. Daniel hesitated. Tomorrow then? Yes, Mick couldn't see any reason why not, he'd tell the boys at lunch time, he'd ring back if there was a hitch. Eight o'clock at the Alte Krone? Prima, prima, and now here was a lance-corporal cook with a rupture and advanced impetigo.

A day lost. But did it really matter? He was free—legally free—to leave Göttingen when he chose. The devilish thing about his previous detention had been that "they" had contrived to make use of official sanctions. Now he was officially released, and if there should be the slightest reason, during the next thirty-six hours, to anticipate being molested, he would seek official protection. Besides, if he went off too quickly, Earle and his colleagues would think that he was panicking because he had something to hide; but if he hung about a bit, he would be behaving consonantly with the attitude which he had always tried to maintain, that he had nothing to tell and therefore nothing to fear. So he would spend this afternoon and this evening tidying up his room in the University building and saying good-bye to von Bremke, tomorrow he would take a last long walk in the country for old times' sake, and after that he would dine his friends and catch the midnight train. A good way of ringing down the curtain. This settled, he left his lodgings, stopped at a travel agency to book his seat on the flight from Hamburg (as he had supposed, there was nothing at a suitable time from Hannover), stopped at the Alte Krone to book a table for six at eight p.m. the next day, and went on to a friendly Gasthaus for a lunch of assorted sausage and beer.

". . . And so you're leaving us, Herr Dominus?"

"Yes, Herr Doktor. Tomorrow night."

Von Bremke produced a clean handkerchief, pursed his lips, and wiped them carefully.

"You would be free to dine with me at my home before you go? This evening?"

"As it happens, yes. But—"

"—Very well, then. Here is my address."

He handed Daniel a card.

"But Herr Doktor. Your wife. You said—"

"—My wife is dead, Herr Dominus. You will be doing a lonely man a kindness. My hour is seven."

When he left von Bremke, Daniel went to his own room. There was little enough to do there. The filing cabinet was empty save for a few discarded and useless notes. He went through the drawers of his desk and found nothing of interest except a forgotten request from Robert Constable, which had been addressed to him c/o the University, to give an approximate date for his return. This he could now answer in person quite soon enough. There was nothing to keep him. He stood up and waved farewell to Archimedes. Earle Restarick came in.

"Well?" Earle Restarick said.

"I'm off . . . in a day or so."

"Nothing to tell us?"

"There never was anything. And now I'm free to go ..."

"I suppose so. Care to have dinner? For old times' sake. Tonight?"

"I'm engaged."

"Tomorrow?"

"Engaged."

"The next night?"

"I shan't be here."

"I suppose not," Earle Restarick said. "Well, remember this, Danny. I *did* like you when you thought I did. Those weeks in the spring ..." He went towards the door. "You coming now? We could take a little walk."

"Sorry," Daniel lied, with an easiness which, even a few weeks before, would have appalled him : "I've got some more stuff to clear up in here."

Ten minutes later, while Daniel was looking at Archimedes to pass the time until Restarick should be well off the premises, Leonard Percival came in. Apart from their brief conversation on the telephone, this was the first Daniel had seen or heard of him since the dinner with Pappenheim in the deserted mess.

"Long time no see," Percival said. "So you're off?"

"Tomorrow night."

"And you weren't even going to say good-bye?"

"Our brief acquaintance hardly required it."

"Perhaps not. Who," said Percival pointing at Archimedes, "is your friend?"

Daniel told him.

"I remember. Displacement of liquids. Killed by soldiers while working out a problem in the sand. Which reminds me. You can't really imagine," said Percival sadly, "that they're going to let you disappear just like that?"

"They've no way of keeping me."

"I grant you they've had a spot of bad luck. No one could have known that Captain Fix-it, M.P., would come along. But after all, they're bound to have a few more nasty little tricks ready to try."

"What makes you think so?"

"Word gets around in my profession. And after a time you get to know the other fellow's style. This last stunt was typical. Typical of clever but retarded minds with strong romantic impulses aggravated by schizoid tendencies. All fascists suffer from a basic fantasy. They see themselves as knights of the round table. Swords and armour. They have ludicrous ceremonies and they swear blood-curdling oathes. They're like a gang of children... but you know how *persistent* children can be."

"You all seem like children to me. And now that Nanny's restored order, I'm going to leave the nursery and return to adult company."

"You're making a silly mistake, Mond. You may find it difficult to take Pappenheim very seriously, but he understands the issues, he doesn't wallow about in fantasy, and by and large he wants what is right."

"In your opinion. But just whom do you represent?" Daniel said. "And how did you get into this anyway?"

"Have I told you about my uncle Rupert? An interesting man with influence in the most peculiar places. He got me into this, but just what he got me into I'm not at liberty to say. All you need to know, Mond, is that Pappenheim and I are (a) 'goodies' and (b) sane. The other lot are (a) 'baddies' and (b) as mad as dervishes, and they'll stop at nothing to get what they want out of you. So I'm giving you a last chance: tell us what you've discovered here and then let us get you out of Germany. Because you won't get out on your own."

"There you are, you see. You're as mad as they are: you keep insisting that I've got something to tell."

"I *know* you have. It's not just what those librarians have told us— Yes, yes, yes," he said as Daniel opened his mouth, "we've used exactly the same sources as the other side. It's a recognised licence in the profession, one which we often adopt, by common consent, to save time. But I'm not going on what those librarians say. They can't know much. I'm going by the *the look on your face*. On the few occasions I've met you, Mond, I've looked very carefully, through my very powerful glasses"—he tilted them so that they flashed straight into Daniel's eyes—"into your moody, sensitive, intellectual face. And now I'd stake ten years' pay that there's something behind that face, something that's given you a most unpleasant shock and which Pappenheim and myself and the very sane interests we represent want to hear about with no more ado."

"I don't give a damn," said Daniel, "for you or Pappenheim or the sane interests you represent or the psychopaths with whom you compete. I'm a free man with a British passport, I'm leaving for England tomorrow night, and if anyone lifts a finger to stop me, I shall yell for the police."

Leonard Percival sighed.

"All right," he said. "I wish you and your British passport the best of British luck."

". . . So you see," von Bremke said, "I was so much looking forward to your arrival in Göttingen. I had hoped to know you well, to be of help perhaps. To talk, from time to time, of England, of which I have good memories. But just before you came my wife's illness was found to be other than we had hoped, and I was much preoccupied. And now it is too late."

They were sitting in von Bremke's modest but pleasant garden just outside the town, in a summer-house, to which an elderly and uniformed maid, who had served the indifferent dinner, now brought coffee, a candle and three kinds of liqueur on a big brass tray. Von Bremke thanked and dismissed her very formally, then started to pour the coffee.

"Now you are going," he said, "and it is too late."

"I'm so sorry about your wife."

Von Bremke shrugged.

"Kümmel, cointreau or aurum?"

"Aurum?"

"An Italian Liqueur made of oranges. You should try it if you have never done so. It has a most beautiful colour. That is why it is here. My wife loved the colour."

He poured. Daniel examined the colour in the light of the candle, sniffed, sipped and nodded politely. It looked and tasted like an inferior curaçao.

"My wife," said von Bremke, "died of the same disease as Professor Dortmund. It is to talk of him that I have asked you here tonight."

God, thought Daniel, shall I never hear the last of him? Then, be patient, he told himself : be kind to this sad old man. Only another twenty-four hours or so, and you'll be on your way. Listen to von Bremke and part friends.

"The Dortmund papers," von Bremke was saying, "were my first failure. Until then I had enjoyed every success and might have looked for the highest esteem of all. But when I set my hand to the Dortmund papers, I found that they were in a class which I could never enter. I was . . . second-rate."

"Just unlucky?"

"Second-rate. But of course I refused to realise this at the time. I insisted for many years that because the papers meant nothing to me they could mean nothing to anyone. Before the war, and again in 1944 when they sent people here to enquire, I insisted that the papers were the product of a disordered mind. I even said this to you some weeks ago."

"I remember."

"That was because I was jealous," said von Bremke sedately. 'You had solved part of the problem, and I was jealous, and so I told you that the rest would just be madness distilled from pain. Yet even as I told you, I knew that this was not true. For as I watched my wife die, there was no madness. She remained very clear. And anyhow I knew, I had always really known, that Dortmund's illness had not affected his work. Rather, it was the other way. His work, what he found, had hastened his illness."

Von Bremke lit a small cheroot and poured himself the last of the aurum.

"And so now I ask myself," he went on, "what is it that you have found? I am no longer jealous, I am simply curious. Would you care to gratify a lonely and curious old man, Herr Dominus? After all, I too have worked at this, so that we are partners, in a way. I should think it a great kindness if you would tell me what I failed to find."

"There is . . . nothing," said Daniel miserably.

"I cannot believe you. Whenever I have seen you lately, you have had an . . . excitement . . . about you, such as does not belong to men who find nothing."

"Anxiety, that's all."

"Yes, but also fulfilment. Oh, I quite understand, Herr Dominus, that you would not wish to tell me the details of your work. But it would give me great pleasure to know, very roughly, what you found at the end of it."

Just for a moment, Daniel wavered. Be kind, he said to himself : part friends. What harm can it do if I give him a very broad idea? He could never learn how to *use* the method; even if I told him what it was for, he could never work through the intricate steps by which I came at it. He does not even know how to read Dortmund's notation. And yet, Daniel thought, there is something not quite right here. Von Bremke is playing on my sympathies, exploiting his own loneliness and bereavement, in a way that I should not have expected and which degrades his dignity. If he can bring himself to do that . . . And besides, if once he was told the conclusion, he might, just might, be able to work back from it, piece the method together, solve the notation. Better not risk it; better fob him (politely) off.

"There are great uncertainties," Daniel said. "When I get back to Cambridge, when I've had time to check and confirm, then I will write to you."

"I see," said von Bremke coolly. "You are leaving Göttingen, leaving the papers, before your work is properly confirmed. Unwise, Herr Dominus; unsound."

Daniel stiffened. He had laid himself open to this imputation, he knew, but it was still an affront to his professional pride. He was on the point of justifying himself, then pulled back; vanity was the oldest trap of all.

"There is no more, Herr Doktor, to be said."

"Yes, there is. One thing. Please do not be angry with me, and please do not think I am angry with you, for withholding confidence."

Good. They would part friends after all.

"But do one favour for me instead," von Bremke was saying. "Professor Dortmund was buried, by his request, in the mountains. But it is not far, and before you leave you should, I think, visit his grave. A gesture of respect, And besides," he said to the puzzled Daniel, "you will find something to interest you."

"An inscription? A statue perhaps?"

"Something to interest you. You will go?"

"If you ask it."

Why not? Part friends, humour the old man's whim, give an aim and end to tomorrow's expedition.

"The grave-ground in question is not so easy to find," von Bremke said, "but I have made a little map."

"Thank you . . . And now, Herr Doktor, if you'll excuse me. Tomorrow will be a long day. My very best thanks for all you have done."

"You have not finished your aurum."

Daniel drained the sticky liquid. When von Bremke was satisfied that the last drop was gone, he led his guest, in complete silence, to a door in the garden wall and bowed him into the suburban road outside.

Von Bremke's map had some instructions at the bottom. According to these, Daniel's best plan was to take a coach into the mountains as far as Goslar and thence a local bus to a hamlet called Erding. Prominent in Erding was the Gasthof Frühlingsgarten; here he must turn to the right and follow a road which after half a mile formed a T-junction with another and rather more important road. If Daniel turned left at the T-junction and walked for something under a mile, he would find the "grave-ground" which he sought lying at the end of a footpath which branched off the road to the right.

Since he had the whole day before him and since it was a delicious September morning, he decided to walk the five odd miles from Goslar to Erding. Though he still regarded von Bremke's request as somewhat peculiar, he was exceedingly glad he had come. It would be nice, he thought, to look back on a last day of tranquillity among the mountain forests. Although there would be other good things to recall about his sojourn in Germany, they were not very many, most of them having been cancelled out, as it were, by disagreeable events which had in some way stemmed from them. The splendid days he had spent with Earle in the spring—how could he remember these with pleasure when all the time Earle had been concealing such treacherous intent? Even the hours he had passed with Fielding and the Dragoons were tarnished by the memory, which had become more sickening as the occurrence receded and so could be seen in a proper perspective, of von Augsburg as he staggered to the ground, the blood bubbling through the fingers with which he clasped at his mangled throat. Von Augsburg (who would now, they said, recover) had probably deserved everything he got; but the welling blood, Fielding's knowing remark, the look of satisfaction on Glastonbury's face . . . these were associations which must leave an ugly blot on all memories of those concerned. All in all, Daniel thought to himself, this day in the mountains is perhaps the first and only day I have spent in Germany which has not been somehow contaminated.

And after all, was von Bremke's request so very odd? Was it not appropriate that he should pay his respects at the tomb of the man whose secret he had been probing all these months, whose secret he (and he alone) now shared? There was a bond here, however distasteful, which must be acknowledged. Besides, there was . . . "something to interest you". It might even be something spectacular; for von Bremke had not indicated the position of Dortmund's grave in respect to the rest, and it was therefore reasonable to suppose that it possessed some immediately visible, some unmistakable distinction.

But whatever this might be, it could wait a little. Daniel was hungry and thirsty after his walk; he decided to have an early lunch at the Frühlinsgarten before he completed his journey. After he had eaten, he spent some time enquiring, in his phrase-book German, what time he could get buses back to Goslar. At last it seemed tolerably plain that a bus left Erding at half past three and would arrive at Goslar in good time for him to catch another back to Göttingen at four o'clock. He could be back in his lodgings by seven at the latest, with ample leisure to bath and finish off his packing before he met Fielding and the rest at eight. Having thus established his line of retreat (a phrase and a conception which he owed to Fielding), he walked slowly through the high afternoon to the T-junction. It was now just before two: an hour, say, for the walk to the graveyard and back, half an hour, more than long enough, to admire the Dortmund monument and indulge in suitable reflections.

When he had turned left, in obedience to von Bremke's instructions, at the T-junction, he found that the road on which he now was led along the bottom of a valley, the two sides of which were rapidly closing in. By the time he had walked half a mile further, the fir-crowded slopes were so near on either side that as soon as one set a foot off the road, one must start to ascend. Presumably the footpath he was looking for led up to a cemetery set in a clearing on the right-hand slope—a clearing, then, which must surely be visible at any minute now. But as he walked on down the road he scanned the slope ahead in vain. Another quarter of a mile: still nothing. Another furlong. Of course, the trees were very thick . . . and here at last, on the right, was his footpath; it must be, though track would have been a better description. There was something familiar about it, and as he climbed he remembered : he had come this way before but much quicker, which explained why he hadn't spotted it sooner. When the slope grew suddenly steeper, he was certain. In a minute at most he would breast a little ridge and be looking down from a sandy bank, down into the "Warlocks' Grotto".

So this was it. This was what von Bremke, who had never used the word cemetery, had meant when he spoke of Dortmund's "grave-ground". A grave-ground with one grave: the slab of stone in the centre. Well, and why not? If Dortmund wanted to be buried up here, and if the authorities had allowed it, who was Daniel to complain? He walked down to the centre of the bowl and stood over the stone. Somewhere away in the woods a dog barked and others answered it. "Something to interest you." Just the setting? Or the eccentricity of Dortmund's choice? Or was there something inscribed here, some lapidary pronouncement on human vanity which von Bremke had thought would be to Daniel's taste? But there was nothing. Nothing to be seen on the rough surface of the stone, either on top or along the sides. More barking, nearer now. The Germans, he had heard, were keen huntsmen, with elaborate codes and ceremonials. What did one hunt in September? Wild boar? Daniel thought not. Hare, things like that? What was it to him? He would sit here, on the soft pine-needles by Dortmund's tomb, for ten

minutes, and then walk back for his bus. But was it Dortmund's tomb? or just a joke of von Bremke's? The joke
would have no point; but if it was a grave there must be
some mark. He looked again. Nothing on top. Or on either
of the longer sides . . . but *here*, at the further end from the
entrance to the grotto, just above the carpet of pine-needles,
a tiny Maltese cross; and underneath—scrape away the pine-
needles, how mournful that barking was—carved in small,
very plain letters, *Dormiat Dortmundus:* Let Dortmund
Sleep.

Appropriate and even dignified (despite the pun), but
hardly worth a long expedition. Not that he was sorry he had
come. How interested Trooper Lamb would be to know what
was in the grotto he had named. Those dogs couldn't be more
than a few hundred yards away. But he wouldn't be seeing
Lamb again, he supposed, so he must remember to ask Fielding to tell him. Funny, the barking (baying?) seemed to be
coming from all round. Trees made for very odd acoustics.
Why a Maltese cross? Hadn't someone once told him they
were unlucky? Something to do with the Knights Hospitaller
and their practice of black magic? But wasn't that the
Templars? Witch-craft and sodomy. Something in Spencer
about it: "There whilom wont the Templar Knights to bide,
Till they decayed through pride." He had better get up and
go before he fell asleep. Like Dortmund. Dormiat Danielus.
Let Daniel Sleep . . .

His head nodded, he dozed, snored loudly and woke himself up. This really wouldn't do. Slowly he rose to his feet,
shook his head, brushed some pine-needles off his trousers,
started towards the entrance to the grotto. A man standing
there, a man dressed in green, with a dog. A tree. Then
another man, another dog, another . . . He turned his head
to look round the grotto. Filling every gap in the trees was a
man in green, green jacket and kind of green plus-fours, and
with every man a dog, the man standing, the dog sitting,
tongue out, panting, otherwise silent, looking at Daniel.

Hunting wild boar? No: hunting filthy, Jewish, homosexual pig.

"A reminder, Daniel," said one of the green men in the voice of Earle Restarick. "A reminder that you can't get away from us. If you try to leave Göttingen tonight, we shall stop you. We shall hunt you down. For the rest, we're giving you another week. Seven days from today I shall come to you and it will be time for you to tell us what you know. Now, come up here beside me."

Daniel climbed the bank to Restarick's side. The green man at the entrance to the grotto (grave-ground) opened a satchel and produced something furry, which he set on the down-slope of the bank. It scampered down to Dortmund's stone and sat there, sniffing, scratching, whimpering, giving an occasional furtive glance from side to side. Trapped. There was a high whistle. The dogs bounded down the bank; the hare hopped up on to the stone slab, sat there, for perhaps a third of a second, in a begging posture, and was then engulfed.

"They're very hungry," Earle explained with a seraphic smile, "but very well disciplined."

There was another whistle in a slightly lower key. Each dog scrambled back to its master. On Dortmund's grave the half-eaten hare, still just alive, twitched its legless rump and screamed. Earle Restarick turned, and within ten seconds every man and every dog had vanished into the trees.

PART VI
INTERLUDE

"**D**ANIEL, what on earth . . . ?"

The diners stared at him as he shambled across the floor of the Alte Krone.

"There was an animal in pain. I didn't know how to kill it, I could hardly bear to touch it, so at first I just sat there . . . trying to comfort it. I thought it would never die. So eventually I picked it up and . . . smashed . . . its . . . head on Dortmund's grave."

Daniel's guests exchanged glances.

"You were so late," said Fielding soothingly, "that we started without you."

"That's all right. I . . . I . . ."

"Hadn't you better go and wash before you eat," Fielding said. "There's rather a lot of blood."

But Daniel sat down in the empty chair at the end of the table and started to cry. Fielding nodded at the three subalterns (his subalterns now), and they rose to go. Mick Motley also rose.

"Please don't go. I'm so sorry about this. I . . . You must help me," he blubbered, "I'm not strong. Fielding . . . Julian . . . I'm not strong."

Fielding nodded again. The three subalterns, with very odd looks on their faces, trooped out of the restaurant.

"I'll be in the bar upstairs if needed," Mick Motley said. "Drink a little wine, Daniel. At once. Then eat."

After Daniel had drunk two glasses of hock, which reduced his outburst to a quiet snivel, Fielding ordered him some soup and his favourite dish of sole, and then said :

"If you're to leave tonight you'll have to eat up and get going. Done all your packing?"

"I'm not going."

"Oh?"

"I can't go. They ... showed me what they'd do if I tried. Until today I thought, this is a civilised country, with laws and policemen, nothing can keep me here now. God, how silly I was. Naïve. If I so much as set foot on Göttingen station, they'll ... they'll ..."

"Daniel. Drink that soup and then try to explain."

Daniel did so. By the time he had finished his sole, he had given Fielding an adequate if disordered account of his situation, and had once again implored his help.

"I must say," Fielding said, "this business of Leonard Percival is as odd as any of it. I always thought he was rather interesting for a Fusilier, but *this* ... You're sure he's not having you on?"

"I can't be sure of anything ever again. But he seems to know so much. He always knows what's happened, he always finds me when he wants me."

"I wonder whether he knows about this afternoon. Has it struck you," Fielding said, "that Percival and this other fellow, Restarick, have never—well—never clashed? It's almost as though they'd agreed between them that when one of them was doing his stuff the other should stay well clear."

Daniel shook his head stupidly.

"But that," said Fielding, "is by the way. The immediate point is this. If you think Percival's on the level, why not hand yourself over to him and Pappenheim and do what they ask?"

"No."

"They'd get you out. Your secret would be in good hands."

"No, Fielding. I can't trust them with it. Even if they're all they say they are, I can't trust them."

"Convince me, Daniel. Convince me that what you've found is so terrible that no one else must know it. Come on," said Fielding in a hard voice : "convince me."

"How can I ?"

"By telling me."

"But then—"

"—If you want my help, Daniel, you'll have to convince me that there's no other way. Percival and Pappenheim, you say, have offered to lay everything on for you. But no, that's not good enough for you, you've come to me instead. It's going to be very difficult for me, Daniel; but I'll do what I can—if, and only if, you first convince me that it's necessary. And the quickest way of doing that is to tell me what you know."

"How can I be sure you won't pass it on? After all, you're in the Army, you support that kind of people, you—"

"—For Christ's sake. The rest of them, Daniel, are asking you to hand all your stuff over and tell them mathematical chapter and verse. I'm not asking that. I couldn't understand it, for a start. I only want a rough idea of what's so terrible about it all. That couldn't help anyone much even if I did pass it on."

The same old argument, Daniel thought, as von Bremke had produced.

"It might," he said wearily. "They might be able to work back."

"Very well, Daniel. I swear to you," said Fielding in a strained voice, "on my honour as an officer and a gentleman, that nothing you tell me will go any further."

An oath. But what did it mean? Captain Detterling, when the question of perjury was raised, had brushed it aside as a "trivial difficulty". He had further remarked that in this regard Fielding Gray would do and say exactly what he was told. If this was the attitude which held, among Dragoons, of an oath to be given before a court, why should Daniel believe in the oath which Fielding had given him now? Between them all they had destroyed any basis for truth or trust. Something of this he now faltered out to Fielding.

"You are failing," Fielding said, "to draw an important distinction. To me an oath sworn on the bible, itself a pack of lies, means little or nothing, particularly if it conflicts with the interests of a friend. But the oath I have just sworn to you was sworn on what I live by. The honour of an officer, I dare say, is an outmoded notion, the honour of a gentleman even more so, and I can hardly expect you to take them very seriously. But they are what I live by, *all* that I *can* live by. Will you accept that?"

"What does it mean, this honour? In what does it consist?"

Fielding thought for some seconds.

"It means," he said at length, "that I can never betray someone if once I have undertaken care of him. As an officer, I am bound to undertake care of the soldiers entrusted to me. As a gentleman, I am bound to undertake care of those who have a just claim on me. But first I am entitled to make sure that the claim *is* just. That is why you must tell me what you know."

"Very well," said Daniel : "I'll tell you."

"Good. Now pay the bill for dinner and take me to where you live."

As soon as they reached Daniel's lodgings, Fielding said :

"How much luggage have you?"

"Two large suitcases."

"You must manage with one."

"My notes take up most of it."

"You must still manage with one. The rest of your stuff stays behind, as if you were just away for an odd night. So pack what you can into one suitcase, Daniel, and while you do so, pay me your journey money."

Daniel jammed a comb into a hair-brush, wrapped them

in newspaper, and started, rather jerkily, to put things into
a sponge-bag.

"You remember," he said, as if talking of a past almost
infinitely remote, "what I was telling you on that train to
Hannover? A particle makes a strand on its journey through
space. We follow this strand back, little by little zeta by zeta,
so that we never lose it. Where do we finally arrive?"

"At the . . . origin . . . of the particle?"

"Theoretically, yes. At the origin of the particle, and so
at the origin of matter. But this would take us too long. One
cannot go nosing back through all eternity. But, Fielding, we
can come at other secret places. We can come at the crisis
points of the particle's existence. Have you heard of the elec-
tronic leap?"

"When an electron changes orbit inside an atom?" .

"Yes. It happens suddenly and without warning, so that it
is impossible to make accurate observations. But suppose we
knew that it had happened recently. We could tag on, so
to speak, to this electron and follow it *back* to the precise
moment of the leap. Such a leap is completed almost instan-
taneously—during a zeta of the strand/particle's development. With this new method of Dortmund's we could analyse
the particular zeta. The crisis point. We could find out exactly what happened and how."

Daniel picked up a bedroom slipper.

"Now do you understand?" he said.

Fielding's face showed a sense of anti-climax.

"No. Clearly it would be very interesting. Terrible . . .
no."

"Fielding . . . A crisis point in a particle's existence often
indicates a crisis point in the atom to which that particle
belongs. It can mean a structural change in the atom itself.
And the atom's structure, remember, is normally bound together by the most tremendous forces."

"You mean," said Fielding, in a bored way, "that vast
amounts of energy are involved? That here we have the

means of making bigger and better atomic explosions? I always rather thought it would add up to that."

"Well, it doesn't," said Daniel crossly. If he was to tell what he knew, he wished to be heard with suitable respect and interest. "The technique for producing atomic explosions is comparatively crude. Let me remind you once more: by using the Dortmund method we shall be able to examine —what no one has been able to examine before—the precise behaviour of particles at the exact instant of fundamental change."

"What you're saying," said Fielding slowly, "is that the method which you've discovered—"

"—Which Dortmund discovered—"

"—That this method gives you a new insight into the forces which bind matter together."

"Bind the whole universe together. It's an absolutely basic concept. These are the forces which regulate the behaviour of matter, which see to it that everything holds together and proceeds according to the rules. If once you start tampering with these forces, you are tampering with the foundation of existence. What does the expression 'chain reaction' mean to you?"

"That a single atomic explosion might set off others, and these in turn—"

"—Exactly. As things are now, this could never happen, because the elementary explosions which we're capable of producing, and these only from a very special kind of atom, do not affect the stability of other atoms. But if once we understood the inner forces which maintain this stability, if once there were exact examination of the way these operate, then sooner or later someone would discover how to undermine or divert them, and then to start off a chain reaction would no longer be impossible. Don't you see, Fielding? Nature's stability could be infiltrated, its basic and binding principle corrupted. There would *not* be bigger and better explosions, as you put it: there would be ... dissolution."

Daniel folded his pyjamas, put them on top of his dressing-gown, tried in vain to close his suitcase, and sat despairingly down on his bed.

"Let me." Fielding removed the dressing-gown and threw it on to the floor. There were two sharp clicks, and Daniel's packing was finished. "You really believe it could go as far as that?"

"People are mad enough for anything."

"I don't question that. I mean, do you really think that this knowledge could produce—well—this result?"

"In time, yes. Up till now scientists have been pottering about on the outer edge, but Dortmund's method could take them right to the heart of it all. It's a kind of magnifying glass, which would enable them to see, down to the last little detail all those vital things which so far they're only guessing about. What really happens, for example, when the electron 'jumps'. And from these they could learn the first and last secrets of all, Fielding—what is substance, what is the fundamental essence from which God—"

Fielding held up his hand as if to close the subject.

"When you asked me for help," he said, "what did you suppose I could do?"

"I don't know. I thought you might get hold of Captain Detterling. He's a friend of yours, he'd listen to you. And somehow I'd feel safe with him."

"You have a point. But it wouldn't do to draw attention to him. If we were to summon him here, they'd guess what we were up to before he was half an hour out of Baden Baden, and by the time he was here, you wouldn't be. Better, don't you think, to deliver you safely to him?"

"I don't follow."

"Ah, my dear, but you do. From now on you follow all the time."

"I don't—"

"—I'm now going to ring up for a taxi. In case anyone's listening, I shall tell the driver to take us to the station, but

in fact we shall go straight to the barracks. In my room is a
camp bed, all ready for use on Apocalypse (which, you may
remember, starts in three days' time) and very handy for
you to spend the night on. In the morning there will have
to be adjustments. They will not be entirely to your taste—"

"—I can't under—"

"—But they will guarantee your safety, which at the
moment is a more urgent problem than your comfort. And
in three days' time—"

"—Fielding. Do please try to make sense."

"I'm making the best of sense. Where's the telephone?"

"This is Squadron Sergeant-Major Bunce," Fielding said.

"How do you do?"

"Sir."

"And this is Squadron Corporal-Major Chead. He's our
equivalent of a Colour Sergeant."

"What's a Colour Sergeant?" Daniel said.

"Stores, sir—all that. Pleased to meet you."

"And Trooper Lamb you already know."

They were all in Fielding's office: the Sergeant-Major,
who was tall and very thin; the Corporal-Major, who was
tall and very fat; Trooper Lamb, whose acne was redder
than ever; Daniel, still rather bemused after a rough night
on Fielding's camp bed; and Fielding himself, who seemed
to be enjoying some deeply satisfactory private joke.

"Sit down, please, gentlemen . . . Now," Fielding said, in
the placid but slightly arch voice of one who is telling a child
a bed-time story, "my friend, Mr Mond, has to be got out
of Germany. For the next two days we must look after him
here in the barracks. Then we shall take him with us on
Apocalypse, and either hand him over to Captain Detterling
at Baden Baden—if we get near enough—or else make such
other arrangements as circumstance may suggest."

There was a puzzled silence.

"So Captain Detterling's in on this?" said the Corporal-Major eventually, in a tone half of affection and half of apprehension. "You never served under him, did you, Basil?" —this to Sergeant-Major Bunce.

"I've heard a bit about him," said Bunce gloomily.

Daniel had a feeling that Detterling's name in these circles, like that of Jupiter among the ancients, had weight rather than respectability.

"Captain Detterling," said Fielding firmly, "is not immediately in question."

"I can see that, Captain Fielding," said Bunce more gloomily than ever; "what I don't quite see is in what capacity your friend here is to accompany us."

Interesting, thought Daniel: he has very sensibly asked how but no one has thought to ask why.

"Mr Mond will travel in the Land Rover with Lamb and myself—acting as my servant."

"Time for a change, eh?" said the Corporal-Major, and laughed with unnecessary loudness.

"That will do, Tom," said Bunce. "What about your man Lewis, sir? Soldier-servant is all he's good for. There's nowhere else I can fit him in."

"Trooper Lewis," explained Fielding, "will be excused the manoeuvre by courtesy of the M.O. He is at this minute in the M.I. Room, where Dr Motley is diagnosing a mild case of shingles. Lewis will stay in barracks with the rear-guard. Mr Mond will take his place on Apocalypse—and take it to the extent of possessing his identity card. I've already given Lewis a certificate saying that this has been withdrawn from him for an administrative check, and here it is."

He placed a folded and filthy piece of paper on his desk.

"Does he look like me?" asked Daniel. "I mean the photograph?"

"The description fits quite well. That's all that matters."

"A private soldier's identity card," explained Corporal-Major Chead to Daniel, "does not have a photograph.

They'll get round to it one day, but just now only sergeants
and above have faces."

"The important thing at the moment," said the Sergeant-
Major bossily, "is that Mr Mond will have an official identity
if questioned. And questioned he may very well be, if
left alone for ten seconds, seeing as how there is a certain
delicacy in his appearance which is not consistent with his
role."

"I rely on the three of you to see to that," Fielding said.
"I want Mr Mond kept out of the Fusiliers' way—and that
means he'll have to be moved out of the Officers' Mess—
I want him accepted without comment by the squadron, and
I want him turned out as a passable Light Dragoon—and
a passable soldier-servant—by early Friday morning when we
leave for Apocalypse. Until then I don't want to see him at
all—I'm sorry, Daniel, but if you think you'll understand
why. Can you cope? Mr Bunce?"

"Whatever you say, sir," said the Sergeant-Major, with a
kind of constrained gaiety, as of a governess at the family
picnic.

"Corporal-Major?"

"At least he ain't got shingles," said Chead, and wheezed
with laughter.

"Trooper Lamb?"

"I can teach him to cook up the field rations and keep your
kit straight, sir. He'd better bunk-up with me in the spare
parts shed."

"Good idea."

Fielding rose from his desk. All except Daniel immediately
rose too.

"Lesson one, Mr Mond, sir," said the Sergeant-Major,
and heaved Daniel gently but firmly to his feet.

"Right," said the Corporal-Major in the squadron stores,
"Lamb here can nip down to the mess for your luggage, and

we'll start dressing you up a credit to the squadron. Mugger?"

A long, yellow face peered round a pile of unappetising blankets.

"Denim trousers, denim blouse, field-smock, gaiters, boots ammunition, and beret with badge."

There was a brief noise as of a burrowing dog, and Mugger was standing by Daniel with the items ordered.

"Who's this then?" Mugger said.

"Trooper Lewis."

"Don't look like Lewis to me."

"What's in a name?" said the Corporal-Major.

"Stoppages. That's what's in a name," said Mugger didactically. "If I put this lot down to Lewis, they'll stop him three quid, four and a tanner."

"Put it down to the Captain."

"Who's going to sign?"

"I am," said the Corporal-Major, and forged Fielding's signature immaculately on to Mugger's ledger. "Saves the Captain being bothered," he explained to Daniel. "Like to try this lot on?"

"I had rather hoped . . . cherry trousers?"

"Walking out only. And from what I 'eard there's no walking out in store for you."

"That is certainly true," Daniel said.

"Make the best of these then. Don't be shy. Mugger and me, we're married men. What about some char, Mugger?"

Mugger went behind a counter and came back ten seconds later with three enamel mugs, villainously chipped, full of a hot, sweet, oddly invigorating liquid.

"Tea-bags," Mugger said, "and nicely laced with issue rum. Made it off the Fusiliers on the night exercise. Swapped our empty jar for their full one. Their C.O. never lets 'em have a rum-ration, see," he said to Daniel, "in case they all lose what little sense they got. So they won't ever find out. Not until some long-nosed fucker from Brigade comes round with a dip-stick at the annual inspection. They'll find out then all right."

"You rotten sod, Mugger," said Tom Chead easily. And to Daniel, "Them boots all right?"

"A bit . . . unfriendly."

"Just have to wear them in, that's all. Let's see you in that beret."

"It does something for 'im," said Mugger, after they had explained that the badge should be worn over the left eye rather than the right.

"Yuss . . . Do you know," said Corporal-Major Chead to Daniel, "when we're fitting out a new recruit, when we put the old skull and coronet up on his bonce for the first time, do you know what we say? 'You can polish all you want, friend, but that skull will keep on grinning.' That's what we say."

Later on, Lamb took Daniel to have his hair cut by the squadron barber, who was a chirrupy and middle-aged little man called Geddes.

"Who's your friend, dear?" Geddes said to Lamb.

"New man for Squadron H.Q."

"Well, it's a real pleasure to have some hair to work on for a change. You see, dear," he said to Daniel as he settled him in the chair, "one takes a pride in one's work, but it's not very easy when there's no material, which in the Army there usually isn't. Not with Sergeant-Major Basil Bunce about— he sends the boys along for a chop if there's so much as a teeny-weeny whisker within three inches of anyone's lughole. But with you there's a lovely lot to come off."

Already the thick, black chunks were raining on to the floor.

"Might one ask, dear," said Geddes, "what your name is? I like to know the names of my clients."

"Trooper Lewis," said Lamb.

"Going to be rather *confusing*, isn't it, in Squadron H.Q.? I mean, this one having the same name as Captain Gray's batman?"

"Lewis the batman's gone sick. Shingles."

"Over-excitement, I wouldn't wonder. Fancy being batman to heavenly Captain Gray. Tidying his *things* and that ... Get a look at yourself in the mirror, dear," Geddes said to Daniel. "Lovely job, though I say it myself."

Though disconcerted to find that his neck was now naked as far up as the tops of his ears, Daniel was pleased to see that he looked much younger. More than this, he now looked pathetic and defenceless to a degree which, although he had always cultivated a meek demeanour, astonished even him. No one who now came across this shorn and shabby little figure in the ill-fitting denims would give it any attention beyond a glance of pity or contempt.

"If you've done admiring yourself," said Lamb, "we'll go and get some dinner."

Midday dinner in the Dragoons' section of the other ranks' cookhouse was a social event. Gossip was exchanged, plans for the evening mooted or confirmed, wagers struck. Everyone was there and everyone was in something of a hustle; it was therefore, as Daniel realised, an ideal opportunity for Lamb to perform an important part of his mission, which was to introduce Daniel into the Squadron at large without at the same time arousing curiosity.

"We'll sit over there," Lamb said. "Not right in the middle and not in a corner. When they see you with me, they'll take you for granted. Those that are near enough will ask a question or so, but no one'll come over specially."

"Then why not the corner? The fewer questions the better."

"We mustn't seem to be avoiding the blokes. They don't like a new man to push himself forward, but they don't like him to be stand-offish either. They expect him just to be there, like everybody else."

The event proved Lamb to be right. The two or three men who were already at the table at which they sat down nodded with friendly indifference. One said,

"Just in time for the Apocalypse lark, eh, mate?"

"Yes," said Daniel shyly.

"Where've you come from then?"

"Transferred from Regimental H.Q.," said Daniel, in accordance with Lamb's earlier instructions.

This provoked neither surprise nor comment. Daniel looked at the mess of Shepherd's Pie on his tin plate and resolutely began to eat.

"Sounds like one of them failed officer candidates," he heard someone whisper further along the table.

"Runty little bloke. Like a worried rat."

"Don't you worry about them," said Lamb softly, "but try to finish your grub. You're used to it by now, remember."

Since the grub was not as nasty as it looked, and since the morning's activities had given him quite an appetite, Daniel cleaned his plate off creditably enough.

"Good," said Lamb as they left the cookhouse. "Word 'll go round that there's a new lad arrived who's got an officer voice but failed for a commission. There's plenty of those about these days and you look the part—all brain and no muscle. Now then. At fourteen-fifteen hours we're due with the Sergeant-Major . . ."

"Come to attention, Mr Mond," the Sergeant-Major said, "when you enter my office. Heels together, stomach in, chin up. That's it. Now sit down please. From now on, sir, I shall address you as Trooper or Dragoon, since we may as well begin in the way we mean to go on.

"Well then, Trooper Lewis. The act of coming to attention before your superior implies formal recognition of his right to give orders and your readiness to obey them. Once you understand that, we shall agree very well. Indeed, once you understand what the formality signifies, the formality itself is dispensable. With intelligent men this is usually the case: only fools need to be constantly reminded of their subordinate status, because only fools forget it. It follows that discipline is often soundest where it is apparently laxest, as in this Squadron. So do not be mislead by our laxity, Dragoon Lewis. It is only permitted because each one of us has an exact understanding of his place, or perhaps I should say his *area*: each one, that is, knows exactly how far he can go in any given direction. Within this limit we are allowed great freedom of manners and procedure. But once that limit is passed, Trooper Lewis, once a man forgets his place or his area, then our whole structure is threatened and we get very firm. Much firmer than regiments which employ a stricter discipline in the normal course. I believe you've met Major Glastonbury, lately our Officer Commanding?"

"Yes."

" 'Yes, sir,' or 'Yes, Sergeant-Major.' A courtesy, Trooper Lewis. Courtesy is always desirable if formality is not. The distinction is important . . . Well then. Major Glastonbury is famous among us for shooting a sentry who was asleep on active service. Few regiments these days would forgive such a proceeding. We accept if we hardly welcome it. *That sentry had finally forgotten his place*, and we realise, since we are allowed such freedom within our places, just how unforgivable that is."

"But this freedom is an illusion, Sergeant-Major. In return for minor privileges you've sacrificed the most important liberty of all—liberty of choice."

"If liberty of choice means a sentry is free to go to sleep and endanger his comrades, Trooper Lewis, then we're well rid of it."

"I mean that in all essential matters you are bound to defer."

"No. In all *military* matters we are bound, ultimately, to defer. How else would you run an Army?"

"Military matters like haircuts? I hear you're very keen on those."

"Tiresome but necessary. If senior officers from outside see long hair, they get suspicious, and then they come poking and prying and interfering. If you want to be left in peace in the Army, you must conform in the small things, Trooper Lewis. Just like if you're having it off regular with another man's wife, you keep your fly buttoned as long as he's still in the house."

"All right. But my complaint is that you leave no area of moral choice."

"In private affairs we leave morals pretty much to the soldier concerned."

"But if a moral conviction conflicts with a military decision?"

"A political attitude, Mr M——Dragoon Lewis, if I may say so. If you're sitting in an armchair sticking flags in a map of campaign, you can afford moral convictions. If you're lying in a ditch dodging bullets, you cannot. Because bullets, Trooper Lewis, don't share your moral delicacy ... even supposing you have it, which most of us don't."

"You're evading the issue, Sergeant-Major."

"I don't need you to tell me that, Trooper Lewis, but I'm too busy just now to say any more. Now then. Captain Fielding says we get you out. I don't ask why, because that would be beyond my place. It's either private or it's hush-hush, and so to know about it is beyond my place. What I do, Trooper Lewis, is help to get you out. While you are being got out, your place is that of a soldier-servant. You wait on the Captain, as you will be shown how by Trooper Lamb, you address all your military superiors—which in your case means every living soldier, Trooper Lewis—with courtesy, and you do just what they ask of you, though it'll be mostly me and the Corporal-Major that does the asking. That's your place,

Trooper Lewis, and if you stay inside it you will receive nothing but kindness and respect. Move out of it, and God help you."

Later that afternoon Lamb introduced Daniel to the accommodation which they would share for the next two nights in the "spare parts shed". This was a large shack at the back of a hangar in the Motor Transport Lines. Since these latter were at the extreme upper limit of the barracks, the shack afforded its occupants, as Lamb remarked, a degree of privacy rare at his level in the military scale. It also afforded little enough space, being crammed with shelves and crates which contained anything from tiny screws by the thousand to large and jagged sections of armoured car; but Lamb had cleared a pleasant alcove for himself under a window with a view of the fields to the south-west, and he now found room to erect a camp bed for Daniel alongside his own. Other attractions, tucked away behind a kind of wardrobe in which hung a comprehensive selection of pistons and Lamb's dress uniform, were a basin with running cold water and a gas-ring. The former did for what Lamb called "ablutions and a pisser", the latter for the occasional "cuppa and fry-up". No need to go out for anything short of a shit. Lamb was very proud of being so self-contained.

"How come they let you live up here?" Daniel asked.

"Security of classified equipment. All this stuff's worth a packet, so someone's meant to watch it during after-duty hours."

"But surely you don't stay in every evening?"

"Well, it's all rather a fiddle really. That security business —the Corporal-Major thought it up. We're friendly, you see ... Anyway," he went on quickly, "it's cosy living here and I'm sorry we're not staying for the winter. There's a smashing stove the other side of those machine-gun brackets."

Winter-quarters, thought Daniel dreamily, remembering a

word from the grammar books. Snow piled outside the window, Lamb and the Corporal-Major drinking tea over the stove, one or other occasionally leaving the warm circle for a piss in the pisser and hurrying back . . . Yes, it would be cosy to be a Trooper with no worries, living among spare parts.

"Time for a few lessons," Lamb said, "before tea. I'm going to take that camp bed down again and show you how to put it up. Then I'll show you how to take care of the Captain's webbing and the rest. I stood in as batman when Lewis was last on leave, so I know all his little fads . . ."

That evening the Corporal-Major visited them in the shack, bringing a bottle of whisky.

"Came to see how you'd settled in," he said. "Get us a pot of char, Lambkin, and we'll spike it with a spot of this."

"Get the tea, Danny," said Lamb, "and show him how well you're learning."

To the accompaniment of muttering and giggling on the other side of the wardrobe, Daniel made the tea.

"Not bad, Dan. What do you say, corpy?"

"Not bad at all . . . So we're calling the Captain's friend by his Christian name, are we?"

"I'm just the batman," said Daniel. "The Sergeant-Major made that very plain. So what else should he call me?"

"Aye." Chead looked hard at Daniel. "Bit of a rum do, eh?"

"Very rum, Corporal-Major. I'm afraid I can't tell you."

"No more I should have asked. If we were meant to know, we'd have been told."

"You accept that? You're happy for information to be given or withheld as someone else sees fit?"

"Suits your book just now, don't it?"

"Yes. But I'm surprised you take it so easily."

"Well now," said Tom Chead meditatively. "You remem-

ber we were talking about Captain Detterling this morning,
and I said as how I'd served under him?"

"I remember."

"Well, Captain Detterling had a word he often used—
Necessity. It was an old Greek idea, he used to say. Necessity
was what was there and couldn't be changed, see, or not by
the like of us. It was a kind of framework for things, like
Standing Orders. So the best way to go on, Captain Detterling used to say, was to accept these orders, this Necessity,
without kicking up a fuss, and then wait and see what happened next. He was quite right, you know. Never a dull
moment, so long as you can wonder what will happen next;
and the less you know about it first, the more fun it is when
it happens."

"But you surely miss a lot of ... fun ... by not knowing
why?"

" 'Why' is something for officers to know, Danny boy,"
the Corporal-Major said. "It gives 'em ulcers and break-
downs and Field Marshals' batons. I'll settle for my stripes
and a good laugh, now and again, at other people's expense.
And now I'll be getting home"—he glanced regretfully at
Lamb and then at Daniel— "to my old woman. She's a bit
of Necessity if ever there was."

The next afternoon it was decided that Daniel was ready to
undergo a test. He was to go along to the Guard Room by
the main gate, report to the Fusilier Guard Commander that
the spare parts shed would be unoccupied during Apocalypse,
request him to make a note of this for the information of the
officer commanding the rear-guard, and then return to Lamb
in the M.T. Lines.

"But," said Daniel, "Fielding—Captain Gray said I was to
keep away from the Fusiliers."

"Yes. But the Sergeant-Major says we've got to make sure
you can cope with 'em if you need to. Now don't forget: any-

thing with badges on its shoulders—salute it like I've shown you."

As Daniel walked down to the Guard Room, he considered the problem of the only Fusilier who really concerned him, Lieutenant Leonard Percival. So far there had been no sign of him; but then so far Daniel had been kept very close. Once given the conditions which would prevail during Apocalypse, the constant liaison and interaction which their role surely required between Fusiliers and Dragoons, it seemed unlikely that he could avoid Percival's notice all the way from Göttingen to Baden Baden. And if Percival spotted him, what would he do? Expose him as a fraud? Threaten such exposure unless Daniel agreed to accept his protection and his terms? And for that matter, where did Percival, to say nothing of Earle Restarick, think he had got to now? They must both have been trying to track him down since his disappearance from his lodgings. In the barracks, he was probably safe from Restarick, even if the latter knew he was there; but he was not safe from Percival, who was officially qualified, who had an official duty, to denounce him. Furthermore, once on the march he would be safe from neither. An unexpected break-down perhaps (he imagined a remote cross-road with a little shrine), or a rendezvous at night, Michael Lamb and himself waiting hour after hour for Fielding, and then at last the baying of the hounds through the forest . . . But surely Fielding would have given thought to all this. No point in anticipating difficulties. Wait and see, like the Corporal-Major said : it was more "fun" that way.

He paused in the doorway of the Guard Room, came creditably to attention, concentrated on the protocol which, Lamb had instructed him, was required in dealing with Fusiliers.

"Leave to fall in, Sergeant, please."

"Yes please, Dragoon."

"With your permission, I have a message to deliver."

"Please state your message."

Daniel did do.

"Thank you, Dragoon. Fall out, please."

Daniel turned smartly to the right and marched out.

"Come here," bellowed a voice : "that Dragoon."

Dimly, Daniel was conscious that a car had passed him and gone out through the gate.

"Failing to salute the commanding officer in his car," howled the voice.

A wrist with the royal arms on it brandished what looked like an enormous pair of wooden scissors under Daniel's nose.

"Sergeant of the Guard," roared the voice.

"SIR."

"Escort at the double to put this idle Dragoon in a cell."

"Excuse me, Regimental Sergeant-Major Holeworthy," said Basil Bunce's voice from somewhere over to the right, while Daniel, remembering Lamb's instructions for emergencies, stood stock still and stared straight ahead.

"*Well*, Squadron Sergeant-Major Bunce?"

"I witnessed the incident, Mr Holeworthy. The colonel's car had almost passed the Guard Room as this man stepped out of the door. He couldn't possibly have seen it in time."

"Is that what you saw, Mr Bunce?"

"It is, Mr Holeworthy."

"Well, I saw something different, Mr Bunce. I saw this sloppy idle soldier wandering out of the Guard Room like a mental deficient in the family way. *I* saw—"

"—I'll request you not to insult my men, Mr Holeworthy."

"This thing isn't a man, Mr Bunce. It's a heap. Look at its dress. Those denims would be a disgrace to a Jewish Armenian nigger boy digging shit-holes in the Corps of Pioneers."

The Sergeant of the Guard and two men with rifles formed up facing Daniel.

"Escort . . . Two paces forward . . . *March*."

"If you insist, Mr Holeworthy—"

"—I do insist, Mr Bunce—"

"—Escort ... A-bout ... *Turn*—"

"—Then I think you should know, Mr Holeworthy—"

"—Prisoner and escort .... double ... *march*—"

"—That this man is certainly a Jew, though not, I think, Armenian or Negroid."

"Prisoner-and-escort-halt," rapped the R.S.M. "A Jew, are you?"

"SIR," bellowed Daniel.

"Then I don't suppose you could know any better. Escort-fall-out-and-double-awayeee. Now, you from the Dragoons. Repeat after me. Next-time-I-see-the-Commanding-Officer-in-his-car ..."

"Next-time-I-see-the-Commanding-Officer-in-his-car ..."

"I'll-salute-so-smartly-that-I-rupture-myself."

"I'll-salute-so-smartly-that-I-rupture-myself."

"Rupture-myself what?"

"Rupture-myself SIR."

"That's better. Good afternoon, Mr Bunce, and thank you for tending your explanation."

"Good afternoon, Mr Holeworthy, and thank you for respecting it. You come along with me," said Bunce to Daniel; "we don't want any more trouble."

They marched away at a stiffish pace, Daniel finding the same embarrassment in keeping step as he did when he walked with Jacquiz Helmut.

"I'm sorry to have been a nuisance," he said.

"Not your fault, just bad luck. I was afraid something like that might happen, so I followed you in case."

"Thank you."

"We shouldn't really have risked it," the Sergeant-Major went on, "but we had to give you some practice in taking care of yourself. I thought you came through it very well."

"It's just a matter of knowing the idiom."

"Like I've told you before," said Basil Bunce, "it's the small things that count. Saluting and saying 'sir'—if you only do that at the right time you can plot a mutiny and no one the wiser. Etiquette, that's what you've got to watch. And that's why he let you off—he'd gone further than etiquette allowed, and he knew it, and he let you off."

"Just how far, Sergeant-Major, does etiquette allow him to go?"

"As far as he likes short of personal malice. And he's not a malicious man. Just stupid."

"What would have happened," said Daniel, "if I'd been put in a cell?"

"If they hadn't rumbled there was something wrong about you, you'd have been kept there for two hours, then released under open arrest, with a charge laid against you for neglect to the prejudice of good order and military discipline. Later on, you'd have been brought up in front of Captain Gray. Since the Fusilier R.S.M. would have been witness against you, etiquette would have required Captain Gray to punish you severely. Seven days confined to barracks, I'd expect."

"How can one be confined to barracks on Apocalypse?"

"Your punishment would have been postponed until you got back."

"I'm not coming back, Sergeant-Major."

"No more you are," said Bunce; "I almost forgot."

That evening Michael Lamb took Daniel to the NAAFI. They drank very thin beer and listened to a jangling piano on which someone was playing, over and over again, the theme tune from The Third Man. When Daniel went to buy his round of beers, the manageress, a young and beautiful German, told him that she could not accept Deutsch-marks. You had to pay in something called, apparently, "Baffs".

"British Army Field Vouchers," Lamb explained, "what they pay us with. Sort of joke money, like you have for Monopoly. No use except in Army canteens."

"Can't you get paid in marks?"

"We can, but they don't like it, so they make us give two

weeks' notice. It's policy, see? They want us to spend our money in barracks, not down in the town."

"I'm afraid I can't get you a drink."

"I'll get us all the drink we want, Danny. Your turn when we're out on Apocalypse. Okay?"

"Okay."

So Michael Lamb bought more thin beer, and the piano jangled (Porgy and Bess now), and the air became vile with cheap cigarettes and sweaty denims. And Daniel remembered reading somewhere that a soldier's real home always remained his regiment (even long after he had grown old and left it), and he thought to himself that he was beginning to understand why. There was peace of mind here, that was what it amounted to. Even the foul-mouthed R.S.M. Holeworthy, so far from destroying it, somehow guaranteed it. He might shout you into the ground, he might put you in a cell or even in irons, but in the last resort he was there to protect you. No stranger would come through the barrack gate without R.S.M. Holeworthy knew his business; no one would come knocking on your door at night without *his* say-so first. Such a man (not malicious, just stupid) and others like him meant safety here.

Safety here. (Home, home on the range, the soldiers sang.) But tomorrow it would be different. Tomorrow they would leave the NAAFI and the spare parts shed and head out into the open. Would the soldiers carry their peace of mind, their sense of home, with them wherever they went? Would Holeworthy and Bunce continue to guard them, and Daniel with them, against the world? Or would they all, once out of the barrack gate, be raw and vulnerable, at the mercy of the intruder in the dark? Nothing the like of him could do about it, as Corporal-Major Chead might have said: wait and see.

PART VII
APOCALYPSE

A T A STEADY twenty-five miles an hour the column of Dragoons made its way down lanes and side-roads, proceeding west from Göttingen towards the spa-town of Bad Salzuflen.

"It's ten miles odd from Bielefeld," Fielding had explained to the assembled Troop Commanders before they left, "Bielefeld being the centre of the Assembly Area. We shall be sitting just outside Bad Salzuflen for about twenty-four hours, while they make the final preparations before ordering the advance."

The Land Rover which contained Fielding, Lamb and Daniel was followed by a large truck which contained the Corporal-Major in the front and Mugger with miscellaneous stores in the back. Much of these consisted of emergency field rations, since the Dragoons would sometimes be well in advance of the Fusiliers on whom they were theoretically dependent for supplies of food. Behind the truck came twelve armoured cars (three Troops of four), and behind these another truck which carried a technical Sergeant and a selection of tools and spare parts. Followed yet another armoured car—the one in which Fielding would ride when actually leading his Squadron in battle. Last of all came a second Land Rover in which were Sergeant-Major Bunce, his driver and also Trooper Geddes the barber, the latter's function in current proceedings being, to Daniel at least, obscure. To this Land Rover was attached a large trailer which contained "administrative stores" in the form, preponderantly, of drink.

"As you all know," Fielding had said to the "O" Group, "This is different from our usual order of battle, but it's what they think best for us in the courier role. I've no real complaint, except about one defect which has become more and more obvious in exercises over the last month. They refuse to allow us our own decontamination unit. This means, among other things, that we must draw our anti-radiation suits from the Fusiliers, which could cause serious muddle and delay."

He says it as earnestly as if it were real, Daniel had thought as he stood listening with Lamb beside the Land Rover. He's enjoying the make-believe of death and devastation; part of him, just a small part, wishes that it *were* real. Perhaps a small part in all of us does. Chaos, anarchy, an end of responsibility and law . . . A new kind of freedom when the old kinds have grown so stale.

"Still, it's too late to bother about that. I've told them but they wouldn't listen. The upshot is that we shall be issued with our anti-radiation gear by the Fusiliers when, and only when, we have received orders to proceed to a contaminated area."

"Can't they dish the stuff out while we're waiting in Bad Salzuflen?" Julian James had said.

"No. It's still very much on the secret list and they don't want it paraded round one moment longer than is strictly necessary for training purposes . . . By the way, the Fusilier officer in charge of issuing it is Leonard Percival." For a split second Fielding's eye had caught Daniel's. "Try to be nice to him and then perhaps he won't keep us hanging about . . . Trooper Lewis "

"Yes, Fie— Sir?"

"Please go over and ask the Corporal-Major if he's happy about the emergency rations. If he's ready I think we all are. Any questions, gentlemen?"

And now, at eight o'clock on a blue morning which carried

a light bright chill of autumn, the column was winding through the woods and fields *en route* for its parody of war. Fielding, who had not seen Daniel for two days, had at first addressed him only with sparse and official briskness, possibly to hide embarrassment; but now that they were well under way, he was beginning to relax.

"What's Michael managed to teach you, Danny?" he asked.

"Most of the things which I shall need to know. But I'm still not too sure of myself with that field cooker. It has a malignant disposition."

"Not to worry. Whenever we can we shall eat in German pubs or restaurants."

"With official blessing?"

"Very much not. We're meant to imagine war-time conditions and live down to them. But as far as I'm concerned, since the whole thing's imaginary, the discomfort may as well be too."

"A sound philosophy of training?"

"A matter of personal taste. We're prepared to risk our necks but not to live like pigs."

"Funny," said Daniel. "When you were talking to them about decontamination units, you seemed to be treating it all quite solemnly. Yet now you're laughing at it."

"I was talking about a problem of logistics," Fielding said, "and I was taking it more or less solemnly because I'm interested in such problems. I am not interested in sleeping in a slit trench or eating hard-tack."

"But surely," Daniel insisted, "you're meant to be training yourself to do just that?"

"I find this ascetic strain in your character rather out of keeping, Daniel."

"You're evading the question."

"Pass me that map-case, would you? We shall not be popular if we get on the wrong route and tangle with other units."

The same technique, Daniel thought, as the Sergeant-Major had used the other day—pleading urgent official duties as a refuge when faced with disagreeable truths. To Lamb he said,

"I forgot to tell you, Michael. That Warlocks' Grotto of yours—there's a man buried there under the stone."

It was a measure of his confidence in his escape that he was now able to think of the Grotto without distress.

"I always knew that," said Lamb unexpectedly. "I saw the little cross."

"Oh?" said Fielding, looking up from his map. "You never mentioned it."

"I liked the place," said Lamb, "and I thought it might put you off going there."

"Why, Michael?"

"You don't like the dead, sir. I've seen the way you screw up your face—when we pass a cemetery or stop for a funeral."

"Now that," said Daniel, "is very interesting."

Fielding turned his head from where he sat in the co-driver's seat and looked back at Daniel.

"I find you rather trying this morning," he said. "You'll oblige me, both of you, by keeping your mouths shut unless first addressed by me."

By the time he had established his Squadron Headquarters in two adjoining suites of the Schwaghof, a commodious hotel four kilometres outside Bad Salzuflen, Fielding had recovered his good humour.

"Pity we're going to have such a short stay," he said.

"Even so, won't it cost rather a lot?"

"No. These rooms have been 'requisitioned'. The bill goes in to Divisional H.Q."

"Will they pay it?" Daniel asked.

"Normally not. But just now there's one of our chaps, Ivan

Blessington, doing A.D.C. to the General. He'll see it's taken care of—he'll pop it in with the General's expenses."

"So we're here by courtesy of the tax-payer?"

"Do stop grumbling, Daniel. If your conscience bothers you, you can put up a tent in the car park. Now, I'm going into Bielefield to find Ivan Blessington and get some advance gen. about what's going on."

Fielding went off with Michael Lamb. Julian James and Piers Bungay came in with the Sergeant-Major and started to pin an enormous map on the wall. There was a whistle from the car park underneath the window.

"Fusilier C.O. playing up on the wireless," came Trooper Geddes' fluting tones. "He wants to know our exact position, and he wants to talk to Captain Gray on the set."

Sergeant-Major Bunce stuck his head out of the window and said,

"Give him the map reference, and tell him that Captain Gray's been sent for by the General's A.D.C. Mr Bungay, as 2 i/c, is coming to the set."

"Must I, Sergeant-Major?"

"You must, sir."

Piers Bungay went crossly out. Julian lifted a telephone and started, in a thoughtful voice, to order luncheon—"a selection of cold delicacies for up to ten people"—and a case of hock. Daniel began to unpack Fielding's valise, this being what he was there for.

"I hope Piers won't say anything too silly on the set," said Julian when he had finished telephoning. "Where *are* we meant to be, by the way?"

"About a kilometre down the road, sir. Captain Fielding said that no one would notice the difference."

"They'll spot it when they're given the map reference. It'll be about six figures out."

"I think not, Mr Julian. Trooper Geddes has clear instructions about where we really are as opposed to where we are really, if you take my meaning."

"Jolly good, Sergeant-Major."

Daniel laid out Fielding's blue silk pyjamas. Four waiters arrived bearing a table covered with Julian's cold delicacies, a fifth brought in a case of hock, and a sixth a tray of glasses. The manager came beaming up behind and said that payment could be made in any currency, including whisky and coffee. Julian took him on one side. The Corporal-Major came in and without a word to anyone heaped a plate with the most delicate of the delicacies; then he joined Julian and the manager in the corner where they were busy muttering words like "cocoa", "blankets" and "parafin". Daniel, mystified, laid out Fielding's shaving things and helped himself to sour cream and red caviar. Piers Bungay returned from the wireless.

"Well, sir?" said the Sergeant-Major.

"He was really very awkward. First he said that if we were where we said we were, that is where we ought to be, then he should be able to see us from where he was, which he couldn't. So I said we'd taken great trouble with our camouflage, but somehow he didn't seem convinced. Then he dished out what he called Security Orders for Overnight Encampment. He said that no one was to have anything to drink; that Bad Salzuflen was out of bounds to all ranks and so were all German villages, hotels, restaurants and shops whatever; that there were to be no lights or fires after dusk, when everyone must go to bed anyway, except for a thirty per cent picket; and that everyone was to stand to in full equipment every two hours during the night. Do you think he could be going potty?"

"I don't think we need worry, sir. I doubt whether he'll have time to come bothering us."

"I wouldn't be too sure of that. He sounded jolly officious to me. After all, you know, we are technically under his command. And that's another thing. He wanted to know why Captain Gray had gone off without getting his permission."

"What did you say?"

"At that point I just gave up. I said he'd have to ask Captain Gray himself but that for the life of me I couldn't see it mattered."

"Unwise, sir?"

"He certainly seemed a bit put out, I must admit ... I say, some greedy pig has woughed all the smokers. Daniel, ring down for more smokers, there's a dear. One gets very hungry with this sort of rubbish going on."

Daniel rang down for more smoked salmon. The Corporal-Major put down his empty plate and went conspiratorially out with the manager. Jack Lamprey came in and said:

"The Fusilier Colonel's down in the car park. He's looking rather batey."

"I knew this would happen," Piers said. "Get rid of him, will you, Sergeant-Major? I really can't bear any more."

The Sergeant-Major drank a bumper of hock and went out. Looking down from the window, Daniel watched Mugger carrying an enormous crate of something straight into the hotel under the fascinated gaze of R.S.M. Holeworthy and the Fusilier Colonel, both of whom were draped round with so many items of military equipment that they looked like a pair of Christmas trees. Sergeant-Major Bunce, who now emerged unarmed save for a riding switch, had, by contrast, a somewhat dilettante air. Having saluted smartly, he murmured something into the Colonel's ear, whereupon, to Daniel's astonishment, the Colonel beckoned to Holeworthy and positively slunk away to his jeep. Thirty seconds later Mugger slopped out of the hotel entrance buttoning a large wad of money into his breast pocket, exchanged a friendly word with Bunce, and walked over to the stores truck, which the Corporal-Major was zestfully disembowelling.

"I hope," said Jack Lamprey who had now joined Daniel at the window, "that they're not overdoing it. During Broomstick they got careless and sold all my bedding. There are limits, as I had to remind them rather sharply."

"We shan't see *him* again for a bit," said the Sergeant-Major as he rejoined them.

"What did you tell him, Mr Bunce?"

"The simple truth, Mr Piers. The area which he allotted us in his orders is an open meadow with a mound in the middle of it. On top of the mound is a memorial notice saying that three hundred and thirty-nine political prisoners were shot and buried there on May 10th, 1944."

"How on earth did you know that?"

"I always carry that notice around with us, sir. It comes in handy if we don't fancy going where we're told."

After this, since there was plainly nothing to be done until Fielding got back from Bielefeld, the Sergeant-Major went to sleep while Daniel and the three subalterns made up a four at Bridge.

That evening, after Fielding had rung up to say that he was dining in Bielefeld and wouldn't be back till late, the Corporal-Major proposed to Daniel that they should run into Bad Salzuflen for a change of air and a bite of supper. Although Daniel was not sure how wise this would be in his predicament, his confidence had been so far restored in the last few days, and he was so heartily sick of the hotel and the three subalterns, that he accepted the invitation. After all, he thought, not much harm could come to anyone who was accompanied by Corporal-Major Chead.

The Ratskeller in Bad Salzuflen, to which they were conveyed (Mugger driving) in the stores truck, was heaving with soldiers of apparently every regiment in the world, Dragoons, however, being predominant among them. There were even, despite their Colonel's edict, a number of Fusiliers, these latter of a seasoned if not criminal appearance. The Corporal-Major, after surveying the crowd with genial distaste, selected a quiet table in a corner and studied the menu with ceremony. After they had all three ordered Russian Eggs to be followed by Ox-tail stewed in red wine, with a pricey hock and beer for Mugger who preferred it, the discussion turned on money. Mugger deposed that the takings for the day's sale of stores to the hotel manager were DM.512 Pf.20.

"And very handsome," said Tom Chead. "All gash kit? There won't be no trouble with the books?"

" 'Cept with those self-heating tins of soup. They're experimental, see? They was meant to be issued only when an officer said, and a signed report sent in about them when we got back."

"Mr Bungay's acting as second in command, so he's the man to do that. In return we'll put another twenty marks on his cut—poor little bugger's always short. By the way," said Chead, handing Daniel a ten mark note, "Here's yours."

"What for?"

"You was there when it was fixed up. We like to keep everyone happy."

"I shan't report you," Daniel said huffily, "if that's what you think."

"It's the principle of the thing, Danny. If you give everyone a cut, you make for a cosy feeling of loyalty all round. Sodality, Mr James calls it."

"I'd much sooner not—"

"—Take it and hold your tongue," said Mugger. "Responsible people like me and the Corporal-Major, we've got enough to worry about without you airing your morals. Now then, corpy. Distribution. Forty marks to Mr Julian James, who first got the manager talking—"

"—He won't want it. He's got plenty and he only does it for laughs."

"Sodality," said Daniel primly. "Make him take it."

"Quite right," opined Mugger. "Sixty marks to Mr Bungay as 2 i/c—that's without the extra twenty for this report he's got to write. Forty for Mr Lamprey, though he was no help, but we've got to keep him sweet after that balls-up with his bedding on Broomstick. Ten for Danny here, fifty for Basil Bunce, leaving two hundred and—"

"—Well, well," said a wheezy voice. "if it ain't my dear friend Mugger."

A diminutive Lance-Corporal of Fusiliers, who had a face like an intelligent herring's, was standing behind Mugger with a hand on both his shoulders.

"You great long thieving streak of luke-warm yellow piss," said the Lance-Corporal. "Where's our fucking rum?"

"I don't know to what you allude," Mugger said.

"That rum what you pinched on the night exercise. It took me over a year," said the Lance-Corporal, blinking his eyes at Daniel, "to make that jar of rum, being as how our mob are so close with it. And then up comes this bleeder on a dark night, talking as smooth as the serpent in the garden—"

"—I'll tell you what," said Tom Chead, "you're upsetting my digestive juices, that's what. We don't want none of your insolence, nor we don't want your rotten rum. So just move on, soldier, before I send for the management."

"Pardon me, my lord."

The Lance-Corporal gave a piercing whistle, and a row of Fusiliers appeared behind him, cutting off Daniel and his friends in their corner.

"Now then," the Lance-Corporal said. "No one puts it over us, not even Earl Hamilton's light-fingered, cherry-arsed Dragoons, nine-month bellies and all. We'll have that rum, or else."

"Baaah," went Mugger like a demented sheep; "baaaaah."

Four things then happened in quick succession. First, several Fusiliers, howling, battered Mugger's head with empty beer bottles; whereat a line of Dragoons rose like a wave from the centre of the room and crashed down on to the Fusiliers from the rear; a few seconds after which, thundering down the wide stairs from the streets with a furicano of whistles, came a mixed squad of British Military and German Civilian

Police; whereupon Fusiliers and Dragoons and all else present turned to make common cause against a common foe.

"Sweet Jesus Christ," said the Corporal-Major.

He picked up the prostrate Mugger, slung him over his shoulder, seized Daniel with his spare hand, and made for the swing doors which led to the kitchen, emitting a high and wavering "Ta-whit-ta-whoo" as he went. Several Dragoons instantly broke away from the central mêlée and followed. In five seconds flat they were all through the kitchen and out in a little yard which opened on to a back street.

"How many of our boys left in there?" called the Corporal-Major.

"Least six, corpy."

"They'll have to take their chance." But even as he said it three more men dashed out into the yard. "Form up into two ranks, the lot of you. You two, carry this poor bloody Mugger. Picket . . . Picket, *shun*. Right turn. Quick march."

Led by the Corporal-Major and followed by Mugger's stumbling bearers, the two files marched sedately down the side-street and across the square, at the far side of which they were halted at the entrance to another side-street, where Mugger had parked the stores lorry. This was now being watched over by a Sergeant of Military Police and four attendant red-caps.

"Right," said the Corporal-Major. "On the word dismiss, the picket will take a smart run to the right and mount the rear of the three tonner. Picket . . . dis-*miss*. Trooper Lewis, up front with me."

"What's this then?" said the red-cap Sergeant out of a brutal and broken-veined face.

"Town Picket from the 10th Sabre Squadron, Earl Hamilton's Light Dragoons. Thank you for watching our truck, Sergeant. You may fall out."

"Who are you telling to fall out?"

"I'm telling you to fall out." Tom Chead pointed to the

three stripes, surmounted by a crown, on his upper arm. "Corporal-Major they call me. Equivalent of a Colour Sergeant or Staff Sergeant, which is one up on you, matey, so many thanks for your kind enquiries and good night."

"Town Picket, you say," said the Sergeant without moving; "and what's that man being carried for?"

"Drunk. Which is what Town Pickets are for. Sweeping up drunks."

"No one told us you were mounting a picket."

"All aboard?" called Tom Chead, ignoring the Sergeant, and swung into the driver's seat.

"Just a minute," said the Sergeant. "Driving your own picket are you?"

"Usual driver of the vehicle indisposed."

Tom Chead pulled the starter. The engine turned over several times but didn't catch. A second and longer attempt produced the same result.

"You can sit there pulling all night if you want," the Sergeant said. "I've removed the rotor-arm, a precaution which you should have taken yourself and neglect of which is a chargeable offence. Now then, Corporal-Major: your name and number if you please."

The Sergeant of Military Police, with his men grouped behind him, was standing on the pavement; and since the three-tonner was parked on the left-hand side of the street, the conversation between him and Chead was now being conducted across Daniel, who, true to Michael Lamb's advice, was staring straight ahead. As he did so, a man crossed the street from the other side, paused on the pavement about ten yards from the Sergeant, and stared back at Daniel through the wind-screen. Although his appearance was not familiar, Daniel knew him, or rather, knew that he knew him. Just where he had met him or in what circumstances, he could not have said; but met him he had, if only once, however briefly... Where? When? The man, who was stocky, hatless, short-haired and wearing a smartly cut

mackintosh, continued to stare quietly up at Daniel, without
moving, without giving any sign of recognition.

"All right," said Tom Chead, leaning across Daniel, "two
hundred marks for that rotor-arm back."

"It is an offence to attempt to—"

"—Three hundred."

"Make it four."

"There's some of my blokes still caught back there in the
Ratskeller," said Chead. "Get them out, and you can have
four."

"Five."

"Done. C.O.D."

The Sergeant took his men over the square at the double.
The man in the mackintosh continued to gaze placidly into
the cab of the three-tonner.

"Narrow thing," said the Corporal-Major. "All our profit
gone. And all because of bloody Mugger and his baahing."

"Why did that annoy them so much?"

"Old soldiers' tale. Wessex Fusiliers means country boys,
see, and country boys means shepherds, and shepherds means
fun and games with sheep. Just before the war they caught
one of 'em at it—in the middle of a manoeuvre on the Salisbury Plain. So ever since then, when anyone wants a rise out
of 'em . . ."

Where had he seen that man before? And why did he just
stare like that? Daniel wiped the sweat from his forehead
with the sleeve of his field-smock.

". . . Same with the Cumberland Light Infantry," Tom
Chead was saying, "only in their case it was a cow. In India
too. You know what a fuss them Hindus make about cows,
so when they found this squaddy on the job there was a
perishing riot, so there was, and they had to call reserves in
to squash it. Well, the only spare troops near enough was a
Brigade just about to sail home from out of Bombay, so they
got this Brigade off the troopship, and very nearly had a
mutiny on their hands for good measure. You never saw

such a pig's breakfast. And here's that bloody red-hat, and not before time . . . five hundred I said, matey, and five hundred it is."

Chead passed the notes to Daniel, who passed them to the Sergeant, who licked his thumb before counting them. Four rather bedraggled Dragoons were then released and climbed into the back of the truck. The Sergeant did them the honour of replacing the rotor-arm with his own hands and waved them on their way like royalty. As they passed the short-haired man on the kerb he swivelled his head to follow them.

"Nothing they won't do for money, them red-caps," said the Corporal-Major. "You take the Italian campaign. They drew protection money out of every cat-house from Syracuse to San Remo. The Mafia wasn't in it . . . Anything the matter, Danny? You don't look so good."

"I'm all right," said Daniel desperately. "What was that noise you made down in the Ratskeller? Like an owl."

"Calling the boys off, that's all. We've always used that call in the Squadron. It means trouble coming, watch your-selves, pack it in. A look-out's call. 'Ta-whit-ta-woooo . . .' And talking of look-outs, Danny boy, there was someone watching you in that street back there. I saw him and so did you, which is why you're looking like a land-mine went off under your crutch."

"I . . . I don't know who it was."

"Never mind. You're all right with us."

Perhaps, thought Daniel; but when it came to the point, you all got out of the Ratskeller quick enough and left the Fusiliers to face the music. Neatly done, I grant you, and of course it would have been asking for trouble to stay; the fact remains that it was the Fusiliers ("Baaah") who stood their ground and who are now, doubtless, sitting in cells.

The three-tonner drew up in the car park of the Schwaghof.

"Two of you stay in there with Mugger," the Corporal-Major shouted back; "the rest of you go and get some kip.

I'll have to take Mugger on to the M.O.," he told Daniel: "he was looking even worse than you do. Want to come?"

Daniel nodded. The idea of seeing Mick Motley gave him comfort. Motley, while his behaviour might be erratic, was a man who helped other people, as opposed to hitting, bribing or tricking them, and so in a small way served the cause of decency. Just now, Daniel thought, a little decency was what he needed.

They drove down the road for another mile, looking for the Fusilier encampment.

"That'll be it . . ."

Chead turned the three-tonner through a gate on the left. What seemed to be about fifty men sprang out of the ground with rifles trained on the driving cab. R.S.M. Holeworthy loomed out from among them.

"Turn those head-lights off," he yelled. "Do you want the entire enemy air force to know where we are?"

The Corporal-Major sighed and doused his lights.

"With your permission, R.S.M. A sick man for the M.O."

"Leave the truck and carry him."

Led by a terrified Fusilier who clearly did not know the way, Chead and Daniel and the two Dragoons carrying Mugger stumbled down row after row of tents which were pitched with parade ground exactness. During the third time round Daniel tripped over a tent peg and went sailing into an enormous net which turned out to be camouflaging Mick Motley's ambulance. Inside the doctor was drinking whisky by candle-light with a morose Staff Sergeant.

"Guesties," said Mick thickly. "Drinkies?"

"No thank you, sir. We haven't had any supper yet. On account of Mugger here what's fallen down and bust his napper."

Mick looked sillily at Daniel.

"Seen a ghost, boy? Staff, get them all some soup, poor sods. Didn't you hear? They haven't had any supper."

By this time Mugger was arranged on one of the bunks.

Mick stood over him, staggered slightly, shook his head as if to clear it, and then bent down fairly steadily to make his examination.

"Fallen down nothing. He's been hit . . . hard."

" 'Fraid so, sir. Bottles."

"Then why lie about it? Hard enough to cure a man without being told lies. But that's what it is in the Army. Lies, lies, lies."

The Staff Sergeant, who had been pouring soup into cups from a saucepan, distributed it among the Dragoons. An acceptable kindness, Daniel thought. Everywhere else in the Army you either got much more than you wanted or else nothing at all, according to somebody's whim. But here in Motley's ambulance . . . Motley . . . ambulance . . . *"Get an ambulance and fucking quick."* The rubble in Hannover. The tubby man who had guided them from the hotel and had the black bag ready. The man in the street in Bad Salzuflen. So.

"Jesus, Mary and Joseph," Mick Motley said. "They've half killed the poor bastard. Who did this? There'll have to be an enquiry. Which of you were there when it happened?"

Daniel looked at Motley, who looked at the Corporal-Major, who looked back.

"No," said Motley. "No enquiry if we can help it. I'd say, Corporal-Major, that he took a nasty toss in the stores lorry, sustaining serious damage to the scalp as he fell, and probably upsetting a box of tins, some of which fell on his head and face and caused the minor injuries. But since he was alone in the back while you were on the move . . . ?"

"Alone," confirmed Chead.

". . . Then no one except himself can tell us."

"Will he be all right?" said Daniel.

"I'm not certain. Not till I've had him X-rayed. You, Staff, get these men to help you shift that camouflage net. We've got to get him to B.M.H. in Bielefeld."

"The R.S.M. won't like us driving through the lines at night, sir. Enemy aeroplanes—"

"—Are you mad, Staff?" And then, very low, to Daniel, "I'll cover up as best I can, but if he dies there'll have to be an enquiry. So you'd better start thinking now . . . Take your men home when they've moved that net, Corporal-Major. There's nothing more you can do."

Five minutes later the Dragoons and Daniel stood by as the Ambulance started. R.S.M. Holeworthy came screeching through the night.

"Mr Motley, sir, do you want every aeroplane in the enemy air force to hear you?"

"Emergency, R.S.M. For hospital in Bielefeld."

"But there's no way out of camp, sir. You're bang in the middle of the tent lines."

"You pitched tents round my ambulance?"

"I never knew you'd want to use it, sir. After all, this is only an exercise."

"Well, unpitch them, do you hear? You must clear a path for me to get this ambulance out. NOW."

"But the only way is through the officers' lines, sir. They're mostly asleep."

"I think," said the Corporal-Major, "that our lot had better push off."

As they climbed into the stores truck at the gate, Daniel heard noises of rapidly swelling turmoil from the centre of the Fusilier camp.

"Poor old Mugger," said Corporal-Major Chead, "how he'd have enjoyed it. I hope the poor bleeder don't die. There'll never be a storeman to match him. Crafty he was, to the very depths of his rotten old soul."

Fielding returned from Bielefeld very late and told them that the next day they would be driving on to Kassel, which was to be the central point of the east-west Start Line from

which their army would begin its advance. As he had expected, Ivan Blessington was possessed of information which
he was not meant to pass on and which gave a pretty fair
idea of how the manoeuvre would develop. They could be
more or less sure, Fielding said, that from Kassel the army
would advance due south, the division to which they themselves belonged being deployed on the extreme right-wing,
nearest, that was, to the Belgian and French frontiers. Since
the enemy was advancing from the east, their division would
be the last to make contact; and it was most unlikely that the
Fusilier/Dragoon "Courier" services would be required until
several days had passed. Although the exact route which they
would be told to take from Kassel was uncertain, the proba-
bility was that they would proceed straight down the arterial
road through Marburg, Bad Homburg and Frankfurt, and
then on to Heidelburg.

When Fielding was told something of the row in the
Ratskeller he was displeased with all concerned, and the more
so when Basil Bunce observed, albeit with great tact of
phrasing, that it was Fielding's own fault for leaving the
Squadron leaderless for so long. A telephone call to the
British Military Hospital in Bielefeld revealed that Mugger
was on the danger list and made Fielding's temper less stable
still; but the Corporal-Major pulled things round with an
idiomatic account of the confusion in which they had left
R.S.M. Holeworthy and the Fusilier encampment. After four
brandies—large ones which he did not, Daniel noticed, drink
slowly—Fielding was entirely restored to good humour. He
listened sympathetically to Daniel's tale of the watcher in
Bad Salzuflen, pointed out that this was a very good instance
of just how safe Daniel was (for had not the stocky man been
powerless to act?) and then dismissed his entourage to bed.

The next morning, very early, Fielding was summoned by
the Fusilier Colonel to hear his official instructions for the
drive to Kassel. They were to proceed by the direct route *via*
Paderborn, Fielding told his "O" Group on return, and to

make their camp in a bombed area near the autobahn. The Colonel was most emphatic that this time he would not tolerate any variations on his orders: hotels were out. They would be in Kassel for between twelve hours and twenty-four.

After the drive had begun, Fielding told Michael Lamb and Daniel that he had rung the B.M.H. again before they left. Mugger, though still ôn the danger list, was doing well.

"And a good job," Fielding said to Daniel. "If Mugger's all right, they'll probably accept this tale the Doctor's thought up about how he fell down in the back of the stores truck. Certainly, those Fusiliers who hit him will keep quiet, and so will Mugger: honour among thieves. The only trouble is that the Fusilier C.O. wants to kick up a fuss. He's heard that some of our chaps were in the Ratskeller, and he wants to know why they weren't arrested by the M.P.'s as well as his own. I told him that Dragoons were clever at taking care of themselves in these situations, but that didn't help matters. He's not very keen on me at the moment. And if he did stir up the shit, it's always possible that you might be among those that fell into it. Which in the circumstances would be less than happy."

"Surely, nothing much can happen while the manoeuvre's still going on?"

"No . . . Unless Mugger died and some busybody got hold of it. They'd have to cover themselves jolly quickly then."

"Busybody?"

"We have them."

"I'd got the impression there was nobody you couldn't fix."

"Nobody important. The trouble comes from the very small busybodies—the self-righteous National Serviceman who writes to his mother who writes to her Member of Parliament. The latter we can probably cope with—but by that time it's also gone to the press. Meditate on this, Daniel: in our society the big rows are always started by small people—the ones who have nothing to lose and are glad of a little attention."

"But in this case?"

"No one in the Squadron will say anything. That's all I can promise."

"But you seem quite confident about it all."

"What else? Do you expect me to go round crying?"

They were coming into Paderborn now. Daniel looked up at the crazy roof of the cathedral and remembered how he had been there (it seemed ten years ago) with Earle Restarick in the spring. Then he looked down at the main entrance and saw a group of men with red armlets, among them Pappenheim.

"Official observers," said Fielding. "They'll be a lot of pressmen too."

"German?"

"English. The lot. Liddell Hart & Co. This is the biggest thing in the military year."

"I thought the generals were trying to keep it quiet."

"Until it happened, yes. But they can't keep the journalists out of a show like this."

"Pappenheim was there with the observers."

"Why should you worry?"

"First that tubby man from Hannover, now Pappenheim."

"He probably didn't even see you."

"The tubby man did. He knows where I am."

"What can he do about it?"

"They said they'd hunt me down. Anything, an accident, the sort of thing that happened to Mugger. Oh, Christ."

"Stop it, Danny," said Michael Lamb. "We're here with you." He gestured over his shoulder at the column behind. "We're all here with you."

But Daniel had changed the mood of the morning, and little more was said until, two hours later, they reached Kassel.

After they had been in Kassel three days, the Dragoons began to be jumpy. They had been warned to prepare for a stay of up to twenty-four hours, and twenty-four hours, amid the dismal ruins of the flattened slum to which they were allotted, would have been long enough. But first one day went by and then another; unit after unit rolled past them and away to the south; at last even the neighbouring Fusiliers departed; and still the armoured cars and their attendant crews stood idle and without orders among the rubble.

"I can't understand it," Fielding kept saying. "The theory is that we must be well up with the attacking forces so that we can do our stuff the moment someone lets off an atomic shell. And until then we're meant to stay close to the Fusiliers for liaison. They've been gone for over twelve hours now."

The autumn weather, so brilliant when they left Göttingen, had turned grey and damp. A fire had been contrived from old packing cases and assorted debris; but fuel was now exhausted, and only a last poor ghost of warmth came from the black pile of ash.

"Send out a party to collect logs, sir?" said the Sergeant-Major. "There's those woods the other side of the autobahn."

"No," snapped Fielding. "We may be told to saddle up at any moment. We don't want to have to hang about for anybody."

"They ought to be occupied, sir. Just sitting here's getting them down. Inter-troop football, sir, all against all, three matches. If we can clear a pitch out of this rubbish."

"Just as you think best, Sergeant-Major . . . I can't understand it at all," Fielding said.

The Sergeant-Major moved off to organise a clearing party. There was a sceptical but good-humoured cheer, and then the work was quickly and keenly under way.

"How easy it is to keep them happy. As long as they have something, anything, to do. You know," Fielding said, "I drove round the town this morning to see if I could pick up any news from anyone. Even Div. H.Q. was packing up to move forward. The General and Ivan had already gone, otherwise I might have learnt something. As it is, I honestly believe we're the last unit left in Kassel. One wonders if they've simply forgotten us."

"Didn't the Fusilier C.O. say anything before he left?"

"Just that we were to stay here until we received further orders."

The sun broke through and immediately went in again. The remains of a rotting ceiling collapsed on to a jagged pile of bricks. Fielding and his three officers moved away from the dead fire and started giving desultory encouragement to the soldiers who were clearing the football pitch. Over the waste land came a small, round man wearing a duffle-coat, a haversack and an enormous trilby. Daniel shuddered, thinking that it was the tubby man of Hannover and Bad Salzuflen; but as the figure drew closer he saw a kind smile across an innocent and unknown face.

"Alfie Schroeder," said the little fellow: "of the Billingsgate Press."

"You'd better speak to the Squadron Commander," Daniel said.

"I'd much rather speak to someone like you."

"I don't know anything about what's going on."

"Neither do I," said Alfie Schroeder. "Our military correspondent's got the piles, so they sent me at the last minute."

"You won't learn anything here. The war has passed us by, it seems."

Alfie Schroeder gave Daniel an odd look, and said,

"I'm sticking to the human angle. I heard a little tale about one of your chaps being taken off half dead to the military hospital in Bielefeld. That's why your lot's still here—so's they can put a hand on anyone who might help with the enquiry. Care to tell me about it?"

"How is he? Mugger?"

"Neither better nor worse, they say." He gazed solemnly at Daniel. "I've seen your face before. In the paper."

"Impossible. My sort don't get into the paper."

"I've got a long memory for faces. Let's see ... Unofficial strike leader? No. Criminal offence? No. Pools winner? No, but warmer—I've got it, by God I have. Winner of the Spinoza Prize for Mathematics. April, 1951. 'Daniel ... er ... er ... Mond, receiving the award from the Chancellor of Cambridge University in the Senate House.' What are you doing here, boy? National Service?"

"What else?"

"They must be mad, wasting a chap like you as a private soldier. There's a story in this if you'll go along with it."

"I'm not allowed to talk to the press."

"Balls to that. A winner of the Spinoza Prize can talk to anyone he wants to."

Michael Lamb came up.

"Who's this, Danny?"

Daniel introduced them.

"Mr Schroeder's interested in Mugger."

"In Mr Mond," said Alfie.

"He says," Daniel went on desperately, "that we're being kept here in case there's an enquiry about Mugger."

"Bugger Mugger. People get hurt every day. It's not every day I find a Spinoza Prize winner arsing about as a common soldier."

"Watch it," said Lamb.

"No offence meant. I'm a Labour man myself. But you see what I mean."

"No," said Michael Lamb, "I don't. This man's called Trooper Lewis and he's got an identity card to prove it."

Daniel produced Lewis's filthy piece of paper.

"Lewis, Edward Paul. Which explains why your friend here calls you Danny, I suppose. There's more in this," said Alfie buoyantly, "than meets the eye."

"Danny's just a nick-name."

"Tell that to your Auntie Flo. I'm never wrong about a face once I've seen it."

"You only saw a photograph," said Daniel.

The Corporal-Major joined them.

"Bloody fire out? That's all we need. Who's this then?"

"Schroeder of the Billingsgate Press," said Alfie. "Perhaps you'd like to tell our readers what it's like to give orders to a ruddy genius."

Tom Chead looked at Daniel and then at Alfie.

"Forget it, matey," he said. "Run along and forget it."

"I've got my job to do."

"And I've got mine. You leave my soldiers alone. You've no business poking your nose in."

For answer Alfie opened his haversack and took out a box brownie which he trained on Daniel. There was a ponderous click.

"Pardon me," Alfie said, "but I've got a duty to my public. They'll be very interested to see a photo of Mr Mond here all dolled up and collecting his Spinoza Prize, along with another one of him in his denims doing his National Service just like anybody else. It's the sort of thing which keeps them happy in a democratic age. Keeps my editor happy too. Though he may have some questions about why Mr Mond says his name is Lewis. Anyone got any answers?"

"Yes," said the Corporal-Major. He twisted Alfie's arm until the camera fell on the ground, and then stamped on it.

"My brownie," said Alfie softly. "Years I've had it."

"I told you. Leave my perishing soldiers alone. Busting in here, you and your camera, you might be anyone at all."

Alfie bent down and picked up the crumpled camera.

"My brownie . . ."

"Security," blustered the Corporal-Major. "How do I know you're what you say you are?"

Alfie held out a press card.

"You only had to ask."

"Schroeder. What kind of name is that?"

"Good enough to stir up the Billingsgate Press when they see it at the end of a telegram. They're going to be very upset when they hear what you've done to me and my camera.

And they're going to believe what I tell them, even without a photo. You should have let it go as it was. You haven't helped Mr Mond, not one bit."

Alfie turned and walked away across the waste land, holding the brownie in front of him with both hands. Daniel went after him.

"Mr Schroeder, I'm so sorry . . ."

Alfie walked straight on.

"He didn't mean it. He's a kind man, really, but he's my friend, you see, and he thought— Mr Schroeder. You've got to keep quiet about me. You must. *Please*."

"That's better," said Alfie, stopping and facing Daniel. "Now. Why have I got to keep quiet?"

"If you tell anyone who I am, it'll be very bad for me . . . and for those who are helping me."

"Why?"

"I'm on the run."

"What have you done?"

"Nothing. Nothing wrong, that is."

"If you told the Billingsgate Press about it, we could—"

"—No. I can't tell anyone about it. If I did, they might— well—find out a whole lot more. Or there might be new pressures on me. I can't explain."

"Mr Mond," said Alfie, "you're talking in riddles, but it's obvious there's something big here. If I tip off London, even the little I know, something big's going to come of it and they're going to be very pleased with Alfie Schroeder. I want them to be pleased, Mr Mond; I need their pleasure."

"I need your silence."

"Then you'll have to show me that your need is the stronger."

For some seconds Daniel cast about for ways of doing this; then he thought of Fielding Gray and what he had said during that last dinner at the Alte Krone.

"On my honour, . . ."

"What honour, Mr Mond?"

"My honour ... as a Jew."

Alfie Schroeder removed his trilby, blew into it several times, and replaced it. Then he handed Daniel the broken brownie.

"So you take it," he said. "You'll find the film still inside. It would have been all right, because I'd wound it well on. It would have come out, that picture. Shalom, Daniel Mond."

The little figure walked on over the waste land. Daniel returned to the Corporal-Major and Michael Lamb.

"He's gone, Danny? Good riddance."

"He left me his camera. With the film in it. Undamaged."

"Oh," said the Corporal-Major and turned heavily away.

"But what's the good?" said Daniel. "If we're just stuck here until they call us back for an enquiry, what's the good?"

Fifty yards away a football thudded against a wall and a roar went up from the spectators. A despatch rider bumped over the rubble from the direction in which Alfie Schroeder had disappeared.

"Captain Gray?"

"Fetch him, Danny."

When Fielding opened the envelope, he said :

"At last. But it's not the route I thought. We're to go back to Paderborn and south-west to Bonn. And there's another thing. They think Mugger's going to die."

At least, thought Daniel, they're not keeping us here, they're letting us advance.

"So they're sending a Special Branch man to Bonn to meet us," Fielding went on : "he'll want to interview anyone who knows anything about it."

Since the order to start had been received late in the afternoon, it was nearly dark by the time the Squadron reached Paderborn, where they turned left down the main route for Dortmund.

Dormiat Dortmundus.

This time the Squadron Sergeant-Major was riding with them in Fielding's Land Rover, as Fielding wished to consult him over the *affaire* Mugger.

"We'll have to take our line from Dr Motley, sir. From what Tom Chead tells me, the doctor's prepared to support this tale about Mugger falling over in the stores truck... unless Mugger dies."

"What difference does that make?" said Fielding crossly. "No need to make difficulties just because the poor chap's dead."

"The doctor's a Catholic, sir. He probably thinks that murderers should be brought to book."

"But that would mean Daniel here giving evidence. And then where should we all be?"

"I dare say the Corporal-Major's evidence would suffice, Captain Fielding. Again, it all depends on the doctor. If he refrains from mentioning that Daniel... Mr Mond... Trooper Lewis was mixed up in it ..."

"But where is the bloody doctor? How can we know what he's going to say?"

There was no answer to that. The doctor had last been seen retching from his ambulance window as the Fusilier convoy drew out of Kassel. Heaven alone knew where that lot had got to by now.

"Anyway," said Fielding, "the doctor himself won't know what he's going to say till he knows whether or not Mugger's really going to die. So if this Special Branch chappie catches up with him while it's still in doubt, what's he going to do then?"

"I really couldn't tell you, sir."

"What was your impression, Danny? You were there— damn it."

"Just what Mr Bunce says. Mick knows we don't want an enquiry since I'm mixed up in it all, but if Mugger dies that won't count. Mick's very firm over some things." Decency, he thought; he could destroy me with his decency.

Night was now down. A thin drizzle was slanting across the headlights. A huge German truck with trailer overtook them, the trailer lashing back within a yard of their bonnet as it passed and chucking mud all over their windscreen.

"Bastard," said Michael Lamb. "He must have overtaken the whole Squadron."

"Not very hard, the pace we have to travel," said Fielding. "My God, how boring these treks are. Got that whisky there, Danny? In the small pack."

Daniel passed the whisky forward. Fielding took a long swig and didn't pass it back. Sergeant-Major Bunce, next to Daniel, stiffened slightly in the darkness.

"First halt due, sir."

"To hell with that." Fielding took another long drink. "We'll be lucky to make Bonn by midnight as it is."

Bunce lent forward and quietly took the whisky bottle from Fielding's lap.

"You won't be wanting more of that, sir, not till we've halted for a brew-up. We didn't eat before we left Kassel, remember."

"Quite right, Mr Bunce. Sorry."

"Nothing to be sorry about, sir. If I might suggest . . . There's a good wide margin of grass just here by the look of it."

Lamb drew off the road on to the grass. Fielding jumped out with a torch and walked back, signalling the other vehicles into the side.

"Cook him something quickly," Bunce hissed at Daniel, "and don't let him have that bottle."

Bunce went off down the column. Daniel opened some tins of stew and emptied them into a saucepan, while Lamb got the oil-burner going. The drizzle, thicker now, swirled all about them, although they were huddled in the lee of the Land Rover.

"The Captain's working up for one of his moods," Lamb said.

Geddes the barber came out of the dark.

"Hello, cookie," he said. "Bas Bunce says to mix these up in the Captain's din-din."

He passed six tablets of what looked like codeine across to Daniel.

"Crush them into the gravy, dear. Oh, and there's letters for you, Lambkin. Came in with the mail yesterday, but I clean forgot. By-ee for now."

While Daniel served the stew into mess tins and crushed the codeine tablets into the portion intended for Fielding, Michael Lamb went round in front of the head-lamps to read his mail.

"Message for you, Danny," he said in a puzzled voice. "Just says, 'Tell Daniel we hope he's enjoying his outing with his nice friends, and we look forward to seeing him when it's over. Earle.' Who's he? What's he mean?"

Fielding and Bunce reappeared together. Daniel tried to pick up two mess tins for them, but his hands, shaking and wet with rain, slipped helplessly along the handles. Anyway, which was Fielding's?

"Come on, for Christ's sake. We haven't got all night."

Calm now, calm.

"Here you are. I'm sorry."

All four of them wolfed down their stew. Ten minutes later the convoy was on the move again.

"Fielding ... There's been a note from Restarick. They must be following."

He repeated the message.

"There's nothing they can do. So long as you stick with us."

"I don't like the sound of it."

"Neither do I," said Fielding savagely. "One bloody mess after another. You're at the bottom of it all, and it's no good your whining. Pass up that whisky."

"Sir?" said the Sergeant-Major.

"For God's sake don't be such an old woman, Bunce. I've eaten, haven't I?"

All of a sudden drowsiness overwhelmed Daniel. Those tablets, he thought; couldn't even get that right; one bloody mess after another.

"Whisky," snarled Fielding from a thousand miles away.

Daniel just had strength to glance apologetically at the Sergeant-Major, and then sank down into the dark.

When Daniel awoke, stiff, cold, foul-mouthed, he and Lamb were alone in the stationary Land Rover.

"Where . . . ?"

"Bonn. They've gone to find out where we're meant to go to now."

"What happened after I went to sleep?"

"Buncie threw the bottle out of the window, and told the Captain he was ashamed of him, being nasty to his friend and getting all worked up about nothing at all."

"And then?"

"And then," said Lamb reluctantly, "the Captain started to shout. He was never appreciated, he said. He did all this for you and just had you grizzling at him for his trouble. He'd given up his university career to be in the Army (not quite true from what I've heard), and all the thanks he got was louts like Basil Bunce telling him his manners. Then he stopped as quickly as he started, said he was sorry about thirty times, and that was it. All over till the next time. It's always like that."

"Often?"

"About once a month. Generally when things get niggling. Not really rough—he seems to like that—but niggling, like this business of Mugger. Untidiness, he calls it."

Untidiness was now much in evidence. When Fielding and

the Sergeant-Major returned to the Land Rover, they were both jittering with rage.

"Leave us without orders," the Sergeant-Major said, "all on our tod for days, and then bawl us out for being late."

"And shunt us all round Bonn because they still don't know what to do with us . . . We'll leave the column here, Mr Bunce, and go and find someone who makes sense."

"Begging your pardon, sir, the Staff Captain said the column was cluttering up the street."

"What does he want me to do? Dump the whole lot in the river? Daniel, go down the column and find Piers Bungay. Tell him I'm going to Div. H.Q. with the S.S.M. to get proper orders, and that he's to keep the Squadron right here till I get back."

The Land Rover thundered off. Daniel wandered down the line of vehicles, until eventually he found Piers Bungay and Jack Lamprey, who were lolling against one of the armoured cars and sharing a bottle of hock with the Corporal-Major.

"Hullo, Daniel. What's the news?"

Daniel told them and gratefully accepted a glass of hock.

"I say," came a young and haughty voice from the darkness, "who commands here?"

A guardsman's hat with the circumference of a cart-wheel and a peak which thrust down like a vizor swam through the murk towards them. It was supported on a column of battledress just over five foot high, the whole having the effect of a malignant toad-stool.

"Who commands here?" repeated the toad-stool.

"I suppose I do for the time being," said Piers.

"Look here, then. I'm the Staff Captain, and I told your Sergeant-Major, *myself*, to get all your infernal tank-things—"

"—Armoured cars—"

"—Armoured car-things out of this street. The B.M.'s livid. This is Brigade Headquarters, he says, not the Odeon car park."

"But my Squadron Commander told us to stay put until he got back. We don't know where to go, you see."

"I can't help that," said the toad-stool, petulant, "you can't stay here."

Julian James lounged up.

"Hullo, Bagger, you old chiz," he said to the toad-stool. "What's the trouble?"

Bagger squealed with annoyance.

"Your bloody tank-things are blocking my street."

"Your street, Bagger? He was always knocking off things at school," said Julian to the assembled audience, "but we can't let him get away with a whole street."

Trooper Geddes arrived, waving a piece of paper.

"Mappy-reference just come over the wireless," he announced. "We've got to go there straight away."

"Who sent it? Captain Gray?"

"No, sir. Divisional Intelligence."

"I can't think what it's got to do with Intelligence."

"What does that matter?" wailed Bagger. "You've been told where to go by your wireless-thing, so for God's sake get out of my street."

"But when the Squadron Commander comes back, he'll wonder—"

"—No, he won't. Someone else will have told him—"

"—Someone at Div. H.Q.—"

"—Supposing he doesn't find Div. H.Q.—"

"—Coming back here, expecting to find us—"

"—All alone in the dark—"

"—With nowhere to go—"

"—No one to talk to—"

"—I thought the S.S.M. was with him—"

"—Look, gentlemen all," said the Corporal-Major. "Mr Bungay can take the Squadron on to this mappy-ref— map-reference. I'll wait here with the stores wagon for Captain Gray. That's if the Staff Captain here will kindly permit one vehicle to stay in his street."

"I suppose so," said Bagger ungenerously.

"Right," said the Corporal-Major. "Now let's just take a look and see whereabouts this map reference is."

"Good idea," said Bungay. "Who's got a map-thing? . . . Ta. I can never remember: is it *up* first or across?"

"Allow me, sir . . ."

After a few moments the Corporal-Major said:

"I don't want to disappoint anyone, but that map-reference, it means this here street."

"Bagger's street-thing? There you are, Bagger, we've been ordered to stay in your str—"

"—Not to stay here," shrilled Geddes, "but to come here, the wireless said."

"Well, now you've come here and you can bloody well go. The B.M.—"

"—But no one's told us where to come next."

"Just take this bloody circus away, that's all."

A fierce, black-jawed little man, wearing a green beret and swishing a black cane with a silver knob, was suddenly inside the circle and revolving like a run-away light-house. Bagger saluted. No one else did.

"Now look here, whoever you are," Jack Lamprey said, "why not try to be a little more helpful?"

"I'm the Brigade Major, that's who I am."

"Splendid," said Piers. "Perhaps you can tell us where to go. You see—"

"—Don't you address field officers as 'sir' where you come from?"

"No. Now it seems that you and Division between you have made a perfectly ghastly cock-up about our—"

"—Captain Hennessy, I want this officer arrested for insolence." And to Piers, "you're arrested, do you hear me?"

"Yes. Now about our—"

"—I won't talk to someone who's been arrested."

Fielding's Land Rover drew up. Fielding got out, took it all in, saluted the Brigade Major, and said:

"Mr Bungay, Mr Lamprey, Mr James, Corporal-Major. The Squadron will move off in one minute flat. Main road south out of Bonn, right turning at 064279, thereafter halt on signal."

"You can't take him," screamed the Brigade Major pointing at Bungay. "He's under arrest."

"Galloping paranoia," said Julian, loud enough for everyone to hear.

"Be quiet," said Fielding very sharply. Then, grasping Piers by the collar, "I'll take full responsibility for this officer. He will be available to face your charges at any time—if," said Fielding looking meaningfully at the large audience of Dragoons around them, "you can find any evidence to support them. Thirty seconds, gentlemen."

He flung Piers away from him like a puppy dog in disgrace, mounted his Land Rover and drove on, leaving the Brigade Major frothing and Daniel unheeded.

"Come in the Sergeant-Major's Land Rover, dear," said Geddes: "the one down there at the back."

Gratefully, Daniel accepted. As they left Bonn, he could just make out a river on their left and, on the right, a slope with imposing houses; then he fell asleep. Some time later he was jolted awake by a bump in the road, and saw that the rear lights of the column in front of him had formed a long red path as of slowly twisting tracer which seemed to be working like a corkscrew into the now unbroken blackness ahead. He cried out at the beauty of it, thinking it must be a dream, and slept once more.

When the dawn roused Daniel, he found that they were in a little park which was dotted about with band-stands and clumps of trees, and criss-crossed by streams that burbled under willow-pattern bridges.

"Bad Neuenahr, dear," said Geddes. "Spa-town. But they don't seem to have got round to patching it up yet."

And indeed the band-stands were scabby with dead paint, the paths overgrown with weeds, the grass scarred with nettles. A royal garden, Daniel thought, in the last days of Byzantium.

"Brekker, dear? We've got a nice tin of skinless sausages."

"No, thanks. I ought to get back to the Squadron Commander."

"Suit yourself. He didn't seem too anxious for your company last night."

Pondering this remark, Daniel walked slowly to Fielding's Land Rover, which was a hundred yards away, beside a pond and a miniature waterfall. Lamb was sitting on the bank by himself and singing "September in the rain."

" 'Lo, Danny. We'd better get some breakfast ready for the Captain. He's gone to talk to the Fusiliers." Lamb gestured down a long double avenue of trees. "We're together again."

They cooked up a pan of fatty bacon. Fielding came down the avenue with Mick Motley.

"Give him some breakfast," Fielding said. "He has good news."

"Mugger's going to be all right," said Mick. "The Special Branch man moved into the Kurhotel last night and had me go over. Just as he was starting in, he had a phone-call from Bielefeld. Mugger was sitting up and taking nourishment. So off went the dick to get his story from source."

Nevertheless, Mick seemed worried about something.

"Had you told him anything?"

"Luckily not. So now it's up to Mugger."

"He'll think of something plausible and harmless," said Fielding. "We've heard the last of this."

"How long have you been here?" Daniel asked Mick.

"Since yesterday. We've been half round the world since we saw you last. They couldn't decide where they wanted us. Or anyone else."

"Ivan Blessington said something about that last night,"

Fielding told them. "There's some muddle about the Division which is impersonating the enemy. They changed direction when they weren't meant to, and no one's known what to do since."

"In that respect at least," said Mick sourly, "the manoeuvre bears some relation to probable reality."

"Si-irr," came Geddes' voice, panting and fluting down the line of vehicles, "green alert. Just came over the set."

"Decision at last," said Mick Motley. "I shall be sorry to leave this ridiculous kurgarten."

But that alone could not account for his evident uneasiness as he chucked away the remains of his bacon with a bad-tempered flick of the wrist and sloped off down the avenue which led back to the Fusiliers.

"He might have waited for a lift," said Fielding, who soon after drove off with Lamb in the same direction. "Don't forget," he shouted back at Daniel: "draw suits for me and Michael."

Still too drowsy to be sure what this could mean, Daniel was hustled by the Corporal-Major into a crowd of soldiers, told to right turn, and marched off with the rest over the thick wet grass. After they had left the kurgarten and shuffled a short way down an elegant street, they were called to a halt by a large glass door, on which was blazoned SPIEL BANK. Through this they were fed by files into a thickly carpeted corridor and then up some stairs to where Leonard Percival was presiding over three roulette tables, all of them covered with what looked like diving suits made of fish scales. Leonard Percival looked straight at Daniel and nodded affably. Then he flicked his fingers, and three Fusilier Sergeants, one to each table, began to distribute the diving equipment.

"I want three please," said Daniel when it was his turn.

"Three, laddie?"

Fusiliers, it seemed, were less formal on manoeuvres.

"That's right," said Percival, who had come up behind

the Sergeant. "Trooper Lewis here is Captain Gray's batman. The third one's for the driver, I expect."

He flashed his spectacles at Daniel.

"Sign here," said the Sergeant; "name and last three."

"Last three?"

"Last three figures of your number," prompted Percival kindly.

"I ... er ..."

"Nine-two-nine," said Percival to the Sergeant, who looked surprised. "Good morning, Trooper Lewis. See you later, I expect."

Laden with the three suits, Daniel stumbled down the casino staircase to the corridor below, where people were trying the things on. Watching the others carefully, Daniel did the same. After some officious person had pulled a zip at his rear, he found that he was totally encased and looking out through a small window of perspex, feeling much as he had felt (stifled and humiliated) when he had first worn his gas-mask as a child. In a matter of seconds the perspex filmed over and resisted all his efforts to wipe it clear. It then occurred to him that the film had of course been caused by his breath on the inside; but he could think of no way of dealing with it, other than by pressing the perspex on to his nose and waggling the latter like an internal windscreen wiper. Since this seemed foolish and was making him very short of breath, he tried instead, but without success, to find the rear zip that would release him. If only he could have air ... AIR. Then some angel of mercy, who must have seen his struggles, unfastened the zip and helped him, from behind, to work the suit off his shoulders.

"Thank you," panted Daniel, turning to his rescuer.

"Think nothing of it," said Leonard Percival; "but you might find it advisable, next time you put this on, to adjust the oxygen regulator"—he tapped Daniel's left breast—"as an alternative to suffocation."

With a gay wave Percival passed on down the passage.

Daniel, feeling depressed, nervous, and much in need of his after-breakfast evacuation, gathered up his three suits and went through a door marked *Herren*. Just inside it sat an old woman who was wearing a long black dress and had a dish in her lap which held several silver pieces. Doesn't she know, thought Daniel, that the gamblers have all gone home?

He made to pass the old woman, but she trust her saucer in his path. Daniel fumbled for his purse and found the only change he had was a five mark piece. Ludicrous; he couldn't give her nearly ten shillings. But he must get to one of the guarded cabinets. Now. He placed the five mark piece in the saucer and took up four silver pieces in exchange. One mark was quite enough. Evidently the old woman thought so too, for she rose, went into one of the cabinets, busied herself inside, then emerged and held the door open for Daniel. As he went in, she made to take the suits from him, but he shook his head, remembering what someone had said, that these were a new pattern, still very secret. Security, he thought, piling them on the floor. What a bloody nuisance they were; he would now have to lug them all the way back across the park.

"Danke," he said when he came out of the cabinet.

But the old woman was gone. He passed through into the corridor, which was empty. They've gone and left me, he thought. The lights had been turned off and heavy curtains kept out the day. Left me in the dark with no one to talk to. He began to run down the corridor, the anti-radiation suits scratching at his face, twisting between his legs. As he ran, stumbling, sightless, sobbing, an arm came out to stop him.

" 'Ere we are at last," Tom Chead said: "keeping the whole ruddy Squadron waiting."

The leading elements of the enemy had penetrated as far as Worms, or so it appeared; whereupon Worms had had two "tactical" atomic missiles pumped on to it and was now a devastated area, whither the Tenth Sabre Squadron, followed at some distance by the Fusiliers, was hastening to tidy up the mess. As they drove south the countryside became flatter and flatter, its hedges receding over the brown fields like enormous spokes which would all meet at some infinitely distant hub. Along the lonely little roads a house, even a lone tree, constituted definite events. An inn was a sensation, and near one such they halted at midday.

"Stand us a beer, Danny?"

"With pleasure."

He pushed a coin over the bar to pay. The landlord shook his head and pushed it back. On the upper face, Daniel now saw, there was an unfamiliar design. And a date ... Quickly he scooped it up and paid with a note instead.

"Steady with that beer, Danny? What's the matter?"

"Someone's passed a useless coin on me. That's all."

Some hours later they made their base two miles outside Worms. Before they had been there long Mick Motley appeared in his ambulance and announced that he had come on ahead of the Fusiliers to set up a Rehabilitation Centre.

"So find me someone to rehabilitate," he said.

But it seemed that neither Fielding nor anyone else had any very clear notion of what to do next. Exercise Broomstick, hitherto their most important experience of such matters, had been a carefully prepared affair in a quiet corner of the Harz; by means of prior briefing and appropriately planted notices some impression of a "devastated area" had been created, and this had enabled definite tasks to be allotted which bore a discernible relationship to a theoretical situation. Here in Worms there was no such situation. Undoubtedly one would have been contrived and imposed by the umpires, had not the enemy's irresponsible behaviour thrown the whole manoeuvre off balance and left the umpires marooned, without information, about a hundred miles behind the invaders' front. They were still probably at least as far away as Stuttgart.

"And so," Fielding was explaining to anyone who could be got to listen, "until the umpires turn up there's no basis for action at all."

"What will these umpires do?" Daniel asked.

"They'll announce that such and such areas are considered impassable and tell us to arrange diversions. That so many people are littered about dead or half alive, and what are we going to do about it? That kind of thing."

"I want someone to rehabilitate," said Mick, who had been drinking rather a lot since he arrived.

"Oh God . . ."

"What's more," said Mick, "I'm going to take my ambulance into Worms and find someone to rehabilitate."

Despite the tactful protests of the medical Staff Sergeant, the ambulance went roaring off.

"What we do know, sir," said the Sergeant-Major, "is that Worms has been destroyed by atomic shells. So oughtn't we to put on these here radiation suits?"

"And walk round looking like a load of farts with nothing at all to do?"

Daniel recognised the peevish tones he had heard on the road to Bonn.

"Well, sir, we can assume that so many thousand people are dead and look around for burial sites. We can—"

"—Look," rasped Fielding. "Just down that road is Worms, a prosperous centre of the wine trade and looking every inch of it. I'm going to assume nothing until someone comes and tells me to. It's not my job—or yours."

"Imagination, sir? The city's a smoking ruin, the geiger counters are clacking away like castanets, the people—what's left of them—are wandering crazily round like damned souls. There's looting, rioting, rape, mayhem, parties of peasants with perambulators crowding all the roads—"

"—That will do, Mr Bunce."

Basil Bunce looked dejected. The ambulance came roaring back and Mick leered at them out of the driver's window.

"I've found someone to rehabilitate," he said.

He tottered down from the cab, then climbed into the back and shut the doors with a crash.

"Whatever can he be up to?" said Piers Bungay.

"Well, if we're not going to do anything else, sir," said the Sergeant-Major, "we may as well brew-up."

"Anything to keep you happy, Sergeant-Major."

Bunce went away to organise the brew-up. Fielding lit a cigarette, puffed it, flicked at it impatiently and threw it away. Julian James, having set up a folding table and four camp stools, summoned Daniel, Bungay and Lamprey to Bridge. Just as they were picking up their hands, a large motor-coach drew up.

"Crikey," said Julian. "The official observers."

Led by a fat and cosy brigadier, official observers and journalists of every shape and complexion began to climb down from the coach. A Japanese gentleman was there, two Indians (quarrelling with each other), and several grinning Negroes; an obese Turk, palpably drunk, was there and also a tall Englishman whom Daniel recognised as a distinguished military historian; Pappenheim was there and so was Alfie Schroeder. Fielding saluted the Brigadier, who, though obviously a tolerant and amicable soul, was showing signs of displeasure.

"These gentlemen are all interested in observing the new Courier Team in action," said the Brigadier, panting slightly as though from incipient indigestion.

"Well, we're the advance guard."

"I know. We rather thought—well—perhaps you'd be wearing your radiation suits—"

"—I desire very much," said the obese Turk, "To see the fornication suits."

"—And, well, sort of doing your job." The Brigadier looked reproachfully at the Bridge four which, although now standing up to show respect for his seniority, was still bidding briskly.

"We're having our tea," said Fielding, "and awaiting instructions."

"Four no trumps."

"Is there nothing I can show these gentlemen?"

"Five hearts . . . Perhaps," opined Julian without being asked, "they would be amused by the Rehabilitation Centre."

He pointed to Mick Motley's ambulance.

"Rehabilitation Centre?" said Alfie, winking at Daniel. "What's that?"

"It's where we take care of civilians and others badly affected by radiation."

"That sounds interesting," said the Brigadier doubtfully.

"Five no trumps. We are playing Blackwood, partner?"

"You. What is your duties?" said the Turk to Daniel.

"I'm the Squadron Commander's personal servant."

The Turk kissed his fingers and started prancing obscenely about.

"Do you mind? There may be a slam on here."

The Turk looked at Julian as though about to order him shot, then joined Alfie and the two Indians by the ambulance.

"Damned impertinence. Six hearts . . ."

There was a scream from inside the ambulance. Alfie, standing by the rear doors which he had just opened, was blushing violently. The two Indians were holding hands and tittering, while the Turk's face was swollen with prurience.

"The Rehabilitation is instructive?" whinnied the Japanese, and skipped over to have a look for himself.

"Of course, of course," the military historian was saying: "the old system of the field brothel under medical supervision. I'm delighted to find it restored—keeps the men clean and morale high. In an atomic war, you see, there'll be no bloody bishops to complain. They'll all be dead," he concluded with relish.

"Six no trumps."

"I like very much the rehabilitation."

"I'm afraid," said the Brigadier to Fielding, "that I'll have to report all this."

"That ambulance is nothing to do with me, Brigadier. It's on loan from the Medical Corps to the first battalion of the Wessex Fusiliers."

"But I mean, all this slackness. Bridge and all that. What will all these frightful foreigners think?"

"Sir, oh sir," came Geddes' deplorable falsetto, "message on the set. They've made a mistake. The atom shells haven't fallen here at all."

"Where have they fallen?"

"They're trying to find out."

"You see, Brigadier? If I'd committed my men in Worms, it'd have taken me hours to pack up again and start for the real trouble."

"Of course, dear boy. Sorry I was cross. The fact is that this little party is rather a strain ... Come along, gentlemen, please."

The Turk lingered lustfully by the ambulance.

"Come along, Colonel Haq."

The Turk still lingered.

"Colonel Haq, there's a bottle of whisky waiting in the coach. If you don't come now, those journalists will have drunk it all."

The Brigadier made a clucking noise and the last of his charges boarded the bus. As it drove off, Pappenheim stared blankly back out of the window and Alfie Schroeder waved his enormous hat.

Fielding went over to the wireless set, where he spent several minutes. Then he said something to the Sergeant-Major, and the cry went ringing down the line :

"Prepare to mount in three minutes. South—for Baden Baden."

"The trouble, of course, is the Americans," Captain Detterling announced.

The sun was shining in Baden Baden, and Fielding, Daniel and Detterling were sitting in the garden of the Brenner's Park Hotel.

"I must be getting back," said Fielding uneasily. "I've a lot to do, and I'm not meant to be here at all. Officially the whole place is a radio-active inferno. Can I leave Daniel with you? His luggage is in the hall."

"As I was saying," Captain Detterling said, "it is the new American clientele which is ruining everything. The reason is that Americans simply cannot understand servants. Their sickening affectations of equality, alternating with bouts of persecution mania, have destroyed discipline. One minute they are simpering over the chamber-maid as though she were their adopted daughter, the next they go into a fit of paranoia because they have realised that it is not their love which she wants but their money. All of which is very unsettling for the staff. This hotel has always been famous for its calm and elegance, but how can you have either when at any moment some rabid matriarch from the middle-west may start squealing that the barman has cheated her of sixpence?"

"Look," said Fielding "I'm really in a terrible hurry to get back to the Squadron. I've brought Daniel here to deliver him into your safe keeping. Can I take it that you'll see him safely over the frontier?"

"And then," said Detterling, "they refuse to understand food. This hotel has only just reopened for the first time since the débacle. Herr Brenner has made heroic efforts to ensure that the cuisine should be what it always used to be —the most refined in Europe. So naturally it is very upsetting for him to discover that he now has to entertain a class which goes in either for footling vegetarian fads or else for enormous hunks of raw meat."

"I'm due for a final briefing from the umpires in under an hour," Fielding wailed. "I must know what you're going to do about Daniel."

"I am not a difficult man to please," Detterling said, "but I do like to receive what I'm paying for. Last night at dinner I was told I could not have a Bearnaisse sauce because there was no tarragon. Why was there no tarragon? Because some wretched American woman, the wife of a manufacturer of cheap brassières, had an allergy to it. If any came within a hundred yards of her, she was subject to uterine frenzy. So her husband had ordered that all tarragon be removed from the hotel, and he was obeyed because he had booked twenty-five suites for a four day business conference next November. A business conference in Brenner's Park Hotel. It passes belief."

"Will you take care of Daniel?"

"No," said Detterling, "I will not. I've already put up with enough inconvenience because of the follies of your damned Squadron. Think of all the time I sacrificed to sorting out Giles Glastonbury's nonsense. After a row like that, I should have thought you'd have more sense than to stick out your neck in this ridiculous way. Think of the trouble there'll be if someone finds out what you've done. Passing off a civilian as a Dragoon—it's an insult to the Regiment."

"I've already explained the circumstances."

"All Mond had to do was to hand himself over to Pappenheim and Percival. I've met Percival's uncle—a very sound man. If Mond will make stupid difficulties, why should I put myself out?"

"I don't know," Daniel said. "I just had a feeling I could rely on you, that's all."

"Of course," said Fielding, "if you're afraid . . ."

"I am merely refusing to put up with unnecessary inconvenience. I came through my entire military career without a day's discomfort or annoyance, so you can hardly expect me to incur them now because of some silly scruple of Mond's."

"His secret—"

"—Whatever his secret may be, it is his patriotic duty to hand it over to responsible people. I know something of these matters, and I know that Pappenheim and Percival are suitable recipients."

"Come on, Daniel. We're wasting our time."

Fielding and Daniel rose to go.

"Sit down," said Detterling crossly, "and listen. If you're determined to see this through, I suppose I must help you. *Res Unius*, et cetera, even if Mond is only a fake."

Detterling lifted his left ankle with his right hand, placed it carefully on his knee, and then put his fingers together.

"I can't actually escort Mond myself," he intoned, "because I'm going to the races this afternoon with Max de Freville and I've got my cousin Canteloupe coming to dinner. But the answer's so simple I wonder you haven't seen it for yourself."

"It isn't simple at all. Earle Restarick's people will be keeping a watch, both for Daniel Mond *and* Trooper Lewis, at every likely crossing place on the frontier. Now, we're going to be fully occupied here in Baden doing our courier stunt at last; and even if I could spare the whole Squadron to escort Daniel, there's no end to the dodges they might try to stop him getting across. That's why we were relying on you. There'll be a lot of good reasons why they won't want to tangle with a British Member of Parliament. If Daniel were once firmly under your protection, they'd probably call the hunt off."

"I've already told you," said Detterling, "that I'm not at leisure for the task. Baden races only happen once a year, and one can't afford to miss anything. However, it is all, as

I was saying when you interrupted me, exceedingly simple. Listen carefully, and I will tell you what you must do..."

When they left Detterling, Fielding and Daniel collected Daniel's luggage from the hall of the hotel and put it back in the Land Rover. Then they were driven by Lamb down a broad avenue, past the Kurhaus and the many coloured terrace of the Trinkhalle, and up to the left on to the slopes which overlooked the town. All about them, as they went, leaves rustled and water glistened; while the hill which they must climb to reach the Squadron resembled nothing so much, with its little pavilions and carefully drilled trees, as a toy scene set down as a background for a child's model railway.

As they drove no one said anything at all until they had almost reached the camp at the top of the hill. Then Daniel murmured,

"I'm sorry you won't be there... at the end. After we've come so far."

Fielding shrugged.

"You had to leave us sometime. We'll miss you, Daniel. But it's also rather a relief."

At the Squadron camp the umpires were already waiting to brief Fielding. Daniel, in an end of holiday mood, went round saying his good-byes. But since the Sabre Squadron was at last about to go into action, no one had much time to spare for him.

"See you at Lancaster some day," said Julian James; "I must pay the old place a visit."

"Don't forget," said Basil Bunce gloomily, "to send back Lewis's identity card."

"Don't forget," said Tom Chead, "that you owe the Captain nearly four quid for that kit you're wearing."

"Don't forget... don't forget us," said Michael Lamb, and went back to checking his engine.

A little later an order was shouted down the lines and everyone started to put on his anti-radiation suit. Daniel put his on just by Mick Motley's ambulance, in which his suitcase was already stowed.

"Typical of the Dragoons," Mick Motley was saying: "they have all the bright ideas and leave others to do the dirty work . . . Anti-mist solution for the eye-piece—here."

"I'm sorry to be a nuisance."

"I don't mind, Danny. I'm glad to help. The fact remains that when the chips are down, so to speak, the Dragoons have always quietly disappeared. With the best of excuses, of course."

"Detterling hadn't even a good excuse. Only that he was going with a friend to the races. He just said, 'Motley's your man—and tell him I said so'. He seemed to think he was doing you a favour."

"They're clever at giving that impression . . . Don't forget to check your oxygen rate every fifteen minutes."

"How long does the oxygen last?"

"About three hours. But you and I will be out of these things long before then."

After that Mick's Staff Sergeant zipped up their suits and there was no further conversation.

The Sabre Squadron, with the ambulance in the middle of the column, wound down the hill, turned right along the wide avenue past the Trinkhalle and the Kurhaus, and then right again. Daniel peering through the port-hole in one of the rear doors, saw a sign which said "Schwarzwald". The Squadron, he knew, would set up a base-headquarters somewhere on the edge of the Black Forest, and would then return to proceed with its task of purifying and disciplining a theoretically devastated Baden Baden. Meanwhile, Mick would stay at the base in the forest and set up his Rehabilitation Centre; and it was on the functions of this that Daniel's final escape would depend.

Slowly the column rumbled on. Daniel looked out of the

porthole at the armoured car just behind. This, he knew, was the leading vehicle of Piers Bungay's Troop and contained, among other things, Bungay, to whom he had not had time to say good-bye. This was sad, as Bungay was not the sort of person he would meet again. Julian, yes, Fielding, yes, and even Captain Detterling. But not Piers Bungay, who was now locked away from him for ever inside his anti-radiation suit. Daniel hated to leave people for ever without saying good-bye; it was like forgetting to close an account which one meant never to use again. For year after year, he felt, his name would be set, on the first of every month, at the top of a new page in a ledger; but at the end of every month the page would still be blank, and the shop-keeper would shake his head sadly, wondering what he had done to offend his client. Quite untrue, of course. For most people in this world, whether shop-keepers or Bungays, did not sorrow over the empty page, they just put a line straight through the name at its head; but this too was sad, even sadder than reproachful remembrance. "Don't forget us," Michael Lamb had said; but how soon would Michael forget?

The ambulance came to a halt. Daniel, in accordance with his instructions, sat still in the back; until eventually a radiation suit opened the doors and beckoned him down. He could not even tell whether it was Mick or the Staff Sergeant. Whoever it was lumbered up into the ambulance and arranged some blankets on stretchers; then he opened a cupboard and dragged out what looked like a small deflated barrage balloon. With surprising deftness he tied a pair of cords round a fir-tree, tied two more round another fir-tree, and then gave the silver material a brisk shake, whereupon it unfolded itself and dropped a gleaming curtain to the ground, thus forming a small bell tent the apex of which was secured by the lines of cord stretched between tree and tree. Other such tents, sending out a susurration as of pliant tinfoil, were unfolding all round them; until the scene resembled an engineer's drawing which Daniel had once been shown of an envisaged settlement, crowned with domes, turrets and cupolas, on the moon. The figure in the suit took him by the arm, shook him out of his rapt contemplation of the miracle that was making around them, and guided him, through a complexity of overlapping flaps, into the tent. There he unzipped himself and Daniel, and worked his suit off his shoulders. It turned out to be Mick.

"Magic gadgets, these," he said. "This is where I live and examine my patients in ray-proof security."

"Except that every one of them that comes in will bring contamination with him. To say nothing of what we've brought in ourselves."

"They're experimenting with some kind of spray to deal with that. They're also planning lighter and more flexible suits in which it will be possible to work—even to perform surgery—so that one need never take them off."

"Except to eat and defecate."

"Stop making difficulties, Daniel. It's early days yet. Eating will be reduced to swallowing pills, and as for the other thing, they're planning a built-in chemical unit."

"Charming."

"Anyway, as things are we've got this tent, and you'd better make the best of it because there may be a long time to wait."

"Can't we go out? It's such a beautiful day."

"Not without wearing our radiation suits. The umpires would stop us. They're going to be swarming all round here —we're part of a very important experiment."

"I do believe you're preening yourself, Mick."

Outside there was a grinding of engines.

"That'll be the main body of the Squadron going back to Baden. They should be bringing in my first patients in about two hours."

"Who will these patients be?"

"Spare soldiers from the umpiring units with tickets describing their supposed condition. I give them temporary treatment and then put the necessary admin. machinery in motion to deal with their cases. Which reminds me. We'd better make out a ticket for you."

While Mick scribbled on a writing pad, Daniel looked out of a perspex panel in the wall of the tent. The observers' charabanc drew into his field of vision and emitted the observers. The Brigadier at their head was beaming and gesticulating; the obese Turk, just behind him and still plainly drunk, got stuck in the door and had to be pushed through by Alfie Schroeder.

"Here you are," said Mick, handing Daniel a sheet of paper. "Don't lose it."

"What does it mean?"

"You'll see . . . Oh God. Not them again."

The two Indian observers had come giggling into the tent.

"No nice lady today, doctor sahib?"

The Japanese scurried in behind them.

"Ah, the rehabilitation gentlemen. The rehabilitation is not so instructive this morning."

Pappenheim came in, glowered at Daniel, and went out.

"Come along, gentlemen," clucked the Brigadier outside: "we shall be returning to the Rehabilitation Centre when it's in action later on."

Noises of giggling, clucking, chirruping, panting and complaining faded away among the trees.

"I think," said Mick Motley, "that we'd better have some lunch and get a rest while we can. You're going to need all your strength, Daniel. Yes, indeed. All your strength."

About two and a half hours later the first of Mick Motley's radio-active "patients" began to come in. These were cases so badly affected that they could not walk and had been ferried to the base on improvised stretchers strapped to armoured cars. They were one and all prescribed "deep sedation", after which they were laid in rows under the trees to die. They would be finally disposed of by working parties from the Fusiliers, who were expected to arrive that evening.

The official observers and journalists took considerable interest in this grisly charade, the journalists at least apparently feeling that some protest was called for. Although Mick Motley explained patiently that all those so far "treated", being beyond hope, would in any case die in a few hours and painfully, this was not considered a good enough answer. The public conscience, it appeared, required radio-active humanity to live to the last gasp even if it would prefer not to.

"Look, gentlemen," said Mick desperately : "this is euthanasia, mercy killing."

"Mercy killing," said a hatchet-faced man in a tweed suit, "is for animals. Surely medicine can do better than that."

"Not yet it can't," said Mick. "The only hope left for that lot is God's grace."

Alfie Schroeder, who was standing near Daniel, thought this so funny that he cackled with laughter; whereupon the Brigadier, who was looking rather distraught, led his charges away to their picnic tea.

"What's with you?" whispered Alfie to Daniel, lingering.

"The doctor's fixing something to get me out . . . How long is your lot staying here?"

"I don't know. Why?"

"It would be better if that German, Pappenheim, didn't see what happens."

"What harm can he do you?"

"I'm not sure. But I think it would be better if he didn't know what's done with me."

"I'll do my best." Alfie grinned and produced a packet of laxative chocolate. "Of course, if he doesn't like chocolate . . . One thing. If ever you can talk about all this, you'll talk to me first, won't you? You probably don't think much of the Billingsgate Press, but one good turn deserves another."

"Agreed."

Half an hour later, some less seriously afflicted patients arrived, straggling on foot in a long column which was guarded by two armoured cars. Daniel watched through the perspex panel as they were lined up outside the tent. A group of five men staged a breakaway; a machine gun chattered; an approving umpire made a note on his mill-board.

"Now then," said Mick. "I'm going to mix you in with that lot. When you leave here you'll be a soldier from the first battalion of the Cumberland Light Infantry, which is one of the umpiring units, and you'll be impersonating an enemy casualty captured in the ruins of Baden Baden. All right?"

"Surely one of the umpires will see that something's wrong? They're watching every move."

"No. The assumption is that enemy casualties, as opposed to civilian ones, may have been wearing protective suits at the time of the explosion."

Mick pointed through the perspex. Several of the "casualties" were indeed wearing anti-radiation suits.

"We're going to pass you off as one of them," Mick said. "Shock case."

"My luggage?"

"Don't worry about that. Don't worry about anything. Remember, Daniel: no one ever interferes with an ambulance, wherever it's going. Get the idea?"

"Restarick's people would interfere with a hearse, let alone an ambulance."

"Not unless they had reason to suppose you were in it. We're going to take care of that now."

Mick helped Daniel with his suit and then zipped him in. He produced a pair of pliers and did something rather strenuous to the zip. After this he took the casualty ticket which he had written out earlier for Daniel, added something at the top, and handed it back.

"This is your passport," he shouted into Daniel's ear. "Don't lose it. Now wait."

The first casualty came into the tent. Mick examined his ticket, said something which Daniel could not hear, endorsed the ticket, and gestured the man out. The second casualty to enter was one in a radiation suit. This time Mick took considerably longer reading the ticket. Then he showed the man a corner of the tent, indicating that he was to wait there; after which he looked slowly up at Daniel and nodded his head towards the way out.

Once outside, Daniel was approached by two men in radiation suits, who looked over his ticket and led him off towards a group of ambulances which had accrued, Daniel supposed, during the course of the afternoon. They all seemed identical with Mick's. As he went, Daniel had a brief glimpse of Pappenheim, who was disappearing rapidly into a clump of bushes. Full marks to Alfie Schroeder of the Billingsgate Press . . . though surely, Daniel thought, there could no longer be anything to fear from Pappenheim. From the others, yes; but there had been no sign of them since the note addressed to Lamb. Helped by his two escorts, he clambered into the back of an ambulance and was relieved to see his suitcase where he had left it. Presumably there was to be a convoy and Mick's ambulance was to make part of it. His guides raised their right hands in a kind of admonitory salute and stalked away.

A few minutes later he was joined by two more casualties, neither of them in radiation suits, who looked at him curiously but said nothing. Someone climbed into the cab in front; twice the engine failed to start, then the ambulance drew slowly away through the wood and bumped on to the road. So soon, Daniel thought; there could be no question of a convoy then. For the first time it occurred to him to look at the ticket which Mick had made for him. This, being written in a typical doctor's hand, was barely decipherable; but at the top Daniel could just make out the word "encased" and the interrupted phrase "suit only removable by". Remembering Mick's business with the pliers, Daniel felt behind him with his gauntleted hands and failed to locate the thong of material which operated the runner on the zip. So that

was it : no zip, probably other damage as well; so that no
one could identify him or question him until he was cut out
or otherwise released from his sheath of this new and secret
material, which would doubtless require expert handling.
"Suit only removable by." He had the best protection in the
world : he was entombed.

And for all he knew betrayed. Who were these two men sitting with him? Who was *driving*? Where were they going?
Hitherto he had assumed without question that Motley was
on his side; that he had been told a certain amount by Fielding, had guessed as much more as he needed to know, and
was therefore, out of his natural decency, lending assistance
which only he could give. But why should this be so? Why
should not Mick Motley have his own axe to grind? Almost
everyone else seemed to have one. He could be sending
Daniel anywhere—to Percival or to Restarick or to the Devil,
for all Daniel knew, and not a thing he could do about it.
He could move only with difficulty. He had forgotten to
apply anti-mist solution to his perspex eye-piece before putting the suit on again (why hadn't Motley reminded him?)
and by now he could hardly see. When his supply of oxygen
ran out, as it would do in about three hours (according to
the estimate Mick had given him) he would not be able to
breathe. Suit only removable by . . . And if whatever or whoever was needed was not available? *Dormiat Danielus.*

Come, come. This was paranoia, this was panic. Unworthy
of a Dragoon. Be calm. The ambulance, which was now
going very fast, swung round a corner so sharply that all three
of the rear passengers fell in a huddle on the floor. One of
his unencumbered companions helped Daniel back to his seat
and said something inaudible with an ugly twist of his lips.
Daniel looked stupidly back and nodded inside his helmet.
The ambulance, having picked up the speed it had lost on
the turn, went faster than ever—apparently, thank God,
down a straight road now. Daniel tried to peer out of one
of the portholes, but his eye-piece was too misty for him to

make out anything except an unwinding riband of grey. Calm. Of course Mick Motley was his friend. Then why did his two companions look so grim and threatening? Sheer fright, perhaps, at the speed. After all, one of them had helped him up very kindly; there was no reason to suppose they were his enemies. No reason at all. As for his oxygen, he had enough for about two hours and three-quarters. Of course someone would be available to release him long before then. Of course Mick knew what he was doing. Of course he was being taken to a safe place. Yes, but where? Well, it was his fault if he didn't know that, he should have asked Mick. Why hadn't he? Because he was bewildered, because he hadn't been thinking, because he had trusted Mick implicitly; and of course he was right to do so. Of course. Calm. Be calm.

After twenty minutes of driving dead straight and always at the same high speed, the ambulance made a long turn to the right, and then proceeded rather more slowly than before, taking occasional bends. After five minutes of this, Daniel was suddenly conscious of a noise like a telephone ringing in a distant room. The warning bell, he decided; they must be coming into a town. At this point the ambulance stopped. For ten minutes, twenty, nothing happened. "No one ever interferes with an ambulance," Mick had said. Thirty minutes, forty... For Christ's sake. Less than two hours of oxygen now, much less. The rear doors opened; a jaw with a cigarette clamped in it was thrust into the ambulance and two beady eyes looked at Daniel. The cigarette waggled, a yellow claw snatched his ticket, a forehead narrowed, a pair of shoulders shrugged in spiteful resignation, and the claw, having returned the ticket, was raised to a hat in mock salute. A round hat; French.

After a further wait of twenty minutes the ambulance drove on, sedately now, its bell ringing no more. Again it stopped, again the rear doors opened. Below them Daniel could see a blur of white. Two smaller blurs detached themselves, turned into orderlies as they came closer, took Daniel efficiently by either arm, helped him out of the ambulance, across some gravel, up some steps, down a corridor and into a room. Daniel thrust his ticket at them, gestured frantically at the back of his suit and at the left breast where the oxygen control lay. One of them took the ticket, shrugged, gave it back, grinned at his colleague and followed him out of the door. Daniel rushed after them but the door was locked.

By his calculation (and if Mick had been telling the truth) he had just on an hour's supply of oxygen left. *An hour?* He hadn't allowed, he suddenly remembered, for the time during which he had worn the suit between leaving the camp above Baden and arriving at the forest base. That had been —oh God, God—at least forty minutes. He had perhaps a quarter of an hour left. He clawed behind him at the useless zip. He thumped on the locked door. He even yelled aloud inside his armour. Then he sank to his knees on the floor, weeping and praying to a God in whom he did not believe to send him succour; and at the end of his prayer the door duly opened to reveal Leonard Percival in battle dress and just behind him Earle Restarick.

For some moments both of them stood grinning down at Daniel. They've got me where they want me now, he thought. And then, why are they together? But what difference did that make to him? The deal which they would offer was already plain. They'd leave him inside the suit but set him up somehow with more oxygen—under constant threat of withdrawing supplies. Only when they knew what they wanted would they release him from his prison ... or perhaps just leave him to die. But this was France, this must be a French hospital, surely ... No. To judge from their triumphant smiles there could be no escape. It was all quite clear. Tell us or suffocate : your knowledge or your life.

Daniel was still on his knees. He must get up or they would think he was imploring their mercy. With an immense effort (the oxygen must be very low now) he rose to his feet, staggered over to the wall and with his right gauntlet traced an enormous NO. Then he turned and faced them, standing very upright. For perhaps ten seconds he confronted their still smiling faces through the sweaty perspex; then the dark came up and swallowed him whole.

When Daniel recovered consciousness, he was in bed in a large and pleasant room the ample window of which framed a row of sunlit poplar trees. On either side of his bed sat Leonard Percival and Earle Restarick.

"You've no idea," Percival said, "the trouble they had cutting that suit off you. They jolly nearly had to use a blowtorch. You ought to be exceedingly grateful they got you out in time."

"Gratitude's not my forte at the moment."

"Come, come. Things might be a lot worse. Did you really think, Mond, that you could put an end to all your troubles just by leaving Germany? Didn't it occur to you that the sort of organisation which Restarick here represented would have resources that transcended a simple frontier?"

"I was putting my trust in England. A man can be safe there. In England. In Cambridge."

"Maybe," said Earle Restarick, "and maybe not. Anyhow, you're still a long way from England. In Strasbourg, to be more exact. How do you feel about putting your trust in the French?"

Daniel did not reply.

"Tell me," said Earle, "if you had got away . . . to England . . . what would you have done? When all the dons said, 'Welcome home, Daniel Mond, and what have you brought back from Göttingen?', what would you have done?"

"I should have told them that I'd failed."

"Even if it meant giving up your chance of a Fellowship and leaving Lancaster College?"

"Rather than tell anyone what I knew," insisted Daniel,

"I should have told them that I'd failed with the Dortmund Papers."

"Why?"

Daniel shrugged against the pillow.

"Do you think I might have something to eat? I don't know how long I've been asleep, but I'm damned hungry."

"You were out for sixteen hours. They stuck a needle into you to make sure you had a nice long rest."

"To get my strength back for whatever's coming next, I suppose."

Earle twitched slightly and pressed a bell. A little while later a black nun came in with a tray of rolls and coffee.

"You know," said Percival, "we admire you. You've given us a lot of trouble, and you're just about as wrong-headed as you can be, but we really do admire you. So as a measure of our appreciation we're going to tell you a story. A story with a moral," he said, flashing his spectacles. "You'll like that, won't you?"

Earle looked away and Daniel went on eating.

"The story started," said Percival, "when certain inquisitive gentlemen in Whitehall heard that Dirange was sending someone out to have a go at the Dortmund Papers. Now as it happens, and although you didn't know it, quite a few people had a rough idea of what these were about; but since no one had ever been able to do the sums properly, it wasn't the faintest good. What was needed was someone to do a pukkha job of working it all out, in the hope that this would confirm and add to what little had been surmised and, most important of all, enable the knowledge to be applied. And now here was wonder-boy Mond about to have a crack, and the betting was that he'd succeed."

"Whose betting?"

"Let's just say the experts'. These days, Mond, people like you go on record very early in your lives. In your case, when you won the Spinoza Prize. You'd already become a valuable national property, you see. So we knew all about your capacities—but we also knew you were a bit quirky. All this left-wingery and stuff. You being you, it was clear from the start that if the secret was the sort of thing we thought it was, then you'd do your damnedest to supress it when you found it."

"How right you were."

"So we had to think up ways of bringing pressure to bear on you."

"I wonder you didn't fit up a wheel and a rack."

"We're not allowed to torture people," said Percival, as though the suggestion had been entirely serious; "not English people anyway. Not yet. It has to be psychological. So we consulted some of your friends at Lancaster—"

"—*What friends?*"

"It would hardly be fair to tell you. You'll just have to live with that."

Jacquiz? Robert Constable? Was no one to be trusted any more?

"So we consulted some of your chums," Percival was saying, "and we found out that you had a very affectionate and dependent nature. If there was one thing which would really knock you flat, it was the withdrawal of love. So at this stage we made a very simple plan. Restarick here was to turn on his affection and then turn it off again; you were to be left in loneliness for some weeks; and then Restarick would come back, full of love after all, and you in your relief would tell him anything he asked you."

"A good plan," said Daniel bitterly; "you don't know how good."

"But," said Earle, "it went wrong. Just when you were nicely softened up, those Dragoons hit town. So no more loneliness. A new friend called Fielding Gray. Months of work wasted."

"You knew so much," said Daniel, "didn't you realise the Dragoons were coming, and that Julian James had been at Lancaster, which made it at least possible that I'd get to know them?"

"Blind spot," said Percival sadly. "The very last thing any-one thought of was that you'd become pals with the military. So no one had checked on the Dragoons. An endearing ex-ample of British inefficiency . . . Anyway, there it was. Change of plan required. Love was out. The next best thing was fear."

Percival rose and went to the window.

"There was nothing personal," he said bleakly.

"I dare say not."

"The same goes with me," said Earle. "I've told you before and it's true. I really was fond of you, Daniel."

"But that didn't stop you later, did it?"

"Look," said Percival, swinging in from the window, "we're not going to apologise. Restarick and myself and the rest of us, we were acting on behalf of the free powers of Western Europe and of Great Britain among them. We needed what you knew."

"And the way to get it," said Daniel, "was through my fear."

"Right. So we started to frighten you. Up till then I'd just been keeping an eye on things. I sat up on that hill, a humble Lieutenant of Foot, receiving reports from Restarick and von Bremke—"

"—So he was in it too?"

"Holding the ring, you might say. Among other things, he was meant to keep an eye on your progress, and to play on your obstinacy by telling you the job couldn't be done, that Dortmund was off his nut anyway—in the hope that you'd turn round and show him just how wrong he was. But that's all by the way . . . As I was saying, there I sat in those bar-racks, and if things had gone right you'd never have known I existed. But when a new plan had to be hatched up, my help was needed. We had to convince you that you were in danger. We had to set up a myth of goodies and baddies and make you believe in it. So I took the first possible oppor-tunity of introducing myself and Pappenheim as agents of the Saint George department, and we created a whopping great dragon : an entirely fictitious neo-Nazi conspiracy. With a bit of American aid thrown in because you, as an anti-capitalist, were sure to swallow that. Fear is like beauty, Mond; it lies in the eye of the beholder."

Percival sat down on the foot of the bed.

"You won't need me to spell it all out from there. The technique was to have the dragon puff flame increasingly near your backside, and every time he did so renew St George's offer to come to the rescue—on his terms of course. But then something else went wrong. Captain Detterling upset our little scheme whereby Restarick's 'neo-Nazis' were to have prevented you leaving Germany. Still, we were in high hopes. The dragon stepped up his puffing and your pants were getting hotter and hotter—till suddenly you vanished."

"So that at least was genuine," Daniel said. "The Dragoons really were helping me?"

"For what use it was, yes."

"It's important to me to know. Fielding Gray and the rest —they weren't just part of the pretence? They really did try to rescue me?"

"In their casual way."

"At least their friendship was true."

"Yes. But it didn't take us long to find out where you were —and we guessed what they hoped to do with you. Hand you over to Detterling, M.P., for him to do his fix-it act all over again. So we decided to let you get that far—indeed to make sure that you did. We persuaded the brass-hats to switch the atomic attack from Worms to Baden. It took some doing, and we were nearly refused, but at the last moment someone very important indeed weighed in on our side. The whole manoeuvre was switched, Mond, to get you unsuspecting to Baden Baden; you must have cost hundreds of thousands of pounds."

"I'm flattered."

"Meanwhile, someone had waited on Captain Detterling

and told him, very firmly, what he was to do about you when you arrived. He didn't care about being told, but he's a responsible man, he has his country's interest 'at heart, and so, after a few things had been explained to him, he agreed to obey our orders. He would advise Captain Gray to hand you over to Dr Motley for the last leg of your escape. And now I'm afraid you're going to be very disillusioned to hear that Mick Motley had his instructions too."

"But you said ... you said that the Dragoons were genuine, that they were what they seemed to be."

"The Dragoons of the Sabre Squadron, but not Detterling, and not Dr Motley. One of the things I sniffed out during my peaceful days in the barracks was that Motley, having made a corporal's wife pregnant, was reluctantly compelled to abort her. So it wasn't too hard to persuade Motley to come in on our side. I broke the sad news to him at Bad Neuenahr, while your lot were still in Kassel, and from then on he was running for our team. Don't think too harshly of him. He's got an old mother and about ten unmarried sisters to support."

"And so ... Motley imprisoned me in that suit and sent me on to you. You know, when I saw a Frenchman at the border, I really thought I was safe."

There was a long pause.

"Listen to me, Danny," said Earle. "Someone's going to find out this secret of yours some day. Like Percival says, we already have some idea of what it's about. Why don't you just tell us and be done?"

"Decency," said Daniel, gathering all his strength. "Someone else may find out, as you say, and he may tell you, but it won't be me. To tell you would be to destroy what I live by."

"A good answer, Mond," said Percival austerely. "But do you remember, when we started this explanation, I told you that the story had a moral? The story's not over yet."

Percival smiled blandly, and assumed a didactic air.

"When you got here yesterday evening," he said, "our intention, as you seemed to realise, was to make you talk by refusing you oxygen if you didn't. As I've told you, we're not allowed to torture people; but in this case we were covered, because it had all been rigged to look like an accident. Damaged suit, oxygen supplies exhausted, etc., etc. The French had agreed to co-operate, to make sure of their share of the secret; and in actual fact those radiation suits are the very devil to deal with. So we were going to torture you under the pretence of being unable to cut you free. Rather like the man in the iron mask. We'd have fixed up the oxygen and communicated with you by writing. As it happened, you passed out. But we could have fixed you up with oxygen just the same, left you in the suit, and then started our little game when you came round. But here you are—free. Haven't you wondered why?"

"Because I made it plain that I wouldn't surrender?"

"No. It was a good gesture, Mond, but you wouldn't have gone on writing NO for long, I promise you that."

"Perhaps you are preparing some other kind of beastliness."

"How many times do I have to tell you that we're not allowed to torture you? Our effort with the anti-radiation suit was our only chance in that line. Why, Mond, do you suppose that we've already abandoned it?"

"Look, Danny," said Earle. "Tell Percival what he wants to know. Tell him now, before it's too late. Otherwise he's going to tell *you* something—something which will really hurt. More than torture or anything else. Far more than the loss of your decency."

Bluff, thought Daniel. They daren't go ahead with the oxygen treatment—probably someone higher up stopped them—so now they're trying to bluff.

"Believe me, Daniel. It will be better if you tell him."

"As I understand the matter," Daniel said, "there was never any real threat, even in Germany, and there certainly isn't now. I'm in a hospital in Strasbourg, and I'm free to leave for England any minute I choose. Of course, you can always turn childish—hide my passport, steal my money— but if you think that will help you, after all I've been through, you're even sillier than I thought. So kindly send for my luggage. I'm going to get up."

"You haven't answered my question," Percival said. "We had you just where we wanted you in that radiation suit: why do you think we let you go?"

"I don't know and I don't care. I imagine that you or your superiors thought better of murdering me. Now please send for my luggage."

"We let you go, Mond, because we thought of a better way. The oxygen game had its risks. The French doctor was nervous about keeping you in that suit. It might affect you mentally, he said. You might go into a claustrophobic frenzy and suffocate yourself. Or he might get the pressures wrong and kill you by mistake. And of course you're much too valuable to lose. Nevertheless we'd have gone ahead, Mond, had Restarick here not pointed out that, *you being you,* there was a very much simpler way, so simple that it hadn't even occurred to me."

Percival sniffed several times, then removed his spectacles and wiped his watering eyes with a handkerchief. He was, Daniel realised with horror, crying with amusement.

"Your friends in the Sabre Squadron, the only real friends you've had all along. I tested you about them just now, said they were casual and so on. But you insisted, and you were right, that in their way they were true. They helped you, and they didn't ask for anything back. Fielding Gray and his officers. Sergeant-Major Bunce, Corporal-Major Chead, Michael Lamb. Mugger, now happily convalescing in Bielefeld. Your friends.

"Now, if you don't tell us about the Dortmund Papers, Mond, your friends are all going to be ruined—just because they helped you. They aided you in impersonating a serving soldier, bad enough in itself. But what is far, far worse, they thereby made you privy to important official secrets: those suits, those special tents, the whole general method of a Courier Team's operation. *Not* things which you are entitled to know, Mond, but things which they enabled you to study, at close quarters, for over a week. Gray and the officers will be cashiered, Mond; Bunce and Chead will be reduced to the ranks and dishonourably dismissed. All of them, along with Lamb and Mugger, will go to prison. That's what will happen, Mond, unless you come across with what you know. Which brings me to the moral of this story: there's weakness in numbers. If you'd stayed on your own, Mond, you might have kept your secret. There was very little we could do to you—I've told you that. But when you asked other people for help, you were recruiting your own enemies. Every hand raised to help you, in the long run, was a hand raised to drag you down."

For some minutes Daniel said nothing. Then,

"You'd better send for my suitcase. I shall need the notes which are in it. And who must I explain to? You or Earle could never understand."

"There'll be someone here in an hour. Try to be ready by then."

Earle and Percival went out. Five minutes later a black nun came in with Daniel's suitcase. Oh dear, he thought, oh dear, oh dear, oh dear. He got out of bed and looked through the window. A short drop on to flower beds: no good that way. So he went to his suitcase, rummaged about for a time, and then found what he was looking for, tucked in a side-pocket with his supply of pencils. Oh dear, oh dear. "They helped you," Percival had said, "and they didn't ask for anything back." Fielding, Michael, Mugger. Basil Bunce and Tom Chead. My comrades of a week, my Dragoons, my Sabre Squadron. Yet even to save these he could not tell what he knew, for to do so would be indecent; it would be to murder the God in whom he did not believe; it would be to destroy his honour as a Jew. But perhaps there was a way (so simple that it hadn't even occurred to Leonard Percival) of keeping silence without also ruining his friends; for after all, Percival and his colleagues were interested in his secret, not in taking revenge. Or so he could only hope. And so he did hope, as he opened the pocket knife which he kept for sharpening his pencils and then (asking grace of the God in whom he did not believe) urged it towards his throat.

FIELDING GRAY

EXTRACT FROM FIELDING GRAY'S WORKING NOTEBOOK.

May 23, 1959.

This evening I have just taken my old journal out again. Originally it consisted only of scattered incidents and observations, but I put it all into coherent form while I was stationed on the island of Santa Kytherea in 1955. Although I took another look at it last year, while I was in hospital after that Cyprus business, and tidied it up a bit for the sake of self-respect and the honour due to the English language, I never thought that it would have any value, other than as a private reminder of what I would really have done much better to forget. However, Gregory Stern is prepared to pay me handsomely to turn it into a novel. Though he has never seen it, he seems to have a very strong hunch about it, and all that on the strength of a chance word or two—for I very nearly didn't mention it at all. I thought of Christopher, and I was going to keep quiet; but then again it all happened a long time ago now, and Gregory Stern, on whom I must be largely dependent for years to come, was very pressing.

In any event, there it is. I've undertaken to turn this journal into a novel ... a work of 'fiction'. I suppose the first step is to read it through once more ...

The Journal of Fielding Gray ...

THE JOURNAL OF
FIELDING GRAY

ON THE SECOND SUNDAY after the war in Europe ended, we had a service in the school chapel in memory of the dead. As many old boys as could be reached at short notice had been told about it, and the visitors' pews were crowded with uniforms. While all of us were wearing scruffy grey flannels and patched tweed jackets, the champions of England were hung about with every colour and device in the book. There were the black and gold hats of the guardsmen, the dark green side-caps of the rifles, kilts swaying from the hips of the highlanders, and ball buttons sprayed all over the horse artillerymen; there were macabre facings and curiously knotted lanyards; there were even the occasional pairs of boots and spurs, though these were frowned on in 1945 because of Fascist associations.

At first the service was in keeping with these sumptuous appointments. A spirited rendering of 'Jerusalem', the political implications of which escaped most present, set up a smug sense of triumph; and that passage from the Apocrypha which they always have at these affairs, though it paid a decent tribute to the rank and file, left us in no doubt that what really mattered was material wealth and traditional rule. I myself had a place in the Sixth Form block which commanded a good view of the visitors, and I could see, by this time, that the magnificent officers were openly preening themselves, as if the whole show had been got up solely in their applause. Indeed, when the role of the dead was called (a proceeding which took some time), there were unmistakable signs of boredom and pique; there was much fingering of canes and riding whips, much fidgeting with Sam Browne belts; the warriors were not assembled, it seemed, to listen at length to the achievements of others. At

the very least, they appeared to feel, the list could have done
with some discreet editing.

'Connaught la Poeur Beresford,' boomed the Senior Usher,
'Lieutenant, the Irish Guards. Died in a Field Hospital of
wounds received at Anzio. Previously awarded the Military
Cross for gallantry in the Libyan desert.'

Well, *that* was all right: even the supercilious cavalier in
the cherry-coloured trousers could hardly find fault with that.
But : —

'Michael John Blood. Corporal, the Royal Corps of
Signals. Died of pneumonia in the Military Hospital at
Aldershot.'

That, of course, really would not do at all. Or rather, it
would do well enough provided that no one called attention
to it. There was no need to drag it out in public, a sentiment
evidently held by a young and marble-jawed major, who
was obsessively stroking a huge hat of khaki felt. Watching
the major sneer, I felt a guilty pang of sorrow for Michael
John Blood, who had been scrofulous and bandy to the point
of caricature but who had never sneered at anyone. R.I.P.
Who was this major to spit on the pathetic grave?

But then again, who was I to be critical, even of a sneering
bully like that? Shutting my ears to the grinding rehearsal of
mortality, I reflected that my own state of mind, while perhaps less invidious than that of the gathered junkers, was
comparable and quite as selfish. ('Norman Isaac Cohen.
Captain, the Parachute Regiment' ... *Cohen*?) For the only
feeling of which I was really conscious, on that beautiful
summer's evening in the first Maytime of peace, was one of
relief : relief that no one was going to kill me, that I could
now proceed without let into a future which promised both
pleasure and distinction. There was, for a start, a whole
summer of cricket before me; and after that I was to stay on
at school a further year, during which time I would be Head
of my House (perhaps of the entire school) and would
attempt to convert the Minor Scholarship, which I had won
to Lancaster College the previous April, into a full-blooded

Major Award. Thus a place at Cambridge was already awaiting me, and since my father was well provided with money
(if not exactly generous), I could enter the contest with an easy
mind as one whose motive was honour and not necessity.

'William King Fullworthy. Sergeant, the Intelligence
Corps. Somewhere in the Burmese jungle.'

Somewhere in the jungle. It only went to show. Fullworthy,
who was scarcely two years older than I was, had won, before
he went for a soldier, the most brilliant of all the brilliant
awards that Lancaster had to offer. But Fullworthy, it
seemed, would not return to claim it: situation vacant.
Whereas I, Fielding Gray, had only to step outside into the
evening sun, and on all sides the world would lie serene about
me, to bring me knowledge, sing my praises, yield me joy.

And so surely, I thought, in the face of this dispensation
I must at least try to show gratitude. But to whom? To
what?

'Tobias Ainsworth Jackson. Lieutenant-Colonel, the Royal
Army Ordnance Corps. Died of cardiac failure while commanding the 14h Supply Depot at Woking.'

Died of drink. Everyone knew the story, as Woking was
not far away and Colonel Jackson, bored with running what
was in effect a military funeral parlour, had frequently and
calamitously visited his old school. No, I could not be grateful
to him for the future which had been restored to me. But
to whom else? To dead, bandy Blood? Distasteful. To the
rose-lipped Cornet of the Blues, who was poutily languishing
opposite? Ridiculous. To the sneering major? Never. To
God? He shouldn't have let the whole thing start in the first
place. To Fate then? Perhaps. Or to Luck? That, surely,
was nearer the mark. One's gratitude was due to Lady Luck,
who would resent, one might presume, too much concern
for those she had deserted. Prudence dictated that Fullworthy,
somewhere in the jungle, should be left to rot unwept.

'Alastair Edward Farquar Morrison. Captain, the Norfolk
Yeomanry. Killed on the beaches of Crete, having first conducted himself with great courage and devotion to duty.

Captain Morrison, being pinned down by machine-gun fire . . .'

It was very difficult not to weep for him. Alastair Morrison
had been a man if ever there was one. Like his younger
brother Peter. Very slowly I turned my head until I could
see, further down the row, the large round face and sturdy
trunk of Peter Morrison.

'. . . Upon which Captain Morrison waded back into the
sea, dragged one man to safety and then returned for the
other. He was shot dead a few yards before he reached
shelter. Posthumously awarded the Victoria Cross.'

Peter's face, as I watched him, seemed to crumple slightly;
he blinked once, then blinked again; after which he sniffed
firmly, folded his arms over his chest, and resumed his usual
aspect of calm, good-humoured authority. Over the years
I had learned to love that look; but now, very soon, Peter
would be gone—not across Styx, like his brother, yet assuredly
into a different world. For Peter, a year older than myself
and at present Head of our House, would leave at the end
of the summer; and although I was heir apparent, I would
have preferred my friend's company to his title.

'Hilary James Royce. Major, the Royal Fusiliers. Killed
in the retreat from Tobruk.

'Percival Nicholas de Courcy Sangster. Second-Lieutenant,
the Rajputana Rifles. Killed in the defence of Singapore.

'Lancelot Sassoon-Warburton. Brigadier, formerly of the
Ninth Lancers. Killed during the evacuation of Dunkirk . . .'

Who would there be, I wondered, to replace Peter when
the summer was over? There would be, of course, Somerset:
Somerset Lloyd-James, my exact contemporary, who was now
sitting just behind me, nostrils bubbling and spots glowing,
as they always did when he was amused or excited. But
Somerset, though ə clever and entertaining friend, could
never mean the same to me as Peter; for all his shrewdness
he showed little understanding. And besides, he was in a
different House. Even if he could and would help, he was
not always available. Whereas Peter . . . Peter had always
been there when wanted, for his home was not far from mine

and we had known each other since we were tiny children.

'Cyprian Jordan Clement Willard Wyndham Trefusis, tenth and last Baron Trefoil of Truro . . . Trelawney, Squadron-Leader . . . Trevelyan . . .'

By this time the old boys were very restless indeed. The marble-jawed major was clawing ferociously at his felt hat. The cherry-trousered legs of the blasé cavalier were being crossed, re-crossed, positively entwined. Sufficient unto the day, I thought, the evil thereof. I would worry about Peter's departure when it was nearer—there were, after all, nine weeks to the end of the quarter. And there was, too, someone else. Not just Somerset Lloyd-James. Someone very different.

'The Honourable Andrew Usquebaugh, Midshipman, the Royal Navy . . . Valence . . . Vallis . . . Vazey . . .' Would it never stop? All right, so they're all dead. What good will it do them or anybody else to carry on about it? 'Alan George Williams . . . Derek Williams . . . Geoffrey Alaric Williams . . .' Dear *God*.

Yes. There was someone else all right, and he would still be in the school next year. Christopher Roland, who was sitting on the other side of chapel, beyond the choir in the Fifth Form block: short wavy tow hair; square creamy forehead; mild eyes, wide-set, and soft nose; full lips curved slightly downwards; dented chin. My own age and my own House. Not clever, but easy to talk to. Not handsome, but good to look on. Strong build and bones, but a gentle skin. 'Godfery Trajan Yarborough . . .' X, Y, Z. Surely there was no demise to record under Z?

'Zaccharias,' bawled the Senior Usher, 'Pilot Officer, the Royal Air Force.

'And lastly, Emanuel Zyn, Private, The Pioneer Corps. Died of tuberculosis in the hospital of Colchester military Prison, where he was a member of the maintenance staff.'

Although the fate of Private Zyn provoked the contempt of all present, the hymn which now followed put them in better accord with the proceedings. 'For all the Saints', though nominally about the dead, was too brisk in metre and bracing in tune to have reference to any but the living. Joyfully, the heroes in the visitors' pews mouthed their own praises, while the boys, courteous to their guests and glad to be on their feet for a change, added their loyal support. I sang with ironic relish (or so I told myself), Peter Morrison, along the row, joined tunelessly but solidly in, Somerset Lloyd-James behind me lisped away with spirit; and from the Fifth Form block Christopher Roland turned towards me, caught my eye and smiled. One way and the other, 'For all the Saints' restored optimism and good humour all round; so that when the Headmaster mounted the pulpit during the last rollicking verse, he was assured of a friendly audience for his address.

The audience did not remain friendly for long.

'Already,' the Headmaster said, 'the expected voices are to be heard among you. "It is all over", the voices are saying : "victory has been secured. Statesmen have wrought and politicians have intrigued; industrialists have been enriched, general officers have been ennobled; humble men have died and (we trust) will not be soon forgotten, and moralists have moralised assiduously on all these and other accounts. But now it is all over and we can return to the business and pleasure of the old, the real, life. We have endured six years of bereavement, danger, discomfort and official interference; and now we will have recompense in full".'

Now I came to think of it, this was exactly what everyone around me had indeed been saying; and to judge from the faces of the warriors it was a fair assessment of current opinion in the Mess. And what else, I asked myself, could the head man expect? Wars were fought either to annex or to preserve. This one, as we had all been told to the point of vomiting, had been fought to preserve freedom, and freedom, to all present in the chapel, meant a return to life as it had been before the struggle started. What they wanted, what I wanted, was a return to normal : an end of rationing, of regulations, of being bossed about by common little men in offices, and of depressing notices about duty all over the place.

We all wanted, we had all earned, some fun; and who better to pay the bill than the ill conditioned louts who had made all the trouble in the first place?

'This,' said the Headmaster, 'is what the expected voices, the voices of common self-interest, are already saying. It is my duty to tell you, both you who have fought and you have been made to sit helpless while your friends and brothers went out to die, that there can be no recompense and no return to the old life. This truth is both economic and political: England at present affords no substance for prizes, and the people of England (to say nothing of the world) will no longer tolerate what most of you here would mean by "the old life". But it is not on an economic or political level that I speak now. I must speak as a Christian. And as a Christian, I am to tell you that past inconvenience does not entitle you to present repayment, least of all at the expense of others, our so called enemies, who have suffered worse. "But", the expected voices will cry indignantly, "it was their fault." Their fault? The fault of ignorant peasants and misguided artisans, of children of your own age, who are at this minute starving among the rubble of their homes? *Their* fault? And even if it were, shall there be no forgiveness... no charity ... no love?'

There was precious little love to be seen on the faces in the visitors' pews. There was anger, pride, incredulity, sullenness, boredom or greed: no love. And really, I thought, why should there be? People who started wars of aggression, particularly with the British, deserved everything they got; it was no good asking my sympathy for the Germans, leave alone my love. Clearly, life must go on its way, and if luck had destined me for the comfortable courts of Lancaster rather than the ruined backstreets of Berlin, then there was no point in making myself miserable about it.

'And as for a return to the old life,' the Headmaster was saying, 'I tell you, again as a Christian, that what has happened cannot be dismissed as though it had never been. You cannot say, "The war is over; let us forget it and do as we did before." The enormity has been too great; the residue of guilt is so vast that we must all bear our share of it. We cannot retire into our pleasant gardens to sit at leisure while the world's wound festers outside our wall. It is not merely a question of feeding the hungry, or curing the maimed and diseased, though these offices will be important: it will also be required of us to acknowledge and to understand a cosmic infection of hatred and evil, which must henceforth be purified and for which the least of us here present must atone.'

As the Headmaster descended from the pulpit and began to walk back down the aisle towards his stall, I could hear a low and resentful muttering among the officers. One of them gestured obscenely, looked for a moment as if he were going to shout at the Headmaster's retreating back, was checked by a sharp but sympathetic nudge from his neighbour's one remaining elbow. The Headmaster was notorious for subjecting others to the exaggerated demands of his own conscience, but just this once, I felt, he might have been more tactful. Doctor Bunter at the organ, scenting trouble, broke prematurely into the introductory bars of the final hymn, with the result that half the congregation failed to find the place in time and 'The Day Thou gavest, Lord, has ended' started off like a bucolic round rendered by six hundred lugubrious drunks. But when, half way through the second verse, proper control was achieved, the sad, familiar song began to take effect. The officers relaxed and sang with restrained solidarity. The boys bellowed happily away in a sentimental trance. There was now a feeling, all through the building, as of souls melting and mingling into one another to form one huge and quivering spiritual colloid. It was a communion on the lowest possible level, a common agreement to wipe out an intolerable debt with the liquid of a few easy tears.

And Doctor Bunter had thought up a fitting climax, a final outrage of titillation. As the voices proceeded with lachrymose satisfaction through the last verse ('So be it, Lord; Thy Throne shall never/Like Earth's proud kingdoms pass away'), the organ was reinforced by the drums and bugles of the school J.T.C., symbolically stationed behind the 1914–18 Memorial Screen; and as the last echoes of the hymn were yet fading, a roll of kettle drums was succeeded, irresistibly, by the soaring notes of the Retreat. Cheeks moist, eyes shining, all listened to the call that announced the end of the day: the end of the day for the last Trefoil of Truro and for Private Zyn, for scrofulous Blood and knightly Morrison; the end of the day for boozer Jackson; for scholar Fullworthy, whose elegiac verses had been so delicate; for Connaught la Poeur Beresford; for Williams (A.) and Williams (G.); for Vallis, who had made the winning hit on another evening long ago, and for little Usquebaugh who had always funked his tackles; the end of the day for Sangster and Sassoon-Warburton, that promising young brigadier; for Royce, who had died alone in the desert, and for Vazey, one of fifty suffocated in a submarine; for Captain Cohen, who had been circumcised by a Rabbi, and for Captain Yarborough, who had been circumcised by a bullet: for all these, the end of the day. Tell England with the drum and with the bugle: these, your sons, are dead.

Yet plenty, after all, remained alive; and these, having given thanks for their preservation, mingled in a grand passagio up and down the terrace which overlooked the 1st XI cricket ground.

'And what,' said Peter Morrison, 'did you think of the head man's sermon?'

'Typical,' I told him. '*They* all sat around while this horrible mess was cooking, and now they tell us we've got to clear it up.'

'The mess is there,' said Peter. 'Something must be done.'

'Of course. But need they be so mealy-mouthed? If they just said, "We're sorry, but it's happened, and now we need your help", then all right. But no. It seems we have to feel *guilty* as well.'

'Everyone has to feel guilty,' said Somerset Lloyd-James, who had just joined us; 'ever since Adam ate the apple.'

'And what,' said Peter, 'were you doing at a Church of England service? I thought you went to some foul little place in the town. Incense and images.'

'I had special dispensation,' lisped Lloyd-James, 'in order to hear the head man preach. I was anxious to ascertain his views.'

'The official line?' I said aggressively. 'Well, now you know it. Sackcloth and ashes.'

'You might have known for yourself,' said Lloyd-James, 'that your life would not suddenly become one long round of pleasure just because the war was at an end.'

'Of course I knew. I simply hoped that there would be some prospect of pleasure, that's all. Not people lecturing me about my guilt for a war which started when I was eleven.'

'Good evening, gentlemen,' said the Headmaster behind us. 'I should like you to meet Major Constable. You especially,' he said to me. 'Major Constable has been appointed Tutor of Lancaster. He is being prematurely released from the Army to take up his duties.'

Out from behind the Headmaster stepped the Major who had clawed his felt hat in chapel.

'You?' I said stupidly.

Major Constable did not seem surprised.

'Yes, me,' he said. His voice was mild, his face, as in chapel, ferocious.

'I'm sorry, er—er—Major Constable, I—'

'—Mister,' said Major Constable; 'or to you, as a future Lancaster man, Tutor. I shall be out of the army by this time tomorrow. The college is anticipating rather a rush.'

'I'll be getting on,' the Headmaster said: 'you'll write, Robert, as soon as you're settled in Lancaster?'

'Yes Headmaster,' said Constable, as intensely as if he were going to send a new instalment of the scriptures, 'I'll write.'

The Headmaster stalked off.

'He seems rather agitated today,' I said.

'He is a busy man,' Somerset Lloyd-James put in sternly.

'We're all going to be busy,' said Major-Mister Constable with an air of dedication. 'You heard what the Headmaster said in his sermon.'

'You didn't,' I said carefully, 'seem to be agreeing with him at the time.'

'On the contrary. Any emotion I showed sprang from a sense of the urgency of what he said. There has been far too much complacency these last few days.'

'Perhaps, sir,' said Peter softly, 'it's just a feeling of relief?'

I laughed in the cynical and disillusioned manner which I had been carefully cultivating ever since first reading *Dorian Gray* three months before.

'I don't know,' said Major Constable unctuously, 'that the subject is one for laughter.'

Clearly I was losing marks.

'Tell me, sir,' I said wildly, 'what is your subject?'

For a split second he wore a look of outraged vanity, as if it were unpardonable in me not to know.

'Economics . . . You, the Headmaster tells me, are a classical man. Might one ask what you had in mind for the future?'

'I'm hoping to become a don . . . a Fellow of the college.'

Constable twitched violently.

'Why?' he demanded.

But at this moment the Senior Usher appeared, ushering before him the cavalryman in the cherry trousers.

'I thought,' said the Senior Usher, 'that you'd all be interested to meet Captain Detterling. The only boy in the history of the school ever to make a double century in a school match.'

Detterling was not in the least like a schoolboy hero. Though elegantly got up, he had a stringy physique, an unhealthy colour, and a morose mouth. Although the evening was warm he shivered frequently. His hand, when I shook it, was very damp.

'I must congratulate you,' the Senior Usher was saying to Constable with open distaste, 'on your new appointment to Lancaster. Let's hope'—with heavy sarcasm—'that you'll get things back to normal without delay.'

'One must look forward rather than back just now ... You'll excuse me, gentlemen. I have a train. It's nice,' said Constable dubiously, 'to have met you.'

'A dreary man, that,' said the Senior Usher loudly before Constable had gone ten yards. 'I can't conceive what Lancaster is thinking of. He's not even a good economist. If he were, the authorities would have found him something more important to do during the war than running around with a lot of black men.'

'Gurkhas,' Captain Detterling said languidly. 'They're not really *quite* black, you know.'

'Perhaps,' said Peter, 'he wanted to help with the fighting. He seems to be a conscientious man.'

'Conscientious?' the Senior Usher snorted. 'He's as red as Detterling's ridiculous trousers.'

'Oh I say, sir.'

'Look forward rather than back, indeed. Before you can turn round, he'll have that college changed into an *institute*. He'll put a cafeteria in Hall, he'll sell the port to endow bursaries for the sons of dustmen, and he'll grow cabbages on the front lawn.'

'As it happens,' said Somerset Lloyd-James, 'he comes of a very good family. They were Hereditary Constables and Knights Banneret of Reculver Castle. Hence their name.'

'Much comfort that'll be to Gray here when his college has been turned into a night school.'

The Senior Usher sailed on his way and Detterling trailed off behind him. Peter, Somerset and I walked slowly down the steps on to the cricket ground and then towards the square at its centre. The crowd on the terrace grew thinner and the sun was low.

'The head man,' said Peter after a long pause, 'was right

about one thing. The hungry must be fed and the homeless sheltered. Forget the guilt, as I propose to, and there is still a lot to be done.'

'What will you do, Peter?' I said.

'I shall grow food.'

'And you, Somerset?'

'I shall advise people for their own good,' said Lloyd-James coolly. 'Giving advice is going to be very much the thing to do. I shall be an expert in an age of experts.'

'What will you be expert about?'

'Whatever people think they are most concerned about.'

Somerset was always slow to commit himself.

'And what,' said Peter Morrison, 'are you going to do, Fielding? Your turn.'

'You heard me say. I want to be a don.'

'What sort of don?'

'A wining and dining don. A witty, worldly, *comfortable* don.'

'All that,' said Peter, 'is incidental. What will be at the centre of it?'

'Too soon to know.'

'I disagree. To me, fertility is the central object, fertility for my land—it will be mine now Alastair is dead—and also for myself. To Somerset, if I am not mistaken, the central object is power. What, Fielding, is yours?'

A bell jangled in the distance.

'I must go and count heads,' said Lloyd-James.

'So must we ... Am I to have an answer, Fielding?'

'I think ... that I want truth.'

'A tall order?'

'Not about everything. Only in my own small way. In some small corner I shall try to establish the truth.'

'Limited and limiting,' said Lloyd-James.

'Satisfying. If only to myself.'

Peter said nothing but nodded carefully. Then we separated, Lloyd-James to assist at *adsum* in his House, Peter and I to do the same office in ours.

This is a story of promise and betrayal. I am writing it, some ten years after it was enacted, on the island of Santa Kytherea, in a small white house between the mountains and the sea. I am doing so, first because there is very little else to do (the routine duties of the Squadron will be quite adequately supervised by Sergeant-Major Bunce), and secondly because I wish to establish, once and for all, what went wrong in that summer of 1945. 'Promise and betrayal.' I have written above, implying that I was the golden boy who received the traitor's kiss. But was it really like that? And if so, what, exactly, was promised, and who or what betrayed?

FIRST THINGS first. How did it all begin?

I have already described Christopher. Imagine him, then, on a winter's afternoon, running home from the Fives Courts: cheeks flushed, stockings down over ankles, gym shoes spattered with mud, shorts (because of clothes rationing) noticeably outgrown. It is nearly tea time and it is just getting dark. I am coming the other way, clumping along in gum-boots, having spent the afternoon drearily gardening (to help the War Effort). Our paths meet where we must both turn off for our house. Christopher waves, smiles, runs on ahead, and I just stand there, while God knows what desires are stirred inside me. And yet this was not lust—I swear it. I had had a vision; after three hours of grinding tedium among oafish and tetchy boys I had seen someone graceful and kind and gay, someone, moreover, who had waved me a share of his grace, smiled me a portion of his gaiety, as he passed in the evening light.

And that was how it all began, in December 1944, about five months before the day of the Memorial Service. And in the meantime? Outwardly just good friends, as the papers say, playing our games and gossiping our gossip, much as we always had since we first met as new boys some years before; but inwardly, as far as I was concerned, there was now a deep longing to protect and to cherish, to fondle (but only as a comforter) and (as a brother) to embrace. That smile had roused my soul. But how was I to tell Christopher? And what would he reply?

The problem was the more difficult as Christopher was a creature of very little brain. This is not to say that he was half-witted; on an everyday level he managed his affairs competently enough; but he was a boy of very conventional outlook and not pervious to ideas or books. To embark on an exegesis of Platonic love (for such this surely was), its history and implications, was therefore impossible. He would have thought I was mad. On the other hand, the fact that he was so conventional did hold out a slight hope; for convention at our school took in, as an abiding if scarcely a wholesome element in school life, the notion of the 'pash' which any boy might entertain for another, usually a younger one. With some such notion Christopher was undoubtedly familiar. But yet again, the concept of a 'pash' was so set around with petty guilt and assorted silliness that this was not at all the level on which I wanted to proceed. 'Christopher, I've got a pash on you.' No, definitely no. Whatever it was I felt for Christopher, love Platonic or love Romantic, agape, eros or caritas, it was altogether too serious to be demeaned by the idiom of the lower fourth.

Yet in the end everything turned out much easier than I had thought possible. For the truth is that Christopher had a sensibility (if not an intelligence) which I had underrated; and on the evening of the memorial service, after five months of mere cerebration on my part, he simply took the initiative himself.

Despite the severity of the Headmaster's sermon, he had proclaimed a modest concession in honour of victory. After seven o'clock *adsum* there would be no Sunday prep. and each House might conduct its own celebration, in such manner as seemed fit to its master. In our House, the Headmaster's own, a seemly sing-song was ordained. I shall never know quite how it happened, but at some point this innocent entertainment suddenly took on a grotesque, a Lupercalian licence. One moment we were all singing 'The Lincolnshire Poacher'; the next—memory recalls no interval—the monitors' gramophone was playing 'Jealousy', and the elder half of the House was coupled with the younger in a shambling, sweaty tango. Even Peter Morrison, enveloping his study fag, was performing elephantine steps across the dining-room floor. I myself was dancing with a pert and pretty little new boy, who was writhing from his hips as if his life depended on it—when a hand descended on his shoulder, there was a gruff 'Excuse me', and Christopher had taken his place.

'What's happened to everyone?' I said.

'I don't know, but it's all right. It's because the war's over. Just this once, it's all right.'

Although he did not come close, he gripped my hand and my shoulder very tight.

'All right for you being the girl?' I said fatuously.

This he ignored.

'Your hair's in your eyes,' he said.

He let go my hand and moved his own towards my forehead.

'Auburn,' he said oddly. 'That's the word, isn't it? Auburn.'

The music stopped and he quickly withdrew his hand. Someone put on 'The Girl in the Alice Blue Gown', to which we now began to waltz decorously. Christopher was a good dancer, light, yielding, following without effort as no doubt he would have led. But the choice of record was a bad one and dispelled the satyr spirit that had briefly descended. Peter Morrison released his study fag, stopped the music, banged on the panelling for silence.

'Tidy up for prayers,' he called, dismissing the incident for ever; 'and look sharp about it. The head man will be through in ten minutes.' So that's that, I thought. 'Just this once, it's all right . . . Your hair . . . auburn.' And then the music stopped.

But late that night, as Christopher and I were walking upstairs to bed, I felt the back of his hand brushing against mine and then his fingers curling round my own. Together we walked down the long row of cubicles, until we reached his. It was quite dark. Everyone else was asleep, or should have been, for these were junior cubicles, of which we had joint charge, and the occupants had been sent to bed two hours ago. In any case, provided we were quiet no one would realise if we both went into Christopher's cubicle; no one would interfere. The darkness was all ours and we knew it; and knowing it squeezed hands the tighter—and said good night.

For Christopher I cannot answer. For myself, it was fear which made me leave him when I did. I only wanted to be with him and hold him; but this might lead to other desires, on his part too, perhaps, and these, I thought, might end by provoking his disgust. That night outside his cubicle I loved him so much that the thought of incurring his anger or distaste made me sick with terror. What did he want? He gave no sign, I could not tell, I must not gamble; so I let go his hand and slunk away, cursing my timid heart, to my solitary school bed.

Early in June I made a hundred against Eton on our own ground, a triumph which was all the sweeter as Christopher had been batting opposite me much of the time, himself making a very decent 47. The occasion was marred, however, by the presence of my parents. When I was out I put on my blue 1st XI cricket blazer and went to join them; and hardly had I sat down before my father started getting at me. No congratulations about my century, just grinding and grudging ill humour from the moment he saw me. Since I might have been spending the time with Christopher, it was very hard to bear with.

'All that blue,' said my father, eyeing my blazer and costing it to the nearest sixpence: 'anyone would think you were playing for the 'Varsity at Lord's.'

'And so he might,' my mother said, 'if he goes on like this.' She paused and twitched slightly. '*You* never made a hundred,' she said; 'you never even played for the first eleven.'

'The standard was higher in my time,' said my father, part whining, part vicious. 'In those days the eleven played like grown men. This is just boys' stuff.'

'Old Frank,' I told him, referring to the retired professional who still attended every match, 'says this is one of the strongest elevens he can remember. Frank was here in your time, I think?'

'Frank's getting too senile to judge properly. I'm telling you, in my day we had teams of men. Men who would have been serving their country in time of war, not playing games at school.'

'The war's over,' said mama.

'Not in the East.'

'I shall do my time in the Army,' I said, 'when and as they call me.'

'When all the fighting's done.'

My father had served in the recent war with the Royal Army Ordnance Corps and had been released early as his business was of industrial importance.

'What does the Headmaster think?' said mama nervously. 'Will you have to go into the Army before or after you go up to Lancaster?'

'No one knows yet.'

'And what's so certain,' said father, 'about him going up to Lancaster?'

'But, Jack, he has a scholarship . . . And if he makes it into a better scholarship next spring . . .'

'Scholarships don't pay for everything. Who finds the difference?'

'If you're going to be like this, why did you decide that Fielding could stay on at school another year?'

'Because that Headmaster of his gave me some drinks and got round me. Said some very flattering things, I must say . . . So I gave my word, that my son would be needing his place here for another year, and I shan't go back on it.'

'Then why not make the best of it?' said mother.

'So I shall—for another year. If they don't call him up before,' said father gleefully.

'They won't,' I said. 'That much at least is certain. As a candidate for a further University award, I am deferred at my headmaster's request until August 1946.'

'Very nice too,' said father. 'Dreaming about Latin and Greek while others do the fighting. But hear this. After you leave this school, I'm not paying for any more Latin and Greek. If, *if* I send you to Cambridge, it'll be to do something useful.'

And so on. The usual bullying by my father, the usual pathetic or ill timed remonstrance from my mother, the usual pouts, sulks and flashes of open revolt from me. After a time Peter Morrison, who was a great favourite with my mother, came up to pay his respects.

'Not playing yourself?' said my father brutally.

Peter, who was a goodish player and had only just failed to get a place, was used to my father and took this very well.

'Too good a side for me,' he said.

'But I've just been telling him'—my father stabbed a bitten finger nail at me—'this is children's stuff. If any of 'em were worth anything, they'd have been off at the war by now. Like me.'

At this point I couldn't bear it any more. I made up some lie about having to help, because of shortage of staff, with the arrangements for tea; then hurried away, ignoring Peter's reproachful look. Christopher was sitting at the back of the scoring box, and when I sat down beside him, he pressed his knee hard against mine. The white flannels he wore were soft and warm and very slightly damp with sweat. The contact, so childish and innocent, was of a sensuality poignant beyond desire. Thigh close against dewy flannelled thigh, chaste yet rapturous, we sat through ten minutes of indifferent batting and an eternity of love.

'Leaving me and your mother like that,' my father said before they left the next day: 'no bloody manners any more than you've got guts.'

But it would have taken more than my parents' visit to spoil that time of happiness. Dispassionate memory records that the June of 1945 was a damp, cloudy month; but another kind of memory can recall only blue, bright mornings and golden afternoons.

One such morning. Early morning school: Catullus.

'Vivamus, mea Lesbia, atque amemus,' boomed the Senior Usher,

'Rumoresque senum severiorum

Omnes unius aestimemus assis . . . Now, those verse translations I asked you to make . . . Gray.'

> 'Come, Lesbia, let us live and love
> And at a farthing's worth we'll prove
> The sour talk of crabbed old men.
> The suns which set can rise again:
> But we, once set is our brief light,
> Must sleep an everlasting night.
> Give me a thousand kisses, all your store,
> And then a hundred, then a thousand more—'

'—Thank you, that will do. I gather you approve the sentiment?'

'Yes, sir.'

'So, with qualifications, do I. This poem states briefly and without compromise the essentials of the Pagan position. A dignified if melancholy acceptance of the extinction which will follow death, accompanied by a whole-hearted relish of the available consolations.'

'And the qualifications you have, sir? Are any needed?'

'Yes. Catullus was dead and buried some fifty years before the birth of Christ. Christianity proposes a different ethic.'

Ah.

'It's not . . . compulsory . . . to accept the Christian ethic, sir. Lots of prominent men in the last two thousand years have rejected it.'

'But this school, Gray'—dryly and not unkindly—'does accept it. Christianity has the official sanction here. Individuals may have their own ideas, but they must nevertheless conform with the official ones. It is a condition of belonging.'

'And if this condition is based on what is doubtful or untrue, sir?'

'You are only asked to conform. Not to believe.'

The Sixth Form stirred, scenting heresy in high places.

'But why conform,' I insisted, 'if one does not believe?'

'It is convenient to run this institution, any institution for that matter, on certain assumptions. One assumption here, as enjoined by our founder, is that Christ was the Son of God and that the morality which he preached is therefore binding. This is the basis of our rule. We cannot compel you to believe in it, indeed many of us would not wish to, but we can and must compel you to act by it. Otherwise our whole careful structure will fall apart. So for our purposes, Gray, you should behave, *not* as though you were heir to perpetual night, but as though you had an immortal soul which you may not jeopardise by showering your kisses upon Lesbia. Unless, that is, you care to marry her first.'

And suppose I wanted to shower my kisses upon Christopher? One thing was certain from what I had read: Catullus ('dead and buried some fifty years before the birth of Christ') would have seen no objection.

And one such afternoon. In the squash courts with Christopher. Squash was not much played in the summer, so we had the place to ourselves. After the game, a cold shower. Christopher under his shower (the drops clinging to the light fair hairs on his legs) displaying the whole length of his body. The young Bacchus . . . no, the young Apollo. Christ, how beautiful.

But Christopher leaving the shower as soon as its function is done. Christopher drying himself, without undue haste, certainly, but without lingering. Christopher dressed. Sun beating through the skylight.

'This place is like an oven. Let's go.'

'Christopher . . .'

'We'll be late for tea. Let's go.'

But as we walked up the hill, he put his hand in my arm, ran it down to hold my hand for a few paces, then brought it back to the inside of my elbow.

'Christopher . . . When you still did Latin, did you get as far as Catullus?'

'No, Fielding.'

'Do you know what he wrote about?'

'No.'

'Passion.'

Christopher looked puzzled.

'Dirty-minded lot, those Romans,' he said at last.

No, it was no good trying to communicate what I had to say in words. This beautiful, ignorant child would never understand them, unless they were the plain, crude words he knew, words which I neither wanted nor dared to use. So I squeezed his hand in the crook of my elbow, and his hand squeezed back. Hand against arm on the way home from the squash courts—the poor, stifled language of our love.

'Love?' said Somerset Lloyd-James, as we walked by the river some days later. 'I should have known we wouldn't get through the summer without that nonsense coming up.'

'I didn't say I was in love with anyone,' I said. 'I was just asking what you thought about it in theory.'

'You must distinguish, for a start, between several commodities all of which are loosely called by the same name. Do you want to know about desire, affection, charity, passion or infatuation?'

'Somerset is having practice in being an expert,' Peter Morrison said.

'Well,' I persisted, 'do you believe, in the first place, in the state which is known as "being in love"?'

'That,' said Somerset promptly, 'comes under the heading of infatuation.'

'Expand.'

'A superficial physical attraction which deliberately conceals its own triviality under layers of romantic accretion.'

'How,' asked Peter, 'does it form these... layers of romantic accretion?'

'It seizes upon anything to hand which may have poetic connotations. A sunset, say, or a bottle of wine. It seeks to arrogate to itself the splendour of the former, the legendary tradition behind the latter. A kiss at sunset receives the blessing of the departing Apollo; a giggle over cheap sherry is associated with the wildness and beauty of the young Bacchus.'

'Somerset seems to know a lot about it,' said Peter. 'I wonder whether he has ever been infatuated.'

'Of course not,' said Somerset coolly. 'I have far too clear a head.'

We passed old Frank, the retired cricket pro, who was fishing with a crony. He answered our salutes by pointing at his float and shrugging.

'Frank says he catches an average of two fish a year,' said Peter, who had enquired into the productivity of the river.

'A peaceful occupation,' I ventured.

'Pointless and debilitating,' said Somerset sternly. 'Which reminds me. What are you both going to do during the holidays? Not much more than a month to go : one cannot begin to plan too soon.'

'I shall be on our farm near Whereham,' said Peter, 'until my call-up papers come through. Which should be early in September.'

'And I shall be at home at Broughton Staithe,' I said gloomily, 'as usual.'

'A pleasant place to do some work?'

'Not with my parents around. Though they'll be going away for some of the time.'

'Without you?'

'If I have any say in the matter.'

'And of course,' said Somerset, 'you will have Peter close at hand at Whereham. I think, yes, I think I shall make a tour of the East coast to inspect you all. When shall your parents be away?'

'Late August to early September.'

'Perfect. I shall come to stay. Bringing my ration book, of course. We can comfort Peter during his last days of freedom.'

'I'm not scared of the Army,' Peter said. 'Will your parents let you come? Just like that?'

'They trust me and they pay me an adequate allowance. Within the limits imposed by their money and their trust, I am free to do as I please.'

At the top of the hill from the valley up to the school we came in sight of Founder's Court: on three sides the inelegant but oddly satisfying buildings reared in the 1860s, when the school had moved from the City; the fourth side open towards the valley; and in the middle of the grass a robust statue of the Elizabethan crook who had started the place.

'Sir Richard,' I said, indicating the statue, 'is rather like my father to look at. And they have other things in common. Greed and obstinacy for a start.'

'What a one you are for your obsessions. First love, then your parents. Tell me,' Somerset continued, 'if your father is so very unsympathetic, how did he come to choose such a nice name for you? He doesn't sound like a reader of *Tom Jones*.'

'My mother chose the name. An old friend of hers who'd been killed in the first war...A keen cricketer who was nicknamed "Fielding" since his surname was Legg. It always pleases her when I do well at cricket—as much as it annoys my father, who is jealous of the man.'

'Jealous of a man dead thirty years?' Peter murmured.

'I told you. He is both greedy and obstinate. He stores things up.'

'Quite a chapter of family history,' observed Somerset. 'Clearly, obsessions run in your blood. I think I shall come to Broughton Staithe a little early and evaluate this man.'

'Come whenever you like. My father enjoys having my friends to stay. He uses their faults as ammunition against me after they are gone.'

'Which I suppose explains why I've never been asked before. Are you sure you can risk it now?'

'Yes,' I said. 'I'm learning at last how to deal with him.'

'How?' said Peter.

'Whenever he's unpleasant, simply get up and go away. It's the only way to cope with bullies ... until you're big enough to hit back.'

'So long as you don't let him bully me instead,' Somerset said.

'You're not bullyable ... you've got the evil eye.'

And so it was arranged that Somerset should come to stay with me at my home in Broughton on about August 20, and that we should both go on to Whereham to spend several days with Peter before he was claimed for the service of the King.

Early in July I was summoned by the Headmaster, who was also, as I have said, my Housemaster. It was in both capacities, he remarked at once, that he wished to talk to me. He gestured me into a chair, and coiled his own shambling frame into one which was opposite me and had its back to the evening light outside.

'It is time,' the Headmaster said, 'for certain things to be made plain.'

'Sir?'

'Next quarter you will be head of this House. By next cricket quarter you may well be head of the entire school. Nor could anyone say that you lacked the abilities needed.'

Outside the window the evening deepened. For some days it had been intensely hot, and now thunder threatened. A dark cloud was spiralling out of the valley; there was a drop of sweat in the cleft of the Headmaster's chin.

'No,' the Headmaster said; 'your worst enemy could not say you were unequal to such responsibilities. But. But.'

'But what, sir?'

'I wish I knew more precisely where you stood. Outwardly

you do us every credit: your work, your games, your ostensible behaviour. But what what is your ... your *code,* Fielding? On what do you base your life?'

'It's a little early to know.'

'Well,' said the Headmaster, 'there's one particular thing we must both know now. What is your ... attitude ... with regard to Christopher Roland?'

So that was it. Steady now.

'The same as it always has been. I've known him for nearly four years and I'm very attached to him.'

'Yes. But now there is something about the two of you ... when you are together ... which makes me uneasy.'

'There's no reason why you should be, sir.'

'Can I accept that assurance? Can I be really certain that you are a suitable person to be my Head Monitor?'

Outside the dark cloud was swiftly growing, like a huge genii called out of its lamp. The Headmaster leaned forward in his chair and shook himself like a large, worried dog.

'You haven't been confirmed,' he said. 'Where do you stand—the question must be asked—in respect to Christianity?'

'Not an easy question, sir ... I find it hard to understand its prohibitions, its obsession with what is sinful or wrong. The Greeks put their emphasis on what is pleasant and seemly and therefore right.'

'Christ, as a Jew, had a more fastidious morality. And as the Son of God He had authority to reveal new truths and check old errors.'

'Did he?' I said.

There was a long silence between us.

'The Greeks stood for reason and decency,' I said. 'Isn't that enough?'

'Reason and decency,' the Headmaster murmured, 'but without the sanction of revealed religion ...? No, Fielding. It isn't enough. What you ignore or tolerate, I must know about and punish in order to *forgive.* Please bear the difference in mind.'

'It is a radical difference, sir.'

'Let us hope it will not divide us too far . . . Will you come,' he went on abruptly, 'and stay with us in Wiltshire? Some time in September? You and I both, we shall be too busy to talk much more this quarter. But there is more to be said on the subject we have just been discussing. Not to mention practical arrangements for the autumn.'

'I should be glad to come, sir. Any time after September the seventh.'

I explained about Somerset and Peter.

'Good, good,' said the Headmaster, uncoiling himself to dismiss me. 'Meanwhile, please remember. I do not say that your position is dishonourable. Merely that it is rather too fluid for my comfort. Good night, Fielding.'

'Good night, sir.'

Lightning flashed through the window.

'Ah,' said the Headmaster; 'I always enjoy a good storm.'

We both turned to the window. A second trident of lightning forked into the valley below.

'I nearly forgot,' the Headmaster said, 'what with the very general tone of our argument . . . Please let me see you less . . . or at any rate less conspicuously . . . in the company of Christopher Roland.'

'He says we're not to be seen together so much.'

Thunder outside the window of my tiny study. Rain dashing out of the dark against the glass. Christopher sitting in the armchair to the left of the door, myself at the desk, upright, as though interviewing him for employment.

'Why not?'

'He didn't really say. He was uneasy, he said . . .'

'Uneasy about what, Fielding?'

'I don't know. Yes, I do. You see, Christopher, I'm . . . I'm . . .'

'Yes, Fielding?'

Such a small word, and yet I hadn't the courage to say it.

'I'm . . . Both of us . . . We're conspicuous people here. We must be discreet, that's all.'

'But I like being with you.'

'Same here. But we must be careful. For the sake of peace, we must be careful. Good night, Christopher.'

The thunderstorm did not clear the air. For days the heat was moist and heavy, while clouds lurked angrily round the horizon as if waiting for the moment to move in and kill. One afternoon Peter Morrison and myself, accompanied by Christopher and another boy called Ivan Blessington, took our bicycles and went for a swim in the Obelisk Pond, a sand-bottomed lake in the middle of a nearby wood, kept clean and sweet by a stream from the Thames and taking its name from a grotesque monument which an uncle of Queen Victoria's had erected to his morganatic wife.

We were not the only people there. A party of soldiers, battledress blouses flung aside, collarless shirts gaping, lolled about on the sandy shore smoking cigarettes and staring at the girls from a local private school, who were decorously bathing from some huts a hundred yards down the bank. When we arrived, the soldiers looked us over briefly, as if afraid of possible rivalry, then sneered and turned back to the bathers. An edgy mistress called to two or three girls who were swimming eagerly away from the huts as if in response to the soldiers' gaze. The girls turned back; the soldiers shrugged and swore; the four of us went into the trees to change.

When we came back, the soldiers were dressing themselves and very slowly, at the command of a rat-faced corporal, forming themselves into ranks. Bored, sweating, heavy-lidded, denied the recently promised view of young female flesh, they consoled themselves with whistling ironically at Christopher and myself, who were the first of our party to pass them. The rat-faced corporal, not above currying favour and seeing a difficult afternoon ahead, joined in the whistling, then looked anxiously at his watch.

'Eyes front,' he called : 'say good-bye to the pretty ladies.'

Chuckling morosely, the men prepared to receive orders. I walked on quickly. Christopher, trembling but resolved, turned to face the corporal.

'I'll have your name and number, please,' Christopher said.

'Who might you be?' snarled the corporal.

'A member of the public who is going to complain about your behaviour.'

'So you're going to complain about my behaviah, are you? Just you piss off double quick, my lad, before I—'

'—Will you give me your name and number?'

The corporal preened himself, inviting the squad to share his coming triumph.

'No, my lord Muck, I won't give you my name and numbah, howevah much you disapprove of my behaviah, hah, hah, and you can just run away and play with yourself —if you've got anything to play with.'

Peter, all muscle and chest, and Ivan, who had black curling hair from his neck to his navel, had now walked down and were standing behind Christopher.

'That won't help you,' Peter said coolly. 'I know your unit. Your commanding officer comes constantly to our cricket matches. It will not be difficult for him to find out which of his men were training in these woods this afternoon. And who was in charge of them.'

'Now, look here, mate,' began the corporal with an in-gratiating whine, 'it was only a joke, see, only—' But Peter, Christopher and Ivan had already walked on down to the water. The corporal looked after them, twitched, spat, turned back to his men, and began mouthing instructions in a quick, uneasy sing-song, looking over his shoulder from time to time to grin and shrug in our direction.

'Shall you report him?' said Christopher.

'Yes.'

'I don't know. Perhaps I'd sooner you didn't.'

'Then you should have ignored him. Whatever you begin

with men like that must be finished. Otherwise they think they can get away with things.'

'But he'll get into trouble.'

'Exactly. Why else should you have asked for his number?'

We began swimming, black Ivan in the lead, towards the girls along the bank. Rubber-capped heads turned quickly in our direction, turned away, turned back again with intent, interrogatory looks. Ivan, twenty yards in front of the rest of us, skimmed the water with his hand and splashed the nearest girl.

'Jolly warm, isn't it?' he called.

The edgy school-mistress, who had regarded the invasion with mistrust, smiled with relief as she heard Ivan's safe public school voice. Nevertheless,

'Only two more minutes, girls,' she shrilled.

Myself, I duck-dived and swam under water until my ears roared. Now then; surface: what would I find? Miscalculation; I had come up short. Ahead of me some girls were standing in a ring round Ivan, who was floating on his back (the black hair on his chest and belly curling and glistening) and explaining how you could float for ever, if you only relaxed and got your breathing right, could eat your meals, wait for rescue, even sleep. Peter was swimming in a circle round a tall, slender girl with ripe breasts, talking gravely up to her as she stood and nodded. Christopher, like me, seemed somehow to be in the margin; peevish, he swam a noisy thirty yards on his back; petulant, he aimed a splash at one of the youngest girls, laughed raucously, went deep red as the child winced and backed away, her lips quivering.

'All out,' howled the mistress.

The girls withdrew. Ivan's group waved and giggled. Peter's solitary maiden walked in backwards, her eyes fixed on his round, solemn face. Christopher and I swam away fiercely and professionally, as if to indicate that the serious business of the afternoon was only now to begin.

Later, as we all lay on the strip of sand by the shore, Peter said:

'A pleasant change.'

Proud, easy, the well oiled male, fully equipped for his role.

Ivan nodded and grunted, then turned his face to the sky and laughed.

'They didn't believe a word of what I told them,' Ivan said, 'but they looked at me as though I'd been John the Baptist come to preach in the river Jordan.'

'One of their traps,' I said snappishly. 'Their biological function is to entice the male and then smother him, so that they can breed from him without fear of revolt. A little simulated worship is a well tried bait.'

Peter and Ivan grinned tolerantly.

'Who's been listening to Somerset Lloyd-James?' Peter said.

Christopher looked across at me.

'I left my watch up with my clothes,' he said. 'Those soldiers . . . I'm going to make sure it's still there.'

'I'll come with you,' I said.

Peter and Ivan assumed carefully neutral expressions. Christopher and I walked slowly and silently towards the trees. Even in the shade the afternoon was very hot . . . hot, damp, urgent. As Christopher bent down to look for his watch I put my two hands on his bare neck and started to scratch him lightly with my finger-nails. He shivered and went on searching.

'Here it is. Quite safe.'

He turned to face me, then rested his cheek against mine.

'Come on, Fielding. We must go back.'

'Let's stay here. Just a little.'

'No.'

'Why not?'

'Peter and Ivan . . . they'll think it funny.'

I turned my head and kissed his cheek. He stood quite still for perhaps ten seconds. Then he shivered—just as he had when I massaged his neck—and slipped away from me.

'Back to the others.'

I followed, wildly elated by the kiss, scarcely resenting the evasion. This must be enough, I thought tenderly, for he prefers it so. Don't be greedy. Don't ask for any more.

Back to the lake.

'Peter . . . Ivan . . .'

'Watch all right?'

'Watch?' said Christopher. 'Oh . . . yes, thanks.'

'Good. I thought you looked rather flustered.'

'Of course I'm not flustered.'

'Of course not,' said Peter serenely, 'if your watch is all right.'

A double file of schoolgirls was now trotting home along the opposite shore of the lake. Peter raised himself on one elbow to wave, and was answered by a gust of giggles, which passed across the water and into the trees like birdsong.

That night I couldn't sleep.

Vivamus, mea Lesbia, atque amemus . . . The words went round and round in my head.

Give me a thousand kisses all your store,

And then a hundred, then a thousand more.

Don't be greedy, I told myself. You've had one kiss and when the time is right you'll be allowed another. That's enough. Don't go and spoil it all.

'And so,' said the Senior Usher, 'we are to be governed by the Socialists. How pleased that dismal man Constable will be.'

The rest of the school was out on a Field Day, which both myself and the Senior Usher had managed to evade. We were celebrating our holiday with what he called a 'discreet luncheon' accompanied by that great war-time luxury, a bottle of Algerian wine.

'How will it affect us here, sir?'

'A lot depends on whether or not they get in again in five

years' time. Just now they've got much bigger fish to fry than us. But by about 1950 the supply will be running out. And then . . .'

'But surely, sir, they can improve the state system of education without wrecking ours? Why don't they just leave us alone?'

'Socialists,' said the Senior Usher, 'can never leave anything alone. That's the trouble. They start with one or two things that badly need reforming, and jolly good luck to them. But then it gets to be a habit. They can't stop. And that's what'll do them in. As Macaulay has it, we can make shift to live under a debauchee or even a tyrant; but to be ruled by a busybody is more than human nature can bear.'

'So how long do you give them?'

The Senior Usher took a long swig of Algerian.

'Not much more, I hope, than four years. By which time a lot of people will have stopped being grateful for the benefits and started to resent the preaching. Particularly if it is suggested that their socialist duty requires them to share their new prosperity with their less fortunate brothers in other lands.'

'And that'll be the end of the socialists?'

'For the time being . . .' The Senior Usher looked suddenly glum. 'This foul wine,' he said, 'is not improved by a thunderous atmosphere . . . Yes, for the time being the end of the socialists; and, I hope, of our dreary friend Constable. But just at present he's in the ascendant, and I must give you a solemn warning.'

'Warning, sir?'

'Yes. Although you made none too good an impression on him back in May, he was interested by your ambition to become a don. So he has written to me to enquire about you. He may hate my guts but he respects my judgment. In his way, he's a very *just* man.'

'What did you tell him?'

'That it was early days yet but I thought you showed great promise. I added that I should be very surprised if you didn't turn your minor scholarship into one of the top awards next April.'

'Thank you, sir. But what has this to do with a warning?'

'Ah. Because of your behaviour when he met you, Constable has got it into his head that you are frivolous. He suspects your motives. He thinks you want to be a don because it is a pleasant way of life.'

'There's a lot in that,' I said.

'Of course there is, and no one but a prig like Constable would resent it. But as it is, you're handicapped—doubly handicapped. As an economist, Constable in any case tends to regard us classical scholars as parasites. And here *you* are cheerfully admitting to the status.'

'But I don't admit to the status.'

'You admit—to me—that you're out for enjoyment?'

'Among other things.'

'Then by Constable's standards you are a self-acknowledged parasite.'

'What am I meant to do? Exterminate myself?'

'You must try to disguise the fact that you are enjoying yourself. For Constable's benefit, you must turn scholarship into a duty. You must regard a fellowship as a high vocation.'

'But surely, sir, Mr Constable's not typical of the entire college?'

'No. But he holds an important office in it. Now I've had time to think about it more closely, it's clear that Lancaster have been very shrewd in appointing him. It's clear that they saw the way the wind was blowing and installed Robert Constable as a valuable piece of camouflage.'

'Mixed metaphor.'

'Don't be pert. Their scheme is that Constable, as Tutor of the College, should go through a conspicuous routine of labour and sorrow for the benefit of the socialist authorities, while the rest of them are left in peace to pursue their own amusements.'

'Then they'll be on my side?'

'Likely enough. But they won't put themselves out to

protect you from Constable. He's got too important a function to fulfil: he's both a concession to and a defence against the demands of the socialist conscience. For the time being they'll let him have his way.'

'Like you said that Sunday? Let him sell the port and grow cabbages on the front lawn?'

'I doubt,' said the Senior Usher, 'whether they'll go as far as that. But they certainly won't make an issue over *you*.'

As the days went on the clouds on the horizon continued to sulk there and hour by hour the air become heavier with their threat.

'Bad for the nerves,' Peter Morrison said. 'And now, Fielding, a word in your ear.'

We went to Peter's study. Although the window was wide open, the little room was like an oven and smelt, very faintly, of Peter's feet, for it was his custom to work with his shoes off.

'Your little thing with Christopher,' said Peter. 'I don't want to seem censorious. It's happened to us all at one time or another. But that's the point. In your case the time has now come to stop.'

'Nothing's really started.'

Peter shook his head in gentle reproof.

'Something's started all right,' he said; 'the only question is how to stop it before it's too late. It's not a question of morals, Fielding. It's just that you're now too important a person to be found out. At this stage whatever happened to you would affect everybody. Corruption in high places: drums beating, heads rolling. It's bad for the House, that kind of thing. It distracts people. Disturbs good order.'

'You're preaching to the converted,' I told him. 'I don't want trouble any more than you. And I've done nothing to cause it.'

'I know how easily the converted can relapse. Take myself . . . Well, no, perhaps we'd better not do that.'

Peter smiled, rather obliquely.

'If you were going to offer any practical advice...' I prompted him.

'Practical advice of any value is hard come by in this particular field. But there's one important thing I want you to get into your head. People make a lot of fuss about all this. They talk of boys being perverted for life by their experiences at their public schools, and they then maintain that this is why, quite apart from any question of abstract morality, it's so vital to keep the place "pure". But what they can't or won't realise,' Peter said, almost angrily for him, 'is that it's not what two boys do together in private which does the permanent damage, but the hysterical row which goes on if they get caught.'

'I'm not quite with you.'

'Well then. Two boys disappear into the bushes. Once, twice, twenty times. They get a lot of pleasure from one another, but other things being equal it does not become a permanent taste, because they grow up and go out into a wider world which offers richer diversions. All right?'

'All right.'

'But supposing they're found out. Drama, tears, denunciation, letters to parents, threats of expulsion, endless inquisition: when, how often, with whom, where, how ... And by the time that little lot's over, what would have been just a casual experience, not much more than an accident, has become ... momentous, obsessive. It has been branded on to the very core of memory and feeling. It has become something which is always with you, like a wound which will be there and keep reopening for the rest of your life. A trauma, I think the psychologists call it. But the wound was not inflicted, in most cases, by the original incident, only by the savage insistence ... by the vengefulness ... of those who chanced to find the secret out. And indeed the reactions of authority can be so extreme that they affect not only the boys immediately accused but anyone else round the place who has ever done the same thing himself. Even, perhaps, those who are completely innocent. The whole atmosphere is charged with guilt, fear and fascination. It's like this thunder hanging over us now. Can you wonder that the public schools turn out so many . . . so called . . . homosexuals?'

'You seem to have gone into it with some care.'

'It was no more than my duty. When I became head of this House, I had to determine how I could meet my responsibilities, how I would cope with whatever might crop up—this included.'

'And you decided that the best way was to leave people to amuse themselves in peace?'

'Let's just say that I wished the topic to be as unobtrusive as possible. Which is why I am so anxious that you, a person of prominence, should not run the risk of stirring up a conspicuous scandal. Others, you should remember, are less tolerant than I am.'

'Others?'

'In a place like this there are always inquisitive people. You don't need me to tell you.'

'No. I don't. Because I told you a long time ago—and it's still true—that I've given up . . . games in the woods. I've done nothing with Christopher. Nothing whatever.'

'Keep it that way,' said Peter briskly; 'that's all.'

Peter's warning was obviously well meant, and it set me thinking. From the age of thirteen and a half, as Peter well knew, I had amused myself with a variety of boys and without any ill effects. But I had been lucky never to be found out, and knowing this, I had turned over a new leaf, for purely practical reasons, when I had become a monitor— 'a person of prominence' as Peter put it—a few months before. At this stage one simply could not afford trouble. There was also another point : ought not one to be putting away childish things by now and graduating towards women? But what might have been a firm decision never to touch a boy again had been weakened almost from the start, by two further considerations: first, that there were not, as yet, any women towards whom to graduate; and second, that it was now quite clear to me, from my reading of Greek and Latin literature, that one could have the best of both worlds. If Horace, Catullus and countless poets of the Greek anthology could have boys as well as girls, then why shouldn't I? It was of no use for the Senior Usher to point out that these authors had been superseded by the Christian morality, for that morality, with its nagging and its whining, I merely despised.

Nevertheless, for the last few months prudence had prevailed. The only danger of relapse had been Christopher, and since he was clearly resolved to impose strict limits the danger did not seem to be very serious. I was far too fond to force him (for that matter I had never forced anybody) and I was unwilling (don't be greedy) even to try to persuade him. Peter, who was very shrewd and knew both Christopher and myself very well, presumably realised this. Then why his warning?

It could only be, I decided, just *because* he knew us so well. Perhaps my prudence was a frailer vessel than I thought, and Peter had spotted this. Even so, that still left my terror of offending Christopher. Yes; but could it be that Peter had also spotted something else, in Christopher this time, that gave him cause for worry? Was this the reason for his warning—that Peter had seen, as I had not, signs that Christopher, for all his delicacy, might give way after all? Signs that determination was softening into mere reluctance, and that this in turn . . .

And so it was that Peter, by warning me against what I had in any case thought to forgo, first taught me that it might yet be achieved.

'Busy, Christopher?'
'Trying to get ready for this exam tomorrow. Geography.'
'I'll just sit here and keep quiet.'

'All right. But I *must* work.'

So I perched my bottom on the little bookcase behind his chair, put my hands on his neck, and started to massage his shoulder blades.

'Please don't.'

'Just go on with your work, Christopher. This will soothe you.'

'It doesn't. It ... I'm sorry, Fielding, but please go.'

'All right. Can I come back later?'

'Come back and talk to me ... *talk* to me, Fielding ... after adsum. If I've finished this.'

'And if you haven't?'

Christopher sighed, very gently.

'Come anyway,' he said.

Exams.

' "Cum semel occideris, et de te splendida Minos Fecerit arbitria :

Non, Torquate, genus, non te facundia, non te Restituet pietas." '

' "When once you are dead and Minos has pronounced his high judgment upon you, not your lineage, Torquatus, nor all your eloquence—nor even your very virtue will bring you back again".'

I paused, I remember, and I thought : now for it, now let 'em have it straight. Then I wrote :

The passage is crucial. Moralists of the sternest persuasion would readily agree with Horace that neither high birth nor clever words can recommend the soul in the face of final judgment. But then the poet puts in his hammer blow :

　　　　　'... non te
　　　　Restituet pietas.'

Not virtue itself is going to be any help. *All*, in fact, is vanity : not only gold and silver, not only worldly fame and accomplishment, but duty, faith and purity too. The highest moral character can procure one no preference among the shades.

I handed in my essay paper (I remember) and walked outside. There was an end of the year's exams, from which, with luck, I would pick up a prize or two. The results would not be known until the last day of the quarter. Meanwhile, there were seven days to pass and nothing to do except enjoy them. There would be a cricket match between the Scholars and the Rest, the finals of the House Matches, the junior boxing and swimming. And other sports? Ever since Peter's warning I had been watching Christopher with new eyes. It *was* possible, I was almost certain of that now. And without offending him? Yes; my body did not offend him, I knew that, he was simply nervous because it had never happened to him before. If I chose the right moment, went about it the right way, all would be well. And without scandal (Peter's voice insisted)? But no one need ever discover. And one thing above all was certain : no amount of chastity would prolong the passing summer or bring me back from the shades.

That night, at last, the storm broke, clearing the air and the sky. The next day's sun dried out the cricket pitches for the carnival matches that would close the season's play; and the weather was now set fair (or so it seemed) for ever and a day. From being sluggish and sullen, everyone turned warm-hearted and gay—except for Somerset Lloyd-James, who had never been known to be either and was in any case brooding over some problem which for the time being he declined to reveal.

The Scholars versus the Rest of the School was to be a full day's match. So far from being a traditional fixture, this contest had never occurred before and had been promoted this year largely by the efforts of the Senior Usher (a great cricket fancier) on the strength of the unusual number of good players in his Sixth and Under-Sixth Classical. He was said to have backed the Scholars heavily at odds of two to one laid by the Master of the Lower School; whether this was true I never found out, but if so the odds were fair, for the Scholars, while distinguished by style and promise, were opposed by a much tougher and more experienced team which included eight members of the School XI.

The morning's play was dull. Batting first in easy conditions, the Scholars fiddled and finicked around for a full hour, at the end of which they could only show 30 runs on the board for a cost of three wickets. At this stage I went in myself and managed, with the steady support of a young scholar called Paget, to put on fifty odd in the same number of minutes—only to be dismissed, just as I was very well set, by a gross full toss which I mistimed and lobbed straight into Christopher's hands at mid-on. Soon afterwards the players came in for lunch in the pavilion, the Scholars' score now standing at 120 for 5—which, since the wicket was plumb and the out-field fast, was at best an indifferent performance.

Lunch, with a barrel of beer, was put up and presided over by the two pedagogues whose money allegedly rode on the match. It was a good lunch (as lunches then went), and to add to the pleasure of the occasion several distinguished non-playing guests had been invited, among them the two external examiners of the Sixth Classical, the Headmaster, and, as the school 'personality', Somerset Lloyd-James, who was sitting next myself. Always a greedy boy when opportunity offered, Somerset now rapidly emptied three pots of beer and inspected me with the glazed look in his eye which meant (as I knew from four years' experience) that he was after help or information of more than usual importance.

'It would appear,' he said a bit thickly, 'that the biggest prize of all lies between you and me.'

'*What* does?' I said, somewhat inattentive, as I had just seen the Senior Usher point me out to one of the examiners, a tubby and voluble Warden from Oxford, and start whispering in his ear.

'The position of Head of the School next summer. The place is taken until April. After that it will be between the two of us.'

'Will it? Who told you?'

'I have my sources.'

'Why do we have to talk about it now? April's a long way off.'

'I thought you'd like to know.'

'And I suppose you want to know something in return.'

Somerset's eyes went more glassy than ever.

'If you've any ... views ... on the situation?'

'Well, I shan't grudge you the crown if you get it. And I hope you can say the same. All right?'

Apparently it was, for Somerset now started shovelling food very fast into his face, and I became involved in an uptable conversation with the tubby Warden, who wanted to know about the reaction of my contemporaries to the Fleming Report on the future of the public schools. Having acquitted myself as best I could, I started to think again about the very odd exchange which Somerset, à propos of nothing at all, had introduced, and was just about to take the matter up with him, when commotion arose at the far end of the table. Old Frank, one of the umpires for the day, had collapsed on to his plate.

The Senior Usher, as principal host, took immediate command. Without moving an inch from his seat and merely by giving quiet and terse instructions to those near him (including the Headmaster and the Warden) he had, within ten minutes, established that Frank was seriously ill, administered immediate succour, procured an ambulance, despatched Frank, arranged a private room for him in hospital, comforted Christopher (to whom the old gentleman had been talking when he collapsed), convinced everyone that there was nothing more to worry about, and appointed Somerset, who was a pundit if not a performer, to be umpire in lieu. Part dismayed by the event, part titillated by guilty excitement and part overcome by admiration of the Senior Usher's expertise, I clean forgot the peculiar turn in Somerset's conversation (for I had never been much interested in the topic itself, only curious as to why it had been so inappropriately broached) and did not give it another thought for several weeks.

After lunch, the game went better for the Scholars than we had dared to hope. Paget, a sturdy fifteen-year-old, received three loose beery balls in the first over and treated himself to two straight fours and a beautiful leg sweep for six. Before the Rest, still dazed by the refreshments and the drama offered at lunch time, had realised what was happening, he had put on forty quick runs; while his partner, a skinny and intelligent child from from the Scholars' Remove, stood his ground against the very few balls he was allowed to receive and simply blocked them dead.

After twenty minutes of this (score now 160 odd for 5), two quick bowlers were brought on to break up the stand—and at once had every kind of ill luck. The skinny boy ('Glinter' Parkes he was called, because of his knack of flashing his spectacles) snicked two straight balls through the slips for four; Paget, failing to keep a square cut down properly, was criminally missed at gully; and the better of the two bowlers then tripped over his own shadow, did something to his ankle, and was hauled groaning from the ground. What with all this, and what with the malaise, compounded of drowsiness, indigestion and accidie, which always assails fieldsmen at this time of the afternoon, the morale of the Rest fell apart like a rotten mackerel. 175 for 5 . . . 180 . . . 190 . . . 195 . . . The target, on such a day, was 300 or more; but anything over 270 was very acceptable, and anything over 230 would leave us with some sort of chance.

205 ... 210 ... and some more smart runs from Paget. But now, with the score at 224 for 5, Peter Morrison was put on.

Peter bowled slow off-breaks which never failed to turn at exactly the same pace off the pitch and at exactly the same angle. Paget, having sent the first off-break past mid-wicket for two off the back foot, decided to do the same with the next. And there it went, bowled with Peter's usual action, flying at Peter's usual height, pitching at Peter's almost invariable length; and there was Paget, bat up and body poised —only to find that by some grotesque failure of the natural laws the ball, instead of turning in towards him, had gone absolutely straight on to hit the top of his off stump with a melancholy clack.

226 for 6—and very nice too, when one considered the state of play before luncheon. But not so nice when the next batsman spooned his second ball to square leg, and his successor, trying to hit a six, was brilliantly caught on the long-on boundary. 226 for 8; and neither of our last two players could so much as hold his bat properly. In five balls (Peter's of all people's) we had ceased to be dominant and come to a case in which we needed every run we could scrape.

It was now that Glinter Parkes, the skinny boy, justified himself as scholar and cricketer both. After our No. 10 had somehow survived the last ball of Peter's over, Glinter faced up to a goodish 1st XI bowler of medium pace leg cutters. Instead of blocking the first of these or leaving it alone, as he would have done at any time during the last hour, Glinter placed his right foot just wide of his wicket and daintily dropped his bat on to the ball as it passed, sending it mid-way between the two slips for four runs, as pretty a late cut as ever I saw. The bowler, considering the stroke unrepeatable, bowled the same ball twice more, and was much put out when the same stroke was twice repeated. The fourth ball of the over, a quicker one on the middle-and-leg, Glinter parried with determination; off the fifth he took a short run to an indolent mid-on; and the sixth was once again survived by No. 10.

Batting now against Peter's rubbish, Glinter, who did not have the strength to hit it, once again resorted to intelligence. He stepped right across his stumps and dribbled the expected off-break down to the deserted region of fine leg, a stratagem which brought him two runs off both the first two balls. Peter then moved mid-wicket down to stop this annoyance, whereupon Glinter played the ball firmly through mid-wicket's former position and took another two. In such thoughtful fashion he pushed the score past 240 to 250 and a few runs beyond, and would probably be there yet, a little Odysseus of the crease, had not the doltish No. 10 declined an easy short run at the end of one over and been dismissed at the beginning of the next. No. 11 survived with ignominy for two balls more, and then the Scholars' innings was closed for a total, passable but far from ample, of 256.

The trouble with the Scholars' side was that we had no reliable fast bowling. Although Paget could send the ball down quite quickly for someone of his age, his pace alone amounted to very little against fully grown boys and he did nothing much with the ball either in the air or off the pitch. Other bowling consisted mainly of medium or slow medium off-breaks and in-swingers, in no case with any kind of edge. However, one thing all our bowlers could do was to keep a steady length; and although the Rest found no difficulty in playing this stuff, their rate of scoring was slow.

Stumps would be drawn at half past six. By tea time (four-fifteen) the Rest had been batting just under an hour and had made only 57 runs for two wickets, both of these having been thrown away in sheer impatience. Thus the Rest needed exactly 200 to win and would have just on two hours to make them. A hundred runs an hour was nothing out of the way on our ground if once the batsmen got going; the only question was whether our bowling, uninspired as it was, could continue to contain the opposition by the exercise of patience and accuracy. The answer, unfortunately, was almost certainly 'no': for even if the bowlers did not tire of such plodding work, the Rest had players to come who were very quick on their feet and would make our medium pace good length look like any length they pleased.

The first to do so was Christopher. He came in at No. 5 only ten minutes after tea (No. 4 having carelessly allowed himself to be yorked by a half-volley from Paget) and set about his business with classical precision. A nimble mover with a long reach, he simply came to the pitch of our careful good-length bowling and drove it away where he would. Before very long, the bowlers tried dropping the ball a little shorter, but this was a common practice on our fast wickets and Christopher knew the answer: since the bounce of the ball was absolutely regular in pace and height, he could hit it, hard and almost without risk, on the lift. During his fourth over at the crease he slashed two fours through the covers and then pulled a short and sleasy off-break right off his middle stump for six, to bring the score to 94 for 3.

Christopher was a sight to see that afternoon. Hair bleached by the sun (he never played in a cap), arms brown and smooth, fair, delicate skin showing through the cleft of his unbuttoned shirt; legs moving gracefully down the pitch, bat swinging with the easy strength which only timing can give, eyes flashing with pleasure as he struck the ball full in the meat. I thought of Keats's Ode and wished, for Christopher's sake, that he might be arrested in time for ever, just at that thrilling moment of impact when the hard leather sinks, briefly but luxuriously, into the sprung willow, and the swift current of joy quivers up the blade of the bat and on through every nerve in the body. For my own sake too I wished that time might stop: so that I might stand for ever in the sun, while the trees rustled and the young voices laughed along the terrace, and watch my darling so beautiful and happy at his play. But time slipped on, and my darling started to sweat like a cart-horse, and the Scholars were faced with shameful defeat.

For by half past five the Rest had scored 183 for 4 wickets and nothing, it seemed, could save us now.

'Rather disappointing,' said Somerset Lloyd-James, as he moved, between overs, from the wicket out to square leg.

'I don't know,' I said. Then, seeking what consolation I could and finding it very sweet, 'At least Christopher's enjoying himself.'

Somerset looked at me with attention.

'That pleases you so much?'

At the end of the next over, he said :

'Why not give young Parkes a chance to bowl?'

'It is not the umpire's province to offer advice.'

'Since you yourself are deriving a certain pleasure from your defeat'—he glanced down the wicket at Christopher—'you might at least let some of your own side share it. It would please Parkes to bowl, and with the mess you're in it can't do any harm.'

Well, and why not? Just about everyone else had had a go. So two overs later, when the score was 210, I threw the ball to Glinter Parkes.

With modesty and concentration, Glinter requested some changes in the field. Then he took three steps to the wicket, gave a little twitch of his narrow behind, and bowled. From somewhere about his person the ball issued out in a steep parabola, reached its apex, and started to descend; meanwhile the batsman (Christopher's partner), having disdainfully plotted the curve, waited below, licking his lips. At some late stage in the ball's descent, however, it unaccountably departed from its ordained path, landed a good twelve inches shorter than it should have done, broke very sharply from the leg, and removed the puzzled batsman's off bail. Glinter blushed, and there was some embarrassed applause from the other scholars. 210 for 5.

'Natural flight, that boy's got,' said Christopher, and went to warn Peter (No. 7) who was now approaching the wicket.

'You've made 69,' Peter told him : 'watch out for your century.'

'And you watch out for Parkes's bowling,' Christopher

said : 'it comes down short of where it should. About a foot short.'

Glinter listened carefully, and glinted. His next ball started the same as the one before. There was ample time to see Peter carefully working out where the ball should land and then allowing for its being a foot short. The only trouble was that this time it came down where it should have come down, so that Peter played all round it and yelped sharply when it landed (almost vertically) on the toe of his back foot.

'How's that?' said Glinter.

Somerset Lloyd-James jabbed a finger down the wicket, and away went Peter. 210 for 6. We were back in the match. Only just, but we were back.

'This is ridiculous,' Christopher said.

'A perfectly sound decision,' said Somerset huffily : 'the ball struck his back foot, which was in a direct line between the wickets.'

'I know. I meant that it just shouldn't get wickets, this kind of thing. That's all.'

'What warning are you going to give the batsman this time?' enquired Somerset with malice.

But Christopher said nothing to No. 8 as he came in, and perhaps for this reason the rest of the over passed without incident, except for a clumsy scoop of No. 8's between mid-on and mid-wicket for two runs.

Christopher then faced one of our stock bowlers from the other end and took 16 runs off him. 228 for 6. Since No. 8, (despite his horrid scoop off Glinter) was a very fair player, as was the one who would succeed him, our chances were really negligible again ... unless Glinter could produce another of his disgraceful surprises. This he promptly did, by substituting for his usual ballooning delivery a low, quick ball which knocked down No. 8's stumps while he was still looking for it half way to the moon.

'This nonsense has got to stop,' Christopher said.

He intercepted No. 9 and spoke to him very low and earnestly. No. 9 took guard, watched Glinter like a cashier on guard against a stumer cheque, stepped right back, patted the ball slowly towards cover, and called for an easy single. Christopher then demonstrated how harmless Glinter's bowling was, if you only hung on to your wits, by advancing down the pitch and firmly hitting three successive balls full toss for four. From the last ball of the over, which he mistimed slightly (nearly giving a catch to mid-on), he only made two, bringing his own score to 99 and that of the Rest to 243.

At this stage two things happened. First, No. 9 informed us that it was now definitely known that No. 11—the bowler who had hurt his ankle earlier—was too lame to bat, which meant that we only had two wickets instead of three still to take; and secondly, No. 9 then proceeded, off the first ball of the next over, to put up one of the easiest catches in history to short leg. Fourteen runs to be got and only one wicket to fall; and No. 10, now last man in, well known for the futility of his batting.

Nevertheless, he managed to block out the rest of the over; and now, with Christopher to face the bowling, the problem was whether or not to continue with Glinter Parkes. It was true that he had taken three priceless wickets; it was also true that he had been derisively treated by Christopher. But then so had everyone else. Anyway, I wanted Christopher to get a hundred and in my heart of hearts I wanted him to carry his side to victory. So let things take their course, I thought. I threw the ball to Glinter.

Glinter's first delivery was a very high full toss. 'This is it,' I thought; 'he must get a single off this.' But it was so high and droopy that Christopher, remembering the catch he had nearly given at the end of Glinter's last over, simply stopped the ball with his bat and let it drop dead at his feet.

'May I?' he said, and bent down towards the ball.

I nodded. Christopher picked up the ball and threw it to Glinter.

'How's that?' Glinter said to Somerset.

'Don't be a silly little boy,' I said: 'I gave him permission.'

Somerset looked at me, smiled and shook his head at such naïveté, and jabbed his finger down the wicket at Christopher.

'He's still out if there's an appeal,' Somerset said. 'No one can give a player permission to break the rules.'

'That's what I thought,' Glinter said.

'Now you look here, Somerset—'

Somerset smiled and removed the bails.

'A narrow thing,' he said.

In this way did the Scholars defeat the Rest of the School in the high summer of 1945, the first time and (I believe) the last that the match has ever been played.

'It doesn't *matter*, Fielding. It wasn't your fault.'

'But you were so close to your century.'

'I hope there'll be other chances. Next summer . . .'

'What a way to win,' I said.

'I should have known better than to handle the ball.'

'Somerset was just being bloody.'

'Somerset was going by the rules. That's what an umpire's there for . . . What shall we do now? It seems funny having the whole evening free.'

'Yes . . . How did your exams go, Christopher?'

'I think I just got by.' But at the recollection his face sagged, and suddenly a surprising amount of loose flesh was hanging under his chin. That's how you'll look in twenty years' time, I thought. *Non te restituet pietas.* Piety (yours or mine) will not preserve your beauty.

'You must be tired,' I said. 'Sit down there.'

He looked at me carefully, then sat down in the chair at his desk. I sat on the backcase behind and placed my hands on his shoulders.

'You played wonderfully today,' I said, and started to rub the top of his spine with my thumbs. 'I could have watched you for ever.'

'Easy bowling,' he grunted; his body relaxed in the chair.

'But you must feel stiff after all that batting.'

'Yes.'

'Where?'

'Everywhere.'

Don't be greedy. Kiss him, if you like, then take him to watch the Junior House Tennis in the garden. Or take him along to Peter to talk about the match. Or go to the Monitors' room and play him a record. Don't spoil it now.

'Here?'

'Yes.'

'And here?'

'Yes . . . *yes.*'

'Better now? Better, Christopher?'

'For Christ's sake, Fielding. TAKE ME SOMEWHERE SAFE.'

There was a path which led through the woods along the lip of the valley, and about half a mile down it, standing in a clearing near the edge of the trees, a group of abandoned farm-buildings, from which, long ago, they had farmed what were now our football fields. Among these buildings was a hay-loft, which was still used to store the hay from the fields each summer. Later in the year the hay would become dry and prickly, but in July it was still sweet. A fine and private place, and thither I now took him.

We came back separately. Peter met me as I came in through the door by the boot-lockers.

'I've been looking for you,' he said. 'Frank died in hospital. Half an hour ago.'

That at least, I thought in bed that night, could not be blamed on me. Frank was an old man, and now, after a long and contented life (as far as could be known), he was dead. Unconscious to the last, they said. The best way to go.

That Christopher and I had been together in the hay-loft when he died was neither here nor there. There could be no connection, no guilt . . . not on Frank's account. But oh dear God, what had I done to Christopher?

As soon as we had climbed up the ladder into the hayloft, he had looked at me very redly, as if to say, 'What now?' I took my coat off and he took off his; I lay down in the hay and he lay down beside me. By now I was almost more nervous than he was—far too nervous to have any sexual feeling—and so desperately anxious not to upset or disgust him that I could hardly bear to touch him. However, I undid the buttons of his shirt, loosened the top of his trousers, then stroked his hair and kissed him lightly.

'Let's get undressed,' I said.

He turned away from me, pulled off his shirt and trousers, and kept his back to me while I too undressed. When he judged that I had finished, he turned slowly back. Rather to my surprise, I saw that he was very excited indeed. Since I was still too nervous to be in the least aroused, and since I was afraid lest he might notice this and perhaps be hurt, I moved right up against him and hugged him to me, the whole length of my body against the length of his. For ten seconds we lay like this, ten seconds during which I realised that all I wanted was to hold him in this way, close and without movement, without being roused myself or further rousing him, simply feeling his warmth and knowing he felt mine. I put my mouth to his ear and kissed it.

'I love you,' I said.

Then, very slowly, I moved my knuckles down his spine : not to demonstrate or stir desire but to soothe, to try to tell him to be still, just to lie against me and be still. But hardly had my hand passed down between his shoulder blades, when his whole body seemed to jerk and stretch as though pulled by a rack and I felt him coming against my belly.

'Oh,' he whimpered, 'oh, oh, oh.'

I did what I could. I held him very tight and stroked his hair until he finished. And then I eased him away from me.

'Lie still,' I said, 'lie quite still, and soon you'll feel all right.'

But his whimpering had passed into little sobs of distress. He turned away and started, still lying down, to put on his clothes.

'Lie still,' I said. 'It doesn't matter. It often happens like that.'

'You'd know,' he sobbed, and huddled into his shirt.

'Christopher, please . . .'

'I never wanted this,' he blubbered. 'You made me want it by fingering me, messing me about. You went on and on until I couldn't help it.'

'I only wanted to show you how much I . . . How fond of you I was.'

'Then why didn't you? Why didn't you talk to me the way I asked you to? That was what I wanted—oh, so much— for us to be real friends. There were so many things you could have told me.'

'But I did, I tried—'

'—No, you didn't. You thought I was stupid, and you told me nothing. You patronised me, Fielding. Patronised me and played about with me, until it all had to end in this.'

'But nothing's ended. If only you'll lie quiet . . .'

I reached for his hand, but he snatched it from me, scrabbled through the hay, thumped down the ladder and was gone. The next time I saw him was at lock-up adsum. He was very quiet and his face was all puffy. Thank God, I thought to myself, they'll think he's been crying for Frank.

And now, as I turned in bed this way and that, I had a sense of loss that lay in my stomach like a lump of jagged iron. But surely, I thought, I can make it up to him. I can go to him, ask to be forgiven, and talk to him in the way he wants. Then everything can start again. I had a comforting vision of Christopher and myself walking arm in arm across the cricket field. 'What a lot of things you know, Fielding,' Christopher was saying as he looked into my face and smiled: 'now please tell me . . .' Start again? And where would it end this time? Suddenly I had a different vision— of Christopher as he had been that evening when his body suddenly stretched against mine: 'Oh . . . oh, oh, oh.' And now I felt the desire which had deserted me in the hay-loft, and my hand moved down my own flesh.

'What have you done to Christopher?' Peter Morrison said.

'Nothing.'

'Don't lie to me, Fielding. I saw him last night at adsum, and so did everyone else. He looked heart-broken.'

'That was because of Frank. He was always fond of him, and he was sitting next to him when he collapsed.'

'Let's hope that's what the rest of 'em think. I know better. I saw you going off together.'

'Well, if you're going to *spy*—'

'—I was just looking out of the window, and I didn't suspect anything—until I saw him later. Do you know the damage you may have done?'

'No one need find out . . . if you don't say anything. Even if you do, no one can prove it.'

'Let's just think of Christopher. The damage to Christopher.'

'But,' I said, 'you told me that it did no harm provided no one found out and made drama.'

'Certainly I told you that, and it's usually true. But there's a special condition here: Christopher is very fond of you, he near worships you, so he'll make his own drama. Get it? When you feel like that about someone, it's very hurtful to be *used*, Fielding. You didn't think of that, did you? You simply decided that you'd have your bit of fun.'

'That's not true,' I said. 'I did think and I did try very hard . . . not to do it. It just happened, and I couldn't help it.'

'All right,' said Peter kindly, 'I accept that. If he wanted it too, and if it wasn't deliberately planned by you, then it could have been all right. But evidently something went wrong. What, Fielding?'

I told him.

'I see,' Peter said. 'So on top of everything else there's loss of control . . . humiliation . . . in front of the one person in all the world whom he wants to impress. What are you going to do?'

'Ask to be forgiven. Tell him it was all my fault, that he's got nothing to be ashamed of, and then ask him to take me back.'

'You'd better make it good. It would be a great pity if Christopher did something . . . unexpected.'

'What do you mean?'

'Guilt, disgust, and humiliation. Quite a burden. So if he got desperate and tried to off-load some of it, it would make a very nasty mess.'

'But if I can manage him?'

'Least said, soonest mended. If Christopher's all right, who am I to complain? I only hope you've learned your lesson and that it won't happen again next year.'

'Thank you, Peter.'

'But just one more thing, Fielding. I hope that Somerset Lloyd-James wasn't looking out of his window at the same time as I was looking out of mine.'

'Somerset?'

'Yes. You must be careful of Somerset.'

'But he's our friend.'

'Somerset is growing up fast. Somerset is getting ready to break friends and influence people. There have been all the signs, even if you've been too busy to notice them.'

'I can't believe that Somerset—'

'—Just keep your eyes open, and you'll soon know all you need to and more. And that, Fielding, is my very last piece of advice. I now resign everything into your hands. When we meet in Whereham next month, you will be head of this House, I shall be a recruit under orders to join the colours. The king is dead and rather relieved to be : long live the king.'

*   *   *

'. . . Don't grovel, Fielding. It doesn't suit you.'

'Christopher. I'm trying to say I'm sorry.'

'There's nothing to be sorry about. You were very kind.'

'But you looked so awful last night. And all those things you said, about my messing you about, never talking to you properly. All that.'

'That was last night. I'm all right now.'

He looked it too. Just perceptibly older, perhaps, and certainly a little more thoughtful, but no longer ashamed or distressed. He was as bright and beautiful as ever. And yet something was missing. I did not know what it was, I only knew that something which I'd always cherished in Christopher was no longer there for me.

'You see, Fielding, I've been thinking. Yesterday was the first time for me, ever. So naturally I made rather a mess of it.' He laughed. 'Next time it'll be better, I promise you.'

'Next time?' I said stupidly.

'I could hardly sleep for thinking of it. I nearly came to you in your cube.'

There was no hesitation in his voice. Always before there'd been diffidence or deference, even when he was trying to be firm. Now he was sure of himself. And of me. I was being taken for granted.

'You see,' he said, 'I always thought that I'd hate it. Then, when it happened like that, I did hate it. But later . . . when I started to remember what you looked like, how it felt having you against me . . . I longed for you so much I could hardly bear it.'

There was candour in all this, candour and honesty. But what was it that had left him?

'Fielding, let's go there. Now.'

He smiled, or rather, that's what he thought he did. But his smile had changed: although the mouth and the lips were the same, there was a new look in the eyes, a look of invitation. It was no longer a smile, it was a leer. So that's what's gone, I thought: innocence. And then this look, which would have been so welcome in many others as a herald of casual pleasure, filled me, for a moment, with loathing. In others I should have thought it saucy, sexy, enticing; in Christopher I found it an obscene parody of something which I had once —only a day before—held almost sacred.

'Look,' I said: 'Peter suspects something. We must be careful.'

'We can go different ways and meet there.'

'Christopher . . . we must be sensible. Next quarter I'll be head of the House. There's too much to risk.'

'There wasn't yesterday,' he said.

But yesterday you had your innocence.

'I've already said I'm sorry about that.'

His face sagged, just as it had the previous evening when I asked him about his exams. His look was no longer obscene, only pitiable. I can't just desert him, I thought. And when it comes to it, I still want him all right . . . if only as an appetising bundle of flesh. The same as all the rest of them now, but a lot of fun to be had (if only it can be safely had), a super twenty minutes in the hay. And after all, I thought, I owe him that.

'Listen,' I said. 'On the last night of quarter the door by the boot-lockers is left open all night for those with early trains. So we can go and come back in the dark and it'll be absolutely safe. Let's wait till then.'

His face brightened.

'All right,' he said. And then, 'Will you come and stay with me in the holidays? We shall be left alone most of the time. Will you come?'

'Yes—no—I'll have to think. My parents . . .'

'Of course. When can you let me know?'

'In a day or two. Before we break up.'

Don't desert him, not just like that. Play for time, and ease out gently. Don't let him be hurt.

'And on the last night of quarter,' he said, 'what time?'

'After Somerset's party.'

'I shall think about it every minute.'

*   *   *

Tumescence, detumescence, retumescence.

But I don't think it was that simple with Christopher. I think that he was hoping for a whole new world of physical pleasure. Despite his misfortune at the first venture, he had caught a glimpse of a strange and brilliant terrain; he had seen enough, if only just enough, to promise wonders. How far he expected me to help him in his exploration would be hard to say; but for the time at least, since I had guided him in his first foray, he would want my company.

But what had I to offer? Although the magic had gone—that much was certain—might there not still be friendliness and a little cheerful lust? But then again, prudence was quickly reasserting itself. It was one thing to take risks in a daze of love, quite another to take them for a momentary and familiar pleasure.

'Sixth Classical,' announced the Headmaster from the platform: 'First, Smithson: Brackenbury Leaving Bursary, Pilch Prize for Classical studies. Second, Higgs: Brackenbury Leaving Bursary, Liddell Prize for Greek Verse. Third, Gray: Lewis Prize for Latin Elegiac Verse and Wilkinson Award for Classical Literature. Fourth, Warmsby, Fifth, Scott-Malden: Muir Prize for most improved scholar of the year . . .'

So that was it. I had beaten everyone in my own year and all but the two oldest in the year above me. The Wilkinson Award was worth twenty guineas. The academic year had ended well.

According to a pleasing custom which the Headmaster detested but suffered, on the last night of the quarter senior boys would visit and entertain each other in their different Houses. Peter and I called on Somerset Lloyd-James, who had pompously invited us, some days before, to take a little wine with him. When we arrived, Somerset was dispensing Woodbines and Gimlets.

'I sent for some hock from home,' Somerset explained, 'but my father says that war-time Railway workers cannot be trusted. Next year, when things are back to normal . . .'

'Never mind. What shall we drink to?'

A full moon looked disdainfully through Somerset's window.

'Departing friends.'

'Departing friends,' said Somerset, and hiccuped.

Six more people crowded in, among them Ivan Blessington and Christopher.

'I ordered some rather good hock,' said Somerset to the new arrivals, 'but it's finished. Gimlets on the table.'

Christopher raised his glass to me when he thought no one was looking.

'The toast,' said Somerset thickly, 'is departing friends, not returning ones.'

'Departing friends,' everybody said.

'When the Gimlets are gone,' said Somerset carefully, 'I think there is some sherry.'

'The Gimlets *are* gone.'

'Get the sherry.'

'And now,' said Peter, when everyone had poured himself some sherry, 'I shall propose another toast.'

'Good old Peter.'

'The School,' Peter said, and emitted something between a sob and a sneeze.

'Don't cry, old chap. You'll be back, you'll come and see us.'

Somerset sat down, put his head on the table, and was sick.

'I knew that sherry was a mistake. Time to go.'

I wrote a note which said, 'See you at Broughton on August 20', and propped it against the sherry bottle for Somerset to see when he recovered.

'After that exhibition,' I said to Peter on the way across

Founder's Court, 'I don't see that Somerset needs much watching.'

'Somerset can take time out,' said Peter, 'like anybody else. Five bob to a skivvy to clear up the mess, and tomorrow is another day.'

'Home tomorrow,' shouted Ivan, who had kind parents and several jolly siblings.

'Shush. The head man hates a row.'

Christopher touched my elbow. We fell behind.

'The hay-loft,' he whispered; 'I'll start now and wait.'

But my head was humming and the moon, I thought, was dangerously large. When we reached the House, I left the rest abruptly, lay down fully dressed on my bed, and did not wake until the first light was showing and Christopher, his face drawn and dirty, was standing over me.

'You never came.'

'I fell asleep.'

'Will you come in the holidays?'

'Come where?'

'To stay with me. You said you'd let me know.'

My head ached and there was a thick sweat all over me, under my crumpled clothes.

'I still don't know myself. I'll write.'

'When?'

'In a few days.'

'I mean, when would you be coming?'

'It's difficult.' I gagged nastily and a spurt of pain flared from the base of my skull. 'Somerset's coming to me, and he mustn't get to know . . . about us.'

'Why should he get to know?'

'He sniffs things out. Peter's been warning me about him. God, I feel awful. Please go away.'

'I wish you'd be more definite.'

'How can I be? Somerset—'

Suddenly my mouth was full of a nauseous sherry-flavoured bile. Out of sheer pride I managed to swallow it back.

'Somerset's just an excuse,' Christopher was saying. 'The truth is you've finished with me. That's why you didn't come last night.'

'All right, I've finished with you. Now for God's sake go away and leave me in peace.'

'Good-bye then, Fielding.'

'*Good-bye.*'

A few seconds later, realising, despite my discomfort, what I had done, I raised myself on my elbow to speak some word of kindness. But by then Christopher had gone.

This afternoon, when the weekly mail reached the Squadron here on the island, there was a letter for me from the Senior Usher. He has been retired for some five years now, and his leisure, despite the demands of his reading, eating and drinking, extends to an abundant correspondence with old friends. But as it happens, this is the first letter I have had from him for some months; which intermission he excuses by explaining that he has been on a cruise.

... And unlike some of one's friends, whose first concern on leaving England is to notify their entire acquaintance of the fact, I regard such expeditions as 'time out', as periods during which one's countrymen and their affairs simply cease to exist. I neither write nor receive letters; I do not even read a newspaper. What, in heaven's name, is a holiday for?

Even so, my dear Fielding, at one stage I found myself being very strongly reminded of you. We were making a three day call at the Piraeus, and I decided to go to Delphi, where there was to be a performance (alas, in one of those hideous demotic versions which are now so popular) of Sophocles' Antigone. As soon as Antigone appeared on the stage, I could not but think of you. It was not so much a matter of physical likeness, though there was that, as of— how can I put it?—an aspect bestowed on her by her destiny. From the first second that the actress, a very good one, lifted her face to the audience, it was clear that Antigone was doomed, that the gods had grown bored with her and were going to have her blood. And this ... this aura of impending disaster which hung about her reminded me of you, of you ten years ago, when you appeared, with your hangover, to say good-bye to me on the last morning of that cricket quarter in 1945. You had about you the look, almost the smell, of one who is shortly to be defeated. Unlike Antigone, you had no good reason to expect this—quite the reverse, for the quarter had ended for you in every kind of triumph and the next year, as it then seemed, must hold many more. Nevertheless, and whether or not you knew it at the time, your star had turned hostile and its new malignity was reflected in your eyes.

I hope you will pardon this piece of hindsight ...

Did I know, that morning after Christopher left me, that already my fortunes were turning sour? Certainly, there were several causes for disquiet:—my father's attitudes, the Headmaster's fussy moralism; the Senior Usher's suspicions of Constable and Peter's suspicions of Somerset; Christopher's distress, and my own uncertainty in the whole realm of love. But if there was a warning latent in all of these, there was urgency in none. I remember feeling no more than rather sad and sick that morning, as I left the Senior Usher's Lodging and walked down the hill to my train.

WHEN I ARRIVED home in Broughton Staithe, late in the afternoon after my drunken awakening, my mother announced that we were to go out to dinner to celebrate the beginning of the holidays. A restaurant had been chosen which was a few miles down the coast and known for its resourceful use of cheap local sea-food. At that time one might spend only five shillings a head on a meal, exclusive of any beverages which one might be lucky enough to obtain, and eat only one main course of fish or meat. The proprietor of The Lord Nelson had overcome these difficulties by combining mussels, prawns and cockles into a variety of stews and sauces; he could thus provide a full-scale Bouillabaise under the pretence of serving 'soup' (officially a minor course) and garnish a plate of chicken with a rich crustacean compote ('white sauce') which made of the 'main' course a banquet by the standards of the day.

The dinner was mama's idea. My father, who grudged the petrol needed to get there, was in any case mistrustful of what he called 'mucked up' food; and since he was also indiscriminately greedy, he liked his plate to be set before him within a few seconds of sitting down and resented the delays consequent upon the subtle attentions which were paid to the cuisine of The Lord Nelson. Knowing this as I did, being, besides, tired after my journey and feeling, almost to tears, my painful parting from Christopher, I could hardly relish the treat in store for me, the less so as I had the additional burden of simulating pleasure for my mother's sake.

Despite all this, I flatter myself that I played my part quite well. During the drive along the coast I did my best to amuse my father, whose greeting had been civil, with a non-tendentious account of the closed quarter. I played down my own successes, though urged by mama to describe them in detail, made light of the important position which I was to assume the next September, and concentrated on mildly derogatory tales, which I knew from experience to be acceptable, of personalities who survived from my father's time at the school. But my father was not one to be fobbed off with a quiet evening when he was in the mood for drama. My return made it imperative for him to assert this own talents and importance, lest mama should be in danger of forgetting them, and indeed he had probably consented to come to The Lord Nelson only because the money he must pay out there entitled him, in his view, to more attention than he would have received at home.

In any event, by the time we were at table it was clear that I had made the mistake of holding the floor too long.

'It's very pleasant,' said my father self-pityingly, 'to come home after a long day with the firm at Torbeach and listen to someone who lives in a different world.'

During the ensuing silence, while mama and I assessed the quality of this gambit, a waitress removed the soup plates.

'Bring the next course quickly,' snapped my father, 'and don't worry about the frills.'

He surveyed his wife and son, waiting for comment. Since we were too experienced to volunteer this, he reverted to his original tactic.

'As I was saying,' my father said heavily, 'it's nice to know that my boring efforts in Torbeach, which neither of you want to know about, produce the means of financing a more gracious existence for my son.'

Mama and I maintained our practised silence. The waitress returned with three plates of chicken blanketed in the famous sea-food sauce.

'What's all this?' said my father, waving his hand over the plates. 'I said no frills. Take it away and bring us plain roast chicken. Plain food for plain people.'

The text-book answer to this was, once more, to say

nothing and let the waitress do as my father had ordered. But I was fond of the sea-food sauce and did not see why I should be dictated to in the matter. This, of course, was the state of mind which my father's technique was calculated to provoke. He went on and on probing from different angles, until finally his opponent, however strong his resolution to keep silent, was compelled to make some protest, if only in order to prove to himself that he was still alive. And once that protest was made, however reasonably and un-emphatically, my father's art would in no time inflate it into an act of treachery or rebellion.

'If you don't mind,' I said, with a sense of throwing away game, set and match, 'I'll have it as it is. It makes a change.'

'I mind?' said my father. 'Why should I? All I've got to do is pay for it. And what about you, dear? Do you share your son's preference for messed up nonsense? Or mine for honest food?'

The waitress hovered awkwardly. Mama looked at her husband, her son, and lastly at her plate. Whatever she said now, the damage was done; she was indeed fond of sea-food sauce, but knew that what was coming would prevent her from enjoying that or anything else. Seeking for a neutral factor, she glanced at the waitress.

'It seems unkind to send it back,' she mumbled: 'after all that trouble . . .'

Mama had made the fatal mistake of referring to the convenience of someone other than her husband.

'You are quite right,' said my father dangerously: 'one must not be inconsiderate. It is still war-time when all is said and done. That will be quite all right,' he said, grinning fiendishly at the waitress, who took her chance and was off. 'And so,' he continued, 'I find myself eating the kind of food I detest because my family refuses to back me up against a waitress.'

'Why not give it a chance?' I said. 'You knew what kind of food they have here when you arranged to come.'

'I arranged to come because your mother was so keen.

She said, and I agreed, that some sort of celebration was in order to welcome you home. I simply hoped that I might be allowed to order the kind of food I like when we got here.'

Even now, perhaps, the situation was not past mending. But the sight of my father, as he messily scraped the sauce to one side and then munched great mouthfalls of chicken and potato with eyes and cheeks bulging, was too much.

'You seemed fierce enough,' I said, 'to make us have what you thought fit. If, just for once, the tables have been turned, it bloody well serves you right.'

Not clever, I thought to myself despairingly, not witty, not even effective; just raucous and crude. Here was another element in my father's technique: he induced such anger that one lost one's head; one answered with a blind violence which, alien from logic and justice, could express only personal animus.

'Thank you for that. Thank you, Fielding my son, for letting me know how you feel about me.'

'Jack, dear, he didn't mean—'

'—I know very well what he meant. That it doesn't matter what I want, because I'm only his stupid father, who doesn't care for Latin and Greek and is only fit to grind away in his factory at Torbeach and produce the money you both spend so freely.'

My father thumped his fist on the table with deliberation and looked quickly over his shoulder to see what impression he was making on the other diners.

'Bring me beer,' he shouted at the decrepit wine-waiter; 'I never really wanted this wine in the first place.'

He snatched the half-full bottle of South African hock off the table and thrust it at the terrified old man. My mother, who loved wine of all things, followed it with miserable eyes.

'Let me tell you this,' said my father, gleefully noticing mama's discomfiture over the wine. '*I* built up that business to what it is, and *I* hold it together, and *I* keep and feed you both. What I expect in return is a little loyalty and support.

Do I get it? No. I get hate. Pure, bitter hate, which I can see in your eyes. I come out to a restaurant, hope for a nice evening—'

'—Please be quiet, Jack. Nobody hates you.'

'They simply,' I said, 'despise you. You've done nothing, at Torbeach or anywhere else, except bully people about and think how marvellous you are.' I had made a great effort to collect myself and my argument, and my matter was certainly well grounded. 'You haven't built that factory up : it's exactly the same as when you inherited it. *Inherited* it. You don't hold it together : your manager does. You don't feed and keep us. Grandpa's money does that. And as for support, your ideas are so mean, so vulgar, so contemptible that you deserve none. So for God's sake shut up and let us eat our meal in peace.'

My father did not mind being answered back in anger : this was necessary if a scene was to proceed at all, and he liked scenes to proceed for some time before people actually cringed. What he did not like was being told home truths; and the set which I had just advanced, to the prejudice of the fantasy in which he figured as an able and deserving self-made man, caught him on the quick. My father, when really caught on the quick, ceased to bluster and became dangerous, cunning and cool.

'There is something in what you say,' he now calmly remarked.

The wine-waiter brought his beer.

'Please bring back that wine after all,' he said : 'I think my wife would like some . . . Yes,' he went on, 'there is something in what you say, Fielding. What you must remember, however, is that the factory, inherited or not, is now mine, and that the money is also mine. I can use it how I wish. Now, I was thinking of settling a little on you. A nice little sum, the income to help you through Cambridge, the capital to become yours when you finished there and to help you start up in whatever you chose to do. Because I know you don't fancy the business and I wouldn't dream of compelling you to enter it against your will. So, I thought, I'll give him a nice little sum to start him off. But after what you have just said this evening since it seems you hold me in such contempt . . . I don't suppose you will want to take my money. No. You have made your position clear. I'm very sorry that you won't allow me to help you.'

'You showed no signs of doing so last time we discussed the matter.'

'Ah. I thought again. There was something to be said, I decided, for the arguments which you and your mother put forward. But now . . . now that you have decided to turn spiteful and insolent . . . I see that I must change my mind once more.'

My father took a long envelope from his pocket and pulled out the contents.

'A cheque for £10,000,' he said meditatively, laying this on the table : 'instructions to Japhet the solicitor to hold this in trust for you until the day you graduate as Bachelor of Arts, and in the meantime to pay you quarterly the income it will yield from careful investment. Four per cent, let us say. A pity I've had the trouble of writing this letter for nothing.'

'I'm not too proud to accept £10,000 of Grandpa's money, if that's what you mean.'

'My money,' said my father wistfully, and slowly tore up the cheque. 'Since you despise me so much, you obviously can't accept it.'

I shrugged. All three of us at the table knew that had the evening gone peacefully, had no one risen to my father's bait, then the cheque and the letter would not have appeared and would simply have been destroyed in secret or kept for another occasion. But the fact that the cheque was only a stage prop did not mean that my father could not issue such a cheque if he chose. We all knew this too. And so there was always just the outside chance that this time he had really meant it . . . Ten thousand pounds, an income, a nice bit of capital later . . . Despite myself, I was sweating as at the loss of a genuine offer. Abruptly I pulled myself together: to dwell on this was to play my father's game for him. Best simply to be grateful that now the process of self-assertion had been gone through there would probably be peace for several days. Mama and I would be left alone—until passing time again brought father's self-esteem to the pressure point of orgasm.

At breakfast next morning there was a letter for me. I recognised Christopher's writing on the envelope and left it unopened until I was alone in my own room.

Dear Fielding (Christopher *wrote from his home in Tonbridge*),

I am so sorry for making such a silly row before I left this morning. Of course I understand why you couldn't come last night. And why you are uncertain about coming to stay. If Somerset Lloyd-James is coming to stay with you, even though you told him nothing about staying with me, I think he might sort of sniff things out, as you say. I know this sounds silly, but lately I've felt that there's come to be something rather sinister about L-J, not that I know him very well. I feel that he's the kind of person who wouldn't hesitate to use anything he knew about people, if it could help him, and at the same time would pretend to be doing it because it was his duty or something. Roman Catholics have an odd way of seeing double, I mean of bringing their religion into things when it suits them and otherwise not.

But even so, if you came here, say just for a night or two, either well before or well after Somerset came to you, need he ever find out? Do think it over and try to come.

          Love from Christopher.

P.S. I thought you might like the enclosed. It was taken during the Eton match.

My shabby treatment of Christopher had made me feel

very guilty; and twenty-four hours' absence from him had revived a raging lust. Now, sooner and more easily than I had any right to hope, both problems were settled. Immediately I sat down to reply. I could come to him any time before August 14, I said, but must be back in Broughton not later than August 16 to allow three clear days before Somerset's arrival. For there was a strong chance that he would write or ring up just before the 20th to confirm times and dates; and if I failed to answer his letter, or if my mother told him on the telephone that I had gone to Tonbridge, then he would instantly become suspicious and start probing when we met.

... So let me know quickly, Christopher, and the sooner I can come, the better, for every possible reason. Much love and many thanks for the photo ...

In truth, however, the photograph was rather an embarrassment. The picture itself (Christopher in cricket kit, grinning, sweaty and dishevelled) was more or less all right; but on the back he had written, 'To Fielding with all my dearest love from Christopher. Please come soon, or I shan't be able to bear it.' Not the sort of thing to leave about, I thought : best tear it up and shove it down the loo. But just then I heard my mother coming down the passage towards my room, so I stuffed it at the back of my shirt drawer for future disposal.

My father was genial over the family supper.

'I met an old friend in the club house today,' he said, 'who has just come back on leave from Southern India. He may know just the thing for Fielding.'

Mama and I remained silent.

'He's a tea-planter. He says there are splendid openings. He's coming in later to discuss it.'

'Discuss what?' said mama, biting her lip.

'The openings on tea plantations in Southern India. You don't need a degree or anything, he says.'

'Then it would be a waste of Fielding's.'

'Don't you see? He needn't bother to get one. He could just do his Army service and then go right off.'

'To Southern India?' said mama.

'To Southern India. The Nilgri mountains, to be more precise.'

'And waste his place at Cambridge?'

'When a splendid chance like this comes up . . . At his age, I'd have been off like a bullet. Steady money, open air life, plenty of servants, jolly good chaps to work with. What more could anyone want?'

'I could tell you,' I said, 'but I haven't the strength.'

I was bored to death. Although four days had passed since I wrote to Christopher, there had been no answer. That afternoon, desperate to talk to someone of my own age, I had rung up Peter, who had been out when I rang. So now I had put on my Dorian Gray act, which at least (I felt) made something sophisticated, even significant, out of my frustration. ('Why am I so bored, Henry?' 'Boredom, my dear Dorian, is the privilege and burden of a sensitive spirit. Coarser natures are immune.')

'What's that?' said my father.

'I don't think the life would suit me. One must get up early because there is so much to do, go to bed early because there is so little to talk about.'

Well, it would serve.

'I suppose you think that's clever. When you know more about life, you'll realise that it's practical common sense which counts, every time. Every time.'

'I'll settle for uncommon sense. As the term implies, it is rarer commodity.'

'You don't know what you're talking about.'

'All I'm trying to say,' I said, my pose dissipated by extreme irritation, 'is that I'm damned if I'll be shunted off, on the unasked advice of a complete stranger, to plant tea with a pack of whisky-swilling boobies from cheap board schools.'

'Bloody little snob. *Intellectual* snob. I suppose you'd sooner sit on your behind in Cambridge for three years, talking arty nonsense while I pay the bills. Anything rather than do a proper day's work. Sometimes I think I've got a woman for a son.'

'That's right. A woman with a first eleven batting average of 37.62.'

'They haven't asked you to play for the Rest against the Lord's Schools, I notice. Or shouldn't I mention that?'

'They never asked you to play for any team at all. Or shouldn't I mention *that*?'

Mama twisted a handkerchief in her thin hands.

'You must both help me with the washing-up,' she said, with all the firmness at her command, 'or your friend will be here, Jack.'

This was not to be denied. Father declared truce by rolling up his napkin, after which, in absolute silence, we carried the dishes to the kitchen.

Mr Tuck, the tea-planter, got smaller as he got taller. His feet were huge, his legs ample; but his hips were ungenerous, his chest meagre, and his head like a wizened grapefruit. Mr Tuck was very sure of his opinions, which coincided in most respects with my father's, and he laughed loudly and constantly out of a mouth like a frog's which seemed almost to meet at the back of his head.

'I've brought Angela,' said Mr Tuck on the doorstep.

Father looked puzzled, as though he had not heard of Angela, who was a real dish. She had what Browning's bishop called huge, smooth, marbly limbs, of which a pair of shorts revealed all but an inch and a half. Her breasts were prominent but not outrageous, her skin was gold with a suggestion of silver down, her hair (blonde) fell over her shoulder like Veronica Lake's, and she had teeth sound enough to chew a raw elephant. Her nose turned up exquisitely. Her ears, when they appeared from behind the curtain of her hair, issued a pressing invitation to insert one's tongue into them, and then slyly hid behind her hair again. Her eyes were the light blue of a summer's dawn. (They were also her weakest feature, being slightly crossed and rather close together.) All in all, she could not have been much more than twenty, and the turned up nose took two years off. I gaped, my father gaped. It was left for mama to restore order.

'Oh, how nice,' she said. 'Please come in, Miss Tuck.'

'*Mrs* Tuck,' said Mr Tuck, and brayed like a donkey.

'Oh . . . I'm so sorry.'

'That's all right, dear lady. I don't need to be told how lucky I am. I acquired this six months ago on local leave in Oute.'

We all trooped into the drawing-room, Mrs Tuck looking vaguely annoyed, possibly at having been 'acquired' in Oute. When she sat down her shorts rode up another inch. Has she I wondered, got anything on underneath them?

My father absent-mindedly poured quadruple whiskies all round (rather stingy singles were his usual form) and conversation of a kind began.

'So this is your young hopeful,' said Mr Tuck. 'Your father says'—turning fiercely on me—'that you've got brains.'

I concentrated on keeping my eyes away from Mrs Tuck's loins.

'What are you going to do with yourself?' Mr Tuck continued with a snarl.

'It's uncertain. The Army for a time, of course. And then Cambridge. Or Cambridge,' I stammered, 'and then the Army.'

'I told you,' my father said: 'he's got Cambridge on the brain.'

'He has a scholarship to Lancaster,' said mama defensively.

'What in?' asked Mr Tuck with contempt.

'The classics. Latin and Greek.'

'Never went in for that sort of thing myself. Keener on practical things.'

'That's what I always say,' my father said.

Mrs Tuck, looking bored, set her empty class firmly down.

'More whisky?' said my father.

Mrs Tuck nodded and said nothing.

'Ice, dear?' said mama, then seemed to think she had somehow used the wrong idiom. 'Ice, Mrs Tuck?' she emended.

'Call her Angela,' said Mr Tuck. 'I call her Ange,' he added aggressively, as though warning everyone that the privilege was exclusive; 'don't I, Ange?'

Mrs Tuck took a long drink of whisky.

'Your father tells me,' said Mr Tuck turning back to myself, 'that you might like to join us. We're looking for young chaps with the right background.'

'What background is that?'

'Well, you know, decent school, decent parents ... all this,' said Mr Tuck, gesturing round the room at two water colours by mama and some hunting prints which father had bought cheap in a sale. 'Solid,' Mr Tuck expanded; 'nothing flashy. Reliable young chaps who can do a sound job of work. And keep the Indians in their proper place.'

'Won't they be wanting their plantations back fairly soon?'

'What gave you that idea?'

'There seem to be suggestions of that kind in the air just now,' I said.

'They can't do without us, and they know it. Why only the other day I was talking to one of *their own chaps*—'

'—Jesus Christ,' said Mrs Tuck, speaking for the first time, 'you do bore me. I think you must be the biggest bore in the world.'

She got up, put down her empty glass, and retreated to the French window.

'Steady on, old girl,' Mr Tuck began.

But his mem-sahib was trying the handle.

'Let me,' I said. I slipped the catch and held the door open for her. 'I'll show you the garden.'

'That's right, dear,' said mama, 'you show Angela the garden.'

'But what about the discussion?' my father complained.

'It'll keep for a minute,' said Mr Tuck. 'Let 'em go out for a blow. Leave us old fogies to the booze.' He paused for a moment. Then,

'Old Ange often blows up like that,' he said hilariously, and started to laugh more loudly than ever, straining out guffaw after guffaw as though he was taking part in some kind of endurance test.

'I'm glad you gave me an excuse to get out of that,' I said to Mrs Tuck as the laughter died behind us.

'What have you got to complain about? At least you're not married to any of them.'

Mrs Tuck was plainly too full of her own woes to sympathise much with anyone else's. We walked down a well kept lawn, the pride of my father, who was an assiduous amateur gardener, and then through some prettily arranged shrubs to a little pond. Mrs Tuck sat down on a stone seat. She put her hands on her elbows and straddled heavily.

'No need for you to hang about,' she said.

'I'd like to. If I'm not in your way.'

Mrs Tuck shrugged, not unkindly, then patted the seat by her side.

'I dare say,' she said after a little while, 'that you're surprised at me for making a scene.'

'We have them all the time in our family.'

'At least you're not hooked. You can leave any day you want to.'

I let this pass.

'Can't you?' I said.

'Daddy,' she remarked abruptly, 'was a colonel in the Indian Army Pay Corps. One day they found his accounts were rather odd. So they took him away to arrange a Court Martial and I was left alone in the bungalow. With all those spiteful women—you know the sort—coming in all the time to ask if there was anything they could do. "You poor creature",' she mimicked badly, ' "you must think of me as a mother." I had to get out. And then Tuck turned up, on leave from his plantation. Just my luck. It was Tuck or nothing,' she said, as though it were a line in a repertory play which she was repeating for the seven hundredth time.

'And your father?'

'Dismissed the service. Some old friend found him something in Hong Kong. God knows what he'll get up to there.'

You ran out, I thought: as soon as things got tough, you ran out. And you didn't even have the sense to look where you were running.

'It was lovely up there before Daddy got into trouble,' she was saying: 'race meetings, dances, golf. They had a real grass course. New people on leave all the time. And I had to get Tuck.'

'Why?'

'What do you mean, why?'

'With all those other people passing through on leave?'

'The word had gone round about Daddy. But Tuck was so potty for a juicy young woman that he just didn't care.'

So you took advantage of him and now you're being well paid out.

'If you're keen on golf,' I said, 'perhaps we might play? The course here is very good. And very beautiful. Between the sea and the saltmarshes.'

'You're rather sweet,' she said. Was it my imagination, or was her knee pressing against mine?

'Fielding? Fielding?' It was mama from the lawn.

'When?' I said gruffly.

'When what?' said Mrs Tuck, and withdrew her knee unhurriedly, leaving me in doubt whether or not it had been there by accident.

'Golf. Tomorrow?'

'Not before Wednesday.'

'That's nearly a week.'

'I know.' She patted my hand. 'I don't want Tuck to be jealous. If we make it too soon . . .'

Delicious thought.

'All right,' I said : 'Wednesday. Half-past-two?'

She nodded. 'I'll look forward very much.'

'*Fielding.*' Mother was growing urgent.

'We must go,' said Mrs Tuck softly, and held my hand until we came in sight of my mother on the lawn.

'There you are, dear. Angela too . . . I'm afraid you must come in, Fielding, because Mr Tuck wants to ask you some questions. About your School Certificate and things.'

'For Christ's sake, mother. Father must know I won't go out there.'

'Yes, yes, dear, but if you could—well—humour him till he gets over it. You know how he is. If you pretend to fall in with the idea, he'll forget it almost at once.'

'What's the matter with going out there?' said Mrs Tuck, puzzled.

'Nothing, I suppose. But I've got other plans. Cambridge.'

'Well, if that's what you fancy . . .' Mrs Tuck shook her head, as if troubled by a fly. 'India can be great fun, you know.'

'I'm sure. But it's not for me.'

Mrs Tuck looked at me blankly, then smiled a smile that turned my inwards over.

'I'll go on home,' she said, moving away easily on her strong, lovely legs. 'Tell Tuck to stay out as late as he wants so long as he doesn't disturb me when he gets in.'

'Yes, dear,' said mama, rather shocked.

Mrs Tuck turned to smile once more.

'Wednesday,' she cooed back at me, and was gone into the night.

Dear Fielding (Christopher wrote),

Sorry I've been so long answering your letter, but something awkward's happened. As you know, I only just managed in my exams, and the head man's suggested to my parents

*that I ought to have tuition during the holidays. They've
found someone from Oxford who's to come and stay and be
my tutor for three or four weeks in August. It's really a good
idea, I suppose, but I do wish to God it wasn't happening
because it means you can't come until September. I mean,
there'd be room all right, but my parents think I ought to
concentrate on this tuition, and anyhow it wouldn't be the
same. I'm miserable about this, but there's nothing to be
done.*

*I remember you saying that you were going to stay with
the head man in Wiltshire on September 7 or thereabouts.
Why not come here for a few days before going there? It's
not far out of your way, only ¾ of an hour from London,
which you'll have to pass through anyway. I feel ghastly
about putting you off like this, and terribly disappointed, but
what can I do?* Please *let me know that you can come in
early September.*

All my love,
Christopher.

*P.S. (Two hours later.) The new tutor's just arrived. He
seems quite decent, but he's very ugly, rather like Somerset
L-J, though no spots. Also, I'm afraid he's rather an oik,
and he seems very intense. Oxford Group or something?
Keep your fingers crossed for me.*
Christopher.

This letter was a blow, but perceptibly less of a blow than
it would have been had I not now met Angela Tuck.
Although there had been something ambiguous about the
encouragement which she offered me, encouragement it had
certainly been; and she had made it very plain that her
marriage was not to be regarded as an inhibiting factor.
Angela, in a word, was fair game; even if nothing came of
the chase, the days would pass the quicker when it started.
Meanwhile, I looked forward to our golf match with a
mixture of acute nervousness and unbridled reverie.

*　　　*　　　*

Although I had politely answered Mr Tuck's questions and even filled in a form, thereby seeking to deny my father that sense of being opposed which alone gave spice to his activities, we still hadn't heard the last of the tea-planting scheme.

'I want to get it all settled,' my father said. 'A definite application must be made. I want to see more keenness.'

'But Jack dear, Mr Tuck said we couldn't do anything more until we knew about Fielding's Army service.'

'Well, what about his Army service? Is he trying to find out? There must be people he could go and see.'

'I've told you,' I said: 'I've been deferred for another year because I'm a candidate for a University award.'

'But if you're going to India,' said my father with relish, 'you won't need a University award. Therefore you needn't be deferred. Why,' he said, clapping his hands spitefully together, 'we might even be able to get you into the Army this autumn. And as soon as that's out of the way you'll be free to leave for India at once.'

'It's too late to get me undeferred,' I said, uncertain whether or not this was true. 'Anyway, the Headmaster's made all his arrangements on the understanding that I'm coming back. And apart from anything else, you haven't given notice, so they'd charge you at least one quarter's fees for nothing at all.'

This argument told.

'By God, we'll see about that,' said my father, slapping his hands together once more. 'I just wouldn't pay, that's all.'

'Then they'd sue you and you'd look a frightful fool.'

My father gave a grunt of rage.

'And anyhow,' I went on, 'you said you wouldn't go back on your word. About next year.'

'These days we have to take our chances when we see them. It's all very well for that Headmaster of yours, dreaming away about Latin and Greek all day long. What does he know about the *practical* things?'

'Enough to administer a large school, and act as a housemaster, and sit on several commissions in London, and get an important book written, all in the face of a horrible war and a crippling shortage of staff and materials of every kind.'

'What's the book got to do with it?'

'Nothing. That's the point. He just managed to get it written as well as coping with all the practical things, as you call them.'

But the point was lost on my father.

'Well, one thing I can do,' he said, grinding his teeth, 'is to write to Lancaster College and tell them that you won't be wanting your place there.'

'But Jack dear, supposing this tea thing falls through?'

'That's just what you'd both like, isn't it? *I'll* see it doesn't fall through. You can rely on that.'

The next day we heard that after two bombs of a new and hideously powerful kind had been dropped on cities in Japan the Japanese had surrendered unconditionally. Good, I thought: quite a chance now that I won't have to do any Army service at all.

... And so, the Headmaster wrote from Wiltshire, you need have no worries about Lancaster. They're not interested in your father's plans, about India or anything else, only in yours. It is true they will want to know where their fees are to come from; but all sorts of systems of government subsidy are now being mooted, and I've no doubt at all that your case will be covered—though it might mean doing your Army service before you go up, which is perhaps the better choice anyhow. (Incidentally, I don't think the end of the war in the Far East will make much difference to your military liabilities.) However, just in case your father's letter should cause the college authorities any doubts, I've written to Robert Constable the Tutor (you met him last quarter, I think?) to reassure him and to set everything straight. I

*know it must be tiresome for you to put up with this kind
of behaviour, but you must try to remember that your
father is a busy man and is no doubt suffering from the
strain of these last years.*

Lolling about boasting in RAOC messes.

*This is black news (the Headmaster continued), from
Japan. It is tempting to let relief, that the war is now finally
over, oust any other emotion. I hope that you will not make
this mistake. An element more terrible than any I could have
thought possible has now obtruded itself into our lives, and
I do not see any limit to the potential horrors which may
develop from it. And this is to take only a selfish view. What
has already been done to the people of Japan, and done
in our name, is horror enough.*

That's all very well, I thought; but then no one was going
to send *you* out there to risk your neck in the jungle.

*My wife and I (the letter concluded), are looking forward
to seeing you about September 7. Perhaps you will write and
let us have an exact date? By the way, I've written to
Somerset Lloyd-James and asked him to join us if he can. I
felt he would make an interesting addition to the party.*

The hell he will, I thought. If I go to stay in Tonbridge en
route for Wiltshire, as Christopher suggests, then Somerset
will smell out my state of sin the first moment he sees me.
Or will he? For Christ's sake be reasonable. We're all beginning to go on as if Somerset had a crystal ball. And anyway, all that can be forgotten for the time being, because this
afternoon is golf with Angela Tuck.

*   *   *

Mrs Tuck was rather late, but she was impeccably dressed and turned out to be a thoroughly competent player. She declared her handicap as eight; and though at first sceptical of this, I found myself two down after the first five holes.

'I never thought you'd be so good.'

'Why not? They say women need big bottoms for golf, and I'm well equipped there.'

She hit her ball straight down the fairway the best part of two hundred yards. I squared up to mine, hit too hard and lifted my head, struck the ball with the heel of the club, and saw it hop fiercely into a bunker twenty yards away and forty-five degrees to my left.

'Bugger,' I said, and apologised hastily to Mrs Tuck, who smiled and shrugged.

Excited by this tolerant behaviour, I took my No. 8, walked into the bunker, sent my ball flopping out in a cloud of sand, and yelled blue murder.

'Whatever's the matter?'

'Something's got in my eye.'

'Come here then.'

As she examined my eye, she came very close; her splendid breasts brushed against my shirt, her belly pressed up against mine. For about ten seconds she stayed quite still; then she made a quick dab with her handkerchief and stood back.

'All right?' she said.

'I'm not sure it's really out.'

'Aren't you now? I'll have another look ... later.'

At the end of the hole I was three down.

'Your father's been on at Tuck about your job,' Mrs Tuck said a few holes later on. 'He wants to know what the next step is.'

'There isn't a next step.'

'You really don't want it?'

'I've told you. I want to go to Cambridge.'

Mrs Tuck sighed gently.

'But you filled in that form, didn't you?' she said, and put her ball dead from fifty yards.

'Only to keep my father quiet. I didn't suppose your husband cared much either way.'

'Oh but he does, Fielding. When Tuck came on leave, he was told to recruit suitable young men over here. Promised a bonus if he did well at it.'

'In a few months there'll be ex-officers at a penny a score.'

'Not just any young men. Young men from good schools, to give the place a bit of tone...and young men whose fathers have money to invest.'

'Just let Tuck try getting money out of my father.'

'Tuck,' she said softly, 'has more ways of persuading people than you might think.'

I took my No. 6 for my chip shot and hit the ground some inches behind the ball. It described a flaccid little arc and fell lifeless, still twenty yards short of the green. I looked at it stupidly.

'Is there any way,' I said at last, 'of calling your husband off?'

'It could mean promotion for him. Important promotion.'

'What do you care?'

'Since I'm stuck with Tuck,' she said, placidly but very firmly, 'I'd sooner it was for richer than for poorer.'

She plopped in a twelve foot putt.

'Five up,' she said, 'and nine to go. I could do with a rest.'

We sat down on a sand dune, from which we could look across an empty beach to the sea. The breeze whispered through the scattered, spiky grasses; the sand was warm.

'Lonely,' said Mrs Tuck, and shivered slightly despite the sun. She moved closer. 'Let's have another look at your eye,' she said.

With her left hand she held the lids apart, while with the fingers of the right she gently massaged my scalp.

'That's all right,' she said. She withdrew her left hand from my eye, then ran her finger nails down the bare flesh of my arm and on down my flannelled thigh.

'Ooooh, Angela,' I said, and reached out greedily for her.

'No,' she said, pushing me away; 'you're very sweet, but no.'

'Then you shouldn't have done like that with your nails.'

'It's not that I don't like you, Fielding. I think that you're very attractive.' A hand rubbing my knee. 'It's just that . . .'

'Just that what?'

'I can't really be at ease with you as long as we're at cross purposes.'

'What on earth do you mean by that?'

'You're quite sure you want to go to Cambridge?'

'Of course. I've wanted nothing else ever since I can remember.'

'And I suppose I can understand that. But,' she said regretfully, 'it does place a barrier between us. Me brought up in India, you see, and you despising it like this.'

'I don't despise it.'

'But you refuse to go there, Fielding. I find that . . . rather hurting. I find it makes it very difficult for me . . . to get to know you better.'

'You mean . . . *You mean* that if I fall in with this sch—'

'—Don't spell it out,' she said kindly; 'it would only spoil things.'

There was a long silence while she went on rubbing my knee.

'Come on,' she said at last, taking my hand to pull me up, 'we can't sit here all day.'

I lost the match by eight and six.

The first rocket soared and sprayed over the fair-ground in the Tuesday Market Place; there were cheers, gasps, moans; the V-J celebrations in Lympne Ducis had begun.

Lympne Ducis, which was about twenty miles up the coast from Broughton Staithe, was an ancient town with modern facilities for shipping. It had a beautiful fifteenth century Customs House and also a small but well equipped harbour which had been working to capacity during the war.

Although the summer fair, which was traditionally held in the Tuesday Market Place, was limited in scope by war-time restrictions as to fuel and power, the proprietors, knowing there was a lot of good money in the town and victory to grease it, had strained the regulations to bursting. The old-fashioned roundabout and the tower slide were there as usual; but for the first time since 1940 there was also a big wheel and a dive-bomber, a ghost-train and bumping cars. The stalls were crammed with food and prizes, with waffles and cockles and 'Victory' sausages, with teddy bears and goldfish, with hats which bore the legends 'Blighty', 'Britannia', 'Tipperary', 'Tobruk' and 'Hiroshima'. There were lights, after the years of darkness, wreathes and festoons of lights; and as the rockets swept arching up over the gabled houses, every bell in Lympne Ducis rang out in triumph over the evil little yellow men beyond the sea.

'How exciting,' said mama; 'I wish your father had come.'

'He might at least have let us have the car,' I said.

'You know how it is, dear. This hateful petrol rationing.'

'There's always enough when *he* wants to go somewhere . . .'

And now the outlines of a huge set-piece were visible high over the market place. The myriad points of light crackled and whirled and fused, formed themselves into gradually distinguishable features. Surely . . . it must be . . . yes, oh God of Battles, *yes*, George King and Emperor, his Queen, his daughters, all smiling serenely out of the spurting flames. The noises of the fair died, music came from the loudspeakers hung round the square, and fifteen thousand voices took up the chant:

LAND OF HOPE AND GLORY,
MOTHER OF THE FREE . . .

'I think, dear,' said mama, 'that I should like to sit down somewhere.'

With some difficulty, I made way for my mother through

the rapt singers and led her into the lounge of the Duke's
Head. With even more difficulty I fought for and won a glass
of whisky in the bar.

'There, mother. Make you feel better.'

'Thank you, dear. Don't let me spoil it for you, though.
You go out and join in, and collect me later.'

'If you're sure, mama . . .'

But I turned away without waiting for an answer. Outside was a vast sea of vocal euphoria.

> God, that made thee mighty,
> Make thee mightier yet . . .

Not only us, I thought; not only us in our privileged
chapel : all these people too.

GOD, *THAT MADE THEE MIGHTY*, MAKE THEE MIGHTIER YET.

The music died, the cheers faded, the fair-ground chorus
resumed. The roundabout organ; laughter, screams. A man
in front of me was sick, another slipped in the mess, staggered
against two young girls who were walking arm in arm, and
fell violently to the ground.

'Two bloody little 'ores,' the man said.

The girls looked distressed. Pale and vulnerable, irresistibly
pretty and pathetic.

'Bloody, fuckin' little 'ores,' the man shouted from the
ground.

The dense crowd seemed indifferent.

'Come with me,' I said, and taking them both by the arm
I swept them through a gap in the crowd to a stall which
sold waffles.

'Have a waffle?'

'No, reelly . . .'

'What's your name? Mine'—'Fielding' would sound too
ridiculous in this company—'mine's Christopher.'

'Chris . . . I'm Phyllis.'

'And I'm Dixie.'

Phyllis was a well set up but commonplace blonde; Dixie, who wore a 'Hiroshima' hat, was a brunette with spotty but interesting features, a weak mouth, a tilting nose.

'Have a waffle?'

'Well, all right.'

'Three waffles, please. With syrup.'

'Ooooh . . .'

It was not an evening on which to rebuff invitation. All round us, set free in the name of victory, excited by the singing, made bold by the pealing bells, people were confronting one another, breaking the rule of a lifetime for this one night. Hand reached for hand, even heart (briefly) for heart; stranger clung to stranger and called him brother. Phyllis and Dixie could be no exception. We all went on the roundabout, the dive-bomber, and the tower slide, at the bottom of which the girls' skirts flew up to reveal brown, ample thighs. We went on the bumper cars; we fired air guns and threw darts; Phyllis won a goldfish in a bowl.

'The ghost-train. The ghost-train.'

'Phyllis is feared of the dark.'

'Then you come, Dixie.'

'Yes, you go, Dixie, love. I'll stand here and mind my fish.'

Into the car and through the double gates.

'Ooh, I'm so feared, I'm as bad as Phyllis, hold me tight.'

'I'm here, Dixie. Kiss me.'

Spider webs trailing in the dark. Dixie's tongue meeting mine, keen, wet, inexpert. An enormous phosphorescent skull. Into the huge mouth went the car and into Dixie's went my probing tongue.

'Hold me tighter. More. More.'

Diabolical laughter. A sudden turn, throwing me right across her. My hand on her breast—how did it get there?— a little whimper, part of guilt and part of joy.

'Chris, Chris, Christopher. Kiss me again.'

Rattle, jerk, bang, and out into the lights.

'Round again, please. Two.'

'No, Chris. Phyllis. She's waiting.'

'Just once more. I've already paid.'

Crash through the double door. *Now*. Tongue between her lips, left hand over her shoulder and cupping her breast, and with the right hand . . .

'No, Chris. No.'

'Yes, Dixie. And when we get out, we'll give Phyllis the slip and we'll—'

'—No, Christopher. No, no, *no*.'

But her legs parted slowly to admit my hand into a warm, moist country where I had never been before.

'Oh, no . . . Oh . . . Oh . . .'

'Dixie. We'll give Phyllis the slip. And then . . .'

I moved my hand to part her legs yet wider.

'I can't, I can't, I can't. She's my *sister*.'

Using both her hands, she thrust mine away from her, away from the paradisiac country. Panting and whimpering, she strained away from me. The whimpers mounted and coalesced into hysterical weeping. Christ. Christ, Christ, Christ.

'Dixie, *please* . . .'

A heavy, rending, choking, unquenchable cacophony of sobs. Rattle, jerk, bang, and out into the lights.

Run for it.

Out of the car and down the steps, just missing the astonished Phyllis (crash went the goldfish bowl—'Oh Chris, my poor little fish'), straight through the crowd, round the tower slide and behind the stalls. Would they follow? Would they call the police? Would they collect a mob? A whistle from the distance. Could that be . . . ?

Into the Duke's Head.

'Quick, mother. We'll miss the train.'

'But Fielding dear, I thought—'

'—No, no. There's no time at all.'

'If you say so—'

'—Please be *quick,* mother. This way, out of the side door . . . Down this street. It's a short cut.'

'Really, dear, anyone would think the police were after us. You know I can't hurry too much.'

'Taxi . . . *Taxi.*' By God, what a bit of luck. There weren't more than three in the whole town. I blocked the road, waving frantically.

' 'Ere, 'ere. I don't take no more fares, master. I'm off 'ome. I've used my quota for the day.'

'But the lady's ill. Just to the station.'

'Ill, be she?'

'There'll be a whole pound for you if you take us.'

'Ill she be. In you get, missis . . .'

When we were in the train, which was not due to leave the station for another thirty minutes, mama said:

'If you ask me, dear, you ought to be a little more careful of your money. A whole pound.'

'It was for you, mama.'

'Was it, dear?' said my mother equably. 'Well, if *you* think it was worth it . . .'

'Why is it,' said my father the next morning, 'that I never get any co-operation?'

'Co-operation, dear?'

'Yes, dear, co-operation, dear. I've had a letter from the so called Tutor of Lancaster College, in which he acknowledges mine and begs to inform me that any instructions about Mr Fielding Gray's place at the college should be sent by Mr Fielding Gray. Don't they know that I'm his father? And that he isn't twenty-one?'

It was unlike my father to own publicly to a snub. He must have something up his sleeve, I thought. Nevertheless the opportunity to gloat was too tempting to be missed.

'It is a popular fallacy,' I said to my father, 'that parents have a legal right to dictate to their children until they are twenty-one. Provided a person pursues a responsible course of life, he can leave home and suit himself as soon as he is sixteen.'

'Then leave home and suit yourself,' my father said. 'Go on.'

'Jack, dear—'

'—I will have co-operation. And I'll tell you how I'm going to get it. Either you do as I say,' he said, thrusting his face into mine, 'or there'll be no more money for you until you do. You can live here and have your meals, since you're still under twenty-one, but there'll be no money at all for anything else.'

There was a long silence.

'Does that set you straight?' my father said.

'While we're talking of money,' I said, trembling all over, 'let me tell *you* something to set you straight. Mr Tuck is not offering me this job to do you a favour, but because his boss in India is after some extra capital which they think you may be persuaded to provide. His wife told me all about it. They don't love you, they don't think you're marvellous, they simply want your cash.'

After this I locked myself into the lavatory and burst into tears.

...*I must say* (Peter Morrison *wrote from* Whereham), *you seem to be having a most unpleasant holiday. I expect it will be a relief when your parents go away. Meanwhile, I only hope your father stops being so silly over this tea-planting business. I don't see you as a sahib.*

Which reminds me. I'm as glad as you are that there's now no prospect of getting killed in the Far East; but I don't think we should be sanguine about this bomb they've thought up. The terrible thing about it is that it makes its possessor infallible. It does away, you see, with any margin of error or need for selection. In the old days you had to aim at your target. Now, in order to be sure of destroying what you want to, you can simply destroy everything at all. Suppose such a weapon were entrusted to a man like your father (or even Somerset) who knows he's right?

But I expect you are depressed enough without my raising additional nightmares. I hope things improve, and I look forward to seeing you and Somerset on the 24th or 25th. Please let me know which ...

So at least that was all right—though quite what was to happen about money, since my father's threat, was still obscure. One could only hope for the best, I thought; and anyhow, mama would be sure to wangle something. So I wrote to Peter to tell him that Somerset was definitely arriving at Broughton (as I had now heard) on August 20th, and that we would be coming on to him on the 24th. After that, I wrote to Christopher :

... So that all being well I can be with you in Tonbridge on September 4 or 5 and stay till I leave for Wiltshire on the 7th.

Oh Christopher, how I wish it could be sooner. I've been so lonely without you. I expect you've been lonely too (in a way, I hope you have), but at least you're busy with this tutor of yours. There's a line from a poem by a man called Auden which keeps running in my head—

'I think of you, Christopher, and wish you beside me ...'

If only it was that afternoon of the Eton match again, when we sat next to each other in the scoring box ...

Having posted these two letters, I settled down to read *Dorian Gray;* but the afternoon was very hot and the book a sickly bore. Every ten seconds I was interrupted by memories of Christopher in the hay-loft : 'Oh ... oh, oh, oh.' Oh Christ, those long smooth legs with their fluffy down.

And then I thought of another pair of legs. Angela Tuck's. Why not go to the Tucks' bungalow and say to Angela, 'All right. I'll sign on with your husband's plantation provided you'll come to bed with me in exchange'? That was the deal she had held out, so why not take her up? Not in so many words, of course, ('Don't spell it out,' she had said) but in the same veiled terms which she had used on the golf course, so that later on I could always wriggle out of the bargain. They meant to exploit me; why shouldn't I exploit them? All these adults ranged against me made for inequitable odds; I was entitled to any little victory I could win, however treacherously, in their despite. Superior strength in the opposition (as the Senior Usher had once observed) absolved one from obeying the Queensberry Rules.

Mr Tuck had gone to London for a few days. My father, having apparently taken my point about Tuck's motives, had sent the wretched man to Coventry; so that Tuck had doubtless felt it expedient to try his talent for recruiting elsewhere. Angela had been distant. But if I were now to present myself and make my offer? She couldn't eat me, after all, and anything was better than hanging around in the house with Dorian Gray gone stale on me.

I went to my room, washed my hands, face and feet, slicked my hair down with water, and substituted my blue 1st XI blazer and scarf for my ordinary coat and tie. Then I walked the three quarters of a mile to the Tucks' one-storey bungalow near the quay.

The curtains of one room were drawn. Angela must be having a siesta (Indian habit). On the whole, good. I was about to knock on the front door, when I reflected that she might be cross if woken up and dragged through the hall to answer. Better surprise her, quieten her as she lay vulnerable on the bed, and then introduce my business. 'I've been thinking over what you said about India, and I see that I've been very silly. It's not a chance to be missed.' Something like that. Whatever else, she could hardly pretend to be shocked.

Very quietly, I tried the front door. The catch was evidently up, for the door opened. The excitement of what was virtually house-breaking had now replaced desire. As the door opened yet further, apprehension replaced excitement. I was about to turn and run, had indeed already turned. Too late.

'Who's there?' said Angela's voice from inside a half-open door a few feet along the hall. My lips were parting to reply, when :

'Nobody's there,' said my father's voice. 'How could they be? I fastened the front door.'

'I thought—'

'—Don't be a silly girl, Angie. Your old Jackie will see you're safe.'

'And Jackie will be a good boy about you know what?'

The voice was childish, wheedling, without irony.

'I'll see that little beast signs up with Tuck. After that . . .'

'If Tuck was in a position to say that you'd guaranteed to invest a few thousand—'

'—Why can't that wait,' said my father crossly 'until the Army's finished with the boy and he's free to join?'

'Now the war's over, they're anxious to expand as soon as possible. If Tuck brings in new money *now*, they'll be very grateful.'

'Well, I'll see. If Angie's nice to Jackie, Jackie will see what he can do.'

The bed creaked.

'No. Jackie must promise Angie.'

Sweaty and furious as I was, I nevertheless had a clear mental picture of concupiscence struggling with avarice in my father's face.

There was a great wail of randiness.

'All right. Tuck can tell his boss I'll invest five thousand. Perhaps a little more if things go well on the market.'

'There's a dear, *good* Jackie.'

If she knew him as I do, I thought grimly, she'd get him to sign something this minute. But perhaps she too was keen to start. After all, I'd heard people say my father was a hand-some man.

'Jackie. Oh, Jackie.'

A different tone now, all childishness gone. A woman

speaking. Either she was a good actress or she was very much
in earnest.

'Christ, Christ, Jackie, Christ.'

She was in earnest.

I heard my father's breathing mount. Wait. Time it carefully. You swine, Jack Gray, you disgusting swine, with your
hot, panting breath.

'Soon, Angela, *soon* . . .'

'Oh *yes*, Jackie.'

Now. I opened the front door to its full extent and then
pulled it to with all the strength in my body.

Having slammed the door on the repulsive idyll in the
Tuck bungalow, I went for a walk along the beach in order
to calm myself. For a long time I thought, with a mixture
of lust and apprehension, of Dixie in the ghost-train. Supposing she or her parents tried to raise a complaint?
Suppose the police came making enquiries? In the end, however, I persuaded myself that the police would have neither
time nor good reason to look as far afield as Broughton
Staithe, and that in any case Dixie probably wanted to forget
the whole episode as much as I did. Though there was one
aspect of it I could never forget: my first, brief visit to the
lotus country of a woman's loins.

Having, with some difficulty, dismissed Dixie, I reverted
to the problem of my father. He had now given Angela a
definite promise that myself plus £5,000 would be signed,
sealed and delivered over to Tuck. It was always possible
that my father had no intention of trying to keep his bargain;
but equally, why should he not? The £5,000 would probably
be quite a sound investment; the arrangement would get me
off his hands for good; and more than all this, he would have
had the satisfaction of destroying my most cherished plans
and ambitions.

Quite why my father was so set against Cambridge, I was
unsure. It was not, I suspected, just a simple matter of mean-

ness about money or jealousy of my success; there was an intensity in his attitude, an element (however perverse) of morality, the clue to which, I thought, might possibly lie in something that I had once been told by the Senior Usher.

'If there is one thing people cannot stand,' the old man had said, 'it is that someone should achieve happiness and distinction by doing work which they despise. Their indignation is grounded in genuine moral feeling : it is like the resentment which dully married women feel at the success of a famous courtesan.'

'And why,' I had asked, 'are you telling me this?'

'My dear Fielding. You propose to spend your life doing intellectual work. You may as well learn now as later that many people—most people—regard such work as effeminate and degrading.'

Yes, I thought now, it fitted near enough. '. . . effeminate and degrading.' 'Sometimes,' my father had said, 'I think I've got a woman for a son.' My father clearly regarded Cambridge and all it stood for as immoral or at least unmanly; the work was not proper work at all (it was far too pleasant, for a start) and no son of his was going to make a living by it. So much, I thought, for diagnosis. But what, in heaven's name, was I going to do? If my father wanted to cut off supplies, no one could stop him. The Headmaster's talk of government grants and subsidies was all very well; but hitherto I had been accustomed to ample provision and I now shrank from the prospect of going through Cambridge on a meagre official pittance, of which, in any case, I had yet to be definitely assured. And quite apart from all that, if my father persisted in his present intention it would mean no last year at school, and on this I had set my heart.

Calmer than when I had set out but even more depressed, I arrived at our front door. Just inside the hall, on a hard chair by the telephone, sat my mother, looking very peculiar indeed.

'Mama . . . Why on earth are you sitting out here?'

'Something rather funny has happened,' my mother said.

Her eyes glinted weirdly, part in amusement and part in shock. 'Angela Tuck rang up. Your father's just died of a heart attack.'

Quite how much my mother knew or guessed, I never found out for sure. The official version, which mama apparently accepted, was that my father had gone to Angela to ask where he could get in touch with her husband in London, as he wanted some more information about the tea-planting scheme. Angela, while entertaining him to a cup of tea, had suggested that I myself might make difficulties about this; upon which father had flown into a rage, choked, gone into violent spasms, and then relapsed into kind of coma. Angela had rung for a doctor, but by the time he arrived my father was dead.

This seemed to me a very convenient version of the affair; inaccurate but on the whole equitable. I was glad that I myself was mentioned as in some sort contributing to father's demise; for since I had good reason to believe that this might indeed be the case, some reference to me, however wide of the actual facts, was both ironic and just. Guilt I felt none; my father had been a pestilential bully and now, by a happy accident, had been permanently removed. Even if one assumed that my own act of slamming the door had been the mortal factor (and who was ever to say that this was so?), the act had been excusable and its consequence unforeseen.

To Angela I did not speak of the matter. If she suspected that I had been the intruder that afternoon, she had yet to give any sign of it. For my part, my feelings towards her were unaltered, save that they now included considerable admiration of her resource : she must have had a most difficult and disagreeable job rigging the scene into decency against the arrival of the doctor. No doubt about it : a slut she might be but a slut to be reckoned with.

The coroner was soon satisfied that death was due to

natural causes, and arrangements for the funeral were briskly made. Mama, once she had had a few hours to get over her surprise, showed more efficiency and character than in all the years I could remember.

'Tell the undertaker,' she instructed me: 'opening time tomorrow.'

'Opening time?'

'As soon as he opens his shop or whatever he calls it. No point, Fielding dear, in hanging about.'

Or again, while kneeling in the church before the service.

'The people from the firm,' she decreed, 'must come in for drinks afterwards. But not the soaks from the golf club.'

'Some of them were friends of father's.'

'You mean they'd let him buy them drinks. Not that he was so quick to do that.'

'They'll resent it, mother.'

'I don't doubt it, dear,' said mama, as she concluded her devotions and resumed a sitting position: 'but since I never want to see any of them again, it doesn't matter, does it?'

The Rector, irritated by the flippancy with which mama had convened the ceremony, cut his address to a minimum. Even what little could be said in favour of the deceased he threw away rapidly, like a bored actor whose new mistress was waiting for him in his dressing-room. 'John Aloysius Gray,' he snorted, 'served from 1940 to 1945 as captain, later major, in the Army Ordnance Corps.' An undistinguished record, it now sounded infamous.

After John Aloysius Gray had been fed to the worms, the widow stood to receive condolences. Last in the line was Angela Tuck, to whom mama was more than gracious.

'You're not to feel it was your fault, Angela dear.' (Did she then know more than she let on?) 'You come home with me and Fielding. And when I've got rid of those nuisances from the firm we can all have a nice talk.'

From that day on my mother seemed increasingly eager

for the company of Angela Tuck. Since Tuck himself was still away, presumably recruiting, Angela was free to indulge mama, and was indeed invited to be present on the most intimate occasions, such as the family discussion with little Mr Japhet, the solicitor from Lympne Ducis, about my father's will.

With the exception of a few minor bequests to old friends and senior employees of the firm, everything was left to my mother, with the suggestion that she should 'take what steps she thought fit' as to the education and subsequent provision of myself. Although this was broadly in accordance with bourgeois custom, I was disconcerted that no more definite arrangements had been made. Knowing my father as I did, I had expected either to be provided for under some restrictive form of trust, or, quite possibly, to be spitefully disinherited : what I had not expected was that the will should be merely casual. (Here, of course, I had badly misread my father's character : I should have realised that he would have seen no point in restricting or spiting people by means of his will, as he himself would not be there to enjoy their discomfiture.) Again, quite apart from the vagueness of the immediate arrangements, my father had shown a disquieting unconcern for the future : there was no kind of entail, no stipulation that mama should regard myself as her heir, indeed nothing whatever, as far as I could see, to stop her giving away the whole lot that very afternoon. While I did not doubt her good will, I had no very high opinion of her good sense : mama was simply *not* a person who should be allowed to control a fortune.

Little Mr Japhet clearly thought the same and was busily trying to persuade her to put her affairs entirely in the discreet hands of himself and the bank manager. But mama, true to the spirit which she had shown since father's death and strongly supported by Angela, was being difficult.

'You say,' she said, 'that after death duties there'll be about £50,000 in cash and investments?'

'That's right, dear lady.'

'And what's the firm at Torbeach worth?'

'To you, dear lady, about £5,000 in a good year.'

'I don't mean yearly profits. I mean lock, stock and barrel.'

Mr Japhet looked shocked. My stomach stirred uneasily.

'Surely, mother—' I began.

'Don't interrupt, dear,' said mama. 'Now then, Angela. Tell Mr Japhet what you were telling me yesterday.'

'Just at the moment,' said Angela, 'there's more money around than materials or plant. It follows that a going concern like this one, fully staffed and equipped and with half a century's good will behind it, would fetch an abnormally high price.'

Shrewd enough, I thought; but I wish you'd mind your own business instead of ours.

'But,' continued Angela, 'the seller's market won't last for ever. As soon as things settle down again and they start producing more modern kinds of machinery, your bucket shop at Torbeach will be a back number.'

'*Bucket shop?*' said Mr Japhet.

'That's what it makes, doesn't it? Buckets?'

'General hardware, madam.'

'What the hell,' said Angela.

'Anyway,' said mama, quiet but firm, 'I've made up my mind. Sell the firm . . . for money down. Not for shares in anything else or deferred bills or whatever they call them, but for money down. I've been living in the shadow of that factory for twenty years, and I never want to hear of it again.'

'But,' said Mr Japhet primly, 'it is a family firm. The employees of the factory are also the loyal employees of your family. They will be distressed.'

'I doubt it,' said mama. 'Loyalty to families is going to be a thing of the past, if my newspaper is anything to go by.'

Despite my uneasiness, I had to admit that my mother and Angela between them had made some telling points. Now I must put in a word for myself.

'Excuse me, mother,' I said politely, 'but while Mr Japhet

is here, do you think we might come to some firm arrangement about my allowance? Could it be paid into a bank every month or something?'

'Your *allowance*, dear?' said mama softly. 'I thought your father gave you pocket money?'

'Yes, mother. But now . . .'

'I think the same sort of arrangement will still do very well, dear. For the time being . . . And now, Mr Japhet. In a day or two I propose going away on a little holiday. I've got a lot of things to think over, and I need a change and a rest. You can arrange, I think, to have money placed at my disposal in the bank?'

'The bank will allow you to draw as you wish,' said Mr Japhet, 'against repayment when we obtain probate.'

'That,' said mama dismissively, 'will be exceedingly convenient.'

'Mama?'

'Yes, Fielding dear?'

'Would you like me to come with you? On this holiday, I mean?'

'Oh no, dear. I wouldn't dream of asking you to put yourself out. Not that you would, would you?'

'What can you mean?'

'Simply that there's a lot of your father in you.'

'If you want me to, I'll put off—'

'—No, dear. I'll do very well by myself for a while. What day is your friend coming? Somerset Lloyd-Thing?'

'Lloyd-James. Thursday.'

'Then I'll be off on Wednesday so as to be out of your way. How long will Somerset Lloyd-Thing be staying?'

'Lloyd-James. Only a few days. Then we go to Peter at Whereham.'

'Such *nice* manners Peter always had. How kind of him to ask you.'

'And then, later on, I'm going to stay with the Headmaster in Wiltshire. So you see, mother—'

'—The Headmaster? I should have thought he saw enough of you in term time.'

'He wants to discuss arrangements for next year.'

'Does he?' said mama blankly.

'Yes. So you see, mother, I'm going to be away a lot and I shall need some money.'

'But you'll be staying with people all the time.'

'Yes, but fares and so on . . .'

'We mustn't be extravagant, dear, must we? And if the Headmaster wants to talk to you, perhaps he might be the one to pay your fare.'

'For Christ's sake, mother.'

'It's not Christ's money, dear, but mine. So I'll write you out a little cheque. But you do understand—don't you?— that just because your father's dead you can't automatically have everything you want. As it is, there'll be the extra food for Somerset Lloyd-Thing.'

An unsatisfactory letter from Christopher at Tonbridge. He was enjoying his tuition, it seemed, as his tutor from Oxford was a very kind and interesting man. He was looking forward to telling me about some of the things they had discussed. Until when, he was 'yours ever'.

If that was all he had to say, I could see no reason why he had written at all. He hadn't even remembered to confirm the dates which I had suggested for my stay in Tonbridge. So I wrote him a quick note, repeating that I could be with him on September 4 or 5, even a day or two earlier if he liked, and asking him to reply at once as I was anxious to have it settled.

Angela dined with mama and me on both the last two nights previous to mama's departure. Indeed, I gathered that had not Tuck's return been daily expected, Angela would probably have accompanied my mother on part at least of her holiday.

Up to this time, I had been no more than vaguely irritated
by this new friendship, putting it down to the loneliness of
the two women. But on the night before my mother left, I
began to feel almost as if the association were turning into a
league—a league against myself. The women paid me none
of the deference which the senior male in a household, however young, is usually accorded. They were deaf to my small
requests and combined to disregard my preferences. The off-
hand manner which Angela had lately adopted towards me
had now become something more like contempt; while my
mother's old self-effacement now seemed nearer to indifference. All in all, I was relieved that they were about to
part; their influence on one another was clearly unwhole-
some. Yet I saw no need of worry. My mother would return
from her holiday rested and in her right senses (in so far as
she had any); and Angela, no doubt, would soon be swept
back to India by Tuck. Meanwhile, I was to see Somerset
and Peter again: at last, the longed for company of old
friends.

*This afternoon, when the mail-boat arrived, I received
a copy of a London weekly to which I subscribe. On the
second page is the announcement that the Editor, Mr
Somerset Lloyd-James, will shortly contribute a series of
five long articles about the current state of our national
finances; so Somerset, it seems, has realised his ambition
to become an authority. At the head of the announcement
is a photograph, taken, I should surmise, while he was
still up at Cambridge, not so very long after I last saw him.
Yet the face on the page before me might as well belong to
the devil for anything it recalls of my schoolboy friend. And
indeed, even when he arrived in Broughton Staithe that
August of 1945, he had already changed a great deal. The
change, of course, had been taking place the whole of the
previous quarter, but since it had been gradual, and since I
had seen him daily, I had hardly noticed it (despite the*

comments of Peter, who, seeing him rather less often, had been more aware). But now, after I had been nearly a month away from Somerset, the metamorphosis was plain: he had matured, I might almost say he had aged, and his knack of spreading a defensive glaze over his eyes was now more than ever pronounced. Had we not still had a number of friends and interests in common (and even these were now discussed by Somerset in a new spirit, a spirit which was grudging where before it had been merely guarded), and had it not been for certain familiar tricks of manner and idiom, I should scarcely have recognised the boy who had walked with me over the cricket ground in May.

'I WAS SORRY,' said Somerset as soon as he was out of his train, 'to hear about your father.'

'You needn't be.'

'I should have been interested to meet him. Your mother too.'

'She thought we'd sooner be left to ourselves.'

'Considerate of her,' murmured Somerset. 'As it happens, I do have one or two rather private things to say to you.'

'Fire ahead.'

'Not yet.'

'Why not?'

'Your mood is not propitious. I must wait until you are more receptive.'

'And when is that likely to be?'

Somerset was silent for several seconds. Then he said :

'Before I can tell you what I'm going to, I must first establish the new relationship between us.'

'The new relationship?'

'Yes. Hitherto I have been the ugly but amusing boy befriended by the glamorous school hero. I have been philosopher, clown and client. This is a role I am no longer willing to sustain. I must assert my claim to equality—in some respects to dominance.'

'For heaven's sake, Somerset. I've always regarded you as an *ally*.'

'No, you haven't. Whether you knew it or not, you always condescended.'

'Well, if so I'm sorry. I never for a moment—'

'—No need to be sorry,' Somerset said. 'I bear no rancour. But from now on things must be different. When I'm sure you fully understand that, I shall be ready to speak more plainly.'

A taxi appeared at last in the station yard. We piled into it with Somerset's luggage, and sat side by side in silence until we were home. There was about Somerset, I thought, the air of a scrupulous duellist—of one determined to ensure, before shedding his opponent's blood, that everything was entirely *en règle* at the outset. It was as though he were giving me fair warning, enough to let me know that combat was about to begin, not enough to let me into the stratagems which would be used. Yet if he was after my blood, why should he trouble to give warning? Perhaps his Catholic conscience would not allow him to omit this, or perhaps he was obeying some atavistic notion of chivalry, such as might have deterred his remote ancestors from 'striking horse' in a tournament. But whatever the refinements might be, an instinct told me plainly, amid much that was in question, that Somerset meant business and meant it soon.

'The atom bomb,' said Somerset at lunch, 'is just another element in the situation.'

'Peter and the head man seem to think it's too colossal to take into account. That it's beyond our control.'

'Nothing which we ourselves have made can be beyond our control. It is simply another problem which requires thought.'

'So what would you do about it?'

'To start with,' Somerset said, 'I'd put a stop to all this so called moral protest. The atom bomb *exists*. We may as well accept the fact without whining.'

'All right. I accept the fact without whining. So what am I to do next?'

'You should remember that as far as you know only your side can make it. No one else has the secret . . . yet.'

'And so?'

'And so you should establish dominance before it's too late. Before your enemies too can make atom bombs and so achieve parity.'

'Somerset . . . You don't mean we ought to use the thing?'

'One would hope that the mere threat, the *unambiguous* threat, would be enough.'

'And who,' I asked, 'are our enemies?'

'Those who wish us ill—about three quarters of the world's population.'

'So you would establish a series of atomic bases all over the world and then hold it to ransome?'

'For its own good,' said Somerset, 'to say nothing of ours. Unfortunately, however, we can't afford it and our American friends, who can, won't finance such an undertaking. They would regard it as wicked.'

'They might not be alone in that.'

'No doubt they will have the sentimental support of all who, like themselves, are ignorant of history. The historical lesson is quite plain : if you are lucky enough to discover a new weapon, you should make full use of it. Because if you don't somebody else will, and almost certainly at your expense. A melancholy truth,' said Somerset with satisfaction, 'which applies, *mutatis mutandis,* in all human activities.'

For three days nothing much happened. We went for walks by the sea, we prepared meals and ate them, we talked of neutral topics, and we read. Somerset said no more of 'the private things' which he had to communicate; nor did he make any signal of impending battle. But always the threat was there, and I became more and more impatient for its open declaration.

On the fourth evening of Somerset's visit, having dinner at the local hotel, we saw Angela Tuck. She waved in a friendly way, and when she had finished her meal she came over, unasked, to join us.

'Introduce me to your fascinating friend,' she said.

I introduced her.

'Tuck is back tomorrow,' she announced.

'And we are off—to a friend at Whereham.'

'Then you must come round to my place,' Angela said, 'and have a drink.'

We all went down the road to the Tuck bungalow by the quay.

'Drinkies,' said Angela. She bustled out and bustled back with a tray, three glasses, and, incredibly, two bottles of champagne.

'Don't ask me where I got it from,' she said, and opened one bottle with a few expert movements.

Somerset coyly dabbled some of the wine behind his ear.

'Twenty-one today,' sang Angela raucously, and knocked back the glass in one.

'Literally?'

'Literally. I hope Tuck brings me something nice from London. He hasn't even sent a telegram, the rotten sod.'

'Let's hope he's had good hunting,' I said. 'It might make him more generous.'

Angela gave me a sly look and seemed about to reply. But by now Somerset was on his feet proposing a toast.

'To our charming hostess,' Somerset said, 'now that she has acquired the key of the door. May she always be free with it.'

'Whoops,' went Angela, and tucked into her fizz. She sat down on Somerset's lap and started to stroke his cheek.

'Little Somerset,' she said; 'and where did he learn to say such pretty things to the ladies? Open the other bottle,' she ordered me, rather sharply, and deposited a sploshing kiss on Somerset's spotty forehead.

What in God's name is she up to now, I wondered. I opened the bottle with clumsy, unfamiliar hands, while Angela went on kissing Somerset. The cork popped and a great gout of champagne shot over her dress.

'When it rains, it rains bubble-juice from heaven,' Angela sang. 'Lucky we've got some of mother's ruin for when that's gone. Better put on something dry.'

She tottered out.

'I can't understand it,' I said: 'she's usually got a head like a rock. I mean, whatever she does, there's none of this *childishness.*'

'She's been drinking all day,' said Somerset coolly.

'How do you know?'

'She's got fresh blisters on her fingers where she's burnt them with cigarettes. Drunks always do that.'

'How clever of you to notice.'

'There've been quite a few drinkers in my family.'

Angela came back in pyjamas.

'Tell you what,' she screamed: 'birthday gamies. Let's all have a birthday gamey.'

'Willingly,' said Somerset, hiccuping and helping himself to the last of the champagne.

'Get the gin first,' said Angela, throwing out her bust like Volumnia.

'Where is it?'

'Kitchen.'

Somerset clumped off.

'What do you mean . . . gamies?' I said.

'Cardies.' She swayed over to a desk and came back with a pack. 'Forfeits. You'll see.'

Somerset came back with the gin and poured out stiff measures all round. Remembering the scene on the last night of the quarter, I wondered whether Somerset would be sick again: certainly drink effected a rapid change in his demeanour, a change decidedly for the better, I thought.

'Forfeits,' announced Angela.

She dealt each of us a card, face down.

'Whoever has the highest card can claim a forfeit from the one with lowest,' she explained with surprising lucidity.

'What kind of forfeit?'

Angela shrugged.

'Turn 'em up,' she said.

Somerset had the highest card, Angela the lowest.

'I claim a kiss from Angela,' Somerset said.

'You've already had some.'

'This will be a *special* kiss.' Somerset's spectacles were crooked and his lisp pronounced.

'That's the thpirit,' Angela mimicked. She crawled along the carpet to the side of Somerset's chair, knelt there and held her face up to him. Somerset took his spectacles off, leaned down, missed her mouth, and kissed her on the end of her turned up nose.

'You need your gig-lamps.'

She picked them off the arm of the chair.

'Don't meth about with my thepectacles.'

Too late. Angela had keeled over and crunched the glasses against the hearth stone. Blood came from her hand.

'My glathes,' wailed Somerset.

'Angela's hand . . .'

'Never mind my hand *or* anybody's rotten glasses. Deal the cards.'

'Luckily I remembered to bring another pair. But they're not so comfortable.'

'*Deal the cards.*'

I dealt. This time Angela had the highest card, Somerset the lowest.

'Take your trousers off,' said Angela briskly.

Knowing that Somerset was too mean to buy himself underpants from his allowance, I started to smirk. But Somerset was equal to the occasion. Having got his trousers off swiftly and with dignity, he tucked the tail of his shirt between his legs.

'Not much meat,' said Angela, pinching one of Somerset's thin white calves and leaving a trail of blood. 'Deal the cards.'

Somerset dealt. This time I won with a ten, while both Angela and Somerset had eights.

'Forfeits for both of you,' I said hilariously. 'Let's have your shirt, Somerset. And as for you, *Angie*, the top half of your pyjamas.'

Angela complied poker-faced: Somerset seemed reluctant. When he had removed his shirt, he was naked save for his shoes and socks, and he did not strip prettily. He placed his hand over his groin, Angela inspecting him closely as he did so. Am I trying to humiliate him, I wondered; or do I, in some unbelievably perverse way, wish to be . . . associated with him?

'Cards,' said Angela, excitable no longer but grave and purposeful. She dealt each card with ponderous care; after which she turned up an Ace, Somerset and I both Kings.

'Ace high,' said Angela; 'forfeits from both.'

She looked carefully from Somerset to me and back again.

'You,' she said to Somerset, 'are interesting. Ugly and skinny, but interesting. I claim you. You,' she said rounding on me, 'are just a sexual cliché. Peaches and a little frothy cream. From you I claim privacy.'

'The game's not over yet,' I said sullenly.

'This is my house, and I'm telling you to go away and leave us alone.'

She wiped her bloody hand casually over her breast, then bent over Somerset, who was looking myopic but composed.

'Do as the kind lady asks,' said Somerset.

This time, I thought furiously, he is not going to be sick.

'I think,' said Somerset with deadly softness, 'that I shall be able to find my own way back . . . even without my glasses.'

He lay back in his chair. Angela took his hand and lifted it away from his body.

'Get out,' she hissed at me; 'and don't slam the door.'

Inland from the sea, on the way to Whereham, the fields shimmered and drowsed. The bus, almost empty, nosed along the lanes and through clumps of complacent trees, made long stops in market places or in front of tiny post offices, which displayed in their windows pre-war Christmas annuals, knitting magazines and toy magic lanterns.

At one such post office I dismounted and sent a telegram to Christopher. 'Please confirm September 3, 4 or 5 for visit.

Anxious to hear. Fielding.' After all, I thought, Christopher must have had my last letter at least five days ago; he should have answered by now.

When I returned to the bus, Somerset, who had hardly spoken since we got out of bed, enquired with bland interest:

'What was all that about?'

'Just a wire to the charwoman. Something I forgot to tell her.'

'It could have waited, surely, until we reached Peter's house?'

'I suppose so. I just felt restless.'

'So I noticed. You know, I think the time has come ... now ... for me to speak to you. After what happened last night, I fancy the conditions are favourable.'

'Then make yourself plain, Somerset. For God's sake be plain and be done.'

'Very well.' Somerset took a deep breath. 'There's one thing I want,' Somerset said, 'which I don't propose to let you take from me or to spoil for me after I have it. Eight months from now, next spring, they will need a new Head of school. I propose to be that Head and I don't propose to allow you, as a subordinate Head of your own House, to challenge my authority. Nor do I propose to allow you to discredit that authority by making a mess of things in your own little area. Mismanagement or scandal in your House would also mean mismanagement or scandal in my *school.*'

'People have been warning me about you for some time,' I said slowly, 'and I sometimes thought that it might turn out to be something like that. But then I told myself, calmly and reasonably, that it simply couldn't be, because no one as sensible as you could care about anything so trivial. I'm *disappointed* that I was wrong. *Why*, Somerset?'

'You have so much already,' said Somerset, almost humbly. 'Surely you wouldn't grudge me this?'

'You can have it and welcome. I shan't stand in your way or make rude noises when you ascend your throne. But the choice isn't ours. It will be made by the Headmaster.'

'If the position is offered to you, you must refuse.'

'The head man would think it very odd.'

'You must put him off as best you can.'

'I've told you,' I said, irritated at last. 'I don't care either way and I wouldn't dream of pushing myself forward. But if the head man *should* call on me, then I'm damned if I'll grovel about saying, "No, I am not worthy, choose Somerset instead." You can't expect it.'

'Can't I? You know, Fielding, I've been following up one or two little rumours about you. About you and Christopher Roland. I don't suppose you'd much care for them to be brought to the Headmaster's attention.'

'The head man already knows I'm fond of Christopher.'

'But does he know *how* fond? He can be very sensitive, the head man, about that kind of thing. He has to be in his position.'

'There's nothing to be sensitive about.'

'Isn't there?' Somerset paused, and then proceeded with the solemn manner of one dictating his terms. 'What's happened, Fielding, was no affair of mine. I'll let the past rest, and gladly, provided you do as I say. That's the first point. By-gones can be by-gones if you'll let them be.'

'Generous of you.'

'But secondly, remember this. If I get a hint of anything in this line starting up again, *next year* . . . I won't have it, Fielding. Any more of that, with Christopher or anyone else, and *I'll get you sacked.*'

'Is it pride talking, or morality?'

'Let's just say that anything of this kind would offend my sense of good order.'

'Pride.'

'Seemliness.'

'*Obsession.*'

The bus drew to a stop. I spotted Peter, who was waiting for us in front of a brick chapel of improbable denomination.

'Have it which way you will,' said Somerset, taking his case from the rack. 'Those are my terms—quite easy terms, don't you think?—and if you still want to be there wearing your pretty blue blazer next summer, you'd better keep them.'

Peter's father, an immense brown man with a trace of Norfolk in his voice, was seldom seen save in the evenings, when he liked to discuss the prospects for county cricket now that the war was over; and Peter's mother, a grave woman with an enchanting smile, was called away to a married sister's sick bed the day after Somerset and I arrived. So the three of us were left, as I had hoped we would be, to amuse ourselves. Since Somerset was prone to hay fever, Peter did not suggest that we should help in the fields. Instead he took us on long, leisurely tours of his family demesne; drove us in a farm car to markets, or in a trap (petrol being tight even for farmers) to have picnics where there was a castle or a church, a village cricket match or a summer fête. It was a time of happiness and truce. Peter gave himself up to serene enjoyment of his last few days as a civilian in his own place; Somerset was clever, affable and modest; and I myself, while conscious of the new threat posed by Somerset, was in good part reassured by the wholesome presence of Peter and lulled by the simple pleasures of his country. So the kind days of the late summer and the new peace passed, until, one morning shortly before Somerset and I must leave, we all set out for Whereham Races, along with Peter's father, who had taken a rare holiday to watch one of his own horses run.

The main event of the day was to be a three mile steeplechase, carrying a prize of one hundred sovereigns and open to any gentleman or yeoman who, during the war, had farmed his land in the shire or borne arms for his King. Mr Morrison's contestant for the prize, Tiberius, was to be ridden by a young tenant who had recently returned from Germany, Mr Morrison himself being disqualified by a weight of eighteen stone. Tiberius, an ageing black stallion much loved by Peter and known for many miles around, was second in the local betting. Favourite was Lord Blakeney's Balthazar, a young, clever and quick-tempered horse, who, it was said, would worry Tiberius by his aggressive manner and finally defeat him by sheer speed and skill.

But hope stood high with the Morrison faction, and the sun shone, and the mid-day provision of food and drink, which many of Mr Morrison's friends and tenants had been bidden to share, was ducal by the standards of the time. Flushed faces came and went, ate and drank, whispered into Mr Morrison's ear or boomed at him across the tankards; during which time Somerset condescended to those about him in his best country manner, I was euphoristic and inclined to show off, and Peter, anxious for his beloved Tiberius, was hospitable but preoccupied. We watched the first race, a mediocre affair over which Somerset contrived to win a little money on the outsider, who was ridden, as he remarked, 'by the only jockey whose knees inspire confidence'. After this there was more drinking. Then came the second race, again poorly contested, again yielding money to Somerset but not to myself. By now, what with the sun and the cider, I had already lost more than I had meant to risk on the entire meeting, but this was no time for counting losses: for next on the card was the great race of the day, and any moment now Tiberius would appear in the paddock.

Peter rejoined us after a visit to the ring.

'How do they bet?' asked Mr Morrison.

'Even money for Balthazar, sir,' said Peter, who always addressed his father by this style: 'two to one Tiberius. Five bar.'

'Lay this down the line,' his father said, producing a thick wad of white five pound notes. 'Slowly now. Don't go sending them into a panic. And put at least a score of it with the tote.'

'Thee be sure then, 'squire?' said a wizened old man who wore a vilely dirty cloth cap and had drunk perhaps two gallons of cider since our party arrived on the course.

'Nay,' said Mr Morrison, 'how should I be? But it's a

while since I had a good bet these last years, and the price is fair.'

'Shall I take less than two to one, sir?' asked Peter.

'Go down to six to four, my dear,' his father said; 'then take the rest to the tote. And not less than twenty on the tote, mind, howsoever they bet.'

'Best be to work, master,' said the cloth cap to Peter: 'there'll be a pile of money come in for the black 'un.'

'Come with me,' said Peter to Somerset and myself. 'We'll watch by the water-jump.'

While Peter disposed of his father's money Somerset wandered off 'to see,' as he put it, 'if he could get a price'. Myself, feeling that faith was the only logic of the day, I put ten of the twelve pounds I had in my pocket on Tiberius, getting one of the last offers at two to one: if he won, then I should recoup my losses and be fourteen pounds to the good; if not . . . well then Peter or Somerset would have to help. But it seemed as if I were on to a good thing: although Balthazar was still favourite, his price was stretching as that of Tiberius shortened; and likely enough the prices would meet before betting was through. Peter, looking strained, came away from the tote tent and put his hand into my arm; Somerset materialised from nowhere.

'This way,' Peter said.

'Don't you want to look at him in the paddock?'

'No. This way. He'll be all right when he's out on the course, but the crowds make him nervous. I can't bear it.'

We crossed the course from the stand and walked down over the meadows towards the water-jump, which was in a slight dip some three hundred yards after the first turn. I reflected that Peter's unwillingness to watch Tiberius in the paddock amounted almost to a dereliction of loyalty, something so unusual as to indicate that he must be very strung up indeed. I could feel the palm of his hand sweating into my arm; I must find comfort for him.

'Betting go off all right?' I said.

'Betting? I suppose so. I got twos over quite a bit, then

seven to four for all but thirty. I took that to the tote.'

'Quite an investment of your father's,' Somerset said. 'Did you have anything for yourself?'

'No,' said Peter shortly: 'it would be like blackmail.'

'What about you, Somerset?'

'I found rather a nice price,' said Somerset, smug but vague: 'really rather nice.'

And now we were at the water-jump, an inoffensive natural ditch and guarded only by a foot of fence, but tricky because of the downward slope which led into it and a brief marshy patch on its far side, which might make it very hard for the horses to gain the firm footing they needed in order to make a proper onset at the sharp up-hill gradient immediately beyond it. Tiberius and the rest would have to take this jump three times. Starting in front of the stand, they would go away for two hundred yards, which included one easy plain fence, then turn, very sharply, over one hundred and thirty degrees, take another plain fence after a hundred yards, and run downhill to the water-jump; after which the course looped away, round and back, over three more fences and through two more dips, till it turned into the home run. This was about quarter of a mile from turn to winning post, included two more jumps, and completed a circuit of just on a mile. Peter had barely finished a rather jerky account of all this, when the first of the horses appeared on the course and started to parade slowly in front of the stand.

'He seems all right,' said Peter, looking through his glasses. 'I'm worried about Johnny Pitts in the saddle though. He's only been back from the Army a few days and he can't but be a bit strange to it. Blakeney's man, Georgie Owen, didn't go to the war ...'

The ten horses circled in front of the stand, then one by one tailed off to stand sedately behind the starting gate.

'Well behaved bunch,' Peter said. 'I wonder we've not had trouble from Balthazar.'

A white flag went up by the starting gate.

'Orders . . .'

Then there was a great cheer from the stand and all the meadows around, for the flag was down and the field away. After the first hundred yards, it was the brown Balthazar, with the Blakeney cerise and argent up, a clear leader by four lengths; the rest were in a close bunch, nothing to reckon.

'I hope he gets clear of them,' Peter mumbled; 'he doesn't like being jostled.'

And after the first fence, the bunch behind Balthazar began to string out. Two horses stayed neck and neck, second and third, while Tiberius, a length and a half behind them, was going a placid, uncrowded fourth, a position he retained without effort round the terrible angle of the bend, to negotiate which it was necessary to slow down to an extent that made the impatient Balthazar shake his head and prick his ears in anger. Over the second fence and down the slope to the water-jump; Balthazar going very fast—'Too fast, Georgie Owen ought to know better'—but proving his cleverness by a jump which cleared the treacherous morass beyond the ditch and sent him racing up the hill the other side, to go seven lengths clear of the pair behind him, who were in turn a good three in front of Tiberius.

'There's my good boy,' called Peter softly, as Mr Morrison's light blue and black sailed easily over the ditch and beyond the marsh. For a moment it seemed to me as if the horse turned his head very slightly to acknowledge the call; but then Tiberius was galloping serenely away up the hill, gaining, little by little and without any forcing, on the two horses between him and Balthazar.

'It's when they start jumping short, late in the race,' said Peter, pointing to the patch of marsh : 'once land in that . . .'

By the end of the first circuit, Balthazar was ten lengths in front of the second and third, outside and just behind whom Tiberius was running with a confidence which implied he would pass just so soon as he judged fit. Of the rest of the field, three had fallen on the loop, two were badly tailed off, but one, a little grey animal with a short, humorous face, was going very trimly some five lengths behind Tiberius.

'That grey,' Peter said. 'Fancy Man ... There's a lot of running there.'

Once again, as he rounded the great bend, Balthazar pricked with annoyance. Once again he came down the slope at a very smart pace, cleared stream and marsh, and thundered off up the hill. Second and third ran more cautiously; but the second horse took off too soon, landed with hind legs almost in the ditch, slipped, kicked, veered, kicked again, and interlocked a leg with the third horse as it landed. In a moment there was a writhing, snorting mass on the ground which seemed to block the entire course. Tiberius having switched suddenly to the far side to avoid it, rapped his right rear leg sharply against the fence post as he jumped. Landing just inside the marsh, he had to struggle and change step to get going, by which time he had lost another two lengths to Balthazar and been substantially gained upon by Fancy Man, who, apparently unimpressed by the melée and giving it the smallest possible margin, improved his position yet further by jumping like a bird.

'Never mind, boy,' called Peter. 'There's a long way to go.'

And indeed it was now apparent that Balthazar was feeling the pace. Round the loop, back into the straight, Tiberius, unworried as it seemed by his mistake at the water, tracked him with an easy, fluid action and was visibly making up ground. The gap shortened to ten lengths and then to seven; Balthazar's jumping was beginning to lose its rhythm, while Tiberius's was still as smooth as paint; but always, three lengths behind Tiberius and giving the impression that at any moment he could an if he would, came the perky little Fancy Man. And so, when they passed the post for the second time, it was a three horse race ard an open one.

'Take two to one, Tiberius,' a bookie's call floated across the meadow.

'Will you now?' muttered Peter, whose eyes had been

fixed into his glasses. Now he lowered them to talk.

'I don't like it,' he said; 'he's hurt. He's hiding it, bless his heart, but he's hurt. That rap last time over here...'

And again he lifted the glasses. Looking towards Somerset, I saw that the expression of casual condescension, which he had worn all day, had somehow deepened to one of sagacity and power.

'What are yóu looking so pleased about?' I said.

'I'm glad Tiberius is shortening the gap.'

Which he was still doing. This time, as he rounded the bend, Balthazar seemed glad to relax his speed; he took the plain fence clumsily and came towards the water-jump without enthusiasm. Meanwhile Tiberius kept to the same powerful and, as it were, routine stride which he had used throughout the race; and always the little Fancy Man came skipping daintily behind.

'He's hurt,' mumbled Peter again and again; 'I know it.'

At the water-jump Balthazar checked, jumped nervously, landed with rear legs in the morass, floundered, panicked, threw Georgie Owen back into the ditch. Tiberius jumped gamely; but weariness (or was it pain, as Peter said?) showed through his immaculate style; he too landed in the marsh, kept his footing only with a desperate effort ('Good boy, my sweetheart, that's my good boy'), and was off, oh, very slowly, up the hill. He had beaten Balthazar; but Fancy Man, who had jumped both ditch and marsh as sharp and clever as a flute, was now gaining rapidly. For all the wear he showed he might have been at the beginning of the day.

'He can't keep him off. Even if he wasn't hurt...'

But as Fancy Man drew up to Tiberius the brave stallion seemed to find new heart. A slight check in his beautiful action showed that he was indeed hurt; but he found new pace from somewhere, and even though Fancy Man was gaining it was no longer with ease. There were now five fences left. Over the first Tiberius stayed clear; then down into a dip where they could not be seen; out of the dip and over the second fence Tiberius still had his shoulders ahead;

then down into another dip. Out of this and over the third fence—which was also the third from home—it was neck and neck. Into the home straight.

'Now, boy. Does it hurt? Does it hurt you, boy? Does it hurt?'

The second fence from home was an artificial and heavily guarded water-jump. Tiberius, amidst applause that rang back from the sky, took it with all the grace and skill he had shown at the very start of the race. Fancy Man pecked slightly, lost half a length, but he was over safely, his nose still level with Johnny Pitts's thigh. And now, once more, with the last fence a hundred yards ahead, he started to gain.

And this was when Johnny Pitts, forgetful after four years of driving a tank with his famous cavalry regiment, made his one mistake. For the first time in the race, he took his whip to Tiberius.

'Oh God,' moaned Peter, 'oh God, oh God . . .'

For a few yards more the horses were more or less level; then Tiberius faltered and, as Pitts thrashed more and more desperately, seemed to skid to a halt. For a moment he stood upright, shaking his head slowly, then knelt (as though to pay Pitts the final courtesy of allowing him to dismount), then subsided on to his flank and lay still. Pitts, puzzled, stood looking down on him; Fancy Man prinked over the last fence and past the post; the crowd responded with a low murmur and a turning of backs; and Peter, the tears pouring from his eyes, lowered his glasses and faced his friends.

'It's no good,' he sobbed. 'It's the whip that has broken his heart. Not the pain, the exhaustion, the defeat. But the whip . . . the whip has broken his heart.'

While Peter and his father attended to the disposal of Tiberius, Somerset left me in the drink tent on pretence of wanting a pee. Watching from the entrance to the tent, I saw him go up to a bookmaker and collect a handsome wad of notes. I stood and looked straight at Somerset as he walked back.

'Yes,' said Somerset, putting a cool face on it, 'it was not for nothing I was reared in the country. I liked the look of that little grey. Seven to one . . . My family has always had an eye for horses.'

'Well,' I said, swallowing my anger in my need, 'you can lend me some of it. I'm almost out of money and I don't want to bother Peter just now.'

'Try him tomorrow,' Somerset answered, putting his money carefully away. 'He'll have got over it then.'

'It's the least you can do.'

'I don't lend money, Fielding. It makes me brood, wondering when it will come back. Peter will let you have what you want. He has stronger nerves than I have, and a more generous disposition.'

'Of course,' said Peter the following afternoon. 'How much will you need?'

Somerset had gone home. 'See you at the Headmaster's,' was all he had said to me before he left. No further reference to what had passed in the bus. Happily, Peter had asked me to stay one more night, so that there was now a chance to say a great deal which would otherwise have been impossible.

'How much will you need?' Peter said.

'Fifteen pounds, if that's all right. To see me home, then down to the head man's place and back. I'll send it on to you as soon as my mother gets home from her holiday. About September the fifteenth, she said.'

'You'd best send it to the bank for me. Barclay's, Whereham. I shan't want fifteen pounds where I'm going.'

'Even in the Army one gets time off.'

'Not recruits.' He went to a drawer and produced a bundle of notes. 'So that's settled. Now what is it you've been so anxious to tell me these last days?'

'You've noticed?'

'I've noticed. Let's walk.'

As we left the house, I told Peter the substance of what had been said on the bus.

'Don't say I didn't warn you,' said Peter when I had finished. And then,

'I don't suppose for a moment you've got anything you could throw back at Somerset?'

'I have, oddly enough. But no one would believe me.'

I told him about the spree at Angela Tuck's.

'You're right,' Peter said. 'It's all too remote. It might just as well have happened in Timbuctoo. They won't believe you, and you can't prove anything, and Somerset knows it. Whereas what he's got on you . . . He probably can't prove it either, but it's so close to home that he might make things very awkward.'

'I know. What shall I do, Peter?'

We were walking down the old smugglers' path, which made straight as an arrow over the ten miles to the sea. The way was between high banks which were topped by over-shadowing trees. It was dusty and rutted but it was also cool and secret, a fitting place to consider threat and devise counter.

'Ignore the whole thing,' Peter said at last. 'Treat it as a bluff. Somerset may make himself a bloody nuisance, but unless he's got absolute proof he can't do any more. So ignore Somerset and ignore his threat. But from now on make doubly sure you keep your nose clean. You'll remember, I hope, what I said to you last quarter about that.'

Peter sat down against the bank and I sat down beside him. The leaves rustled listlessly over our heads. They were still green, the leaves, but they already looked tired, as though they would be glad to fall in a week or two and rot away to nothing in the earth.

'Tomorrow,' said Peter, 'you must leave here. A day or so later I go to the Army. So for the time, perhaps for a long time, we are parting; and since this is so, I want you to promise me something. I want you to promise me, Fielding, for all our sakes, that you won't hurt Christopher again.'

'What happened wasn't my fault. And I've made it up with him.'

'Yes. But what have you got in mind for him this time?'

'To be friends. To give him what he's always wanted.'

'You're telling me the truth, Fielding? You promise that you won't . . . take advantage of him?'

'I'm going to be to Christopher exactly what he wants me to be,' I said. 'I shan't ask for anything more.'

I shan't need to, I thought.

'Good,' said Peter. 'I was afraid you might still be greedy; it's always been your trouble, you know. But now I can go away without worrying. And if you stick to what you've promised me, you'll have nothing to fear from Somerset or anyone else.'

'I'll stick to it,' I said : 'to the last syllable.'

So I returned to Broughton Staithe, to make ready for Wiltshire and the Headmaster; and Peter, three days later, packed one small bag and went for a soldier of the King. I felt sadder, more oppressed, at this parting than at any time since the morning I had left the school at the end of July. My ally, my old counsellor, was now gone; and I felt as some early Englishman might have felt, as he watched the long line of Romans file down to the ships, bound for tottering Rome and leaving England unmanned to face whatever might come out of the misty North.

THE FIRST THING I saw, when I unlocked the front door of the empty house at Broughton, was a sprawling heap of letters. Three were for me; one of them from Christopher.

Dear Fielding,
No, I'm afraid you can't come and stay on your way to Wiltshire. It's no longer possible. I can't explain now.
        Yours,
            Christopher.

Unfriendly, not to say mysterious. I read the other two letters: one from my mother, saying that she was having a nice holiday and confirming that she would be back on September 15, just after I myself returned from Wiltshire; and one from Ivan Blessington.

... Was passing through Tonbridge the other day and called on Christopher for tea. He looked ill and very nervous. I know my arrival was unexpected, but it can't have been that. He seemed upset that his tutor, who'd been there for most of August, was now gone; but again, it can't have been just that. There's something very wrong there, I don't pretend to know what, but you if anybody should be able to find out and help ...

Blunt, imperceptive Ivan. If he had spotted something wrong, then something wrong there must certainly be. I didn't care for the dictatorial tone, but Ivan surely had a point. Not only was it within my power to help, it was my

plain duty. But how could I help when I had just been so
brusquely warned off the grass? After some thought, I wrote
to Christopher and suggested that we should meet in London
for lunch and a film on the sixth of the month; we might
even have dinner together, I added, as I should be staying in
a hotel overnight and the journey back to Tonbridge was a
short one . . . or so he himself had once said. Even if this
failed to flush Christopher, I thought, it must at least elicit
some account of what was doing.

Dining that night in the local hotel, I saw Mr Tuck and
Angela. They seemed morose but oddly in concert. I began
to wonder, not for the first time, how and where my father
had originally made Tuck's acquaintance. Tuck was indeed
the dreadful sort of friend I would have expected my father
to have, but I could remember no reference to him, over the
years, until the evening early in the holidays when his impending visit had been announced. On the one hand, my father's
knowledge of Tuck had been sketchy, for he had not known
about Angela until she appeared on the doorstep : on the
other hand, he had apparently had sufficient confidence in
the man to accept his tea-planting proposition at face value.
Driven by renewed curiosity about this odd couple and bored
by the prospect of a lonely evening, I suppressed the
embarrassment to which memories of my last meeting with
Angela inclined me and approached the Tucks, rather warily,
while they were drinking coffee in the lounge.

Tuck was affable, Angela off-hand. When I asked if I
might drink my coffee with them, no one seemed to care
much either way, so I braved their indifference and sat down.

'Sorry to hear about father,' Tuck said.

'It was certainly sudden . . . Tell me, when did you first
know him? You'll forgive me saying so, but until a few weeks
ago neither mother or I had ever heard of you.'

'Good point,' said Tuck. He laughed loudly, as though
it were also a cracking good joke. 'Let's see now. When did
I first meet your old man? Early in the war, it must have

been. He was with some kind of Ordnance outfit in Kalyan —big transit camp near Bombay. We just met by accident in the old Taj one night. Got talking over a peg, saw a bit more of one another ... Then he was posted away. That's how it was in those days. You were just getting to know a chap, and he'd be posted away.'

He lit a particularly foul cheroot.

'And you didn't see him again until this summer?' I said. 'That's it.'

'And yet he spoke of you as an old friend, and was prepared to pull my entire career to pieces on your suggestion.'

'Your old man,' said Tuck, 'knew a good thing when he saw it.'

'Perhaps,' I said, with a glance at Angela. 'But India wouldn't have been any good for me.'

'That,' said Tuck, 'remains to be seen.'

'What do you mean?'

'Do you suppose,' Angela said, 'that this hole can produce a drink?'

'No harm in trying,' said Tuck, and rang a bell.

'What do you mean? What remains to be seen?'

An indignant woman in a tweed skirt appeared.

'Who rang the bell?' she snarled.

'I did,' Tuck snarled back, 'because I want some service. What is there to drink?'

'No drinks in the lounge,' she said with relish. 'There's been a war on, or hadn't you heard?'

'I'd also heard it was over.'

'No drinks in the lounge,' the tweed woman repeated spitefully, and marched out.

'Jesus Christ,' said Tuck, 'whatever is this bloody country coming to? You may find,' he said to me, 'that India's not so bad after all. At least the servants do what they're told.'

'Would you please tell me,' I said, 'what all this is about? I neither have, nor ever have had, any intention of going to India to plant tea. And now my father's dead—'

'—But old Ange,' said Tuck complacently, 'had quite a

few talks with your mother before she went away. Didn't you, Ange?'

'So you've been getting at her? I suppose you want our money for your damned plantation.'

'*Her* money,' Angela emended. 'She's very concerned, you know, about your future. So are we all.'

I rose to go.

'That's very kind of you,' I said, 'but I don't need your interest. Nor does my mother.'

'No?' said Angela. 'She's very lonely . . . and very grateful for advice.'

'She's weak, if that's what you mean. Too weak to get rid of hangers-on.'

'Now then,' said Tuck : 'you're being most impolite to my wife.'

'Your wife,' I shouted at him, 'is a common whore and you're a common crook.'

Not until I was half way home did it occur to me that Tuck had almost certainly connived at, had probably indeed ordained, Angela's infidelity with my father. That it had failed so ludicrously of its object was mere bad luck. Now they had started on my mother instead. And Somerset? Had that been just a whim of Angela's, or had she decided that Somerset too might somehow come in useful? What had they spoken of together, I wonder, that night after I was dismissed?

Dear Fielding (Christopher wrote),

I can't come to London to meet you for lunch or anything else. I'm sorry, but please don't write to me again until I've first written to you.

Christopher.

I walked along the empty beach. It was a grey, blowy day, not at all like the afternoon, a month before, when I had sat in the warm sand hills with Angela. Autumn was coming to expel the few holiday-makers who had braved the barbed

wire and the gun-sites, war-time relics which, though already
rusted and crumbling, brought a lingering hint of violence
to the lonely dunes. Violence; savagery; threat. Somerset;
my mother; Tuck. And Christopher. Christopher too seemed
to betoken the same residual sense of menace as the jagged
concrete and the rotting ration packs. What did he mean—
'don't write to me again until I've first written to you'?
Everything had been made up between us. If he really
couldn't have me to stay (parent trouble?) what could be
more pleasant and obvious than a day together in London?
What the devil was going on? Nervous, Ivan had said, and
also upset because the tutor had gone. But it wasn't just that.
'Something very wrong there... you if anyone should be
able to help.' But Christopher had refused my help. Should
I go there despite that, force myself on him, make him tell
me about it? Oh hell, I thought, and kicked an empty tin :
his letters had been plain enough; if he didn't want me, he
didn't.

But for my own sake I must find someone else. I thought of
Dixie quivering in the ghost-train; of Angela's finger nails
on my bare flesh. Both of them had sent me away unappeased.
I must be appeased, I must *know*. Now that it was over with
Christopher, I must be admitted, at long last, into the Lotus
Country.

Thoughtfully I counted my money. Ten pounds and odd
were left of what I had borrowed from Peter. I must pay for
my railway ticket, also for meals and so on during the
journey; and then there would be the hotel bill for the
night in London—but this, as my family was known to the
hotel, could always be sent to my mother. Yes, I told myself :
there would be, there had to be, enough.

Piccadilly, struggling back to the gaieties of peace;
coloured lights which I hadn't seen since I was a child in
1939, tawdry, pathetic, out-dated : museum pieces.

Scott's, Oddenino's, Del Monico. The little streets between
Piccadilly and Shaftesbury Avenue, the broken glass awnings

for the cinema queues. No lack of choice, numerically. But in point of quality, all much the same: young enough, but tired, bitter, all with the angular look of predators, or (worse) with the angles blocked out by slabs of make-up.

Now or never. Choose one. This one; of the angular variety, rather too thin in the leg, a little older than the rest, but with a discernible air of kindness.

'Please, could you tell me the—'

'—Like a nice time, dearie? Only just round the corner. A pound.'

'A pound?' (Surely it was more than that, admission to the Lotus Country?)

'Can't do it for less, dear. Professional, pride, you know.'

'All right.'

Over Shaftesbury Avenue and down another little street.

'Rather young, aren't you? I'm not sure I ought to be going with you. Ah well. In here.'

Up three flights of stairs. Little room, big bed, bare dressing-table. Ashtray by the bed full of lip-sticked cigarette ends.

'Pound first, please, dearie. And five bob for the maid.'

'For the maid?'

'Someone's got to clean the place up, haven't they? Ta.'

Skirt up round middle. Rather nice thighs above gartered stockings. Dixie. Angela. Christopher . . .

'Just let me get the doings, dearie . . . No, don't take your shirt off. Just let your trousers down . . . There . . . Oh my, my . . . *There's* a naughty boy.'

Rubber sheath. The woman sitting on the side of the bed. Reaching forward with her hands.

'Can't we get properly on the bed?'

'Don't want much for a quid, do you?'

Knees suddenly raised and thighs part wide; hands under knee joints; feet hanging limply, high heels near buttocks.

'In you go, dearie.'

'I . . . I . . .'

'Be a man and get on with it. What are you gaping at?'

'I . . . *Where?*'

'For Christ's sake put it in.' Indicative fingers. 'There.'

Easy enough too. Nice, soft.

'Not bad, darling. Now, come on.'

Nice, soft. Crutch straining forward to meet mine.

'Come on, darling. Come . . . Come . . .'

'Oh . . . Oh . . . There . . .'

'Finished? That's a good boy. Not bad, was it? We'll just . . . get . . . this . . . off you.'

Into the ashtray with the lip-sticked cigarettes.

And so now I knew. It had been, as my companion put it, not bad. Which was about all one could say. Not bad; just about worth a pound (and five shillings for the maid). Now back to the hotel quickly for a thorough wash.

The Headmaster's holiday retreat was in one of those little valleys which, cosy and tree-girt, are tucked away like oases in the military wilderness round Salisbury. Somerset, I was told when I arrived, was in bed at home with a chill and would not be joining us till the morrow. After an ample supper (the Headmaster's wife, besides being a capable amateur philosopher, qualified as a *bonne femme*) the Headmaster took me to his study.

'There's something,' he said, 'which I don't wish to discuss in front of Elizabeth.'

'Oh?'

'Roland,' said the Headmaster, 'Christopher Roland.'

Oh my God, had Somerset already opened his mouth? Or someone else? Or Christopher, in an agony of repentance (hence his unfriendly letters), written to confess?

'What about Christopher, sir?'

Commendably cool, on the whole.

'It's very odd and very sad. It seems he was reported to the Tonbridge police for hanging about a nearby Army camp and . . . and what they call soliciting.'

'Oh my God.' Horror. Relief. Nothing to do with me at any rate.

'I can understand that you're shocked. I wondered, though, whether you could . . . cast any light on the matter. After all, the two of you were very close.'

'I don't think so, sir.' Play this one with care. 'It explains, of course, some rather curious letters I've had lately.' I told him what Ivan Blessington had written, and about the two curt notes of refusal I'd had from Christopher himself. 'I was puzzled and hurt. But if this had already happened . . .'

'It happened about ten days ago. Because of his youth and the good standing of his family the police have agreed to take no action, provided his parents keep him in strict supervision and arrange for him to have psychiatric treatment. He cannot, it goes without saying, come back to us next quarter.'

'I suppose not.'

'No question of it. But my duty lies, not only in taking preventive measures for the future, but in investigating any damage that may already have been done. It occurred to me . . . that you might help me there.'

'But look, sir. You say he was suspected of soliciting. It can't have been more, or else the police would have acted—family or no family. So on the strength of mere suspicion, Christopher is to be confined at home, messed about by psychiatrists, and forbidden to return to school—disgraced. Can't you see the terrible injury this must do to him?'

'I have six hundred boys to consider. I can't risk contamination.'

'Where there are six hundred boys, there's bound to be contamination already. You know that, sir.'

'I can't, knowingly, add to it.'

'But what do you know? What did Christopher *do*?'

'He hung about . . . with his bicycle . . . near the entrance to this camp. When the men came out, he used to smile at them, try to enter into conversation.'

'There could be a dozen explanations. He could have had friends serving there, friends from school perhaps.'

'Among the private men?'

'Everyone starts in the ranks these days.'

'In special training units. Not in a serving battalion. Besides, Roland was given every chance to provide just such an explanation. His only response was to sulk. They could think what they pleased, he said.'

'Dignified.'

'Petulant. I can understand, Fielding, that you are concerned for your friend. I am too; but I must put my public duty first. And I must therefore ask you, directly, to tell me anything you may know about Roland's previous behaviour, so that any damage he has done may be undone.'

'By removing more people on mere suspicion?'

'That was not worthy,' the Headmaster said wearily.

'I know, sir, and I'm sorry. But Christopher is a very dear friend and this has been a shock. Can nothing be done?'

'The psychiatrists will do all they can.'

'The shame of it will destroy him.'

'I gather lots of people these days submit quite willingly to psychiatric treatment.'

'Not people of Christopher's kind.'

'But is there anything so special about him?' said the Headmaster gently. 'He always seemed an ordinary boy to me. Pleasant but ordinary.'

'He was very proud in his own way, very . . . fastidious. This kept him away from the others and made him lonely. He wanted love.'

Careful; don't go too far.

'For someone who was fastidious he seems to have gone a very peculiar way about getting it. So I shall ask you once again : how was this wretched boy corrupted? And has he corrupted anyone else in my charge? As we both know, Fielding, you were intimate with him.'

'Yes, I was, sir. And as far as I am concerned, he was innocent. His innocence . . . that's what I prized most of all.'

'But now . . . after what's happened?'

'I can't begin to understand or explain it, sir, and there's nothing more I can say.'

And that must be enough for him, I thought. After all, what I *had* told him was true enough. I certainly couldn't understand what had happened; and from where I stood, Christopher was neither corrupter nor corrupted. The terms were meaningless.

'I think,' said the Headmaster heavily, 'that Elizabeth will have coffee ready now.'

Thinking it all over in bed that night, I suddenly realised that I was glad. Despite my protest to the Headmaster, despite my genuine indignation at what had been done, I could not really have wished it undone and Christopher restored. Where Christopher now was he was truly lovable, because he could be contemplated as the image of vanished beauty : if brought back again, he would only become what he had threatened to become in July, a common pastime, to be casually lusted for, and later a common nuisance. Christopher's downfall, then, was both convenient and poetically apt. Best get such people out of the way before they lost their charm and grew ugly, boring, irrelevant. These things are so . . .

Somerset arrived the next afternoon, looking even more pasty-faced than usual as a result of his chill. After tea, however, he felt strong enough to walk with the Headmaster and myself to inspect a nearby church, the tower of which, as the Headmaster explained, had once been used for an interesting local variant of the game of Fives.

'A custom more common further west,' Somerset commented : 'in my part of the country we once had as many kinds of Fives as there were convenient church towers.'

'When was it given up?' I asked.

'Early nineteenth century,' Somerset said. 'Ball games against church walls did not suit middle-class notions of propriety.'

'It went deeper than that,' said the Headmaster. 'Even

early in the nineteenth century, it was already plain that Christianity was to be dangerously attacked. Not just by irreverent ironists, as in the previous century, but by dedicated men of science and intellect and high moral principle. The threat was so serious that the church could no longer afford to be associated with everyday pleasures: the parson must cease to hunt, the layman from playing his games in the churchyard. Frivolities like these could be tolerated only in an age of faith, when the church was so firmly entrenched that even ribaldry in its own ministers could do it no damage.' He gestured amiably. 'In an age of faith, immorality itself could be seen as joyous. But once let there be doubt, and severity, even in the most trivial things, must follow. It is the first line of defence.'

'So evangelism, like the Inquisition, was a reaction against rational enquiry?' I said smugly.

'There is something in that, though a stricter study of dates would discourage so glib a summary... There is a box-tomb which I should like you both to see. Twelfth century.'

The Headmaster led us over a small mound, through a clump of yew trees, and down into a little hollow. The tomb was of a curious faded red; it had sunk unevenly, so that on the side nearest us, which was badly cracked, it was about a foot high while on the far side the tilting slab that topped it almost dug into the grass.

'A tomb of importance,' Somerset remarked. 'One would have expected its occupant to be buried inside the church.'

'Ah,' said the Headmaster with relish. 'This tomb belongs to a renegade. Geoffery of Underavon he was called, and he was given this manor as a reward for knight service in one of the minor crusades. But Sir Geoffery had come home through Provence, where he acquired the habits and graces of the Troubadors. The arts he had learned proved only too effective in this unsophisticated part of the world, where bored wives and daughters were very grateful for a little pagan zest. His songs and addresses made him notorious and then infamous: until finally, one summer afternoon when he was riding by the river, without armour and on his way to an assignation, he was set upon and murdered by six visored knights, none of whom displayed either pennant, crest or coat of arms. Or so said the one attendant esquire, who had made off at the first sign of trouble. The deed was approved by the local clergy, who were keen to curry favour with injured husbands, and it was decreed that the Lord Geoffery should not be buried inside any church of the diocese. However, he could not well be denied burial in holy ground, and hence this tomb, out here in a lonely corner of the churchyard.'

'Lord Geoffery of Underavon,' I murmured, touched by the tale, 'martyr for poetry. Do any of his songs survive?'

' "Ver purpuratum exiit",' said the Headmaster in his soft, deep voice.

> ' "Ornatus suos induit,
> Aspergit terram floribus,
> Ligna silvarum frondibus".'

'Sir?' objected Somerset politely.

'I know, I know. Sir Geoffery would have sung in French or Provençal. In any case, that verse comes from the Cambridge Collection and so was probably written by a clerk. But it is my fancy to imagine Geoffery singing something out of the kind. Since,' said the Headmaster sadly, turning to me, 'the answer to your question is "no". None of his songs has come down.'

A flowered meadow by the river. The chirrup of the grasshopper, to remind him of fiercer afternoons when he had pursued the same errand in the Midi. The long robe, the lute, the two prancing heraldic dogs, the esquire riding a few paces behind. 'Will you not sing, my lord?' 'For you, boy? Why not? A song of the season.' The tone of the lute, plangent even in celebration. 'Ver purpuratum exiit...' The coloured spring is forth ... Then six men, six black helmets, and down goes poet and lover, vulnerable in the soft robe which he wears for his tender mission. No, his songs have not come down to us. He could not even be buried in his own church. He has lain in the shadow of the yew trees for eight hundred years.

'Martyrdom,' observed Somerset, cutting into my reverie, 'is a powerful expression. Not to be used of those who dally with the arts and their neighbours' women.'

We all three circled the tomb warily.

'Still,' said the Headmaster, 'at this distance in time Sir Geoffery makes an attractive figure.'

'A joyous sinner in an age of faith, sir?' I suggested.

'If you like. He fits so beautifully, somehow, into his background.'

'So beautifully that he was murdered.'

'Then let us say,' said Somerset, 'that his story fits beautifully into his background. He was deservedly punished for importing heresy and vice.'

The Headmaster looked vaguely troubled at this. The sentiment did not match with his notion of Sir Geoffery as a Chaucerian sinner; it implied something altogether more sinister; it was, he might have said, unworthy.

'I think we can afford to be more tolerant than that,' he remarked, bending down creakily to examine a crack in the side of the tomb.

'*We* can, sir,' said Somerset, 'because it all happened so long ago. But could they?'

'Some songs and a few love affairs,' I said; 'not very injurious.'

'Scandal,' said Somerset, 'and disorder. Injurious enough.'

'So we are to equate poetry with disorder?'

'As did Plato.'

'Who has ever since been discredited for doing so.'

Our voices rose acrimoniously. The Headmaster smiled and put a finger to his lips.

'Hush,' he said, 'you will disturb the Lord Geoffery. His

sins and his songs are both forgotten now. We must let him lie in peace.'

When we got back for supper, the Headmaster's wife handed him a slip of paper. He went into his study to telephone and reappeared, very grave, fifteen minutes later. He nodded apologetically to his wife.

'Supper in twenty minutes, my dear. Please come in here, Somerset, Fielding . . . It's Roland,' he said, when he had closed the door. 'The poor boy's killed himself.'

'Oh, Christopher,' I said stupidly.

'Why should he do that?' said Somerset, looking ingenuously from me to the Headmaster.

The latter told him briefly of the police complaint and Christopher's confinement.

'It seems,' he added, 'that he found a pistol of his father's, also some ammunition. He put the pistol in his mouth—'

'—I told you,' I interrupted angrily, 'I told you it could only do harm.'

'It had to be done,' said the Headmaster sternly. 'And what I must now say to both of you is this. So far, nothing in this wretched affair directly concerns the school : the whole sequence of disaster has begun and ended in the boy's own home and during the holidays. But questions may be asked, and so I must ask you : do either of you know of anything in the boy's activities at school which might have bearing on all this? Do you?' he said, turning to Somerset.

'I didn't know him very well, sir,' said Somerset, with a hint of smugness. 'Perhaps Fielding can be more helpful.'

'I've already told you what I know, sir. As far as I'm concerned, he was lonely and innocent. Which I suppose could explain what has happened,' I said, gulping back the tears which now threatened.

Briefly and viciously, Somerset smiled at me.

'A martyr to innocence?' he said.

The Headmaster looked at Somerset with a curious cross between disapproval and admiration.

'It seems there is no more to be said,' he remarked flatly; 'we must not keep my wife waiting.'

The tears which had nearly overcome me had not been for Christopher. They had been tears of vexation that there should be such unseemliness in things, that a convenient pattern should have been so crudely torn. Christopher confined had been someone who could give no more trouble and was at the same time a source of pleasantly nostalgic memories. Christopher confined had been like a well loved book, to be taken down and replaced at will. But Christopher dead was something that had to be explained, by myself to myself and, perhaps, to others as well: in either case an abiding source of concern and nuisance.

'You see now,' said Somerset later that night in the bedroom we shared, 'why I am so averse to disorder. This is the kind of thing which results.'

'You're not blaming me?'

'No,' said Somerset equably, 'I'm not. Even if I did, what's past is past, and my concern, as I've already told you, is with the future. But perhaps all this will serve to remind you that I meant what I said the other day: I will have nothing like this happen while I'm in charge, and in charge I still intend to be.'

'You mean, you'd still make use of Christopher against me?'

'If you stand in my way.'

'Even now . . . after *this*?'

'Let's not be sentimental. What you think of as Christopher Roland will soon be a mass of maggots. What survives him has gone to account elsewhere. Neither the spirit nor what's left of the flesh will worry about any use which I might make of their past.'

'I thought perhaps *you* might worry.'

'No more than you would,' said Somerset cheerfully, and turned out the light.

The inquest, so the Headmaster was able to tell us three days later, established that Christopher had taken his life while the balance of his mind was disturbed. There would be a funeral service in Tonbridge in two days' time, after which the body would be cremated. Gently but very firmly the Headmaster insisted that I myself, as Christopher's closest friend, should attend these ceremonies with him. This would mark the end of our little house party. Somerset would return home when the Headmaster and I left (by car) for Tonbridge; the Headmaster's wife would close the house and proceed to the school, where the Headmaster would join her after the funeral; and I would return from Tonbridge *via* London to Broughton Staithe.

'It's a long way to Tonbridge, sir,' I said hopelessly. 'Are you sure you'll have enough petrol?'

'I get an extra allowance. For special duties.'

'I see, sir . . . I don't at all want to come with you. I've already been to one funeral these holidays.'

'It will please the boy's parents.'

'How? I mean nothing to them—or they to me.'

'Then let us say,' said the Headmaster, 'that I myself shall value your support.'

There could be no answer to that.

'But that's not until the day after tomorrow,' the Headmaster said, his eyes brightening. 'Tomorrow is the last day of your visit, the last of my own holiday. In the midst of death we are in life. Tomorrow, yes, tomorrow we must do something memorable. We will walk to Salisbury Cathedral, like pilgrims, over the plain.'

'Somerset?' I whispered in the dark.

'Well?'

'What was . . . it . . . like with Angela?'

'Very pleasing,' said Somerset. 'Angela,' he added conceitedly, 'thought so too. I rather hope we'll get together again before she leaves for India.'

'You've arranged to meet?'

'We correspond.'

So Angela thought Somerset was worth keeping in touch with.

'But what,' I resumed, 'was it actually like? I mean, I always thought it was something quite incredibly different. But in fact . . .'

'What do you know about it?' said Somerset crossly.

'As much as you.' Piqued by Somerset's tone, I told him of my adventure in Piccadilly. Perhaps, I thought, I was being rash, but I wanted to tell somebody, and Somerset could never use this against me any more than I could use Angela against him. We were on neutral territory, territory so remote, as Peter had put it, that nothing which happened there could count.

'But buying women,' said Somerset, 'is not at all the same thing. Besides, there's a nasty shock in store for those who consort with street-walkers.'

'Oh?'

'The Lazar of Venice,' Somerset said with relish, 'the French Worm. Otherwise known as the Raw-boned Knight of Germany, the Neapolitan Bone-Ache, the Spanish Sweat, or, *tout court*, the Pox. It covers you with sores, removes your nose, rots your brain—'

'—For God's sake. We used one of those rubber things. And I washed jolly carefully.'

'Some kinds of dirt cannot be washed off,' said Somerset sententiously.

'Come to that, Angela's not exactly chaste.'

'At least she's amateur.'

'I wouldn't be so sure,' I muttered spitefully.

'What's that?'

'Nothing. Get back to the point, Somerset. Did you find it . . . well . . . the revelation one's been led to expect?'

'Candidly,' said Somerset, 'no. But then I never expected a revelation. Did you?'

'I think I expected something rather remarkable.'

'Just like all sensualists. You expect far too much of bodily amusements, and then complain when you're disappointed. Ungrateful lot.'

'I'm not ungrateful.'

'You will be,' said Somerset happily, 'if you get the Spanish Sweat.'

'I'm merely surprised that everyone makes such a thing about it.'

'There you have a point. It needs putting in its proper place. As for me,' said Somerset complacently, 'if Angela makes herself available again, I shall be well content. If not, then at least I shall be spared the trouble of making my confession.'

We walked towards Salisbury by way of the Race Course. As we passed the empty stands, I told the Headmaster about Peter and Tiberius.

'We shall miss Peter Morrison,' the Headmaster said, his eyes lowered towards the cathedral spire beneath us. 'I must write to tell him about Christopher Roland. I'm afraid it will come at a bad time, just when he's starting his Army life, but I feel he should know.'

There was a long silence as we started to descend over the downs. The cathedral spire, always visible except when we walked among trees, pointed straight up out of the close like the finger of an Archangel. I accuse. At any moment, surely, the huge finger would point or beckon. 'This was my beloved son, and because of you he is now a mass of maggots. State your defence.' Please, he was so attractive. That firm body, those golden legs with the silver down . . . 'What's that got to do with it? God delighteth not in any man's legs, nor in any woman's for that matter. But we'll say no more of that for the moment. Why did you desert him when he needed your love?'

'There is something,' the Headmaster broke in on this

dismal fantasy, 'which I have been meaning to say to you both. A trifle awkward. The question of which of you I shall choose as Head of the School next summer.'

Somerset went poker-faced. The grey sky started to drizzle.

'I think, sir,' I said, 'that Somerset—how shall I put it?— has more appetite for the job.'

'With due respect and without prejudice, that does not necessarily make him the better man for it.'

'I shall be very busy,' I added, 'with cricket and so on.'

None of this was said to placate Somerset or from fear of his devices. Having what I already had, I did not really want more, and I was glad to make this plain. There would be quite enough, by way of business and pleasure, to occupy me next summer.

'By the beginning of May,' said the Headmaster, 'you will have been to Cambridge and either succeeded or failed in improving on your award. I cannot see that you will be as busy as all that.'

'Then let us say that I am not particularly keen.'

'That,' said the Headmaster, 'does not unfit you for the task. It might even mean that it would be very good for you. What do you think, Somerset?'

'I think, sir, that Fielding is not much concerned with whether a thing is good for him or not.'

'And does that unfit him for the position we are discussing?'

'No. I think Fielding would be a good Head of the School, if rather off-hand. I also think that I should be a better one, because I should be more . . . more dedicated.'

'To the responsibilities? Or merely to the concept?'

'To both, sir.'

'Well,' said the Headmaster, 'we shall have to see. Meanwhile, I have only raised the point in order to receive your assurances that this will not make for bad blood between you.'

'Not for my part,' I said.

'I'm sure,' said Somerset, 'that I shall have no cause to show ill will.'

As we walked on in the silence imposed by increasingly heavy rain, the huge finger once more seemed about to point at me and the voice of the Archangel spoke again, the more resentfully, I thought, for having been interrupted.

'Why did you desert Christopher when he needed your love?' I didn't desert him : I was going to him, and then he told me not to. 'But you weren't going in love; you were going there to use him.' He wanted to be used. 'He wanted to be loved.' *Whatever* he wanted he forbade me to go to him. That wasn't my fault.

'Perhaps not; but you'd already withdrawn your love and made up your mind to exploit him; so you'd already betrayed him.' *He* didn't know. 'Didn't he? And what about the relief you felt when you heard he wasn't coming back to school—because that meant he couldn't be a nuisance later on? How's that for betrayal?' He certainly didn't know about *that*. 'Betrayal nevertheless. And another thing. When you couldn't have Christopher, you went to a whore instead. How do you answer that?' She'd starve if somebody didn't. 'No good, Fielding.' The voice had now turned into Peter Morrison's. 'I've told you before. It is foolish and dangerous (leave alone the moral side of it) to use people, to take advantage. Look where it's got you. Your mother, whom you've used all these years (don't try to deny it) as a shield against your father—your mother is getting ready to hand you over to Tuck. And what is more'—the voice was balatantly mocking now, no longer Peter's but Somerset's—'that strumpet you picked up may well have passed on the French Worm or the Neapolitan Bone-Ache or (*tout court*) the Pox.'

Tired, wet, soiled, crumpled, bored, disgusted and afraid, I entered with my companions into the clammy and obscene chill of the cathedral. The organ piped a malignant miserere and the skeletal banners of vanished regiments hung in menace over my head. A gargoyle verger snickered into the ear of a raven priest. In some shadow, surely, the Furies lurked; at any moment they would proclaim my guilt, infest me with the sores of the Lazar, hurl my putrefying flesh into the pit.

Regardless of Somerset and the Headmaster, I hurried away up a side-aisle, turned right, left behind a wooden screen, walked, with a cold sweat all over me, into a deep shadow. There was something which looked like a stone altar looming in front of me (surely stone altars were forbidden?); an outcast seeking sanctuary, I lurched forward and snatched at the stone block with my hands. Looking down, I saw the figure of a knight and shivered all through my body.

'Go on,' said a low, spiteful voice just behind me: 'have a good look while you're at it.'

'There's nothing for me here,' I said without turning.

'On the contrary. You've come this far and now you must face it.'

Still shivering, I looked closer. The tips of the prayerful stone fingers pointed up to a mailed chin, above which was a full mouth, turned slightly downwards, a soft nose, and mild, beseeching eyes. Christopher. From behind me the voice laughed, amused and pitiless. I turned.

'You shouldn't have run off like that,' Somerset said. 'It was very rude.'

And now another church. Smaller than Salisbury Cathedral but having the same traditional appurtenances. The banners, the tablets in the wall. And the coffin where the transept crossed the aisle.

'When faced with untimely death,' the unctuous young clergyman declaimed, 'we do well to reflect on the role played by the unexpected in this realm below. An established way of life, worldly goods, intellectual systems and disciplines—none can stand against the blind hand of fate.'

The Headmaster sat beside me, boot-faced.

'But,' said the greasy ministrant, 'even when the careful structures of our lives are shattered, when our hopes and ambitions are laid low, there is one supreme discipline to which we may always turn for comfort and instruction. If, that is, we will only make ourselves humble enough to be received into it. I refer you to the knowledge and love of Jesus Christ.'

I winced and let out a long, hissing breath. The Headmaster turned his head slightly and looked at me with mild curiosity, as if he would be vaguely interested (no more) to see what I did next.

'I deem it no more than my duty,' said the preacher, 'to say that the boy whose death we mourn today had strayed outside the knowledge and love of Christ. His plans and pleasures had ends which were inspired by influences hostile to true religion. He was young, suggestible; so we must hope and pray that he will be forgiven where he goes. But had others, whose duty it was, encouraged him to be stronger in the Way, then perhaps he would have lived to walk down it.'

I rose. 'I'll wait for you outside,' I whispered to the Headmaster, who nodded, agreeably, companionably, as if indeed he himself were only remaining in his seat because he wanted a few minutes more of rest.

'. . . Contagion and blasphemy,' the words followed me down the aisle, 'to which this unfortunate boy must have been exposed . . .'

God, I thought as I reached the open air, that bloody parson's having a go at the head man. I sat down on a convenient tombstone. 'Contagion and blasphemy.' Contagion. What was that sentence of Huxley's I had read earlier in the summer? 'Somewhere in my veins creep the maggots of the pox.' No. *No.* Christ, that poor little coffin. Christopher inside it, the smooth thighs, the full, pretty lips. Cold now, unkissable. Cold and rotting: maggots—though kinder in their way than the maggots of the Pox.

A bell started to toll. On something which resembled an hors d'oeuvres trolley the coffin was wheeled out of the church porch and down the path towards the waiting hearse, the driver of which, having reluctantly stubbed out a cigarette and concealed the butt somewhere in his hat, busied himself

with the door at the back. Christopher, oh Christopher. No
knight's effigy for you. Only the consuming fire. Christopher,
forgive me, for I knew not what I did. The Headmaster
stood over me.

'We must take our seats in the car.'

Confess. Tell him everything. Then there will be peace.

'Sir. There is something I must tell you. Several things.'

'In the car.'

We moved slowly down the path, among the not incon-
siderable crowd that had gathered for Christopher's
obsequies, and watched the coffin as it was handled into the
hearse. I saw a tubby little man with a red, resentful face
help a gaunt yet complacent looking woman into the first
car behind the hearse. Christopher's parents; the thought of
meeting them later made me feel, for a moment, physically
sick. '. . . He often spoke of you. Tell me, Mr Gray, as his best
friend, what do *you* think could have made him do such a
terrible thing?' 'Having two such horrible parents.' 'Interesting, Mr Gray, but we happen to know a thing or two—'

'—Come along, Fielding.'

The Headmaster took my elbow and urged me gently
towards his car, a black 1935 Saloon of a make now defunct
and eminently suitable for a drive to a crematorium.

'Funerals,' the Headmaster was saying, 'are really rather
lowering, as you may have found. Particularly if there is a
disagreeable sermon. You wanted to tell me something?'

'Yes, sir. I—'

'—Please, gentlemen?' said a whining voice.

We turned to see a ratty little man who was in battle-dress,
which was fastened right up to the chin, and huge, wallowing
Army boots.

'Please, I don't know anyone, but you looked kind, and I
wondered . . .'

'You want to come with us?'

'Please.'

'Of course,' the Headmaster said.

Two heavy drops of rain landed on my neck. The Headmaster opened the back near-side door, and the soldier clambered noisily in. I made for the co-driver's door, then, drawn by some lurking sense of kinship, climbed into the back to sit by the soldier instead. The Headmaster made no comment, but heaved himself into the driving seat and settled there with the gravity of a Royal coachman. It was now raining with almost tropical violence; after some difficulty with the windscreen-wiper, the Headmaster set the car cautiously into motion and then, realising that he was already well behind the rest of the procession and did not know the way, put his foot down harder than he meant to and rode over a yellow light.

'You knew . . . Mr Roland?' I said to the soldier.

'I didn't know him. Only I seen him.'

During the pause which followed, I watched the struggle in the man's face between the natural reluctance of the inarticulate to embark on a tricky explanation and the guilty fear that unless he did so he might appear as an interloper.

'I'm not just snooping though,' the man said with an effort.

Touched by this delicacy of feeling, I sought about for ways of helping the explanation to birth, only to realise that this was the first time in my life (since the nursery) that a conversation between myself and a member of the lower classes had been other than merely administrative, and that I had no idea whatever how to proceed with it. The Headmaster, who appeared to share this feeling, maintained a prudent silence and kept his eyes squarely into the rain.

'It was like this,' the soldier said, gallant and tortured. 'I was in detention, see, serving a week in the guardhouse. But being a handy kind of man, they didn't put me on rough work but had me paint the place up and fit new lights and things. Get it?'

The Headmaster and I got it.

'So every day,' said the soldier with growing confidence, 'I was working round this guardhouse, inside and out, and every day there was this young fellow, this Christopher

Roland, used to come on his bike and stop near the gate, like he was waiting for somebody. A lonely little chap like me, see, because although I was getting it light it's no fun spending twenty-four hours of every day round a guardhouse, with only a wooden bed waiting for you in a damp cell.'

'What makes you say he was lonely?'

'The way he kept looking to see if anyone was coming he could talk to.'

'Did he talk to you?'

'No,' said the soldier bitterly. 'He couldn't come in through the gate and I couldn't go out of it. He used to smile at me, though. Every now and then, I'd look up and see him smiling. Specially when someone had been shouting at me, bawling me out to be quick with this or that, then I'd look up and I'd find him smiling, as if to say he was sorry and he hoped I'd come through.'

We were out of Tonbridge and into the country. The rain, no longer violent, had settled into a steady vertical drench.

'Then one day just before my sentence was up,' the soldier went on, 'he didn't come. I was that upset I thought I should have cried. Afterwards I heard why, about the police and all ... It wasn't till then I even knew his name. And now this ...'

The soldier removed the khaki beret from his head and started wringing it in thin, dirty fingers.

'So you see, you must see,' he said urgently, 'what he meant to me and why I'm grieving for him, no matter what he done. Because whatever he came there for, he was good to me. It was him that kept me going, and I can't forget him. Oh, he used to talk to anyone that went in or out—anyone who'd stop and listen—, and there was no doubt what he was after, or so I heard later from the lads. But he never forgot me. Whenever he came or went, he always had a smile for hallo or good-bye. See what I'm trying to tell you, gentlemen?'

Scruffy, sharp yet weak in the face, twitching, undersized, perhaps thirty-five years old, the soldier, I thought, looked like just the sort of man one read about in the Sunday Press. A lonely, repellent little man, who would live unloved and die unlamented, would probably die, indeed, without its even being known, until days or weeks later an employer or chance creditor, scenting something odd, suggested to the police that they might call ... What could Christopher have seen here? Surely to God there were more attractive people in the world who would have been grateful for his smiles?

'So you came to the funeral,' was all I could think of to say.

'Yes. I'm R.C. myself, so I don't hold with this burning but that's none of my affair. I thought ... a prayer for him .... I didn't get dispensation to come to the church, neither, but perhaps God ...'

'God will hear your prayer,' said the Headmaster, speaking for the first time since the procession started.

'You think so?' said the soldier doubtfully.

The engine died and the car stopped.

'Damn,' said the Headmaster vigorously.

'Petrol-pump,' said the soldier. Before anyone could say anything, he was out of the car and had the bonnet up. He administered a brisk tap.

'Press the starter,' he called, 'and we're away.'

As indeed we were.

'But,' said the soldier knowingly, 'once it starts that trick, it goes on. More and more. Till at last you're getting out every fifty yards.'

'And so?'

'New petrol-pump. Ten minutes to fit. Any proper garage.'

The car stopped. Again the soldier went out into the pouring rain and set it going.

'You see?' he said as he got in, smelling deplorably.

After the car had stopped four more times, we came to a small but apparently reputable garage. A sneering, balding man fitted a new petrol-pump.

'That'll be six quid.'

'Robbery,' the soldier said.

'Yes, er, surely—' the Headmaster began.

'Ain't you forgetting something?' the sneering man said, thrusting his face at us. 'Ain't you forgetting that there's been a war, and parts like that are hard to come by, and if you don't want it you needn't have it, because it'll only take me two ticks to whip it out again?'

'But we must have it.'

'Then it'll cost you six quid.'

'A cheque?'

'What do you take me for?'

'But I haven't got that much in cash.'

'Then you haven't got a petrol-pump either.'

The garage man made towards the engine, flourishing a spanner. The soldier slammed the bonnet down and said,

'This gentleman will give you three knicker, which is more than a fair price for the pump and your trouble. If you try to detain us, that is illegal, and we shall be within our rights using force to get away. Get into the car, gentlemen, and start her up.'

The Headmaster and I gaped, then did as we were told. The soldier looked perky and serene. The garage-man scowled and held out his hand.

'Four quid,' he said.

'Three. You give him three, sir.'

The Headmaster gave him three, and once more we were on the road. By this time we had ceased to be strangers, had become companions in adversity and almost confederates in crime. For a number of reasons which I was not anxious to examine, I was finding this complicity irksome.

'I'm very grateful,' the Headmaster said. 'Where did you learn that bit about illegal detention?'

'I'm quite a one for finding out things like that. It helps you get your rights.'

What an abominable little man, I thought. Aloud I said:

'I suppose we're too late. For the cremation.'

A least I should not have to talk to Christopher's parents.

'I suppose so,' the Headmaster said. 'I really can't say I'm sorry.'

With much heavy breathing he managed to turn the car round.

'I was looking forward,' the soldier said, 'to seeing how it worked. The coffin being shot into the furnace and all ... Ah, well. Perhaps you'd drop me at the camp, sir? It's not far.'

When we reached the gate of the camp the soldier said:

'That's where he used to stand with his bike. Just over there by the tree. Poor little sod.'

He waved cheerfully and strutted through the gate, his huge boots spread wide in a waddle. Two regimental policemen descended on him and ushered him into the guardroom.

'He was absent without leave,' said the Headmaster bleakly. 'He couldn't get leave to come to the funeral, I suppose, so he came without. And we didn't even ask his name.'

'Now he'll be put in detention again. And every time he comes out of that guardroom,' I said with loathing, 'he'll look at that tree and think about Christopher's smile.'

The Headmaster, who seemed saddened by this remark, drove slowly but jerkily away.

'What a foul little man,' I said at length. 'How could Christopher—'

'—What were you going to tell me? Before he asked for a lift.'

Silence.

'Well, Fielding?'

'I was going to say,' I said feebly, 'how sorry I was that that clergyman tried to get at you in his sermon.'

'No, you weren't. You were going to make a confession of some kind. You were going to ask for help. And do you know,' said the Headmaster gravely, 'I was rather pleased. So pleased, that however bad it had been I would have seen you through. But now that poor little soldier has annoyed you so much that you are determined to prove that you don't need help. That you are not like him, prepared to give and receive. For a brief moment, when you were close driven, you thought you would look for comfort. But then you realised that this meant humbling yourself, and your vanity took over.'

'I merely want to be my own man.'

'All your own man. *Never* to give or receive. So be it then. I only wish it could have been otherwise.'

'It was nothing that really matters, sir. I was hysterical. That service ... the coffin ...'

'You don't have to protest,' said the Headmaster. 'I'm not accusing you. I'm simply sorry you did not see fit to honour me with your confidence. That way we might have become friends instead of politely disposed strangers. Now it is too late.'

'So you've been with a trollop,' said the Senior Usher. 'Why hunt me down during my hard earned leisure to tell me that?'

We were sitting in the Senior Usher's London club, where, unable to go abroad and heedless of falling bombs, he had for five years spent most of his holidays. My visit there was the result of a snap decision. When I had arrived in London the previous evening, depressed by the day's events and so more than ever inclined to remember Somerset's disquieting exegesis on the Pox, I had made my way to the Kensington Public Library and sought out the medical section. Here I had been still further depressed and thoroughly confused: as far as I could make out, venereal disease might announce itself by exhibiting almost any kind of symptom or even none. Advice must clearly be had. Peter was not available to give it; any reputable doctor, if consulted, would want to be put in touch with school or parents; to wait my turn in one of those East End hospitals advertised in lavatories was unthinkable. I needed a tolerant and knowledgeable man of the world who would not betray me, and for such, remembering conversations past, I took the Senior Usher.

'Why,' he said, 'bring this dreary item to me?'

'I want your help, sir.'

'You've gone and got clap?'

'Not yet. But supposing I did?'

'It'll hurt like hell.'

'And the other thing . . . syphilis?'

'You'd show up all the colours of the spectrum.'

The Senior Usher emptied the glass at his side and signed to a septuagenarian steward for another.

'Let's get this settled for good and all,' he said, 'and have no more worry about it. It's very easy if you only keep your head and put the thing in its proper place. You used a French Letter? Right?'

'Right.'

'Then the odds, the overwhelming odds, are that you won't have any trouble at all. But if your old man starts hurting badly or begins to look like a Turner sunset, there's something the matter and you must go to a doctor and get yourself cured. They've discovered a new drug, I'm told, which is both painless and swift. Unlike the old days.'

He gave a perceptible shudder.

'But what doctor, sir? I don't want any trouble at home . . . or with the Headmaster.'

'Quite right. It would only upset him to no purpose. So *if* anything goes wrong, I'll fix you up with a chap I know who gets his living by not asking awkward questions.'

'Thank you very much, sir.'

'Just remember two things,' said the Senior Usher. 'First, you're not old enough to have whores until you're old enough to cope with the consequences yourself instead of pestering respectable old gentlemen in their clubs. And secondly, don't come running to me the minute you get an itch or a sweat spot. If you've really got it, you'll really know it.'

'But the books say—'

'—Yes, I know they do. So just to be on the safe side, we'll arrange a blood test for you in about six weeks' time. I'll have my chum come down to the school and invite you to meet him in my Lodging.'

'Oh, thank you, sir. It's a great relief.'

'My privilege. Now go away and leave me in peace until next quarter, which God knows will be soon enough.'

So that, I thought, as I caught the train from Liverpool Street, was one matter cleared up. The Senior Usher was quite right : all that was necessary was to keep one's head and look facts in the face, to use one's powers as a rational man. One must not panic, and one must not be tempted (as I had been at Christopher's funeral) to surrender when things got rough. Instead, one must think. Whatever the difficulties which might now ensue, difficulties made by Somerset or the Headmaster, by my mother or the Tucks, all could surely be solved by the power of rational thought.

This morning, just as I was sitting down to carry on with this memoir, I was handed a special signal from the C.O. in Malta. It seems that an all-party delegation of politicians is to tour this area and visit, among other places, this island, and that Mr Peter Morrison, M.P. for Whereham, is to make one of the delegation. It will be interesting to see him again—and also opportune, as I have spent so much of these last weeks thinking and writing about him as a boy. This exercise has suggested certain questions, which were never asked at the time and might now be usefully answered.

WHEN I REACHED home, I found a letter from Christopher which was dated the day before his death.

Dear Fielding,

I want you to know how things are with me. Because they're not at all the same as you probably think. By now you'll have heard from the head man what's happened and how I shan't be coming back next quarter. But it isn't that which is making me unhappy, or not so much. And it's not the psychiatrist either, revolting though he is, putting his hand on my knee, asking me to tell him every last detail about 'the things you did at school'. (Don't worry, Fielding; he's not interested in names.) No, it's none of that, miserable as it all is.

It's this, Fielding. I was afraid, at the end of last quarter, that you'd gone away from me. But then you wrote and seemed so anxious to come here, and I thought, it's all right, he still loves me, those last few days at school were just a bad patch. That was until I started talking to the tutor who came. After a time we got to be friendly; and because I didn't have anyone else to tell I told him about you. He encouraged me to talk about these things, you see, I think he was fond of me and wanted to get closer, and this was the only way I'd let him get close. Anyway, I told him. And he said you weren't coming because you loved me, that was obvious from what had happened, you were coming because you were bored at home and wanted me in bed. At first I wouldn't believe him, but he kept on and on, he said he only wanted me to know the truth. And at last I thought I'd ask you straight out when you came and settle it like that.

Then the tutor left, earlier than he'd been meant to, I

*don't think my parents liked him. It was then I started going
up to that Army camp. At first I just passed it by accident,
then I saw the men going in and out, and I thought . . . well,
you know what I thought. I was so lonely, Fielding, even the
tutor was gone, and I wanted someone, anyone, to be with
and hold them. In the end I didn't find anyone, they were
quite kind, most of them, and just went away without understanding—though I suppose one of them must have reported
me because of what the police said later.*

*But apart from all that, something horrible happened.
There was a soldier under punishment, a horrid little man
with a thin face and hands like claws, who used to be doing
jobs round the gate. He used to look at me with long
imploring looks, and I was sorry for him, in a way, so I did
my best to smile back. And then one day I realised something.
I realised that even if my tutor was wrong and you did still
love me, very soon you wouldn't and I'd be to you what that
soldier was to me, someone loathesome but always there,
someone you had to smile at to keep him happy while all
the time you just wanted him to go away and never come
back. That's what you'd feel about me, perhaps you'd felt it
already, because sometimes I'd seen in your smiles the same
strain, the same hidden disgust which I now felt in my
own.*

*And then there was the police and all the rest which the
head man will have told you. So of course you couldn't come
here and I couldn't ask you whether you loved me or not,
though I knew the answer anyway, I'd always really known
it since after that time in the hay-loft. Ivan Blessington called
in a day or two later, which made things worse, because it
reminded me of everything I wasn't going back to. But it's
not that which has made me despair. It's because of that
soldier, it's knowing, from what I thought of him, what you
really thought of me. Oh, I'm young and nice to look at, not
like him, but in the end that's all I was to you or will be to
anyone.*

So now I'm going out to post this letter—they'll let me

*go that far if I tell them first. I'm sending it to your home,
not to the head man's house in Wiltshire, which is where
you'll be, because I don't want to embarrass you. You can't
say I've ever really been a nuisance yet, and I pray I never
shall be.*

>   *Love, yes, love,*
>   *Christopher.*

Those peaceful days at Whereham, I thought: it must have
been about then that Christopher was hanging round the
barrack gate, waiting. Why hadn't he sent for me if the tutor
had left? Perhaps he didn't want to disturb me at Whereham
('You can't say I've ever really been a nuisance yet'), or
perhaps it was because he already knew all he needed to—
'I'd always really known since after that time in the hay-
loft.' That time in the hay-loft: the one and only time: and
now this.

, I tore Christopher's letter into very small pieces and let the
wind carry them away over the September sea.

'Mama . . . It's nice to see you back.'

'Is it, dear? How have you been getting on?'

'Quite well, thank you . . . Mama, I'd better tell you
straight away. I'm afraid I had to ask the hotel in London
to send on the bill. Two nights.'

'Two nights?'

'There and back.'

'But I thought, Fielding, that I gave you money for all
that.'

'Yes, mother, but it wasn't quite enough. And I'm afraid
I owe Peter Morrison some money. You see—'

'—How much?'

'Fifteen pounds. You see—'

'—I'm not much interested,' my mother said, 'in whatever
story you've thought up to tell me. I shall pay the hotel bill
because I don't want to feel uncomfortable when I go there.
As for Peter, he should have known better than to lend you

so much. He'll just have to wait until you can pay him back yourself.'

'But *mama*—'

'—It's high time,' she said, 'that we got a few things straight, you and I.'

'What things, mother?'

'Your extravagant habits. This idea that you can have what you want for the asking. But just now I'm rather tired. We'll talk about it all later on.'

> 14477929, Pte. Morrison, P.,
> 3 Platoon, 'A' Coy,
> 99 P.T.C.,
> Ranby Camp,
> Near Retford, Notts.
> September 15, 1945.

My dear Fielding,

If any letters are to reach me, they should be addressed exactly as above.

Ranby Camp is the end of the world, but I'm rather enjoying myself. The thing is that all anyone on the training staff here can think about is how soon he will be demobbed. With the exception of a very few regulars, everyone thinks, talks, eats and sleeps nothing but release numbers and priorities, with the result that no one has much time for training or interfering with us. As far as I can make out, the British Army is one vast Heath-Robinson contrivance which exists only to fall apart, and the days pass in an atmosphere of sloth and cynicism which would, I fancy, amuse you.

But of course it's all rather futile. I fail to see why I should spend perhaps three years of my life in dodging what are in any case unexacting duties and listening to repetitious stories of Neapolitan whore-shops. Still, one must make the best of a bad job; and so I've decided to apply for the Indian Army, which could be rather exciting. Nothing's settled yet, but when and if it is I shall hope to come down to school and see you all before I go.

After this, the ink changed colour, and it was clear that what followed had been written some time later.

The head man has just written about Christopher. I haven't time to say anything about it now, and anyhow I don't yet know what I want to say. I suppose we shall have to talk about it when I see you again.

        Ever,
          Peter.

'I'm just off to have dinner with the Tucks,' my Mother said. 'I might be quite late, so don't bother to wait up.'

I sat down alone in the kitchen to a tin of cold spam. There were now, I reflected, just five days before I was due to return to school. I had made all my preparations and only one thing more was needed: that my mother should pay the fees, which had to be sent, at latest, by the day before the quarter started. She might, of course, have done so already. But somehow I thought this unlikely. She had made no mention of the matter since her return two days before; indeed, she had made no mention of anything to do with my future. Her manner was of one who had plans about to mature, of one who would have an announcement to make at any minute. Meanwhile, she watched my preparations without comment and did not commit herself. When asked, for example, to drive me and my trunk to the station, so that I might send it off by P.L.A., she had simply shrugged her shoulders and said that it could wait. And so it could, I thought; but not for long. Tomorrow or the next day I must get her to declare herself; and the best way of doing so would be to remind her about the fees.

But it was my mother who took the initiative.

'It's time,' she said, after breakfast the next morning, 'that we had a little talk.'

'Gladly.'

I lowered my paper. Mama came and stood over me as I sat in what had always been my father's armchair. She looked determined and confident; formidable. In the few weeks since my father's death her body had thickened and straightened, while the drooping lines of discontent round her mouth had become strong, sardonic curves.

'Last night,' she said, 'I had a long discussion with the Tucks.'

'What have they to do with us?'

'There's no need to take that tone. Mr Tuck made some very sensible suggestions.'

'I think I know. They want me to carry on with this absurd tea-planting scheme, and they want you to invest money. The same old story. I wonder you troubled to listen.'

'Angela Tuck has been a very good friend to me. At a time when I needed support and advice.'

'She got at you, mother, that's all.'

'You listen to me,' my mother said, leaning forward and speaking very precisely. 'You think you're going comfortably back to school and then on to Cambridge. All on my money. Well, I'm changing all that. I've written to your Headmaster and told him you won't be coming back, this term or any term.'

'Quarter.'

'It's a pity I had to pay a term's fees in lieu of notice—'

'—A quarter's fees. In that case I may as well get the benefit until Christmas—'

'—But I mean to start as I'm going to go on. No more school. Real life now. No more school and no more Cambridge . . . unless of course you can pay for it yourself.'

'Why, mother? For God's sake, why?'

For a long time I had half-consciously expected this. I had told myself that when the time came my intelligence would show me the solution. But I had been reluctant to envisage more than a token showdown, after which my mother, as she had done for years, would comply with my reasonable requests. I had not considered tactics, I had merely assured myself of my ability to cope with a feeble-minded woman. Now that this woman had made, stated and already acted upon firm plans of her own, I suddenly found myself powerless to do more than entreat.

'Why?' I asked piteously. 'Why?'

'Because I want to see you make a real life for yourself by your own efforts. To see you behave like a man, not sit around, dependent on someone else's money, amusing yourself with Latin and Greek. Latin and Greek'—she mouthed the words grotesquely—'what *use* could they ever be to anyone?'

'But it was all carefully planned. It was to have been my career.'

'Your *career?* A career spent mouldering away under a heap of books, talking arty nonsense to a lot of clever-clever dons, who wouldn't last a minute if they weren't protected from the real world by their cosy college walls?'

My father's voice, I thought.

'It's what I wanted, mother,' I said wearily. 'And you always seemed happy about it.'

'Don't you see?' she said. She was now speaking almost into my ear. 'I had to support you against your father, or you wouldn't have wanted me, any more than you wanted him. And I didn't know what was in his will. If it had been different, if you'd been free to do what you planned, I'd have been forced to make the best of it, or lose you altogether. But now . . .'

She stood back and surveyed me, hands on hips.

'My son,' she said. 'My pretty, arty son. I want a man.'

'Mother. There is enough money for me to do what I want. I'm asking you, pleading with you, to let things go on as we'd always agreed.'

'No. Real life now.'

'Do you hate me so much?'

'I simply want what's best for you. I've listened for too long while you've laughed and been so clever about ordinary people, ordinary sensible things. Now you're going to learn what the world's like for most of us. What it's been like for me these last twenty years.'

So that was it. Part morality, part vindictiveness. She wanted to make me into a 'real man' doing a 'useful job', just like anybody else, compelled to join in with 'ordinary' people and to echo their 'sensible' notions, to be bored, to conform. No good arguing now, I thought. Listen to what she says and then think later.

'So what have you arranged?' I asked.

'I've arranged to invest all the money that would have gone on your useless education with the owner of Mr Tuck's plantation. £5,000, and probably some more later on. You'll do your Army service as soon as possible, and then you'll go out to India to join Mr Tuck, who will take you under his personal supervision. He hopes to be a partner by then, so you'll have every chance to get on. If you work hard and show the right spirit'—Tuck's phrase, surely?—'you'll become an important man and make good money, like Mr Tuck. If you don't . . . well, don't think you can fall back on me.'

Money, money. But no good arguing now. Keep your head, I told myself; be patient and rational; look round for a way out. Don't let her have the scene she'd like, not until you have a weapon to silence her. And what could that be? Never mind now.

'All right, mama,' I said. 'I have no choice. What do you want me to do?'

The first thing I must do, as Mr Tuck officiously explained, was to go to the Registration authorities in Lympne Ducis, there to notify them that I no longer wished to be deferred from call up and would like to volunteer, on grounds of personal urgency, for immediate drafting.

'Now we all know where we are at last,' Tuck said, 'let's get this show on the road.'

Although I had no intention of cancelling my deferment, I was prepared to go through motions enough to stop my mother's tongue for the time, and the next afternoon I took a train to Lympne Ducis. It was, after all, an outing of a kind.

Having gone to the registration office for just long enough to look with loathing at its exterior, I made my way towards the cinema. ('Yes, mama,' I would tell her when I got home, 'they'll do what they can, they say, but it may take some time.') Crossing the empty market place in front of The Duke's Head, I heard a scampering of high heels behind me.

'Christopher ... Chris.'

Dixie. Walk on and pretend not to notice.

But she was up beside me, panting and flushed, gripping my arm.

'Don't run away, please, Chris. I only wanted to say ... I'm sorry, so sorry, for behaving like I did that night.'

'You?' I said stupidly. 'Sorry?'

'Yes. So sorry. I don't blame you for rushing off like you did. But please talk to me now. Say you've forgiven me.'

'But after what I did to you—'

'—I led you on, Christopher. I wanted you to. I don't know why I started on like that. Phyllis ... I don't know.'

I turned towards her and put my hands on her shoulders. The afternoon, gold on the gabled houses, had a chill of dying summer; but it was not this which made me shiver.

'You wanted me to?' I repeated. 'Then why not now? We'll take a bus out to the pinewoods ... Go to the cinema ...'

Dixie drew away.

'No, Christopher,' she said gently. 'Not any more. I'm engaged now, see?'

She held up her hand and the imitation diamonds sparkled in the autumn sun.

'I'm very happy,' she said. 'So when I saw you just now, I wanted for us to part friends like. Say it, Chris. Say we part friends and wish me luck.'

Engaged. To a 'real' man no doubt, who had a 'proper' job. Engaged to grow older and older in a deadly routine

of begetting and boredom and the weekly wage-packet.
Engaged to watch the children grow up and leave, to slobber
through loose dentures at the grand-children on their
Christmas visit, engaged to die and to rot. 'Before I go, I'd
like Clarry's eldest to have my engagement ring. The jewels
always looked so pretty in the sun. I remember one day, many
years ago in the market place . . .'

'Don't they look a treat in the sun?' Dixie said.

'And in the shadow?' (My dear Dorian.)

'Christopher? What—'

'—Never mind, Dixie. Of course I wish you luck. And if
we're to part as friends, you should know my proper name.
I'm called Fielding, Fielding Gray.'

'What a nice name. Funny but nice. Why did you say it
was Christopher?'

'I thought you'd laugh.'

'Not that sort of funny. Thank you for telling me, though.
It means . . . that what you say is real.'

'Real?'

'That I'm not just anybody you picked up one evening at
a fair. Give us a kiss, Fielding Gray.' She pointed to her
cheek. 'There.'

I made to kiss her. At the last moment she altered the
angle of her head and gave me her closed lips.

'I must run now,' she said. 'Ta-ta. Be good.'

The high heels clicked away across the square. Begetting
and boredom. Reality. And warmth. Was that what made
the long years endurable for Dixie and her kind, engaged
only to parturate and die? Michael Redgrave and John
Mills, the cinema poster said: The Way to the Stars. How
Dixie would thrill to the sham title, as she thrilled to the fake
diamonds in the sun. But who was I to pity or condemn?
I, who had only dared to let her know my real name when
I was quit of her for good?

When I came home that evening, there was a letter from
the Senior Usher.

. . . The Headmaster has told me of your mother's decision, and I can well imagine how disagreeable you must find your predicament. Not that the feeling can be anything but salutary: set-backs, once in a while, are excellent therapy. Provided, that is, they are not unduly prolonged and destructive. To come to the point without more ado, I object to waste and I cannot stand by while a scholar of your promise is lost to us at the whim—forgive me—of a foolish woman. There has been enough loss these last years; scholars will be rare; our side, the humanists' side, needs all the support it can get. And so, since I am a bachelor and not a poor one, I propose, if you will permit me, to undertake the expense of your further education: the expense, that is, of another year at the school here and later of whatever provision you may need, within reasonable though not frugal limits, at Cambridge. My motive is not entirely one of highminded patronage; if I wish to keep a scholar, I also wish to oblige a friend. The loss, you see, would be personal as well as academic.

I realise that your mother's attitude will be, to say the least of it, hostile, and that she will withhold money. I enclose an encashable money order for your immediate needs, and I will make arrangements, which we can discuss later, to see you all right during future school holidays. Since I have chosen to interfere, I shall interfere amply, and place you altogether beyond the reach of—forgive me once more—your mother's palpable malice.

The Headmaster, whom I have of course informed of my intentions, is dubious of the scheme but prepared to accept it. I think he is afraid your mother will make trouble, will claim that I have illicitly seduced you away from her control. Legally, however, she can do nothing. You are nearly eighteen; provided your course of life is respectable and you have visible means to support it, you are entirely free to leave her as soon as you wish.

In the present circumstances, I think you would be well advised to do so immediately. If ties are to be cut, they should

*be sharply cut. You will be welcome at my Lodging for the
last few days before the quarter begins ...*

'And so what did they tell you at the Registration office?'
my mother asked.

'Nothing. I didn't go in and now I never intend to.'

'Well, my lord. And what do you intend?'

'To leave here,' I said, 'tomorrow.'

'Very forceful all of a sudden. What will you use for
money?'

'I have a friend,' I said triumphantly, 'a master at the
school, who will see me through my last year there. *And*
through Cambridge.'

'How kind of him. But suppose, just suppose, that I object?
After all, you're under twenty-one.'

'There's nothing you can do. Provided I have proper
means and occupation, I can go where I wish.'

'Yes,' my mother said quietly, 'I expect you're right. We'll
talk about it in the morning.'

'There's nothing to talk about, mother.'

'We'll talk about it in the morning. What time,' she
enquired, 'are you off?'

'Early.'

'But I expect we'll still have time, dear, for a little talk
first.'

Trunk, I thought. That can come with me in the taxi and
go in the guard's van. Stop at the post office on the way to
the station, cash the money order, and wire the Senior Usher
to expect me in the evening. Suitcase: socks, shirts, hanks,
pants; washing things in the morning. All set. Just as I had
told myself: use your brains; wait until you see the way out
and then take it—fast. True, I had been lucky; but I had
kept my head, bided my time, avoided excessive unpleasantness and contrived, though under heavy pressure, not to

commit myself. A victory for intelligence and reason. With the thrill of impending departure in my belly I went to my fitful rest.

'So you think,' said my mother the next morning, 'that you're going to walk out of here just like that?'

'I don't want to part with bad feelings, mother. You've got one idea for my future and I've got another. You can hardly blame me for preferring mine.'

'A mother knows what's best for her son. Don't you see,' said mama, with something of her old whine, 'that I'm doing all this for your sake? The Army will make a man of you, and in India you'll have a job for which any boy should be grateful.'

'The Army will have its chance in any case,' I said. 'But not yet. You know what I want to do, mother—what I've always wanted to do. Let's not have any more argument.'

'I'm your mother.' Self-righteous now. 'It's for me to give you money and help you with your future. Not for some interfering master at that damned school.'

'Then give me money and help me. Stop listening to the Tucks all day long and help me do what I want.'

'I bore you, I brought you up, protected you, fought for you—'

'—Yes, yes, and I'm grateful. But now—'

'—And in return I've a right to have my wishes respected.'

'It's no good, mother. There's a taxi coming for me in ten minutes. Just as soon as you change your mind and try to see things sensibly, I'll be glad to come back to you. Until then . . . well, for heaven's sake let's be nice to each other.'

'Nice to each other. As if you'd ever been nice to me in your whole life. As if you'd ever thought of me at all, except as someone to get money for you out of your father. Well, you're going to think of me now for once. Oh yes. You're going to think of me now, Fielding Gray, because you're going to have to do what I tell you. You're not going back to that school, money or no money, because I'm going to show them this.'

She fumbled in her bag.

'*This.*' She waved a photograph in front of her. Christopher in cricket kit. ' "To Fielding with all my dearest love from Christopher",' she read from the back in an obscene, mimicking voice. ' "Please come soon, or I—'

'—Stop it, mother.'

'—"Or I shan't be able to bear it." That ought to be quite enough, after what's happened. That wretched boy dead, after offering himself to soldiers like a common whore in the street—'

'—STOP IT—'

'—Yes, this ought to be quite enough, I think. Mind you, we knew already what you'd been up to, Angela and I. She's kept in touch with your friend who came here, Somerset Lloyd-Thing—'

'—Lloyd-James—'

'—and *he* told her all about *Christopher*. It's a funny thing, but he seems to want to stop you going back too. Nice friends you have. So when he heard that Angela and I had a plan for you, he wrote back helpfully to tell her about this Christopher . . . only there was no real proof yet, he said. *Until I found this.* While you were slopping around in Lympne yesterday, not doing what you were told.'

'So you were snooping, *prying*?'

'Not at all. Simply doing my duty as your mother and going over your clothes. This was at the bottom of your shirt drawer. Rather careless, rather forgetful for someone so very clever.'

'Mother,' I said. 'Christopher's dead and the whole dismal story's finished. All we want to do, all of us, is to forget it.'

'Oh? I wonder whether Somerset Lloyd-Thing wants to forget it. Anyway, you won't be able to forget it now, because I've got proof and I won't let you. I'm going to tell your Headmaster what I know; and if he lets you back into his school after *that*, then I'll start writing round to the parents

and telling them that their esteemed Headmaster is condoning
sodomy. Sodomy,' she hissed, like a dry tap.

I lurched forward.

'You mean, spiteful bitch,' I shouted. I thrust my hand
out to seize the photograph, but she drew away from me
and brandished it above her head.

'Oh no, my lad,' she said. 'Anyhow Angela's seen it. Even
if you tear it up, we can make such a scandal between us
that that Headmaster of yours will never want to hear your
name again.'

'Bitch,' I screamed, 'bitch, *bitch*, BITCH.'

I lowered the hand which was reaching for the photograph
and hit her with a back swing of my knuckles across her
cheek. Her lips parted and the blood welled up through her
teeth.

'Mama, I'm sorry, so sorry. *Please*, mama. I didn't
mean—'

'—Nasty little pansy,' she lisped through the streaming
blood; 'nasty, vicious little pig.'

The door bell rang. I offered my handkerchief.

'Don't you come near me,' she said. The blood poured over
her chin and dripped down on to her dress. 'You get into
your taxi and run away back to school. And when they turn
you out, you can just come back here. You'll have to grovel,
Christ, how you'll have to grovel, but you're under twenty-
one, so I'll let you come back here.'

Be reasonable, I told myself. It was her fault. She provoked
me beyond bearing, and so I struck her. She threatened the
vilest kind of blackmail to get her way, and so I struck her.
One minute there had been relief, the generous promise of
freedom in the Senior Usher's letter, the next there had been
frustration and despair, jealousy masquerading as mother
love, the hideous desire to control and possess: she was
destroying everything, and so I struck her. But reason could
not encompass the enormity, could not blot out the picture of

the bright blood pouring from my mother's mouth.

The train slunk through the debris into London. I was following my original plan and heading, as invited, for the Senior Usher's Lodging, because I had nowhere else to go; here, if anywhere, lay help and refuge. But not for long now. One or two days at most, as long as it took my mother to convince the Headmaster of what she knew. I looked down at the jagged, carious rubble. Beaten, I told myself, beaten. How were intelligence or reason to help me now?

'When a position becomes untenable,' said the Senior Usher, spreading his buttocks before an ample and illicit fire, 'it is necessary to retreat with good grace to a tenable one. You realise that you can't stay here?'

'I suppose not.'

'You see, as long as your misdeeds were extra-mural, so to speak, I could help you. This business of your trull in Piccadilly—easily seen to. But now that you're known to have sinned within these very portals . . . it's too *near*, Fielding, and it can't be disregarded. You remember what I said last quarter? We don't expect you to believe in the Christian ethic—or at least I don't—but we have to insist that on our own ground you observe it.'

'A condition of belonging, you said.'

'Exactly. We can, of course, exercise some discretion. We can even ignore what we might have suspected—so long as it's safely dead and buried. But your mother has exhumed this unhappy affair, and she has made of this wretched boy Roland a kind of accusing Lazarus. You see, it's the fact of his suicide that finally settles the question. There'd be those who'd say that you were the cause of it. So you must see that we simply can't keep you.'

'I know that. I know I must leave here before the quarter starts. But what am I to do?'

'As I say, dear boy. Retreat to a tenable position. Now then. No last year here, no further award at Lancaster. But you still have a minor scholarship to the college and a place awaiting you. It's more than most people have; so settle for it.'

'But will they still accept me? If they hear about all this?'

'Of course. They are civilised and easy-going men, who do not concern themselves with the peccadilloes of adolescence. In any case, you're now too late to propose yourself for this October, so you'll have to do your military service first; and by the time that's done, the whole thing will have been forgotten.'

'The Tutor . . . Robert Constable . . . he didn't strike me as easy-going. Neither forgiving, I'd have said, nor forgetting.'

'You misunderstand him. He is a bore and a prig, but also a conscientious and progressive left-winger. Vintage 'thirties. Which means that he stands not only for social reform but also for intellectual and sexual freedom. It is, to him, a duty to tolerate your kind of behaviour. Though of course,' said the Senior Usher wryly, 'the more complicated and unhappy you can be about it, the better he'll be pleased. Never let on that you were simply enjoying yourself.'

'And . . . money?'

'I'll stand by what I promised. If you don't qualify for some sort of ex-service grant, I'll see to it you're all right.'

'And meanwhile? *Now*, I mean? These days one can't just take the King's shilling overnight.'

The Senior Usher scratched his rump.

'If you ask me,' he said slowly, 'as things stand you'd be wise to go home and make your peace with your mother. She is, it seems, a dangerous woman. Tell her you're sorry you were rude and you'll do what she asks. Keep her quiet, dear boy, till it's too late for her to do any more damage.'

'What more can she do?'

'On the face of it, none. As I say, Lancaster is run very differently from this place, and nobody there will give a second thought to her story. They keep their chapel going as a decorative museum piece, and that's about as far as the Christian ethic gets with *them*.'

'Well then?'

'One never knows. I still think you'd be wise to calm your mother down and keep her calm till time's done its work.'

'I don't at all want to go back.'

'A little more gratitude would become you, and a little more co-operation. You can't have everything your own way.'

'I'm sorry, sir. I didn't mean to be difficult and I *am* grateful.'

'It'll be unpleasant, I know,' said the old man, relenting. 'But when a woman has a mind to do damage she can be damned ingenious. As you've already seen. So you go off home tomorrow, soothe her down, and get yourself into khaki as soon as possible. Meanwhile, I'll brief Robert Constable and get him to set your mind at rest about your place at Lancaster. And now,' he said, 'I've ordered a nice little dinner in your honour and we will talk, if you please, of something—of anything—else.'

'Good-bye, sir,' I said to the Headmaster.

On the boundary of the cricket ground the damp leaves, whirled and fell still.

'Good-bye, Fielding,' said the Headmaster. 'I'm sorry it's turned out like this. You're not to blame your mother.'

'There's no point in blaming anyone. Would you do something for me, sir?'

'What?'

'When the boys get back and you see Somerset Lloyd-James, tell him I'm sorry not to have seen him to say good-bye.'

'I'll tell him, certainly. I expect he'll be sorry too.'

'No, he won't. You'll see that from his face. Look into his face, Headmaster; look into his eyes. You're unlikely to see anything at all in them, and if you do it won't be tears.'

When I arrived home again, my mother did not, as she had threatened, make me grovel. She was distant in her greeting and received my apologies for having struck her with an ugly shrug of the shoulders; but as soon as I had made it plain (following the Senior Usher's instructions) that I had come home to toe the line, I was treated with consideration and even with affection. Since I was prepared to yield over the big issues, it seemed that I was to be humoured in the lesser ones. Once I had been to Lympne Ducis, accompanied this time by mama, and had signified to the authorities that I wish to be called up as soon as possible, my comfort and preferences were constantly consulted. On the day that I gave Mr Tuck a formal assurance that I would join the company in India as soon as I was free from the Army, my mother handed me a cheque for £15, made out to Peter Morrison, and another, worth twice as much, for myself, and suggested that I might indulge any reasonable fancy during the few weeks before I was posted. (Even a trip to London was sanctioned, and I was able to visit the Senior Usher's doctor friend, who tested and approved my blood.) Life at Broughton Staithe, then, was easy and tranquil that autumn; and not only on the surface: for early in October I received assurance from Robert Constable that my place at Lancaster was indeed still open, so that in the very act of complying with my mother's demands I could reflect, with deep and secret satisfaction, that the last word would be mine.

Dear Gray (Constable had written in his own hand),

I have now learned, both from the Headmaster and the Senior Usher, about the circumstances of your leaving school. They give few details, but I gather there has been some sexual indiscretion. Officially, however, you have merely been withdrawn by your mother, albeit at unexpectedly short notice. This can make no difference to your prospects here; and as Tutor of the College I am pleased to notify you that you may take up your place and your Minor Scholarship as soon as you have concluded your military service.

Yours sincerely,
Robert Constable.

So that was finally settled. When I left the Army I would go to Lancaster, and there was nothing my mother or anyone else could do to stop me. Full of glee at my victory and longing to tell someone of it, I wrote off to Peter to give him a detailed account of my afflictions and of my cleverness in achieving so happy an issue.

'Well,' said Tuck the night before I left for the Army, 'here's wishing you all the best.'

Mama was giving a little dinner party in honour of my departure.

'I expect,' said Angela, 'that you'll look very different when you come home on leave.'

'Fitter,' said Tuck.

'Tougher,' said Angela.

'More grown up,' said mama.

'Where exactly are you going?' said Tuck.

'99 Primary Training Centre. At a place called Ranby.'

'His friend Peter Morrison is there,' mama said, 'who comes from Whereham. Isn't that lucky for Fielding? Such a nice, kind, helpful boy.'

'I don't suppose he'll be there for much longer,' I said. 'Primary Training only lasts for eight weeks, they tell me. After that we go to training units belonging to our own regiments.'

'Which regiment are you going to?' asked Tuck.

'The 49th Light Dragoons. Earl Hamilton's Regiment of Horse.'

'Rather grand?'

'I don't know . . . My school has quite a pull with them.'

'Hmm,' muttered Tuck suspiciously. 'You'll need a bit of extra money if they give you a commission in that lot.'

'Fielding will have an allowance,' mama said. 'And it will be nice for him to be in a regiment with people from his old school.'

Now that she had won her way, my mother apparently

expected no trouble from old associations. A naïvely snobbish woman, she had even encouraged me to make use of school connections in order to enter a smart regiment. As for the money which would be needed, she had already shown herself generous and was prepared to continue so. Truth to tell, mama was not really an unamiable woman; and had she, earlier in her life, received love, she would not now have needed to exercise power.

'An allowance,' Angela said, as though such a thing were beyond the dreams of avarice; 'how very kind of you.'

'So long as Fielding is sensible,' my mother said, 'I shall help him in every way I can.'

'You've got a brick of a mother,' said Tuck when the two ladies had left us.

'You might call her that.'

'I jolly well do. It took her to make you see sense about the plantation. Not many people would have had the patience.'

'She has certainly been very persistent,' I said.

'A pretty cool way of putting it.'

'We're a pretty cool family.'

'Not your mother. She's warm, generous . . .'

'Tell me, if it's not a rude question. How much is she investing in the plantation?'

'Ten thousand. More later, I think. Now the factory at Torbeach has been sold, she reckons she can afford it.'

'I don't wonder you find her generous.'

'It's all for you,' Tuck said.

'Precisely. My father, if you remember, wanted something for himself.'

'Don't play games with me, boy.'

'Never again,' I said : 'I promise you that.'

And so I left for Ranby Camp and the last part of this story. I expected anything up to three years of discomfort and boredom, but if Peter could face it, I told myself, so could I. It had to be gone through sometime; and always there was Lancaster College waiting for me at the end of it. Whatever had been lost, that—and it was much—was still promised.

And now, too, I should be seeing Peter again. He would not be at Ranby much longer, but there he would be. I could seek him out, discuss what had happened, receive his sympathy and applause; then talk with him of friends and enemies in common, of days past and to come. It would be good to see Peter; as the train rumbled over the dreary flats, I cheered myself by thinking of the round face that would be waiting for me and the slow, soothing voice . . .

Today, as for weeks past, the wind has thrust at the island without ceasing. The clouds are coming across so low that the little village on the hill above me has been hidden for hours. Beneath the cloud a swirling drizzle reduces everything to two dimensions and one colour, a drab yellow. But now, just as ten years ago in that train across the Lincolnshire flats, I cheer myself with thinking of Peter, who will be here, in three days' time, with his delegation of M.P.s.

Although the spell still works, it is weaker now than it was then. Then the thought of Peter's calm eyes and kind, clumsy hands was enough to quicken the dull fens to enchantment, to make the blue war-time bulbs, which darkened rather than lit the carriage, shine out for durbar. But now, glad as I am that he is coming here, I know that such reunions do not, as a general rule, come up to expectation.

AT RANBY CAMP they squadded me and kitted me, took away my civilian clothes and sent them home for me, and issued me with a card which entitled me to forty cigarettes a week at special rates. Then, reluctantly and spasmodically, they began to train me. A jolly red-nosed sergeant lectured me on procedure for seeking redress of grievance or applying for leave if my wife were to prove unfaithful; an officer in fur-lined suede boots assured me, in a fluting voice, that the Army's skills would stand me well when I returned to my civilian trade; and a neurotic corporal, who had been broken from sergeant-major for striking a Eurasian pimp in a dance hall in Deolali, opined that a properly cleaned rifle was a better friend to me than my mother.

On my second night, I set out to discover Peter. I sloshed through the mud which lapped round the nightmare archipelago of a myriad Nissen huts and at last found a door which said 'A Coy Office'. Inside, working under a dim light with five tea-cups and five empty plates in front of him, was an immense and flabby colour-sergeant.

'Permission to speak, Colour, please?'

'Put them down on the desk, laddie,' said the colour-sergeant without looking up.

'Put what down?'

'The tea and wads down.'

'I haven't got any tea and wads, I'm afraid. I've come about a friend, Private Morrison—'

'—Not got the tea and wads?'

'I'm from "H" Company, Colour. But I've got a friend called Morrison in this, and I . . .'

The colour-sergeant held up his hand for silence and began to speak in a mildly hysterical manner.

'I took over as C.S.M. of this shower,' the colour-sergeant

said, 'without, I might tell you, being given the acting rank, at 1300 hours dinner time. So I couldn't tell a single one of them from the next, not if it was Jesus Christ Almighty who came round asking. That's why I'm sitting here in the middle of the night, trying to sort out the horrible mess that's been left behind. A tap at the door. Ah, I says, my tea and wads and none too soon. But instead a young gentleman arrives, as bold as the colonel on his horse, and starts asking questions. It makes me want to cry.'

He looked as if he really might.

'I'm terribly sorry. If you like, I'll go to the NAAFI and get your tea and wads for you.'

'But then,' said the colour-sergeant after some thought, 'there'd be two lots. The lot that's been ordered already, see, and the new lot that you got.'

'Better two lots than no lots.'

'Yes,' said he colour-sergeant after further thought, 'I do believe you're right. So you go to the NAAFI for me and I'll look up this mucker of yours and see where he beats his meat.'

'Beats his meat?'

'What hut his wanker's in. What did you say he was called?'

When I arrived back from the NAAFI twenty minutes later with a large tray of tea and wads, I found a stringy and yellow sergeant-major, who was sitting in the colour-sergeant's chair and lighting an eighth of an inch of Woodbine.

'Permission to speak, sir, please?'

After the sergeant-major had coughed till the tears ran down his face, he nodded his permission.

'I've brought the colour-sergeant's tea and wads.'

'Too late, son. I've just taken over from him.'

'Well, would you like these, sir? It seems a pity to waste them.'

'I've been sitting here for ten minutes,' said the sergeant-major after a heroic bout of coughing, 'and three people

have come in with trays of tea and wads. Poor Colour Baines
can't stop himself, you see. Three days at Anzio without a
bite to eat, and now he just can't stop himself, which is why
I've had to take over from him.'

'So where's he gone to now, sir?'

'They've sent him back to the stores. It doesn't matter so
much there, but you can't have it in a company office. What
I *would* like,' the sergeant-major said, 'is a cigarette.'

'I'm sorry, sir. I don't smoke. But I could go to the NAAFI
for you.'

'That's right, son, you do that.'

I went again to the NAAFI and with the aid of my special
card brought twenty cheap cigarettes. I was half afraid lest
someone else might have taken over from the sergeant-major
by the time I got back, but instead there was no one in the
office at all. So I looked in a file called Personnel,' Distribution
of, and discovered that 14477929 Recruit Lance-Corporal
Morrison P., who had applied for and been granted an
Indian Army Cadetship, had gone on embarkation leave the
day before, having been posted w.e.f. November 1 to the
Officers' Training School at Bangalore. He would be back
in Ranby *en passant*, it appeared, in ten days' time. Although
the sergeant-major had not paid me for the cigarettes, I
obeyed an instinct, which twenty-four hours of my new life
had already awakened in me, and decided to leave them
behind.

A week later I was summoned for interview with a visiting
personnage called the Cavalry (Armoured Corps) Selection
Officer. This turned out to be Captain Detterling, the only
boy in the school who had ever made a double century in a
school match. His cherry trousers, which had seemed the
last word in elegance on the school terrace last May, were
rather tactless, I thought, against a background of denim
overalls and mud. He was sitting in a tiny office which was
warmed by a stove twice as big as the only stove we had in
my Nissen hut; despite which he was wearing his officer's

great coat, slung stylishly over his shoulders to resemble a cavalry cloak.

'Permission to enter, sir, please?' I said from the door.

'Good lord,' Detterling said, 'do they still teach recruits to do that?'

'Sir.'

'Well you can knock it off with me, dear boy. After all, we have met before.' He shook hands with me, waved me into a chair and inspected a form in front of him. 'Now let's see. You want to go into the 49th Earl Hamilton's Light Dragoons, it says here.'

'That's right, sir.'

Detterling pondered awhile.

'That's my regiment,' he said, as if he had just remembered, and looked down at his trousers as though for confirmation.

'Sir.' (No other comment seemed possible.)

'Well, there'll be no trouble about that. As you probably realise, a lot of us come from the old school for a start. By the way, I was down there last week. Saw your chum Morrison. He's going to India, he says.'

'So I gather.'

'He's looking forward to seeing you here first. Told me to tell you. I don't suppose,' he continued, almost as if there were some connection, 'that I can interest you in taking a *regular* commission?'

'I'm afraid not. I'm going up to Cambridge, you see.'

'The Army's rather jolly in peace time, you know. I had two years of it before the last show started. Lots of cricket and servants, that sort of thing.'

'Do you suppose it will be the same, sir?'

Captain Detterling looked glum.

'I don't suppose it will ever be *quite* the same,' he conceded. 'But you might like to think about it.'

'I'm sorry. Cambridge...'

'Morrison was talking about that. And the rest of them.'

'The rest of them?'

'The Senior Usher. And the head man. As I told them, you're just the sort of chap we'd jump at, if you wanted a regular commission.'

'I'm sorry.'

'So am I,' said Detterling rather oddly, 'and I'm sorry to keep nagging you like this. But I'm afraid it's my job: trying to interest people in the Army as a career. Not very easy, I assure you. And the trouble is,' he prattled on, inexplicably nervous, I thought, 'that I'm meant to explain what a healthy, exciting, useful sort of life it is for good, keen chaps. As if anyone wants to listen to that. I keep telling the Board, if only there were more talk of hunting and proper dress uniforms instead of all this boring rubbish about tanks, it would make my job easier ... But I mustn't detain you.'

'There's nowhere I'd sooner be.'

'I suppose not. *Tanks*,' said Detterling crossly, 'how I hate them. Hideous, noisy, dirty things, spoiling everyone's pleasure.'

'I do see your point.'

'But I oughtn't,' said Detterling, 'to be talking like this. You keep your nose clean in this horrible dump, and we'll take good care of you when you get to us. We'll fix you up with an emergency commission or whatever it's called in about six months. And there's no harm,' he pleaded, 'in just thinking about making it permanent, now is there?'

Although I was so preoccupied and even diverted by my new way of life that I had contrived to forget my disappointment at Peter's absence, I was eager for his return. The 'A' Company sergeant-major, gratefully remembering the cigarettes though not offering to pay for them, agreed to pass on a message; and at eight o'clock in the evening, two days after my interview with Captain Detterling, I found Peter waiting for me outside the NAAFI.

'Not here,' said Peter at once; 'I know somewhere quieter.'

He was wearing, I now saw, the insignia of an Officer

Cadet: a large white celluloid disk behind his cap-badge and a white tape on each shoulder. He would have been less than prudent to show himself in the NAAFI in a get-up like that.

'This way,' Peter said. 'Sorry about the trappings, but I'm leaving tomorrow and this is what we have to wear on the boat.'

'So soon?'

'Yes.'

He led the way across a football pitch two inches deep in yellow slush, past a coal heap, a cookhouse, two rubbish dumps and a discreetly stinking urinal labled 'Sergeants and Above', and down a path of crazy pavement to a small stone cottage. Above the door a red light-bulb dimly illuminated a text which was surmounted by a Maltese Cross:

THE CHURCH ARMY
I bring not peace but the sword.

'Nice and quiet for all that,' Peter said.

Also warm and cheerful. For threepence each we were both given a cup of thick tea and a spicy sausage roll by a woman with a wobbling bust, who invited us to make ourselves comfortable by a huge coal fire.

'So you're off tomorrow,' I said. 'The Indian Army. How long will it last?'

'For two years perhaps. Long enough for me. I do six months at the O.T.S. at Bangalore. Then the Punjab. I've always wanted to go somewhere like that before settling down.'

He was anything but settled now. There was a long pause, during which he crumbled his sausage roll. Nervous, I thought, upset. Meeting like this only to say good-bye again. It was not a happy thing.

'Tell me,' Peter said, 'wasn't Detterling here the other day? The chap with the cherry trousers?'

'He interviewed me.'

'Did he give you my message?'

'He said you were looking forward to seeing me.'

'Only that?'

'And that you'd all been talking about me back at school.'

'I don't suppose he really gathered what it was all about. You may as well know straight off, Fielding. There's bad news.'

'Bad news?'

'It's very difficult for me.' He leant forward and started to speak very quickly, not exactly with urgency but more as if he were throwing away essential but embarrassing lines in a carefully rehearsed style. 'When I was home on leave,' he said, 'I went to see your mother. She'd be lonely, I felt, and although I hadn't seen you yet I thought she might like to hear about Ranby ... She was always very kind to me when we were younger. You remember?'

'She still speaks fondly of you. Such nice manners, she always says.'

'I was ... am ... fond of her too. She was so proud of you, Fielding.'

'Victorious, you mean.'

'No. It depends how you see it, I suppose, but to me she seemed proud. She kept talking of the 49th Light Dragoons, how she longed for the day when you'd come home with a commission ...'

As Peter talked on, the scene he described flickered in my brain like an old film. Peter and mama, one each side of a fire like the one we sat by now, were mouthing silently at one another, while what they said appeared in white sub-titles at the bottom of the screen.

'... Tell me, Peter dear. What sort of uniform do they wear? In Earl Hamilton's Light Dragoons, I mean.'

'It'll be a little while before he gets to them, Mrs Gray. He has to finish his Primary Training first.'

'I know. But when *does* he go to the Dragoons?'

'They wear cherry trousers, Mrs Gray. Most of these cavalry regiments go in for something rather dashing.'

'Will Fielding have boots and spurs?'

'They're trying to discourage those. After all, they're not much good in tanks.'

'But they look very smart . . . Ah well. How soon do you suppose you'll all be released?'

'Hard to say. Three years . . . Two and a half.'

'Because Fielding's got such a good job to go to. Has he told you? He's been offered a splendid position on a tea plantation in India.'

'I heard about it.'

'I expect you were interested, as you're going there too. Yes, it's all been arranged. One of the partners—well, he *will* be a partner—will take special care of him, and with a little luck he should do very well.'

'Mrs Gray. You must know as well as I do that Fielding will never go to India.'

'What did you say, Peter dear?'

'I heard from him not long ago. Fielding still means, as he always has, to go up to Lancaster College.'

The screen flickered violently, then went bright and blank.

'*Why*, Peter?' I said. 'Why in God's name did you tell her that?'

'It's very difficult . . . I suddenly felt that I must speak up on your account. Set the record straight. I couldn't allow you to deceive her any more; I couldn't let this proud, kind old lady just sit there and be made a fool of.'

'Proud, kind old lady. She's behaved wickedly, abominably—'

'—She's your mother, Fielding. You owed her the truth, however hard it was for you.'

'But she's been vicious, vindictive.'

'Because you couldn't see it right. You never tried to understand. You failed in love.'

'God is love,' said a voice behind us. A bald and snuffling old man, carrying a sheaf of tracts.

'God bless,' he snuffled, putting two tracts on the table between us, 'God bless.'

'Christ,' I said, fingering a tract, 'dear Jesus Christ. So

what happened then?'

'A few days later I went down to the school to say good-bye. The head man had already heard from Lancaster. Your mother had been to see Constable.'

'What could she do there? Constable doesn't give a damn what I've done. He wrote to me and said so. It's just like the Senior Usher says,' I went on wildly: 'Lancaster's not like the school, it's too powerful to be intimidated by some chattering woman.'

'No one was intimidated, Fielding.'

'Well then?'

'You never knew much about Constable. The Senior Usher did, but even he didn't understand him properly. As he now admits. You see, although Constable was a progressive, a liberal—indeed *because* he was those things—he was a man of deep moral feeling.'

'We knew that. But his brand of morality didn't trouble itself about the petty sexual offences of children.'

'No. But it troubles itself about betrayal. When your mother showed Constable that photo which Christopher sent you ... and when he thought about what it implied ... he began to suspect that you had failed Christopher in some way, that you had used him and then deserted him. But he couldn't be sure, and it might not have been your fault, so he was prepared to overlook this—or so he wrote to the head man— had it been an isolated incident. But there was more.'

'What, for God's sake?'

'Constable is a man of honour. A man of his word. You remember when the Senior Usher sneered at him for not getting a good job in the war, for "running round with a lot of black men"?'

'Yes.'

'Well Constable could have had a soft job all right, only he chose to fight because he thought his honour required it. He wouldn't take the easy way out.'

'What's that to do with me?'

'When Constable heard from your mother that you'd first

struck her and then, later on, lied to her—'

'—But the old man told me to lie to her. To stop any more trouble.'

'The old man's standards aren't Constable's. When Constable heard how you'd deceived your mother, letting her think you'd fall in with her plans, drawing a handsome allowance on the strength of it, when all the time you had his own letter of acceptance in your pocket, it offended both his morality and his chivalry. Treachery ... and violence ... to a woman.'

'She was treacherous to me,' I wailed.

'In Constable's eyes that does not excuse you. Nor in mine. I think it is the blow which I cannot bear. You never told me about that when you wrote, did you? And you were quite right. The rest I might have pardoned; not the blow.'

'I never meant to hit her. I was wild with anger and disappointment. I was sorry, terribly sorry, and I told her so.'

'And then went on to express your sorrow by cold-blooded deceit. But my feelings are by the way. To Constable, as he told the head man, all this added up to a pattern of exploitation and betrayal so clear and consistent that he would have nothing more to do with you. He's finished with you, Fielding. You can't go to Lancaster. Ever.'

'He might have written,' I choked out; 'someone might have written.'

'The head man was to have done that. He asked me to tell you instead.'

'But great heavens,' I said, 'if you and the head man and the Senior Usher—if you can all put up with me, why should Constable condemn me? The head man, he's moral enough, God knows, and if he—'

'—The head man,' said Peter patiently, 'like the rest of us, has had time to grow fond of you despite your faults. He's seen the good things, fallen for the charm. Not Constable. He's seen you once and he didn't much like what he saw.'

'God curse Constable,' I snivelled into the fire.

'I did warn you.'

'Yes.'

'Can I help?'

'No. You've done enough. It's your fault. I may have been foolish, but it's your fault. If you'd only held your tongue.'

'It would have come out sooner or later. What did you think you were going to do? Deceive your mother for the rest of your life? Yes, you would if you could. You'd deceive anyone if it suited you, anyone and everyone and all the time. Just as you did Chistopher.'

'I didn't deceive Christopher. I loved him.'

'Until you got what you wanted, perhaps. Then you just kept him on a string. All your talk of scholarship and truth —your whole life was a lie. You had to learn,' said Peter, rising to his feet, 'if only on a practical level, that you can't get away with it. Never mind that you've failed us, failed us all, in love: I don't expect you to understand that. But what I hope you've learned, now, is that if you cheat you get found out. Sooner or later a man like Constable comes along, a man of truth who isn't put off by charm, and he reads the signs and he finds you out. When that happens, the spell is broken.'

'So you hate me too?'

'No,' said Peter, holding out his hand in farewell, 'I can't hate you after all this time. But I've no illusions any more. You've shown yourself as you are this evening. A clever, shallow, charming boy, blubbering with self-pity because he's told a lie and been found out.'

Since that evening I have not seen Peter. Our correspondence, a mere matter of form, trickled, dwindled and then, years ago, ceased. And now tomorrow he will be here on this island. Despite the meagre and long discontinued letters, despite what passed in the Church Army canteen, I am ridiculously, childishly excited. How much will he have changed in ten years? Will time have confirmed his natural gift of sympathy, or will this have yielded, now that he is prominent and even powerful, to self-righteousness and pride?

THE VISIT is over. The Members of Parliament, having expressed themselves interested and gratified by all they have seen, have climbed into their helicopters and departed for Malta.

And Peter Morrison? He was round-faced and solemn as ever; he had always, as I remembered, looked and behaved as though he were shouldering a heavy burden, and the cares of his position have therefore done little to alter his appearance. Nor has time done much. There was still, this afternoon, a bloom in his cheek, a tenderness in his eye which took me back to that summer day when Tiberius died of a broken heart. The years have been kind to Peter Morrison.

When he first saw me, he looked away slightly and waited for our Colonel, who accompanied the delegation from Malta, to make a formal introduction. Then,

'Fielding,' he said heartily. 'You'll excuse us, for a minute or two, colonel? We're old friends.'

The colonel took the hint and pottered off to join another group.

'You've not changed . . . not all that much,' Peter said.

'I try not to let it show.'

'Don't be bitter. Do you like it here? What do you do?'

'I command a Sabre Squadron on detachment. We are responsible for good order on this island.'

'I must say,' Peter said, 'it always surprised me that you chose the Regular Army.'

'What else was there? Cambridge, as you may recall, was out. And I never intended to go to India.'

'I liked it.'

'So you said—in your one letter.'

'Don't be bitter,' said Peter again. 'Why *did* you choose the Army?'

'Because it offered something rather the same as Lancaster. A closed, comfortable and privileged society. Without the intellectual interest, of course; but that, as you know, was never really important to me. I simply wanted to shine in agreeable surroundings. I hardly do that here, but at least I am obeyed.'

'Did your mother not mind? She seemed, I remember, so determined on India for you.'

'My mother died.'

'She was always delicate. When?'

'I wrote and told you.'

'I'm sorry. It's been such a long time. When?'

'About two years too late. Two years after she'd done all the damage.'

'And ... the money?'

'She'd invested a lot of it in that Indian plantation she wanted me to go to. First of all one of the partners—a friend of hers called Tuck—tried to embezzle a lot of the capital. They rumbled him just in time, but he gave them the slip and disappeared ... They hushed it all up to save themselves looking damned silly.'

'But the investment was still safe?'

'At first, yes. But oddly enough Tuck had been a very good manager, the only one of them who really understood anything. Soon after he'd gone the place just ran downhill and packed up altogether at Independence in '47.'

'But there was other money?'

'It was mostly in a merchant bank recommended by Japhet, the family lawyer. That went bust too, just before my mother died. I think it was what finally killed her.'

'So there was nothing left?'

'Just a little. Enough to reassure the Colonel-in-Chief when I applied to have my commission made permanent. But that's gone as well now.'

'How?'

'We won't discuss it, if you don't mind. Tell me about yourself, Peter. Your parents? I always liked your father.'

'Both dead like yours. The land's all mine now.'

'And your land is fertile?'

He smiled. For the first time I had said something which pleased him.

'You remember?' he said.

'I remember.'

'That evening on the cricket ground with Somerset ... I see him a lot, you know. We have political circles in common. You read his magazine?'

'With admiration. Has Somerset,' I enquired, 'got political ambitions?'

'I shouldn't wonder.'

'Then let me give you back your own advice. Watch him.'

Peter gestured amiably.

'I've no objection to furthering Somerset's ambitions,' he said. 'He'll make a very good politician.'

'A better politician than friend.'

'There you wrong him. Somerset values good order, and always did. He never harmed anyone unless his sense of order was offended first.'

'The only trouble was that his sense of order required that Somerset should do all the ordering.'

'Why are you being so tough with me?' Peter said. 'Aren't you pleased to see me?'

'I've looked forward to it for weeks.'

'Then why this hostility?'

A political trick, I thought. He wants to spare himself embarrassment by getting me to say it first. Then the truth will be out, but he can pretend to deny it for the sake of politeness. The important point will have been made without his having committed himself to a single harsh word. He wants it both ways; very well, he's the guest; let him have it so, and then we can part with the appearance of decorum, with a mutual saving of face.

'You've shown me, now you're here at last,' I said, 'that

to you I've become alien, totally alien. I realised, of course,
that I was no longer the person you once knew. But I had
hoped that there might still be ... *something* which remained,
something to which you could respond. It seems that there
isn't. Or rather, there might be, but it's no longer in me, in
myself as I am here and now, but only in memories of the
past.'

I waited for the expected denial, for the formal protest
of continued affection. But Peter nodded briskly.

'That's it,' he said. 'To me you're now alien, as you say.
You have been since that night in Ranby Camp. To me,
Fielding Gray is the beautiful and brilliant hero of the first
summer of the new peace: an illusion, as it turned out, but
a bright and memorable one. After that—nothing.'

He turned and walked away towards the Land Rovers
which would carry the delegation back to their helicopters
down on the beach.

This evening, for once, there is no wind on the island, so
that I can hear the bell from the village up on the hill. Since
it is tolling very slowly, I assume that it rings for a death. To
me it rings for all the alien dead: for my parents and for
Peter's; for Christopher and for the brave Tiberius; and for
Fielding Gray.